STELLA AND SOL

KIMBERLY LOTH

KIMBERLY LOTH

GOD
of the
SUN

FIRST BOOK IN THE STELLA AND SOL SERIES

Stella and Sol

God of the Sun
Volume 1
By Kimberly Loth

For Will
My incredible husband
For believing in and supporting me
Always
Thank you

Prologue

THE BABY

igh Prince Leo of Stella sat down at the large circular table. It was rare for them to eat breakfast in the dining hall of the castle, but the rest of his twelve siblings arrived last night at the behest of his sister, Candace, who had an announcement. Of course, he knew what the announcement would be, they all did, but he played dumb anyway. This would be the first grandchild for his father, and so it warranted a special breakfast.

Bright yellow lights hung from the ceiling, and the floor glowed white. Light flowed from nearly every surface, as the darkness could be suffocating. Thank the stars for magic. Leo looked around the noisy table. Over the last few years, the number of people around the table had grown. When they were children, there were only twelve of them, plus his father and his father's wife. Now, couples were starting to emerge. Three of his older siblings were married, and others had steady relationships. At seventeen, Leo had had a relationship or two, but at the moment he was free. Which was a lonely place to be when his favorite sister was about to announce that she was pregnant. Where in the depths were Ari and Sage? They would keep him entertained. But they were always late.

Candace caught his eye, and he smiled at her. She practically glowed. She wore her deep black hair swept up in a twist. He hadn't seen her wear it down since she got married.

He missed having her around. They were the only two siblings who shared the same mother, and that created a special bond between them. But now Candace was a lower queen and had too many responsibilities to come home often.

A hand thumped him on the shoulder, and his eldest brother, Ari, collapsed into the armchair to Leo's right. He sat with his leg flung over the armrest, his blue hair hanging in his eyes. To Leo's left, his sister Sage sat down, flicking her rainbow-colored hair over her shoulder. She had deep purple bloodshot eyes. She yawned and put her head on the table.

"Late night?" Leo asked.

Sage nodded into her arms. "Has she announced that she's been knocked up yet?"

Ari straightened in his chair and poured himself a glass of juice. "She can't be knocked up if she's married."

"She's only been married for a month. My guess is she's a few months along. That's knocked up," Sage said, sitting up and rubbing her forehead. "Remind me to never drink again."

Ari laughed. "You say that every time we go out. The last time I reminded you, you punched me." He turned his attention to Leo. "How come you didn't come out with us last night? I sent you a few messages."

"I turned off my disc. I wanted to spend some time with Candace. She won't be here long."

"Right," said Sage. "You just don't like to party. Maybe you should go live in Sol."

Leo snorted into his glass of orange juice. "If I have to live in Sol, you two are coming with me."

"They'd kick us out so fast. Ugh, what did I do to my hair?" Sage asked, examining the multi-colored locks. She squeezed her eyes shut, and it returned to the brilliant violet she usually rocked. She dug into her pocket, took out a small bottle, and downed it.

Before Leo could ask what it was, Candace stood, and the whole table fell silent, except for Sage, who was giggling. Candace glared at Sage, and Leo squeezed her knee. She covered her mouth and tried to stifle the giggles. The small bottle clinked next to her plate, and he picked it up. The label said "Giggle."

"That's not nice," Leo hissed at her. "Taking this potion right now. You're going to ruin the announcement." As the tenth child, Sage got away with more than the rest of them, but sometimes she took things too far. This wasn't fair to Candace.

"Sorry." She giggled. "I thought it was Sober. My head is killing me. For what it's worth, the giggling isn't helping."

Candace cleared her throat as the door creaked opened. Every head in the room turned.

An old woman hobbled in. She was large with a pale weather-beaten face, and she wore a bulging tattered coat. An earthy odor emanated from her. She crept slowly to the table and then plucked an apple from a bowl. She took a bite and spit it out, revealing gray teeth.

"Blech, those taste much better in Sol. I need to remember to eat before I come next time." She looked around the table. Her blue eyes pierced Leo's, and he shivered.

The entire table sat in shocked silence. No one moved. Leo had heard the stories about the Old Mother who gave horrible prophecies that required someone to make a great sacrifice. He didn't know anyone who had actually met her. He assumed the rumors were simply scary stories kids told each other.

The old woman cackled and pointed to Candace. Leo's stomach clenched. Not now. Not her. He pushed his chair back, ready to help Candace if she needed it. He crept around the table and made his way toward her.

"A prophecy I have for you. The vipers grow restless. They long for the blood you deny, and they are changing. If the kingdoms of Stella and Sol are not joined by that child's first birthday, then he will die," said the Old Mother.

She stared at each of them in turn, making eye contact. "And he will not be the last. The union must be strong. You must prove to the earth that Stella and Sol will be forever joined, or the vipers will eat you all."

With a poof and a cloud of dust, she disappeared from their midst. Not a sound was heard in the room except Sage's giggling.

Chapter One

THE STRANGER

Screams filled the little house in the middle of the slave village. Zwaantie pushed her white blonde hair out of her eyes and held Mrs. Bakker's hand, making exaggerated breathing motions in the hopes that maybe Mrs. Bakker would copy her and make the birth easier.

Instead, Mrs. Bakker let out another ear-piercing scream and crushed Zwaantie's fingers. Zwaantie's slave, Luna, wiped a white cloth on Mrs. Bakker's forehead. The room was stifling with the wood stove burning. Wilma, the midwife, said it helped the mothers, but Zwaantie thought it just made them hot and irritable. Mrs. Bakker opened her bright blue eyes and stared at Zwaantie.

"I'm sorry, Your Highness," Mrs. Bakker said in between breaths. Zwaantie sighed. She supposed being addressed like that would be the story of her life, as it had for all of her sixteen years, even if she was just trying to do her job.

"Please, call me Zwaantie."

Don't ask for such disrespectful things. No one should call you anything but Your Highness.

Zwaantie nearly rolled her eyes at the Voice, but then she'd get another reprimand. The Voice was always scolding her and everyone else for silly things they said or did. Thank Sol it could not read thoughts. It was a constant chatter in everyone's heads, reminding them of the rules. Solites learned at a young age to tune out all but the most forceful of the words, or they'd never be able to think.

Zwaantie's mother often reminded her that she should be grateful for the Voice, or else their kingdom would be in chaos all the time. God spoke to them through the Voice so they would always know the right thing to do.

Mrs. Bakker struggled to speak. "Of course, Princess Zwaantie."

Solites believed in hard work, and so even as the crown princess, she was not allowed to sit around and be pampered. If she became queen, she wouldn't be able to perform her midwife duties as often since she'd have to attend to the affairs of the kingdom. She hoped that by some miraculous surprise, she wouldn't have to take the throne, because what Zwaantie wanted most in the world was to be normal.

It was unusual for a member of the royal family to pick such a job since it was so demanding. Her younger brother, Raaf, had chosen to learn how to cook. Her father was a master archer, and Mother was a seamstress. Mother had hesitated when Zwaantie declared she wanted to work with the midwife. But after Zwaantie batted her baby blues, Mother gave in. Zwaantie abhorred royal things, so she chose a job that got her as far from the castle as possible. If Mother had refused, her second choice would have been farming.

For the most part Zwaantie loved her job, except she hated wearing the brown dress. All her dresses covered her body from neck to foot, but the brown dresses always seemed more suffocating. They were tighter in the chest and arms so loose fabric didn't interfere with any medical procedures.

"One more big push. You can do this." Wilma gave Mrs. Bakker a wide toothy smile, but it didn't do any good. Mrs. Bakker bore down, her face twisted in pain. She let out another scream and then collapsed. Zwaantie dropped her hand and rushed to see the baby, her favorite part. She left Luna to attend to Mrs. Bakker.

Wilma sat on a low stool and cleaned out the mouth of the tiny boy with inch wide gold bands tight on his wrists and ankles. Those bands marked him as a slave and would grow with him. Wilma rubbed his back, but he let out no cry, his body a deep purple.

"Quick, grab the bottle of Breathe."

Zwaantie spun around to the wood table and dug into Wilma's leather bag, her chest tightening. The Voice blabbered about the immorality of potions, but she ignored it. In the four years she'd been working with Wilma, she'd never seen a baby or mother die, but they did sometimes. She tossed aside Nopain and Bloodstop and finally found Breathe.

Abomination, the Voice said forcefully. Although the Voice abhorred magic, it wouldn't stop her from using the potions. She tuned out its chattering even though it'd gotten loud, unstopped the bottle, and handed it to Wilma, who tipped the contents into the baby's mouth. As soon as the liquid hit his throat, he sucked in a deep breath and let out a cry.

The knot in Zwaantie's chest loosened. They were out of the woods. She collapsed against the table, relief flooding her body. Wilma wiped the baby down, wrapped him in white cloth, and handed him to his mother, who took him with shaking arms.

As Mrs. Bakker nursed her baby, Wilma observed the girls cleaning up. Zwaantie had become fast friends with Wilma when she started her training. Zwaantie wasn't sure how old Wilma was—probably older than her grandmother, but Wilma had an answer for every question Zwaantie ever asked. She loved that because Mother often used the dreaded phrase: "Because I said so." Plus, Wilma never treated her like a princess, and yelled at both her and Luna equally. Working with Wilma was the only time that Zwaantie felt like a normal person.

Zwaantie was still learning, and she found the work incredibly rewarding. She'd never delivered a baby without Wilma present, but she felt she was ready. She was about to tell Wilma as such, but a knock came from the door. Luna rushed to answer it. The rusty hinges squeaked as she cracked it open.

"Come in," she said, stepping back and opening the door. Luna had a wide smile on her face that told Zwaantie only one person could be on the other side.

Sure enough, Pieter ducked as he stepped into the doorway, his sandy blonde head nearly grazing the ceiling of the tiny home.

"The king has called for you," he said with a nod to Zwaantie.

"Tell him I'm working."

You will go to your father. That is non-negotiable.

Zwaantie sighed. They were always summoning her for dumb things, like what color they should use to decorate the grand hall or what to feed the lower kings and queens. Quite frankly, Zwaantie didn't care. But the Voice would keep talking until she did what he commanded. She thought about arguing, but then she'd have to open her mouth. Zwaantie often spoke aloud to the Voice, but she only did that when no one else was around because she thought it looked weird when people walked down the street talking to themselves. Everyone knew they were arguing with the Voice, but Zwaantie didn't want people to see her doing it.

"Pieter, wait. Luna and I will come. Wilma, will you be okay?"

Wilma gave her a knowing grin. "Yes. I'm going to stay here tonight and make sure there are no other complications. Tell your mother we need more medicine. That was my last bottle of Breathe."

"I will, but I don't think there is a whole lot she can do."

"The mage wagon should've been here weeks ago." Wilma wrung her hands together. They relied on those potions and had no way to produce them on their own, and it wasn't like they could go over to Stella and get them. Potions were the only kind of magic allowed in Sol, though the Voice still discouraged it.

"I'll see if she can have a guard wait by the crossing, intercept a carriage, and send a message that we need medicines." It was the most she could do. Someday she would be queen, and she used to think that meant she'd be able to change things in her kingdom, but the more she learned, the more she realized that there was so much out of her control. She didn't want that job or the responsibility.

Pieter held the door as Zwaantie and Luna walked out into the cool morning. Zwaantie flipped up her hood so that no one would recognize her. Their shoes clip-clopped along the cobblestones, breaking the silence. Tiny houses with thatched roofs lined the road, packed tight next to one another. Slaves went to work as soon as the day broke, so even by mid-morning, there were hardly any people around, save a few guards who watched from the shadows. Pieter stayed close to Luna, and Zwaantie saw them brush hands a few times.

"You know, you are allowed to hold hands," Zwaantie said.

A deep blush formed on Luna's face as Pieter intertwined his fingers with hers. Zwaantie let out a sigh and dropped back a few steps. They were adorable. Luna's caramel skin stood out against Pieter's pale skin, but they seemed to fit so well together. The bands on both of their wrists flashed in the sunlight. All slaves had four bands. One on each wrist and ankle. By the time they were fully grown, the bands were about three inches wide and fit snug against their skin. They never came off.

When they were ten, Zwaantie asked Luna if the bands hurt. Luna replied that she barely felt them, but she didn't like the way people looked at her because of them. Being a slave was a stigma Zwaantie wouldn't want.

Though, in some ways, she envied Luna. Pieter had been Luna's choice. No one had told her who she had to marry.

Zwaantie had a choice as well, but her pool was smaller. As heir to the throne of Sol, she'd have to marry a lower prince. The problem was she didn't like any of them. There were only four, well five. But the prince from Zonnes didn't count because he was only four years old. Zwaantie was glad he was the only one who lived in the capital city, or she'd have obnoxious princes at her door every day. As it was, she still had to see the other four lower princes once a month. The lower kingdoms of Ghrain, Sonnenschein, Haul, and Slonce were each at least a day's carriage ride from Zonnes, where Zwaantie lived in the high castle.

The princes were yet another reason to not become queen. Every day she found another one, but most centered around the fact that she wasn't a leader. Not by a long shot. She did what others told her. Except for the Voice. She disobeyed it as often as she could get away with because she was so tired of its incessant chattering and never ending lectures, but she didn't think that was a sign of leadership.

Thankfully her mother hadn't brought up the dreaded "m" word yet. Zwaantie had until her brother took his position as Grand Chancellor. Because Mother said that when Raaf returned, she would have to prepare to take the throne. Which, roughly translated, meant getting married. As much as she missed Raaf, she hoped he had to train for a long time.

Four years ago, the grand chancellor had declared that his time was at an end, and Father chose Raaf to replace him. Raaf was only eleven at the time, but Zwaantie knew he was glad to get the position. Next to the king and queen, the grand chancellor held the most power. He spoke to the Voice on behalf of the people and controlled the guards.

She should've told her mother and father she didn't want to be queen when they chose Raaf to be grand chancellor. Maybe if she'd spoken up then, Raaf would be preparing to become king instead.

Who knew how long it took to train the grand chancellor. At least ten years. Maybe even longer. Was anyone ever ready to face God?

A hooded man pushed past Zwaantie and grabbed Luna's wrist. Pieter shoved him away, and Zwaantie rushed to her side.

"How dare you touch my slave." Zwaantie glowered at the man. She caught sight of his dark face and took a step back. He was from Stella.

"You don't belong here," the man growled at Luna. "Certainly not with those slave bands. Come with me. I will bring you home."

Zwaantie stepped in between them. "Let her go."

The man shoved her, and she nearly lost her balance. "This is none of your business."

Zwaantie stalked to him and lowered her hood. Two guards came running as she knew they would when they recognized her. She hated being reminded that without her royal title she was nothing. She couldn't even protect her friends without using her status. She was pathetic.

"Is there a problem, Your Highness?" one guard asked, glaring at the man. The other guard pushed the man against the wall of the nearest house. "Filthy Stellan, what are you doing in our land?"

Zwaantie needed to play this carefully. She didn't like the way the man talked to Luna, but this was the first Stellan she'd seen in weeks, and they needed medicine. Curse the stars. She should've stayed hooded. She could've talked to the man without having him fear her. Now she was steps away from getting him arrested. She never thought before she acted.

"No, no problem. I apologize if I alarmed you," Zwaantie said.

The guard released the man, and he shook out his arms, his black eyes trained on the guards.

"I could have you arrested," Zwaantie said. "But I won't. We are nearly out of medicine. Please return to your kingdom and let the traders know we will pay handsomely for any they bring."

The man narrowed his eyes at her. "What's in it for me?"

Zwaantie bristled. Stellans never did anything unless they got something in return. Everything about them was barbaric and uncultured. That was what happened when there was no Voice. If this man had been a Solite, he'd have jumped to help Zwaantie.

"One month of merchant food." Stellans never took anything for payment except food.

"Two."

Zwaantie rolled her eyes. "Fine, two. Hurry, please."

She addressed the guards in full princess mode. "Would you please make sure this man is given two months' worth of merchant food and is escorted to the border?"

"Of course, Your Highness."

Zwaantie waited until the man was out of sight before they continued on their walk. She let out a breath and replaced her hood. She'd think twice before she showed her face next time. Crime was rare in Sol, and Zwaantie had never had to use guards before.

Pieter held tightly to Luna's hand. The words the man spoke bothered Zwaantie. Luna had been with her for so long that she often forgot Luna didn't belong in Sol. She was from Stella.

"You don't want to go back, do you?" Zwaantie asked, scared that maybe her best friend and slave was unhappy here.

Luna gave her a smile. "No, of course not. I barely remember Stella."

"How could he have gotten you through the wall anyway? The Voice wouldn't let you go," Pieter said.

Solites were forbidden to cross the border, and once Luna's mother signed the slave contract, Luna became a Solite, at the age of four.

"I don't know. It doesn't matter. This is my home. I have no desire to return to the dark." She clung to Pieter and looped her other arm through Zwaantie's. "Besides, I wouldn't have you two there."

As they exited the tiny village, the castle came into view, winking in the sunlight. Its spires reached high into the sky. It was the grandest building in Sol. A smaller castle sat off to the side for the lower king and queen of Zonnes. A handful of fields with an occasional farmhouse separated the slave village from the castle. Merchant homes were on the other side of the castle.

They strolled along the road in the middle of the fields, watching the animals graze. Zwaantie loved the farms, in spite of the smell. They were the lifeblood of their kingdom. Maybe in another life, she could've been a farmer's wife. She'd like that. It was simple and rewarding.

Just before Zwaantie entered the door of the castle, she closed her eyes and turned her face to the sun, letting it warm her face. Thank Sol she'd been born here, where it never got dark, instead of Stella, where the sun never shone.

Chapter Two

THE UNEXPECTED RETURN

They hiked up the long winding stairs to the king's chambers. Pieter pushed the door open, but there was no one there. Luna's mother, Ariel, came running down the hall, her shoes clattering on the floor.

Ariel stopped short in front of them, breathing hard, and she put her hand on the hard stone surface of the wall to balance herself. "What took you so long? Everyone has already gone outside."

"Why?" Zwaantie asked, confused.

Ariel clapped her hands together. "Your brother is returning. Come, they should be here soon."

Luna's face broke out into a wide smile, but Zwaantie's stomach fell. Her brother was coming home. His training was over, and that could only mean one thing for Zwaantie. Marriage.

They followed Ariel down the long hall. Zwaantie dawdled on purpose. She wasn't ready for this. She paid close attention to the portraits that hung on the walls. Normally she raced by them, but today she noticed how the children always smiled but the kings and queens did not. They bore the weight of the kingdom on their shoulders. The last portrait was of her grandparents and her father as a child. Zwaantie had never seen him smile like that. She barely knew him. Mother spent time with her and Raaf, but Father always was too busy. She didn't want to do that to her own children. Ariel held the door open and waved to Zwaantie.

"Quickly, child, they'll be here soon."

Luna and Pieter stood directly behind Ariel, waiting for Zwaantie. She sighed, gathered her skirt so as not to catch it on the door, and stepped out into the sunlight.

She blinked against the bright light. Her eyes adjusted, and she stared out over fields and villages in the distance. Soon this would all be hers.

Zwaantie's mother and father stood near the top of the outer stairs, holding hands. Zwaantie was a spitting image of her mother, with the same blue-green eyes, long blonde hair, and heart-shaped face. Father was tall and broad, with graying hair and a perpetual scowl. Zwaantie took her place next to her mother. Their slaves stood a few steps behind them. Mother nodded to Zwaantie, a small smile playing on her lips. Zwaantie supposed she was excited as her only son was coming home. A son she hadn't seen in four years.

Zwaantie bounced on her toes, the nerves finally getting to her. She hadn't seen her brother in so long. Would they still be friends? His letters had gotten sparse in the last year or so.

"Would you be still? You're acting like a child." Mother gave Zwaantie a disapproving glare. Zwaantie stilled. Otherwise, the Voice would tell her off, but she was having trouble not fidgeting.

Zwaantie didn't understand how Mother could be so calm. They hadn't seen Raaf in four years. He'd sent letters of course, but beyond that, she'd had no contact with him. She missed him like crazy. He was her best friend. Had he changed much, or was he still her Raaf?

Her dread at his return dissipated a bit. Raaf was coming home. She couldn't wait to hear about his training, and she could tell him about her work with Wilma. Plus, she had to fill him in on all the princesses. If she had to get married, then so did he. She wanted him to marry Princess Cornelia from Haul. She was loads better than Princess Luus here in Zonnes.

The sound of horses clip-clopping on the drive came just before the carriage rounded the corner. Four white horses pulled the bright yellow carriage, and Zwaantie squealed.

Hush. Behave like a princess.

Zwaantie sobered. Stupid Voice. She had to listen to it. She had no choice, but it was a real killjoy sometimes.

Okay, all the time.

Zwaantie folded her hands in front of her like she was trained and stood with her head tall and an impassive expression on her face. But the Voice couldn't stop the racing of her heart. Luna brushed at something on Zwaantie's shoulder and smoothed her hair. Zwaantie figured she was having trouble staying still as well.

The carriage came to a stop, and Zwaantie had to restrain herself from running down and ripping the door open. She waited impatiently for the footslave to open the door.

Raaf came out first. He'd grown about a foot, and he'd cut his hair. He used to wear it long, because Mother loved the rich red color. But now it sat just below his ears. His face was stony, which was unusual. When they were kids, the smile never left his face.

"Mother, may I go greet him?"

Mother nodded. Zwaantie took slow steps so not to appear too eager, but she was sure the huge grin on her face would give her away. Luna kept herself so close that if Zwaantie were to misstep, Luna would bump into her.

Raaf moved away from the carriage.

Zwaantie beamed at him. "Welcome back."

"Thank you. Have you been well?" His voice had dropped at least three octaves. He no longer sounded like her Raaf. She bounced in front of him, itching to give him a hug, but knowing that would be inappropriate.

"I've missed you. We need to catch up tonight. I want to hear about your training." She spoke louder than normal and way too fast. But she couldn't help herself. Raaf was home.

He frowned. "I can't tell you anything. I'm sorry."

Another figure emerged from the carriage, and Luna lost her composure.

"Phoenix," she squealed and threw herself at him, nearly knocking her brother over. They were from Stella and much more affectionate. Zwaantie didn't even hug her own mother and was sure the Voice was chastising them, but they didn't seem all that bothered. Phoenix held her tight, and Zwaantie studied him.

When they were children, the four of them were inseparable. They played in the woods on the castle grounds together as if they were all siblings. The only difference was the bright gold bands Phoenix and Luna had on their wrists and ankles that marked them as slaves. That and their deep caramel-colored skin.

Zwaantie never realized what that meant until she was older. There were hundreds of slaves in the castle. Almost all of them were pale Solites. Stellans were rare in Sol, and most were traders who hurried back to Stella the first chance they got. As far as Zwaantie knew, Luna and her family were the only Stellan slaves in Sol.

The year Zwaantie turned twelve, Raaf went off to train in some secret location in the middle of the mountains, and Phoenix went as his personal slave. It was natural for Luna to become Zwaantie's slave. She and Luna were like sisters, and she was sure Raaf and Phoenix had a similar relationship even though Phoenix was a few years older. Zwaantie didn't see how they couldn't, being trapped in the middle of nowhere with no company except stuffy old chancellors and a few guards.

Unlike Raaf, Phoenix had a huge grin on his face that would charm the stockings off most girls.

He'd changed as well. His black hair had grown and fell in loose curls to his shoulders. His face was no longer pointy and sharp, but had matured into a strong jaw.

He let go of Luna and bowed to Zwaantie, and she couldn't help but notice his wide shoulders and the muscles that moved under his gray linen shirt.

His dark eyes sparkled. "Princess, it is good to see you."

Zwaantie's chest tingled as she appraised him. She was expecting children to return, but instead they became men. Extremely good looking, in Phoenix's case.

Phoenix had always been exotic, but she'd never thought of him much different from her brother. She had no business thinking of him now. He was Luna's brother and a slave.

But with his deep piercing eyes, full lips, and caramel colored skin, he was stunning.

Luna beamed at him. "I can't believe you came back. Just in time too."

His eyes danced as he looked down at her. "Just in time for what?"

She pouted and swatted him. "You got my letters. Don't play dumb."

"Well, my baby sister isn't getting married until I approve, and I have less than twenty-four hours to give you my blessing. Where is this Pieter you've been going on about?"

"Standing behind the king. You'll have to wait until tonight to talk to him, but I'm sure you'll love him."

Phoenix glanced at Mother and Father. "He's awfully tall."

"So?" Luna asked with a frown.

"Nothing. Just an observation."

Raaf still hadn't said much. Zwaantie looked at him cautiously. She was jealous of the easiness of Luna and Phoenix. Even if she and Raaf had never been affectionate, they had been extremely close, but now Raaf seemed uncomfortable. Slaves bustled about hauling trunks off the carriage. The horses snorted and stomped their feet.

"Would you like to have tea in my rooms and catch up?" Zwaantie asked him.

He shook his head. "No, we have work to do. Tomorrow I become grand chancellor. Come, Phoenix."

Phoenix gave Luna a sad smile and followed Raaf up the stairs. Raaf stopped for just moment and greeted Mother and Father, but then he swept into the castle.

Luna looped her arm through Zwaantie's and laid her head on Zwaantie's shoulder. "I can't believe they're back. I'm so happy."

Zwaantie kept her eyes on Mother and Father. They had their faces close together and appeared to be discussing something in earnest, but were smiling.

A sinking feeling fell in Zwaantie's stomach. She wasn't happy. Not at all. Raaf was no longer himself. This was what happened when people grew up. Mother would start asking when Zwaantie was ready to take her crown. One that she could only take on in marriage.

Mother glanced up and glared at them, and Luna moved away from Zwaantie.

"Sorry," Luna whispered. She shouldn't have had her head on Zwaantie's shoulder.

Mother spun around and clomped into the castle. Zwaantie waited until she was out of sight. There was nothing wrong with Luna having her head on Zwaantie's shoulder, but Mother thought it was inappropriate. She wondered how long it would be before the Voice would start yelling at them for that too. It seemed like anytime Mother thought something was wrong, the Voice suddenly did as well.

"It's okay. Let's go inside and see what we can find to do with ourselves," Zwaantie said.

Chapter Three

THE GRAND CHANCELLOR

Zwaantie was having trouble mustering up excitement. Two of her favorite people were hitting huge milestones, and she should be thrilled for them. In some ways she was. But in other ways, she felt like they were moving on without her. Plus, they were both getting what they wanted. Zwaantie never would. Because what she wanted was to not be royal.

She woke up late, which was normal. Her curtains were still shut, blocking out the bright light. She'd given Luna the morning off. Usually by the time she got out of bed, Luna had her room tidied and a bath drawn.

She sat up and stretched. Zwaantie liked her room, decorated like the summer sky. Her quilt was bright yellow, and her bed had sky blue hangings. Soft green rugs adorned her floor.

She slipped on her morning shoes and padded her way across to her closet where she fingered the dresses, trying to find one she could put on herself. They were all styled the same. Solid colors with long, flowing sleeves. Sometimes they were shaped to fit the body, but they mostly felt like giant tents. The loose dresses were easier to put on than the fitted ones, especially with the slip and petticoat underneath. The fitted dresses had far too many strings for Zwaantie to do them on her own. She wasn't used to doing this by herself, but she wasn't about to let Luna work on her wedding day. The door flung open, and Luna burst in, breathing heavily.

"I'm so sorry, Your Highness. I know what a big day this is for you."

Zwaantie put her hands on her hips and frowned. "I told you not to come. It's your wedding day."

That is not your place to tell her.

Luna gave her a sad smile and closed the door. "Sit down. I'll find your dress. I know you told me not to come in, but the Voice forbids it. We don't get days off."

"But you're getting married. The Voice needs to get a life."

Watch your words.

Zwaantie rolled her eyes.

And your actions.

The Voice was obnoxious. Always bossing her around. And everyone else too, but she was only annoyed when it bossed her. And her slave. It wasn't fair to Luna. She should be able to relax and prepare for her own wedding.

Zwaantie sat and watched Luna flip through the rainbow of dresses. "Find one that will match your colors at your wedding."

"You're still coming?" Luna furrowed her brow.

"I wouldn't miss it. You're my best friend." Plus, this was the one opportunity she had to grant her best friend a gift. If it were up to her, Luna would live in the castle with Zwaantie, like a princess, but like she was so rudely reminded, the Voice wouldn't allow slaves to live like that. But anytime a member of the royal family attended a wedding, a gift was given. The bride and groom could ask for anything under the royal member's jurisdiction. Kings and queens rarely attended weddings because the risk of the couple asking for something too big was there. But princes and princesses didn't have as much to lose.

"What about Raaf?" Luna asked.

"His ceremony should be long over by this afternoon. I'll make sure Phoenix can come too. I'd try for Ariel, but you know how my mother is. She'll never let her go. Now what color will best match your wedding?"

"You mean, the gray I'm wearing?"

Zwaantie scowled. She'd told Luna to pick out one of her old dresses weeks ago.

"You're not getting married in gray." Luna was pretty good at following Zwaantie's instructions. She had to be. If not, the Voice would give her a thorough telling off.

Luna lowered her eyes. "I tried, Your Highness. I did. But every time I went to put on one to see how it would look, the Voice intervened."

"What did it say? Don't steal the princess's dresses? It must have heard me tell you to take it."

"No, it didn't say anything about stealing. It told me that I was not allowed to wear anything but gray. Colors are above me."

Zwaantie clenched her fists. When she was queen, she'd have words with Raaf about what was and what wasn't allowed. Especially with the slaves. A day off now and then and the ability to choose their own clothes should be allowed. After Raaf became grand chancellor, he would be the only one who could influence the Voice. Though Zwaantie had no idea if the Voice would listen to him or not.

"Fine. But you will take my ribbons for your hair and pick a few flowers out of the queen's garden. That's an order. You tell the Voice you'll be disobeying me if you don't."

You cannot tell her to disobey the Voice. Ribbons and flowers are fine, though.

Luna gave a small smile and nodded. "Thank you, Your Highness."

Luna pulled out a purple dress. "This will look striking at the ceremony this morning."

"I think you're right. Purple is very royal, isn't it?"

Luna helped Zwaantie into the dress, did up the laces in the back, and then brushed out Zwaantie's long blonde hair.

"Are you nervous?" Zwaantie asked. She couldn't imagine what it was like to be getting married, though soon she'd be marrying too. There was absolutely no one she wanted to marry. Her mind strayed to the way Phoenix's face lit up when he saw Luna. She could handle waking up to a smile like that. He was a slave though, and marriage to him would be forbidden.

"A little. But mostly I'm happy. Pieter is going to make a good husband."

Zwaantie shuddered. "Seventeen seems too young to get married."

Luna tugged at Zwaantie's hair and gave her a grin in the mirror. "I'm only a year older than you. Careful, I'll bet the queen will be looking for your husband soon."

Zwaantie shook her head violently, and her braid went flying. "I told Mother that I wasn't ready last month when she tried to sit me next to one of the lower princes at dinner." Now that Raaf was home, Mother would be even more insufferable. Zwaantie was too young. She had to find a way to stall her mother.

"Your mother was married at fifteen. She probably thinks you're long overdue."

"She was deeply in love." Zwaantie hoped her mother would let her marry for love. Mother had been a merchant's daughter. Father was the high prince and fell in love with her on sight. The problem was that she wasn't ready to start the search now.

"I hope so. For your sake. Love is pretty amazing." Luna's eyes got that dreamy look she had every time she talked about Pieter. Zwaantie wanted that. She wouldn't settle for anything less, and she certainly didn't want to think about it for at least another two years. Maybe even longer. Mother and Father could still rule for a few years. Surely she didn't literally mean as soon as Raaf returned. Maybe she could talk her mother into letting her wait.

Luna fixed the braid, and Zwaantie spun around. "Okay, you've done your duties with me today. You don't need to do anything else. Go home and get ready for your wedding. I'll see you just after noon."

Luna nodded. "You don't have to come. Really."

"Of course I do. You're my best friend."

Luna gripped her hands. "Thank you."

Luna slipped on her shoes and clip-clopped out the door. Another slave appeared in Zwaantie's doorway only seconds later.

"You're needed in the great hall, Your Highness."

Zwaantie hurried out of the room. Her steps were loud, but then so were all the rest of those bustling about. Zwaantie saw people from all the lower kingdoms. The lower prince of Haul chatted with Princess Luus. Good, maybe he'd marry her, and he'd be off the table. She glanced around for Princess Cornelia to reintroduce her to Raaf, but couldn't find her.

Apparently, a new chancellor was a big deal. Though, Zwaantie thought, this was dumb. Everyone knew the Grand Chancellor had no real power. He was a face; that was all. Someone who let people think they actually had a choice. Someone to advocate for them with the Voice. But the Voice did whatever it wanted anyway.

The Voice did more than just scold. For small indiscretions, it would shame, and for larger ones, it would create physical pain. Most times the pain went away on its own. Bad things still happened on occasion because the Voice had no warning that the person was going to steal or lie. They would confess to their local chancellor when the pain got bad enough, and he gave their name to the grand chancellor, who would plead for the poor soul's sanity with the Voice. Sometimes the Voice listened, and sometimes it did not. Zwaantie had never done anything bad enough to have to confess. Which was good because now she'd have to confess to her brother. She didn't want him knowing the things she'd done. Though she had thought about doing bad things from time to time.

Zwaantie entered the grand hall from the back of the room. Sunlight streamed through the glass on the ceiling. Large white banners with the symbol of the sun hung from rafters. Zwaantie wove her way through the throng of people to the front. Most didn't even notice her, thank the stars. Because if they did, she'd have to make awkward conversation and submit to their fake bows and suck ups.

She climbed the stairs to the thrones. Mother and Father were already seated. She gave a quick curtsey to both and then took her seat in the smaller throne next to Mother.

"There are a lot of people," Zwaantie said.

"A new grand chancellor is an exciting time. We're so proud of your brother. He's really stepping into his role. You could learn a thing or two from him."

Zwaantie rolled her eyes.

Stop that.

Now that Raaf was back, Zwaantie would have to endure the constant comparisons. She was quite aware that her parents wished Raaf had been born first. Then he could be king. Which meant she would've been free to do what she wanted since chancellors were all men. Her life would've been easier. There would've been no expectations.

"Yes, Raaf will do an excellent job. Where is he anyway?" He'd barely said a word to her since he arrived home yesterday. He was at dinner, but spent most of the time talking to Mother and Father about boring politics.

"A few last-minute ceremonies. What they do out here is simply for show. The real act of passing on the chancellor's staff is done in private."

"Well, maybe the Old Mother will come and spice things up."

Mother gasped, and Father shook his head at her.

Do not speak of such things.

Zwaantie gave them a cheeky grin. She made the same comment every time there was a ceremony of sorts. The Old Mother was a legend who everyone feared. Zwaantie had never met her or even met someone who had, but the legend was that she would show up at grand events and make a terrifying prophecy that could only be avoided if someone made a great sacrifice. Luna told her they had the Old Mother legends in Stella as well. Zwaantie supposed that was why she was so fascinated with the stories. They crossed the borders.

A hand came down on her shoulder. "Nice color, Zwaantie."

Zwaantie smiled at her brother. He was handsome with his own purple robes. His face had relaxed. Maybe he had just been nervous about today and would turn back into her Raaf after this.

She looked to Phoenix and gave him a small smile. He returned it, and her heart fluttered. She let out a breath. His smile was going to be the end of her. She focused on Raaf.

"You ready?" she asked.

He nodded. "I hope so. This is just a formality."

He moved past her, his stony face back, bowed to his parents, and took his seat. Phoenix stood behind him. Pieter stepped through a door and stood behind her father.

"What's Pieter doing here?" she hissed to her mother.

"He's your father's slave. Why wouldn't he be here?" Mother cocked her head at Zwaantie like she couldn't understand why Zwaantie would even think such a thing. Zwaantie often sent Luna home early or gave her breaks during the day, but Mother never did the same for Ariel. She had that poor woman working from the time the gray skies cleared until thirty minutes before everyone had to be locked in their rooms.

"He's getting married today. He should have the day off."

Mother shook her head. "Your father will release him after the ceremony."

Zwaantie frowned. "And then he'll be back for dinner, right?"

"Of course. All the lower kings are here. Your father needs help dressing for dinner, and he needs a slave to attend to him during the meal."

Zwaantie had meant the question sarcastically. She couldn't believe her father expected Pieter to come back. She supposed if he had many personal slaves like the lower kings and queens, it wouldn't be an issue, but Mother and Father always thought that was too extravagant.

"Can't someone else attend to him tonight? Maybe Phoenix."

"Phoenix will be busy with your brother. Don't be silly. They're slaves, dear. They understand. This is their life."

Normally Zwaantie didn't have issues with the slave system. It was set up so people didn't starve, and for the most part, the slaves were treated well, but times like this she didn't understand why they couldn't even give them a small break. The system was implemented a few hundred years before. Zwaantie didn't know how it even started.

Her father stood, and the room hushed. With his broad shoulders and brilliant red robes, no one could mistake him for anyone other than the king. Zwaantie always admired the way he led the people. He was beloved. She would not be. She didn't know how to be a good queen.

He held his arms wide and gave the crowd a smile he reserved for his kingdom. Every eye in the room was on him. Zwaantie stared into the crowd. Every color imaginable was represented. Clothes in Sol only came in solid colors. Royalty chose whatever they wanted. Nobility wore every color but purple. Merchants were not allowed to wear red. Peasants wore only yellow and blue. Slaves wore gray.

"Welcome to Zonnes on this glorious occasion," Father said. "It isn't often we get to see the chancellor staff passed on. The last time was when I was but a child. I'm more than pleased to see this honor bestowed upon my son. Thanks be to Sol."

"Thanks be to Sol," Zwaantie and the rest of the crowd repeated.

Father took his seat and the current grand chancellor stepped in front of them. He wore bright white robes and carried a large golden staff.

"Sol has been good to us and the Voice benevolent."

Mother nudged her. She'd zoned out, and now Raaf held the staff, and they were all standing. Stars. What had she missed?

She brought her hands together to clap for him with the rest of the crowd. Most people had smiles on their faces, and she supposed she should be happy for him too, but this was just one more thing that would take him away from her.

Chapter Four

THE WEDDING

Zwaantie hated mingling. She never said the right thing, and she hated talking about the affairs of the kingdom. Just once she'd like one of the princes to ask if she'd read his favorite story or ask about the babies she delivered.

She was much happier just hanging out with Luna. Plus, at things like this, she always felt like people were just talking to her because she was the future queen. She never voiced her thoughts out loud. That would be rude.

She glanced at the glass ceiling. The sun was nearly at high noon. She searched the crowd and found Father. Pieter still hovered behind him.

"Father," she asked, interrupting his conversation with the lower king of Sonnenschein.

You shouldn't interrupt.

"Yes, dear?" He gave her his full attention. That meant he didn't like the conversation he was currently in, because this was rare.

"Pieter is getting married at noon. Don't you think you should let him go?"

Impertinent girl. Do not talk to your father that way. A small pain flashed across her head.

Father pursed his lips and cocked his head. Then he raised his eyebrows. "Uh, yes. I forgot. Pieter, you may go. Be in my rooms by five to help me dress."

Pieter bowed to Father. "Yes, Your Majesty."

Behind Father's head, Pieter mouthed "Thank you" to Zwaantie and disappeared. One boy rescued. Now she had to rescue another. She'd be lucky to get to the wedding on time. She found Raaf deep in conversation with the previous chancellor. Zwaantie tapped him on the shoulder, the earlier chastisement for interrupting still stinging.

He turned to her and gave a forced smile. "Hello, dear sister. What can I do for you?"

The old chancellor leaned on his walking stick. His face was wrinkled, and his eyes sunk so far back that they nearly disappeared. No wonder he was ready to give it up. She hoped the position wouldn't be as hard on Raaf.

"I'm going to Luna's wedding."

"Thank you for letting me know. I'll see you at dinner."

Zwaantie frowned. "I think you should come with me."

He glanced down at her. "Why? It's a slave wedding. I've got better things to do." This was not like him at all. What was going on?

"Because she was your friend too."

Raaf sighed. "She was my playmate when we were children. Honestly, Mother should've known better than that."

Zwaantie clenched her fists. She wasn't going to win this one. "Well, I'll take Phoenix with me then. He'll be back in time to help you dress for dinner."

Raaf glared at her. "No, you won't. I need Phoenix."

Zwaantie's voice rose a couple of notches. "Why the dark would you do that? He's her brother. He needs to attend her wedding." She stomped her foot. This was ridiculous.

Calm down.

She seethed. Now the Voice wouldn't even let her be angry.

"Careful with your speech, Zwaantie. Someone might think you grew up on the streets of Stella. I need my slave. He's not coming with you. You better go if you want to get there on time."

"Fishbrain," Zwaantie muttered under breath.

That was not appropriate. A small pain flashed across her forehead, but it was worth it.

Raaf grabbed her arm. "You will not use that foul Stellan language in my presence again. I am the grand chancellor, and you will treat me as such."

Zwaantie ripped her arm out of his grip. "I thought you were my brother."

His eyes flickered, and for a second, she saw remorse. Good. Maybe he needed to be reminded.

She stomped away and didn't breathe again until she hit the hallway. She squeezed her eyes shut for a second. What was wrong with Raaf? He was not the same person who went off to train. She couldn't think about that right now because she had a wedding to attend and couldn't be late.

She raced to her room and grabbed her green cloak. Merchants wore green cloaks, so she wouldn't stand out. She didn't want to ruin Luna's wedding by turning the attention on herself. Having the crown princess at a slave wedding would make everyone forget who was getting married.

The air outside was getting cooler. Fall was on its way. Zwaantie loved the leaves changing color and the nicer temperatures. Plus, the mage wagons came over from Stella. That was her favorite thing. They came twice a year and brought new potions, but they also always had fun magic, things that weren't technically allowed in Sol; yet, they somehow got away with.

She made her way through the fields to the slave village. The chapel stood in the middle of the little neighborhood. Zwaantie had never been in this one before.

She stepped inside and was surprised to hear the sound of laughter. Though the royal chapel was brighter, it was always a quiet, peaceful place—laughter was forbidden. Plus, slaves were normally somber and quiet. Luna wasn't when she was around Zwaantie, but that was only when they were alone. Everyone in the pews was engaged in conversations with those around them. The atmosphere was happy, in spite of the dull gray color that permeated the room. From the clothes they wore to the bare rough stone walls.

Zwaantie looked to the tinted window in the ceiling, and stared at the sun. Windows were perched over the top of the chapel, so no matter what time of day, you could find the sun. You could generally tell what time it was by what window the sun was in. It was high noon, so the sun was in the north window.

"Sol be with me," she muttered and closed her eyes, as was custom when one looked at the sun.

Zwaantie took her place in the back of the chapel and sat, her hood on. She already stood out as everyone else was wearing gray, but no one said anything to her.

The sounds in the chapel died, and Zwaantie turned. Pieter and Luna stood at the back holding hands, a ribbon tied around their wrists. It was a brilliant blue and was striking against the gold bands. Zwaantie rose, and as Luna passed her, she smiled.

The minister stood in front of the tiny crowd and turned his face to the sun.

He recited the wedding sermon, and Zwaantie watched Pieter and Luna. Pieter had only been at the castle for a year, but he and Luna had eyes for each other from the moment he showed up. She and Luna had many giggles in the evening when Luna would tell stories of her courtship. Zwaantie wasn't surprised a month ago when Luna declared she was getting married. Zwaantie had hoped Luna wouldn't rush things, but such was the way in Sol. When her mother decided that Zwaantie should get married, her own courtship would be only three or four months.

The ceremony was short, and at the end, Pieter kissed Luna. Zwaantie felt a small pang of jealousy. No man had ever looked at her that way. Would she ever find love like that?

Zwaantie followed the crowd out of the chapel and waited behind others to congratulate the couple. She lowered her hood, revealing herself. Immediately everyone dropped to the ground and pressed their faces to the dirty street. Zwaantie grabbed both Pieter and Luna before they could bow as well. She hadn't wanted to reveal herself, but if a royal gift was to be given, it had to be public.

"Stay," she said to Luna and Pieter.

Luna took a deep breath and made no move, so Zwaantie let her go. Pieter nodded as well.

The rest of the crowd was still prostrate on the ground. She wouldn't be able to convince them to stand. No matter how much she pleaded. The Voice was stronger than her command.

"As is custom, when a member of the royal family attends a wedding, you are allowed to ask for a royal gift. What do you wish from me?"

Luna opened her mouth and closed it again. "It is possible..." She frowned. Then she squeezed Pieter's hand. "Your choice."

He cocked his head for a moment. "We'd like our own home so we don't have to share with my family."

"It is done. I'll speak with the housing master when I return to the castle. Now, I must go and let you attend to your festivities. Congratulations."

Zwaantie was troubled. Luna was about to ask for something, but didn't. Zwaantie wanted to know what that was and why she didn't ask for it.

Chapter Five

THE BOY

Zwaantie was almost to the palace's back door when she ran right into Phoenix. He bowed deeply, his black curls falling into his face. Zwaantie had the sudden desire to brush them away.

"Forgive me, Your Highness. I wasn't looking where I was going."

Zwaantie waited for him to come out of the bow and meet her gaze. His eyes were beautiful. "It's okay. Where are you going in such a hurry?"

"I was hoping to make it to the wedding. If you're heading back, I'm guessing it's over."

"It is. I'm sorry. But if you hurry, you can probably catch some of the after party." She didn't stay because no one would relax around her. It wouldn't be fair to Pieter and Luna. She imagined their parties were much more fun than the royal ones. Stars, she hated being a princess.

He creased his thick eyebrows. "What after party?"

"All weddings have parties, right?"

"Not slave weddings. We don't have time. There is a reason it was held during the noon hour. A lot of slaves get lunch then. Most of them are probably back to work by now."

Zwaantie wasn't sure what to think of that revelation. "Well, since you couldn't attend the wedding, would you like to go for a walk with me?" Zwaantie was missing her youth. Her brother was now the grand chancellor, and her best friend was married. Phoenix was the only one left who had no other responsibilities, other than serve her brother. Soon he would be the only one.

He hesitated for a moment. Then a tentative smile spread across his lips. "Sure."

They followed the path to the queen's garden. The flowers smelled heavenly. Birds played in the fountains, and butterflies fluttered around her head.

"I'm sorry you had to miss your sister's wedding."

He shrugged. "I knew it was a possibility. I'll congratulate her tonight after dinner."

"How did you get away from Raaf?" Raff'd been such a turd about letting him go, and now here he was.

"He said he had things to discuss with the old chancellor in private, so I left. That happened a lot when he was training. I hung out with the guards quite a bit. As long as I'm in time to help him dress for dinner, he won't miss me."

Phoenix smiled at her, and Zwaantie was again struck by the fact that he was no longer a boy. Working out with the guards must've been how his muscles developed. He looked at her, his dark eyes sparkling, and her heart skipped a beat. She dropped her eyes, embarrassed at her thoughts.

"Now that Luna's married, will you be next?" she asked, hoping for a reason to deflect her feelings.

He laughed. "Oh, no. Not even close."

"Why not?"

"Because I'm not ready for that."

She could completely relate. They came to a fork in the path. One route led deeper into the garden and the other to the woods. "Do you ever miss the times when we were kids, running around in the woods?"

He gave a small laugh. "You and Raaf would get in such trouble when you came back covered in dirt and grass."

Zwaantie chuckled. "And somehow you and Luna didn't."

"Our mother didn't care."

Zwaantie played with the petals on a pink rose. "I miss it. I miss being kids. I don't like how everyone is growing up."

Phoenix shoved his hands into his pockets. "I know. Raaf and I were close until we left for his training. He doesn't even talk to me anymore."

"Me either."

Zwaantie's heart swelled with the unfairness of it all. Life was moving too fast. She looked out past the flowers and saw the pond they used to play by.

"Let's be kids again," she said.

"What do you mean?"

"Meet me by the rock after dinner. Let's play tag in the woods. Just one last time."

Phoenix frowned. "Zwaantie, we're not kids anymore."

She took a couple of steps closer to him. He held his breath, and his eyes bore deep into hers. She wondered what kind of effect she was having on him. "I know. But we can pretend. Just for one night. Please?"

He let out his breath. "As long as Raaf lets me go at a reasonable hour."

She squealed. "Oh, this is going to be so much fun. It almost makes dinner with the lower kings and queens bearable."

Phoenix shook his head. "Not quite."

He left her in the garden a few minutes later, and she wandered by a fountain, deep in thought.

Earlier today, her mother made sure she talked to at least two of the lower princes. Zwaantie cringed at the idea of even considering a life with them. Phoenix though, just the thought of spending time with him made her giddy. That was probably because she was just excited to play again. Though her thoughts were not on how they used to play, but about how he looked at her so seriously.

She shook away the thought of his beautiful face. He was a slave. She made her way to the castle and found the housing office.

The squat housing master greeted her. "How can I help you, Your Highness?"

"I granted a gift at a slave wedding this afternoon. Luna and Pieter would like their own house. Can you make that happen?"

"Of course."

"Thank you. Please outfit it with the best furniture, the kind you would use in the castle, and fill the cupboards with the finest dishes and linens. Also, fill the pantry and icebox with food. Can you do that before this evening?"

The housemaster looked skeptical, but he gave a tight smile. "Of course, Your Highness." Zwaantie knew that was short timing, but she'd seen her mother ask for more, and they always pulled through.

"Thank you. You can deliver the key to my room during dinner."

Zwaantie didn't know what Luna really wanted to ask her for, but she'd make sure her gift was the best she could give.

Zwaantie had several hours before dinner, so she slipped out the side door and down the rocky path to Wilma's cottage. She didn't bother knocking. By now this was practically Zwaantie's second home.

She found Wilma in the tiny kitchen washing herbs in a large ceramic pot. She marched into the kitchen, and Wilma turned.

"I thought I heard you. Did you ask your mother about the medicines?"

Zwaantie leaned on the counter and inhaled the scent of basil and lavender. Wilma's house always smelled amazing.

"No, but I met a Stellan and paid him two months of merchant food to send someone as soon as possible."

Wilma dropped the lavender into the water. "Two months? That seems steep."

"We need the medicine. I'm hoping that by overpaying he'll be honest about it."

Stellans couldn't produce food because they had no sun, so they traded their magic for food. It worked well and provided Sol medicine and other things that made life easier.

Zwaantie didn't want to lose the sun, but she often wondered what it was like on the other side of the wall. Most Solites wouldn't even dream of wanting to see Stella. Almost all the stories of the Stellans painted them as barbarians, but Zwaantie had Phoenix and Luna, so she was more curious than horrified.

"How was the ceremony?" Wilma asked.

"Raaf or Luna?"

Wilma shook out the lavender, sending water everywhere. "Both."

"I enjoyed the wedding more. Raaf seems different." Zwaantie fiddled with a spoon.

Wilma brought her bowl of herbs to the table. "How do you mean?"

"I don't know. He's barely said anything to me. I was looking forward to having my brother again."

Wilma handed her several stems of basil. "Pull the leaves off these and put them in the bowl."

Wilma preached that the best medicine for the mind was work. Zwaantie should've known that if she came here whining, Wilma would put her to work. She did as she was told though because if she stayed long enough, Wilma's advice would be worth it.

"I've known both of you since you were babies. Raaf's always looked up to you. When he left, you were children. Do you remember how he cried?"

Zwaantie did. It was the only time she'd seen him do so. He could barely say goodbye to her. She'd been bawling too, but that wasn't so unusual for her at the time. She was better at controlling her emotions now.

"That's what I don't get. Shouldn't he be more excited to see me?"

"You're not kids anymore. He knows you're about to become queen. When that happens, he'll have to answer to you. That's not easy for someone who was once your best friend."

Zwaantie accidentally shredded a few leaves. Wilma growled at her and handed her another stem. "Try not to ruin these. I don't have an unlimited supply."

"Sorry. I still want him to be my best friend, but he seems so distant."

"Have you talked to him in private or only while your parents are around?"

"Only when Mother and Father are there."

"Try getting him alone. I bet you'll be surprised by how much he missed you too."

"Maybe." Zwaantie wanted Wilma to be right, but she wasn't sure. Raaf felt so far away. She wasn't comfortable with all this change. Adulthood was being forced on her, and she wasn't ready.

Chapter Six

THE COW: PART 1

Luna returned before Zwaantie had to get ready for dinner. Zwaantie protested, but Luna reminded her that Pieter was working anyway, so there was no reason for her not to attend to Zwaantie. On the way to dinner, Mother caught up with them in the hallway.

"Tonight you will be seated next to the prince of Sonnenschein."

Zwaantie groaned.

Stop that. She's your mother. You will listen to her.

"Yes, Mother." Zwaantie wrung her hands. "Is this necessary? I'm not ready to think of marriage. Especially not with Vache. He's horrible."

Mother sighed, but her eyes softened. "I know. Like it or not, the time has come. I know it's scary, but this is just the beginning. Your brother is grand chancellor. It's time for you to start exploring your options. Sonnenschein is a good city and the largest outside of ours. They know what it takes to run a large kingdom. He's smart, and he'd be a good match for you. Be charming."

Zwaantie rolled her eyes.

Stop being disrespectful.

"Yes, Mother." It was easy for her to suggest him. She wouldn't

47

have to look at him every day. He looked like a cow. She and Luna followed Mother to the dining room.

Several tables had been set up in the room in a u-shape so that all could see the king and queen. People sat on the outer edges and slaves served from the other side. Zwaantie took her place next to the cow-man, and he smiled at her. Vache had huge green eyes, wide nostrils, and a fuzzy white patch on his cheek. He was maybe a year or two older than her.

"Crown Princess Zwaantie, it's a pleasure to sit with you." His voice was surprisingly high for a young man his size. Zwaantie had forgotten how annoying it was.

This was going to be a long night. He and his father always made their view of her intelligence clear when they attended the monthly meetings. Vache wanted to be high king and didn't give a piggy's teat about her. Of the four possibilities, he was on the bottom of the list, but the most eager to make a match.

The prince tugged at his collar and adjusted the vest that strained against his girth. They must eat a lot more in Sonnenschein than those in the capital city. Zwaantie had to admit, though, the best cakes and cookies come from Sonnenschein.

Vache spoke again, startling her once more with the high pitch. "You have a lovely home."

"Thank you," she replied, irritated. He'd been to her home dozens of times. Surely he could come up with a better conversation starter.

A serving slave stood before her. "Wine or water?"

"Wine, please." There was no way she would get through the evening tonight on water. The wine was weak, but it relaxed her all the same.

Vache cleared his throat. And then began talking. He talked for the next two hours. Even when his mouth was full, he was jabbering on about something. Watching cattle graze was more exciting than listening to him. There was no way in the dark sky she would marry this prince.

Zwaantie looked around the room so she wouldn't fall asleep. Raaf was seated several people away, and Princess Cornelia was next to him, thank the stars. They looked like they were having a better conversation than she and her wretched prince. Mother and Father sat at the head where everyone could see them. Behind Father, Pieter stood tall, his eyes locked on Luna. Zwaantie didn't know what it would be like to feel that way about someone. To love them so much that you couldn't take your eyes off of them. Slave or not, Zwaantie was jealous of Luna's life.

Vache reached for his goblet and brushed Zwaantie's arm. She jerked away. She needed to stop this right now even if it meant getting into trouble. Then Mother would see that she was too immature to entertain suitors and become queen. This man was a cow, and Zwaantie intended to prove it.

She sat tall, pursed her lips, and with a perfectly straight face said, "Moo for me."

A giggle escaped Luna.

"Excuse me?" Vache scowled. Zwaantie didn't even flinch, just repeated her request.

"I would like you to moo for me. You know, like a cow. Moo." The Voice was going berserk in her head.

Stop being disrespectful.

Apologize to him.

Stop this.

Vache's eyes went wide, and for a half second, Zwaantie thought he'd actually do it. But she was to be disappointed.

"No. I will not be disrespected like this." His chin jiggled.

Apologize.

A pain shot through her forehead. She didn't have the energy to fight it. Everything about tonight made her tired.

"You are right. I don't know what is wrong with me. The wine must've gone to my head. Forgive me."

Zwaantie pushed her chair out and escaped toward her room. She had stayed long enough that her departure didn't draw any unnecessary attention. Luna followed.

Zwaantie flung herself down on her couch and covered her eyes with her arm. She'd screwed up this time.

"Your mother is going to have your tail for that one," Luna said.

"I know. Worth it." Zwaantie gave a grin that she didn't mean, but she couldn't let Luna see her pain. Raaf was grand chancellor. Luna was married. Mother wanted her to take the crown. She would have to be responsible for the entire kingdom. The thought made her physically ill.

Luna sighed and folded down Zwaantie's bed. "If you say so."

A knock sounded on the door. Mother was fast. Zwaantie wasn't ready to face her, but Luna answered it.

"A delivery for the crown princess," Luna declared, shutting the door.

Luna brought her a small box wrapped with a deep green ribbon. Zwaantie opened it carefully. Then she grinned. "This isn't for me. It's for you."

"What is it?"

Zwaantie handed her the box. Luna opened it and pulled out a key with the number fifty-four etched on it.

"It's your new home. I hope you like it."

Luna clutched at the key. "Thank you. You've been too kind to us."

Zwaantie waved her hand. "Nonsense. You're my best friend. I should've done more." Zwaantie hesitated for minute. She wasn't sure if she should ask or not, because she suspected there was more that Luna wanted. "Can I ask you a question though?"

"Sure." Luna was still staring at the key.

"You were about to ask me for something different at the wedding. What was it?"

Luna shook her head and placed the key back in the small box. Then she tucked the box into the pocket of her faded gray skirt.

Zwaantie sat up straight. "Tell me. I won't be mad, I promise."

"It's nothing, really. The house was so generous."

Zwaantie grabbed Luna's hands and met her dark eyes. "Tell me. Please"

Luna let out a breath. "I was going to ask if our children could be born free."

Zwaantie's heart stilled. Then she did something she'd rarely done before. She stood and pulled Luna into a tight hug. "I'm sorry. I can't do that. I wish I could."

Luna nodded into her shoulder. "I know. That's why I didn't ask."

The bondage bands were magical. Once placed upon a slave, it was a hundred-year sentence for the slave and all of his or her posterity. Luna's mother was the first, and so there would be at least two or three generations before the bands would fall off. Zwaantie couldn't change that.

Luna pulled away and wiped at the tears on her face. "Come on. Let's get you dressed for bed."

Another knock sounded just as Zwaantie opened her mouth to argue.

Three guesses who was at the door. Mother. Mother. Mother.

Luna opened the door wide. Mother stalked into the room, her thin lips in a tight line.

"You asked him to moo for you?" She raised her eyebrows. "Honestly, Zwaantie. Could you have been any more disrespectful? Didn't the Voice tell you to keep your mouth shut?"

Mother sat in a dainty white chair. She seemed perfect for the chair, her grace and poise filled but did not overwhelm it. She was the ideal queen, something Zwaantie realized she would never be. She hated the proper stuff.

Zwaantie sank onto the couch. "I don't want to marry. I can rule without a husband."

"But what about heirs?"

Was Mother really going there? Fine. Zwaantie was ready to end this once and for all.

"Raaf can have them. I'm sure he'd be thrilled with the idea that his kids will one day rule all of Sol. I'm not ready to discuss this. Besides, do you think that I can honestly love that man?"

Do not speak to your mother in such a manner.

"Honor is more important than love." Mother spoke with so much conviction. Like it wasn't even possible to consider the other side of things.

Zwaantie was so sick of that argument. If it wasn't about marriage, it was something else. Honor was more important than friends. Honor was more important than self. Honor was more important than pride. Now it was more important than love. Fine. She'd do the honorable thing and become queen, but she was going to control some aspect of her life. She couldn't just give her entire self away.

"I don't see how I can be a dishonorable queen if I don't marry."

"It's your duty to the people of Sol to present them a queen who will give them an heir. Besides, the people expect you to have a husband."

"Love, Mother, I want love." And freedom, but she couldn't express that out loud. She was just as trapped as Luna, if not more.

"You can marry for love. Is there a merchant's son you would rather have?"

"I thought you wanted me to marry a prince."

"I do. But I don't want to see you unhappy."

Couldn't she see that Zwaantie simply wasn't ready to think about that? But...since Mother brought it up.

"You are saying I could marry whomever I like?" Zwaantie couldn't help her thoughts. Phoenix filled her mind. She'd be queen a thousand times over if Mother would just let her control this one small aspect of her life. She wasn't expecting Mother to be reasonable about this though.

Mother sighed and brushed a hand through her hair. "Yes, of course. We are not opposed to marriage outside the royal ranks. We just thought you'd be happier with someone of your own kind. Now who do you want to marry?"

"Suppose I wanted to marry a slave. Then what?"

Stop being ridiculous.

Sometimes Zwaantie hated having two mothers.

"That's impossible." Mother dismissed the idea with a wave. She was right of course. Zwaantie just wanted to hear her say it. "Now you are being silly." Mother stood and crossed her arms. "It's time for you to grow up. You will be queen, and I recommend finding a husband who will be a good king, like the prince you just insulted."

Zwaantie resisted the urge to stick her tongue out like a child.

"Also, I'm entertaining the lower queens and princesses in my rooms late this evening. Your presence is required. You will give the queen of Sonnenschein an apology."

"Yes, Mother."

Mother left without saying anything more.

"I want to be alone," said Zwaantie. If she was going to go play in the woods, she needed to get rid of Luna.

"But what about your mother? You'll need me to attend to you."

"I'll be fine."

Luna left quickly. It was her wedding night. Zwaantie hoped Father let Pieter off early as well.

Zwaantie had no intentions of going to the see the queens and princesses. She had two hours until midnight, and she had every intention of making the most of it. She'd pay for it tomorrow, but tonight, she was going to be a child. Responsibilities were for those who actually wanted to be queen.

Chapter Seven

THE POND

Zwaantie shut her door with a click and looked around. The dark hallway was empty. She snuck down the hall and turned a corner. A slave with arms full of tablecloths scurried by but didn't look up. Soon she was at the back door. She creaked it open and slid out into the garden.

It's late. Go back to your room.

"Oh, you shush," she told the Voice. "I'm not doing anything wrong, just going for a walk. I'll be in before midnight." She could never figure out how the Voice could sometimes scold her for things that weren't wrong at all. There was never pain associated with it, just words, but it was still annoying.

The smell of the flowers overwhelmed her. She loved early fall. Except for the rain. The ground was always squishy and wet. She kept to the stone path where her wooden shoes clacked against the ground. She thought about taking them off because of the noise, but no one was around. Plus, she didn't want to get her socks wet. Not that she planned on staying dry this evening. Every adventure in the woods ended with someone being soaked from the wet ground or an accidental trip into the pond. A smile crept upon her lips without warning. She felt a little rebellious sneaking out to play with Phoenix.

The path wove farther and farther into the garden. She came to a fork and took the left one. The right path would lead to the queen's garden, which was filled with peonies and mums and usually people. The left path led to a pond that smelled like dead fish. Though Zwaantie didn't like the smell, that was where they played as children because no one else was around.

When she arrived, Phoenix was already there, sitting upon a large rock, watching the sun slipping toward the gray. His back was to her, and she paused to watch him. His dark hair settled just above his shoulders. A small thrill buzzed in her stomach. What would it feel like to run her fingers through those curls or have him stare at her with those deep brown eyes?

She squished her way across the grass to him. He heard her and turned. He smiled wide and patted the rock. Zwaantie's dress pulled at her neck as she climbed up. She hiked up her skirt so the dress wouldn't strangle her. She envied the people of Sonnenschein just a little because their clothes allowed a bit of the neck to show. Here in Zonnes, they covered the entire neck. Most of the time it didn't bother Zwaantie, but when she climbed rocks or trees, her clothes tried to kill her.

"You ready to play?" she asked.

"In a minute. I like watching the sky from this rock. When we were kids, I sat out here all the time, even when you three weren't around."

"Why?"

"It's peaceful."

She settled next to him and put her hand on the rock so her fingers barely touched his. He didn't react, but she shivered. She was playing with fire. But she hadn't done anything wrong yet, so the Voice couldn't say anything.

"Where do you suppose the sun goes?" he asked. After midnight, the sun disappeared into the clouds and a deep gray settled across the sky, but it never went completely dark.

"I've no idea. I've always wondered what the stars look like."

"They're amazing. I miss them," he said.

"You remember? Tell me about them."

"Millions of tiny dots in the dark, dark sky. They make me feel like anything is possible."

"Maybe someday you'll see them again."

"Yeah, right," he said, pointing to his bands.

Zwaantie let out a deep breath. She didn't want to be reminded of his place. She wanted him to be her equal. "Tell me a story. A funny one."

"Since when did you become so demanding?" he asked with a wide grin.

"Because I miss laughing. Everyone has been altogether too serious today."

"Sorry, I'm out of funny stories," he said with a grin.

"You're telling me my brother didn't do one stupid thing today?"

"Nothing worth telling a story over. However, I heard his sister got herself into some trouble." He winked and chuckled.

Zwaantie sat up straight. "How did you know about that?"

"We were with your mother when that oaf of a prince came lumbering over. Did you really ask him to moo for you?" Phoenix raised a brow at her.

Zwaantie let out a bellow, and Phoenix laughed.

"Okay, no funny stories if that's all you've got." Zwaantie hopped off the rock and challenged him. "If you can catch me, you can do whatever you want with me." This was a game the four of them played a lot as kids. The one caught would often be tickled or have their socks stripped off and have to step into the pond.

He crossed his arms and smirked. "Anything?"

Zwaantie nodded and took a half step away from the rock. She kicked off her shoes and pulled off her socks. The grass was soft and squishy.

Put your shoes on. Your feet will get dirty.

Zwaantie ignored the Voice and felt a dull ache behind her eyes. It was bearable. Phoenix eyed her bare ankles and grinned.

"Even throw you into the stinky pond?"

He wouldn't do that. It was a joke they played a lot as kids, but no one ever actually threw anyone into the filthy pond. "Yep, even that."

"You're on." He stood, and she ran. He hit the ground a few paces away from her. She raced toward the woods. He was better in the trees than Zwaantie, but she wanted him to catch her. Though, she didn't want to go into the pond.

The ground in the woods was soft and warm, coated with damp

leaves. Zwaantie darted around a couple of trees and then noticed she couldn't hear him. He must've taken his shoes off.

She snuck around a wide old oak tree. Phoenix was nowhere in sight. She dashed out and ran across a small clearing. Something crashed into her from the side, and she went flying. Zwaantie hit the ground on her hip and rolled, but he pinned her down.

"Gotcha," Phoenix whispered into her ear. She giggled as he picked her up and threw her over his shoulder. She liked the feel of his arms wrapped around her legs. The Voice sighed, but didn't say anything. Technically, they'd done nothing wrong, so it couldn't find anything to lecture her on.

"Where are you going?" Zwaantie asked.

"Back to the pond."

"You're not really going to throw me in there, are you?" A tiny bit of fear crept into her stomach.

"You said anything." He laughed, and the motion shook his whole body. Zwaantie struggled against his arms, but he held tight. He wouldn't throw her into the pond. Would he?

She smelled the pond before she saw it. She couldn't see much from his back.

"Ready?" he asked.

"No."

He laughed and swung her off his shoulder. He laid her on the ground and straddled her, holding both of her wrists in one of his hands. The wet earth seeped into her back, but she barely noticed. His strong grip on her hands, the way his legs felt on her sides, the pressure of his body on her stomach, warmth flooded her body, and her heart raced.

His chest rose and fell in rapid breaths, and he gave her a devastating grin. She wanted to kiss that smile right off his mouth, wanted to run her hands up his chest and embrace him.

Phoenix leaned down so that his mouth was inches from Zwaantie's ear. "You didn't really think I'd throw you in there, did you?"

She shook her head, not daring to speak in case she accidentally said the things she was thinking. She loved the feeling of him pressed against her.

His breath was light on her ear. "But I am going to tickle you until you pee your pants."

Zwaantie squirmed and squealed. His hand found her ribs, and she couldn't help but laugh. He proceeded to torture her for the next few minutes.

"Stop. Please." She could barely get her words out through her laughter.

Then he released her and rolled to the side. Zwaantie propped her head up and faced him. Her hair fell across her hand and into the grass. Luna would kill her tomorrow; Zwaantie's hair would be in thick knots. The blonde would probably be streaked with green from the grass.

Zwaantie reached across and placed her hand on one of Phoenix's. This was a risky move. She didn't even know what she was doing, but she had to do something to appease the desire in her chest.

"We should go. Midnight will be here soon." Phoenix stood. His rejection stung.

"I don't want to. We could just stay here." Zwaantie sat up and searched his eyes for any indication that he agreed with her. She saw the conflict in his face.

"You know the punishment for being caught out of bed after midnight."

That depended on Raaf's mood. And he wouldn't behead Zwaantie or Phoenix, which was the normal punishment. After midnight, the Voice turned off, so anything could happen. The chancellors always assumed the worst. Why else would someone stay out? Or at least that was the reasoning of the chancellors. But whatever Raaf chose to do to them still wouldn't be pleasant.

"No one will catch us out here."

Phoenix grinned. "You have a point. But who knows what we'll do after midnight. We could go crazy and murder the guards."

She stood and brushed off her skirt. "You don't honestly buy that bull that they feed you about what happens after midnight? Have you ever stayed awake?"

"Yes," he replied.

"Then you know you don't go crazy. You just think differently and nothing seems wrong."

"But the guard would notice if I wasn't there to get locked up, and I would be in serious trouble. Plus, it's not safe. You know this." It was true. Because the Voice turned off, anyone could do anything without repercussion. As children, they were warned about the evil that lurked in the midnight hours.

"I know. I'm just not ready to go in."

"Me either. This was fun. Would you like to meet again tomorrow?" he asked.

"I'd love to." She smiled at him, and he returned the smile. Her insides tingled. The things she could do with that boy after midnight. Thousands of thousands of kisses. She grabbed his hand and squeezed. He squeezed back without looking at her and then disappeared down the path.

Judging from the color of the sky, she had about twenty minutes. It would take her at least fifteen to get to her room. It was light enough to see outside, but inside the castle, it got pretty dark. Because of the constant sunlight, they didn't use candles often.

Zwaantie hesitated, wondering what she would do if she chose not to lock herself in her room. Hide out somewhere, probably. Those stories she was told as a child still lingered in her mind. After midnight she could be raped or murdered.

Time, Princess. It is time to go in. You don't want to be caught outside after midnight.

Zwaantie obeyed reluctantly. The headache wouldn't be worth it. She gathered her shoes and socks and meandered down the path barefoot.

As she turned the corner toward her room, she saw a guard marching down the hall locking doors. She hurried. The Voice urged her to run. She settled on a light jog. All over the kingdom, guards were locking doors of homes to protect the people from those who stayed out. It was the only time of day that the Voice couldn't protect them.

The guard waited by her door. "Cutting it a little close, aren't we, Princess?"

"But on time."

"Dangerous out there after midnight. People do crazy things."

The clock tower began its twelve o'clock strike. Zwaantie felt a change in the air. The sun had slipped into the gray, taking the Voice with it. The guard's eyes went ice blue, and he looked at her differently, like she was no longer a princess but a girl who was beneath him. The midnight hour had come. Zwaantie slid into her room, shut the door, and waited to hear the door lock from the outside. After a few seconds, it did, and she was safe from the night. From both the guard and herself.

Most nights Zwaantie stayed awake and contemplated all that was wrong with the world. Tonight, she just wanted to sleep. She searched for the laces in the back of her dress to undo it. Her fingers fumbled for a few moments and finally gave up. She crawled under the covers with her dress on and fell into a deep sleep.

Chapter Eight

THE GAME

The next day Zwaantie woke feeling giddy. She'd never felt this way before. She clung to it, desperate for the freedom it promised. Falling for Phoenix was dangerous, but for now, she didn't care. She rolled out of bed and tried to ignore Luna's disapproving glare.

"Mud, grass, and sticks. How old are you?" Luna tugged the dress down and tossed it into a basket. Then she took in the bed.

"Next time you decide to go rolling around by the pond with my brother at least take your dress off before you get into bed." She pulled the cover over the grass and dirt on the white sheets. "I'll take care of this later."

"How'd you know I'd been with Phoenix?"

"Because he came home looking just like you. I'm not dumb."

"I thought you had your own house now."

"I do. But it's closer to the castle than mother's house, and so Phoenix stayed with us. He didn't think he'd make it home on time. Zwaantie, what are you doing?"

"It's not like we did anything. I was just missing my childhood. We played tag."

Luna sat Zwaantie down in front of the mirror and frowned.

"You know, we're not kids anymore. It's probably not a good idea to go sneaking around the woods together. Besides, I thought you were supposed to be with your mother and the lower queens."

Zwaantie spun around. Luna was trying to take away the only thing she had control over. Plus, they were growing up way too fast. They should do more running around in the woods. "That's ridiculous. There's nothing wrong with trying to hang onto our youth. In fact, you and I are going to dig out Sticks and Serpents and go play with Raaf and Phoenix this afternoon."

Luna motioned for Zwaantie to turn around, and continued her brushing. "Are you sure? I don't want you to be disappointed if Raaf says no."

"Wilma said that maybe I just needed to get him on his own for a bit. It's a good way to ease into a conversation. I miss him." She did. Part of her just wanted to see Phoenix, but she was also doing this for her brother. She needed him too. Maybe she could put her life back together on her own, and then she'd have allies to help her figure out how to avoid becoming queen. Raaf was an important ally.

"I know you do. Now come on, let's get you dressed, or you're going to miss lunch."

"Is it that late?"

"Yes. You know, when you become queen, you won't be able to sleep in anymore."

Every time Zwaantie turned around, someone was reminding her of her place. She was so sick of this.

"Hopefully I won't have to think about that for a long time."

Zwaantie arrived to lunch a little late. The lower royal families had gone home. Mother scowled at her.

"I expected to see you in my room last night."

Zwaantie picked up her napkin and spread it across her lap. "I know. I'm sorry. I closed my eyes for a few moments and didn't wake up until my door had been locked."

Mother sighed. "Zwaantie, you need to start taking more responsibility. You'll be queen soon."

Zwaantie didn't bother to argue. That was the problem. Mother couldn't see that she wasn't responsible enough to be queen.

～

RAAF HAD MENTIONED AT LUNCH THAT HIS AFTERNOON WAS FREE AND he was hoping to catch up on his paperwork, whatever that meant. Zwaantie planned on making him put away his paperwork for her.

An hour after they ate, Zwaantie and Luna stood at Raaf's door with Sticks and Serpents in hand. Luna knocked, and Phoenix answered. Zwaantie saw his face and had to suppress her smile.

"Zwaantie would like to talk to Raaf."

"Of course, come in. I'll go get him." He went through a side door. There were all kinds of hidden and side passages throughout the castle to make it easier for the royal family to get to their offices.

Zwaantie and Luna entered. Zwaantie stopped short. She hadn't seen his room since he'd returned. Before he left, it was decorated in blues and greens, and toys were scattered everywhere. Now it was stark white. Everything from the comforter on his bed to the stiff couches near the fireplace.

Zwaantie and Luna sat on the horribly uncomfortable couch and set the game on the table. Phoenix returned a few moments later and grinned at the game.

"Oh man. We haven't played that in years."

"I know. I'm going to talk Raaf into playing."

Phoenix met her eyes for a second. "I hope you're successful. Raaf could use a few more laughs."

Moments later Raaf collapsed into the chair across from her. "A game, really?"

"I thought you could use a break."

His stony face changed into a grin. "You have no idea. You know what four years of training and a few days on the job has taught me?"

"What?" Zwaantie asked, her eyes flicking to Phoenix. She couldn't stop looking at him.

"Being grand chancellor is boring."

Phoenix chuckled. "Being your slave is no party either."

Raaf shoved Phoenix's shoulder. "I can give you more work if you want. Have you seen my shoes? They're filthy."

Zwaantie snorted. "Being queen will be duller. Have you ever been in on those monthly meetings?"

Raaf shook his head.

"Oh yeah, I didn't start going until after you left. Well, I'm sure you'll go now because the old grand chancellor always did. Not exciting in the least."

"I have to prod her to keep her awake," Luna said.

"What are you waiting for? Let's play," Raaf said.

Zwaantie opened the box with relief. Maybe she'd been mistaken on how much Raaf had changed. Raaf dealt out the cards. Zwaantie peeked over hers at Phoenix. His brow was furrowed as he looked over his cards. He was adorable when he was thinking.

They started to play. Zwaantie had picked this game because it allowed for a lot of talk time.

"What exactly did you do in training anyway?" Zwaantie asked.

"I read a lot of books."

"Really, that's it? Why did you have to go so far away?" Zwaantie still didn't know where he'd gone. Only that letters took a week or more to get to her.

"I asked that question a time or two. The only answer they gave was that I would concentrate more if I didn't have any distractions. Most of the time, it was just me and a chancellor locked in a room. The lower chancellors rotated every week, and the grand chancellor came a few times a year. But I learned everything I never wanted to know about the Voice and Sol. Some of it was interesting, but most of it was boring."

"Tell us something interesting," Luna said.

Raaf set down his cards and tapped his chin. "Did you know that the Voice can actually force you to do something?"

"What do you mean?" Phoenix asked.

"Well, our only experience with the Voice is that it scolds and causes pain. But sometimes it will stop people from doing horrible things after they start. So if someone started beating someone, the Voice can force them to stop."

Zwaantie shivered. She hoped the Voice would never force her to do anything she didn't want to do. That seemed dangerous.

Phoenix picked up a serpent card. "You know, no one actually knows what a serpent looks like, but I don't think this is it."

"Are you saying serpents are something different?" Zwaantie asked.

"Yeah, we had them in Stella, but they only come out after

midnight." He paused for a second. "The Voice doesn't want me talking about that. Sorry."

Zwaantie rarely heard Phoenix or Luna voluntarily talk about Stella. She supposed Luna didn't remember much, but Phoenix might. He was two years older than his sister.

"Why did you come to Sol anyway?"

"Our dad died, and mom didn't have many skills. She failed out of mage school. Mom's sister was a trader and married a Solite and settled down here. She told mom to come on over, and she'd take care of her."

Luna stiffened next to her, and Zwaantie wondered how bad this story was going to get.

Phoenix set down a few cards. "When we arrived, we discovered she'd married a cruel man, and after a month, he threw us out on the street. We had no way to get food, and by then we'd been in Sol long enough that the Voice wouldn't let us go home. Mom had no choice but to become a slave."

Zwaantie felt sick to her stomach. She didn't want to know this story.

Raaf cocked his head at Phoenix. "How could he be cruel? The Voice wouldn't let him."

Phoenix sneered. "The Voice is not all knowing. There are a lot of things a person with a sadistic nature can still do."

"Like what?" Raaf asked. "The whole point of the Voice is to stop people from doing bad things. I just spent the better part of four years learning about this. It's not possible for someone to be evil."

"Yes it is. You're not allowed to starve your children, but you can give them only a tiny amount of food so they'll never feel full. I can't hit my sister, but if I were to tease her and play a little rough on purpose, the Voice wouldn't be able to tell the difference. Those kinds of things. Plus, all bets are off after midnight. The guards can lock you in your homes, but what happens behind closed doors stays behind closed doors."

Raaf frowned, and Zwaantie wondered what he was thinking. She'd known that was possible. She couldn't figure out why he hadn't. Maybe it was because she tested the Voice often. Perhaps Raaf never walked the line. Never tried to see what he could get away with.

Luna threw down her cards. Ten sticks and ten serpents. "Ha, I win."

They played three more games, and the conversation turned lighter. It was relaxing and fun. Zwaantie took every opportunity she could to watch Phoenix, and she noticed him doing the same. She hoped that no one else saw. She was falling fast.

Chapter Nine

THE COMPLICATION

Thoughts of Phoenix bothered Zwaantie all week. She kept losing track of what she was doing and couldn't stop thinking about the way his eyes met hers or the smile that formed on his lips every time they crossed in the hallway. This had never happened before. They'd met every night except one when he had to stay with Raaf. Was he thinking of her too?

She and Luna spent the day hiding out in Wilma's cottage sorting potions and cutting herbs. She didn't want to risk running into Mother and discussing her duties or the princes. Last night Mother had offered to travel to Haul to visit with the prince there. She said Raaf wanted to see Cornelia anyway. Zwaantie wasn't going to give Mother another opportunity to make her go away. She wanted to stay here in the castle where she and Phoenix had a refuge. A place to be together, but not together. He was on her mind constantly, and that unsettled her.

She couldn't shake her thoughts. After dinner, she practically ran to the rock by the pond. She beat him this time, climbing onto the rock and watching a couple swans in the pond. There was clean water just on the other side of the hedges, but the swans wanted to play in the dirty water. Maybe they were hiding from others as well.

She'd been so focused on the swans that she hadn't heard Phoenix arrive. He touched her shoulder, and she jumped, nearly falling off the rock. He grabbed her, wrapping his arm around her waist, and when they steadied, she found her face inches from his. His lips were so close. She leaned closer, wanting to feel them on hers, but he backed away.

She let out a breath of frustration.

"Are you okay?" he asked, his eyes serious.

She straightened her dress. "Yes. But you shouldn't sneak up on me like that. I nearly fell off."

"I wouldn't let you fall. How was your day?" he asked.

She shrugged. "Boring."

"Mine as well. Your brother spends more and more time alone."

"Don't a lot of people come to visit him to confess?"

"Yes, but he only takes confessions for a few hours a day. He spends time in the evenings with the guards, but that's it."

She grumbled. "He's doing all this grown-up stuff. Soon I will have too as well. I'm not looking forward to that."

"I can picture it now. You in those meetings with all the lower kings and queens, bossing them around."

"Oh no. I don't want to attend those stupid meetings. Maybe I can delegate that to my husband." The word was out of her mouth before she could stop it. She would have a husband. She didn't want to think about a possible spouse. Because that person wouldn't be Phoenix.

Phoenix wiggled his eyebrows. "Any idea who it might be?"

"No. Not yet."

They both went quiet. She looked down and saw his hand splayed on the rock. She wanted to hold it. His fingers were long, and she wondered what they would feel like woven in with hers. This would be brave and daring, and she would risk a headache and a thorough telling off, but maybe, if she was careful, the Voice wouldn't even notice.

She moved her hand so their fingers were touching. He didn't move. This was a good sign.

"Have you seen Luna's new house yet?" she asked.

Phoenix nodded. "Yes. I stay there a lot. The beds are nicer."

Zwaantie slid her fingers across the top of Phoenix's. Neither said anything for a long second. Then he flipped his hand over and wove his fingers into hers. A thrill buzzed in Zwaantie's chest.

She was surprised the Voice wasn't berating her. Physical touch was discouraged, but holding hands wasn't forbidden. She supposed the Voice could find nothing wrong with this.

"Princess, you know that I am a slave."

"Yes. I do."

"Then why do you..." His words trailed off, but Zwaantie understood. He couldn't say anything. He didn't want to bring their clasped hands to the Voice's attention any more than she did. If Phoenix made a big deal out of their hands, the Voice might decide it meant more.

"Because I like your hair. And you have nice eyes. And you're sweet and kind, and sometimes feelings can't be helped." She'd said too much. Any second now, the Voice was going to tell her that she wasn't allowed to say nice things to slaves.

He grinned. "No, I suppose they cannot. Can I ask how long you've felt this way?"

"Not long. Maybe just last week."

He laughed out loud. "Well, Princess, I can tell you I've felt this way far longer."

He looked deep into her eyes and brushed away a stray strand of hair.

"How long," she asked, her voice barely above a whisper.

He dropped his eyes. "I don't know. Since shortly before Raaf and I left. I thought of you constantly. I just assumed I'd have to watch from afar."

"You've never said anything before today. Why?"

"I'm a slave. You're a princess. It's treason."

He jerked his hand out of hers and gripped his head. Zwaantie placed her hand on his shoulders. "Are you okay?"

He took a couple of deep breaths and then shook his head, his dark curls flying around.

"I'm fine," he said, blinking his eyes. "That one hurt."

Zwaantie watched him carefully. "Did the pain go away, or will you have to confess?"

"It went away. I should be okay."

Zwaantie wondered how far this would go. She felt so powerfully about him in such a short time. Maybe the feelings would fizzle just as quickly. She hoped not. Her skin tingled at the possibilities. Their relationship would be forbidden by both the Voice and her mother. She didn't want to see Phoenix in pain. She had to find a way to make this okay, if not with Mother, then at least with the Voice.

She needed to know the rules. Was it actually wrong for her to love a slave, or was that just Mother's idea? There was a difference between tradition and true right and wrong. Zwaantie had never thought about this before. It was time to find out.

Chapter Ten

THE WAGON

Zwaantie was on a mission. One that involved escaping the castle for a few hours with Luna, Phoenix, and Raaf. Things had been easier with Raaf since they played Sticks and Serpents, but she hadn't been able to spend a lot of time with him.

Slow down. This is not appropriate.

She stopped running and cursed the Voice for interfering. She settled on a brisk walk, her shoes clip-clopping on the floor, and ignored the slaves bowing to her as she passed. The castle seemed filled to bursting with them today. Odd.

She rounded a corner and knocked on a door. Phoenix opened it. Her lips twitched into a small smile. "I wish to see my brother."

Phoenix frowned. "Now's not a good time, Your Highness. Please come back later."

A high pitch wailing came from inside his room. "What's going on?"

"Just chancellor business, please come back later."

"No," Zwaantie said and pushed the door open.

Sprawled out on Raaf's floor was a merchant child, probably around ten, flailing around, screaming. A woman, whom Zwaantie assumed was the girl's mother, hovered over her. Raaf ran into the room from a side door. He tried to calm the child, but she continued to flail.

"Speak, woman. What did she do?"

"She hit her father. I've never seen pain come on so fast. Help her, please."

"You lie. If a child hits a parent, they may have pain strong enough to confess, but not this. Tell me, what did she do?"

The woman pressed a hand to her forehead, and she sank to the floor.

"No, you don't," Raaf said, his voice rising. He was still attempting to calm the child, but wasn't having any success. "You need to tell me what she did."

Tears flowed down the woman's cheeks. "She picked up a butcher knife and tried to kill her father. The pain took her down before she could make contact." Zwaantie brought a hand to her mouth. She'd never heard of such evil from a child.

Raaf's mouth dropped open, and he stood. "Phoenix, help me bring the child to another room. Zwaantie, can you stay here with the mother?"

Zwaantie nodded. "Of course." She spun around to find that Luna wasn't with her. She'd forgotten she'd sent Luna off to gather a few things for their afternoon. Zwaantie guided the mother to the couch. Then she went to a side table and poured out a goblet of wine for the woman. She handed over the wine, and the woman took it with shaking hands.

"I'm sorry, Your Highness. I've imagined meeting you on many occasions, but never quite like this." The woman continued to tremble, her voice weak.

Zwaantie forced a smile. "Don't worry about it. Would you like to tell me what happened? Get it off your chest?"

Silent tears flowed down the woman's cheeks. "I've never seen Hilde behave like that before. She was so angry. We all were, but Hilde took it the worst."

"Why was she angry?"

"Hilde's the youngest and is a pretty little thing. She'll never understand what it's like to not be wanted. But her oldest sister, Ina, she just didn't stand a chance. We tried for three years to find a good match for her. But you know after twenty, the good ones are gone. We even searched for a farmer's son, figuring that would be better than nothing, but no one wanted her. She is too ugly. We had no choice."

Zwaantie couldn't understand what the woman was saying.

"What did you do?"

"We did what any parent does when they have an unwanted child. We gave her to the slavemaster."

Zwaantie recoiled. This was unheard of. No parent would do that to their children for such a stupid reason. Maybe she wasn't telling Zwaantie everything.

"Was she a strain on your family financially?"

"No, but what else were we going to do with her? She's our responsibility until she's married. She couldn't marry. We had no choice."

Parents were responsible for the care of their children until marriage. If a child never married, they had no responsibilities. To turn your child to the slavemaster was beyond wrong. But allowed, according to the Voice.

They waited for what seemed like a long time but was probably only a few minutes. A knock came on the door, and they both jumped. Zwaantie cracked it open. She wasn't used to opening doors on her own.

"What's taking you so long?" Luna asked.

Zwaantie stepped into the hall. "Raaf is taking care of someone. I need you to run an errand for me though. Hopefully by the time you get back, Raaf will be done. Go to the slavemaster and inquire about a girl named Ina. Tell him I want her assigned to the castle. A good job."

Luna nodded and rushed down the hall.

Several minutes later, Raaf finally emerged with Phoenix, who carried the unconscious child.

The woman wailed and rushed to his side. "Is she okay?"

"Hilde will be fine," Raaf said. "She's exhausted, but I managed to convince the Voice to remove her pain. She will probably have a residual headache for some time to remind her of her extreme deed, but after a few months, it should go away."

Phoenix handed the child to the mother, and she staggered under the weight. Phoenix immediately took the girl back.

"Find a castle slave to carry her home. Then come back here," Raaf said.

Phoenix nodded and followed the woman out of the room. Raaf collapsed onto the couch.

"That was brutal, huh?" Zwaantie asked. Her mind was still spinning. She'd never realized Raaf's job could be so difficult. She wondered how often he was awakened or interrupted for extreme cases.

"Yep. First time I have had to deal with attempted murder. Normally they'd be executed. But I couldn't do that to a child."

"Was it hard to convince the Voice to let the pain go?"

Raaf shook his head, and Zwaantie waited for him to elaborate, but he didn't. She took a deep breath. If time wasn't so short, she wouldn't bother asking this now, but they'd already wasted a good half hour. Who knew how much longer they had.

"The mage wagon is here. We're going to see the show. Do you want to come?" The mage wagon was one of her favorite things to see. They always did magic that was typically forbidden in Sol.

He wrinkled his nose. "No, why would I want to do that?"

Her stomach clenched. She and Raaf had always gone to see the mage wagon together. He lay on the couch with his eyes closed. His hair was a mess, his jaw still tense. He was probably still upset by the child. He could use the time to get out and relax.

"We always go together." The last time they went was right before he left for his training. That year the mages brought fireworks. Even in the bright light they were spectacular. Raaf chased her around with a sparkling stick, laughing. She missed his laugh.

"When we were kids. Don't you think you are a little old to be doing things like that? What will the people think, seeing their soon-to-be queen frequenting such a questionable venue?"

She shrank away, hurt. Sure, the Voice always gave small warnings when they got close to the wagon, but she didn't think it was that bad.

For a half second she debated starting the argument they'd gotten into at dinner last night, the one about the virtues and vices of magic. If Raaf had been the heir to the throne, he'd rid the kingdom of all magic and seal the border so Stellans couldn't trade with them. Good thing she was the heir. That was one thing she was looking forward to. She'd allow more magic.

Time was slipping away. The mage wagon never stayed long.

"Can Phoenix at least come with us?"

"Yes, but act like a princess," he said with a glare.

He was in a bad mood. She stood and left the room before he said anything more.

She waited down the hall for Phoenix. He came around the corner, and Zwaantie couldn't help but smile. He was so handsome.

"Raaf said you could go to the mage wagon with us."

They took off down the hall, and Zwaantie resisted the urge to grab Phoenix's hand. The Voice would give her a thorough telling off, and she wasn't in the mood to listen to it and feel the pain that would follow.

Luna stood by the side doors with a basket under her arm.

"No Raaf?"

"Nope. Everything go okay with the slavemaster?"

"Yes. She'll be working as a serving maid."

"Thank you." Relief placated some of Zwaantie's guilt. It was strange, feeling guilty without the influence of the Voice. She wasn't sure why she felt guilty. It wasn't her fault the woman sold her daughter off to the slavemaster, but she still felt responsible for some reason.

They'd planned on walking to the wagon, but sitting just outside the front doors was a royal carriage, complete with a footman.

Zwaantie rolled her eyes. Raaf. He'd make sure she acted like a princess.

Fine. She put on her best smile and took the outstretched gloved hand of the footslave. They would arrive at the wagon with fanfare and announcement. They'd be lucky if it was still there by the time Zwaantie showed up. Certain magic was allowed in Sol, but the mage wagon always bordered on breaking the law. The mages wouldn't want the rulers of Sol watching them.

The wagon arrived with great fanfare and fun, probably so that all the merchants would know they were there. They came twice a year and negotiated with the merchants for food in exchange for potions and a few other things. The rest of the year, the merchants waited by the wall for unmanned carriages. They would unload the goods and fill the carriage up with food to send back.

They rattled along the cobblestoned street and passed small homes and farms. The horses frolicked in the fields, and the cows mooed unceremoniously, but the people on the streets dropped everything when the carriage approached, knelt, and pressed their faces to the ground.

As the carriage got closer to the wall of mist, the houses grew farther and farther apart. Farmers didn't like their cattle wandering too close to the wall between the two kingdoms. They disappeared too often. Sometimes because of their own stupidity and sometimes because of Stellan bandits. The wagon was set up in an empty field about a hundred yards from the mist. Zwaantie only saw the wall a few times a year. It always took her breath away.

The wall extended the length of Sol. No one ever found the end of it. Explorers tried on occasion, but none ever returned. The wall disappeared into the sky, inky black and swirling. Wisps of black smoke occasionally shot out about ten feet. If it caught a person, it would drag them into its depths and make them go mad with memories. Eventually, the mist would spit out those it captured, but they wouldn't have any memory of who they were or where they came from.

Stellans crossed the barrier, but only if they clung to the Rod of Lost Memories so they wouldn't lose their way or spend too long inside. Solites never ventured to the other side. The Voice forbade it.

The sun was high in the sky when they arrived at the field. Though aside from the midnight hours when the sky went gray, the sun was always high in the sky. Sweat appeared on Zwaantie's forehead almost immediately. It was warmer near the border than by the castle.

The carriage stopped next to the edge of the field. Luna, Phoenix, and Zwaantie climbed down the stairs. Zwaantie sighed as she took the hand of the footslave.

People sank deep onto the ground as Zwaantie strode past. She wished she could hide amongst the slaves like Luna and Phoenix, but she was cursed with royalty.

The wagon in the center of the field appeared stranger than normal. A shimmering clear bubble surrounded it. People entered the bubble like it wasn't there. How odd. The Voice berated Zwaantie as she got closer.

Evil things reside in there. Go home.

"I'm not doing anything wrong," she said. Luna looked at her funny, and Zwaantie pointed to her head. Luna nodded.

True, but you are flirting with an act of disobedience. Go home.

"How would you know? Now be quiet until you have something real to berate me for."

Zwaantie walked straight through the bubble without hesitation, followed by Luna and Phoenix. She stopped short just inside, and Luna ran into her.

Everything was dark, and she couldn't see. Fear clutched at her throat. She hated the dark. She inched forward and felt Luna grab for her hand. It was virtually silent inside the bubble.

After about thirty seconds, Zwaantie's eyes adjusted and shapes appeared. It wasn't completely dark. It only appeared that way because they'd come out of the sunlight. A small light ball hung in one corner, and thousands of other tiny lights were scattered along the bubble.

The wagon sat in the middle with a few magic lights floating around it. Luna gasped and sunk to the ground.

"Oh, stars," she breathed.

"What?" Zwaantie asked.

Then she understood. The bubble was a replica of the Stellan sky. The stars glittered against the blackness, and the moon provided more light than Zwaantie thought was possible.

She sat on the ground next to Luna, her eyes wide, and let out a laugh.

"Luna, it's the stars."

Luna smiled.

Phoenix settled on the grass on Zwaantie's other side. She wanted to grip his hand, but she wouldn't risk that in public.

"I never thought I'd see them again," Phoenix said.

"I never thought I'd see them at all," said Zwaantie.

All around, people entered the bubble and had similar reactions. They fell to the knees, and mouths dropped open.

"It looks the same. I'd forgotten, but this brings back many memories," said Luna.

"Yes, it does. Do you ever want to go back?" Phoenix asked, his shoulders relaxed and a lazy grin on his face.

She snorted. "Yeah, right. Like that would be possible."

Zwaantie's stomach churned. They weren't allowed to go home. Ever. Of course she wasn't allowed to go over there either, but at least she was in her own home.

"Is it like this in Stella?" Zwaantie asked, pointing at the stars.

"Sort of. These are so close. In Stella, they feel much farther away. But the patterns are the same. Look, there's Orion's belt. He was always my favorite gaw—I mean star."

"Is it this quiet in Stella too?" Zwaantie wasn't used to the peace.

Luna scrunched her nose. "It's not that quiet right now."

Phoenix pointed to his head. "She means in here."

He was right. It wasn't physical noise Zwaantie couldn't hear, but the Voice was gone. She scrambled to her feet. It was common knowledge that the Voice didn't exist in Stella. The hair on her neck and arms stood straight up, and she shivered. If they could create a way for Stellans to be in Sol without hearing the Voice, then they could attack Sol. Sure, it was a weird magical bubble, but that didn't mean they couldn't use the magic.

A couple of hundred years ago, the Stellans tried taking over Sol, but as soon as they crossed the barrier, the Voice commanded them to stop. They stood there like cows waiting for the butcher. The Solite soldiers slaughtered them, and an uneasy truce formed. Now Stellans only crossed the border when they needed food.

Zwaantie left Phoenix and Luna watching the stars and approached the wagon. Most of the magic the Solites purchased from Stella consisted of potions. Spells didn't work unless they were first cast in Stella. Unless a spell was in the form of a potion or attached to an object, it wouldn't work in Sol. The wagon usually pushed the boundaries of magic allowed in Sol. The Voice allowed potions, but discouraged them. If someone tried anything more, they'd be in pain for a week from the Voice. Only the bravest Solites purchased spells from the mage wagons. But this was also where the majority of their medicines came from, so it was allowed.

Zwaantie couldn't find a mage anywhere. She hadn't planned on buying anything other than potions, but now she wanted to make a very big purchase. Low voices floated around from the back of the wagon, and she stopped to listen.

"We can't sell these with her here. She'll go snitching to the king." The voice was soft, female.

"We spent months perfecting them. They are our money makers this year." This came from a male with a deep voice.

"Let's figure out what she wants to buy and get her out of here so that we can start trading," the female said.

Zwaantie peeked around the corner to see if she could make out what they were arguing over. What could they possibly want to sell that was so bad they didn't want her to see? Zwaantie came every time they were in town. That was no secret.

The male mage took a handful of necklaces from the female and shoved them in his pocket. Zwaantie hurried around the wagon.

"I would like to purchase one of those," Zwaantie said.

Both mages looked up with eyebrows raised. The male recovered first. "One of what?"

"Those necklaces."

He reached for a different necklace from the wagon. It was made of jewels and glowed. "This necklace is a rare piece of work. It will light up any dark room."

Zwaantie placed her hands on her hips. "Not that one, one that you have in your pocket."

"I'm sorry. I don't know what you are talking about." A bead of sweat appeared on his forehead, but he kept his body relaxed. He was good.

"You shoved a bunch of necklaces into your pocket. I want one of those."

He reached for his pockets and turned them inside out to show her that he had nothing. Sneaky little devil. She'd lost this one. But then she remembered why she'd come looking for them in the first place.

"I want to buy the stars. I'll give you one year of royal food."

"This dome? You want to buy the dome?"

"Yes. And I'll give you an extra half year if you come set it up for me."

He glanced at his companion. She shook her head. "It's not for sale."

"Do you know who I am?"

"Of course, Your Highness, but this is just an illusion. It only works for a short amount of time. By the time we got it to your home, it would be all but gone. And we don't feel right taking such a large sum of food for something so fleeting," the girl said with a sigh. She meant she didn't want to get her tail handed to her when she came back to town. "However, we do have something else that might interest you. Something that will last longer."

She snapped her fingers, and a table appeared in front of her. Zwaantie's heart stopped for a second. "You can't do magic in Sol."

The mage's face fell, but she didn't miss a beat. "Of course not. But the illusion allows us to perform magic under the dome. Again, it's temporary. The table, Your Highness."

At Zwaantie's feet sat a low table, oblong in shape. The surface gleamed black. It appeared to reflect the dome above with sparkly stars and a crescent moon.

"It's a reflecting table?" Zwaantie asked.

"No, it's a replica of the sky. The moon will change shape with the actual moon."

Oh, this was good.

"Yes, I'll take it. Half a year of royal food?"

"Three quarters," countered the male mage.

"Done."

"But we'd like to be paid in merchant food," he replied. Royal food was higher quality but by using merchant food, they'd get more.

"Of course. Phoenix," Zwaantie called.

"Yes." He appeared at her side almost instantly.

"Go fetch the footslaves to gather my new table. It's time to go." She would inform the trade master of her deal, and they would make sure the food was delivered throughout the year.

Zwaantie looked over her shoulder just before she left the bubble. Both mages watched her. She was insanely curious what those necklaces were that they were going to sell, and she worried what it meant. Stella usually didn't pose a threat, but today not only did they find a way to turn off the Voice, but they were selling objects they did not want her seeing. Perhaps Stella was more of a threat than she originally thought.

Chapter Eleven

THE TASK

The Voice looked around the crowded workroom and at the discarded lists he'd picked up from the box outside his door. The room was tall, three or four stories. Glowing orbs hung in the air like thousands of tiny suns, filling the space all the way up to the ceiling. The orbs ranged in size from pebbles to the carriage-sized bright white ball that hovered a few inches off the ground. A few tables were scattered along the walls, piled high with papers. The orbs moved out of the way as the Voice moved through the room.

This was the only place in all of Sol where spells could be cast. Though the magic was quite different than that of Stella. Stellan magic was wrong and went against nature. Through the Voice, Sol's magic ensured the obedience and passivity of the people. It provided order.

The Voice controlled it all. The ball in the center, the one the size of a carriage, managed the collective conscience of Sol, but the other smaller ones influenced individuals. Earlier today the Voice had been given a list of people who needed whispers added to their balls, but the list lay on the table forgotten. During the years the Voice had been in control, not one other person had ever found or entered this room. It should've been impossible. But today, the Voice had a visitor.

She delivered a life-changing message that was as vague as it was apocalyptic.

"Zwaantie," the Voice commanded, and Zwaantie's orb, along with those who were close to her, zoomed toward him.

The Voice studied her glow. She wielded more influence than she realized. She was beloved by those around her, but the Voice made sure she stayed humble. She'd been a challenge to restrain, but the Voice had done a good job growing her into the right kind of queen for her people. One that listened and was not overly confident. The Voice loved Zwaantie more than she knew.

Now she threatened everything.

Though the visitor had been cryptic, one thing she'd made clear was that the Voice would die.

Unless Zwaantie died first.

The Voice did not want Zwaantie to die, but sometimes sacrifices needed to be made to save the kingdom. If the Voice had an orb, it would be among those closest to her. Zwaantie's death would be difficult, but the Voice would do what was necessary.

Murder would be unheard of in Sol. The Voice would have to be careful so that it would not appear as if the Voice lost control of a person. Zwaantie's death would have to be carefully planned. The Voice moved around the orbs that surrounded Zwaantie. It would also have to be someone who was compliant and eager to follow the Voice's command.

The Voice smiled at the orb that circled closest to Zwaantie. That one would be perfect.

Chapter Twelve

THE PROBLEM

On the carriage ride home, Phoenix chatted easily about his memories of Stella. Under normal circumstances, Zwaantie would've been all over their conversation, but right now she was distracted. She stared out the window as the small houses and shops passed by. This was her kingdom. One she would be in charge of someday. A task she didn't want. Especially now.

The Stellan mages found a way to do magic inside Sol. They said it wouldn't last long. But they could do it. And if they could do magic inside Sol, then they could attack. Casting the spell was entirely different than potions. It wasn't possible in Sol. At least not until now. And those necklaces—they must've been something evil as well. What was so bad about them that they thought she'd tell her father?

Once back at the castle, the footslaves took her table to her room. Luna and Phoenix followed her through the front doors. Zwaantie normally took the back doors, but she had to talk to Mother and Father, and this was the easiest way to get to them. She held up her skirts and marched up the stairs. As she neared the top, slaves opened the doors, and Zwaantie strode through the empty grand hall and out a side door to the meeting room.

Her mother and father would be in there taking care of something mundane like how to increase the production of chicken eggs. The hallway outside the meeting room was crowded with slaves, their bands reflecting under the sunlight that streamed in through the skylights. She found Ariel standing next to the door.

"What's going on?" Zwaantie asked her.

"It's the first of the month."

Oh Sol, Zwaantie had forgotten. Why in the dark didn't the Voice warn her? It was usually so good at reminding her of things she didn't want to do. She was late, probably by a couple of hours. Raaf could've reminded her too. Brat. He probably wanted her to miss the meeting, thought it would be funny. And here she was thinking he'd gone stuffy. She'd pay him back for this one for sure.

Zwaantie turned to Luna. "How's my hair?"

Luna smoothed out a few stray strands while Ariel brushed dust off Zwaantie's dress. Phoenix smirked next to them, and Zwaantie had to resist sticking her tongue out at him.

"I'll see you later," Zwaantie said to Luna, but her eyes were on Phoenix.

A slave opened the door. Zwaantie pressed her lips together and entered the room with her head held high.

A group of nearly twenty people sat around the large oval table. The men stood as she walked into the room, and she racked her brain for an excuse. They would demand one.

She took her place next to her mother and avoided her eyes. Father and Raaf sat on her other side. The rest of the people at the table were lower kings, queens, and chancellors of various villages. Every month they gathered at the castle to discuss problems and solutions. Zwaantie hated these meetings because they were insanely dull. She thought she was too young to attend, but Mother insisted.

Speak, demanded the Voice.

Every eye in the room was on her. She'd hoped they would just continue like she hadn't come in extremely late. But she had no choice. Zwaantie stood.

"Please forgive my tardiness. A group of Stellan mages entered our borders a few hours ago, and I went to investigate."

A cough came from a few chairs over, and she knew it was Raaf trying to cover a laugh.

"And what did you find?" asked Mother. A few snickers came from around the table. No one expected anything good out of Zwaantie. She was the disobedient daughter of the high king and queen. The one who would rather run with slaves than other princes and princesses. The one, who, when she thought no one was listening, sounded like she came from the streets of Stella. But she blamed that one on Mother, who gave her Stellan playmates when she was young. What did Mother expect? Today though, Zwaantie would surprise them all.

"They have discovered how to turn off the Voice."

A gasp escaped most of those who sat around the table.

Raaf recovered first. "That is impossible. The Voice rules over Sol. It cannot be turned off. It is what keeps us safe. If they can turn it off, then they will invade."

"I witnessed it for myself. They created a bubble, and the minute I stepped within the bubble, the Voice went silent. Everyone noticed. The Voice can summon them here to witness if you don't believe me. But if you do believe me, we need to decide how to fix this."

Mother stared at her, stunned. But being the high queen, she went into action mode. "And how do you propose we do this?"

"We start by having spies at the border, and the next time a mage enters, we question him until he explains."

A voice came from across the table, the lower king of Ghrain.

"You had the authority to arrest them. Why didn't you?"

For a half second Zwaantie had thought that maybe she could do this. Be queen. But once again her inadequacy was thrown back in her face. She could've brought the mages in to be questioned by Raaf. Another reminder of why she wouldn't be a good queen.

"I don't know," Zwaantie said, sinking down into her hard chair. She kept her head up because that was expected of her, but she wanted to bury her face in her hands. She kept her eyes trained on the tapestry of an apple orchard hanging above the king and queen of Slonce.

The lower king sniffed. Conversations flared up around the room. Zwaantie wallowed in her own self-pity while the rest of the leaders of Sol decided how to protect her country since she obviously couldn't. Maybe now Mother would entertain thoughts of Zwaantie giving up the throne.

After the meeting, Mother caught up with Zwaantie and Luna in the hallway.

"Tonight you will be seated next to the prince of Ghrain."

Zwaantie groaned.

Stop that. She's your mother. You will listen to her.

"Yes, Mother, but last time was a disaster. I don't expect tonight to go any better."

"Well, try harder this time, and so help me, if I hear one word about mooing, I'll have your tail. The prince is the one who suggested we increase the guard at the barrier."

Anyone could have suggested they increase the guard. Even the slaves would've thought of that. Zwaantie rolled her eyes.

Stop being disrespectful.

"Yes, Mother."

The prince from Ghrain was older than her by about six years. He was good looking and charming. But also condescending.

That evening, Zwaantie settled into her chair before the prince arrived. Luna stood behind her, smoothing her hair as he took his seat with a flourish.

"I see your mother made you sit with me. Are you finally deciding to choose a husband?"

"My mother thinks so." Zwaantie looked around. Where were the drinks?

"Well, you will obviously be picking me. I don't see that you have other options."

What an arrogant jerk.

"You are mistaken. I have plenty of options."

"Where? Sonnenschein? I heard you ran him off awfully fast. I'm not quite as easily deterred."

Zwaantie almost asked him to moo for her, just to prove a point, but decided against it. She needed wine and fast.

A serving slave stood before her, pale as the clouds in the sky. The tray the girl held shook. "Wine or water?"

"Wine, please." Zwaantie reached for the wine, but before she could take the goblet, the slave collapsed onto the floor, convulsing. The cups clattered to the floor, the wine leaving a dark stain on the stone.

Zwaantie was out of her seat in seconds. She knelt by the girl's side, the floor cold underneath her knees. It was a slave she was unfamiliar with. She'd probably seen her around the castle before, but didn't know her name. The girl's face was pale, and her lips had a strange blue tint. Blood trickled out of her mouth. Zwaantie touched the girl's neck. Nothing.

Luna knelt down next to her and put her arm around Zwaantie's shoulder. "Zwaantie? Are you okay?"

Zwaantie shook her head.

"Move, girls." Wilma stood next to them. They scooted over but did not stand.

Wilma moved her fingers over the girl's lips and opened her eyes. Zwaantie did not look. She was already afraid of the nightmares that would come from this experience. This poor girl had just died right in front of her. Why?

Dead," declared Wilma to the waiting crowd. "You," she said, pointing at a slave boy. "Go fetch a couple of diggers."

Zwaantie still hadn't moved. "What do you think happened to her?"

Wilma shrugged. "It's hard to say. From the looks of it, she bled internally. It could be any number of things. Especially if she had trouble earlier and didn't tell anyone. Death is the way of the world, and it happens, even to the young."

A few minutes later, two men arrived in dark brown tunics and took the girl away. The dinner conversation had been hushed during the ordeal, but no one made to leave. As soon as the diggers and the girl were gone, Mother motioned for the slaves to serve them dinner. Zwaantie looked at her mother, hoping against hope to convey that she wanted to go to her room. But her mother just nodded to the prince behind Zwaantie, which she took as a sign that she was to take her seat at the table.

Luna pulled Zwaantie up. Zwaantie's legs shook as Luna helped her to her seat. After she sat, she placed her hands in her lap and stared down at them. Those hands had just touched a dead body. What if she was contagious and Zwaantie would be the next to go? No one else seemed concerned about that. Another slave girl brought her a warm wet cloth, and Zwaantie used it to wash her hands.

She glanced at the prince. "Excuse me. I'm afraid I've lost my appetite." She rushed from the room, Luna on her heels.

She collapsed onto her couch.

"Are you okay, Your Highness?"

Zwaantie shook her head. "A girl just died right in front of me."

"Yes. She did."

"Did you know her?"

"A little. We weren't close."

"Everybody acted like we're just supposed to continue with dinner, like nothing was wrong."

Luna shifted. "I suppose they thought she was a slave, and it didn't matter."

Zwaantie cringed. "That's not right."

"It is the way of life. Why don't you take a bath, and I'll brush out your hair? That always soothes you."

"Yes, that would be nice. Thank you."

Luna had just finished helping Zwaantie put on her night dress when mother entered.

"You left early."

"I did. The death was too much for me."

Mother sank down onto the couch. "You know, when you're queen, you will have to carry on even if you run into hard situations. That wasn't smart running out like that. You'll make the people believe their queen is weak."

Zwaantie was tired of being reminded of her duties. Tired of thinking of marrying a man she'd never love, tired of being queen, and she hadn't even become one yet.

"What if I don't want to be queen?" There she finally said it out loud.

Take it back. This is treason.

A hand flew to her mother's breast. "How could you say that?"

Zwaantie exhaled and twisted her hands together. "Because it's true. I don't want to be queen. Raaf can have the throne. Please, Mother, you must see that I will not be good at this."

Treason. There is only one punishment for traitors. Zwaantie expected a pain in her forehead after a declaration like that, but none came.

"Raaf is already the grand chancellor. Besides, Sol demands that as the oldest heir, you be queen. If you choose not to, you will be sentenced to death. There is no abdicating."

"What?" Zwaantie had never heard this before. No one ever talked about what would happen if she didn't take the throne.

"I may be queen, but we answer to a higher power." Mother pointed out the window to the sun. "You are called by Sol to become queen."

"And if I run away?"

STOP THIS RIGHT NOW. The pain began then, just behind her eyes.

"Then that is between you and Sol, but I doubt you'd survive more than a couple of weeks. This is ridiculous."

This would be irrelevant if Stella found a way to take over. Then she'd be a slave like Luna and Phoenix. Though that might fix her problem. Maybe Zwaantie shouldn't have warned her mother and father about the way the Stellan mages turned off the Voice.

She shook her head. What was she thinking? Sol was her home. She should be concerned about her people, not helping the enemy.

Mother didn't say another word as she swept from the room. Luna sat on the couch with her and held her hand.

"I never knew," she said.

"I know. I'm sorry. I just feel so trapped in my life."

Luna gave a snort. "I can relate."

"I shouldn't compare my life to yours. I'm sorry. It's just that I want to be a midwife. Not queen."

A knock came at the door. Luna answered it. Phoenix poked his head in, and Zwaantie couldn't help her smile.

He sat in the seat Luna had just vacated, and he took her hand in his. "Are you okay?"

"Of course. It was strange watching that slave die, but I'm fine. How did you get away?"

"Raaf sent me to check on you. He wanted to come himself, but he was tied up. I was happy to help."

Luna hovered over them, glaring. "You should leave. I need to help Zwaantie get ready for bed."

Phoenix didn't say anything. He just brushed a strand of hair out of Zwaantie's eyes. She shivered at his touch and let out a sigh.

The door clicked shut, and Zwaantie met Luna's eyes. Her face was hard. "You're playing with fire."

It sure felt like it. Zwaantie's chest burned every time she saw him. Luna was worried about her brother, and Zwaantie supposed he could get hurt in this, but the truth was that she was the one who would likely end up in flames.

Chapter Thirteen

THE PLAN: PART 1

The Voice was trying hard not to lose his temper. He stood among his glowing orbs and muttered to himself. The orbs would absorb some of his words, and right now a very confused farmer was being told he was an idiot and he had to try harder next time. But at this moment, the Voice didn't care. He slammed his fist down on a long table that sat next to the wall. A few lists slid off the table. He picked them up and read the first one.

The following people of Haul need to have their guilt removed.

Sjabbo, farmer, confessed to the sin of moving his fence and encroaching on another's property.

Mina, shopkeeper, confessed to the sin of purposefully keeping the change she owed her customers.

Bastiaan, student, sixteen years of age, confessed to kissing a girl.

This was his job. He was to remove the guilt whispers from their orbs so they could be free of the pain associated with it. There were a half a dozen lists sitting on his table, and he hadn't attended to a single one. He clutched at his hair. How was he supposed to think about these mundane things when he was about to lose his power because of the princess? He had to get rid of her so he could focus on doing his job.

Shoes clattered on the floor in the hallway behind him. He was about to have another visitor.

The door opened, and in she strolled. He left the orbs behind him so none would pick up the conversation. The woman's face twisted into a sneer, and she wasted no time getting in his face.

"That was stupid and foolish. You could've exposed the plan to kill her before even getting a decent shot at it. You're lucky most of the kingdom doesn't recognize the signs of poisoning. Not to mention the fact that an innocent victim died. You can't let that happen again."

"Relax, woman. It was just a slave girl. You don't seem that concerned about Zwaantie's life. Why are you worried about a slave?"

She took two deep breaths and then snapped her fingers. Every orb in the room blinked out.

The Voice's stomach clenched, and his hands went ice cold. This woman just turned off the magic of Sol. "Turn it back on." He couldn't think of anything else to say. Not until the orbs were glowing again. He fought the rising panic in his chest.

"No. Not until you hear what I have to say. If you fail, this is the result. Everything goes away. No more magic, no more Voice, and chaos in the streets. I have seen all the possible futures. The only ones in which the Voice still remains in power are the ones where Zwaantie dies. Unless you want this to be a reality, she must die, and you cannot make any more foolish attempts like today. Find a way to do it now, because the beginning of the end starts tomorrow."

She snapped her fingers once again, and the orbs glowed, like they'd never been turned off in the first place. The Voice sank to the ground, grateful a crisis had been averted. The old woman put a gentle finger on one of the orbs nearest her, and the Voice resisted the urge to swat her hand away. He'd never even touched them.

"Do you ever wonder how it all started?" she asked.

"How what started?" He couldn't concentrate on the conversation. His mind was still with her declaration of all the possible futures. How powerful was this woman anyway?

"This room. The Voice."

She wasn't making sense. "I am the Voice."

"Of course you are, but you haven't always been."

"I know that, but there is no beginning. The Voice originates with the creation."

The woman cackled. "Oh, you fool. It began as a spell. A good one too. I was there."

The Voice furrowed his brow. This couldn't be true. He was the Voice of God. This woman was blasphemous.

"You lie."

"I do not. Let me show you. Call to you the orb of the Bakker child. He's an infant and won't remember or understand our words."

The Voice didn't want to listen to her, but something about the way she spoke made him follow her directions.

He called Philip Bakker's orb to him. His mother, father, and sister's orbs flew with it, but he waved them away. The orb floated between him and the old woman. Her eyes sparkled as she examined it.

"Now before I show you, I'd like to know how much you understand. How does the Voice work?"

"The Voice exists inside the head of every Solite."

"But are you present?"

"No, I simply give the orb instructions, and it acts of its own accord. I would go mad if I was in everyone's head all the time."

"Very good. Essentially, you don't know what anyone has done until the chancellor delivers you names of those who need guilt and pain removed."

"Right, and I can choose whether or not to remove that pain. Once an instruction has been given, only I can modify or change it. I can also choose how strict the Voice is with individuals. Slaves are dealt with most severely while the royal family is given some leniency."

"How do you force someone to do something?"

"I have to allow my consciousness to enter their orb, essentially seeing everything they are doing. In that instance I have total control over their actions if I choose. I can do that to all of Sol at once if I wish."

But he wouldn't ever enter the entirety of Sol. After forcing someone to do something, he always felt exhausted and a little dirty inside. He didn't like being in other people's heads. He didn't know what would happen if he tried to enter the collective conscience.

The woman waggled her finger in his face. "I wouldn't try that if I were you. You have a better understanding than I thought you did. Now to the creation."

She brought her hands together on Philip's orb, and it disappeared into mist.

"What have you done?" The only time orbs disappeared was when someone died. "Did you just kill him?"

"Relax. He's fine. He simply has no 'Voice' at the moment. He doesn't need one. Now watch."

She spun her finger in a circle. Silvery threads dripped out and formed a new ball. She stopped moving her finger, and the orb floated in front of his eyes.

"There, Philip has a new ball. No gods involved, just magic."

Chapter Fourteen

THE PLAN: PART 2

Zwaantie was alone. It didn't happen often, but Luna was off getting one of Zwaantie's dresses fixed, and Mother was having lunch with her sister. Zwaantie didn't like alone time. It allowed for too much thinking. She picked up a tapestry she and her mother had been sewing together and worked on a tree in the corner.

She had a lot to think about. Phoenix had stolen her heart, and she didn't even know that was possible. The thought of marrying anyone else filled her soul with dread. She wanted Phoenix. Committing to him meant marriage and kids were impossible. If they ever had children, they'd be born slaves. Because if anyone married a slave, their children were automatically slaves.

Zwaantie thought through the possibilities. She could refuse to marry, and she and Phoenix could just be lovers. She snorted. Yeah, right. The Voice would never allow it. Maybe love was possible in the Stellan fairy tales Ariel told her when she was younger, but in Sol, love was only possible in marriage.

She could become a slave. But who would do that? Besides, then she'd have to face the wrath of Sol. That wasn't possible.

If only the Voice wasn't so obnoxious. Zwaantie sat up straighter. That was it. The Voice. Her brother was the grand chancellor. He could talk to the Voice. He could fix this. Zwaantie dropped the tapestry. She couldn't believe she hadn't thought of this earlier.

Pick it up.

She stared down at the tapestry lying on the floor. It seemed such a dumb thing to berate her for. She had grand problems, and the Voice was telling her to clean up her messes. She picked it up and slammed it on the table.

She strode quickly down the hall and knocked on her brother's door.

Phoenix opened it. A smiled formed on his lips as he looked her over. She kept her face straight. He would probably be angry with her when this was over.

"I need to speak with Raaf."

"Of course, Princess, come in."

Raaf was sitting on a chair staring into the fire. She sat across from him, and he jerked his head up.

"I need your help," she said.

Raaf picked up the glass in front of him and took a sip. "You always need my help."

"You love me. Right?"

"You're my sister. Why would you ask a question like that?"

"Because I have to know I can trust you."

Raaf set his glass down and leaned forward. "You know you can trust me. I've never told Mother and Father anything you've done. And, Zwaantie, you've broken more rules than anyone I know. I don't know how you aren't in here pleading with me every day. Or is that what you need? Have you finally done something so bad that the pain won't leave?" He cocked his head and gave her crooked grin.

She scowled. "No, my head is fine. But you can't tell anyone. I'm actually here to try to prevent a scolding from the Voice."

Raaf waved his hand. "Continue. You have my word."

Zwaantie let out a deep breath. "I'm in love."

Phoenix stood behind Raaf, his hands clenching the back of Raaf's chair. Zwaantie met Phoenix's eyes. He glared at her and shook his head.

Raaf shifted in his chair, and Zwaantie refocused on him. This was for the best even if Phoenix didn't think so.

He picked up his glass and took another sip. "It's about time. Mother will be thrilled."

"It's more complicated than that. Mother won't approve." Zwaantie clutched her hands together. She was scared of what Raaf's reaction would be. Phoenix's as well.

Raaf gave her a small smile. "Give her a little credit. She just wants you to be happy."

Zwaantie forged on, knowing if she didn't, she'd never get it out. "But I'm in love with Phoenix."

Foolish notion, girl.

Raaf dropped his glass, and it shattered. Phoenix hurried to clean it up. Zwaantie couldn't see his face, but his shoulders were tense and his motions jerky. Was he angry with her? She was trying to fix this.

Raaf covered his eyes and then ran his hand slowly down his face, pinching his lip. He closed his eyes and gave his head a slow shake. "Zwaantie. I can't help you. You have to know that. You've put yourself in an impossible situation." He rubbed his forehead.

Zwaantie wrung her hands. The anxiety in her chest was building. "But there has to be a way. We could run away. I could become a slave. We could find a way to remove Phoenix's bands. There has to be."

You've gone too far. Respect the system.

"Removing the bands isn't possible. As for you becoming a slave, only Mother and Father have access to the bands, and you know that won't happen. If you run away, the Voice will make you come back."

Zwaantie jumped. This was the opening she'd been waiting for. "But you can fix that, can't you. You talk to the Voice. Tell him what we need. He listens to you." The Voice was strangely quiet. She expected something more.

Raaf let out a snort. "It doesn't work like that."

"What do you mean? You tell the Voice all the time to remove pain and guilt."

"Actually, I don't. You know, grand chancellor is little more than a pretty face."

Zwaantie frowned. "What do you mean?"

"I mean, I listen to the people's pleadings, write down their requests, and leave them in a box outside the Voice's chambers. Every day the lists are gone. Most of the time the Voice does what I ask, but sometimes it doesn't. I have one man who visits me every day begging for the pain in his head to be removed, but the Voice never listens. I have other duties as well. Ones that don't involve the Voice. The guards answer to me, and I interrogate those caught in possible crimes, but my interaction with the Voice is about the same as yours."

"But the little girl."

"In emergencies, I can slide a note under the door. But even then, I think we got lucky."

Zwaantie sat back in her chair defeated. She thought for sure this would work. Phoenix took his place behind Raaf again, stony faced. He wouldn't look at her.

"Well, what do we do now?" Zwaantie asked.

Raaf craned his head around to look at Phoenix, but Phoenix just stared at the door.

"I don't know. Move on. Your love story won't have a happy ending. I'm sorry. I wish there was more I could do to help. Besides, Zwaantie, you know as well as I do, that it's your responsibility to become queen. Anything else would be dishonorable."

Zwaantie wanted to argue. What about responsibility to herself? Since when did honor trump everything including her own happiness?

"Will you keep our secret?"

"Of course, but I would highly advise you to cut it off. This won't end well."

～

PHOENIX WAS ALREADY AT THE ROCK WHEN SHE ARRIVED. SHE CLIMBED next to him, but he made no move to touch her.

"You should've talked to me first," he said as she settled herself.

"I thought Raaf could help us."

"But he couldn't. This is a mistake, Zwaantie. I think we need to stop seeing each other."

Zwaantie put her hand on his tightly crossed arms. He didn't react. "No. Please. You know how I feel."

"Raaf is right. This will not end well."

Zwaantie felt like she was about to cry. She hadn't realized how much he meant to her. The thought of just ending it broke her up inside. "We can figure out something." They had to.

"No, this is too risky."

Zwaantie laid her head on his shoulder. "I'm willing to risk anything to be with you." A small pain started in her forehead.

Remember your place, Princess.

He scooted away from her. "No. This has to be the last time."

Zwaantie felt something break inside of her. "Phoenix, please."

"Don't make this any harder than it has to be." His face softened. "Tell you what, let's make this count. Your turn to catch me."

Without a word, he jumped off the rock and ran into the woods. Zwaantie worried that if she didn't go now, she'd never see him alone again. She raced after him, trying not to think about this being the last time. She refused to believe it.

It took her a while, but eventually she caught him. Somehow she ended up pinned underneath him with his fingers tickling her ribs. At first she laughed, but her feelings quickly changed from amusement to desire. She loved the way his fingers pressed into her sides and lingered on her stomach. Phoenix leaned down and whispered in her ear.

"You need to keep laughing or else..."

She was certain he was about to say, "Or else the Voice will know." So she laughed, but her heart wasn't in it. Especially when he looked at her with serious eyes. She knew his feelings changed for her as well.

When she couldn't stand it anymore, she wiggled out. "We should go in."

"We should."

They were silent as they traipsed to the castle. The sky was rapidly turning gray. This was the closest she'd ever cut it. She couldn't hurry though. She had too much on her mind.

The thrill of desire crawled up her spine. It settled into her chest and abdomen. She'd never felt this way about anyone before. The need to be close, to hold, to touch, to kiss. Phoenix squeezed her hand and went his separate way. She watched him saunter away for a long minute. This was the end. She fought tears as she stalked to her room.

She got to her door at the same time as the guard. His normally friendly eyes had taken on a hard stare. That was strange. The midnight bells had not begun to ring yet.

She pushed on her door, but the guard grabbed her arm and spun her around. Pressing her against the wall, he had his sword against her throat. Zwaantie couldn't breathe. The guard's eyes bored into hers. She tried to move, but found herself paralyzed with fear. She couldn't scream. The sword was pressing too hard. He was going to slice open her neck. This wasn't possible. She had so much to live for.

The confusion in the guard's eyes was clear. She clutched at the sword cutting her hands. But the guard held it fast.

"Why?" she whispered.

A shadow appeared around the corner just as the clock began its nightly midnight strike. Phoenix rushed for the guard and jerked him away. The guard dropped the sword and looked at both of them with bewilderment.

Phoenix shoved her into her room, and she clutched at him. "No, stay with me."

"Yes," said the guard. "Stay and protect her."

Zwaantie didn't understand what was going on. Ten seconds ago, this man wanted to kill her, and now he was telling Phoenix to protect her. Zwaantie tugged at Phoenix's hand and pulled him in. The guard slammed and locked the door. They wouldn't be able to get out again until morning.

She felt her neck. There was a dent where the sword pressed, but at least he hadn't drawn blood. She might have some bruising in the morning, but nothing worse than that. Her hands were another story. Blood dripped onto the floor.

"Sit," Phoenix commanded and ran for her washroom.

He came back with a few wet cloths. He gently washed her hands and wrapped them with dry ones.

"Are you okay?" he asked, his dark eyes full of concern.

"That depends. Physically, I'm fine, but my guard just tried to kill me. Why would he do that?"

"I don't know. Did you notice how he stopped when the bell rang?" The bells signaled the midnight hours. As soon as they stopped ringing, the Voice turned off.

Did that mean that the Voice was trying to kill her? Why? No. That was absurd. The Voice kept them from doing bad things.

"We'll have Raaf deal with him tomorrow. Maybe he'll have some insight on what happened. Let's get you to bed."

Zwaantie glanced sideways at him. "You know, there is no Voice."

She wrapped her arms around his waist and pushed herself into him. The sheer physical contact was exhilarating. Zwaantie could stay there all night.

He held her tight. She brushed one of the curls out of his eyes. They sparkled at her.

"We should still get you to bed."

"You're coming with me."

The torment in his face was heartbreaking.

"What? The Voice won't know."

"But I will, and I will ache for you afterwards. Zwaantie, if I'm to have you, I want you all the way. I can't have you tonight and then never again."

Zwaantie's breath caught in her throat, and she didn't know what to say. "Where are you going to sleep?"

"I'm not. I'm going to make sure some murderous guard doesn't try to break in here."

"Okay, I'm going to change."

Zwaantie's hands shook as she changed into her night dress. Phoenix stood at the door and watched her with smoldering eyes as she climbed in bed.

"Come tell me a story," Zwaantie said.

He chuckled. "I'm not your nursemaid."

"I still want to hear a story. Something from Stella."

He sat down on the edge of her bed. "I don't remember much from Stella. I miss the smells though. I lived on an island, and the smell of the sea was my favorite."

"What does it smell like?" She'd heard of the sea, but had never seen it before. It was on the other side of the mist.

"A little like salt, but different. I don't know. Someday see if you can buy a shell from a trader. They smell like the sea."

Zwaantie gripped his hand, and he squeezed back. "Tell me something else."

"The food was awful."

"Really?"

"Truly. They can't grow fresh food, but you already knew that. But imagine eating fruits and vegetables that are days or weeks old. They use magic to preserve it, but it still doesn't taste like the food here."

"Will you lay with me? Just until I fall asleep. Please."

He ran a finger along her jaw. "Yeah, scootch over."

She pressed her back into him, and he pulled her tight against his body. As she drifted off, she realized she'd never been more comfortable. How could she ever sleep without him again?

Chapter Fifteen

THE VISITOR

Zwaantie woke the next morning to a squeal. She sat straight up and found Luna with her mouth hanging open. A hand snaked around her waist and pulled her tight. Oh no.

She pushed at Phoenix's shoulder. "Wake up."

He groaned and then slid out of bed. Then he fell to the floor holding his head.

Zwaantie jumped up and hovered over him. "What's the matter?"

Luna came over and tugged at his arm. "What's he doing here? Help me get him up."

Zwaantie pulled at his other arm, and he stood, but was hunched over holding his head.

Luna glared at Zwaantie. "In less than ten seconds, tell me what happened."

"My guard tried to kill me. Phoenix rescued me and stayed with me to make sure the guard didn't return."

Luna creased her eyebrows. "Okay, I'm going to take him to Raaf. You stay here and don't go back to bed."

Zwaantie paced back and forth in front of the fireplace and waited for Luna to return. Why did the Voice punish Phoenix, but not her? She didn't understand what was going on. Especially with the Voice. Luna returned and clicked the door shut.

"Will he be okay?" Zwaantie asked.

"Raaf was going to the Voice to plead for him right away, but it's up to the Voice."

Zwaantie collapsed into a chair next to the fireplace. "It's all my fault. He was going to stand by the door all night."

"Don't say anything else. He had a completely good reason to be in your room. The Voice will see that."

"Why are you here so early?" Zwaantie asked, realizing that the day just began. She was going to crawl into her bed and sleep for another three hours. Luna went and opened the curtains, sending sunlight streaming into the room.

"Because someone is coming to visit the castle."

"Well, whoever they are they can come back later. You know I don't function until after noon. Close the stinking curtains." Zwaantie found her covers, pulled them to her neck, and put a pillow over her face.

"Your mother is going to be here in fifteen minutes. I should've had more time, but your guard was missing, though now I understand why. I had to go track down the head guard for the keys. Now, unless you want to explain to her why your hair is a mess, you'll get up."

Zwaantie sat up, and the bright yellow duvet settled around her waist. "What does she want?"

"To make sure you are prepared for the guest."

"Did the head guard say what happened with my guard?" She rubbed her neck, the memory of the steel fresh in her mind.

"He killed himself. It happens after midnight sometimes."

Zwaantie didn't know how to process this new information. Something must've been wrong with him.

"He tried to kill me."

Luna dropped her voice. "Let's not tell anyone. We don't want to draw attention to Phoenix. Raaf will keep the secret."

"What secret?" Zwaantie's mother asked from the doorway.

Zwaantie jumped and blushed because she stood in only her underdress. Zwaantie's mother hadn't seen her this undressed since she was five years old. Zwaantie spun around so her mother couldn't see the mess of grass in her hair.

"Oh, just that I stayed up too late. I'm not used to being up this early."

Mother crossed the room, sat in a chair by the fireplace, and studied her. Zwaantie shifted her feet. Her underdress wasn't sheer, but it was pretty close. Plus, without a dress on, her breasts were plainly visible.

"You are to be on your best behavior today. Or I will see that you marry Prince Moo-For-Me. Do you understand?"

Mother had never threatened Zwaantie before. Whoever was coming had to be someone important. But Zwaantie and her family were the most important people in Sol. The lower kings and queens visited all the time.

"Who's coming?" Zwaantie asked.

Mother played with the lace on the edge of her collar, her jaw tense. "A high prince. I want you to wear your red dress, the one with the sequins. And Luna, will you put her hair in a fancy braid? He should be here within a couple of hours."

Luna curtsied. "Of course, Your Majesty."

Mother got up and nearly swept out the door before what she said registered. "Mother, wait!"

"What?" she asked in exasperation.

"What do you mean, a high prince? Raaf's the only high prince in Sol."

"Yes, I know that. The high prince is from Stella."

Zwaantie sank down onto her bed. Luna sat in the chair Mother just vacated.

"Stella," Luna uttered, her eyes staring off into space.

"Stars. That prince has stars." Zwaantie pulled her bright yellow blanket up to her shoulders and wrapped it around herself. "Why do you think a high prince from Stella is coming here?"

Luna pulled her off the bed. "Your guess is as good as mine. Maybe he's coming to seek your hand in marriage." Luna's eyes sparkled, and Zwaantie knew she was joking, but that was actually one of the more sane reasons. He had another thing coming if he thought she was going to marry him.

"This is unheard of." The royal families hadn't spoken to each other in over two hundred years. The only Stellans they ever had contact with were traders.

Luna led Zwaantie to a steaming tub of water. "Get in. We'll talk while I'm fixing your hair."

Zwaantie undressed and slipped into the water.

"Mother can't possibly want me to marry him. The people from Stella are barbarians. They don't wear decent clothes, and they have no rules. And no sun. How could I live over there? I want to see the stars, but not at the expense of the sun."

"Even if he is seeking marriage, your mother wouldn't hear of it. She just wants you to behave while he is here. Believe it or not, I think your mother might feel threatened by his presence. Stella leaves us alone most of the time. What if his visit isn't friendly? After all, they do know how to turn off the Voice."

Zwaantie hadn't thought of that. "But then why does Mother want me to behave?"

"I'm not even going to answer that."

Zwaantie's face was scrubbed clean, and then she stepped out of the tub. Luna dressed her in a bright red dress and pulled the laces tight. Then she braided Zwaantie's hair.

The trumpets blared to announce the arrival of a visitor, and Zwaantie made no move to go down to the great hall. She wanted the prince to meet Mother and Father first. Truthfully, Zwaantie was hoping she wasn't necessary for this visit. She didn't want to meet him. What if Mother made Zwaantie marry him? Then she would leave Sol. And Phoenix.

No, she couldn't make her do that.

"Should we go?" Luna asked, startling Zwaantie out of her thoughts.

"No, we'll wait until we are summoned."

Luna and Zwaantie didn't talk while they waited. Thoughts buzzed in Zwaantie's head about why a prince from the dark side, would be in Sol.

He could show her the stars. In spite of herself, she was excited to meet him. She wondered if he were old or young. It was always hard to tell with princes. Would he be dressed like them or would he wear garments from his own kingdom? People in Sol believed that if no skin was shown, the temptation was less. But Zwaantie disagreed. The more that was covered the more curious she was to see what was underneath.

Luna told her that in Stella they wore whatever they wanted, and sometimes they didn't wear anything at all.

Ten minutes later Raaf appeared in the doorway with Phoenix at his side. At least he wasn't still racked with pain. He didn't even glance at Zwaantie. She hoped he wasn't ashamed of the previous night. She certainly wasn't. She warmed at the thought of his arms around her.

Raaf scowled. "What are you doing? The prince will be here any minute."

"Waiting to be summoned. I'm not that excited to meet him."

"None of us are, but Mother wants you next to her when they arrive."

"Fine."

Luna fussed with her hair a little more, and then they followed the boys to the entrance hall. What would the prince think of her home? Was it like his in Stella? They'd never had a high prince set foot in their castle before. Would he find it impressive or lacking?

The grand hall was wide and the ceiling tall. Mother and Father sat on thrones directly across from the enormous front doors. Sixty guards lined the path from the door to the thrones. Twice as many as normal. Zwaantie wasn't the only one skeptical of this dark prince.

Zwaantie stood next to Mother, with Luna taking her place behind them both, next to her own mother. Raaf and Phoenix went to stand by Father. Behind Father stood Pieter, tall and stoic. A few of the lower kings and queens had many personal slaves, but in the capital city they didn't believe in extravagance. One or two was sufficient. That left the rest of the slaves to attend to the needs of the kingdom. They took care of the roads and kept the streets clean of debris and sewage. They prided themselves in the cleanliness of their city.

The doors opened just as Zwaantie took her place next to her mother.

Chapter Sixteen

THE PRINCE

Two men entered and sauntered up the path to the thrones. They didn't seem awed or nervous of the guards. A little too cocky for Zwaantie's taste.

Both men were dressed identically. They had on dark pants with leather boots. They wore white billowy shirts that opened at the neck with a necklace that rested on the hollow of their neckline. It was a simple necklace, with no jewels. Just a silver disk attached to a leather thong. They wore bright multi-colored vests over their shirts.

Just before they reached the stairs to the thrones, they stopped and bowed. It became clear who was the prince and who was the slave. While the prince bowed deep and low, the slave was more cautious. He eyed the guards next to him with suspicion, and he never took his hand off the hilt of his sword. This was no ordinary slave. He was also his guard. A good one from the looks of it.

The prince rose from his bow and looked at Zwaantie's father.

"High King Geert, High Queen Janna, I bring the greetings of my father, High King Ajax. He wished to come himself, but found that he's unable to get away from his current duties. I hope you will forgive his absence. High Princess Zwaantie and High Prince Raaf, it is a pleasure to meet you."

His voice was rich and lilting. The speech was obviously rehearsed, and he appeared to stumble over the names. The smile never left his dark face. She could see the similarities between him and Phoenix. They had the same devastating smile, rich caramel skin, and dark piercing eyes. But the prince's face was a little sharper. His hair was spiking instead of long and curly. He was definitely striking. Cow poop. She was hoping he was old or ugly.

He bowed once again, a short quick bow, and then spoke. "I am High Prince Leo, the fifth son of High King Ajax of Stella. I have come to see if it would be possible to join our kingdoms."

Father glared down at him. That was a bold statement for a prince in foreign territory. "How exactly would we join our kingdoms?"

His eyes met Zwaantie's. "Through marriage of course. I have no kingdom of my own. Marriage would create a partnership that I think we have both longed for."

Luna sucked in a breath, and Zwaantie flicked her eyes to Phoenix. He stood expressionless, but Raaf was frowning. Zwaantie's heart raced, and her palms began to sweat. She had no idea how her parents would react to this. Would they force her to marry him?

Father continued to glower at the man. Zwaantie let out a breath of relief. This was absurd.

After a long beat, Father waved his hand. "We have no desire to join with Stella. Zwaantie will be marrying a Solite prince."

For once Zwaantie didn't want to argue with him. She didn't want to marry a prince, but one from Stella sounded downright terrifying.

Leo appeared confused. "Did the princess not send a message stating they were desperate for medicines? If Zwaantie and I join in marriage, then we could have free and open trade."

Father stroked his beard. "We would be open to exploring additional trade agreements, but marriage to my daughter is out of the question."

Zwaantie let out a breath. She was in the clear. She watched the prince for a reaction. His face fell slightly, but he forged on.

"Very well. May we stay and discuss possible agreements? I will not be able to finalize anything, but after our discussions, I can take the agreements to my father." He flicked his gaze back up to her again. She averted her eyes. What was he doing?

"Of course. Where is the rest of your party?" Father asked.

Leo grinned, once again looking at her instead of Father. "My guard, Hunter, is the only one who accompanied me. We like to travel light. We hope you will be able to accommodate us. Also, we brought gifts from our home. Do you have servants who can help us fetch them from our carriage?"

Father snapped his fingers, and ten slaves appeared. They followed the prince's guard out the front doors. The prince looked around the great room, examining the tapestries and windows. He glanced at Zwaantie a time or two, but always averted his eyes when he caught her staring back. He was quick to agree to the trade possibilities, but he didn't seem to keep his eyes off of her. Perhaps he wasn't easily deterred. This could be a problem.

She took the time to study him. His angular face was different from theirs. The people of Sol were more round faced and jolly looking. His eyebrows were thick and dark, and he had an unbelievable amount of eyelashes. His eyes were a deep brown. In Sol, their eyes were usually blue or green. Occasionally gray, but brown eyes were rare.

The guard returned, and the slaves followed, carrying large trunks.

Leo opened the first trunk and took out a bottle.

"For the queen, I bring new medicines to better the health of your people. You will find that they are most effective in curing minor diseases and discomforts. There are also potions to enhance beauty, not that you need those." He grinned and closed the trunk. Two slaves lifted the trunk and placed it in front of Mother. She thanked him with a smile and raised her eyebrows at Zwaantie. Zwaantie gave a sharp shake of her head and watched as her mother stared at Leo. Was Mother considering his proposal?

The prince opened another trunk. This one was long and slender.

"For the king, I bring magically enhanced weapons." Leo pulled out a sword, and Father's eyes went wide. "This sword will never dull or chip. It is razor sharp and will slice through any opponent with ease. There are twenty of these."

Father gave Leo a rare smile. "Thank you. That is most generous. You know the way to a king's heart."

Oh Sol. Now Father was having second thoughts as well. If Prince Leo kept this up, they'd be forcing her hand within a day.

He replaced the sword and pulled out a small black box. He held it up for Father to see. "This is one of our newest inventions, a backsnipe."

Father pursed his lips. "That is no weapon. It is just a small box."

Leo grinned.

"Ah, but it is indeed a weapon. It performs much like a crossbow. Do you see this small button?"

The king nodded.

"When I press this button, the bolt will shoot out from the end and will pierce whatever I aimed it at. We are working on accuracy spells, but haven't perfected them yet. Right now, if you are a good shot, this would be the best weapon you've ever used. May I demonstrate?"

The king whispered to a slave. The slave scurried from the room and came back carrying a pedestal. He set it down by the door and placed an apple on it.

The prince pointed the small box at the apple and pushed a button. A six-inch bolt shot out of the end of the box. It went through the apple and lodged in the door.

A collective gasp filled the room. We had no weapons like that. Stella would slaughter them in a war. Leo turned to Father who clapped his hands.

"That is extraordinary. We shall go hunting while you are here. I want to see those in action. Also," he said, waving over a slave. "Go down to the kitchens and tell them we have a rare opportunity to impress the Stellans. I want a grand lunch."

Zwaantie looked at Mother, who still studied the prince with an intense gaze. Zwaantie wondered why no one else was suspicious. For years she'd heard how horrible the people of Stella were, and now here was her father and mother treating them like exalted guests.

The prince gave a small bow and put the backsnipe into a larger box.

"There are ten of those. May you use them wisely."

The prince opened a third, smaller trunk—about the size of a large jewelry box.

"I had heard Prince Raaf became the grand chancellor. This is a weighty position that requires great wisdom and carries responsibility."

He removed a leather throng like the one he wore.

"This disc is imbued with much powerful magic. In Stella, we all have them, and each is unique to the wearer. Mine protects me, and also increases my ability to observe, as I am an academic mage. I'm constantly looking to learn new things. We modeled yours off our head mage's disc, as she is the closest thing we have to a chancellor. When you wear this, your decision-making skills will be improved. We have created twenty so that you may share them with all of your lower chancellors."

The Stellan prince approached Raaf and handed him the necklace. Raaf put it on. He looked at the prince in awe. Now he would want her to marry Leo as well. This prince was making a very good impression on her family, but she wasn't convinced. Not yet.

"Finally, for the princess. It was difficult for me to know what to bring, having never met you before, but I had my sisters' help. First, I present you with a necklace that carries an amethyst, the gemstone of your birthday. Our magicians imbued it with many protection charms. While you wear it, you can never be harmed." He paused for a moment, putting the necklace back in its box. "This was my choice. My sisters, on the other hand, insisted I bring you dresses."

He lifted one out. The material flowed across his hands like water. But it was missing many important pieces. Like sleeves. And the neckline plunged down so far that her cleavage would show. No one but Luna and her mother had ever seen any part of her breasts. Leo was not going to change that now.

Filthy dresses. Don't even think about wearing them.

For once, Zwaantie agreed with the Voice. She gathered her skirts together and got ready to depart. She couldn't stay here anymore. This prince came waltzing in here asking for her hand in marriage and presenting her gifts she could never accept.

Zwaantie spoke. "High Prince Leo, it was a pleasure to meet you. But I'm afraid I'm not interested in your dresses. Now if you'll excuse me, I have a headache."

Zwaantie fled from the room, Luna close on her heels. She didn't bother to look at Mother before she left. Zwaantie didn't want to see the disappointment on her face.

Zwaantie had no intention of leaving her room again that day. She didn't have a headache, but she could pretend. Sleep would be wondrous. Maybe Luna could even find some of that magical medicine the prince brought.

Luna caught Zwaantie before she climbed into bed and wrapped Zwaantie in a hug. Zwaantie froze. There were times where Luna forgot she was in Sol and not Stella. Luna's instinct was to comfort Zwaantie, which she did a lot when they were kids, but she'd withdrawn since she became Zwaantie's slave instead of her playmate.

Luna whispered fiercely in Zwaantie's ear. "Are you okay?"

Zwaantie shook her head. "They all loved him. I know Father said I didn't have to marry him, but he's charming them. Did you see how Raaf was drooling?"

Luna pulled back and laughed. "Then Raaf can marry him. Sit," she said, pointing to Zwaantie's couch. "I'll change your sheets, and then we can get you into bed."

Zwaantie sat and stared at the star table. The moon was in a crescent shape and moved slowly across the table. For years Zwaantie had dreamed of traveling to Stella and seeing the stars. She wanted to see what Stellan magic was capable of too. But her dream was always to travel there, never live. Never leave her own home and become part of Stella. In spite of her annoyances with the Voice, she wanted to stay in Sol, marry Phoenix, and live on a farm.

In Stella they had magic. No need for fireplaces or lamps. They had blankets that warmed you and bright lights. But no sun. The dark terrified her.

"Come on, Princess, let's get you to bed." Luna undid Zwaantie's laces and helped her out of the dress. Zwaantie closed her eyes and pretended to sleep. A few minutes later she heard rustling at the door.

"She is asleep, Your Majesty. Her head ached terribly," Luna said. Zwaantie couldn't have asked for a better slave. Luna would do just about anything for her.

"Wake her up. She's never embarrassed me quite as badly as today."

"The princess is rather difficult when she's woken up. I can send her to you as soon she wakes."

"Luna, who am I?"

"The queen." Her voice quivered.

"Wake up my daughter, now, or you will be dismissed and will have to work with the sewage slaves."

Luna would never work the sewage route. Zwaantie sat up.

"I can hear you, Mother. What do you want?"

Mother crossed the room in three angry strides. Her face was beet red as she thrust it into Zwaantie's.

"How dare you. That is a high prince from Stella, and you...you..." Spittle landed on Zwaantie's face as Mother struggled to find the word.

"I rejected him, Mother. I'm sorry. You said I didn't have to marry anyone I didn't want to. He repulses me." It was a lie, but she needed to be dramatic for her mother's sake. Zwaantie kept her voice deliberately calm. Mother lost her temper occasionally, and if Zwaantie yelled back, it would just make things worse.

Mother's face softened, and she sank down on the edge of the bed. "Did you not hear your father? You don't have to marry him."

"But you were so excited by the things he had. I've never seen you look at a prince like that. How long will it be before you decide he's a good match?"

Mother stroked Zwaantie's cheek. "Oh dear girl. I don't want you to marry him. Not at all. We do need the things Stella can give us though, and this is the first time in centuries that we've had an open conversation with any member of the royal family. This will be a good thing."

Zwaantie relaxed just a little. "Thank you, Mother."

"But it is rude that you walked off like that. Especially after your father completely shut him down on his proposal. If perhaps we could announce your engagement, then Prince Leo will understand and be more open with our agreements."

"To who?" Zwaantie didn't want to think about this. She couldn't even wrap her mind around marrying someone. She was quickly falling for Phoenix, but marriage seemed so permanent. Especially since she'd never be allowed to marry him.

"There are four eligible princes. Pick one."

"What? Mother, no." She didn't know what she'd been expecting to hear. But she hadn't expected her mother to have an answer ready.

Mother's face hardened. "Zwaantie, I don't get it. What do you want?"

"To not think about marriage for a long time. Then in five or ten years, I want to marry for love." Zwaantie thought about telling her about Phoenix, but she could still see the fire in Mother's eyes and knew she'd never go for that.

"Fine. Then you will be Prince Leo's escort while he is in town. Show him the villages. Be good company. He plans on staying for two weeks. You may rest until dinner, but then you will come and be pleasant."

"Why? I don't want to." Everything about this prince made her nervous. She wanted to stay as far away from him as possible.

"Because after you left, he requested you to show him around. I think he thinks if he can spend time with you, you will choose to marry him even though your father said no. This is important."

Zwaantie gripped the sheets in her bed. Perhaps Mother and Father would force her to marry him in the end. He was from Stella though.

Mother left with one more disapproving glare.

"Luna, would you go find me some medicine? Something that will make me sleep."

"Of course."

A half hour later Zwaantie was lost to dreamland. No more thoughts of darkness and a loveless marriage.

Chapter Seventeen

THE WALL

A hand roughly shook Zwaantie out of her peace.

"Zwaantie, wake up. Wilma needs you. Now."

Zwaantie jerked awake and stared into the fearful eyes of Luna.

"What time is it?"

"Four-thirty. Come quickly. I have your brown dress ready."

Oh. No. The brown dress could only mean one thing.

"But I'll miss dinner. Mother is going to kill me."

"Well, then she is going to have to kill you. Wilma needs you. Perhaps you'll be done by seven. You'd be late for dinner, but you'd still make it."

"You know as well as I do that babies aren't born in three hours." But Zwaantie dressed quickly and followed. They found Wilma in her cottage bustling about gathering materials.

"Three women," she shrieked. "Three decided to have their babies now. I don't have six arms. How do they expect me to do three?"

"I'm here, and so is Luna. We'll both take someone."

"No, I want you girls together. Another midwife agreed to help too. She's already on her way to the VanDykes. You will take Mrs. Jacobusse. She's already had four babies. This one should come out easy."

Zwaantie had helped deliver Mrs. Jacobusse's last baby two years ago. She was quiet. Zwaantie liked that in a delivery. The problem with Mrs. Jacobusse was the distance. She lived out by the wall. They'd never make it home in time for dinner.

~

THE DELIVERY WENT FAST. THE BABY POPPED OUT JUST AFTER NINE-thirty. Still too late for dinner, but Zwaantie could make an appearance and appease Mother.

Luna followed Zwaantie to the door of the small house.

"Are you sure you can clean up on your own?" Zwaantie asked.

"Of course. Will you be okay walking by yourself?"

"Why wouldn't I be?"

Luna shrugged. "Because you're a princess. It's rare for you to be on your own without me or a guard. Or Phoenix." She smirked.

Zwaantie ignored the remark. "Exactly. I'm not by myself often. I'll enjoy the walk. I'll see you tomorrow."

There weren't many houses out this far. Zwaantie stepped out of the stifling house, and she glanced at the inky blackness of the border between Stella and Sol. Stars, it was big.

Instead of walking toward the castle, she felt drawn to the wall and its whispers. She stood about twenty feet away and listened. The whispers were fragments of conversations and thoughts with no coherency whatsoever.

"The cow, he ran away. I swear it."

"My love. She died."

"What happened to the food? We had so much a few days ago."

Zwaantie didn't know what to make of the conversations. She took a few steps closer and listened some more.

"The pain. I just want it to go away."

"It's so hot."

"I didn't mean it."

A few steps more, and the Voice began its coaxing.

Get closer. You know you want to. Add your own voice to its whispers.

Zwaantie stopped abruptly. "You've always told me to stay away from the wall."

That was before. This is now. Go, step into the darkness, and you will hear them all.

The breeze shifted, and her hair fluttered in her face. She brushed it away and took a few steps closer. "But that would be suicide."

Maybe, maybe not. But don't you want to know what the whispers are saying? Don't you want to understand?

Not really. She also didn't want the wall to grab her, steal her memories, and spit her out in a permanent state of amnesia.

Zwaantie couldn't figure out why the Voice was now encouraging her to go inside the swirling depths.

Go. See what it will tell you.

Zwaantie shook her head and closed her eyes. "No. I will not."

Yes, you will. Go now.

Zwaantie's head pounded with the disobedience. She took a few steps back from the wall. Tendrils of smoke reached for her. One encircled her wrist, and she heard a small child crying. Its cry was soft at first and then turned to a wailing. Zwaantie jerked her hand back, and the smoke withdrew into the wall.

GO NOW. WALK INTO THE WALL.

Zwaantie clutched her head. "NO! I WILL NOT!" She screamed louder than she had ever screamed before. The Voice went silent. She let go of her head. That had never happened before either—the Voice going silent. She stood tall and looked at the wall defiantly.

"You lose," she said.

She trudged to the castle, tired, and arrived home just after eleven. She'd missed dinner.

The whole exchange with the wall made her wonder what the Voice was up to. Why would it coax her into the wall instead of warning her to stay away? Where the Voice came from was a mystery. She'd asked her mother when she was child, but Mother only responded that the Voice was Sol, telling her to be a good girl. Zwaantie doubted Raaf even knew.

Perhaps this was what Mother meant about Zwaantie not being able to escape her duty as queen. Did Sol know she wanted to abdicate and decided to put an end to her before she could do any more damage? Did Sol sense the intent of her heart?

No, the Voice couldn't do that. It could only react to spoken words or actions.

Zwaantie stopped just outside the palace door, realization dawning. She had spoken the words out loud. She told her mother she didn't want to be queen.

Chapter Eighteen

THE SURPRISE

Bright light hit Zwaantie's eyes, and she blinked a few times.
"Seriously, can't I sleep in?" She rolled over and tugged her duvet over her eyes.

"Not when there is a prince from Stella here. You'll just have to get used to the idea. I managed to smooth things over with the queen last night, but she said that you will be showing the prince around Sol today." Luna pulled the cover down.

"Thank you for helping me."

Luna sighed. "I'm used to it. What happened last night anyway? I made it home before you did, and I know for a fact you weren't with Phoenix because he was with Raaf until late."

"I got distracted on my way home." Zwaantie's stomach clenched. The Voice tried to kill her last night. This was the third time someone tried to take her life. At first she had thought it was a fluke with the guard, but now she was thinking it might be more than that. Maybe the slave girl was poisoned, and that poison was meant for Zwaantie.

She shivered and looked at Luna. She wanted to talk to someone, but didn't know who she could trust. She wasn't sure she could even speak the words out loud. Especially if it was the Voice who wanted her dead. She brushed her hair out of her eyes with shaky hands and tried to act like everything was normal.

"What's on the schedule for today?" Zwaantie asked.

Luna bustled about, seemingly unaware of Zwaantie's worries. "You are taking the prince for a walk around the village to show him how we live. Your mother made me promise to talk to you about being charming and not obnoxious."

Zwaantie stuck her tongue out at Luna.

Luna laughed and continued to blather. Which was fine, because as long as she talked and didn't notice Zwaantie was still in bed, the longer she could lie there. If she just stayed here, would she be safe? Was anywhere safe?

Luna threw off the duvet, and Zwaantie curled into herself. "It's cold."

You must get up. You have work to do.

"The water in your tub is hot. Go." Luna pointed to her bathing area. Zwaantie sighed and shuffled to the tub and sank into the steaming water. While Zwaantie soaked, she heard Luna rustling through something. She poked her head around the shade.

"Why don't you wear one of the dresses the prince brought you?"

Luna held up a short yellow dress that wouldn't go farther than mid-thigh. The skirt flared out and had something underneath that made it puffy. The top of the dress was even less sensible, with a neckline that plunged and sleeves that would barely cover her shoulders. While it was pretty, there was no way in the dark that she would put that on.

"You are joking, right?"

She wiggled her eyebrows at Zwaantie. "Phoenix would choke if he saw you in it. Maybe then he'd actually kiss you."

Zwaantie splashed water toward her. "How do you know these things?" Zwaantie's face burned. She did want Phoenix to kiss her, but she didn't realize Luna knew.

Luna ignored the question. "Start your scrubbing. I'll try to find something more suitable for you to wear."

"Something not out of that trunk."

Luna dug around the trunk for a while, gave up, and pulled out one of Zwaantie's yellow dresses. She'd always liked it because it felt sunny.

After dressing, Luna braided her hair, and Zwaantie ate a quick breakfast. Then they went down to the entrance hall.

The prince was already there, dressed exactly like he had yesterday, except he wore flimsy shoes that left most of his feet bare. Crazy boy. Didn't he know that his feet would get soaked in shoes like that? The streets were always wet. Not to mention the dirt and filth. Eww.

Zwaantie kept her eyes trained on the people around her. Could the gardener want to kill her? Or the maybe the woman out beating her rugs. It could be anyone. Except the prince. He'd arrived after the guard had tried to kill her, so it couldn't be him.

He bowed, and Zwaantie inclined her head.

"Princess," he said, taking her hand. "You look lovely this morning."

"Thank you," she replied. She thought about giving him the same compliment, but didn't want to encourage him. Though she was certain he didn't want to kill her, she still didn't want to marry him. They left the castle via the front door, Luna and Hunter following a few feet behind.

As they meandered down the road to the village, Zwaantie wondered what he thought of their town. Was it different from his?

"Your mother tells me that last night you helped deliver a baby, and that is why you missed dinner."

"Yes." Zwaantie noticed everything about the village. The small houses, the cobblestone streets, the slaves and guards who hid just out of sight. What if another guard tried to kill her? Would someone stop them?

"Why do you deliver babies? Isn't that what healers are for?"

"In Sol we believe in being productive members of society even as royalty. My mother likes to sew, my father is an expert with a bow and arrow, Raaf cooks. I decided to train as a midwife. I find the work quite rewarding."

She wished the world was different. That she could be a midwife for real. What a simple life she'd live.

"I would imagine it would be frightening."

"How so?"

"You don't have magic. Don't some women die in childbirth?"

"Sometimes, but with the magic potions we get from Stella, we have less death than we used to. Do your women ever die?"

"Rarely, though occasionally a woman will give birth after midnight. Most of the time they are safe, but every once in a while, one dies. We consider it a great tragedy when that happens."

Zwaantie creased her eyebrows. "How is midnight different in Stella? Here the Voice turns off. But you have no Voice."

"Our magic disappears. It's quite frightening actually." His hands were in his pockets, but his shoulders were tense.

"Then I suppose it's not that much different from Sol at night then."

He gave a tight smile. "Sort of."

This early in the morning, there were slaves everywhere. They were picking up the trash, sweeping the cobblestones, and cleaning windows on the shops. Zwaantie probably should've waited a few hours before venturing out. She wanted to show the prince what it was like when everything was sparkling and brilliant. Not half done.

Each person they passed stopped whatever he was doing and bowed.

"Are your people always this respectful?" Leo asked, watching a slave to his left.

"Yes. Aren't yours?" Quite frankly, it was annoying. Just once she'd like to be able to walk down the street and not have everything stop dead.

He hesitated for a second, like he was debating whether to tell her. "No, they only bow when they come to the castle. Out on the street we are just like any other person. I like it. I can go to the store or a club without being harassed. I usually take Hunter with me for safety, but most people treat me normal."

Zwaantie didn't know how to respond. No one, except for Luna, Phoenix, and Wilma, had ever treated her like a normal person. Most wouldn't even talk to her. Even when she was delivering their babies, they are all "Sorry, Your Highness."

"Must be nice," Zwaantie said.

"It is."

A slave dashed in front of them to pick up a piece of discarded fruit. Zwaantie hadn't been paying attention and tripped over the slave. The prince caught her, and Zwaantie couldn't help notice a whiff of citrus and coconut. He smelled like summer.

In a flash, Luna had the slave by the ear and dragged him to the edge of the street. She would give him a tongue-lashing, and he would never step in front of royalty again.

The prince stared at Luna and the slave for a moment with a frown. Zwaantie wondered what he was thinking. They walked on and passed the bakery with an incredible aroma of bread and cakes floating out.

"Does your village look like this?" Zwaantie asked.

"We call it a city, not a village. It looks nothing like this. Our buildings are tall with bright lights. And there are many more people than here."

They walked in silence for a few moments, and Zwaantie reflected on how different this felt. She had never taken the time to get to know any of the other princes. She didn't want to. A breeze blew, and Zwaantie noticed that Leo's hair didn't move. It was so strange, spiky like that.

"Tell me more about this prince that you're going to marry," he said.

"I haven't decided who I'm going to marry yet. Honestly, I'd rather not marry at all. I keep telling Mother that, but she doesn't listen."

But you will marry. Soon.

Zwaantie paused. She almost told him that she didn't want to be queen, but she wasn't about to say that again for fear of what would happen. The Voice was in her head again, after the wall, like normal. For some reason that brought a strange comfort to her. She wasn't sure she'd like it if the Voice disappeared altogether. Even if she was afraid it was trying to kill her.

She glanced over at Leo, surprised at how comfortable she was talking to him. Perhaps it was because he was temporary. Someone who would disappear in two weeks and take her secrets with him.

"I want to marry for love. The princes are not looking for love. They are looking for a princess. They don't see me. And not one of them has ever even been interested in me for a moment. Including you. You pranced into our palace and announced your intentions without even so much as a glance in my direction."

"What was I supposed to do? Announce that I just wanted to visit Sol and get to know the royal family? They would've been highly suspicious."

"I suppose you have a point, but don't you think the whole process feels so wrong? I mean, what if you totally hated me, or suppose I was ugly and fat. Would you still marry me then?"

"I'm doing what is best for my country. If that means being unhappy with my wife, then I will do that."

Zwaantie didn't know how to react to that. He was braver than her for sure. She couldn't imagine giving up her happiness for the sake of her country. She felt a little embarrassed of herself.

"Well, we've already established that I will not marry you. So you are off the hook."

"Forgive me for being bold, but I haven't given up yet. You are most beautiful and charming. I think I would be happy with you. Is there any way I can convince you to reconsider?"

Oh, he was good. Complimenting her like that and then trying to see what he could do to win her over. Zwaantie did not like where this conversation was going. Time to pull out the real charm.

"Well, the last suitor refused to moo for me. I will definitely not marry someone who won't moo for me."

He looked puzzled. "What is mooing?"

Zwaantie stopped, right in the middle of the street. "Mooing, you know, like a cow."

"What's a cow?"

"A farm animal. Cows, chickens, sheep, goats, pigs, horses."

Leo furrowed his brow. "I've heard of horses and chickens, but none of the others."

"Have you ever eaten beef?" Zwaantie was dumbfounded. Their whole world revolved around those animals. How could he not know?

"Of course. It comes from here. We can't grow our own food, and animals are hard to keep without fields."

"Where did you think beef came from?"

He shrugged. "Never thought of it much."

The village was the wrong place to be. They needed to visit the farm. The royal farm was smaller than most of the outlying farms, but they still had all the required animals. As a child, Zwaantie's favorite thing to do was milk cows and collect eggs. Which Mother put a stop to the day she got her monthlies. After that she had to be a real princess who sewed and visited with other princesses.

"Let's go visit a farm. Though, you'll need to change your clothes."

"Why?" He looked down at his fluffy white shirt, poofy pants, vest, and flimsy shoes.

"Look at those shoes. They don't protect your feet at all."

"These are sandals. What do my feet need protecting from anyway?"

"Dirt, rocks, cow poop. I need to change too."

He pointed at her feet. "Okay, but I am not wearing shoes like that."

"Fine, but you can't wear those either. And don't get mad if you mess up your pretty leather boots."

"Where are you taking me, the swamp?"

"Something like that, but more fun. Let's go change."

Zwaantie was a little excited to show him her world. Plus, he was easier to talk to than she had planned. Maybe it was because he was from Stella. She'd always felt more comfortable with Luna and Phoenix than she ever had with any of her royal friends.

Zwaantie hurried to her room. As she rounded the corner, she ran right into Phoenix. He grinned as he helped steady her. Pieter was with him, and Luna stood on her tiptoes and gave him a kiss.

"Aw, aren't you two cute?" Zwaantie asked, still not letting go of Phoenix. She liked standing there, practically in his arms.

Luna blushed. "Well, the Voice doesn't care anymore if we kiss."

Zwaantie met Phoenix's eyes. "Must be nice."

His gaze burned into hers. She was so very close. A few inches and she'd get a kiss of her own.

Phoenix let go of her and took two steps back. She couldn't help her disappointment.

"Where are you going in such a hurry?" he asked.

"The prince has never seen a farm, so we're going to show him around. I didn't want to get my yellow dress dirty."

Phoenix raised his eyebrows. "Do you like the Stellan prince?"

Zwaantie shrugged. "He's just like any of the others. Boring."

Phoenix gave a sharp nod. "Well, we need to head on. Raaf and the king sent us to fetch the new weapons. They want to play with them."

As they walked away, Zwaantie had a sinking feeling. Someone was trying to kill her. It'd be a lot easier with those new weapons.

Chapter Nineteen

THE COW: PART 2

Leo wrinkled his nose. "What are those things?"

The pigs rolled around in the muck and snorted. Zwaantie loved the farm. If she hadn't chosen midwifery for her contribution, she would've picked something related to farming. Somehow, she didn't think Mother would let her be a farmer even if she'd tried.

"Pigs. We get bacon and pork from them."

He breathed out. "Bacon smells a hellava lot better than that."

"Yes, well, we wash them first," Zwaantie said without cracking a smile.

"With what?" he asked with a frown.

"Soap."

Leo looked at her and smiled. "Bacon doesn't smell like soap either. And I've butchered fish before, so I imagine pigs are the same way. Good thing we don't eat the outside of them, huh?"

So, he wasn't dumb. That was good to know.

He backed away from the pigpen, and Zwaantie followed. She couldn't tell what he was thinking. She wanted him to like the farm, and it bothered her that she wanted his approval. She wasn't sure what she thought of him, but he had to get off the marriage idea.

"Come on." She waved him to the chicken coop. "The chickens aren't quite so stinky. Would you like to gather some eggs with me?"

"Sure. My mother cooked for fun, and she taught me her tricks. She used to create mountains of scrambled eggs for me in rainbow colors. I was twelve before I knew that the natural color for eggs was yellow."

Part of Zwaantie yearned to understand that magic, but part of her was repulsed by changing food with magic.

A slave handed them baskets, and they set about finding eggs. She stuck her hand in a box and withdrew an egg. Leo watched her for a few moments.

He stuck his hand in another box without looking. Maybe he wasn't so smart.

"Yow," he yelled and jerked his hand out.

Zwaantie looked down and saw an angry red mark on his hand. Then she giggled. A hen stuck her head out of the opening of the box and clucked at him.

"You are supposed to check the box before you stick your hand inside. She thinks you are taking her babies." Zwaantie laughed again. He scowled for a second and then smiled at her.

"Can we cook these when we get back to the castle?"

"The slaves will do it. Though I doubt they know how to make it pretty colors."

"You never do any of your own cooking?" he asked, checking another box before sticking his hand in and pulling out a small brown egg.

Zwaantie watched him. "A few royals do. The ones who decide to make it their hobby. I chose midwifery, so I've never cooked anything."

"Ah, Princess, you are missing out. When you come to Stella with me, I will teach you how to cook."

Oh, he had some nerve. She frowned at him. "What makes you think I'm coming to Stella with you?"

His smile faltered, and he blushed. Good. He was too sure of himself.

"I'm sorry. I got carried away. I really like you. I mean, I know I just met you, but you are truly the most beautiful girl I've ever seen."

Now it was Zwaantie's turn to blush. Her stomach buzzed, but it also made her nervous. She was in love with Phoenix. Guilt gnawed at her insides. Her stomach shouldn't be fluttering for anyone else.

Leo glanced over to Hunter and Luna. They seemed to be enjoying a lively conversation. At least they were getting along.

"Come, I want to introduce you to the sheep." She handed off the eggs to a couple of slaves, and Leo strolled next to her through the field.

"Why do your people wear bondage bands?" he asked.

"They are slaves."

"I don't understand. The only people who wear them in our kingdom are prisoners. And they wear them only so that we can know to not trust them. But you have so many. Even your maid wears them."

"She is a slave. Her mother chose to become a slave."

He stepped around a sheep and wrinkled his brow. "What is a slave, exactly?"

"When our people cannot feed themselves, they choose to become slaves. They agree to serve in whatever capacity the city needs in exchange for food, shelter, and basic clothing. The bondage bands are placed to make sure they follow the agreement. It lasts one hundred years for themselves and any posterity they have. After a hundred years, the bands fall off."

"How is that fair?" he asked, his frown deepening.

"They do work hard for what they are given, so it is fair to the kingdom." She'd been questioning some of the slave practices recently, but the system was efficient, and while it wasn't the best for some individuals, the overall practice was necessary.

His face went beet red, and he stopped abruptly. Hunter came running. "Your Highness, is something wrong?"

"I'm fine. But there is something seriously twisted here."

Leo grabbed Luna's arm and shook her band in Zwaantie's face. "Your slave didn't choose this life. Her mother did. How is it fair to her that she should have to live like this? And her children and grandchildren? This is a sick system."

Zwaantie squared her shoulders and raised her head. "They live good lives. At least ours do. If we didn't have the system in place, they would starve." This was her home, and she wasn't about to let a snotty prince from Stella tell her how to run her kingdom.

Leo stalked off across the field toward the castle. Zwaantie followed but didn't get the chance to warn him before he stepped in a pile of cow poop.

"Oh, for the love of all the stars!" he yelled and held his foot up. "What is this?" he asked, pointing to the steaming crap with a wrinkled nose.

She giggled. "Cow poop."

He muttered under his breath and wiped his foot on the grass. He held onto a tree to steady himself.

"Why do you like it out here?" he asked as she drew nearer to him.

"I told you. The cows."

"I still have no idea what a cow is."

Zwaantie smirked as a cow walked up behind him and bellowed in his ear. He jumped and stormed away. Zwaantie, Luna, and even Hunter laughed.

Leo was sulky and silent all the way to the palace. Just before they got to the entrance, he stopped Zwaantie.

"I'm sorry. We don't have slaves in Stella, and the idea just seems so horrific to me. And then I stepped in, well, you know. Forgive me?"

She shook her head. "No, you ruined my afternoon. But if you do something for me, I will." She was wicked, but she couldn't help herself.

"Whatever you want." He said and bowed extravagantly, a crooked smile on his face.

"Moo for me."

Luna giggled behind her.

Leo's face was impassive. She had no idea what he would do. But without warning, he let out a huge bellow and grinned at her.

"Thank you," she said, genuinely pleased.

"I'll see you at dinner," he said. Then he leaned over and kissed her on the cheek.

He and Hunter sauntered into the castle. Luna's face had gone pale. Zwaantie had just been kissed for the first time in her life by someone other than her parents.

And it wasn't Phoenix.

The Voice immediately began its assault.

You filthy girl. How dare you let him do that to you? You should go scrub your face with acid to burn off the filth. Filthy, filthy girl.

Chapter Twenty

THE KISS

Zwaantie didn't go into the castle. She marched away and down the street. She ignored the slaves and merchants who fell to the ground in a bow.

Filthy girl. A small headache formed between her eyes, but it wasn't bad. The Voice continued to call her all sorts of names.

She stomped inside Wilma's cottage. Wilma looked up from a book she was reading. "Goodness sakes, child, why are you making such a racket?"

"That prince," she fumed. She paced in front of Wilma.

Wilma closed her book, took off her reading glasses, and watched Zwaantie. "What did he do?"

"He kissed me," she spat.

Wilma laughed. "I'd take a kiss from him any day."

Zwaantie glared at her. "Well, you can have him. I hope the Voice is yelling at you, by the way. This isn't funny."

"Honey, he's a doll and probably your future husband. What's wrong with him kissing you?"

Zwaantie stopped and shook her finger in Wilma's face. "Take that back. He will not be my husband. I don't love him. And he's from Stella. How dare you even suggest it."

"Most marriages aren't for love. He's a good choice, better than any of the Solite princes."

"He's from Stella." Zwaantie couldn't believe Wilma was actually suggesting she marry the prince. Sure, Zwaantie enjoyed the magic from Stella, but they were too different. Their culture of touching and kissing and obscene clothes.

"So?"

"So, they're...they're barbarians. He kissed me!"

Wilma stood and pointed at the table. "Let me make you a cup of tea and help you calm down."

"I don't want to calm down."

Wilma bustled about making tea. Zwaantie sat at the table fuming. Not only was Wilma unsympathetic, but she actually thought Zwaantie should marry that creep. At least the Voice stopped berating her. Maybe it realized the kiss wasn't her fault.

Wilma brought two steaming cups to the table.

"When is the wedding?" Wilma asked with a grin.

Zwaantie glared at her and sipped her tea. It burned going down, but Wilma's teas were the best. This tasted of lavender and vanilla.

Wilma was altogether too eager to see her marry Leo. Time to change the subject.

"Did you hear about my guard?"

Wilma sat across from her. "The one who jumped off the bridge? Yes. I did."

"And did you know how that girl died the other night at dinner? Was it possible she was poisoned?"

Wilma shrugged. "Maybe. Why?"

Zwaantie hadn't wanted to admit this out loud. But she was starting to see patterns. "I think someone is trying to kill me. Or rather. I think the Voice is."

Wilma took a sip of her tea and stared into her cup. "Why would you think that?"

"Because I told Mother that I didn't want to be queen. She said Sol wouldn't let me abdicate. What if this is Sol's way of making sure I don't?"

Wilma raised her eyebrows. "By killing you?"

"It sounds stupid, I know. But that girl died, my guard tried to kill me, and the Voice tried to lure me into the wall."

"I checked the girl out, and it did not look like poison to me. Though I will admit poison can be hard to detect. The wall though, you didn't tell me about that."

Zwaantie explained how the Voice tried to make her step into the wall.

"Now, that's easy. You were too close to the wall. That wasn't the Voice at all, but the wall trying to trick you. As for your guard. Obviously, he was going mad. Otherwise, he wouldn't have taken his own life. Does that ease your fears?"

Zwaantie nodded, but she still felt uneasy about the whole thing. Something was off.

Wilma looked out the window to the sun. "You must go. I don't think your mother will let you miss another dinner."

~

THE SLAVE CHEFS CREATED QUITE THE FEAST FOR THE PRINCE. Everything was super fresh, from the greens to the sausages. The prince seemed so in love with the food Zwaantie was surprised he even had time to carry on a conversation with Raaf.

Zwaantie wasn't speaking to Leo, which he took in stride, but she listened to his conversation with Raaf.

"Do you have many siblings?" Raaf asked.

"Yes. I only have one full sister. But through my father I have ten additional siblings. My mother also has three more sons, but I don't see them much."

Zwaantie didn't understand. She wanted to ask, but didn't want to talk to him. Having siblings without the same parents seemed so foreign. It happened occasionally when someone died, but he had half siblings from both parents.

"What do you mean?" Raaf asked. "Does your father have more than one wife?"

"Oh no. My mother and father never married. My mother married her current husband after she had me."

Raaf seemed speechless. "Do you plan on having children before you are married?"

"Of course not. Only the king does that. Well, officially anyway. Several of my siblings are already married. One of my brothers on my mother's side married a Solite, actually."

Zwaantie nearly broke her vow of silence, but Raaf beat her to it.

"How is that possible? Solites are not allowed to cross the wall."

"I don't know. Like I said, I'm not close to that brother. He lives in a different city. But he brought his wife to the castle to have my father remove her bondage bands. I thought she must've been a prisoner. But now I understand she was a slave."

Raaf went quiet, and Zwaantie cursed him. She wanted to hear more. But then Raaf changed the subject and waxed on about Sol's discipline system, which seemed to fascinate Leo but bored Zwaantie to tears.

The strawberry shortcake arrived, and Zwaantie was grateful dinner was almost over.

"This is amazing. I've never had strawberries that taste like this. How do you do it?" Leo asked her.

A direct question. She wasn't sure she could ignore that. Zwaantie pointed up. "The sun."

He nodded. "So why are you mad at me? I've been trying to figure it out, but I'm lost. I mooed for you."

"You kissed me." She shuddered at the thought.

A crease appeared in his forehead.

"I did?"

"Yes, on the cheek. No one has ever kissed me before."

"That was highly inappropriate," Raaf said. "Didn't the Voice warn you?"

Zwaantie glared at her brother. "No, it didn't warn me. I didn't know he was going to do it. But the guilt was horrid."

Raaf speared one of his strawberries. "I wasn't talking to you. I was talking to Leo," Raaf said.

"No, the Voice didn't warn me. Why would it?" Leo scratched his forehead.

"If the Voice can tell that you are about to do something wrong, it will warn you so you don't do it. Surely it could tell what you were doing."

"I'm sorry. The Voice said nothing to me." He faced Zwaantie. "What did the Voice say after I kissed you?"

She blushed. "I don't want to tell you, but it made me feel bad about the kiss, and it's your fault."

Leo picked up his fork again. "It was a simple kiss on the cheek. I often give my sisters the same. I'm sorry if I offended you, but in Stella, kissing on the cheek is considered a polite form of greeting. Probably why the Voice didn't warn me. It's not wrong for me."

Raaf frowned. "That's interesting. The ways of the Voice are mysterious. I wonder what else you can do that we cannot because it is not forbidden in Stella."

Leo shrugged. "You must teach me how to get food like this in Stella. We try with magic, but it doesn't even compare."

After dinner, Zwaantie escaped out to the rock where she and Phoenix met. She needed to think. Phoenix wouldn't be there for an hour at least, and she wanted to be alone. Voices came from the other side of the hedge. Zwaantie listened for a moment. It was Leo and his guard. She crept toward the hedge.

"She is gorgeous. This is bloody awful," Leo said. Zwaantie's stomach buzzed again. She shouldn't react to the fact that he thought she was beautiful. She loved Phoenix.

"How is that a bad thing?" Hunter asked.

"She's funny and beautiful. What do I have to offer her that no other suitor has? Especially since her father has no interest in entertaining the thought."

"You are a high prince. From Stella, which is a hellava lot better than here. And no offense, she's pretty and all, but not gorgeous."

"You're just saying that because you are over the moon in love with Candace. If you weren't, you'd agree with me."

Zwaantie crouched down so she could see them. They sat with their backs to a tree. Hunter pulled an apple out of his bag. "Speaking of Candace, do you remember that she promised to castrate you if you didn't have me back in time for the baby? So whatever you need to do, do it quick." He took a big bite of the apple. "Stars, the fruit here is amazing."

"Father will kill me if I don't return with her. But I made a complete ass of myself today."

"Yeah, you sort of did. The cow dung didn't help. At least it doesn't smell as bad as dog poop."

The prince smiled. "I miss Molly. Have you noticed they have no pets here? No cats, dogs, or birds. Just cows and pigs and crap."

Hunter shrugged. "Maybe we can bring her a kitten or something. That might work. We'd have to go back home first though."

Leo grimaced. "That will take too long."

"Focus. We aren't going anywhere until you get the princess to marry you. What are you going to do?"

"I don't know. This shouldn't be that hard."

Hunter shook his head and swallowed. "You are a prince. Woo her. Don't they teach you that in prince school?"

Leo slugged Hunter in the arm. "I have an idea. Let's go talk to her servants and find out what she does when she thinks no one is looking. I'll find a way to win her heart."

They ran to the castle, and Zwaantie rocked back on her heels. Leo wasn't interested in any trade agreements. He wanted one thing and one thing only.

Her.

The question was why. He'd given no good reason, but he said his father would kill him if he didn't marry her. What was so special about her?

The problem with Leo was that he was incredibly charming. If he convinced Father and Mother that he was a good match, Zwaantie might not have a choice.

She had to figure out how to get out of this. Because unless she was walking down the aisle with Phoenix, she didn't want to do it at all.

Chapter Twenty-One

THE DECLARATION

Phoenix joined her on the rock an hour later. "Missed you last night," he said.

"I know. I had to help deliver babies. I didn't get home till nearly gray. Besides, Luna said you were with Raaf anyway."

"I got here late and just assumed you didn't wait for me."

They sat in silence for a few moments. Then Phoenix spoke. His voice was low and quiet. "I saw the prince kiss you outside the castle. Did you agree to marry him?"

Zwaantie's chest burned. "No. I didn't ask for any of that. I'm not going to marry him." She took his hand. "I love you more than anything. I'm going to marry you. I don't know how or what it will take, but I will."

The Voice went bananas. Take that back. Foul girl. You know your place.

A pinch started in her forehead. But her declaration was worth the pain. Zwaantie figured while she was at it, she might as well give the Voice something to really berate her for. That cow-hole Leo had already kissed her cheek, and she was going to be damn sure he didn't get one on her lips before Phoenix did.

She hopped off the rock and motioned for him to join her. He landed right next to her. "Who's chasing who?" he asked.

"No one."

She grabbed both of his hands and wove their fingers together. He smiled at her, and she took a step closer. So far, the Voice didn't seem to notice anything out of the ordinary. Zwaantie met his smoldering eyes. She should've kissed him when he was in her room. She was done waiting.

She stood on her tiptoes and pressed her mouth against his. His lips were soft against hers, but he didn't react. Just stood there still as a maple tree. Zwaantie pulled away, her chest tight.

"I'm sorry," he said with sad eyes. "I couldn't do it. I love you though."

Filthy, filthy girl.

A blinding pain overtook her forehead, and she knew that for the first time in her life, she would have to confess to her brother.

Chapter Twenty-Two

THE FAILURE

The Voice called over Zwaantie's orb and removed the guilt. He thought about just letting her suffer and maybe allowing that to drive her mad. In the end though, he was afraid that would lead to questions about him. A peasant or slave with unending pain was one thing. The princess was quite another.

A clatter sounded behind him. Oh Sol, she was back again.

He spun around.

"She's onto you," the woman said.

"Excuse me?"

"Zwaantie. She knows it is the Voice."

"How would you know that?"

"I overheard a conversation between her and one of her friends. She knows. Need I remind you what happens if you don't stop this? The prince from Stella plans on winning her heart. I daresay he's almost succeeded."

The Voice laughed. "No. He's not. Trust me."

"Regardless. She suspects you. What are you going to do about that?"

"Does it matter if she suspects me or not? I got close last time."

"With the guard?"

"No. The wall. Though the guard was a near miss. If Zwaantie had come home even ten minutes earlier, he would've killed her, but she was too close to midnight, and my influence ended before he had a chance to finish. The next one will work."

"And what, pray tell, is the next one?"

"None of your business." This woman had done nothing so far to help him. He wasn't about to reveal his plans to her.

"It is my business. I need her dead as much as you do."

"Trust me. She doesn't have a single person dear to her who won't attempt to kill her before this is all over. The whispers are planting seeds."

The woman pounded her fist on the table. "You cannot fail. If she even gets close to crossing the Stellan border, I will intervene, and you won't like my methods."

Then she turned on the spot and disappeared.

Chapter Twenty-Three

THE SNOOP

The next morning, Mother summoned Zwaantie to her room. She probably just wanted an update on how things were going with Leo. Zwaantie could report that she'd been a good girl. Usually Luna would accompany her when she visited her mother, but she'd sent Luna off to find out if Wilma would need her later. She was looking for an excuse to not have to be with Leo.

She knocked, and Ariel peeked out.

"My mother sent for me."

"Yes, come in." Ariel opened the door wider, and Zwaantie swept into the room. She saw Raaf sitting in another chair, Phoenix standing behind him.

She didn't look at Phoenix as she approached the chairs. She was afraid her face would betray her.

She took her seat carefully and smiled. "How are you, Mother?"

Mother scowled at her. "Tell me, Zwaantie, are you in love?"

"Of course not. Who would I possibly be in love with?" Zwaantie hoped against hope that this wasn't the moment where Mother decided she marry Leo.

Mother shook her head. "I was taking a stroll in my garden yesterday, and it was stuffy and crowded and I wanted to be alone so I wandered a little to the west. To my surprise I overheard the most interesting conversation."

Zwaantie paled. She tried to keep her expression neutral.

"Oh, and what did you hear?"

"My daughter, the crown princess, swearing her undying love for a slave. She even promised to marry him. Can you imagine how shocked I was to hear such a conversation?"

Phoenix squeezed his eyes shut.

"Mother, I can explain."

Mother narrowed her eyes. "No. You cannot. I understand now our previous conversations. I have given you options, Zwaantie. I have been nice about this, but no more. You have been shirking your responsibility, and it's time for you to step up and take your place. Maybe then you'll stop with these foolish notions. Once all of the princes arrive, you will have three days to pick one, or I will see to it that Phoenix is executed for his crimes. Do you understand?"

Zwaantie's chest tightened, and her palms began to sweat. Phoenix had done nothing wrong. What was mother thinking? "What crimes?" she asked with desperation.

"Persuading the princess to love him. For a slave, that is death."

"You wouldn't." Zwaantie squeezed her eyes shut. She'd never thought that far. How stupid of her to not think of Phoenix's life.

"I would."

"Mother, I must protest," Raaf spoke up. Oh, thank the stars, Raaf would save her.

"Excuse me, Raaf, but what does this have to do with you?"

"Phoenix is my slave. I need him. You can't take him away from me."

Mother narrowed her eyes at Phoenix. "What is this sorcery you have done? Have you bewitched both of my children? I cannot believe I allowed you to play with them. That was my mistake. I won't make it again. For now, you will work with the sewage slaves. Zwaantie obviously needs some persuading. But if she doesn't marry a prince, you will see your death. I promise you that. Guards, bring him to the sewers."

Tears fell freely. Zwaantie watched as they dragged him away. Her heart shattered. She wanted to save him, but she couldn't. She tried to hold in the sobs, but they came anyway.

"Now, go to your room. I will summon all of the lower princes to the castle and you will announce your engagement within the month."

Chapter Twenty-Four

THE REVELATION

Zwaantie spent most of the next day crying in her bed. Luna bustled around the room but didn't try to talk to her. She must be upset as well, but all Zwaantie could focus on was the pain in her stomach. Not only had she lost the love of her life, she was now going to be forced to marry someone else. And poor Phoenix. He was in the sewers, shoveling out the muck and refuse. This was her fault.

Sometime after lunch, Luna flung the covers off.

"Get up. I know you are upset, but at this point, our goal is to keep Phoenix alive. To do that, you must choose a husband. You need to go for a walk, clear your head, and be ready to charm the ones who've arrived at dinner."

Zwaantie wanted to hit her. "Who is here?"

"Vache. I heard Ryker will make it before dinner because he was already in town visiting with the lower king and queen of Zonnes. It will take Willem and Isaac a few more days."

Oh Sol, they were already here. Luna was right. Zwaantie had to keep Phoenix alive.

"Okay," Zwaantie said and swung her legs out of bed.

"You need to change first and let me fix your hair. Then, while you are out, I'll clean up this room."

Zwaantie changed and washed her face. After Luna did her hair, she went out to the garden. Phoenix wouldn't be there, but she just wanted to be in a place where they'd been happy.

Just as she started down the path to the pond, a hand gripped her elbow. She spun around.

"Leo, what are you doing here?"

"Taking a walk."

"Where is Hunter?"

"He's training with a few of your guards. I was bored, so I thought I'd check out the gardens. Would you like to join me?"

She wanted to say no, but she couldn't. She took a deep breath, let it out, and tucked her arm into his elbow. They wandered toward the roses. She did not want to talk about herself, so she quickly asked him a question. "What's your family like?"

"Loud."

"You can give me more than that."

"Father's a typical king. Though he spends more time with me than yours does with you, I think."

"That wouldn't be hard. I don't see my father often. What do you do with him?"

"He likes to take me out among the people. We'll go to a bar or restaurant and mingle. Father taught me how to gauge the happiness of our people by how they behave around us."

"Why? You aren't heir to the throne."

He pursed his lips. "No, I'm not. Nevertheless, my father thought it was best to teach me how to handle the affairs of the kingdom. I will likely be a close advisor when my brother becomes king."

A tickle of memory came to Zwaantie. The last time Leo spoke of his father, he mentioned how his father had removed bondage bands.

"Didn't you say you had a brother who was married to a Solite slave?"

"Yes."

"Can your father remove all bondage bands?" Perhaps she could somehow find a way to sneak Phoenix across the border. If that Solite woman did it, then it must be possible. But Zwaantie didn't want to be too hopeful. Not yet.

"Of course. So can I."

Zwaantie's heart stilled. She kept her voice steady as she tried to make sense of things. "Can all Stellans remove them?"

"No. Only a few. I can do it because I deal with prisoners sometimes."

"I thought you said you were an academic mage."

He gave her a wink. "I lied. Sort of."

"What's that supposed to mean?"

"Well, I am an academic mage, but I don't sit around reading books all day."

"What do you do?"

"I work closely with our head mage. She's similar in rank to your brother."

Zwaantie wanted to ask more, but the wheels in her head were spinning. This changed everything. Mother had not been specific enough. She said pick a prince. She didn't say she couldn't marry the Stellan.

Chapter Twenty-Five

THE ANNOUNCEMENT

The next morning Zwaantie woke early, buzzing with excitement about her plan. She spent all night planning how she would pull this off. She'd nearly told the prince she would marry him last night but figured that would be too suspicious. This would be epic.

Luna arrived after Zwaantie awoke. She seemed harried and worried.

"I want my best dress," Zwaantie said.

"Well, you're just going to have to wait," Luna snapped.

Whoa.

"What's the matter?" Zwaantie asked.

Luna shook her head. "I don't feel good. Sorry."

Zwaantie smiled. Luna's foul mood couldn't ruin hers.

"What color dress?"

"The green," Zwaantie replied.

She hauled out the dress and then scowled at Zwaantie. "Why are you in such a good mood? Or have you forgotten about my brother?"

Zwaantie felt as if she'd been slapped. "No. Of course not. I have a plan. I found out yesterday that Leo can remove bondage bands in Stella. So I'm going to tell him I'll marry him and then make sure he takes Phoenix with us. Then Phoenix and I will run away in Stella." Zwaantie bounced on the bed. She was pretty pleased with herself.

Luna blinked for a second. "It's a stupid plan."

"What's stupid about it?" Zwaantie was hurt.

"Where are you going to live? Work? You've never worked a day in your life. Do you think you can live like normal people do? Because that's what you'll have to do. And don't think you'll be able to come back to Sol. Your father will have people looking everywhere for you, and then they'll execute the both of you."

She made it seem like Zwaantie hadn't thought about that. Which she hadn't, but that was beside the point.

"I'll just get work as a midwife in Stella. They have babies there too."

Luna slipped the dress over Zwaantie's head. "They have mages who deliver babies. They won't need a midwife."

Zwaantie hadn't thought of that. She could learn. Maybe magic was teachable. Plus, Phoenix was employable.

"We'll figure it out."

"Still stupid. But you never did listen to me anyway. Come on, let's go ruin your life."

Zwaantie paused for a second. "Wait. Something is wrong. Tell me."

Luna rubbed her forehead. "No, it's not. I don't feel good, but I still have to work. I know you're excited about this plan, but all I can see is how many ways in which it can go wrong."

"Say the word, and I won't do it."

Luna gave her a sad smile. "I'm not about to tell the future queen what to do. I think it's stupid, but I'll still support you in your decision."

The prince's room was three doors down from hers. This early in the morning the hallways were empty. Luna knocked, and Zwaantie waited. Hunter opened the door, his hair disheveled. He wore only a pair of short shorts. Zwaantie looked away quickly and felt bad for Luna. She had to look at him.

Luna coughed. "The princess would like to speak to High Prince Leo."

"Of course," he said, "One moment, please."

They heard bumps and bangs from the other side, and two minutes later the door opened. Hunter had managed to put some pants on but nothing else. His chest was distracting.

"Ladies, come in." He gestured into the room.

Luna followed after Zwaantie. Leo stood near the fireplace, dressed as he had yesterday before they went to see the cows. He bowed when he saw her.

"Luna, Hunter, I would like to speak with the prince alone. Will you excuse us?"

Luna hurried out of the room, but Hunter hesitated. He walked over to the prince and whispered something in his ear. The prince nodded and then dismissed him with a wave. He left and looked back just before he shut the door behind him.

"Would you like to sit, Princess?" Leo asked.

He seemed nervous, unsure of himself.

She sat and stared at him for a moment. She took a deep breath. There were a thousand ways this could go wrong, but she had to try. This was the only way she could save Phoenix.

"If I were to marry you, how would that work? Where would we live? What about the wedding? Do you have anything you want from us?"

He seemed taken aback by the question. "I thought that you didn't want to marry me."

Zwaantie fiddled with the lace on her dress and looked down, demure. "Just curious."

"Curious enough to wake me up?"

She shrugged and waited.

"Well, we would live here, obviously. I'm the fifth son. I have no kingdom in Stella. And you are the crown princess. My only request is that we get married in Stella because my father won't risk a visit to Sol. After that, we would need to visit our outlying kingdoms so the rest of the citizens of Stella could meet you. It is customary when a prince or princess gets married. It would take about a year. Then we would come back here, because you are the crown princess. As for me wanting anything, your hand is all I've ever wanted since I've laid eyes on you." The prince pushed his feet against the footrest, which caused the chair to rock back and forth on two legs.

Zwaantie blushed and stared at him from under her eyelashes.

"Sounds reasonable enough. I will marry you."

He toppled over backwards. Zwaantie laughed, and he scrambled up. He picked up the chair and sat down, his face red.

"Ha ha, nice joke," he said.

"I'm not joking."

"Right, ever since I've gotten here, you've done nothing but laugh at me. And scowl occasionally. Besides, you told me that you weren't interested in marrying."

"I wasn't. But I changed my mind."

"Right. And what exactly changed your mind?"

"You make me laugh."

He grinned a little. "Okay, you've had your fun. But I must get myself ready for breakfast. As much as you like to laugh at me, your parents don't, and I need to make myself presentable."

Zwaantie sighed. He still didn't believe her. "Before we announce our plans to my parents, I have a request."

"What plans?" he asked.

"To get married."

He rolled his eyes. "I don't think your parents will appreciate the joke."

"No, they wouldn't if I was joking, but I'm not. I need you to ask them for something. It is customary for the king to offer the groom a gift of his choosing, and I'm asking you to ask for a gift for me, since you said you didn't want anything."

He sank into his chair. "Holy stars, you are serious."

"Yes, I am. Now will you do that for me? Ask them for something for me, but you can't tell them it's for me. You have to pretend you want it."

He squeezed his eyes shut and then opened them again. "Okay, you mean it. You want to marry me."

"Yeah. I do."

"Fine, I'll play along. But if this is some sick joke to anger your parents, I'll never forgive you. And you don't want a high prince of Stella as your enemy."

He stood and paced back and forth in front of the fireplace. He was handsome. Someday he would make his wife happy. But that girl would not be Zwaantie. She almost felt bad for what she was about to do.

"I'm not playing. A year away from home is a long time. I want to bring along Luna. But she won't leave without her brother and husband. So you need to ask for your choice of any three slaves in the kingdom."

His eyes darkened, and his voice grew cold. "We don't have slaves in Stella, and I won't bring any there. You ask for too much, Princess."

"Well, they wouldn't have to be slaves in Stella. The Voice doesn't work over there, right?"

He rubbed his hand over his face. "If I bring them over, I'm removing those bondage bands. They won't be slaves when we come back here."

"That's fine."

"Then I'm not asking for just three then. If we are going to release them, I want to bring more. How many could I ask for without angering your father?"

Now it was Zwaantie's turn to be surprised. "I don't know. We should just stick to the three. I don't think I'm worth more than that."

"You are worth far more than that." He got up and kissed her cheek. "Now, I do need to get ready. We'll announce our engagement at breakfast. Shall I fetch you from your room in twenty minutes?"

Zwaantie nodded, a bit unsure of what she'd just done. She hoped he wouldn't ruin it with his grand plans.

They entered the room together, Zwaantie's arm tucked in his elbow. Mother raised her eyebrows but didn't say anything. Zwaantie tried her best not to act nervous or upset, but until she knew for sure that Phoenix would accompany her, she didn't want to get too excited. Plus, there's the I'm-about-to-announce-a-marriage-to-a-man-I-don't-want-to-marry thing. It didn't matter that Zwaantie knew she wasn't going to marry him. She was still worried about the whole thing.

As soon as they finished eating, Leo took her hand, and they stood in front of her parents. Breakfast had been odd and awkward. She was tense, but Leo was all smiles.

They both bowed. Mother pursed her lips. Zwaantie had surprised her many times by making brash announcements or asking for things she shouldn't. The Voice never warned her against those things. Sometimes, she almost wished the Voice could read her thoughts.

Leo spoke. "As you know, my purpose in coming to Sol was to secure the hand of your daughter in marriage. This morning, she and I discussed the idea at length, and she has agreed to marry me."

At that moment, Zwaantie should have looked at Leo and smiled. Instead, Zwaantie stared at the ground, thinking of Phoenix.

"No," Mother gasped.

Father cleared his throat. "I thought we made it clear that Zwaantie will marry a Solite prince."

"You did. Zwaantie explained to me that who she marries is her own choice. She chose me. She assured me you would be supportive."

Zwaantie met her mother's eyes with defiance. She'd said pick a prince. She didn't say he couldn't be from Stella.

Mother held her gaze for a few moments. "Very well, then we shall begin wedding plans immediately." Mother never lost her composure for long. She knew Zwaantie was only doing this to get back at her, and she would make sure Zwaantie felt the full impact of her choice.

"I'm sorry to disappoint the high queen, but Zwaantie has agreed to get married in Stella so that my father can attend. We would love to have you travel to our kingdom and be present for the wedding. It will take place in three months' time."

Mother scowled, but recovered quickly and smiled. "Before you leave, we must have the traditional wedding ball. We hardly ever get the excuse to have a dance, and I want to use this one. We can have it ready in four days."

Zwaantie gave her a tight smile.

Father had been suspiciously quiet. Zwaantie looked to him. His face was impassive.

"It is customary when a groom chooses a bride to ask the father for anything under his jurisdiction. As high king, all of Sol falls under mine. What is it you would ask for your gift?"

"I would like my choice of fifty of your slaves."

Zwaantie staggered for a moment. "Three," she whispered furiously to him. "I told you three."

He brought his lips close to her ears. "And I told you that you were worth more than that. I almost asked for a hundred."

Father's eyes burned with anger. This would all fall apart. "Perhaps you do not understand how the slave system works. They take care of our city. Keep it free of trash and debris. They also take care of us. Fifty is an awful lot of slaves that we would have to replace. You may have five."

"Do you not think your daughter is worth fifty slaves?"

Father bristled. "Of course she is. But what do you need fifty slaves for?"

"We do not have slaves in Stella. I find I have enjoyed being taken care of. Plus, we could use some cleaning of our streets as well. And your daughter will be gone for nearly a year. Surely she needs slaves to take care of her. But if you do not agree to fifty, then seventy-five will do."

Father stood, his face flushing. "No, absolutely not."

"Then we do not have an agreement." Leo bowed quickly to Zwaantie and stalked from the room, Hunter close on his heels.

Zwaantie raced after them, not even looking up at her parents. They were halfway down the hall to Leo's room when she caught him. She jerked him around and slapped him across the face. "What the darkness were you thinking? I thought you wanted to marry me. Not to mention that my father is a high king. What right did you have to speak to him that way? You're lucky he agreed to the marriage at all. Now you've ruined it. He'll never agree to the marriage."

You should not strike another. A pain flashed behind her eyes, but it quickly disappeared.

He brought his hand to his face, but grinned. "I didn't realize you were so eager to marry me."

"Of course I am. But now you've ruined it."

He grasped her hands and stared down at her with those deep brown eyes. "No, I haven't. Your father will come around."

"He won't come around. You've just made him angry."

"I'll visit with him this afternoon. I promise by tonight, we'll have an agreement. I've done my fair share of negotiating with difficult people. This will not be hard."

He didn't understand Zwaantie's father. No way would he give him fifty slaves. Especially considering her father didn't want her to marry Leo.

Leo was insane.

Zwaantie turned from him and raced to her room. Last night was long, and she needed to rest. And she wanted to forget about her horrible morning. She threw herself down onto her bed and dissolved into tears. Luna sat next to her and rubbed her back, speaking

Luna spoke quietly. "I know you were planning on exchanging your wedding for the release of slaves, but I didn't know you were going for fifty. That was extravagant. Don't you think?"

"I wanted exactly three. The prince is the one who decided we needed fifty."

"Three?"

"Yes, you, Phoenix, and Pieter."

Luna didn't respond, but Zwaantie felt her stiffen. Then Luna leaned across and hugged her shoulders. It wasn't much, but Zwaantie knew Luna was grateful for what she asked for.

~

THAT EVENING, JUST AS ZWAANTIE WAS DRESSING FOR DINNER, LEO came barging into her room. He didn't even knock. He had a huge smile on his face as he swooped her up in a hug and kissed her on the lips.

She didn't respond at first, but then returned the kiss. She didn't want him to be suspicious. Their lips moved easily against each other. It was nice, but there was no fire. No spark.

She pulled away as the Voice berated her. *Filthy slut. Remove yourself at once.*

She gave Leo a fake grin. "I'm sorry, but it's the Voice. It doesn't think we should kiss."

Leo frowned. "But we're engaged. Surely we're allowed to kiss when we're engaged."

"Chaste kisses only. Also, we aren't actually engaged. Father said no."

The pain in her head dissipated.

"Ah, but we have an agreement. Fifty slaves will come with us. My choice."

Zwaantie beamed at him. "I didn't think you could do it."

"Well, I hope you have more faith in me in the future. Are you ready for dinner?"

"Not quite, Luna has to braid my hair."

Leo sprawled out on the couch across from the chair where Luna waited to do her hair.

Leo looked at her. "You know, she did this for you. Besides your husband and brother is there anyone else you'd like to bring with?"

She shook her head. "I've already spoken to Mother. She doesn't want to leave." Zwaantie was relieved by this. She'd have no trouble getting Luna. But the rest of her friends might be more difficult to release. She might get away with Pieter, but asking for the queen's slave as well would be too much.

"Can you do me a favor and find families who want to leave? I don't want to separate any of them. I won't get to choose until Sunday morning when we leave. But here." He handed her a small bag. "The bag contains fifty coins from Stella. Give them to the people who are to come with. Then when the king announces that he is ready for me to choose, I will ask for those coins back. That is how I will know who is coming."

Luna smiled at Zwaantie. "This is a smart one you've got here."

It worried her. If he was so smart, then how was she going to escape? He'd see right through her plan. Leo looked her over.

"Why do you insist on wearing such awful clothes?" Leo asked.

Zwaantie glared at him. "Rude, much?"

"You cover up everything. There is no room for creativity and fun. I brought you a trunkful of dresses. Why don't you wear one of them?"

"Because they are hideous. Not a single one would cover up what needs to be covered."

That's right. Good girl. That was odd. The Voice never complimented her before.

"You mean like your breasts? They are meant to be shown off a little." His eyes twinkled, and Zwaantie knew he was teasing her, but her breasts had always made her self-conscious.

Zwaantie sat down across from him. Teasing could go both ways.

"And why were you looking at my breasts?"

"Why not? Seriously, I just want to see cleavage. I suppose I could just wait until our wedding night, but where's the fun in that? Besides, I made a bet with Hunter, and I want to win."

Hunter grimaced in the corner.

Zwaantie narrowed her eyes at Leo. "What bet?"

Leo ignored her, opened the trunk, and pulled out a shimmery purple and green dress that had no sleeves and would probably show off her underwear if she bent over.

"Why don't you wear this one to dinner?"

"Not on your life."

"Why?"

"Because my mother would kill me. And my father might kill you. We don't wear clothes like that in Sol."

"What is it with you people and rules? Haven't you ever broken one?"

Zwaantie sighed. "Yes, of course I've broken rules. Who hasn't?"

"Then break this one. Wear the dress. Please."

"No."

He sighed, defeated, and sauntered over to Hunter. "I guess you were right. She never has disobeyed mommy." Leo handed him a few coins.

"What the dark?" Zwaantie asked.

"Hunter said you wouldn't do it because you never broke rules. I disagreed. But he won. What a boring wife you are going to be." He raised his eyebrows in a challenge.

"And what an arrogant cow-hole you are going to be. Why did I ever agree to marry you?"

"I've been asking myself that same question since you came to my room this morning. You obviously dislike me, and you have no interest in Stella, so why?"

Oh, he was smart. There was no way she would get away from him easily when they got to Stella. This would take more planning than she thought.

"You wouldn't understand. But I'm not changing my mind."

She stalked out of her room and went to dinner. Leo chatted with Father and Mother, and no one seemed upset by the arrangements that had been made. Hunter sat next to Zwaantie.

"Don't let him get to you. He's just trying to figure out your true motives."

"What?" Now she was nervous.

"He knows you don't love him. But what he doesn't know is why you want to marry him. Don't get me wrong, he's totally okay with marriage for other motives. He's completely smitten, and he was going to marry you no matter what."

Zwaantie sputtered for a second. "What do you mean he's completely smitten? He barely knows me."

"Oh, I've told him the same thing, but he was lost the second he laid eyes on you. I've never seen him look at someone like that before, and we've been friends for a long time."

Zwaantie let out a breath. She wasn't prepared for something like that. She didn't want to think that she'd actually hurt him. It was one thing to leave him if she thought he was just doing this to join their kingdoms. It was quite another if he was in love with her. She'd never love him though. Not the way she loved Phoenix.

"Do me a favor," Hunter said.

"Maybe." Zwaantie wasn't going to commit to anything.

"Just don't break his heart. I don't care what your motives are, but he loves you."

She nodded, not daring to lie out loud. She was disgusted with herself.

Luna wasn't feeling good during dinner, so Zwaantie sent her home. Zwaantie worried about her. She hoped she wasn't coming down with something bad.

After dinner, Leo walked Zwaantie to her room, and Hunter miraculously disappeared. She'd never seen Leo without him. He followed her into her room, as if that was okay.

He sprawled out on her bed and looked at Zwaantie expectantly.

"It will be gray soon," she said. She didn't want him in her room after midnight. Who knew what would happen. Nothing good, that's for sure. Phoenix had been a gentleman. Leo was not.

"We have time," he said drowsily. "Come here."

Don't listen to him. Get him out of your room.

She sat tentatively on the edge of the bed, and pain flashed across her forehead.

You are playing with danger.

"Would you relax?" he asked.

"You are in my room with me alone and are on my bed. Not exactly relaxing for me." Especially with the Voice reminding her how dangerous it was.

"I have no intention of taking advantage of you tonight. I just want to talk. And those chairs of yours are bloody uncomfortable. I won't even touch you, but lay here with me and talk. And take that stupid dress off."

"I thought you said you weren't going to do anything to me, yet here you are trying to get me to take my clothes off."

She gave him a smile to show she was joking and felt instantly guilty. She shouldn't enjoy her time with him. He was a road to Phoenix. That was all.

"Put something else on then. Something comfortable."

Zwaantie escaped behind her dressing screen. But try as she might, she couldn't get the laces on the back of her dress undone.

"Leo, can you help me?"

He nearly fell out of the bed trying to get to her. Probably thought she had less on.

"I can't get the laces. Can you?"

He undid the laces, lingering at the bottom of her spine. His fingers were soft and gentle. "Anything else?" he asked, his voice gruff.

"No, I think I got it."

Zwaantie put on a nightgown, which was just as modest as her dress but more comfortable. She lay down on the edge of her bed. Far enough away that he couldn't touch her, but close enough to talk.

"What do the stars look like?" she asked.

He smiled, and it was a nice smile. "Millions of tiny lights scattered across the navy blue sky. I miss them. It's so bright here all the time. The stars are harder to see in the cities, but out on the ocean you can see them all."

"I think that is what I am most looking forward to. Seeing the stars. Isn't it scary in the dark?"

He laughed. "It's never completely dark in Stella. I mean, we have no sun, but that doesn't mean we have a shortage of light. Sometimes it's brighter there than here. But our lights are different colors."

"How?" Zwaantie asked. The idea of brightness in Stella surprised her.

"Magic. I'll show you sometime how they do it. It's pretty amazing."

They talked for a while about Stella and all the things he would show her.

The midnight hour comes. Get him out.

"It's nearly midnight. You should go."

He sighed. "Why?"

"Because you can't be in here after midnight. We might do something we'd regret."

"We are going to be married. How much could we regret?"

Zwaantie shook her head. "You need to go. Now."

He sat up. "Okay, I'll go, but under one condition."

"And what's that?"

"On Saturday night, the night of the dance, I want you to wear one of the dresses I brought you."

Zwaantie almost argued with him, but midnight was approaching quickly.

"Okay. I'll wear one. But I get to pick."

"Excellent."

He kissed her on the lips and disappeared. The Voice didn't say anything. It must've been chaste enough.

She waited for about ten minutes and then heard her lock click. Locked in for the night.

The Voice in her head cleared with the midnight hour, and she wondered why she didn't want to wear the dresses. She pulled out the trunk and opened it. Each dress was more than one color. She didn't realize that dresses could be that beautiful. In Sol, the clothes only contained one solid color. They may have adornments and things, but the color was always solid.

The first dress she pulled out was a red dress with no sleeves that had a long black ruffled train. She jerked off her nightgown and pulled the dress on. It fit perfectly. Almost too small and it pushed her breasts up. The dress made her feel alive.

She twirled around and giggled. Then she stripped it off and tried on another. Before collapsing into bed, she tried on all of the dresses and picked the one she would wear to the dance.

The dress was a deep black dress with bright blue jewels. It was the dress Mother would hate the worst. No sleeves and way, way too short.

Chapter Twenty-Six

THE DANCE

The evening of the dance, butterflies fluttered in Zwaantie's belly. She and Luna had spent most of the day packing Zwaantie's things because they would leave for Stella in the morning.

Zwaantie pulled out the dress. The material flowed through her fingers.

"That's a little short. And revealing. Are you sure your mother will be okay with that?" Luna asked with raised eyebrows.

"I'm not wearing it for her."

Filthy. You know better. Put the dress back in the trunk and put on one of your own dresses. NOW.

The dress fit well. Zwaantie gave Luna the shoes she had found in the trunk. They had high heels and tiny blue jewels on the toes. They pinched her toes.

Slut. That's what you are. Take the dress off and put on something decent.

A small headache appeared behind her eyes. She didn't want to be in pain the whole evening, but she wanted to wear this dress.

Zwaantie tried to push the thoughts away. Guilt gnawed at her insides, and her headache grew. On her bedside table sat the necklace Leo had presented to her when he arrived. She'd never worn it, thinking it was stupid to need protection because the Voice kept everyone from committing crimes.

Now though, she needed it. Someone was trying to kill her. She wished she'd thought of this earlier. She put it on, and her headache disappeared. A knock sounded at the door, and Luna answered it.

"I don't think this is a good time. Zwaantie is getting ready."

"I don't care. I need to talk to my sister before she leaves." Raaf pushed his way into the room, followed by his new slave. Zwaantie's heart clenched at the site of him. It should've been Phoenix.

"What are you wearing?" Raaf asked and quickly averted his eyes. His slave wasn't quite as discreet. His mouth dropped open. Zwaantie gave him a wink.

"A dress. From Stella. Why don't you sit?"

Raaf shook his head, still not looking directly at her. "Mother is not going to let you wear that."

"By the time Mother sees the dress, it will be too late. What did you want to talk about? We have a dance to attend."

Raaf sat, meeting her eyes. He creased his eyebrows and pulled her hands into his own. He'd never been so affectionate before. "Are you going to be okay in Stella? I can get you out of this marriage if you want. You don't seem happy with Leo."

Zwaantie gave him a sad smile. If he only knew. "Of course this is what I want. When have I ever done anything that I haven't wanted to?"

"I know. But I just want to make sure you'll be okay. Do you need anything from me? We probably won't get to talk much before you leave."

Zwaantie hugged him. "I'll miss you too, baby brother, but I'll be fine. Besides, it's only for a year. Then I'll be queen. That's a scary thought."

He grimaced. "Yeah, it is. Can I escort you to the dance? I won't be able to do that after you are married."

She almost invited him to come with on the tour of Stella, but then remembered that she wouldn't be coming back because she and Phoenix would run away once he had his bands removed. And that made her sad.

Zwaantie entered the grand hall, and her breath caught in her throat. Normally, banners of the sun and bright colors covered the room, but today half of the banners had been replaced with stars and a moon. They stood out in such stark contrast to the bright sun. It was gorgeous.

"I can't believe you're joining Stella and Sol. This is historical," Raaf said.

Zwaantie didn't want to be historical. She wanted to be normal. But she'd do this for Phoenix. Even if they couldn't run away, she had to get him out of the sewers. She would marry Leo if that meant Phoenix could be free.

She searched for her parents. They stood on the opposite side of the hall deep in conversation with the lower king of Sonnenschein. Standing next to them was Leo. He wore light pants made of a shimmery silver material and no shirt. But he wore an open vest that matched her dress. His eyes met hers.

Zwaantie and Raaf approached their parents, and Leo slipped his arm around Zwaantie's waist and pulled her close to him.

"You look amazing," he whispered. "I take back everything I ever thought about you."

Zwaantie's mother turned and looked at her. Her face twisted into a combination of horror and revulsion. In a matter of seconds, Zwaantie could see a thousand different emotions cross her face.

Her mouth opened. Zwaantie was about to have it.

"What do you think of the dress my sisters sent for Zwaantie?" Leo said. "Doesn't she look gorgeous?"

Zwaantie's mother recovered and looked at Leo. Clearly, she'd forgotten he was there. Zwaantie could see her fingers trembling, but she was never one to be rude. "Of course, but I think perhaps she should find something to cover her shoulders."

Leo didn't respond but swept Zwaantie out onto the dance floor. He pulled her close and led her in a dance she was unfamiliar with. In Sol, they didn't touch much when they danced and never like the embrace he had Zwaantie in. But between the choice of facing her mother and dancing close to Leo, Zwaantie chose Leo. Though she felt guilty for enjoying it. She should be thinking of Phoenix. Not Leo.

They danced all night long. Occasionally they would dance the traditional Sol dances, but mostly he held her, and she was bothered that she enjoyed his touch. She fit nicely in the prince's arms. She noticed the Voice was silent. Strange, it never missed an opportunity to berate her.

That night he walked her to her room about eleven thirty. She was sorry to see the night end. She'd had a good time and found that she was altogether too comfortable with Leo. In another life, she'd marry him and be happy. But her heart belonged with Phoenix.

"I'm excited to bring you home. I think you'll like Stella. And you'll love Sage, my sister."

He kissed Zwaantie again, long this time, and her insides tickled. It was sweet, but she couldn't see herself marrying him. But she could see herself being his friend. Although after she betrayed him, she doubted he'd be interested in any kind of friendship.

Chapter Twenty-Seven

THE COMPLICATION

Mother stood next to Zwaantie on the steps as several slaves packed the carriages. There were a few trunks with dresses and personal items, but most of what they brought was food.

Mother frowned at the slaves. "He's taking so many."

Zwaantie shrugged. "He felt I was worth it." She was studying all the slaves. She needed to find Phoenix. He had to be among them. There he was standing near the back, filthy but with a wide smile. His eyes were on her. She smiled back, her insides warming. She was so very close.

Mother followed Zwaantie's line of sight. She gasped and gripped Zwaantie's arm.

"Did you agree to marry the prince so you could get Phoenix? Do you think you'll just run away with him in Stella? Oh, I was such a fool. No wonder you wanted to marry a Stellan."

Zwaantie kept her face straight. She could not give anything away. "No. Mother, that won't be possible, but at least he won't be in the sewers anymore."

Mother pulled her close and whispered fiercely in her ear. "You better be telling the truth, because my reach is farther than you think. If you don't marry the prince, I will find you, and I will make sure

Phoenix dies. And you will watch. Do you understand? You could start a war if you backpedal on this wedding. Why did you think we discouraged it from the beginning?"

"Is everything okay?" Leo asked, causing Zwaantie to jump.

Mother jerked back and gave Leo a sugary sweet smile. "Of course, dear. Zwaantie and I have never been apart. I'm going to miss her so much."

Zwaantie shook out of her mother's grasp and took a few steps down to meet Leo.

"Goodbye, Mother. We'll see you at the wedding."

Mother nodded but didn't say anything more.

"Are you sure you're okay?" Leo asked Zwaantie.

"I'm fine." Her heart raced, but she couldn't tell Leo why she was upset. She hoped she'd be able to get away from Leo before her Mother tried anything.

Luna approached with tears on her face.

"What's the matter?" Zwaantie asked.

"Why is Pieter not among the freed slaves?" Luna asked.

"I was not successful in obtaining the king's slave," Leo replied. "That's your husband, right? We do need to get going, or we'll never make it before midnight. Here, your midnight hours are relatively safe. In Stella, they are dangerous, so we must go."

Zwaantie drew her best friend into a hug. "You can stay here. You don't have to go with me."

Luna gripped the back of Zwaantie's dress and held her close. Then she pulled away, wiping at her eyes.

"We prepared for this possibility. I'll come back to him after, well, after a while. I need to go with you."

"I'm sorry," Zwaantie whispered. "You should go say goodbye to him. Father won't begrudge you for that."

Chapter Twenty-Eight

THE BETRAYER

The horseless carriage was amazing. The seats were wide and comfortable. Soft music played from above Zwaantie's head, and the whole inside was lit in a silvery blue. Leo sat close and put his arm around her. She leaned into him feeling guilty for enjoying it. Again, she waited for the Voice, but it never came. Weird.

Hunter flung himself down on one of the wide seats. "I will be so glad to get home, where things are normal again. No offense, Zwaantie, but Sol is the most uncomfortable place I've ever been. Plus, I miss my wife. She's going to kill you, Leo."

He raised his eyebrows. "Why?"

"You told Candace this would only take a day or two. It's been a week. She's due any day now. If our baby was born while we dawdled here, she will be one unhappy mama."

Leo laughed. "I'm sure I can handle it. Candace has been mad at me before. I thought our timing was pretty swift actually."

Hunter grunted. "Whatever."

Hunter was not a slave, but the way he talked to Leo, it was like he was his friend, his equal. Luna was curt with her sometimes, but they'd been friends before, so Zwaantie allowed it. It had gotten worse since Phoenix, but then Luna was his sister. Phoenix. He would be free in less than twelve hours, and then they could get married. The excitement was almost too much for her.

She was excited for more reasons than one. When she and Phoenix ran away, she'd have something she'd never had before. Freedom. No responsibility. No nagging that she was doing something dishonorable.

The wall came into view, black and ominous. They rode along the road next to the wall for about thirty minutes. Then they stopped abruptly.

"They'll need to hook the carriages to the chains and give instructions to those who are walking how to get across the wall," Leo said, climbing out of the carriage. Zwaantie and the rest followed.

She peered around him to the waiting slaves. "How will they get across?"

"They'll hold to the Rod of Lost Memories. It spans the width of the wall. As long as they don't let go, they'll be fine. But there's more to crossing the wall than just walking across it."

"What do you mean?"

"The wall demands payment. It will take a memory. Whatever you are thinking about when you cross the wall is a memory you will no longer have on the other side."

"So if I think of something bad, I won't have to remember it anymore?"

"Exactly. But it's best to do something unimportant. Bad memories usually have too many other things attached them that don't make sense if you lose the memory. Choose carefully. You also will not remember anything that happens on the journey. It takes about a half hour by carriage. Two hours by walking."

Zwaantie tried to think of something. "And I won't remember the trip or what I was thinking of?"

"Nope. So make sure it is something you can live without. I need to go talk to Hunter. I'll be right back."

Zwaantie stared at the black mist. She crept around the carriage and stood as close as she dared to the wall. The tendrils whispered to her again, but she didn't have the Voice encouraging her to plunge into the wall's depths.

Zwaantie felt a hand on hers. She looked back and found herself face-to-face with Phoenix. They were alone, hidden behind the carriage. Her stomach buzzed.

"You did it," he said.

She beamed at him and placed a palm on his cheek. "I did. A few more hours, and this will be over."

He pulled her close, and she looked at him, surprised.

"Isn't the Voice telling you off?" she asked.

He whispered into her ear. "The Voice is strangely quiet. Maybe I'm too close to the wall."

That didn't seem right. The last time she was this close to the wall, the Voice was louder than ever. It was quiet now, but she suspected that had to do with the necklace Leo gave her.

She wanted to pull away and see if Phoenix had on a necklace as well, but he slid his hand up and around to the back of her neck. She shivered at the touch. He lightly stroked her jaw and tipped her chin so she could gaze into his gorgeous brown eyes.

"You're so beautiful," he said.

Zwaantie smiled. "Thank you."

He leaned down and brushed her lips with his own. Zwaantie reached her arms up and pulled him closer, deepening the kiss. Their lips moved furiously against one another. This was different from Leo. Her whole body was on fire. She pushed into him, wanting to be as close as possible. She'd been waiting for this moment since she first challenged him to that game of tag.

A voice came from behind her. "I can't believe this."

They sprang apart. Leo stood a few feet from her with a frown.

Zwaantie had no words. She had no way to explain. But if Leo refused to take them across the wall, her mother would kill Phoenix. Dammit. They couldn't wait a few more hours? What was she thinking?

Leo shook his head. "I understand now. You found out I could remove bondage bands. This was all some set up. You're going to run away with your slave lover when you get to Stella. I can't believe I was so stupid."

All the blood drained from her face. "This isn't what it looks like." He wouldn't fall for it. Of course, he wouldn't. But she had to try. She turned around to see if Phoenix could come up with some excuse, but he'd disappeared. What the dark?

Leo stalked closer to her. "Oh, don't play dumb, girl. I'm the spymaster of Stella. I can see all the clues. I can't believe I didn't see it before. I was too blinded by my own love."

"Oh, poor Zwaantie, all her plans falling apart."

Zwaantie turned around and found Wilma standing behind her.

"What are you doing here?" Zwaantie asked, thoroughly confused. Wilma wasn't supposed to be here. Not only that, but she was talking to Zwaantie like she was happy Zwaantie got caught.

Wilma tapped her fingers on her lips. "I came to say goodbye. Really, girl, I can't believe you are still alive."

"What do you mean?"

"You were smart, figuring out those connections," Wilma continued. "That silly slave girl was poisoned. That wine was meant for you."

Leo came to her side and stared at Wilma. Would he rescue her now? Or was he too angry? Zwaantie couldn't make sense of her words. "You were the one trying to kill me?"

"Oh, I most certainly wanted you dead, but no, dear. It wasn't me. It was the Voice. But you already know that."

She crept closer to Zwaantie, and Zwaantie backed up. The wisps of the wall slid across her shoulders.

Wilma leaned forward and whispered in her ear. "Before you die, I want you to know who it was that wanted you dead. You should die with the knowledge that someone you loved dearly was behind all those attempts. It will be I who succeeds, but still, you should know."

Zwaantie barely registered the name Wilma uttered. Instead, she spun and shoved Wilma right into the mist. Before she could back away though, Wilma's hand lashed out and pulled her right in.

Chapter Twenty-Nine

THE LOST MEMORY

Leo didn't hesitate or even think. He plunged into the wall where Zwaantie disappeared. She could already be lost to the depths, but he had to try. Even if she had betrayed him.

He hit something solid and wrapped his arms around her waist. She struggled against his grip.

"Calm down, Zwaantie, it's me."

She stilled. "Leo."

He pressed his lips against her ear. "Yes, it's me. Where's the witch?"

"I don't know. She let go of me as soon as we fell. Why did you call her a witch?"

This was good. He wasn't sure where she went, but at least she wasn't with them.

"She's the Old Mother." He almost didn't recognize her. She looked different than she had when she visited, but those eyes were one of a kind.

Zwaantie's grip tightened. "How do you know of the Old Mother?"

"She's the reason I came over to Sol. But I'll explain that later. We need to get out of here."

Zwaantie pulled him back toward the way they fell in. "Thank goodness we aren't far in."

Leo chuckled. "Sorry, Princess, it doesn't work like that. We'll never get out if we try to go back."

"Where are we going then?"

"Toward the Rod of Lost Memories. If we can find that, we'll be able to get out okay. But we can't waste any time. The longer we are in here, the more disoriented we'll be."

He pulled her toward the rod. He had an excellent sense of direction, and if he moved east, he'd hit the rod. If they didn't find it, they'd be lost forever.

"Do you think Wilma will be able to get out?"

"Who?"

"The woman you called the Old Mother."

"Probably. She's the Old Mother after all. Why'd she want to kill you anyway?"

"I have no idea. She was my friend."

Zwaantie went quiet, and Leo pressed through the darkness, his soon-to-be lost memory haunting him.

"Tell me, Princess, how long have you been planning to betray me?"

"You wouldn't understand."

"Try me. We have at least two hours in this mist, and we're both going to forget this as soon as we step into Stella. You can at least do me the service of letting me know why."

Zwaantie tugged her hand.

"Don't let go of me. You'll get lost."

"Why did you come after me anyway?"

"Because I love you. I have since the second I laid eyes on you. I've always thought my brothers and sisters were crazy when they talked about love at first sight, but now I understand. I can't explain it. I'd die for you."

She let out a sigh. "I'm sorry. I don't feel the same way. I wish I did. It would make this so much easier."

"Why did you agree to marry me?"

"You saw how Stella is about slaves. I saw an opportunity to free Phoenix. It was my only option. I didn't plan on falling in love with him, but it happened. Before I fell for him, I didn't even know love like that was possible. I can't imagine my life without him. I didn't mean to hurt you."

Leo almost stopped walking, but he couldn't. Intellectually, he understood what she was talking about. Love was something that grabbed ahold and didn't let go. He felt it for her. But the pain in his chest that she would betray him like that was too much.

They had to keep pushing through the inky blackness.

His hip hit something solid. He reached down and found the steel rod. Thank the stars. They wouldn't perish. The two-inch rod floated at waist level. They could hold on tight and find their way home. Or back to Sol. He wasn't sure which way they'd go, but hopefully they'd exit in Stella.

He pulled Zwaantie over and placed her hand on the cool steel. "Hold onto this. If you let go, you'll disappear. We're lucky we found it. Stay close to me so I don't think I lost you."

"Okay."

They plodded on in silence for several minutes.

"You know, we won't remember anything of our conversations when we step out of the mist," he said.

Zwaantie snorted. "That means I can tell you anything, and you won't remember it."

"Exactly."

"So tell me something true. Something you didn't dare to tell me before," Zwaantie said.

The question surprised Leo. He didn't think she was terribly interested in his life. But since she was asking, he wanted her to understand what was at stake, even if she wouldn't remember on the other side. "If we don't get married, my sister's baby is going to die."

"Why?"

"The Old Mother. She gave a prophecy that said if Stella and Sol weren't joined by the first birthday of Candace's baby, then he would die, and he wouldn't be the last."

"That's awful. Why didn't you just tell me?"

Leo rolled his eyes. "You've got to be kidding me. The minute I walked into the castle, you accused me of having ulterior motives. Do you think you would have just agreed to marry me if you thought I was only doing it for my sister?"

"Probably not. But maybe we could've found another solution. Two minds are better than one. What would you have done if I hadn't agreed to marry you?"

"That's another secret. Your turn to tell me something true."

She was quiet for a few moments. "I don't want to be queen."

"Why not?"

"Because I'm not good at leading people, and I just want to live a normal life."

"Did you want that before you fell in love with Phoenix?"

"Yes. Maybe that's why I fell in love with him. He was my chance at normal. I never was the most obedient child, and I don't like the obligations that come with being queen. If you hadn't come along, Mother would've made me marry someone else who I didn't love. Phoenix or no Phoenix."

Leo didn't know what to think about that. He'd never had to do anything he didn't want to. Sure, he wasn't crazy about going to Sol, but he did that because he loved his sister and wanted to help her, not because he had to.

In Stella, Zwaantie would have freedoms she couldn't even begin to imagine. She might run away with the slave. She might not. She wouldn't remember any of this when they stepped into his land, but stranger things had happened. Even if she did run away with her slave, they'd have a better life in Stella than they would in Sol. If she ran off, he'd have to return to his father, and they'd have to prepare for war.

Stella and Sol needed to be joined. He wouldn't let Candace's baby die.

They walked in silence for a while, both lost in their own thoughts. He wondered what memory she would forget. Probably her fight with the witch if that is what she was thinking about when she crossed the wall. She called the woman Wilma. For Zwaantie's sake, he hoped Wilma was lost in the mist because if not, Zwaantie would still trust her.

After another hour, he was going mad with the thoughts in his head. Thoughts that would disappear the second he stepped out of the mist.

"Tell me something else that you would never tell me if you thought I'd remember," Leo said.

"You're a good kisser."

Leo stopped dead, and she ran into him. That was not what he expected to come out of her mouth.

He spun around, let go of the steel rod, but kept his hip pressed against it. He wrapped his arms around her, pulled her against him. Stars, she felt good.

He leaned down so his face was close to her ear.

"But I thought you were in love with Phoenix."

She snaked her arms around his waist and held him close. He was completely taken aback. She laid her cheek against his chest.

"I am. But that doesn't mean you're a bad kisser. To be honest, if Phoenix had never been in the picture, we'd probably still be heading to Stella to plan the wedding. I like you. A lot more when the Voice isn't whispering in my head. I wish we could've been friends. I bet you would've helped me figure out how to run away with Phoenix."

He chuckled. "Probably. But at this point, even if Candace's baby wasn't in danger, I'm way too in love with you to help you run away with anyone else."

"I know," she mumbled.

He pulled away and found her face with his hands. "We're not far from the edge of the wall. When we step out of the darkness, we'll forget everything that happened in here. I'm going to forget that you are in love with Phoenix and will probably run away with him and betray me. You're going to be happy. But for just a few minutes, can you be mine?"

"Under one condition."

He felt her smile under his hands. "What's that?"

"Will you kiss me?"

His lips met hers, and for several minutes she was all his. He tried not to think about what was coming on the other side of the wall.

He took a step away from her.

"Thank you."

She didn't say anything, but took his hand in hers and squeezed. He kept one hand clasped in hers and one gripped on the rod. Ten feet later he stepped out of the blinding darkness and into the neon lights of Stella.

The End

~

Zwaantie only wanted one thing...

To be with Pheonix.

But he disappears without her.

Now she just wants to go home. Stella is unlike anything she ever experienced and she can't stand it. From the bright lights to the moving pictures—it's all too overwhelming.
But she makes a terrifying discovery.

The voice has followed her and he wants her dead.

Thank you for reading!

KIMBERLY LOTH

PRINCE
of the
MOON

SECOND BOOK IN THE STELLA AND SOL SERIES

Stella and Sol

Prince of the Moon
Volume 2
By Kimberly Loth

For Apollo
For giving up your office and your wife
You have no idea how grateful I am

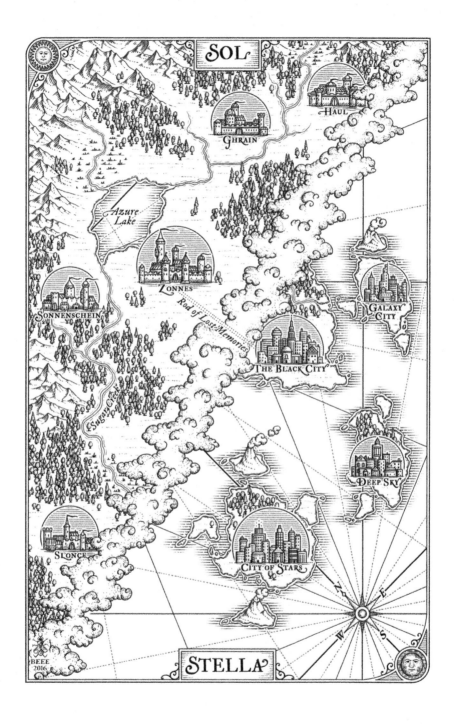

Chapter One

THE BLACK CITY

Zwaantie gasped as she stepped into Stella. Her mind was foggy as Leo pulled her away from the wall. He stopped about thirty feet out. The last thing she remembered was Leo catching her and Phoenix kissing. Now she was on the other side holding hands with Leo. She searched her surroundings.

The sky spread out in every direction, a dark inky black. A few buildings glowed not far from where they stood, but there were no trees or hills. The ground under her feet lit up. Darkness surrounded her, but she was able to see Leo clearly. In the distance small lights shimmered. They looked like the stars, but they were on the ground, not in the sky.

"Are those the stars?" she asked, pointing.

"No, that's the city."

Zwaantie craned her neck around to see if she could spot the stars. She dragged Leo farther away from the wall, trying in vain to find even a single star.

Nothing but blackness.

"You seem anxious," Leo said.

"The stars, where are the stars?" Zwaantie asked.

"We're too close to the city." He pointed at the bright lights off in the distance. "You can't see them as well when there is light. When we get out on the boats, you'll see them."

"Oh." Zwaantie tried to hide the disappointment in her voice. When she pictured Stella in her mind, it was only about the stars, and here she was, and there were none.

She sucked in a deep breath of the heavy air and took another good look around. They were alone.

"Where is everyone?"

"I don't know," Leo replied. He spun around and stared deep into her eyes. "How are you feeling?"

"I'm fine, why?"

"The wall can be disorienting."

"I'm good. I do wonder what memories I lost." She lost whatever happened between the kiss and crossing the wall. She had to find Phoenix and figure out why they were separated. If the kiss was the last thing she remembered, maybe Leo did something to Phoenix. What if Phoenix was lost in the wall?

Leo didn't seem upset about anything, so maybe he didn't remember the kiss. That would be convenient. But still not good. Phoenix might not make it across at all. Then what would she do?

They followed a small glowing stone path. The path was perfectly straight, leading right into the middle of several giant glittering square buildings. Lights floated in the air near their heads, each one about three feet away from the last. The precision was disconcerting. Zwaantie wanted to poke them and see what would happen. She'd never seen lights that weren't attached to a flame of some kind.

Leo kept a tight grip on her hand and pulled her along. After a few hundred feet, they stepped in between the enormous buildings. They were painted with bright colors, and large signs adorned the doors. They had very few windows, but lights still floated in the air.

She and Leo were still alone.

"Where is our group?" she asked, worry starting to set in. What happened in between the kiss and now? Were she and Leo the only ones who crossed? If so, why?

He glanced at the mist. "I'm not sure. It's hard to say if we beat them, or if they beat us." He rubbed the back of his neck. "What's the last thing you remember?"

She had to lie. She couldn't risk telling him if he didn't remember. "I was standing behind the carriage admiring the mist. What about you?"

"I was on my way to find you. I approached the carriage, and then we stepped into Stella."

Zwaantie let out a breath of relief. Leo didn't remember he'd caught her and Phoenix kissing. While this was a good thing, the fact that they were alone in Stella was not. What happened on the other side? What did she forget?

"Why didn't we go through in the carriage with the others?" Zwaantie continued to stare at the buildings. They had no pitched roofs or wooden doors and were at least ten floors tall. The largest building in Sol was the castle, and that only had four floors.

"Who knows? Maybe we fell into the wall or something. Whatever happened is lost on both of us. The wall does that. We'll never remember, but someone else might be able to tell us. I'm just glad we were able to get out. Let's go see if we can find anyone."

"How tall are those buildings?" Zwaantie asked, pointing up at the building next to them.

Leo twisted his head around. "Mm, I don't know. Maybe ten, fifteen stories. Wait until we go into the city. The buildings there are a hundred floors tall."

A hundred? How did they not topple over? Sweat pooled under Zwaantie's arms, and her breath felt heavy. She fanned her face.

"Are you okay?" Leo asked with a look of concern.

"Yes, I'm just hot. The air is so heavy here." The air in Sol was cooler and drier. She wasn't sure she'd get used to this.

"It's the humidity." He tugged on her sweaty hand, and she followed, trying to see into the small windows on the buildings next to her.

"What are these used for? I don't see any people." In spite of not really wanting to go to Stella, she was curious about the way everything worked.

Leo flashed her a grin. "I'm sorry. I forgot you've never seen factories before." He spun around, looking up. "We're in the clothing district. This is where our clothes are made. You won't find any people here because it's after noon. I don't have a disc, or I would be able to tell what time it is. I'm guessing it's about two. Plenty of time to get to the boats."

Zwaantie wondered how a disc could be used to measure time. She always knew the time of day based on the sun. Zwaantie craned her neck again. Nothing but blackness in the sky.

"Where's the moon?" She tried to keep the whine out of her voice, but she wasn't sure she succeeded. She'd gotten a taste of the stars in the mage wagon bubble, and now she was finally here in Stella, and she couldn't see the stars.

"New moon, I think. You can't see it." She stumbled behind him. She couldn't take her eyes off the brightly colored buildings. She'd expected a village much like Zonnes, but magical. So far, there was hardly anything magical and nothing remotely close to her village. Instead it was tall buildings, hard smooth streets, and no grass or trees.

They walked down the softly lit street toward the twinkling lights. Everything was too straight and unnatural. Zwaantie wasn't sure she liked it. She appreciated imperfection. Here, things were flawless with perfectly straight lines. Leo set a brisk pace, and while Zwaantie kept up with him, she winded quickly. The heavy air made it hard to breathe.

Phoenix and the missing group was a problem. Maybe Leo didn't think so, but for Zwaantie, these early moments were crucial. She'd rescued Phoenix from a life of slavery, and now they were going to live happily ever after in Stella. It'd taken so much to get to this point, and she couldn't lose Phoenix now. Where was he?

She stared up at empty buildings. During the day, buildings in Sol were hardly ever empty. This was strange.

"Do your people only work early in the day?" That wasn't very many working hours.

"Yes. I know a lot of your people worked until late in the day. We only work four to six hours a day, until about noon. With magic, we don't need to work long."

Zwaantie creased her eyebrows. "What do you do the rest of the day?"

Leo laughed. "We play. We often take long meals and naps. We've got more magical toys than we do practical magic. Funhouses, clubs, shows. Trust me. You will never lack for something to do in Stella. Honestly, those who create entertainment with magic work harder than the rest of us."

At home, when Zwaantie was bored, she would sew or help Wilma. She would read occasionally. The Voice discouraged idleness, so if she sat still for more than a few minutes, he reminded her of things she had to do. Though she had to admit, her fondest memories were those where she was playing out in the woods with Phoenix. Still, it wasn't right to only work a few hours a day.

"Are all of your people mages?"

"Yes. Though, a few aren't quite adept at magic."

Zwaantie's stomach fell. If she couldn't do magic, how would she make it? She hadn't realized they needed magic to work.

"How do they survive?"

"They work in jobs where magic doesn't matter as much."

"So what will the slaves do when they arrive?"

"They'll be tested for magic ability and then be given jobs based on interest and aptitude. They'll have a harder time with magic since most people begin learning as small children, but they should be able to pick it up with time."

This did not sound good. She and Phoenix would have to find jobs without the prince's help. No matter. They were resourceful, they could figure it out.

After about ten minutes, the twinkling lights turned into brightly lit buildings.

"Oh my sun, those are enormous." Dozens of tall skinny buildings with hundreds of windows disappeared into the sky. They seemed never ending. She'd always imagined living in a farmhouse, but she supposed she could live in one of those buildings if Phoenix was with her. She wondered how many people lived in them. All of Zonnes could fit in that one building.

Leo smiled at Zwaantie.

"The buildings? Yeah, they're much taller than yours."

Zwaantie stopped walking and stared up beyond the buildings to the black sky with no stars. Leo bumped her with his elbow, and Zwaantie spun around. He'd taken off his shirt, and she had a hard time not staring.

He held up his shirt. "Men don't wear these ridiculous things here. Vests sometimes, but it's too hot to wear anything else."

He looked her over. "We've got to get you something else to wear. Appearance is everything in Stella, and people will talk about what you're wearing. We'll need to set up a photo shoot and interview when we get home. Everyone will want to know our story."

"Why? What is it anyone else's business?" This was bizarre.

"In Sol, your people were very respectful of you and your privacy. Here they treat us normal, most of the time, but they demand our stories. It will probably be very strange for you at first, but you'll get used to it. People will be very curious about the princess from Sol."

She'd never been much of a gossip in Sol, but she'd known a few. Was everyone here like that? Leo took her hand, and Zwaantie stared at his back as he moved. She wanted to reach out and touch his shoulder blade. Soon, she'd see Phoenix wear something similar. She smiled at the thought.

They turned a corner and strolled along another street with buildings on either side. These were shorter and squat but lit up like a festival tree. Though candles filled the festival trees in Sol.

The building to Zwaantie's right was glowing blue and had a flashing sign that said *Massage Mage*. A few shops down, another building lit up in red and yellow with words and images winking in its windows promising the best beef sandwiches in town. Even with the brightness, the darkness was oppressive. Zwaantie wanted the sun high in the sky. Everything looked odd in the unnatural light.

They turned a corner, and suddenly the streets were filled with people, and the buildings grew exponentially. Zwaantie craned her neck to see if she could spot the top of one building and found every window covered in moving pictures. The people in the pictures smiled and held up bottles of potions, or strutted around showing off their clothes.

On another building, pictures and moving words played across the entire outside wall. Zwaantie didn't have time to read the whole thing, but she caught a small part of it, Princess Sage hosted another amazing party last night. Singing sensation Alexa made an appearance but quickly left after a few terse words with the host. Everyone is dying to know what was said.

All around Zwaantie, the crowd swarmed. She wasn't sure if she'd ever get used to the sheer number of people. She supposed she'd have to. There was no going back to Sol now. If she went home, the Voice would make her go to the castle and confess her kiss with Phoenix. Then who knows what would happen. Her chest clenched. She'd never see the sun again.

Most of the girls wore sleeveless shirts and short pants or skirts. If they'd been in Sol, the Voice would be screaming inside their heads because of their indecent clothes. Would she have to wear something like that? She missed the Voice. Sure, it had been annoying, but there was a certain comfort to having it guide her decisions.

The people wore sandals like Leo. The other men were dressed similarly, with only lightweight pants. Not one had a shirt on, but a few wore open vests. Though most men weren't pretty. They had hairy chests and large bellies. Zwaantie shrunk into Leo as a particularly fat man squeezed past her. She supposed she shouldn't be surprised by the immodesty.

The crowd cleared, and a few girls squealed. They were nearly identical in sparkly black short dresses, but each had a different color hair. Purple, pink, and blue.

"Prince Leo."

He pulled Zwaantie close to him. "Smile," he said.

"What? Why?"

"Just do it," he said through gritted teeth.

She did as he told her, and the girls pulled out round objects that flashed bright lights in their direction.

"Thanks," the blue-haired girl said. They stared into their devices. "Who's the girl?"

"It's a secret, ladies. Watch the vids tomorrow for an exciting announcement."

He kept Zwaantie close to him as he steered her away from the girls.

"You're going to be all over the Ticker now, and we haven't even announced your name. I need to find a disc and warn Father and Viggo."

Ticker? Disc? He was using words she'd never heard of before. She wasn't quite sure what had just happened. He ducked into a small shop and let go of her.

"Prince Leo," the tall man said from behind a counter.

"Hello. Can I get a disc?"

"Of course."

The man handed Leo one from the dozens on the shelf, and Leo pressed two fingers on it and it glowed white.

"Thank you," Leo said.

"You're welcome." He touched Leo's disc with another one. Zwaantie crept forward, staring at the strange devices. They were paper thin, but shiny. A few glowed, and they came in many different colors. Some even had pictures on them.

Then Leo spoke into his disc. "Viggo."

A face popped out of it, and Zwaantie jumped. "What the dark?" It was as if the guy was in the room with them, but only his life-size head. Except she could see right through it. His features were sharp though, lifelike.

Leo gave her a small smile. "It's just Viggo, my brother. He's on another island, but we can talk to each other this way."

"Hey, Viggo."

The face beamed at him. "You've returned."

"I have. Listen, the Ticker is probably already buzzing with the news of Zwaantie. We've been spotted. I didn't release her name or anything, but you might want to watch, and spin things if needed. We'll do a big announcement tomorrow."

"Of course. Though I've already seen the picture. She's very photogenic, but you have got to get her into different clothes."

"Stars! It's only been two minutes, and she's already up on the Ticker."

"She's big news. It won't take long until she's at the top. I'll do my thing. Get her in some new clothes and take another picture, please. When will we see you?"

"Tonight. We'll do our best. Thanks, Viggo."

"No prob. See you in a few hours." The head twisted and gave Zwaantie a ghostly smile. "Nice to meet you, Princess."

"Thanks," she said, and the head disappeared.

"Let's get you some clothes," Leo said. He nodded at the shop owner and dragged her out of the store. She wanted to ask what this was about, but she didn't even know where to begin with her questions. She had so much to learn. Zwaantie didn't know if she'd ever get used to Stella. She hadn't even been gone five hours, and already she missed home.

Chapter Two

THE OTHER PRINCESS

As they moved along, Zwaantie couldn't help but stare up at the tall buildings. Her head went fuzzy. Everything was surreal.

"Leo!" yelled a girl.

"Not again," he muttered, but spun around anyway. "Oh, never mind."

His face split into a wide grin, and a very pretty, very pregnant girl crushed him in a hug. "You are in serious trouble, mister. You kept Hunter longer than a couple of days."

He laughed. "And you are still pregnant, so I'm not in too much trouble. How's my soon-to-be nephew treating you?"

"Ugh," she muttered with both hands on her enormous stomach. "He needs to come out. Now that you are home, he can. Where's Hunter?"

"I don't know. We had some trouble crossing the wall and got separated. I thought I'd check here first, but since you haven't seen him, then they are probably down by the boats. I didn't know you were in town."

"I've been here since you left. I didn't want to take any chances. I nearly came over to Sol myself, but then Sage reminded me they don't have magic over there, and I'm not having this baby with no magic.

I've heard of women who have given birth in the middle of the night, and they said the pain is worse than death."

She rattled this off in one breath.

"How did you find us?" Leo asked.

"The Ticker. I recognized the store you were standing in front of. I was only a few shops down and quite frankly, I was angry no one told me the second you crossed the wall."

She noticed Zwaantie and raised her skinny eyebrows. She had a regal air about her. "Are you the princess?"

Zwaantie nodded. She wanted this woman to like her. Though she wasn't sure why. It wasn't like she'd ever see her again after today.

Leo gestured toward the girl. "Zwaantie, this is Candace. Lower queen of Deep Sky and my big sister. She's also Hunter's wife." Zwaantie understood now why he and Hunter were so comfortable with one another. Hunter wasn't just his guard, he was also married to his sister.

Candace hugged Zwaantie, the huge belly pushing into her. "It's a pleasure to meet you, but I need to go kiss my husband. We'll talk on the way home."

"Can you help us with something first?" Leo asked, grabbing her arm.

She shook off his hand. "No, I'm going to find Hunter."

"It won't take long. If you do this for me, I'll let you and Hunter have your own boat."

Candace cocked her head for a moment and thought. "As long as it doesn't take too long. What do you need?"

"Zwaantie needs some clothes. That picture of her in this ridiculous dress is already circling. We can't risk any more. All she needs is one outfit to get her home."

Candace glanced at Zwaantie again as if realizing she missed something the first time.

"Wow, you must be stifling. Does everyone in Sol dress like you?"

Zwaantie nodded. "But it's not as warm there."

"Well, this is easy."

Zwaantie wasn't sure what to make of Candace. She seemed friendly enough on the outside, but Zwaantie didn't know if people were different here in Stella. She wasn't sure what was polite or rude.

Leo stayed outside while Candace pulled Zwaantie into a building.

Shirts, skirts, and pants of all kinds of material covered the walls from floor to ceiling. No wonder the clothing factories only operated a few hours a day. Stella had more than enough clothes to last years and never run out of something new. Zwaantie could get used to this.

A few shirts winked and flashed, and others changed color in the blink of an eye. From one rack, soft music flowed from the skirts. They passed another rack of pants that smelled like a garden.

"This is amazing," Zwaantie said, genuinely impressed.

"Yeah, we have good clothes. This is one of my favorite stores. Do you have any idea what you want?"

Zwaantie chewed on her lip. The sheer number of choices was overwhelming. Plus, she was acutely aware that at home, she'd have the most fashionable clothes made, but here she could pick out something awful and not even know it. Somehow, everyone here was watching her. She wanted to know she was wearing the right thing.

She thought back to the dress with the bright blue jewels that she wore at the dance in Sol. Leo seemed to like it.

"Leo likes blue, so maybe something with blue in it."

Candace went to a rack of shirts with small sleeves and simple V-necks and riffled through a few shirts, then turned and glared at Zwaantie. She took a step back. What the dark?

"What's Leo's favorite food?" Candace snapped.

"I don't know," Zwaantie confessed.

"How can you not know these things? I thought you loved him."

"We didn't have much time to get to know each other. I only met him a few days ago. Over time I'm sure I'll learn them." Zwaantie couldn't see how Candace could find fault in that. Though, she couldn't help but feel this woman could see right through her.

Candace's voice dropped low and tight. "I can tell you don't love him. You barely touched him while we were standing out there. When Hunter and I fell in love, Dad used to joke that we would fall over if we didn't have each other to hold onto. Leo only had Hunter gone for a week and half, and I thought I was going to die. And Leo's favorite color is orange, not blue. If you loved him, you'd know these things."

She shoved a plain blue shirt in Zwaantie's hands and then plucked a bright pink skirt off a rack. Her face twisted into a scowl.

"Leo is my favorite sibling. And I have eleven of them so that's saying a lot. You may not love him now, but you sure as hell better by the time your wedding day comes. It should be nauseating to be around you two, or I'll make sure you have a miserable marriage."

Candace stomped out of the store. Zwaantie held the clothes, completely lost. This was ridiculous. She couldn't believe the way Candace had talked to her. Zwaantie would never be mean to anyone. Though, Zwaantie couldn't imagine loving someone the way Candace loved Hunter. It was so passionate and loud. The love she had with Phoenix was quieter. Simple. While she wanted desperately to kiss him again, she didn't need to hang all over him to prove she loved him. But Zwaantie knew his favorite color. It was green.

A tiny woman with spiky purple hair and a t-shirt that fell off one shoulder approached Zwaantie.

"Do you want to try those on?"

Zwaantie nodded, not sure what else to do. Would Candace come back?

The woman pointed to a small room with a curtain. Zwaantie stepped behind it and fumbled with her dress. At least it was an easy one to remove. Once Zwaantie managed to get the laces undone, it fell to the ground, and she slid out of her petticoat. She pulled the pretty blue shirt over her head and reveled at how smooth the material was. She could finally breathe again. The shirt smelled good too, like mint. The skirt was too short, and the Voice would berate her if it were still around, but the skirt still felt nice.

She stepped out from behind the curtain. The shop girl had a pair of orange sandals in her hand. She smiled at Zwaantie. "That looks nice on you. Where are you from anyway?"

"Sol."

The girl laughed. "Yeah, right. Where are you really from?"

"I'm really from Sol. I came over with Prince Leo a few hours ago. You didn't think my clothes were odd?"

The girl's mouth dropped open, and she pulled out her disc and ran her finger along it. She stared at the disc and then at Zwaantie. "It *is* you. No way! What are you doing in Stella?"

"I'm afraid I can't say. Prince Leo wants to keep it a secret. If you don't mind me asking, what are you looking at?"

"Your pic. Here." The girl snapped her finger, and an image floated in front of Zwaantie's face. It was like a portrait, but cleaner somehow. Leo had his arm around her, and they both smiled wide. That must've been what the girls had done.

"Unbelievable," Zwaantie said. She was both fascinated and horrified. Could someone take a picture at any time, and everyone in Stella see it?

"You don't have pictures in Sol?"

Zwaantie shook her head.

"Wow. We haven't had a visitor from Sol in hundreds of years. People will be talking about you for months."

Zwaantie clenched her fists. She'd never be able to run away and hide.

"Here, put on these shoes. You look great. Do you just want to wear them out of the store?" the girl asked.

"Yes, I would. Thank you."

"Okay. Can I have your disc?

"I don't have one of those."

"You don't have discs in Sol either? How do you function? Whatever. We still take coins. It will be twenty diras."

Zwaantie didn't know what to say. They had money in Sol, but she'd never handled it, and she'd only traded food with Stellans.

"I'm sorry. I don't have any coins either."

"Shame. I liked that outfit on you. But I can't let you have it for free."

Zwaantie's cheeks flamed as she slipped into the dressing room. She'd never felt so out of place in her life. Without Candace, she couldn't buy the clothes. She struggled to put her dress on, left the Stellan clothes on the floor, and raced out of there, hoping she wouldn't have to face that woman again.

She spotted Leo just outside the store, surrounded by a small group of people. He beamed when he saw her.

"Where are your new clothes?"

"Candace left before I was done trying them on. I don't have money or a disc."

Leo shook his head, chuckling. "Candace is altogether too eager to see Hunter. I didn't even see her come out. She's probably on the dock with him already."

"Did he say anything about the slaves?" She wondered where Phoenix and Luna were.

"They all made it across okay. We'll head to the docks in a few. But let's get you those clothes. Did you find something?"

Zwaantie nodded, but she really didn't want to set foot in that store. Leo put a hand on her back and led her inside. The woman with the purple hair grinned at Leo.

"Hey, Prince, how can I help you?"

Zwaantie was shocked by how casually the shop girl treated him. He was a prince, and she was acting like he was just another customer.

"My fiancée would like to purchase a new outfit. Perhaps you can help her."

The girl gave Zwaantie a long look. "Fiancée, huh? That's new. The clothes she tried on are still in the dressing room."

Leo handed the girl his disc. The girl's fingers flew across the surface, and then she took another identical device and touched them together.

The girl pointed to the dressing room. "They're all yours."

Zwaantie changed quickly, leaving her dress behind. She had no more use for Solite clothes.

She stepped out of the dressing room, still embarrassed. She had no idea how she would function here. They couldn't do anything without money or one of those discs. She had to get her hands on one.

Leo gave her an appreciative stare. "You clean up nice, Princess. But I already knew that. Come on, let's explore for a bit before we have to meet everyone at the docks."

Leo took her hand and pulled her out of the store.

"What else can the disc do?" Zwaantie asked.

He held out the disc. "We use it for everything. We can communicate with anyone in the kingdom, tell time, pay for things, and do more with magic. I can use any disc, and it will recognize me from my touch. So even if I didn't have mine, I could use another's, and my information would be on there."

"Can I see it?" she asked.

"Sure." He placed it gently in her hand and pressed his finger on it. A number blinked up at them from the smooth black surface.

"What's that?"

"The time. It's just after three."

"Notes," he said to the device.

Words flew up out of the device and floated in front of them.

Who is Prince Leo's mystery girl?

Is the royalty adopting a new style? If so, we need a cold front.

Leo returns from a visit to Sol. Could this mean better food?

"I don't understand," Zwaantie said, trying to make sense of the words.

"It's everything on the Ticker about me. I just wanted to see what people were saying."

"Can I have one?" Zwaantie asked.

"We'll get you set up when we get home."

Zwaantie frowned. She'd need it before they reached the castle. She and Phoenix would have to run away at the first opportunity. "How does money get on there?"

"Oh, it just keeps track of how many coins we have. The bank keeps the money, and it moves from account to account when we spend it on our devices. Hardly anyone uses actual dira anymore."

As they walked the streets, Zwaantie noticed the smell. In Sol, the streets smelled of farm animals or refuse. They didn't have good systems to get rid of the stench. Here the streets smelled faintly of oranges and tulips.

"It smells nice here," Zwaantie said.

"Our city mages do a good job. Most of them do it because they love the magic. Every building is infused with magic. Most of it illusionary, but it makes life interesting. I want to show you something before we head to the boats. But first, let's get another picture with your new clothes." He held out his disc and said "picture."

The disc floated off his hand and hovered in front of them. He put his arm around her and held her close. "Smile one more time."

She did. The disc returned to him. He placed his finger on the disc, and the picture popped up. He touched the picture. "Guess who's getting married. More deets on the vids tomorrow." He took his finger off the picture. "Send to Ticker."

The picture disappeared.

"Much better. I accidentally let slip you and I were getting married to the shop girl. By the time the picture gets there, everyone will know. Viggo's going to be upset because he wanted the announcement to be controlled, but there's nothing we can do about it now. We can relax for a bit. Oh, here it is."

He pulled Zwaantie down a small side street and suddenly they were in the middle of a forest. Zwaantie blinked at the sudden change of scenery. Trees towered over them, and leaves and pine needles littered the ground. Heavy pine replaced the tulip and orange smell.

"What happened?" Zwaantie asked.

"A botany mage created this. It's an illusion of course, but she wanted the people of the city to be able to experience the forest. She's a good friend of my father's. Her house is amazing. Flowers and trees everywhere. And they aren't an illusion."

They kept walking, and a minute later they were back on the street. Zwaantie glanced behind her. No trees, just a shimmer of light.

They wandered in and out of the buildings. Zwaantie loved all the little shops with magical trinkets floating around. She almost forgot she was supposed to be miserable.

Leo's disc buzzed. He glanced down at it. "Oh, stars, I lost track of time. We need to go."

As he dragged her down the streets, she couldn't help but notice the eyes following her as she walked.

"Why are people still staring at me? I thought if I dressed like them, they'd stop."

"You mean besides the fact that you're gorgeous? You're with me. It will only get worse when people find out that you're the princess. I thought you'd be used to it. In Sol, everyone bowed wherever you went. At least here, they're not stopping in their tracks. "

"I didn't go out in public very often, and when I did, I usually went disguised because I hated the attention. I just want to be normal."

Leo stopped short, spun around, and pulled her close. His chest felt so nice against hers. She should be thinking about Phoenix, not Leo.

He stared deep into her eyes. "Zwaantie, you continually surprise me. I need you to understand something, though. You will never be normal. You are special in so many ways. Embrace that."

He kissed her on her forehead, and tugged at her hand. She didn't want to be special. She scanned the crowd, so many eyes on her. She'd never be able to hide in Stella. Her plans with Phoenix were looking grim.

Chapter Three

THE BABY

A few minutes later, a very strange smell assaulted Zwaantie's nose, which was a rude shock from the tulips and oranges.

"What is that?" she asked, wrinkling her nose.

Leo gave her a forced smile. "It's the smell of the ocean. The salt is the briny smell you noticed. You'll get used to it."

He moved swiftly, dragging her along, the tension in his body apparent. The water glittered under the light. Two big boats with wide decks sat at the docks.

"Where are the sails?" Zwaantie asked. Neither of the boats had any masts. There were a few large lakes in Sol, but the boats there had sails.

"We don't need them. They move by magic." His words were clipped, short.

A gruff man stood on the boat. "Prince, we have to go." Others were rushing around them on the docks. "Queen Candace is already on that boat," he said, pointing to the other boat. "The rest of the boats with your party have already left. Please can we move?"

"Of course." Leo tugged Zwaantie onto the boat, worry on his face.

Zwaantie's heart raced. She and Phoenix were supposed to run away before they got to the capital city, but he was already on another boat.

"What's wrong?" she asked.

"We need to get a move on. This will not be a pleasant ride. We dawdled too long in the city."

The captain was a large man, and he wore a deep black vest. Besides him, Leo and Zwaantie were the only ones on the boat. The captain glared at Leo.

"You've risked all of our lives. Go on, get below. We'll move as fast as we can."

How had Leo risked their lives? She hid behind Leo, peering around him. The captain clenched his fists. He looked like he might chuck Leo right off the boat.

"I'm sorry. I lost track of time. We'll stay below. Thank you for your service."

The captain rolled his eyes and moved to the front of the boat.

Zwaantie crawled downstairs and found several large sofas and ottomans. She collapsed onto one that swallowed her right up. Leo chuckled. She was glad to see he had relaxed, but not at her expense.

"Why is the captain mad at you?" she asked.

Leo sat on an ottoman across from her. "Because I've endangered us. I should've been paying more attention."

The boat took off, and Leo nearly fell over. The boat bumped along the water. Zwaantie hadn't been out on boats much, and she was nervous she'd get sick.

"How have you endangered us aside from making sure I throw up on the ride?"

"Sorry," he said and stood. He wobbled along to a small cupboard, pulled out a large bowl, and handed it to her. Then he sat and put his arm around her. "It's just after six o'clock, and it takes about six hours to get to City of Stars. Less if the boats move fast, but we can probably only hope to gain about thirty minutes. If we are out after midnight, we could die."

Zwaantie's stomach rolled as they hit another small wave. "How?"

"All of our magic ceases at midnight. The boats won't move, and the light will go out."

Zwaantie gripped a pillow as the boat swayed. "That doesn't sound bad. Maybe we can just watch the stars."

Leo grimaced. "There's more to it. Monsters come out after

midnight. No one has ever seen one, but anyone who is out dies. A boat is not a place you want to be after midnight."

"If we don't make it in time, we're going to die?"

"Maybe. I've never spent a night out on the water. I don't expect our good captain has either." He frowned.

"Do you know anything about these monsters?"

"We call them vipers. They're some kind of serpent."

"How do you know if you've never seen them?"

"They shed their skin, and so we know their general shape."

"How often do they kill?"

"As often as they can. If you leave a door open or don't quite make it home, they'll get you. A cousin of mine died last year on his way home from a party."

Zwaantie squeezed her eyes shut and tried to ignore her queasy stomach. She was in a land where if she stayed outside after midnight, she would die a horrible death. Just when she thought Stella couldn't get any worse.

"Leo," she said in a cracked voice.

"Yeah."

"Please tell our captain to move faster. I don't care how sick I get."

Leo pulled her tight against him. "Don't worry. He already is. We'll make it."

"All I wanted to do was see the stars," she said, suddenly bereft. Nothing had gone the way she'd planned.

"Don't worry. I'll make sure you get your fill of stars. Maybe after the wedding, we can go spend a few weeks on one of the smaller islands, where the stars always shine."

She didn't want to think about after the wedding with him. He was being so sweet to her, but she couldn't allow herself to feel guilty for abandoning him for Phoenix. There would be no after the wedding. Her own happiness was worth sacrificing his.

"What will happen to the slaves once we get to the capital?"

"I'll free them and find them someplace to stay for a few weeks. We'll integrate them slowly. If they want to go back to Sol, we'll make sure they have passage across the border."

"Where will they stay?"

"I'm not sure. I'll talk to the jobs master. He helps people find jobs. He's very good at what he does."

Zwaantie let out a breath of relief. At least she'd be able to find Phoenix the next day. Though, she had been hoping to run away that night. From what Leo said, the midnight hour would come soon after they arrived, and so there would be no time to find Phoenix or a safe place to stay for the night.

"Will we have time to get to the castle before midnight comes?"

He frowned. "No, probably not. There is a small house near the docks for those who come in late. We'll stay there tonight and go up to the castle in the morning."

Leo's disc buzzed. He pushed a button, and Hunter's face popped out of it and hovered in front of Leo. Zwaantie was still unnerved by this mode of communication.

"What's up?" Leo asked the floating head.

"Candace is in labor. We are too close to midnight." Hunter sounded scared. It was a strange emotion coming from him.

"Where's her birthing mage?"

"In The Black City," said Hunter. "Stars, why didn't we have her come with us? What are we going to do?"

Zwaantie gripped Leo's arm. "Is there anyway I can help?"

Hunter's head swiveled so he looked directly at her. "Unless you can deliver a baby, no."

"But I can. I do it all the time."

"Stopping the boats will take too much time. We can't afford even a small delay."

Zwaantie cocked her head at Leo. "Explain to me how a woman who expected to deliver her baby with magic is going to have her baby on a speeding, rocking boat with no one who knows how to deliver a baby? Both she and the baby could die. Find a way to get me on that boat."

Leo looked from her to Hunter and then stalked up the stairs. Zwaantie wrung her hands. She knew what this meant. This could be a fool's errand. She might save Candace and her baby, but they could die anyway. But if she didn't and something happened, it would haunt her for the rest of her life. She had to help.

The captain stomped down the stairs.

"This is foolishness, girl. We cannot stop the boats."

"Do you want to be responsible for the death of the baby and his mother? Women die without proper care. Thousands of things could go wrong. Do you really want that on your head?"

"You don't understand. If we stop these boats, we are going to die."

"You're telling me no one has ever survived out on the ocean after midnight. Surely it happens."

The captain let out a sigh. "Yes, it happens occasionally. They only survive if they seal up their ships well."

Zwaantie stood straight. "Well, then I guess you better start sealing up the boat."

～

Fifteen minutes later Zwaantie was down in the hull of Candace's boat with her screaming all sorts of Stellan obscenities. The captains had lashed both boats together and were now rushing around checking every seam on the boat and reinforcing the doors. Zwaantie didn't have time to worry about what they were doing. She had a baby to deliver. The boats had stopped moving which would make it easier to deliver the baby, but that meant they were stuck out on the water for the night.

Zwaantie propped Candace up on her bed and spread her legs. The baby wasn't crowning yet, but he was getting close.

"There are things I need to help her with during the birth. Normally we use pain potions from Stella, so I'm assuming you have some of those. I'll need scissors of some kind, clean cloths, and a few bowls. Otherwise I just need you all to stay out of my way."

The captain glowered at her. "I don't have time for this. We're all going to bloody die."

He pulled a bag out of a cupboard with pain potions and the scissors and went to work on the hull door. Leo found Zwaantie a stool so she could sit at the foot of Candace's bed. She handed the pain potion to Hunter, who poured it down the screaming throat of his wife. She quieted a little and sobbed. She would not be an easy mother to deliver. She was scared, a screamer, and this was her first baby.

Zwaantie had delivered scared mothers before, but never when she herself was terrified.

Leo paced around the small room. Then he stopped and leaned down toward her.

"Zwaantie," he whispered.

"Little busy here, can we talk later? Maybe you should go sit down. It's just a baby. She'll be fine." Zwaantie checked Candace again and fully expected to see a crowning head, but nothing.

"No, you need to know a couple of things."

Zwaantie sighed and turned toward him as Candace let out another scream. "What?"

"Do you remember that the magic stops at midnight?"

Oh Sol, she'd forgotten. Delivering a baby in pitch black would be impossible. She'd delivered babies after midnight in Sol before, but the rooms were lit enough that midnight made no difference.

"Thanks for the warning, but I've done this plenty of times. I can do it by sound and touch. It will be good practice."

Bells rang.

Candace let out a scream. Hunter and Leo both yelled. Their words were lost in the confusion. The captain bolted the door behind Zwaantie, and she was so focused on Candace she didn't notice Leo had her arm in a tight grip.

He bent his head toward Zwaantie and whispered furiously into her ear. "You need to listen to me. When the bells stop—"

Zwaantie jerked her arm out from his.

"I have a baby to deliver, and if I'm correct in assuming that as soon as those bells stop, the lights go out, then I need to take care of a couple things first. Leave me alone and let me do my job."

He continued to prattle on, but Zwaantie ignored him. She knew he probably wanted to tell her more about the monsters, but at this point, she didn't care. She checked out Candace once again. A small head was crowning. Thank the stars. This wouldn't take too long.

Zwaantie looked over Candace's knees.

"It's time to push. Your baby will be here any minute."

Candace grimaced, the bells stopped, and the room went pitch black. Zwaantie couldn't even see the hand in front of her face. At first, something like rain pitter-pattered against the boat, but soon the noise was so loud that she couldn't even hear Candace cursing. It was as if a thousand swords were hacking away at the ship. How many monsters were out there? Hundreds? Thousands? Zwaantie's heart constricted. She tried not to think about what would happen if one of those monsters got into the boat.

Candace screamed out. The darkness would be a complication, but she couldn't worry because the baby would be there any minute, and Zwaantie had to focus on Candace. She gripped Candace's knees and shouted over the noise. "I know you are scared, but you have to push. This will be over soon. Are you with me?"

Candace didn't answer, but Zwaantie felt her bear down. A small hand popped out into Zwaantie's hands.

"Almost done, one more big push."

Zwaantie hoped to Sol this baby screamed when he came out because she didn't know if she'd be able to revive a baby with no light.

The shoulders came out, and the rest of the baby followed.

"He's out. Good job," Zwaantie said.

She wrapped him in the towel and flipped him upside down. She cleared out his mouth with her finger and smacked his bum. Silence. Except for that wretched pounding.

"Shouldn't the baby be crying right now?" Hunter asked.

Zwaantie didn't answer, just kept working on the baby. She flipped him over, blew air into his face, and felt his body shudder. He let out a loud scream, and for a few seconds they couldn't even hear the incessant pounding.

Zwaantie cut and tied the cord, cleaned him up, and handed him to his mother, whose sobbing still hadn't stopped. Zwaantie found her shoulder and leaned close to her ear.

"You did great. Now rest. We'll get the mess cleaned up in the morning." Zwaantie tried to still her shaking hands. A rapid thumping came on the door. Now that the baby was here, the monsters seemed more real. Would she and the others survive the night, or were her efforts in saving Candace and her baby useless? Zwaantie was already regretting her decision to come to Stella. She wanted to be home where at midnight there were no monsters and the sun was bright.

Chapter Four

THE CONFESSION

The thumping was louder now, like a thousand hammers pounding nails into a coffin. A hand fumbled for Zwaantie's and gripped it tight.

"It's me," Leo said. "Let's go find a place to sit. We are stuck here until morning."

"How long has it been?"

"Your guess is as good as mine. We should get some rest."

Zwaantie's legs crashed up against something.

"Ouch. I think I found the couch."

She sat down and felt Leo settle next to her. She guessed it had been about three hours, but it could've been longer or shorter. The sheer darkness made it impossible to tell anything.

"Do you think we'll be okay?" she asked.

"The captains did a good job at securing the boat. I think we will. We just need to ride it out. They're manning the door, making sure nothing can get in."

"Do you hear this every night?" she asked.

"We do. It's not as loud when you're in your rooms, but you'll hear them pounding on the doors.

"Holy Darkness, how do you sleep at night?"

"I grew up with it, so I hardly even notice anymore."

Leo scooted closer to her so their knees were touching. "You were so brave. I've never seen someone do something like that before."

"Thanks," she said, meaning it.

"One more reason to love you, right?"

She wished she could see his face to know what he was thinking. When she didn't respond, he went on. "Listen, I need to tell you something."

"What?"

"I haven't been completely honest with you. There is a reason I was so insistent on marrying you. I mean, I totally fell in love, and I know it seems weird, considering how short of time we had, but it happened."

"Really?" she asked because she didn't know what else to say. Her palms were sticky with sweat. Guilt plagued her. This wasn't fair to him.

"Yeah, really. I don't know. You've captured my heart in ways I didn't even know were possible. Watching you with Candace just made it stronger. You're an incredible person, Zwaantie, and you're going to make an excellent queen."

She was grateful for the darkness now as her face flushed with embarrassment. She wasn't going to be queen at all. These things he saw in her were lies.

"Thank you," she finally said.

"I've been deceiving you though, and I need to tell you the truth. The real reason I came over to Sol is much more complex."

Zwaantie leaned forward, curious. "Go on." She didn't know where he was going with this, but it made her feel slightly better that he hadn't been honest with her. Maybe her lie wasn't quite as awful.

"Have you heard of the Old Mother?"

"Yes. We have legends about her." Old stories meant to scare kids.

"Have you ever seen her?"

"No, of course not. She's just a myth."

"She's no myth. She came to see us the day Candace announced her pregnancy. She told us if Stella and Sol were not joined by the baby's first birthday, then the baby would die. So I came to join the kingdoms."

Zwaantie sat back, stunned. "What? Why?"

"I don't know. The Old Mother didn't elaborate."

A sick feeling crawled across her stomach. By running away with Phoenix, she'd ensure a baby's death—the baby she just delivered.

"Why didn't you tell me before?"

"I didn't think you'd agree. You had no reason to want to save my sister's baby." Leo paused, and Zwaantie wondered what he was thinking. He let out a breath. "Besides, there's more. The Old Mother said that after the baby dies, the vipers would kill more people. The entire survival of Stella rests on our marriage."

Rage welled up in her chest. How dare he do this to her? He hadn't even given her a choice or an opportunity to find solutions. Her chest constricted, and anger swelled in her stomach. She felt trapped. She was so close to freedom. To following her heart. She thought for a moment, trying to fully understand the implications. She gripped her head. This was impossible.

The Old Mother. Zwaantie'd studied the rumors. She and Luna used to speculate what would happen if she showed up. It had always been a bit of a joke, but this was no laughing matter. From what Zwaantie understood, prophecies from the Old Mother were insanely complex and often held double meanings.

"Did she specifically say you had to marry?"

"No, but how else do you join two kingdoms? You don't want us to conquer your kingdom, do you?"

"You wouldn't do that."

"To save Candace's baby? You bet we would. We're talking about the life of a child. That's precious, and we will do whatever it takes to save him, even if it means war."

A lump formed in Zwaantie's throat. If she disappeared, not only was she condemning the baby to death, but Leo would attack Sol. Stellans had ways to turn off the Voice. By sheer numbers alone, they'd slaughter the Solites. She squeezed her eyes shut. This wasn't fair. If she refused to marry Leo, she'd either be responsible for death on the Stellan side or the Sol side. Maybe both.

How had this happened? She didn't want to be important. Normal seemed so far away in that moment, and her heart broke a little. A few tears slid down her cheeks. She was once again grateful for the pitch black.

Leo let out a breath. "Please understand. This does not change how I feel about you. I love you. I'm excited to join our lives together. What we're doing is historical, and that makes it scary. But I feel better knowing I'm doing it with you."

Zwaantie didn't say anything. She just listened to the awful thumping on the boat and door. After several moments, Leo's hand found hers. He placed two small pieces of cotton in them.

"I brought you earplugs if you want to sleep."

Like she'd be able to sleep. With the pounding on the boat and the thoughts racing through her head. She took the earplugs anyway. "Thank you."

She shoved the cotton in her ears, which dulled the sound. Leo pulled her into him, and she hated how comfortable he felt. Right now, she didn't like him at all. He'd brought her an impossible choice between her own happiness or the death of thousands of people, but she allowed herself to lay her head on his shoulder. The boat rocked back and forth. Exhaustion overwhelmed her. Today had been too much and certainly hadn't endeared her to Stella. She hated to think what tomorrow would bring.

Chapter Five

THE STARS

A few minutes later, or maybe it had been a few hours, Leo shook her awake.

"You look peaceful when you sleep." He stood above Zwaantie with a huge smile on his face.

The bright fake lights had come on. The night was over and they'd survived. Then the memories came flooding in. She scooted away from Leo. She didn't want anything to do with him.

He gave her a wide smile, but she scowled. His smile faltered. "I convinced the captain to slow the boat down so we could watch the stars for a bit."

Stars. She did want to see them. She sat up and looked around. Blood and fluids covered the floor around Candace's makeshift bed. Both Candace and the baby were sound asleep together.

"We should clean up the mess." One thing Wilma had taught her was to always clean up her messes.

Leo smiled at her. "You've been begging to see the stars. The captain can clean up the mess. He probably won't let you clean it up anyway. A captain rarely allows civilians to touch his boat."

Zwaantie fought to get out of the couch, but it seemed to swallow her up. Leo chuckled and offered his hand. She didn't want to give him any indication she was happy about their current situation, but she was stuck. She took his outstretched hand, and he pulled her up. She immediately backed away from him. She was being rude, but she needed time to absorb what had happened, and the night before had been too traumatic to process anything. Leo seemed unfazed.

"Close your eyes. I want you to get the whole effect at once."

Zwaantie almost ignored him, but she was excited to see the stars, so she did as he instructed. He gently led her up the stairs. He put his lips close to her ear and whispered, "I've put a blanket on the deck. Lie down."

She patted the ground and gripped the soft fabric of the blanket. Slowly, she lowered herself down.

"Now open your eyes."

A whole new world opened up. Tiny dots filled the space. Some were brighter than others, and some were clustered together, and in other places there was only one small dot.

Sound died, and a light breeze blew over Zwaantie's face. She could barely take it in. The sky was breathtaking. Zwaantie could lie there for hours and never get tired of staring up at the stars.

It was amazing.

"Is it everything you hoped it'd be?" Leo lay down next to her. He stared at her, not the sky. How could he do that, when the stars were wide open above them?

"No, it's better. There's no way to imagine this." She was giddy. This was incredible.

"See the bright star right above us," he asked, his finger pointing high in the sky.

"Yeah," she said.

"That's Solaris. God of Light."

"It's just a star."

"Maybe to you. But to me, it's the reason I can do this."

The star suddenly changed to a bright green. Zwaantie gasped.

"Did you just do that?"

"I did."

She propped up on her elbow and faced him. "You can change the color of the stars?"

He laughed. "No, it's just an illusion. A green light in front of the star."

He pointed at the light and moved his finger to the left. The green light moved with his motion.

"Show me how," she said, the excitement overcoming her.

"I wish I could, but this comes with years of practice. You have to be comfortable with your own magic first. Only when you know how to access the magic will you be able to use it."

"But how did you do it?"

"Well, you have to feel the magic inside. Then you envision what you want. That's the hardest part. Anyway, after we envision it, we invoke the god who controls the magic."

"God?" Zwaantie asked. There was only one god. Sol.

"Yes, Solaris is the god of light, so we use him when we want light. We worship the stars. We believe they are all gods."

"That's a lot of gods."

"But we also believe that every time someone dies, they create a new star. Every god controls a different aspect of magic."

"So every time someone dies, a new magic is created?"

"Yes. There is a whole career field in discovering new kinds of magic."

"Wow."

"There are books and books filled with god's names and the magic they control. Sometimes we can just invoke the major god, but it works better if you can be more specific. Potion makers are the best at finding the right god."

"So is there a green light god that would be better than Solaris?"

"Yes, there is." He screwed up his face. "I can't remember what god though."

How odd. Solites worshiped Sol, the sun. He was the only one who controlled the world. Zwaantie wondered how Sol felt about the Stellans worshipping so many different gods. Though, they didn't have the sun, so she expected Sol didn't care much about them.

"Oh look." He took his finger and traced in the sky. His green light connected several stars together. "There's Leo."

"Is that a god as well?"

"No. Just a constellation."

Zwaantie counted for a second. "Seven stars. What do each of them control?"

"Now you're really challenging me. Let's see, Denebola is the goddess of paint, Zosma is the goddess of lilies."

"Just lilies? Not all the flowers?

"All the flowers is Albireo. He's over here." Leo flicked his green light across the sky and then back to his constellation. "Next is Chertan, god of sweets, and then Regulus. He's the god of war."

"Would you have used him if you had to declare war upon Sol?" Zwaantie wanted to understand how far he would've gone.

He dropped his hand, and the green light disappeared. He turned to face her. "I have to do whatever I can to save my kingdom. Can you honestly say you wouldn't do the same?"

She stared out at the stars. This was his kingdom. It was strange and foreign to her. It was scary. But the people were still people, just like in Sol. They cared for one another, and Leo was only doing what he thought was best. He was right. Though she didn't like it, she could understand where he was coming from.

The captain appeared from the hull and tapped his foot next to Leo's head. "It's time to go."

Leo addressed Zwaantie. "Are you ready?"

"Not really." Leaving meant facing reality, and what she really wanted to do was lie here and watch the stars.

When they arrived, Phoenix would be there, and Zwaantie would have to make a decision. Would she stay with Leo and save the baby, or would she follow her heart and run away with Phoenix? She had to do the right thing for both her people and his.

She looked up one last time before she headed down into the hull. The stars were supposed to represent freedom, so why did she feel more trapped than ever?

Chapter Six

THE RUNAWAY

Back in the hull of the boat, Candace was awake.

"Come here, you," she said to Zwaantie.

Zwaantie stared down at the small, peaceful sleeping baby. Her heart swelled at the thought of what she'd done. If they hadn't stopped the boats, Candace or the baby could be dead. Candace reached around and wrapped her in a one-armed hug.

"Thank you."

"You're welcome."

Candace let go. "Leo, we need a picture. Hunter, get over here."

Zwaantie crouched down on one side of Candace with Hunter on the other. A light flashed from Leo's disc.

"Send that picture to the Ticker. You tell them what a brave soul your fiancée is and how she delivered my baby after midnight. People will be talking about it for days. They are going to love her."

Leo nodded and spoke at the picture. The baby had started to fuss, so Zwaantie couldn't hear what he'd said.

The boat came to a slow stop, and the captain yelled down into the hull. "We're here."

Leo waved her over. "I can't wait to show you my home."

Zwaantie gave him a strained smile. She wasn't looking forward to what lay on the other side of the boat. She'd had more than enough of

Stella in the last twenty-four hours than she'd hoped to have in a life-time. Even the thought of spending another night filled her with dread. Those monsters terrified her.

She held onto Leo as they headed up the stairs. She still wasn't certain of her future, but he was the only person she had at the moment. Zwaantie blinked at the brightness. Huge white lights hung over the docks. As Zwaantie's eyes adjusted, she shrunk into Leo. There were people everywhere. Too many. Men yelled at one another on the packed deck and the people on boats.

Leo pulled Zwaantie up onto the dock and kept her close, but people jostled around them. Zwaantie's heart tightened. She was hoping it would be easy to find Phoenix. She had to talk to him and tell him about what would happen if she didn't marry Leo. Maybe he would have ideas of how to make things work. Though now, it seemed impossible.

They squeezed through the crowds and tromped off the docks. Standing in a doorway a few feet away was a man with a black pony-tail. He waved them over. He looked like Viggo, whose head she'd seen floating above Leo's disc in The Black City. Luna stood next to him, an anxious expression on her face.

Thank goodness she finally found a familiar face. Luna was safe. Zwaantie could breathe a bit easier.

Leo embraced the man and Zwaantie looped her arm through Luna's.

"What's the matter?" Zwaantie asked.

Luna looked at Leo and shook her head. Leo stepped away from the smiling man and snaked his arm around Zwaantie's waist. "I want you to meet my brother, Viggo."

Viggo pulled Zwaantie into a hug, and she stiffened. She wasn't sure she'd get used to hugging strangers. He let go of her.

"Congrats on the successful delivery of Candace's baby. You are the kingdom's sweetheart at the moment. Let's keep it that way."

"I have no idea what you mean, but okay."

He laughed. "We met the rest of your party just before midnight. I freed everyone this morning like Leo asked. They are off with the jobs master."

The slaves were free. She and Phoenix would finally be able to have a normal life together. She looked around the group and didn't see Phoenix's face anywhere.

Zwaantie's stomach tightened. "I thought Luna and her brother were going to wait for us."

"Oh, I didn't know," Viggo said.

Luna wrung her hands. "I'm sorry, Zwaantie. I was one of the first ones freed, and a few of Viggo's friends were asking me about Sol, and by the time I went to see what had become of everyone, Phoenix was gone with the rest of them."

"Maybe he didn't realize he was going to stay with us. We should go find him."

"Princess, we've got a lot to do today. Let's get you settled in, and I'll see if we can send someone to find him." Viggo fished out his disc and studied it.

Zwaantie clenched her fist. She wanted to tell Viggo that wasn't good enough. She needed to talk to Phoenix. Maybe if she could just spend a few moments with him, the tightness in her stomach would relax. She needed to touch him. Hug him.

Leo touched her back. "We should get up to the castle. There are a lot of people who want to meet you."

Zwaantie's mind spun. She was so lost. Phoenix was supposed to be here. She was prepared for a hard life. A commoner's life. But not one without Phoenix. Everything had tipped on its side, and she didn't know how to right herself.

"Zwaantie? You okay?" Leo asked.

"No, I'm sorry. I don't feel well. The boat ride didn't agree with me."

Zwaantie's whole insides felt cold and alone, and she wanted to sleep in a warm bed with no dreams. Perhaps in the morning she would awake, and this would be one big nightmare. There were definitely cool things about Stella, but right now, she wanted to go home and forget this ever happened.

At the end of the street several horseless carriages awaited. Zwaantie hardly even noticed when Leo pulled her into one. Viggo and Luna joined them, and he chatted animatedly with Luna, pointing out various buildings. Luna listened to him, but she was still wound up tight. Maybe she missed Pieter. Silently, Zwaantie cursed her father for not letting him come with.

Yesterday, Zwaantie would've found the scenery fascinating and had her face glued to the window watching the buildings as they passed, but now she only wanted to wallow in her misery. Leo put his arm around her and she shuddered. She would have to marry him and accept Stella as her home. A world where they had no rules and clothes were optional. With monsters that came out in the middle of the night to kill them. Who would want this? Zwaantie wanted to be home where she understood the rules and knew what was expected of her.

Maybe there would be a way. Maybe the Voice wouldn't remember her indiscretion when she returned. She had to hope. She couldn't be stuck here forever. Plus, at some point, she'd need to explain to Leo why she couldn't go home.

Luna gripped Zwaantie's hand, and Zwaantie startled. She stared at Luna's red wrists. Yesterday they had been bound, and Luna had been a slave. Today Luna was free. If nothing else, Zwaantie had given Luna the one thing she could never give her in Sol.

Freedom.

Chapter Seven

THE CASTLE

The palace was completely circular, which Zwaantie thought was odd. The castles in Sol had corners and squares.

"The shape is unique, isn't it?" Leo asked.

"Yes, it is different."

Zwaantie craned her head up to see if she could spot the top. It spiraled up, the tip of the castle rising high into the dark sky. It was pearly white with a soft blue glow.

The palace suddenly changed to green, and Luna let out a gasp and then a giggle. "That's amazing." She gripped Zwaantie's arm. "Isn't this incredible?"

Zwaantie gave a small nod, but she was having a hard time finding any part of it amazing. She wondered where Phoenix was now. Was he just as lost as she was? Maybe he had no idea how to find her either.

Leo shifted next to her. "All our palaces are designed similarly. It's to keep out the vipers as best we can. There are seven stories and four layers to each story."

"But it's much taller than seven floors."

"Yes, but that is just the spiral. There are no rooms above the seventh floor."

"What do you mean by layers?" Zwaantie asked, now curious.

"Notice how the outer layer is open? Those are balconies and are open to the outside, so you can sit and enjoy the weather, and people watch. From there you can enter several different rooms depending on where you are on the outside of the castle—the library, the kitchen, the throne room, small dining rooms, and living areas. Those rooms have windows. But the bedrooms are in the third layer—no windows and thick wooden doors so the vipers cannot get in."

"Are you saying the vipers roam the halls at night?" Zwaantie swallowed hard. There was no way she'd be able to sleep with those things banging at her door. She'd often resisted going to her room on time at home, but here she would make sure she was locked in her room a good thirty minutes before midnight.

"Yes, you'll hear them pounding at your door. Earplugs might be good at first."

Zwaantie shared a look with Luna, but Luna was unfazed. Maybe she remembered the vipers from when she'd been a child. It was weird she'd never mentioned them before.

Zwaantie still had trouble believing they had so much magic, and they couldn't find a way to keep the monsters out of their castle.

"What's in the fourth layer?" Zwaantie asked.

"Ah, the heart of the palace. Each level is different. I'll show you them sometime, but now you need to meet my father."

They went under the balcony, through the front door, and into a throne room. The king and queen stood. They hugged and kissed Leo and Viggo. So much touching. These would be her in-laws. She shivered.

A few people stood around the edges of the room with flashing discs. Would every part of her life be on display?

The king bowed, and Zwaantie curtsied. Leo's father was tall like him, with the same spiky hair, but it was graying. The queen was thin and blonde. Zwaantie remembered Leo had explained his mother was not the queen.

"Father and Queen Astrid. May I introduce my fiancée, Zwaantie and her friend Luna?"

They inclined their heads toward the girls. The king and queen must've known they didn't touch much in Sol because Zwaantie expected she would've gotten a hug and a kiss as well.

"Princess Zwaantie, I trust your trip over here was pleasant," the king said.

"Yes," Zwaantie lied. Sure, almost getting eaten by monsters and delivering a baby in the pitch black was completely pleasant.

He held Candace's baby in his arms. Her father would never hold a baby. That was beneath him. Things must be different here in Stella. Her stomach clenched. She wasn't sure she could talk to anyone right now.

"Looks like we had some excitement. I'm glad you were there to assist Candace in her time of need. Would you like to hold my grandson?"

Zwaantie hesitated. In some ways she resented the baby. He was the reason she would have to marry Leo, even though she didn't want to.

Also, in spite of delivering several dozen babies in the last few years, she'd never held a baby except for right after he was born. She nodded, apprehensive.

The king handed her the baby. He was so small in her arms, but warm against her body. His wide blue eyes stared up at her. He was tiny and helpless and so alive. His whole life was in front of him. Someday he would grow up, become whatever he wanted to be, and would make a difference.

Something hit her at that moment. This was who she was fighting for. The life of this baby was at risk if she didn't marry Leo. Her stomach churned at the very thought. She might be trapped, but she was fighting for this baby.

Candace touched her elbow, and Zwaantie startled.

"Shall we go sit while Leo and Father catch up?"

"Sure." She glanced at Leo, who had a sappy look on his face. He was probably imagining her with their own children. She couldn't think about that. Not yet.

Candace led her into a small sitting room with several overstuffed chairs. Zwaantie sank down into one. She dropped her gaze to the baby. He'd closed his eyes and was sleeping.

"What did you name him?" Zwaantie asked.

"We haven't yet. Actually I was wondering if maybe you wanted to pick his name. You saved both of our lives. Thank you."

Zwaantie's breath caught. She'd never been given such an honor before. "I can't do that. He's your baby."

Candace sat on the edge of her chair and leaned toward Zwaantie.

"I don't think you understand. When I realized I was in labor on the boat, I panicked. I knew we wouldn't make it before he came. Even in my pain, I was hysterical. Then here you came, a midwife from Sol to save the day. If you hadn't been there, one or both us could be dead. I'm forever indebted to you. I know I yelled at you about Leo, but now, sister, you come first. You tell me what you need, and I'll do it for you."

Zwaantie thought for a moment.

"What I need is time. I didn't know about the prophecy until after I delivered the baby. You already know I don't love Leo, and it's going to take me time. But I will marry him and save this little guy."

Candace hesitated for a moment. "Will you still name him?"

Zwaantie stared down at the baby in her arms. She had no idea what to name him. After her father? No. Her brother? Yes. He would appreciate that.

"Raaf. It's my brother's name."

"It's different. But I like it. Raaf." The name didn't sound quite right coming off Candace's tongue, but Zwaantie supposed she would never pronounce it right. Ah, well. Raaf will still be pleased.

"Are you going home right away?" Zwaantie asked.

"I don't think so. The lock-in is coming up."

"What's the lock-in?"

"The biggest party of the year. Most young royals attend as well as others who are high on the social strata. We lock ourselves in a warehouse and dance all night."

"But what about lights?" The darkness after midnight was stifling.

"We use gas lamps and natural music. It's so fun. We'll go shopping beforehand and make sure you have the perfect dress."

Zwaantie felt overwhelmed again. Would she have to attend this party? It sounded horrid. Hundreds of Stellans doing Sol knows what.

A knock sounded on the door, and Viggo poked his head in.

"Time to feed the Ticker."

"What?" Zwaantie asked.

"Photo shoot, darling. Let's go."

Candace stood, took little Raaf, and waved Zwaantie away. "Go on. It's time to tell Stella about the Solite princess."

A sinking feeling blossomed her stomach. She didn't want to do this. Her face would be everywhere, and she would have to act like she was happy to be here. Couldn't she just have one day of peace?

Chapter Eight

THE IMAGE

Viggo chattered in Zwaantie's ear as they went down the hall. "We're going to leave you in what you are wearing now. We want this to look authentic, not staged. Two stories are going to hit the Ticker this afternoon. First will be you and Leo and your love story. Second, we will expand on how you delivered Candace's baby. The public is going to eat you up."

Zwaantie's head spun as she tried to make sense of everything he was saying.

"Has Leo already told you our story?"

Viggo shook his head with a laugh. "Oh, no, I'll make it up."

"But if you make it up, it'll be a lie."

"No, sweetie, it's just spin. Leo went to Sol seeking new trade agreements, and he fell in love. Your parents were horrified by their daughter dating a prince from Stella, and so you had to sneak out just to spend time together. In the end, nothing would stop your love. Your wedding will be the biggest event this century."

"But he came because of the prophecy."

He put a finger to his lips. "Only the royal family knows about that."

He pushed open a door to another room, and Zwaantie followed him in, Candace on her heels. Leo was there with his father and the queen. Luna sat next to the queen, talking animatedly. Another man with a larger disc was there as well.

"The princess," he said. He rushed up to her and kissed her cheek. "You are just lovely, aren't you? Come, let's get the Ticker talking. The picture of you in that wretched dress is still floating around, even though Leo posted a few others. Let's see what we can do about burying it, shall we?"

Zwaantie's head began to pound. She didn't understand what was going on.

"First, let's document you meeting the king. A hug, I think."

Zwaantie wanted to scream. This was impossible and wrong. Not only was she going to be on display for everyone to see, but she also had to fake it. She smiled though and went through the motions.

"Perfect," he said at the end. He withdrew into a corner with Viggo. The pictures floated in front of them, and they argued over which to post.

Leo took her hand. "Thanks for being a good sport. Can I get you anything?"

"Just a bed and perhaps a healer. I'm afraid my head is hurting."

"I'll show you to your room. Candace, can you call a healer?"

Candace squeezed Zwaantie's other hand. "I hope you feel better soon."

"Thanks," she said and meant it. She was grateful for Candace and her friendship.

"Come, Luna," Zwaantie instructed. Luna looked up from where she'd been chatting with the king and queen. She frowned at Zwaantie but followed anyway.

They wove their way around the many hallways. It was like a maze. Zwaantie would never find her way around. They stopped at a small door, and Leo pushed a button. The door opened, and he pulled her into the small room. Luna slid in behind them. She was still frowning at Zwaantie, but Zwaantie couldn't think about why. She couldn't think of anything really.

Leo pushed another button with the number six above it, the door closed, and the room moved. Zwaantie clutched his arm, and Luna fell into her as the room lurched. Leo laughed at them, and Luna joined him.

"I forget you're not used to our magics. We call this an elevator. It moves between the floors so you do not have to use the stairs."

"We didn't have these when I was a child. Are they new?" Luna asked with her eyes shining.

"The magic was discovered a few years ago."

Zwaantie rubbed her forehead. "Luna, when we get to my rooms, I need you to go find me some medicine."

Leo frowned at her. "Luna is not your slave anymore."

Zwaantie didn't know how to respond. Her head hurt too bad. "She may not have bondage bands anymore, but she is still my servant."

"Luna will not be your servant. She will stay here as an honored guest, much like you. I can show you how to call for a healer, but I will not tolerate you ordering Luna around like a slave. I told you before. We do not have them here."

Zwaantie was stunned. She had never heard Leo speak with such vehemence and authority. She rubbed her head and nodded, not having the energy to argue with him. He gave her a curt nod.

"Will I be staying near Zwaantie?" Luna asked.

"Yes. My brothers and sisters and I share the sixth story. There are a few extra suites so you two will also have rooms on that floor. Normally guests sleep on the third, fourth, or fifth floors. My father and his wife occupy the seventh floor."

The elevator door opened, and they were once again in a maze of halls. Zwaantie's head spun, and she couldn't concentrate on where they were going.

"This is your room," Leo said.

Her door was painted with a scene from home, a sun and pasture with cows in it. Zwaantie's name was written in the clouds across the sky. It was gorgeous.

Zwaantie squinted and leaned down to look closer.

"Yes, the cows move. Touch one of them."

Zwaantie did, and it mooed. In spite of herself, she laughed. "That's brilliant."

"I'm glad you like it. I spoke with the design mages yesterday before we got on the boat. We wanted to make you comfortable."

He opened the door, and it was like being at home. The air even smelled different, fresher somehow. All of the walls were painted like home. A sun hung in the sky, and Zwaantie's castle perched on a hill, with fields full of tiny moving animals.

Zwaantie smiled at him for a moment, forgetting her misery.

In the center of one wall was an enormous bed with a midnight blue comforter covered in tiny shimmering lights.

"I told them about the table in your room at home. They tracked down the mage who created it and had him make this. Another replica of the starry sky. Later, we'll find the constellations I showed you," Leo said.

It was a nice gesture, but her head really was hurting. He pointed to a dressing screen. Draped across the top of it was a light nightgown.

"I'm going to show Luna her room while you get changed."

She didn't even respond as she escaped behind the dressing screen. It was much easier changing out of Stellan clothes than it was with Solite ones. She slipped under the covers just as Leo came back in.

He sat down on the edge of the bed. "I'm sorry you're feeling bad."

"I think it's the newness of everything. I'm just not used to it."

"You'll find our healers are amazing. He'll figure out exactly what is wrong with you and fix it so you can enjoy your evening."

Just then a huge beast came bounding through the door and leapt up onto the bed. Zwaantie scrambled back so she was sitting up against the wall. "What is that?"

But Leo didn't even hear her. He was busy scratching the beast's ears and crooning to it like it was a baby.

It licked him in the face and then turned its enormous head toward Zwaantie. It crawled across the covers until it was in her face. Zwaantie wrinkled her nose. Warm breath that smelled like liver blew across her face. Its nose was black and wet.

"Zwaantie, meet Molly, my dog."

Ah, a dog. Sometimes the farmers used them to herd sheep, but she'd never met one that crawled into bed with you or was quite as big.

Zwaantie nodded, still a bit speechless. Molly ran her tongue across Zwaantie's cheek and then settled next to Leo, her head in his lap.

"Why is she in my bed?"

"Because she's my baby." He made a kissy face at Molly and scratched her behind her ears. "She sleeps with me. Normally she travels with me too, but I didn't want to bring her into Sol. I didn't know how you felt about dogs."

Oh great, now not only would she be sharing a bed with a man she didn't love, but she'd have to have a beast in the bed as well. Zwaantie wanted to go home. She rubbed her throbbing head.

"Beasts like that belong in the fields with the cows and sheep. Can you get her off my bed, please?"

Hurt crossed his face, but he called Molly down. He sat on the floor with her while they waited.

A few minutes later a healer arrived. He looked a lot like the healers at home, but instead of giving Zwaantie a pill or a foul liquid to swallow, he placed his hand on her forehead and muttered a few words. The pain disappeared.

"Thank you," she mumbled.

"Princess, may I speak freely?" the healer asked.

Zwaantie nodded into her pillow, forgetting Leo was still in the room.

"I sense something wrong with your spirit. Something, or someone, has recently hurt you. Unfortunately, without knowing what happened I can't take that pain away. Can you tell me what happened?"

Zwaantie opened her eyes wide and stared into his. He had a wrinkly brown face and thick black hair. Of course she was in pain. Phoenix left her. Her heart was broken.

"I'm sorry I don't know what you are talking about."

Leo stood behind the healer, looking concerned.

"I would really like to sleep. Can you help me with that?"

He sighed. "Yes, but the pain won't go away until you talk about it and let someone draw the pain out."

He placed his palm on Zwaantie's forehead again, and she felt her eyes drifting closed. Just before she was lost to dreamland, a tiny cow on her wall mooed.

Already she missed home, where she didn't have to do photo

shoots, didn't have to deal with beasts from the field in her bed, and didn't have to marry a man she didn't love.

Chapter Nine

THE TOWER

"**W**ake up, silly girl."

Zwaantie blinked. Luna stood over her.

"I'm not supposed to be your servant anymore, but the prince was worried because you weren't up yet. Come on, get up."

"No," Zwaantie said and rolled over.

"You cannot spend your first full day in Stella avoiding everyone. I know you're upset about Phoenix, and I'm sure you feel completely lost, but appearances must be kept."

"Why?"

"Because I know you plan on running away, and it will be harder to do if they are suspicious."

"I have to marry the prince. I have no choice." She didn't. Not really. She had to save the baby. She certainly didn't want to marry Leo.

Luna sighed. "Of course you have a choice. You always have a choice. Except now. Get out of bed. I've arranged for us to eat lunch together here. Alone."

Zwaantie sat up, grateful Luna had the foresight to let them do something together without dealing with the bright lights of Stella. Luna was dressed in a very pretty white floor length dress with a bright pink flower winding around the bottom. It smelled wonderful.

"Aren't the clothes here amazing?" Luna spun around.

"Yeah, I guess." She didn't want to love Stella. Not right now.

"The dress they picked out for you is the same, except yours has an orange flower. I'm told all the princesses are wearing them today. I feel honored to be among them."

She held up a dress for Zwaantie.

"There is something else you should know." Luna sat tentatively on the edge of the bed.

Zwaantie rolled her eyes. "More bad news?" She was being a brat, but everything was weighing on her shoulders, and right now, the whole world seemed lost.

Luna giggled. Zwaantie hadn't seen her this happy since her wedding day.

"No. I'm pregnant. I wasn't going to tell anyone for a while, but somehow everyone here seems to know. It must be something in their magic. They said it's a girl, which is why I got a pink flower. Honestly, it's why I still came, even though Pieter could not. Our child will be born free, not a slave. If I go home, she will be born with bands because Pieter is still a slave."

She beamed. Zwaantie was happy for her, but still so miserable. Why did Phoenix have to leave? She wanted to have babies too. His babies. Not Leo's. Sure, Leo was nice, but she'd never love him the way she did Phoenix.

Zwaantie slid out of bed, and Luna helped her put on the dress even though she didn't really need to.

Luna pointed at the necklace. "You should take that off. It doesn't match."

Zwaantie fingered the necklace. It was a simple band with a disc embedded with an amethyst. Leo had given it to her the day he came to Sol. Zwaantie hadn't wanted it at first, but the second she had it on, the Voice disappeared. She hadn't taken it off since, foolishly believing it protected her. She didn't need protecting here—the Voice didn't exist—so she slid it off and placed it on her nightstand.

A knock sounded on the door, and Zwaantie let Luna answer it. Zwaantie went into her bathroom and splashed water on her face. She didn't like the look of her skin in the mirror. The unnatural light made it appear washed out.

Your dress shows too much skin.

Zwaantie jumped. This was impossible. She was in Stella.

"How are you here? I'm no longer in Sol," she whispered. She didn't want to draw any attention to herself.

I am everywhere. You chose to block me. Time to go home, Princess, and confess your sins.

A small pain settled behind her eyes. This couldn't be happening. How did the Voice follow her to Stella? She had to put the necklace back on. She jerked the bathroom door open and gripped the necklace.

Oh, come on now, you know you missed me. I won't punish you. The pain behind her eyes disappeared. Please don't shut me out.

She set the necklace down. It was true. She had missed the constant chatter. Her head had felt so empty. Besides, it was nice to have someone tell her when she screwed up so she could fix it. She placed the necklace on her nightstand.

Luna stood beside a small table with a spread of small sandwiches and fruit. The colors were brighter than in Sol, the bread fluffier, and it smelled better. Zwaantie picked up a grape and popped it into her mouth. It was mushy and old. She made a face. Luna laughed. "No more fresh fruits here."

"How do they get by?" Zwaantie asked.

Luna shrugged. "I'm sure we'll get used to it. Sit, let's talk."

The Voice continued to chatter in Zwaantie's head, like it had in Sol. She tuned it out and concentrated on her conversation with Luna. "Thanks for bringing me lunch. I'm still not quite sure about everything here."

Luna nibbled on a sandwich. "So what are you going to do?"

Zwaantie frowned. "I don't know. What do you think?"

"I'm not going home until after this baby is born. But you have to make your own decision. What do you want to do?"

"I want Phoenix, but I don't know if that's even a possibility anymore."

"I think you're overreacting. He got caught up with the other slaves. I'm sure we can find him."

"No, you don't understand. I have to marry the prince. If I don't, his sister's baby is going to die."

Luna cocked her head. "What do you mean?"

"There is a prophecy that says if Stella and Sol aren't joined by his first birthday, little Raaf will die."

"Raaf?"

"Candace let me name him."

Luna didn't say anything. Maybe she was absorbing the news as well. Zwaantie took a bite of one of the sandwiches. The bread was stale and the meat spongy. She'd go home for the food alone. At least now, she knew the Voice wouldn't kill her if she went home. "The right thing to do is marry Leo and save little Raaf."

Is it the right thing though? Maybe joining Stella and Sol would be good for Stella, but it isn't the best thing for Sol. Have you even considered your own kingdom? Is one baby's life worth all of your people? However did you survive without me, dear? You need me to help you become the best queen Sol has ever seen. Time to go home.

The Voice was right. It was time to forget this whole business and go home. Stella could never be her home. It was dark, the food was bad, and there was no way she could spend another day here. The Voice just reaffirmed what she was already feeling, and it was never wrong.

"Maybe I should go home."

That's right. Go home and let Leo figure things out on his own.

"What about the baby?" Luna asked.

That is none of your concern. Your concern is for your kingdom alone.

"He's going to have to find another way to save his sister's baby. He's not going to use me. He doesn't even know if it will work." Even as she said it, a sick feeling settled in her stomach. The Voice told her this was the right thing to do, but something felt wrong.

A knock sounded at the door. Leo poked his head in without waiting for Luna to open it.

"You're up. I was worried." He looked so concerned, and Zwaantie gave him a forced smile. "How was your lunch?" he asked, taking the chair next to her.

"Okay." She wouldn't tell him how awful she really thought it was. She'd give anything for fresh food.

He bounced his knee. "Would you like to go for a walk with me? We can go up to the tower and see the stars."

She did want to see the stars again before she left and gave a curt nod. "Sure. Luna do you want to come?"

Luna shook her head. "I'll give you two some alone time."

Leo held out his arm, and Zwaantie put her hand in the crook of his elbow. The Voice chattered in the background judging everything Zwaantie saw.

"You look beautiful." He looked at her like she was his whole world. She hated that she couldn't give him the same. It wasn't fair to him.

"Thank you," she replied, just as the Voice said. *No, you don't. You look like a slut.*

They walked to the elevator again. Zwaantie shrunk away. Leo chuckled and pulled her inside. He pressed a button that said *Tower.*

"This won't take us all the way up, but it will get us close. We'll have to climb a few stairs."

The elevator opened to a tiny, nearly empty, circular room. Soft pink light glowed from the walls, and a spiral staircase sat in the middle. Zwaantie followed Leo up the stairs. Up they wound, and Zwaantie got dizzy.

After what seemed like ages, Leo pushed open a door in the ceiling and climbed out. He helped her up. Zwaantie gasped. They were at the top point of the castle. Outside. The floor was about eight feet in diameter. If she moved just a few feet, she'd fall right off. They were a thousand feet in the air.

She clutched onto Leo. "Take me inside."

"Are you afraid of heights?"

"We're a thousand feet in the air. If we fall, we die."

"We won't get close to the edge. Though Ari and I let our legs dangle sometimes. Sit. We'll stay in the middle."

She sank down and stared up, so she didn't have to look down.

The Stellan sky spread out before her. She hated it today. Those stars were supposed to be her freedom. Now she was trapped in a marriage she didn't want, longing for a man she couldn't have, and then the Voice followed her here.

Leo pointed to the sky. "See the star there, the bright one."

"Yes."

"That's the God Sarin. When the tower was built, we used him to place a magical shield around it. Even if you tried, you can't fall off."

There is only one God, Sol. This is blasphemous. Tell the prince you want to go home.

That is what she wanted, right? To go home. She let out a breath. "Leo, I want to go home."

He placed his hand over hers. "I know it's different here, but if you'd just give it a few days, I bet you'll love it."

Don't let him influence you. Remember, he is only thinking of his kingdom. You should be thinking of yours.

"No. I want to go home. Now. This was a mistake. I'm sorry. I don't know what I was thinking."

"You're just overwhelmed. I promise it will get better. You know, I was a little overwhelmed when I got to Sol. Remember the cow?"

She almost grinned.

Stand your ground.

"You're not listening to me. I want to go home. Either you're going to help me get there, or I'll do it myself."

He sat up and looked her right in the eye. "Zwaantie, I love you. I'm not going to let you get away." His face was so sincere, so genuine.

"Then let me go."

He shut his eyes for a minute. "What about Candace?"

"You're resourceful. You said yourself it was only one interpretation. Find another one that doesn't involve invading Sol."

He gripped Zwaantie's hand. "What if there isn't any other way? Are you just going to let little Raaf die?"

No. She didn't want that. Not at all, but she had to go home. She had to leave Leo. She couldn't allow the prophecy to influence her decision.

"Yes. I am. Take me home."

His face hardened. She expected him to argue, to tell her she had to stay, but he didn't. His voice was low and soft. "If that's what you really want."

"It is. I'm sorry. I'm not sure what possessed me to think this was a good idea."

Leo looked away from her. "Fine. Can you at least do dinner with my family civilly tonight? Pretend like everything is okay. We can figure out how to get you home tomorrow."

Zwaantie squeezed his hand. "Thank you."

Good girl.

Leo gave a curt nod, but didn't respond. The Voice told her it was the right decision, so why did it feel wrong?

Chapter Ten

THE MISSING PRINCESS

Just before dinner, Candace popped her head in Zwaantie's room.

"You ready to meet the whole family?" she asked, settling on the couch. Zwaantie could barely look her in the eye.

"Where is little Raaf?"

"With a nanny. This dinner isn't really the place for babies. Can I do your hair?"

"It's okay. Luna has already done it."

"It's nice, but I'd like to add a streak of orange. See how mine has blue to match my flower? It will look better in the pictures if we match. Luna, I can put pink in yours if you want."

Luna nodded eagerly. Zwaantie was still uncomfortable with everything. Stellans put way too much emphasis on appearances.

Candace was just finishing the orange streak when Leo came and fetched them. She didn't know why he thought he had to. Candace would've shown them the way. But Zwaantie put on a smile and rested her hand in the crook of his elbow. She only had to keep up this charade for the evening, and she'd be back in Sol by tomorrow night. Safe and sound with the sun. The Voice was still present in her mind, but he hadn't given her a direct command since she'd chosen to go home.

As they moved through doors and descended a few floors, Zwaantie quickly realized they would've never found the main dining room on their own. They wove in out of hallways so they were in the fourth layer, the innermost part of the castle. It was one big circular room.

They were escorted to an enormous round table. There must've been a hundred people sitting around it. The center was cut out, and in the middle of the table waiters came up a stairway with goblets filled with exotic colored drinks.

Luna sat on Zwaantie's left and Leo on the right. About a third of the way around the table sat the king and queen. Beyond them were Candace and Hunter. She smiled at Zwaantie.

"Is this all your family?" Zwaantie asked, glancing at his siblings.

"Most of them. There are spouses, obviously, and a few friends. But mostly family."

"Are all of your brothers and sisters here? You said there were twelve of them."

"They should be."

"Show me."

He pointed first to a young man, who appeared a year or two older than Leo. "Ari is the oldest and heir to the throne. He's not married yet and can't take over until he is married or father dies. He spends most of his time chasing silly girls." Leo rolled his eyes.

Ari was very handsome with thick brown hair, deep-set gray eyes, and thick eyebrows. Zwaantie could see why silly girls would chase after him.

"The next two, Tauro and Jem have already claimed their kingdoms. They are now lower kings."

"I'm confused. They are princes of your city. Why would they be lower kings in other kingdoms?"

"I forgot your succession is different. In Stella, the high king's children become lower kings and queens. We only have four kingdoms. So only Ari, Tauro, Jem, and Candace claim kingdoms. The rest of us stay princes and princesses."

"How is Hunter a king and your guard?" Zwaantie supposed she shouldn't be so surprised. She was a midwife, after all, but a guard seemed a risky position for a king.

"Yeah, I was a bit peeved when she took him from me. I have a new guard, but I trust Hunter more. That's why he came with me. He's still flabbergasted Candace fell in love with him, and he still acts more like a guard than a king, but he'll get the hang of it."

Waiters brought around tiny bowls with hook-shaped food in them and an orange sauce.

"What's this?"

"Shrimp, try it. You'll love it."

It was good. Salty and fishy. Better than the spongy meat she had earlier.

"Who are the rest of them?"

He pointed around the table.

"You've met Viggo. There's Libby, Scorpion, and..." He paused. "Where's Sage?"

He looked all around the table, but he couldn't find who he was looking for.

"Sage is usually with Ari, but I don't see her. She must've gone to some party or something and forgot to come home. If you ever go out with her, be careful what you drink or who you let magic you. Otherwise you could end up in a magical hallucination with unicorns and rainbows that won't end for a week. Don't let her tell you any stories about me either. Sage is wild, but fun."

Zwaantie almost reminded him she would be going home the next day, but decided not to bring it up. It didn't change anything.

He searched the table then continued pointing. "Next to Viggo is Patrice, and there's Aquiles and finally Pius, who more than lives up to his name. We keep telling him to go live in Sol. He'd fit in better."

Poor Pius, he didn't seem to be enjoying his dinner, and he wasn't talking to anyone.

Something was bothering Zwaantie as she looked at all the people, but she couldn't figure out what. She studied his brothers and sisters. None of them looked alike. Some were tall and thin. Others were broad shouldered. Hair color ranged from blonde to purple, but that could've been the magic they used. The other thing, they were all around the same age. Pius looked young, around fourteen or fifteen, and Ari couldn't have been more than twenty.

"How old is Ari?" Zwaantie asked.

"Nineteen."

"And Pius?"

"Sixteen."

"Ari is the oldest, and Pius is the youngest?"

"Yes," he said and took a large bite of his potato "You look cute when you're thinking," he said.

"I'm confused."

"I know. I was hoping we didn't have to talk about this."

"Why?"

"Because life in Sol is so different from here. I'm afraid you'll be upset by this practice. I don't want you to think badly of us. It's really not a big deal."

If he was going through that much trouble to avoid answering a question, which Zwaantie hadn't even asked yet, then it was a big deal. Zwaantie opened her mouth to ask.

"Please don't ask the question. I don't want to have to answer it." His face flushed.

He hadn't learned yet that Zwaantie got what she wanted, regardless of the consequences. "How is it possible that twelve siblings are all born within three years of each other?" Zwaantie wanted to think the best of things. Three sets of quadruplets or something. But she had a feeling the answer would be far different.

"It's because we have different mothers. My father's wife is Ari's mother. But she only had one child."

Disgusting. You shouldn't even be in the same room with such immorality. Zwaantie ignored the Voice, now wanting to understand how this was possible.

"So where is your mother?"

"She lives here in the castle, but that's unusual. The rest of the mothers live on estates in the country or in the city somewhere. Most of them are married with other children, and they're happy."

Zwaantie didn't want to say it, but she had to. "Why would your father do something like that?"

Because he's a horrible, immoral man.

"Because it is expected. High kings traditionally have huge families. Most have forty or fifty kids, but Astrid quickly got sick of sharing her husband, so she asked him to stop after Pius. He is madly in love with her, so he did. I'm not entirely sure he stopped sleeping with other women, but he made sure he never got another one pregnant."

"We don't do things like that in Sol," Zwaantie said.

Good girl.

"I know. The only one who does that is the high king."

"But do most people 'sleep around?'" Zwaantie couldn't keep the ice out of her voice. Suddenly her appetite disappeared. She didn't need the Voice to tell her how wrong this was.

Filth. Disgust. Leave.

He shrugged and took a bite of his fish. The room was too hot, and the air was sticky. The pounding started behind her eyes again. Zwaantie had barely even kissed anyone, and Leo had probably had sex with girls. Lots of them.

Zwaantie stood up and tossed her napkin on her plate.

"I'm going to bed. Send the healer when you have a chance, will you?"

She stormed out of the room. This was impossible and stupid. She wanted to go home where she understood the rules, where once you were married, people were faithful. Love was love and no one messed with it.

Hunter and Candace seemed so enamored with each other. Zwaantie wondered if he slept with other women too. She was halfway to her room when she realized Luna wasn't with her. She had been sitting next to one of Leo's brothers, but Zwaantie couldn't remember which one. Oh sun, Zwaantie hoped he didn't try to sleep with Luna. She wasn't used to attention from attractive men.

Filth. Disgust. Slut. Go home.

Why wouldn't the pounding go away? She hadn't done anything wrong. Zwaantie could barely see as she stumbled along the hallway. She had no idea where she was going. Zwaantie sighed and leaned against the wall and looked around.

A girl with bright pink and blue hair sticking up in all directions came skipping down the hall. She stopped in front of Zwaantie, her figure blurring.

"You okay?" she asked.

Zwaantie shook her head. "I have a headache, and I can't remember where my room is."

She blinked. "Who are you?"

"Zwaantie."

"The high princess?" Sage swayed in Zwaantie's vision.

"Yes."

"Oh stars, the welcome dinner was tonight, wasn't it? Leo is going to kill me. But why aren't you there?"

Zwaantie pointed to her head.

"Oh, yeah, that. Come on, I'll show you to your room, then I'll go apologize to my big brother."

She was surprisingly helpful for someone who looked like a crazed pixie. She helped Zwaantie out of her dress and into bed.

"Can you do me a favor?" Zwaantie asked.

"Sure."

"When you go to dinner, can you make sure Luna, she's my...my friend. Can you make sure she doesn't go to bed with any strange men? Like your brothers."

The girl laughed, a sweet high-pitched sound.

"Sure." The girl paused and picked up the necklace on the nightstand. "Is this yours?"

Zwaantie nodded, her head still throbbing. The girl looped it around Zwaantie's neck and fastened it. Zwaantie didn't have the energy to tell her to forget it.

All of the sudden the Voice cleared, and the pain in Zwaantie's head disappeared. Holy stars it felt good.

The girl dug in her bag and pulled out several bottles. She squinted at the labels.

"Here, this will take away the pain."

Zwaantie didn't want to admit the pain was already gone, so she drank the bright green liquid in one gulp and settled against the pillows. "Will you stay here until I fall asleep?" For some odd reason, her presence comforted Zwaantie.

"Sure," she said and settled into a chair next to the bed. She fiddled with Zwaantie's hair, which Zwaantie found odd.

Zwaantie had a strong urge to tell her exactly what had happened.

"I don't want to marry Leo."

The girl creased her eyebrows. "Why?"

"Because I'm in love with Phoenix."

"Who's Phoenix?"

"He's a slave from home. I told Leo I would marry him so he would take Phoenix here and free him so I could marry him and live in Stella as a commoner." The girl's eyes grew wide, but Zwaantie forged on. "But as soon as we got here, he disappeared, and my heart is broken. And here everyone has sex with everyone, and I find it revolting."

The girl gave a giggle, and Zwaantie paused. She had no idea why she was letting everything spill out. She couldn't help herself.

"I just want to go home. I told Leo as such too, but now I'm not so sure. I'm very confused. Why would I want to go home? I only just arrived in Stella. I'm not giving it much of a chance. Plus, I need to find Phoenix, and he is here, not in Sol."

"Oh stars," the girl said when Zwaantie finished the story. She picked up the bottle and looked at it again.

"I gave you Total Pain Relief. Whatever was causing you pain had to come out. You are going to hate me tomorrow. But I won't tell my brother, I swear. Your secret is safe with me. You should marry him though. He's a good guy. You could do a lot worse."

Zwaantie shook her head, not sure what she was talking about. "You got anything that will make me sleep?"

She grinned all wicked like. "Oh yeah. You'll have the best dreams ever."

Zwaantie quickly swallowed the small bottle of ice blue juice. And then she was floating along a sandy beach, and the sun was beating down on her back and a unicorn appeared in front of her....

Chapter Eleven

THE SECRET

Someone poked Zwaantie's forehead.

"Sage, what in the star gods did you give her?" a deep voice asked. Not Leo.

"Not you too. I already told Leo I gave her something to sleep. I didn't expect her to not wake up. The healer said she'd sleep for a few days, and then she'd be up. Then Father made me give him all my potions," said the girl from the night before. Sage. Leo's wild sister.

"Did you?" the male voice asked.

"Did I what?"

"Give him all your potions."

She snorted. "No, of course not."

"She's pretty," said the guy.

"Oh please, spare me. That's all I've heard from Leo for the past three days. 'She's so gorgeous,' 'Isn't she beautiful?' 'How can I convince her to stay?' If I didn't know better, I'd say she cast a spell on him."

Three days? Zwaantie opened her eyes.

Sage's hair was now green and purple. "About time you woke up. Go fetch Leo," she said to the man sitting next to her. One of his brothers, but his name escaped Zwaantie.

She sat up. "Did that all happen?"

"Your dreams from the potion? Sorry, sweetie, but no."

"No, did I tell you a bunch of stuff?"

"Oh, yeah, but you feel better, right?"

Zwaantie's stomach rolled, and she ran for the bathroom. She slammed the door shut and threw up in the toilet. It was black and nasty. Zwaantie rinsed her mouth out and then sat on the floor next to the door, not sure what to think. Three days. She slept for three days. She hoped Luna was okay.

The bathroom was decorated in soft greens. The tile floor was warm underneath her. It looked similar to her bathroom from home. Though where there should have been a bathtub there was a small room with a glass door.

She heard voices outside her door.

"Where is she?" asked Leo.

"The bathroom," said Sage.

"This bed is comfortable," said the other male voice.

"Stars, Ari, get out of her bed," Leo threatened.

Ah, Ari, the heir to the throne. The one who chased silly girls. Of course.

Zwaantie couldn't hide in the bathroom forever. She needed to face Leo and try to explain she most certainly didn't want to go home. The Voice had influenced everything she thought. She hoped against hope he hadn't told Candace. That would put a strain on their friendship, and she needed her friendship. Sure, she wasn't crazy about life in Stella, and she wasn't looking forward to marrying Leo, but leave? That wasn't her. She would never leave the little baby to die.

That was the Voice talking. Zwaantie had so many questions she needed answered, but she didn't know who to ask or even where to start. How did the Voice follow her here? Why did it want her to go home? Was she the only one who could hear it? She didn't want to tell anyone for fear of what they might think. She fiddled with the necklace. She'd be careful not to take it off again.

She needed to find Phoenix. He was here in Stella, not Sol. There was nothing for her in Sol except responsibility and misery. If she could find Phoenix, she'd feel better about being here. Maybe he could help her figure out what was up with the Voice.

She stood, took a deep breath, and opened the door to her bedroom.

"You look like dog poop," said Sage.

"Thanks," Zwaantie said, running a hand through her hair, suddenly self-conscious.

"No, you don't. You look beautiful. How are you feeling?" Leo asked from Zwaantie's bed. He was lying next to Ari and propped his head up to talk to her. Sage lay on her couch with a pillow over her eyes. They all looked like they were about ready to take a nap. Zwaantie perched on the edge of her bed.

"I'm fine. I wanted to apologize for what I said."

"Which part?"

"I don't really want to go home. I want to stay here and marry you." She hoped it would be enough. She didn't know how much more she could say. It would be so much easier to convince him of her desires if she were able to proclaim her love for him, but she couldn't make herself lie.

He let out a breath. "Oh, thank the stars. I was so worried. Are you sure you're okay?"

Zwaantie gave him a reassuring smile. "Yes, I'm fine. I wasn't feeling good those first couple of days, and so I wasn't thinking clearly. I feel much better today." As long as she didn't take off her necklace, she should be fine.

A hand snaked around Zwaantie's waist and pulled her into the bed. It didn't belong to Leo.

"Hi, I'm Ari." His face was inches from her, and Zwaantie couldn't help but notice how gorgeous his eyes were, a piercing gray.

"Get your hands off of her," Leo growled.

"She needs someone to cuddle. You barely even touch her."

Zwaantie couldn't breathe. His arm wrapped tightly around her waist. Stellans didn't seem to understand personal space.

"He's scared of her," said Sage from beneath her pillow.

Leo had to be mortified. Zwaantie would've been. It almost made her feel bad for him. She slithered out from under Ari's arms and scooted closer to Leo.

He placed his hand in hers. He'd been a lot more affectionate when they'd been in Sol. Maybe his family intimidated him.

"You're really staying here, and you're going to marry me?"

Zwaantie's smile faltered. This is not what she wanted, but it was the right thing to do. "Of course. That's why I'm here."

His face grew somber. "I'm afraid I have some bad news."

"What?"

"I have to leave for a few days."

"Why?"

It didn't bother her in the least that he was leaving, except she didn't know who she would spend time with. Candace maybe. Luna, for sure, but she'd be just as lost as Zwaantie in this big city.

"There has been a viper sighting in Deep Sky. I need to go investigate."

"I thought you said no one had ever seen one." Her stomach clenched. Anything about those vipers made her skin crawl.

"They haven't. But someone got a picture of this one and everything. I'm sorry. I don't want to go, but I have to."

"Why?"

"Because this is part of my job. Sage and Ari will take care of you."

It'd be easier to sneak around and find Phoenix without Leo around. Maybe this was for the best. "Where's Luna?"

Sage sat up. "Oh, man, she's a riot. We've been partying. Last I saw her she was heading out to the movies with Viggo."

Zwaantie stood and crossed her arms. "I thought you were going to keep an eye on her. She's married. And pregnant. She can't be hanging out with other men."

Sage shrugged, not even bothering to meet Zwaantie's eyes. "Relax, Viggo doesn't like girls. I think they've been sleeping together, but only for company. No way would he ever have sex with her. Besides, Luna's old enough to take care of herself."

Zwaantie sank onto the bed. She had so much to learn. This whole world felt so foreign. Even though she didn't love Leo and she was bound and determined to find Phoenix, she didn't want Leo to leave her with Sage and Ari. At least Leo tried to make her feel comfortable.

Ari sat up and put an arm around her shoulder. "Don't worry. We'll take good care of you."

Leo knocked Ari's arm off of Zwaantie's shoulder. "She's off limits. And Sage, I expect you to make sure he keeps his hands off her."

PRINCE OF THE MOON

"I can do a lot of things without using my hands," Ari said with a laugh.

Leo leaned across Zwaantie and punched Ari in the chest. "I mean it."

"Ow. Message received." He rubbed the spot where Leo had hit him. Zwaantie tried to process what was just said. Why would Ari imply he could do anything with her? Ari was delusional if he thought anything would happen between them.

"Make sure she has a good time, though. I want her to see the best Stella has to offer."

"Yeah, of course," Sage said, standing up from the couch. She walked over to Zwaantie's wall and watched the farm animals graze. "She hasn't seen any of the city yet. We've got loads to do. She won't even notice you're gone."

"What about Candace?" Zwaantie asked. She didn't want to spend her time with these two crazy people.

"Deep Sky is my kingdom," Candace said from the doorway, standing there with a short, bald man. "I'm going with Leo."

"That's too bad. I was hoping you could show me around," Zwaantie said.

"Hey," Sage said. "I can do just fine."

Zwaantie was about to apologize. She didn't mean to offend her, but Candace interrupted her.

"This is Janus. He's a communication mage. He'll get you set up for your disc."

Excellent—it was about time. She was curious about what they could do.

Candace came over and embraced Zwaantie. "Thank you for everything. I won't be returning with Leo, but I will see you in a couple of weeks."

Zwaantie returned the hug awkwardly.

"You'll be back for the lock-in, right?" Sage asked.

"Of course."

Sage clapped her hands. "Oh my stars. We should make that Zwaantie's big introduction to society. It would be amazing—the best lock-in ever."

"Make it happen, Sage. I think it's brilliant," Candace said.

Sage leaned against the cushions, and Zwaantie could see the wheels turning in her head. This was awful. She thought by coming to Stella, she'd get away from the spotlight, but now she was being forced right into it.

Candace left the room. Janus sat on a chair and motioned for Zwaantie to join him.

He held up a disc. "This is basically useless without a person's touch. Once we give you one, it will recognize you until you touch another one. So if you lose it, it's not a big deal. Anyone can pick it up, but it will contain his information, not yours."

"Okay." Zwaantie knew that already. "So all I have to do is hold it?"

Janus grinned. "Not quite that easy."

He traced his finger in the air in a circle, and a glowing orb appeared. "This contains all of your information Leo asked me to include. You can use this to pay for anything and call anyone in your circle."

"How does it have money on it? I don't have any money in Stella."

"You're royal, so your money comes out of the king's treasury. All members of the royal family use it."

"What is the limit?"

"There isn't one."

Zwaantie sat back. How could they control how much money was spent? What if someone spent too much?

"Okay, so now what?"

"Now, I need to connect you. Give me your hand please."

Zwaantie held out her hand. Janus pressed his finger against her fingertip, and she felt a sharp pain.

"Sorry, dear," he said. He withdrew his finger, her blood dripping from his fingertip. She looked down at her finger, and the cut wove itself closed.

He dropped the blood onto the glowing orb. Then he snapped his fingers, and the orb disappeared. She let out a gasp. The magic in Stella continued to surprise her.

"Touch the disc please."

She did, and the face lit up in white.

"Call Leo."

"How?"

"Just hold the disc up and say his name."

"Leo," she said.

Leo grabbed his own disc and touched it. His face floated up out of hers. Her own head was floating above Leo's.

"Excellent," Leo said. "Now I can call you." He touched his disc again, and both of their floating heads disappeared.

"Thank you," Zwaantie said to Janus.

"My pleasure." He gave a small bow, and rushed out of the room.

Leo stood. "I need to go. Sage'll take care of you. I'll return as soon as I can. Hopefully this picture of the viper is nothing."

Leo kissed Zwaantie lightly on the lips before he walked out the door. Zwaantie had a sinking feeling in her stomach. Without Leo or Candace, who knew what was going to happen.

Chapter Twelve

THE DESTINY

"**P**rude," Ari whispered under his breath.

"Be nice," Zwaantie said, feeling the need to defend Leo.

Sage snorted. "He's right. I've seen Candace give little Raaf better kisses."

Zwaantie ignored the jibe. "Candace has a reason to love her baby. She could've died in the delivery."

Sage frowned. "I can't believe she had a baby with no pain potions. Did she try to strangle you?"

"She had a pain potion. There was some on the boat."

"Those don't do anything compared to what the healers can do. Most women deliver with no pain. At all. Will you deliver my baby for me? I'll want a healer there too, but it's so cool you can do that."

"Sure," Zwaantie said. "Though you know Leo and I will rule in Sol, not here." She grimaced. How was she going to live in Sol with the Voice? It was making her nervous. She'd always thought the Voice had her best interests in mind, but now she wasn't so sure.

Ari gave her a squeeze. "You don't love Leo. Sage told me about your plans. That's pretty daring for a Solite. I bet Leo just doesn't measure up to Phoenix's lovemaking."

Zwaantie gasped and jumped off the bed. "I never 'made love' to

Phoenix." Then she rounded on Sage. She couldn't believe Sage would tell on her. "I thought you said the secret was safe?"

Sage gave a nonchalant shrug. "Only from Leo. I tell Ari everything. Get used to it. He tells me everything too. So if you have sex with him, I'll know every detail. And you have to live with me, so don't do anything embarrassing."

"I'm not going to have sex with Ari." Zwaantie crossed her arms and pouted.

Ari shifted against her headboard. He looked too comfortable sitting there, with one knee up and an arm slung casually over it.

"Then why did you love Phoenix so much? That's a big chance to take on someone who you didn't even have sex with. What if he's a dud?" Ari asked.

"You've got a lot to learn about love," Zwaantie said.

"Yeah, probably. Can I learn with you?" He wiggled his eyebrows.

Sage giggled and collapsed on the bed next to Zwaantie. "Ari, why don't you get out of here? Zwaantie needs to change."

"I don't see why I have to leave."

Zwaantie tapped her foot. She wanted him out of her room. Sage too, for that matter, but she didn't think that would happen. She needed Luna. She would provide some sanity in this chaos.

"I really want to see Luna. Can you find her for me?"

Ari climbed out of the bed and planted a wet kiss on Zwaantie's cheek. "You really are pretty. Leo was right. And he's not right very often."

Sage rolled her eyes at him. He left without a response and shut the door. Zwaantie sighed and flung herself on her bed. She was only up for thirty minutes, and already she was tired.

"Come on, you need a shower before you can get ready. You stink, Princess."

A shower? "I think you mean I need a bath." She hadn't seen a tub, but maybe it was hidden away somewhere.

"Oh, no a bath would take way too long. They only have tubs in the spas. A shower, come on, I'll show you."

They walked into the bathroom and stood next to the glass closet.

"That," said Sage with a flourish, "is a shower. You probably don't have them in Sol because they involve too much magic."

She motioned Zwaantie into the strange room. "You'll have to take off all of your clothes before you turn anything on, unless you want them soaking wet. When you are ready, you push this button here."

Sage pointed to a blue button on a panel of fifteen or so buttons. "If you want the water hotter or colder, you'll need to push the buttons next to it. Soap for your hair and stuff is inside the cutout. Just stick your hand in there and voila, shampoo."

Zwaantie stared at the panel suspiciously. "What are the rest of the buttons for?"

Sage grinned. "Later. Breakfast with Daddy awaits. But tonight, I'll show you what they can do. We'll take a shower together in our underwear."

Zwaantie tried to shake away the feeling that this was not a good idea. Sage left the room, and Zwaantie stripped off her clothes. She cautiously stepped into the small room, closing the glass door behind her. She pushed the blue button and squeezed her eyes shut.

Huge drops of rain and streams of steaming water flowed over her body. The rain seemed to sooth her nerves. Zwaantie laughed out loud. This shower thing was good. The soap came out as promised, and she scrubbed at her hair and marveled. This was the first time she'd ever washed her own hair. No wonder Stella didn't need slaves; it was much easier to take care of themselves here.

Before she pushed the blue button to turn the water off, she wanted to see what one of the other buttons could do. She pushed a gray one. Soft music floated around the room, echoing off the walls. The bathroom door opened, and Zwaantie yelped.

"No time for the other buttons. Turn the water off and get out of there," said Sage.

Zwaantie wrapped a fuzzy towel around her head and put on a soft robe. Sage sat on the chair by the bed, surrounded by floating pictures and words.

"What's that?"

Sage jerked her head up and pressed a finger on her disc. Everything disappeared.

"Just my notes."

"All good things, I hope," Zwaantie said.

Sage shrugged. "Mostly. I can't wait to attach my name to yours. You are on the top of the Ticker."

"That doesn't sound like a good thing."

"Yeah, it is. Here, I picked out your clothes."

Zwaantie put on the shimmering pink skirt and sleeveless shirt. It was so refreshing to wear something so light and not be bogged down by the weight. No more heavy layers.

"Is this breakfast going to be as large as the dinner?" Zwaantie asked.

"Oh no, just us, Daddy, and maybe Ari and Luna if he can find her. Daddy tries to do something special with each of us. I get breakfast every day. Sometimes it's alone, but most of the time there are a smattering of others. I think he does it to make sure I don't disappear in my partying. If I know I must be back for breakfast, I always am."

"Oh," Zwaantie said, once again feeling uncomfortable with the idea of staying out all night at a party. She needed Luna to help ground her.

They ate breakfast in the king's quarters, not the dining room. There was a small table with seven or eight plates. Ari sat on the left of the king, who seemed to be lecturing him. Sage plopped herself on the other side. Ari beckoned for Zwaantie to come sit by him, but she deliberately chose the chair next to Sage.

The king barely gave her a look as he continued to berate Ari. Zwaantie stayed quiet, not wanting to interrupt. The lecture seemed to involve a young woman who was the daughter of the king's best friend. Once there was a lull in the lecture, Zwaantie jumped in.

"Where's Luna?" Zwaantie asked.

"Out with Viggo, who has turned his disc off. I know his usual haunts. We'll scope them out after we eat," Ari said.

Zwaantie tried to hide her disappointment. She needed Luna.

"Who else is coming?" Sage asked, snatching a strawberry from a bowl and munching on it.

"A few of our head mages. I wanted our princess to meet them." The king spoke with authority, but he wasn't scary like her own father.

Sage raised her eyebrows. "Breakfast, Daddy? Really?" She handed Zwaantie a strawberry. "Here eat. Breakfast will arrive soon. But these are the freshest strawberries in the kingdom. Arrived from Sol this morning."

Zwaantie took a bite and grimaced. The strawberry was rubbery and sour.

"That strawberry is days old, maybe even a week," Zwaantie said. At home, they'd have thrown them out.

Hurt crossed Sage's face, and Zwaantie scrambled to rescue herself.

"I don't mean to be rude, but we eat our strawberries straight from the vine. This is not what I'm used to. You'll have to come to Sol sometime and try them."

"Yeah, well, you have a sun," Sage said and sulked.

Zwaantie creased her eyebrows. "You only get food once a month. How do you keep it from going bad?"

"Magic," Sage said.

Something else was bothering Zwaantie. "There is no way we produce enough food to feed everyone in Stella."

Sage nodded. "We have factories where they can copy the food. But they still need to get fresh food because the spells to multiply food work best with fresh food."

A few minutes later, two men and a woman walked into the room. The woman was taller than both the men, taller in fact than most men. In spite of her unusual height, she didn't slouch or attempt to hide her height. In fact, she stood tall and held her head high.

"Zwaantie, please meet Lyra, our head mage," the king said.

For some reason that woman intimidated Zwaantie more than any other she had met. It wasn't her confidence or height, but her title. Magic imbued every bit of their life in Stella. If this was their head mage, then she possibly held more magic than anyone in Stella, even the king.

She sat across from them. Her gray eyes studied Zwaantie, and she didn't look away when Zwaantie met them.

Lyra spoke, her voice quiet yet authoritative. "Welcome. What do you think of our magic?"

"It's wonderful," Zwaantie said and grabbed another strawberry. She didn't want to talk to Lyra. Something about her made Zwaantie uneasy.

"Yes, it is. Much different from your own, no?"

Zwaantie nodded. "Sol could use some of these conveniences. Lights, for example, would be nice in the evening when the sky goes gray. But most of the people enjoy the simple life we have."

Lyra addressed the king. "When will the ceremony take place?"

He paused for a moment, took a bite of eggs, and did not answer her until he swallowed. "In a month."

"You're certain this will work. What if it doesn't?"

"Then we have eleven months to find another solution."

Eleven months to find what? Zwaantie started to say something, but Sage pinched her hard, and her words came out as a yelp instead.

The conversation at the table stopped. Both the king and Lyra stared at Zwaantie.

"Perhaps this conversation is best postponed until we are alone," said the king with a frown.

The mage nodded.

After breakfast, Zwaantie, Sage, and Ari headed outside. Lights lit up their path, but the sky above was a deep midnight blue. Zwaantie's smile faded when she couldn't see the stars.

"Sorry for pinching you earlier, but you couldn't ask the question you wanted to. Lyra is an evil woman. If you piss her off, she'll haunt you for the rest of your life. None of us dare to confront her. Except Daddy. I'm not sure what he has over her, but he's not scared of her."

"Why's she so scary?" Zwaantie asked.

Ari snapped his fingers. "She can kill like that. Mostly she doesn't because then she'd be implicated in murder. If she wants you dead, you'll die a slow and painful death. Usually a disease the magicians can't cure. And there is no way to trace the magic to her. Of course, there is no proof, but enough of her enemies have died that we know she's responsible."

"But it sounded like she was talking about me."

Sage and Ari shared a look. "Maybe she was," Sage said. "But I didn't want you talking to her before you understood what you were up against. Enough of this serious talk, let's go have some fun."

"We're going to find Luna first, right?" Zwaantie asked. She wanted to see her best friend. If she could just see Luna, she'd have some normalcy.

"Yeah, of course."

Zwaantie couldn't get over the moving pictures on the walls. Everything moved and blinked. They stopped at a large building made entirely of glass.

"What's in this building?"

"Movies. Viggo loves the movies," Sage said.

"What's a movie?" Zwaantie asked.

"Like a play, but on a screen."

Zwaantie nodded.

"We'll have to go sometime. You two wait out here. I'll check," Ari said. "Sage, why don't you try calling him again?"

Sage said, "Viggo," into her device, but nothing happened.

The streets were fairly empty. A few people strolled along, but the atmosphere was much different than when she arrived. Relaxed.

"Princess Sage," a boy called. Sage waved. "Can we get a picture?"

"Of course." Sage latched onto Zwaantie, and Zwaantie didn't need to be told to smile. The boy flashed his disc and walked away.

"Finally," Sage said. "Now maybe I'll be up high on the Ticker with you."

Ari came out. "They were here, but they left. Let's check out the gamehouse."

They didn't walk more than a few hundred feet before they stopped in front of a building with blaring music.

"What's this?" Zwaantie asked.

"A place where we play games. Stay here again," Ari said.

Sage squinted at something on the building. Then she spun around. "How do you and Luna know each other? It seems strange that the Solite princess would be friends with a Stellan."

"She was my slave. I know you guys have trouble with that concept, but she and I were friends from a very young age. She's my best friend. She keeps me stable."

Sage nodded but didn't respond.

Ari strolled out with his hands in his pockets. "They aren't here either. I've got one more idea."

He crossed the street, and the girls followed.

Zwaantie spotted a narrow and tall blindingly yellow building.

Then suddenly it wasn't a building anymore. It was a pencil, and then it was a tree, and a then a frilly dress.

"What's that?" Zwaantie asked.

Ari's eyes sparkled. "A funhouse. You wanna check it out?"

Yes. She did. "But Luna."

"We can find her afterwards. You know you want to."

Zwaantie let out a breath. "Okay. But then we have to find her." She was feeling overwhelmed by everything.

Sage linked arms with her and dragged her over to the building.

Ari chattered as they neared. "Nothing in there is real. It's all magical illusions and changes constantly. Every time I come here I experience something different. Only twice have I entered a room and found it was something I'd done before."

"Okay," Zwaantie whispered, not sure what on earth she'd gotten herself into.

They walked into what should have been a lobby but was completely upside down. Zwaantie froze. Ari stopped and turned to her. "You okay? Sometimes these can be a bit disorienting."

Zwaantie nodded and concentrated on picking up one foot after the other. When she didn't fall, she followed Sage and Ari.

"Ari," boomed a big voice.

"Orion," Ari said. Then the man came out from behind a large desk and threw his arms around Ari.

"I haven't seen you in ages, man. Where you been?" Ari asked.

"Creating fun for everyone. It's a big job." Orion stepped away from Ari and looked over at Sage and Zwaantie.

"What are you doing here today?" Ari asked. "Usually you have your apprentices run this place."

"Yeah, but I had this wicked dream last night, and I wanted to create something new. You'll be the first to experience it, but not until the very end. How many rooms do you want to do today?"

Ari shrugged and looked at Sage.

"Let's do three and nothing scary. I don't want to overwhelm Zwaantie."

"Three it is. And who is this Zwaantie?"

"She's the high princess from Sol, and she's going to marry Leo. Haven't you seen the Tickers?"

He raised his eyebrows. "I don't have time for silly gossip. Leo is a lucky man. Will you be throwing a party to introduce her to Stella?"

"No, she'll come out at the lock-in," Sage said.

"Save me a dance," he said with a wink. "Now, Sol is a strange place. Have you ever been to a funhouse before?"

"No, we don't have this kind of magic in Sol," Zwaantie said.

"I know, but occasionally a traveling band of entertainers will have a room or two you can experience. Did you live in Zonnes?" Orion asked.

"Yes. I always attend the mage wagon, but I've never heard of such illusions."

"Well, come then, experience what magic has to offer."

They followed Orion down a small hall. Just before they entered the first room, Ari pulled Zwaantie aside.

"Nothing you see will be real. Each illusion will last about thirty minutes. If at any time you feel uncomfortable and want out, pinch me. I'll try to stay close."

They walked into a dark room. Ari took Zwaantie's hand and led her to the middle of the room.

"Are you ready?" he asked.

"I guess." Truthfully, she was nervous. This could be anything.

Ari and Sage clapped their hands three times, and suddenly Zwaantie was floating. The air around her sparkled, but it wasn't quite right though. It was too thick. Zwaantie moved her feet because she wanted to turn around and see where the others were, but her feet didn't feel right. She looked down. Her feet were gone. In their place was a fish tail.

She wasn't floating in air. She was swimming in the middle of a fairytale. Mermaids. Ha! Years ago, she'd read stories about the ocean.

Hundreds of brightly colored fish swam below her. Zwaantie dipped her head and swam toward them. They scattered, but the image was still amazing. Something tugged on her tail. She spun and found Ari grinning above her. He waved his hand for her to follow. She laughed out loud, but no sound came out.

They swam into a group of large silver fish with long noses. One butted his head against Zwaantie's thigh, and she petted his nose. He nudged her hand. These fish were just like that dog they had in the castle.

They played with them for a little bit, and Ari waved to Zwaantie again. He swam up, and within seconds their heads popped above the water. They found Sage perched on a rock gazing up at the sun.

The sun wasn't quite right, not bright enough. But Zwaantie supposed they'd never seen a real sun, so what did they have to compare it to?

"Sagie, you've got a whole ocean, and you choose to sit up here watching the sun," Ari said.

Sage shrugged.

"They always give me an ocean of some kind because it's my favorite. Today though, I wanted to see what Zwaantie is missing," Sage said.

Ari tugged at her fishtail. "Come play with us."

She agreed and soon they were chasing bright orange and blue fish.

Without warning, the ocean disappeared, and they were once again in a dark room. Zwaantie patted her skin and hair. Dry.

Ari clapped his hands once more.

This time the room was colored a bright red and orange. Zwaantie couldn't figure out what it was supposed to be, and Sage and Ari looked just as confused. There was nothing but bright colors. Then Ari took a step toward the wall and shot straight up in the air.

He whooped as he came down. He hit the ground again and immediately shot up. He did a couple of spins in the air this time before hit he ground.

"Yay!" yelled Sage. Soon she was flying around just like Ari.

Zwaantie took a small step forward and felt herself propelled upward. The feeling was amazing. She rolled into a ball and didn't quite get out of it before she hit the ground again. She landed on her behind and was again propelled into the air. This time she shot sideways though and hit the wall, and stuck. Zwaantie laughed.

She moved her hand, and suddenly she was flying toward the opposite wall, which she bounced off of right into Ari's arms. He held her close as they fell to the ground.

"This is fun, huh?"

"Yes," Zwaantie admitted. She squirmed against him, wanting out of his embrace. "Will you let me go?"

"Now why would I want to do that?"

"Because it makes me uncomfortable."

"It shouldn't. I'm your brother-in-law."

They hit the ground and shot into the air. Mid-flight he let go of Zwaantie, and she plummeted.

After about fifteen minutes, Zwaantie was tired of bouncing around, so she found the sticky wall and stayed there while she watched Sage and Ari chase each other across the room. Finally, the room faded to black once again, and she fell to the floor. Sage and Ari were breathing hard.

"That was a blast, but I'm bushed," said Ari.

"No kidding," said Sage.

"Time to move though." Ari clapped his hands again. Zwaantie found herself alone in a bright white room. The silence was deafening. There was nothing but whiteness. She sat down, not wanting to go somewhere she shouldn't. She couldn't see Ari and Sage, and that made her nervous. She'd let them find her.

Figures appeared in front of her. They were a bit fuzzy, and they weren't Ari or Sage. Zwaantie squinted and nearly fell over when she realized who they were.

Raaf stood there arguing with Phoenix and Luna. At least it looked like they were arguing. It was hard to tell because the room was still completely silent. Raaf suddenly lashed out and slapped Luna across the face. Zwaantie gasped and stood up to rescue her, but Phoenix beat her to it. He punched Raaf in the nose.

Then as suddenly as they appeared, they disappeared.

In their place stood three smiling men. Each looking at Zwaantie and holding a single rose. Phoenix. Leo. Ari. Weird. They bowed and vanished again.

Now there were three coffins. Zwaantie didn't want to look, but she had to. In one, lay her father, his arms crossed, peaceful in death. She sobbed when she looked in the second coffin. Raaf lay there, blood blooming out of his chest. Very quickly she peered in the last coffin and backed away. In that coffin lay a very young version of

King Ajax. Zwaantie didn't look close enough to see if he had a wound too. She backed away, wanting to get out of this room.

She ran into a wall. If she just stayed there, then she wouldn't have to see anything else. She could wait out the thirty minutes. But the wall disappeared, and she was hovering above a wedding. Her wedding. She smiled as Raaf walked her down the aisle, but she couldn't see the face of her groom. Damn.

The scene lasted only seconds before it shifted again. This time she was in a room surrounded by children's toys. Zwaantie sat next to a little boy with spiky black hair. Together they built a tall tower of blocks. The boy blew on the tower, and it collapsed. He laughed and clapped his hands. A man walked into the room, but Zwaantie could only see his legs. He reached down and pulled her up, but again Zwaantie couldn't see his face. The boy threw his arms around both of their legs.

The room went dark, and Zwaantie thought it was over, but one wall turned various shades of pink, and she could make out clouds. The wall got lighter and lighter until a sliver of very bright light appeared above the clouds. The sun. Zwaantie had heard of sunrises before. A few books had pictures and talked about sunsets, and she dreamed of seeing a sunrise one day. The clouds cleared, and the sun was high in the sky, but the sun on the wall, moved.

Rapidly it rose up the wall and across the ceiling. Then it sank down into the floor on the opposite wall. When it disappeared, the entire room lit up with a moon and stars. Heaven.

Zwaantie lay down on the floor to admire them.

The scene vanished, and the room went dark once more. A door opened.

"Was that wild or what?" Orion strode into the room and clapped his hands once. The lights came on. Sage appeared confused, and Ari looked pissed.

"What in the stars was that?" Ari asked.

"The last one? Your destiny, should you choose to accept it. I brought in a fortune mage to help me create it. Pretty crazy, huh?"

"No, that was not cool. Please tell me that was your idea of a sick joke," Ari said.

Orion cocked his head. "You don't have to follow the path. It was designed to be a future full of honor and adventure. If you don't make the decisions that lead to that future, it won't happen."

"I sure as hell won't be following that path," Ari said.

Ari followed Orion out of the room. Sage looped her arm through Zwaantie's, and they followed them.

"What'd you see?" Zwaantie asked.

"I'm not sure. It was bizarre, like a dream. I couldn't make stars or moons of it. Obviously, Ari's was a bit easier to interpret. What about you?"

Zwaantie thought about Raaf lying in the coffin.

"I don't know. It was a blur." She didn't want to think of a destiny that would cause three men to die. Two of which she loved. That didn't sound like a future full of adventure and honor.

Chapter Thirteen

THE FUTURE

Ari met them outside. "We can head to the beach and see if Luna is there."

"What'd you see Ari? In your illusion?" Sage asked.

"I'm not talking about it."

"Why?"

"It's not important. We should go find Luna now."

Zwaantie nodded. She still wanted to find her. Especially now with the strange vision floating around in her head.

Ari flagged down a horseless carriage. The outside looked like their carriages at home but glowed. The inside was one large wrap-around seat. They scrambled inside, and Zwaantie sunk into the cushions.

"Beach," Ari commanded. The carriage whisked them away. No one spoke of the last room. Though Zwaantie was curious what they saw. She wondered if it was as ominous as hers. About ten minutes later, the carriage came to an abrupt halt.

They stepped out of the carriage and onto soft sand. Sage pulled off her shoes. Ari paid a vendor with his disc and bought a few fluffy blankets. They walked out several hundred feet and spread them out.

"Viggo finally turned his disc on and just sent me a message and said they went back to the castle. Since we're here though, I thought we'd watch the stars. Is that okay?"

Zwaantie nodded. As much as she wanted to see Luna, the stars were more appealing at the moment.

They lay down and stared up into the glittering darkness.

Gazing up at the stars, Zwaantie never wanted to leave Stella. The people made her uncomfortable, the magic was disconcerting, the darkness was stifling, but the stars were its saving grace. She wouldn't feel that way when they were no longer watching them, but for now, she reveled in the sheer comfort of the stars. It was so amazingly quiet it seemed strange a kingdom as busy as Stella could have a place that brought so much peace.

Ari was next to Zwaantie, his bare shoulder against hers. His skin was warm and smooth, and she had to resist the urge to run her fingers down his arm.

Sage pressed up against Zwaantie's other side. "Hey look." She pointed to a group of stars. "There's the constellation I was named after."

"Leo showed me his. Can you color it so I can see it?"

"Sure," Sage said and about a dozen stars lit up with a bright pink.

"Yours is bigger than Leo's."

"Yeah, more gods."

Zwaantie still found it odd they worshiped the stars.

"There's mine," said Ari. A handful of stars lit up with a bright blue.

Ari and Sage argued for a few minutes of which one was better, and after a while, an easy silence settled over them, all lost in thought. Zwaantie worried about marrying Leo. Just because today was fun didn't mean the rest would be.

Ari rolled over so he was facing her, his breath on her cheek. "Have you made a decision yet?"

"What decision?" Zwaantie knew what he was talking about. But avoiding the question seemed appropriate.

Sage snorted. "Are you going to marry Leo?"

Zwaantie sighed. "I told him I would. I don't have a choice."

Ari's breath tickled as he spoke softly into her ear. "Of course you have a choice. Do you want to marry him or not?"

Zwaantie's insides twisted. A few quiet tears escaped from the edges of her eyes and slid down her face.

Ari caught one with his finger. He snuggled closer. "Don't cry," he whispered. "Leo's not that bad. A little on the stuffy side, but since you're from Sol, it shouldn't bother you."

Zwaantie sniffed. "It's not Leo I'm worried about. Marriage is supposed to be about love, and I don't love him. My heart still aches for Phoenix."

Sage spoke, quieter than her normal voice. "What options do you have? Think of it this way. You already like Leo, even if you just view him as a friend. In time, you would come to love him. And if you marry him, then you get us as your family. It's a win, win."

"What about Phoenix?"

"What about him?"

"I love him."

"Then you should find him," Ari said.

"No," Sage argued. "She has to marry Leo."

"But if she never finds him, she'll always wonder. Plus, he could show up at any moment expecting her to run away. Zwaantie needs to make sure she's doing the right thing."

Sage sat up a little. "Since when did you become such a romantic?"

"I'm not. I just want Zwaantie to be happy."

Zwaantie swiveled her head around, and her nose collided with Ari's. She pulled her head back. "Why do you care about my happiness?"

His eyes were serious. "Maybe I just know what it's like to be pushed into a position I don't want."

"If I don't marry Leo, then Candace's baby dies and possibly the rest of Stella. How could you suggest I do something like that?"

"I'm not suggesting you don't marry Leo. I'm just saying you need to find Phoenix and have closure or at least figure out what the best path is for your future."

"If he says he loves me and asks me to run away with him, would you support that?"

"No."

Zwaantie creased her eyebrows together. "I don't understand."

He sat up, staring out over the sea. "In Sol you would never dream of having a lover on the side, but it's very common here. You and Leo could be married and still keep Phoenix around. I can guarantee you Leo will have lovers."

Zwaantie tried not to show the shock on her face. "No way."

"I'm just saying it's an option," Ari said.

Lovers. The idea was preposterous. No, she wouldn't be able to do that.

She would marry Leo because it was the right thing to do. She couldn't imagine doing something that would condemn little Raaf to death. Lovers were out of the question.

"You two will come visit us in Sol right? You know I'll be queen. We'll have to live over there."

Sage squealed. "Duh. But you'll have to come back here to deliver my babies because there is no way in hell I'm going to have them without a healer near. You can visit us, right?"

"Yes, I can come visit. But you must promise to come stay with us sometimes as well."

"Oh yeah. That'll be easy for me. Not so much for Ari."

"Why?"

Ari grumbled. "Because I'll be king. Something I don't want. Father keeps pushing me to marry. I think he's ready to be done."

"Why don't you marry? It's not like your lifestyle would change much. You'll still get to sleep with whomever you want." Zwaantie could barely get the words out, because she was disgusted with the idea. Except, she understood exactly where Ari was coming from. He was being forced into a position he didn't want, just like her.

Sage laughed. "Yeah, he wishes."

"Why is that a problem?" Zwaantie asked.

Ari sulked. It was strange to see him anything other than happy. "It doesn't matter."

"Try me. I just told you about my fears with marrying Leo. You owe it to me to share something."

His eyes flicked to Sage.

"I'm gonna go see if I can find some shells," Sage said and skipped off down the beach.

Ari scooted closer to Zwaantie and dropped his voice.

"Father has always been about duty. You do things because they are expected of you in your position. I've always been what he's wanted me to be."

Zwaantie snorted, and Ari looked at her funny. "Sorry, I can completely relate. I didn't realize you had a sense of duty in Stella."

Ari nodded. "We do. My father has given me enough freedom to allow me to choose most of my own path, and I don't resent him. I like the idea of being a king and the power that comes with it, but the mundane day-to-day things bore the tears out of me."

"Me too. Good thing you and I aren't getting married. We'd both skip meetings all the time. Our kingdoms would fall apart."

He found a shell and fidgeted with it without responding.

"You aren't telling me everything." Zwaantie searched his face until he met her eyes. "You can trust me." Zwaantie wasn't sure why she wanted to know his story or why she wanted him to trust her.

His deep gray eyes bore into hers, and she wondered how on earth all these boys in Stella got such gorgeous eyes and so many eyelashes.

"Mom hated the fact that my dad slept with so many women. She won't talk to any of the kids but me. And Father was not a prolific king. He only has twelve kids. Most have between thirty and fifty. My great-great-grandfather had over a hundred. When I was thirteen, she made me promise that after I married, I wouldn't sleep with anyone other than my own wife."

"I think she's right, but no offense, you made the promise when you were thirteen. If she had waited until now to ask that of you, you wouldn't have promised, right?"

He laughed. "No, I wouldn't have. But if it were easy, I'd use that excuse. But she had the promise bound with magic. I can't break the promise. Even if I wanted to."

"What happens if you do break it, will you die?"

He snorted. "No, all magical bonds promise something different. Mother crafted the whole thing, and she decided if I didn't keep my promise my, uh…" He cleared his throat and looked down. "Well, my best buddy will fall off."

Zwaantie creased her eyebrows together. "Your what?"

He wiggled his finger in front of her face. "You know, my…"

"Your finger?" Zwaantie was so confused. He laughed at her expression.

He dropped his voice to a whisper. "No, my penis."

Zwaantie gasped. "That's horrible. What kind of a mother would do that?"

"The kind that wanted to make sure I would keep my promise to her. She figured it would be worse than death for me. And she was right."

"I kind of hate your mother right now."

"Yeah, I did for a while, but now we're close. We don't talk about it. But I promised myself I would never get married. I didn't foresee the pressure Father would put on me."

"Why did you make the promise then? It seems this whole problem could've been solved if you had simply refused to make the promise."

"I was thirteen, a virgin, and wanting nothing more than to please my mother, who I didn't have to share with anyone. Father spent a good deal of his time with his other children as well, and Mother kept me close to her side. She didn't want me interacting with the other kids. I didn't even meet Sage until a few years ago."

"But you two are so close."

"Yeah, she saved me from a pretty bad decision, and we've been best friends ever since. We both live crazy lifestyles, and we don't judge one another. But I've managed to build relationships with most of my brothers and sisters."

"What changed? I mean when did you realize maybe your mother didn't have your best interest at heart?"

"Three days after Mother made me promise my life away, Father found out about it. He was furious. I'd never seen him so angry. He took me away from her that night, and we spent the next month together. He introduced me to my siblings. During that month, I lost my virginity, and I sleep with different girls practically every night. Father is waiting for me to 'get it out of my system' so I can marry."

He was quiet after that, and she found it difficult to express any of her own thoughts. He further confirmed to her maybe life in Sol wasn't so bad with all the rules. Up until this afternoon she'd never dreamed of sleeping with another man. She felt guilt for simply kissing Phoenix. This utter freedom seemed too much.

"Don't you ever get tired of it?" Zwaantie asked.

"Sex? No way."

"No, I meant different girls. Isn't part of having a lover confiding fears and talking late into the night? If you're with a new girl all the time, how do you even learn about love and sacrifice or even companionship? I can't imagine sleeping with someone just for the sake of sex."

He snorted. "That's because you've never had sex."

Zwaantie didn't answer, and once again found herself staring up at those elusive stars. Two weeks ago, she'd never imagined a conversation like the one she just had. Now she was being told it was perfectly acceptable to be married to one man and take another as a lover. What would become of her?

Chapter Fourteen

THE BAR

Sage skipped over to them and dumped shells onto Zwaantie's lap. "Have you ever seen shells before?"

"No. We don't have an ocean." She picked up one of the spiral-shaped shells. "This looks like the castle."

"I know, pretty huh?"

Ari stood up and brushed sand off his pants. "Ladies, I'm afraid I have to go."

"Wait," Sage said. "We need a picture first."

Sage pulled Zwaantie up and put her in between the two of them. Sage's disc floated out in front of them. After the picture was taken, Sage pressed her finger on the picture floating above the disc. "Showing the princess the fun sights of Stella. We're not going to let her go home."

Then she flicked the picture, and it disappeared.

"Do we have to take so many pictures?" Zwaantie asked.

Sage giggled. "It hasn't been very many, trust me. We want to keep you up in the Ticker. As long as people have something happy to talk about, they won't focus on anything bad."

Ari snorted. "You just embarrassed yourself at the party last night, and you don't want anyone talking about it."

Sage shrugged. "Whatever."

Ari gave a small bow. "Zwaantie, I hope to see you at dinner tonight. I'll save you a seat." He winked at her, and she wasn't sure what to make of it. Sage watched him walking away, and once he was out of earshot, she spun around.

"Did he tell you about his curse?"

"Yeah."

Sage furrowed her brow. "You know how many people know about that? Ari, his mother, Daddy, me, and now you." Sage creased her eyebrows. "He barely knows you."

"Well, he knows my secret though, and so maybe he thought it would be fair."

"Maybe." Sage didn't look convinced. "The day is still young. What do you want to do?"

This was easy. "I want to find Phoenix."

"Okay then. I've heard so much about him. I feel like I already know him. Let's go."

⁓

THEY HOPPED INTO ANOTHER CARRIAGE. BUILDINGS FLEW BY. THE height of the buildings made her feel so insignificant. As they continued to travel, the buildings grew shorter, more rundown, but they were still massive in size. Wide and squat. The carriage stopped abruptly, and Sage popped out with Zwaantie following.

Things were darker here. There was still a lot of light, but it was duller somehow. Less pinks and yellows. More faded oranges and greens. It didn't smell as good either. It didn't smell of refuse, but it had a sterile antiseptic smell. Zwaantie wrinkled her nose.

Sage smiled at an old man sitting on a bench. He returned the smile, half of his teeth missing.

"Welcome to the slums," Sage said.

"Slums?"

"It's what we call areas like this. It's cheap to live, and the people here are usually not doing well financially."

Zwaantie moved away as a young boy with a filthy face and a shirt five times too large brushed past her. Food rotted on the side of the road and glass littered the grounds around the buildings where windows had been broken. "Our slaves live better than this."

Sage frowned at her. "At least the people have a choice. We have a lot of programs to help them. If they want to move up and out, they can."

Zwaantie wasn't sold on the system. At least the slaves were clean and cared for.

Sage pushed open a door, and they entered a room with at least a hundred chairs. Half were full with people wearing bland, ratty clothes. At the far side of the room, behind tables, sat people dressed impeccably.

Zwaantie followed Sage through the room and through another door.

"What is this place?" Zwaantie asked.

"It's the jobs master. People come here when they can't find work. We're going to find out where they sent Phoenix."

They got into an elevator, and Sage pushed the number five. The elevator shook as it went up.

"With all the magic you have, why can't you make the area look nicer?"

"We do, but it never lasts. Why would we put the effort into making something look nice if the people aren't going to take care of it?"

They got out into another dull looking hallway, and Sage pushed the door open that said *Jobs Master*.

A woman in a fluorescent pink suit sat at a desk. The color nearly blinded Zwaantie.

"Hey, Galexia, is Pollux in?"

The woman nodded her head, not taking her eyes off the floating face yelling at her.

Sage pushed open another door, and they found a balding man pouring over a stack of papers. His head jerked up, and a wide smile split across his face.

"Sage, it's always lovely to see you. To what do I owe this pleasure?"

"I'm looking for someone."

His eyes glittered. "You're always looking for someone."

"It's my job."

Zwaantie wondered what it was Sage did.

"Who's this with you?"

"This is Zwaantie. Crown princess of Sol."

Pollux raised his eyebrows. "Ah yes, I've seen the Ticker. You are even lovelier in person. Nice to meet you. Gave me quite a job the other day with fifty freed slaves."

"Thank you for taking care of them."

"It was my pleasure. Nothing makes me happier than helping someone find their mission in life."

"It's one of those slaves we're searching for. His name is Phoenix."

Pollux pulled out his device and yelled into it. "Galexia, get in here."

Zwaantie was shocked by his rudeness. He'd seemed so friendly.

They waited a few moments, and she didn't come in. The silence was a little awkward. Zwaantie couldn't stand it. "What kind of jobs did the slaves get?"

Pollux tapped his chin. "Hmm. They were all over the place. Several tested high for magical ability, so they were sent to the mage training school. A handful were set up to apprentice with various trades. Others are still finding their footing. Where is that damned woman?"

He jabbed at his device. "Galexia, get your skinny ass in here. I haven't got all day." He met Sage's eyes. "You know, she used to listen to me."

Sage chuckled. "Maybe you shouldn't have married your secretary then. Have you tried being nicer?"

He waved a hand. "Of course, I tried. She won't respond unless I get nasty."

Galexia poked her head in, her nose wrinkled, like she'd stepped in dung. "What do you want?"

"I need the lists of the Solite slaves."

She slammed the door shut. A few moments later, she stomped into the room and dropped several sheets of paper on Pollux's desk. "Anything else I can get you?" She glared at him as if daring him to ask for something else.

"That will be fine. Thanks, love." His lips twitched into a smile.

"My pleasure, honey bear." She turned her dark eyes to Sage. "Good to see you, Princess. I hope you find what you're looking for."

She marched out the door, and Zwaantie looked back at Pollux. He had the sloppy grin of a man in love.

"The papers, Pollux," Sage said.

He handed her a list, gave one to Zwaantie, and kept one for himself. Zwaantie read over the Solite names. Most she didn't know. Next to their names was scrawled a job with a salary. Painter. Street maintenance. Magic control officer. Parks attendant. Phoenix's name wasn't on the list.

"It's not here," Sage said, handing her list to Pollux.

"I don't have it either," he said.

"Neither do I. It has to be here somewhere." Zwaantie counted quickly. "There are only fifteen names on each list. That's only forty-five people. Where are the rest?"

"A few decided to go back to Sol. Could he have been among them?"

"No. I don't think so."

Pollux sucked on his lower lip. "Could it be possible he doesn't want to be found?" Then he shook his head at Sage. "What am I thinking? Everyone you search for doesn't want to be found."

"Maybe his name just didn't get written down," Zwaantie said.

"No, we are meticulous. Unless he used a different name, I'm afraid I can't help you. What does he look like? I can ask the person who checked them in."

Zwaantie rubbed her forehead. "He's Stellan, so he has darker skin, gorgeous eyes, and full lips."

The edges of Pollux's lips twitched. "I think I know why we're not finding him."

He pressed his disc once again. "Galexia, you insufferable witch, I need you again."

Zwaantie was still appalled at the way he spoke to her. There wasn't much of a pause before the door opened.

"What do you want?" Galexia asked.

"I need the list of job placements for Stellans on that day as well."

She slammed the door again, and they waited in silence. Galexia stormed in and dropped another couple of papers on his desk and stomped out without a word to any of them.

Pollux picked up the first sheet of paper. "Ah yes, here were go. Phoenix. He's working with the fisherman Hamal. Chances are, he's staying with him and his wife as well. They don't have any children so they have extra room in their house. If you go down to the fishing village, anyone can tell you where to find him. He's one of the best. Phoenix was lucky Hamal's apprentice just got his own boat."

⁓

THE FISHING VILLAGE SMELLED AWFUL. ZWAANTIE COVERED HER NOSE AS they walked along the street.

"Don't they have magic that can fix this?" she asked.

"Sure. But most of them like the smell. Let's check the bar. They usually know where to find everyone."

The bar was packed.

"It's the middle of the day. Why is it so busy?" Zwaantie asked.

"Most fisherman get off just after lunch. They go out early in the morning though. Come on, I want to talk to the barmaid."

A busty woman handed out drinks to smelly fisherman who crowded around the bar. When the woman saw Sage, she beamed and quickly crossed over to them.

"Princess. What brings you here?"

"I'm looking for someone."

"You know I'm always good for that."

Sage pushed a few coins across the bar to her. "His name is Phoenix. He's apprenticing with Hamal."

The barmaid waved a hand in front of her face. "The new hottie? He's got all the girls in a tizzy. They're usually here, but Hamal eats at home with his wife first. Their house is three streets over. On Ling Street. Number twelve, I think. Their name is on the door."

"Thanks, Misty. I knew I could count on you."

Misty tapped the coins. "Anytime, Princess. You know where to find me."

They pushed out of the door and walked along the stinky streets once again.

"How do you know everyone?" Zwaantie asked.

"I like people. Also, I enjoy crossing the boundaries. Hanging with royalty all the time is boring. It's hard to get to know a lot of people." As Zwaantie's best friend had been a slave, she understood what Sage meant.

They found the house easily. Sage knocked, and a tiny woman cracked the door open.

"Can I help you?" she asked with a cautious voice.

"Yes. I'm looking for Phoenix. We were told he'd be here."

The woman's face lit up. "You are the princesses. Yes. He stays here. Come on in."

The woman hustled them over to a small table. "Here, have some tea. Tell me, why are you looking for Phoenix?"

"He came over from Sol with me. I just want to talk to him."

The woman's eyes widened. "The high princess wants to talk to Phoenix?"

"Yes. We're good friends."

"I will tell him you came by. I'm afraid he won't be back for a couple of days. Hamal wanted to take him into the deep ocean."

Zwaantie had been so hopeful. She couldn't help the disappointment that settled in her stomach.

Sage pushed a few coins toward the woman. "This will take care of passage in a carriage to the castle. Please make sure he comes as soon as he returns. It's urgent. Zwaantie and his sister both need to see him."

The woman nodded. "I'll tell him."

Sage stood. Zwaantie followed her toward the door and nearly choked up at the sight of Phoenix's Sol shoes sitting by the door. He was probably wearing those Stellan sandals that didn't protect your feet. It made her homesick for both home and Phoenix.

Chapter Fifteen

THE MURDER

The Old Mother stared at the Voice. He hadn't even looked up when she came in. He'd failed. Zwaantie was now in Stella. The end would come soon now. She'd thought by enlisting the Voice's help, she'd be able to succeed in stopping the prophecy from coming to pass.

It was stupid. No matter what, the future would work out like she saw. It wasn't the first time she'd interfered. But somehow, she never succeeded. She wondered if Zwaantie even remembered the betrayal. She hadn't planned on Zwaantie surviving the ordeal near the wall. She was supposed to be dead. But that wretched prince had interfered, and now not only was she alive, but she was close to marrying the prince in Stella. Part of her was sad Zwaantie had to die. The Old Mother had loved the girl.

Wilma hadn't stayed alive this long though to let one girl's life interfere with her own.

She approached the Voice. He was hunched over a desk scribbling on a piece of paper. She cleared her throat, but he still didn't look up.

"You let her go," she said.

He raised his eyes and glared at her. "No. I didn't. Your fault. I planned on making it impossible for her to cross the wall, but you interfered, and she was able to go anyway."

"You know what this means, don't you? She's going to marry the prince, and you're going to die. You failed."

His incessant scribbling was all she heard.

"I tried to kill her myself, but it didn't work. Now the wall has barred me from going back. I can't cross it," Wilma said. She'd tried a couple of times. Curse her sister. Wilma had never been allowed to cross before. The only time she could get into Stella was when she had to deliver a prophecy, and she was always jerked back as soon as she gave it, and even then, she never actually crossed the wall, she just showed up where she was supposed to be. Maybe the next time she could stall long enough to kill Zwaantie.

Wilma sidled closer to the Voice, knocking his quill so a large streak of ink spread across the paper.

He growled.

"It's over. We're through," Wilma said.

He moved the stained paper and grabbed another one. "No, it's not. You need to calm down. Go back to your hut and deliver babies like you always do. I've got this under control."

She snatched the quill out of his hands. "Do you understand what you've done? You and I, we're both going to die. The future has never been more clear. You had the chance to stop her, and you didn't."

He grabbed for the quill, and she jerked it back. He threw his hands up in the air and huffed. Then he waved a group of orbs near to him.

"You see these," he asked in deadly whisper.

"Yes."

"I still have control over those fifty slaves that entered Stella with the princess. They've been given one command and only one command."

The Old Mother stilled.

"How?" she asked.

"A spell. I was able to bind any Solites who crossed the wall to me. I wouldn't have had to use the magic if you hadn't interfered."

Wilma grinned. The Voice was smarter than she'd given him credit for.

"Smart. Can you control Zwaantie as well?"

"I can. But she's wearing one of those necklaces that blocks me."

Of course she was. She was smarter than anyone realized as well. "What's the command you gave the slaves?" she asked.

"Kill the princess."

Chapter Sixteen

THE SHOWER

The next day Zwaantie arose early. She stretched her arms up over her head. A voice came from her wall, and she jumped.

"Good morning," Leo said. She jerked around and saw Leo's face plastered on one of her walls.

She scrambled out of bed and sat on the couch across from his face. "How did you do that?"

"When I call, I can appear on the wall, unless you turn your wall off. Most people keep them turned off. It all depends on the level of privacy you want."

"That's incredible." He looked so close. "What if I'm in someone else's room?"

"If they have it on, it will work there as well."

"So if I were in Sage's room when you called, you'd show up there?"

"Yep. Did you have fun with Sage and Ari yesterday?"

"I did. They took me to a funhouse."

His face fell. "I was hoping to show you that."

"We can go again. When will you be back?" She wouldn't say she was eager for him to return, but if she was going to marry him, she wanted to get to know him as much as possible.

"A couple of days. The man who spotted the viper is missing. I talked to him yesterday and looked at his picture. He described the viper to me, but now he's gone." His face was pinched.

"What do you think happened to him?" she asked.

"It's possible the vipers got him. If he got cocky about going out after midnight, he might've tried again. I just want to stay and make sure nothing unusual is going on. I don't think this is any cause for concern, but I've been wrong before."

"What do you do, anyway?" Zwaantie asked. It occurred to her that she had no idea.

Her door burst open. Sage and Ari stumbled in. "Zwaantie, there's a meteor shower. We're going to the beach. Let's go."

Zwaantie gave Leo a small smile. "I'm going to go with them."

"Enjoy the meteor shower. See you soon."

He clicked off. Zwaantie was glad for the interruption. Calls with Leo were still awkward.

～

TWO DAYS LATER, DURING DINNER, ZWAANTIE WAS FEELING DOWN. LEO would be returning the next morning, and she still hadn't seen Phoenix. Luna was avoiding her as well. They saw each other in passing, but every time Zwaantie tried to talk to her, she rushed off. Sage and Ari tried to cheer her up, but nothing worked. Her heart was heavy. She was unsure of what would happen with Phoenix. The thought of having him as a lover was growing on her. Could she do that? She shuddered. Of course she couldn't.

"How about I show you how to use the shower?" Sage said with a glint in her eye.

Zwaantie shrugged. "I guess."

"Come on, cheer up. He'll be back soon. You're going to love this. Let's use my bathroom. It's bigger than yours."

Ari followed them. "She's right. There is no way all three of us would fit in your shower."

Sage gave him a look. "You're not coming with."

"Why not?"

"We are your sisters," Sage said with a rude hand gesture.

"She's not my sister yet."

Zwaantie blushed. Ari gave her a wicked smile and strolled to his own room, hands buried in his pockets, the muscles on his back rippling.

Sage's room was two doors down from Ari's. Just before they slipped in, Zwaantie looked to Ari's room. A pretty redheaded girl waited at Ari's door. He turned and stared at Zwaantie before he went into his room. There was something sad in his eyes. It almost made Zwaantie want to stop him and say, *Come play with us.* But he was gone before she could say anything.

"Oh no you don't." Sage grabbed a small gray kitten as it tried to escape out the door. Then she shut it. Zwaantie'd expected bright colors and frilly curtains. Instead the entire room was shades of brown and black. On the far wall, lions and tigers roamed, occasionally growling at the real cats who batted at them. A thick leopard print rug covered the floor.

The cats were everywhere.

"How many cats do you have?" Zwaantie asked.

"Mm. I lost count. Twelve I think."

A black cat rubbed against Zwaantie's leg, and she pushed it away. Cats were good for keeping mice out of the barns, but to have them running around the room was disconcerting. Sage started listing off the names of each cat. Zwaantie recognized most of the names from the constellations Leo had pointed out.

Sage tossed her a couple of small pieces of fabric.

"What's this?" Zwaantie asked.

"A swimsuit."

Swimsuit was an overstatement. Solite swimsuits covered the shoulders and went down to their knees. This was more like underwear. But at least her girl parts were mostly covered. Zwaantie was extremely grateful Sage had not allowed Ari to come with.

"Meow," said the shower door as Sage opened it. A small black and white kitten blinked up at them.

"Andromeda, what are you doing in here?" Sage set the kitten down outside the door and closed them in. "I don't know why she insists on napping in here. She hates water."

Sage waited for a second as if she wanted Zwaantie to say something, probably how cute she thought the cat was, but Sage would be waiting for a very long time. After a few awkward seconds, Sage continued.

"Every button does something different. You'll get used to them the more you use them. You already know this one plays music. If you don't like the kind of music, hold the button down and tell it what you want." She pushed the button and said, "Dance music." The music was loud and bouncy.

"This button will change the scent of the water. Again, hold it and tell it what you want." This time Sage pushed the pink button so it rained and then pushed the blue button. "What smell do you want?"

"Lilacs."

Sage grinned, and the scent of lilacs in the spring floated down around them.

The buttons could be used to create any kind of sensation. The water color changed from blue to green to pink. Other buttons controlled where the water came from and how fast it came down.

Zwaantie felt herself relaxing. She still missed Sol and desperately wanted to see Phoenix, but she was enjoying herself. They messed around for a while, and then Zwaantie noticed there was a button Sage didn't push.

"What's that?" Zwaantie asked.

Sage grinned wickedly. "Push it."

Zwaantie probably should've known better, but her curiosity overrode her caution. She pushed it, and the rain stopped, but nothing else happened. Her feet tickled, and she looked down. A thin layer of white film covered her feet. And it was rising.

"What—"

"A foam bath. The foam will rise until you tell it to stop." Within minutes the foam was up to Zwaantie's knees and then her waist.

"Stop," she said.

The foam stopped. Sage picked up a large handful and molded it into a ball, held it both hands, and then blew on it. The ball floated toward Zwaantie until it stopped above her head. Zwaantie looked up. Sage snapped her fingers, and the ball dropped right on Zwaantie's face and splattered everywhere.

Zwaantie wiped the foam from her eyes and spit out the bit that got in her mouth. She expected it to taste like soap, but it had a light fruity flavor. Sage raised her eyebrows. Zwaantie didn't hesitate. She molded her own foam ball and chucked it right at Sage. Sage ducked, and it missed. Zwaantie laughed and lunged for her, slipped, and buried herself in foam.

~

A COUPLE HOURS LATER, SAGE AND ZWAANTIE WERE LYING ON SAGE'S bed, wrapped in warm robes.

"Will you sleep with me?" Sage asked.

Zwaantie had never shared her bed with her friends. It was a strange question to ask.

"I'm not going to go romantic on you or anything. I just don't like sleeping alone. While Hunter was away, Candace slept with me, and sometimes I sleep with Ari after his girl of the night goes home. Please."

"Okay," Zwaantie said. She was feeling far too comfortable with Sage and with Stella in general. Maybe staying here wasn't so bad.

"Yay," Sage squealed and jumped up. "You'll need to borrow some pj's."

She dug through a drawer and pulled out two very short silky nightgowns. She dumped off the robe, and Zwaantie squeezed her eyes shut because Sage was naked underneath. Although everyone in Stella seemed perfectly comfortable with nudity, Zwaantie wasn't. Sage didn't seem to notice her discomfort. She handed Zwaantie the other pair of pajamas and waited for her to change. Zwaantie took them into the bathroom, shut the door, and was greeted by Andromeda, the kitten.

"Meow."

"I'm not petting you," Zwaantie said and wondered why on the sun she was talking to a cat.

Zwaantie found Sage already buried in leopard print comforters.

"Okay," Sage whispered as Zwaantie crawled under the covers. "Time for secrets. Just one. Something you've never told anyone before."

Zwaantie thought for a moment. "I don't want to be queen." Technically, it wasn't a secret as her mother knew, but it still wasn't something she'd admitted to many people.

"Then you and Ari have the same ambitions. Why don't you want to be queen?"

"Too many responsibilities. I just want to live a normal life."

"Normal is boring."

Zwaantie shrugged, not wanting to talk about it anymore. "Your turn."

"I'm a virgin." Sage turned beat red.

"So am I. That's not a bad thing."

"It is here in Stella. No one else knows, so don't say anything to anyone. If Ari knew, he'd never let me live it down."

"I won't say anything." Zwaantie wanted to ask why, but realized how absurd a question like that was. In Sol, they'd never be having a conversation like this. She took a deep breath. She was nervous to ask the next question, but she shouldn't be. "If being a virgin is so bad here in Stella, then why are you?"

Sage rolled onto her back and stared up at the ceiling.

"I don't know. I mean, it's not like I haven't had the opportunity. It's just never felt right. And now, I guess I've just been holding onto it for so long that it seems stupid to just have sex for the sake of having sex. That's dumb, right?"

"No, that sounds very smart."

Sage turned to face her and giggled. "Of course you'd say that, being from Sol."

"Well, I hope it means something to you when you do lose it."

Sage burrowed into her pillow and gripped Zwaantie's hand. "I'm glad you're going to be my sister. I like you."

Zwaantie's chest warmed. Though the affection shown in Stella was sometimes disconcerting, it made her feel happy. Sage had only known her for a short time, and already Zwaantie could feel her love. Love she should've felt from her own mother or brother, but didn't.

Sage's breathing became slow and even. Two cats fought on the ground next to the bed. She would never sleep with the noise.

A half hour later the twelve o'clock bells rang. Just after the last bell, the vipers pounded on the door. They came every night, but she still wasn't used to them. Every thirty seconds or so another thump would come. Every few minutes there would be a rapid thumping at the door, like someone was knocking. Eventually though, despite the noise, Zwaantie drifted off.

Chapter Seventeen

THE VIPERS

The next morning Zwaantie woke before Sage did. Her sleep was still off. She hadn't slept in late since she'd arrived.

Something on the bottom of the bed vibrated. She sat up and found Andromeda sleeping on her feet. Silly cat. Couldn't she tell Zwaantie didn't like her? Zwaantie pulled her feet out from underneath it and slid out of bed. Andromeda glared at her for interrupting her nap.

Zwaantie wanted to change and take a walk, clear her head and let her have some blessed alone time away from twelve hungry kitties who all seemed intent on garnering her attention now that she was out of bed.

Zwaantie wouldn't dream of wearing any of Sage's clothes because they were too wild and crazy, so she crept silently out of her room and down the five doors to her own. She paused next to Ari's door. He put on such a good act, but Zwaantie knew he wasn't happy with his lifestyle. He needed to find someone he loved. Perhaps she and Sage could help him. It would distract Zwaantie from her own prospect of a loveless marriage. Though people here seemed to take lovers all the time. Perhaps things with Phoenix would work out. She shook her head, startled at the very thought.

The door to Zwaantie's room was open a crack. Odd. She pushed at it, but it wouldn't open all the way. She slipped in and tripped, landing hard on her knees and hands. The room was dark. She reached back to see what she tripped over. It was warm flesh, smooth and dry. She jerked her hand up, stumbled over to the light switch, and pushed the button.

Covering her floor were dozens of creepy, snakelike creatures. Each was about five feet long and six inches round with a triangular head. They had no feet, but had wings tucked away next to their bodies. The tails tapered down to a point.

She screamed.

Louder than she'd ever screamed in her life. Loud enough to wake the dead. Footsteps pounded down the hall. A man shoved at the door, moving the creature that lay next to it. Zwaantie jumped up on her bed. Her foot met the same dry flesh.

Another scream. She scrambled to get off her bed, but then looked at the floor. It was covered in them. She leapt from her bed to the chair opposite it. The door pushed open farther, and in walked several men, including Ari.

She pointed. "What are they?"

No one answered. Their faces had gone stark white.

"You," Ari barked to a man standing by the door, "Go fetch the king and the head mage. Tell them this is the utmost of an emergency. They must come now."

The man nodded and ran off. Ari's eyes met Zwaantie's, and suddenly she was conscious of the fact that she was wearing one of Sage's silky, very short, nightgowns.

"Are you hurt?" he asked.

She wasn't hurt, but she was not okay. "No. What are those?"

"Vipers, I think. Let's wait for the head mage to come. She'll be able to explain it better than I can."

Zwaantie glanced down at the floor where a viper lay not a foot away. The creepiest thing about it was its eyes. They were open, sickly green, and with a vertical pupil. Zwaantie couldn't quite grasp what it was. It wasn't dead. The flesh was warm but none were moving. Each one was a different color with a pattern of diamonds across its back.

"Oh my stars," said Lyra as she entered the room.

"What are they?" Zwaantie asked.

"Creatures of the night. Vipers. I'd heard stories of their appearance, but never seen one."

"Well, now you've seen thirty. Can someone please get them out of my room?"

"How are you still alive?" Lyra asked and poked at one of them with her toe.

"What do you mean?" Zwaantie asked.

"No one ever survives an encounter. Before a few days ago, not a single one had ever been seen. That guy in Deep Sky was first, now this. Somehow, they were trapped in your room. But if you were in here, you should be dead."

"I slept in Sage's room. But now I'd very much like to get out of here."

The mages crept around Zwaantie's room, prodding the creatures with their toes, and a few pulled out long sticks to probe them with. One of the creatures rolled over, and its underside was ribbed with the same sickly green of its eyes. A mage took out his disc. Lyra snapped her fingers, and the disc exploded. The man jumped.

She towered over him, her face pinched. "No pictures. If there is even a hint of this on the Ticker, you will all be executed."

"Sorry," the man said. If pictures like that got out, people would panic, even Zwaantie knew that.

Ari raised his eyebrows and smirked at Zwaantie from the doorway.

"How am I going to get out of here?" she asked. She wasn't about to step on the floor. There were too many vipers.

He held up a finger, turned, and spoke to the king, who'd just arrived, and then carefully skirted the creatures as he made his way across the room to Zwaantie. He paused every once in a while to talk to a mage. Zwaantie sat down and waited for him. A short blonde mage had crawled onto her bed.

"How do you suppose they got in?" Zwaantie asked.

The mage shook her head. "I've no idea. But this is fascinating. I've studied the viper's behavior and killing patterns. Nothing like this has ever been seen before. It's said they can paralyze a victim with a single look."

"But the eyes are open. Why aren't we dead?"

"They're sleeping. They've never been seen before in the daytime, and this explains why. It's almost as if they can't be awake after the midnight hours. I wonder if they will wake again at midnight, or if they have to go to the ocean to rejuvenate. No one has seen one before. Ever." The mage grinned.

Sleeping? As in alive? Zwaantie had to get out of there. She wasn't sure she'd ever be able to sleep in her own room again. Zwaantie shivered, wishing she hadn't had the misfortune to see them. Now she would have nightmares.

Ari appeared in front of Zwaantie. He had no shirt on, and Zwaantie shivered again, but not out of fear this time. He crouched down in front of her.

"I'm going to carry you out of here. I think it's best if you stayed with Sage for a little bit."

Zwaantie nodded, grateful she didn't have to tell anyone she was scared to death to sleep in her own room.

"Oh stars," said the blonde mage.

The viper fell off the bed and the tail whipped across Ari's back. He yelled and careened into Zwaantie. He perched on the edge of the chair like a scared bird. His face was only inches from Zwaantie, and he looked terrified.

The serpent rolled under the bed.

"Sorry," he said and stepped down off the chair.

Zwaantie giggled. "Startle much?" she asked.

He grimaced. "You know I can just leave you there."

She shook her head. "No, I'm not walking out of here on my own. I'm sorry I laughed."

"Well, don't get used it. I don't frighten easily."

He lifted her up, his arms warm on the bottom of her thighs. She blushed again at the lack of clothes she wore. Ari was careful as he tiptoed around the room. Once out, they nearly bumped into the king as he and Lyra spoke to each other in low voices.

"Put me down," Zwaantie said.

He looked down at her like he'd forgotten she was there. "Oh, sorry."

He set her down, and the king looked up. "Are you alright?"

"Yes, sir, I'm fine. I slept with Sage last night, so I didn't get back to my room until after the vipers were asleep. If it's alright with you, I'm just going to stay in Sage's room until Leo returns."

The king nodded, distracted. "That seems like a good idea."

He and Lyra headed off down the hall whispering furiously.

"Now what?" Zwaantie asked Ari.

"Now Leo comes back. This falls under his investigation, so you'll get some good one on one time with him."

"How do you think they got in?"

Ari shrugged. "No idea. Leo will have some insight. He's already been called. He'll return this afternoon."

A small balding man with an enormous shaking belly skirted out of the head mage's way and strolled toward them.

"Ari," the man bellowed, grinning.

"Piscus, I didn't expect you back so soon."

Piscus grabbed Ari's hand and shook it vigorously. "Neither did I, quite frankly, but here I am. And I brought him back, m'lord. He's in your rooms."

"Fantastic. And there's Sage."

Sage stumbled down the hall, her face scrunched up and her hair a mess on the top of her head. "What is all this racket?"

Ari didn't answer. Sage stood next to Piscus for a second and then moved quickly to Ari's other side. "Piscus, what are you doing here?"

He licked his lips. "Just on an errand for your brother. You busy later?"

She grimaced. "Yeah. I am."

"Why don't you two get ready and meet me in my rooms in an hour or so? Sagie, can you have Zwaantie wear the purple and green dress of yours?" Ari asked.

"Why, so she can impress Piscus?" She snorted.

Ari shook his head. "No, but there is someone she'll want to impress. I can't elaborate right now. Just meet me in my rooms."

Chapter Eighteen

THE SLAVE

Sage, still half asleep, took Zwaantie's hand and led her to her rooms.

"What's all the fuss about?" Sage asked.

"They found vipers in my room."

Sage's eyes bugged out. "Vipers?"

"Yeah."

"It's too early for me to process that. Did you really say vipers?" Sage rubbed her forehead.

"Yes. If I'd slept in my room, I'd be dead."

Sage disappeared into her closet and came back out.

"Here put this on." She shoved a bright purple dress into Zwaantie's hands and wrapped her arms around Zwaantie and squeezed tight. "I'm glad you slept with me last night." Then she let go. Her hair was mussed, and she looked like she was about ready to fall over. Obviously not a morning person. Just like Zwaantie.

Zwaantie took the dress into the bathroom and shimmied it on. It was tight and short. But it sparkled in the light, and sometimes it would look green instead of purple. She would never get away with stuff like this at home.

Her hair was all knots and tangles. She ran her fingers through it, and they got stuck. She'd never even done her own hair before and didn't know how to fix it. She was jittery from the viper experience. She had no idea what Ari wanted with her, but this seemed like too much. Zwaantie needed Luna to fix it and calm her nerves.

"Sage," Zwaantie asked, coming back into the room. "Do you know where Luna is?"

But Sage was zonked out on the bed again. Zwaantie opened the door and peeked out, hoping to find a servant. Instead she found Luna, giggling with Viggo as she passed the room.

"Luna," Zwaantie called.

She turned, surprised.

"I've been looking for you," Luna said and gave Zwaantie a big hug. Zwaantie returned the hug, surprised by Luna's statement. She'd been avoiding her.

"Can you fix my hair?" Zwaantie tried not to whine. She didn't want to bring up the vipers and ruin Luna's mood.

Luna frowned. "I'm not your slave anymore. But come with us. Viggo's going to introduce me to the beauty mages. They can do your hair for you."

Zwaantie sighed and followed her. She wasn't in the mood to be primped over, but Sage wouldn't be any help at this hour.

The beauty mages were located on the second floor. They were waif thin and absolutely in love with Viggo.

"Your hair," one said to Zwaantie. "How did it get so long? And thick. My hair would never look like this even with magic. I'm so jealous."

She ran her fingers through Zwaantie's hair, and it smoothed instantly. The knots gone. It would have taken Luna a half hour to get the same results. Speaking of which, she sat in a chair next to Zwaantie, all smiles.

"How did we ever do without magic? I don't think I'm ever going home."

"What about Pieter?" Zwaantie asked.

"He'll come here. We'll find a way. It'll be easy once you're queen."

Zwaantie nodded, not wanting to think of anything that would happen after she became queen.

Fifteen minutes later, Zwaantie was done. Her hair hung in ringlets down to her waist, and the top ringlets were colored a dark purple. Zwaantie's face was painted and her eyelashes elongated. Her own parents wouldn't recognize her.

Ari swooped into the room.

"There you are. I've been looking everywhere for you."

He pulled her up out of the chair and surveyed her.

"You look hot. Though I think I prefer you in longer dresses. This is perfect for right now, though. Come on."

Ari held Zwaantie's hand as he led her out of the room. She almost pulled away. Holding hands meant nothing in Stella. To her, though, it felt like more, and she wasn't sure how to handle that.

Ari jabbered as they walked.

"If anything makes you uncomfortable, you need to tell me right away, and I'll get rid of the prick. But he was a lot easier to find than I thought he would be."

"What are you talking about?" Zwaantie asked.

"I'll show you." He opened the door to his room and pulled Zwaantie in. Seated in a chair across from the fireplace was Phoenix. He seemed utterly relaxed and hadn't looked her way yet. He wore lose fitting pants like most of the men in Stella and a black vest. He'd never looked more handsome.

He wouldn't look toward her. She knelt in front of him, ignoring the way her dress tugged and bunched. She grasped his hands and sought his eyes.

"Phoenix," Zwaantie said.

He jerked his hands out of hers and snarled.

"Get away from me." His eyes narrowed, and his mouth twisted. He looked horrid.

She stood up and backed away, stunned. Ari caught her as she started to stumble.

Phoenix spoke again, his voice full of anger. "I didn't want to see her. Don't you people get that?"

Tears pricked at Zwaantie's eyes, but she blinked them away. "Why don't you want to see me?"

He stood up and paced the room. Zwaantie kept her distance. She'd never seen him so agitated.

"Because, Zwaantie, I don't want to be with you. I never did. The day those bands came off I realized my mind had never been mine.

We speak of magic in Stella, but the magic in Sol is so much more sinister. You bewitched me to fall in love with you, to run away and leave my family and friends behind. And for what? So you'd have someone worship you every day? Have someone who kisses you whenever you ask? If I married you, I'd still be a slave, but to you, not Sol. No way in the darkness would I commit myself to such an awful prospect. You disgust me."

He said the last words with such spite, such malice. Zwaantie fought to keep control in her voice as she answered him.

"I have no idea what you are talking about. But if you didn't love me, you should have just told me instead of leading me on."

"No!" he roared. He came after her and yelled right in her face. Ari made a move toward Phoenix, but Zwaantie placed a hand on his arm.

Phoenix's face contorted as he continued to scream. She didn't move, allowing him this anger. She still loved him, and he deserved the right to express his feelings. Even if she couldn't figure out what he was talking about.

"You will not do this to me again. You forced me to love you with that stupid Voice. The Voice who told me to love you, to want you. And when I discovered what you did, I fled so I would never be bewitched again. How could you do this to me?"

His face relaxed, and his breathing slowed, but his eyes. They still promised murder, but when he looked at her, her heart burned. She still wanted him, and she wanted him to love her. She'd give up anything to be with him again.

She placed her hands on his cheeks.

"But I still love you, and I don't understand."

His eyes flashed with anger, and suddenly she couldn't breathe. He had his hands around her neck, and her vision was going spotty. Zwaantie could see Phoenix's angry face, and then everything went black.

Chapter Nineteen

THE SISTER

"Zwaantie, say something." Ari's face swam into view over hers.

She blinked at him. She wasn't sure she could talk.

"Are you okay?"

She nodded, but the movement felt like her brain was sloshing around in her head.

"Can you sit up?"

She shook her head. More sloshing. Her brain raced through what happened. Phoenix. Why had he tried to kill her? What was wrong with him?

"You hit your head pretty hard when you went down. I tried to catch you, but I was busy making sure Phoenix didn't kill you. I'm sorry. I had no idea he'd do that."

She squeezed her eyes shut. She didn't want to think about what had happened.

"You didn't know. My head hurts." She was terrified by what she saw in Phoenix's eyes and what he did.

Footsteps reverberated on the floor.

Ari barked instructions to the men around him. For some reason his words didn't make sense. They sounded odd and foreign. Zwaantie's eyes would flash open and shut on their own. The room was bright, then dark. Then an odd shade of blue. Nothing made sense.

"Zwaantie, look at me."

She focused on the face above her. His eyes were gray and beautiful. He smiled.

"The healer will be here soon. How can I help until he gets here?"

"Dunno," she muttered. "Everything looks funny." She couldn't keep her eyes open.

"Well, you nearly suffocated."

Something bumped her arm, and she looked up. Another man knelt next to her. He had a kind face and bright red clothes.

"What hurts the worst?" he asked.

"My head. It's sloshy." Her words came out slurred.

"You hit your head when you fell. Here drink this."

He tipped a bottle in her mouth that tasted like blueberries and walnuts. Instantly, the sloshing in her head vanished, and her mind cleared. Stellan medicine was amazing. She sat up slowly, expecting the pain to return, but it didn't.

"That's much better. Thank you."

The healer smiled.

"Sounds like you got lucky. You could've died."

Ari held out his hand and helped her stand up. "What the hell was he thinking? He tried to kill you. Has he ever been violent before?"

Zwaantie shook her head. The tears came without warning. She loved Phoenix, desperately, and he hated her. Enough to want to kill her.

What had she ever done to deserve such hatred? Was she really that unlovable that he had to pretend like he was bewitched into loving her?

Through her tears she saw the healer rummaging in his pockets.

"Here, take this too. It will make you feel better."

She drank it without thinking. She wanted her internal pain to go away. The potion tasted of watermelon, chili peppers, and chocolate. It was such a strange combination. But her insides warmed, and she forgot about being unlovable.

The healer left, and she and Ari sat down on a couch.

"I'm sorry. I didn't know he would behave that way. I knew you wanted answers, but probably not those."

She leaned against the squishy cushions. "I don't understand what he meant. I never bewitched him. Why did he say those things?" Not that Ari would have answers. She just needed to talk, and he was there.

"Your guess is as good as mine. But there have always been rumors about the magic in Sol."

"We don't have magic in Sol."

"It's supposed to be psychological. Mind control. Phoenix spoke of a voice. Did you ever have a voice in your head telling you what to do?"

She sat up. "Of course. Everyone knows about the Voice." Oh Sol, could Phoenix hear the Voice as well? Maybe it was telling him to kill her. Poor Phoenix.

"What are you talking about?" Ari asked, and Zwaantie startled.

"The Voice of Sol. It makes sure we don't do bad things. It comes from God." She rattled it off without thinking. It was what she'd been taught from a child, but maybe she was wrong about the Voice. She'd certainly had doubts in Sol.

Ari shook his head. "I doubt that. You probably have some pretty strong mages you aren't aware of. If I were about to take over as the ruler of my kingdom, I'd want to know who was controlling the Voice."

"Sol is God of the Sun. His Voice is a good thing." Even as she said the words, she wasn't sure she believed them anymore. She didn't want to think badly about the Voice, but being in Stella had her confused.

Ari's eyes sparkled as he leaned forward. "You're telling me you like it better there than you do here?"

"I don't know. But it doesn't mean it's wrong. What I don't understand is why the Voice told Phoenix to love me."

"Maybe it was something else. Could someone impersonate the Voice?"

Zwaantie rubbed her head. "I don't know. I really can't think about this. It's too much." She actually liked his explanation better. If someone was pretending to be the Voice, could it have started in Sol? And if it had, then how did the real Voice let it happen? No, it made more sense that the Voice wanted her dead. Her headache was coming back.

"I still have to go home after I marry Leo. I'll be queen." Where the Voice would likely try to kill her. Maybe she was trapped in Stella forever. She didn't want to abandon her kingdom.

"You'll be able to come back here to visit." Ari shifted on the couch so he was sitting right next to her. "You want to watch a movie?"

"What's that?" Zwaantie asked, grateful for the change in subject. She needed time to process what had happened and maybe even enlist some help in figuring out how to handle the Voice, but for now, she didn't want to think about anything.

Ari gave her a grimace. "No movies? I'm never going to Sol. Do you understand? You come here to visit, but I am not setting foot on that soil."

"No, I'm sorry. I have no idea what they are."

"Well, I know what we are going to do for the rest of the day." He took out his disc and spoke into it. "Sage, get over here. We're going to watch movies with Zwaantie."

Sage's voice floated out, groggy with sleep. "Okay, give me a few."

"What kind of stories do you like?"

"Love stories." Those had been her favorite books, but she liked adventure as well.

Zwaantie giggled at the expression on Ari's face.

"Then Sage should pick the movie. Love stories, really?"

Sage arrived and they watched three movies. The moving stories fascinated Zwaantie. She'd never seen anything like it before. She could stay there for days. She was so absorbed that she forgot about her problems. Near the end of the last one, someone pounded on the door. Ari answered.

"What have you done with my brother? Why is he in prison?" Luna shrieked from the doorway.

Zwaantie jumped up and raced for her.

"How did you know he was in prison?"

Luna held up her disc. A picture of Phoenix floated there. Guards hauled him away. The words next to the picture read, "Former Solite slave arrested and sent to prison. No one will talk about why. Are they all dangerous?"

Ari inserted himself in between Zwaantie and Luna, giving her a wary look. "Your brother tried to kill Zwaantie. We put him in prison so he cannot hurt her or anyone else."

"He wouldn't do that," she shouted. "You let him out!"

Zwaantie pointed to her neck. "Look Luna." She showed her the bruising. "He tried to strangle me. I don't understand it any better than you do."

She glared at the bruising. "Why would he do that?"

"He said I bewitched him. But I didn't."

"He must be out of his mind. He wouldn't do that. Please let him out. Send him home if you have to, but don't let him rot in prison."

Ari stepped between them. "Let's give it a couple of days. He's fine right now. He's being fed and has a bed to sleep in. Then I'll talk to my father about deporting him."

Luna seethed, and Zwaantie kept her mouth shut. She was pretty sure she wanted the same thing as Luna, but she was terrified of what would happen if he got out. If the Voice was telling him to kill her, Phoenix would just try again.

Luna spun.

"Wait," Zwaantie called. But Luna stormed off without a glance. Viggo followed. Zwaantie wanted to chase after her, but suddenly she didn't know her best friend. She'd become a different person since they arrived in Stella. She'd been distant and more confident. Luna stood up for herself more, which Zwaantie was glad for, but it was as if she didn't even want to be friends anymore.

Zwaantie had no idea what would become of Phoenix. Her thoughts and feelings were so mixed up. She wasn't going to lie to herself. She still loved him. Part of her wanted to seek him out and see if he really loved her. Maybe he did. Sol, she was confused.

Another knock sounded on the door. Sage jumped up and pulled it open.

Leo strode in and pulled her into an embrace.

"I've missed you," he said.

This was the last thing she needed. Not only did she have to try to figure out what happened to Phoenix, but she also had to face Leo, another responsibility she didn't want.

Chapter Twenty

THE REALITY

"We'll let you guys have some peace," Sage said, dragging Ari toward the door.

Leo kept his arm around her. Everything about it felt uncomfortable. She would never be happy with him.

"Wait, don't leave. Zwaantie and I will go to my rooms. She hasn't seen them yet."

Zwaantie closed her eyes. She had no idea what he would expect of her. She couldn't kiss him and pretend like everything was normal. Not today. Not when Phoenix had tried to kill her. She had to protect her heart today.

She opened her eyes and met Sage's, who gave her a small smile.

"Why don't you two join us for dinner in my rooms in an hour," Leo said. "I'd like a briefing from both of you on what happened with the vipers. I've already met with Lyra, but I want to know what you think as well."

One hour alone with him. She could do this. He dropped his arm and grabbed her hand. This she could handle. Leo pulled her out of the room and stopped in front of a door that was only four doors down from Ari's.

The room was sleek and very Stellan with sharp lines and dark colors. The wall behind his bed was a large mural of a glowing City of

Stars skyline. On the deep gray bed was Molly, sound asleep. She peeked an eye open when they walked in but didn't move. Stars, Zwaantie was not going to sleep with a dog in her bed. She didn't have to think about that until they were married, but she was sure she and Leo would have words about Molly. The cats were one thing, but the dog?

"She's exhausted from the trip," Leo said.

"I bet you are as well," Zwaantie said.

"Not really. We need to talk about what happened with the vipers."

He pulled her over to his couch, and she sat next to him, but turned so she was facing him. This put some distance between them, but still made it appear as if she was interested in being with him.

"You probably know more than I do. When I woke up, I left Sage's room, pushed open my door, and found it full of vipers."

"Did you leave your door open?"

"I don't think so, but I can't remember. Surely people leave doors open all the time if they aren't in the rooms."

He frowned. "Yeah, they do. Nothing about the vipers is making any sense anymore. I'll talk to Sage and Ari later. They might've noticed something you didn't." He gave her a forced smile. "Have you started planning the wedding yet?" Leo asked.

"No. I'm afraid I don't even know where to start. I'm sure weddings here are different than they are in Sol."

"Maybe tomorrow we'll head to the wedding planner and get things going. The wedding will come fast, and we'll want to make sure we make a good impression on the people."

"Right," Zwaantie said. "So the Ticker will say good things?"

"Yeah. I'll get Viggo to send along a photographer to the wedding planner. It will make a good story."

Zwaantie rubbed her head. More pictures? No thanks. She needed to change the subject. She hesitated. She wanted to understand the way relationships worked here. Ari and Sage had told her some, but would Leo confirm it or deny it?

"I'm learning a lot about the differences in our kingdoms. Tell me, after we are married, will you be faithful to me?"

He sputtered. "Why would you ask me that?"

She noticed he didn't say yes.

"Because it seems as though infidelity is common, even expected here." She almost smiled at his obvious uncomfortableness.

The wall across from Leo lit up, and Candace's face appeared. "Hey, Zwaantie. Hey Leo."

Zwaantie jumped. "How are you?"

"I'm fine. Just checking if Leo got back okay."

"No troubles on the way back," Leo said.

Little Raaf let out a holler, and Candace laughed, holding him up. He'd gained weight and looked as healthy as ever.

"He's adorable," Zwaantie said.

"Are you doing okay? Those vipers must've been scary."

"Yeah, I'm fine. I missed Leo though," she added in the hopes that Candace might take a hint. She grabbed Leo's hand and pulled it into her lap. She didn't have long until Sage and Ari came, and she wanted answers.

Another woman came into the room carrying a toddler.

"Oh, hey, this is my sister-in-law Portia and her son Castor. We're planning an epic party for his first birthday. Maybe you two can come."

"That would be fun."

Leo nodded. "It would be nice to show Zwaantie more of the kingdom. It depends on where my investigation takes me."

Candace leaned forward, her nose going large on the screen. "What's that on your neck?"

Zwaantie's hands flew to her neck, trying to cover it up. Leo touched her neck gently.

"You're bruised. What happened?" Leo asked.

"It's not a big deal. One of the old slaves had a mental break and attacked me. Ari was there, so he protected me." She had really hoped to keep this a secret from Leo. Ari kept the truth out of the Ticker, which meant only the people involved knew what really happened. Something was wrong with Phoenix, and Zwaantie didn't want Leo jumping to conclusions. If he made the connection that it was Phoenix, he might be suspicious since she was so insistent on him coming to the castle to be with Luna. Then he might be suspicious of Luna as well. Zwaantie couldn't have that.

"What do you mean mental break?" Leo asked.

"He went crazy and attacked me. They moved him down to the prison."

Leo eyed her with concern. "Maybe it had something to do with you being the princess."

"What do you mean?"

"Being a slave must've been traumatic for them. They see you as a threat to their freedom. Just make sure you don't go anywhere without a guard."

Zwaantie bit her tongue to prevent herself from arguing. Phoenix's break had nothing to do with being a slave, but she couldn't bring that to Leo's attention. The baby wailed. Candace gave a grimace. "Gotta run. I'm glad you got back okay, Leo. Zwaantie, we'll talk later." The wall went blank.

There was an awkward silence for a moment. Zwaantie wanted to continue the conversation that got interrupted but felt weird just bringing it up.

Leo scratched his head. "What were we talking about before Candace popped in to say hi?"

That was the best opening she was going to get. "Infidelity. Will you have other lovers after we are married?"

A deep blush crept across his face. "I don't plan on it."

Oh Sol. That wasn't the answer she was expecting.

She settled into the couch, ready to get a straight answer. "Really? It seems as if everyone here has one. Why wouldn't you?"

"Because I love you."

"I get the feeling love has nothing to do with it."

"Zwaantie, why are you pushing this? I already told you I won't."

"No, you said you weren't planning on it. I'm from a land of black and white. What are the rules concerning lovers in Stella?"

The door opened, and Sage and Ari came in and plopped down on the couch across from them. Stars, she couldn't get an answer without interruption. Well, Sage and Ari were just going to have to listen to this because she wanted to know.

"What's up?" Sage asked.

Leo looked away from them, and Sage met Zwaantie's eyes. "Uh, oh. Did we interrupt something?"

Ari snorted. "No. If we had, they'd be all over each other. Check out the distance."

"No, it's okay, Leo was just about to explain to me the rules concerning lovers in Stella."

"Oh, yeah, we should go." Sage stood up.

"Come on, it's not like it's a secret," Ari said, pulling Sage down.

Leo sighed and ran a hand through his hair.

"The rules? Lovers are commonplace. I expect at some point we'll both have lovers outside of our marriage. I know right now it sounds barbaric and wrong to you, but over time, you'll change your mind and this won't seem so wrong."

She couldn't face Leo, so she flicked her gaze to Ari. He wiggled his eyebrows, but his eyes were so serious. They bored into her, and she suddenly felt exposed and vulnerable. How could one look be so unsettling?

Their dinner arrived then, interrupting the conversation. Leo talked mostly with Ari and Sage, getting answers about the vipers in Zwaantie's room and Phoenix's attack. Nobody said anything about it being Phoenix, for which Zwaantie was grateful.

After dinner, Zwaantie made to follow Sage out of the room, but Leo stopped her and pulled her close.

"Why don't you stay here tonight? Your room is still a laboratory."

Zwaantie bit her lip. "I think I'll stay with Sage."

Leo's face fell, and Zwaantie felt like she had to do something. She leaned forward and gave him a sweet kiss on the lips. "I'm sorry. I'm still not comfortable with this. Breakfast?"

He nodded, but didn't smile. She felt nothing for him. She couldn't bring herself to do more than that. She only had three weeks to prepare for her wedding night, and she could barely stand to give him a polite kiss on the lips. This was impossible.

Chapter Twenty-One

THE PRISONER

The next morning, Zwaantie and Sage made their way to Leo's room.

"Thanks for coming with me," Zwaantie said.

"No problem. I understand. You will have to be alone with him eventually, you know."

"I know. Baby steps, right?"

Sage shook her head. "I guess. But I'm not coming with on your wedding night."

Zwaantie groaned. "Maybe I can just stay with you."

"No way, sister."

Zwaantie raised her hand to knock, but Sage turned the handle and pushed the door open. Leo rushed around his room, throwing clothes into a bag. He glanced up as the girls entered.

"Oh good, you're here. I have to go."

Sage sat on the bed and pulled Zwaantie with her.

"Where are you going?" Zwaantie asked.

He let out a sigh. "There is a village on the ocean in Candace's kingdom. It's small, only a hundred or so people. It's near where the first viper was sighted. A few fisherman went down there to cast off this morning, and all the inhabitants have disappeared."

"Disappeared?"

"Yes. They are gone."

"Do you think it was the vipers?"

"More than likely. We don't know anything yet. No bodies have been found. I'll let you know when I find out more. This is getting ridiculous. I'll be back for the lock-in. Promise."

"That's ten days away," Sage said.

"Yeah. This is serious. I may return if they discover anything about the vipers in Zwaantie's room, but for now I need to focus on the what's going on in Deep Sky. Sage, you take care of Zwaantie. I mean it."

"Hello. What do you think I've been doing?"

"Let's see, her room was filled with vipers and a slave tried to kill her. I'd say you're slipping."

Sage stood up and glared at him. "She's still alive, isn't she? I'm doing just fine."

Leo shoved another shirt in the bag and jerked it off the bed. He leaned over and gave Zwaantie a light kiss. "I'm so sorry. I'll call you tonight."

He disappeared out of the room with Molly on his heels.

"I thought you were my friend."

"I am."

"Then why did Leo make it seem more like you were my guard?"

Sage laughed. "What do you need a guard for? He's just being paranoid."

Sage's disc buzzed. She pulled it out and then shoved it in her pocket. "Let's go have some breakfast and see what we can find to do this morning. I've got plans this afternoon."

❧

ZWAANTIE FOUND HERSELF ALONE FOR THE AFTERNOON. SAGE AND ARI had both disappeared, promising to be back in time for dinner. Zwaantie didn't know what to do with herself. She couldn't get Phoenix out of her mind. His vehemence was completely out of character. Why did he want to kill her?

Maybe he did have a mental break. Something that caused him to go crazy. She needed to see him to understand. She stood from Ari's couch and looked around the room. She was much more comfortable in here than she was in Sage's. For one thing, there weren't a dozen cats running around. Besides, his room was warm and safe.

She slipped out the door and ran right into Luna, who was in tears. Luna flung her arms around Zwaantie. "Why'd they lock him up? It's not fair."

Zwaantie rubbed her back. "I know it's not. Do you want to try to see him?"

Luna pulled away. "You want to see him?"

Zwaantie nodded. "I think something is wrong with him. We should go talk to him and see what happened."

Luna wiped her tears away. "Yes, let's go see him." She looped her arm through Zwaantie's. "I've missed you."

"Me too. Tell me what you've been up to."

"Hanging with Viggo and his friends. They're so much fun."

"I bet. Ari and Sage are pretty fun too. Part of me doesn't want to go home."

"I can't go home. I saw a healer yesterday about the baby. He says it's healthy. I can't risk going to Sol."

"I know." Zwaantie was glad Luna was talking to her. She'd missed her.

"How do you think we'll find Phoenix?" Luna asked.

"Ari and Sage are both out. Maybe Viggo will take us."

"No, he's out too. I think all the princes and princesses had something to do."

Zwaantie supposed they could just take a carriage like they'd done the other day, but how would they find where he was being kept? They found a guard just as they stepped out of the castle.

"Excuse me," Zwaantie said. The guard glanced up at her suspiciously. She forged on anyway. "I'm looking for the prison where the Solite slave Phoenix was taken. Can you show us how to find him?"

The guard snorted. "Why would you want to see him?"

"This is his sister. She wishes to visit him."

"Sorry, can't help you even if I wanted to. I don't know where they took him."

Zwaantie frowned. She thought about arguing but decided to take things into her own hands. She pulled Luna away from the guard and held her hand out like she'd seen Sage do. A horseless carriage stopped right in front of them.

They climbed inside, and Zwaantie said, "Prison."

Luna settled into her seat. "Well, that was easy."

"I just hope it's as easy to see him once we get there."

Luna ran her hands along the fabric of the seat. "I haven't been in one of these yet."

"Ari and Sage took me to the beach in one."

"I'll have to ask Viggo to take me. Can you believe how easy it is to do things here? We've mostly stayed in the castle. I love watching movies and getting my hair done."

"You should go to a funhouse. It was pretty wild."

"What's that?"

"It's an illusion house. In one room, I thought I was a mermaid under the sea."

Luna's eyes bugged out. "Oh stars, yes. That sounds amazing." She stared out the window for a moment. "Are you okay, Zwaantie?"

Zwaantie let out a breath. "I don't know. I spend most of my days confused. Sometimes I just want to go home, and other times I just want to stay here. I feel trapped. Life was easier in Sol. I didn't have so many decisions to make."

"You mean when I was your slave and did everything for you?" Luna crossed her arms and looked away.

"Luna, come on. I didn't mean it like that. I'm so glad you are free now. I wouldn't take that back, but I don't know how to make sense of anything right now. I just want life to be simple again."

Luna relaxed her shoulders but didn't uncross her arms. "I've never been more comfortable. This is my home, and I didn't realize how much I'd missed it. Are you going to marry Leo?"

"Yes. I don't have a choice. Plus, if I didn't and just went home, who would I marry? Prince Moo-for-me?"

Luna giggled and moved over to sit next to Zwaantie. She laid her head on Zwaantie's shoulder. "I miss Pieter. Promise me that whatever you do, you'll get him over here for me. I won't go back there."

Zwaantie squeezed her hand. "I promise."

The carriage jerked to a stop, and they climbed out. Zwaantie blinked at the sight. Bright orange and red buildings rose up around them. Even the road was a blinding shade of yellow. Everything glowed.

Luna gaped at the buildings. "You would expect a prison to be more dreary."

"You would," Zwaantie said. The prison in Sol was in the dungeons of the palace and was very well-guarded. Zwaantie strode right in the front doors. The entryway was crisp and clean and solid white. There were no chairs or benches, no pictures on the walls, just a small window on the far side of the room.

Zwaantie approached the window, and a tiny woman with a too wide smile greeted them. "Welcome to Stars Detention Center, how can I help you?"

"We are here to visit a prisoner."

"Very well. Name of the detainee?"

"Phoenix. He would've arrived yesterday."

The woman pressed her finger to the wall and said, "Phoenix." Nothing happened.

"Are you sure he's here? We have no record of him."

"We're sure."

The woman pursed her lips. "What was his crime?"

Zwaantie shuffled her feet before responding. "Attempted murder."

The woman brought a hand to her breast. "Excuse me, dear, but we have no such detainees here. If he tried to murder someone, he'll be down at Capital Dungeons."

"I'm sorry, my mistake. Just out of curiosity, what sort of prisoners do you have here?"

"Mostly thieves and potion addicts. Most are released in a matter of weeks after we rehabilitate them. It's rare to see a repeat offender. It's not that way at Capital." The woman shivered. "I wouldn't set foot in there."

"Thank you for your help."

"Good luck, girls. Stay safe, and it's best if you don't try to visit this Phoenix."

As soon as they cleared the door, Luna gripped her hand. "We're still going, right?"

"Of course we are. I'm not afraid of a prison. Come on."

She flagged down another carriage and said, "Capital Dungeon."

Several minutes later the carriage jerked to a stop. Zwaantie could hardly see anything when she climbed out. Darkness hung thick in the air with only a few glowing lights. The building was old and made of concrete. A small sign hung crookedly over the door that said *Capital Dungeon.*

"At least we know we're in the right place," Luna said.

She held tight to Zwaantie's hand as they entered the dim room. The walls were made of metal, and a guard sat behind a desk in front of the only other door in the room. He glanced up from the book he was reading. His face was hard with thick eyebrows and pockmarked cheeks.

"You two are too pretty to be here. I think you're in the wrong place."

He intimidated her, but she wouldn't let him win this one. They were going to see Phoenix. She approached the desk.

"We're here to see a prisoner."

The man shook his head. "No visitors allowed. If you want to leave something for a prisoner, we'll take it to him unless we feel it might endanger others."

"Please, we need to see him. There has been a misunderstanding."

The man let out a laugh. "Sorry, missy, I'm not making any exceptions for you or anyone else."

Luna leaned forward and placed her hand on the guard's arm. She blinked her eyes at him. "Please, we have to see him."

The guard's eyes went glassy, and he nodded. He pushed open the door and strode right through it without looking back at them.

"What did you do?" Zwaantie hissed.

Luna smirked at her. "Turns out, I have quite a bit of magic. Viggo's been teaching me how to use it. I simply compelled him to do what I wanted."

Zwaantie's heart nearly stopped. "Leo explained to me how the magic worked. You can't influence people. It's very physical."

"Right. It doesn't work unless I touch them." Luna took Zwaantie's hand. "Don't tell anyone. No one knows I can do this. But I'll show you my other tricks once we get back to the castle."

Zwaantie didn't say anything. She supposed she wouldn't be able to say anything now anyway, since Luna had basically given her a command like she'd done with the guard. Zwaantie couldn't help but think how similar this was to the way the Voice worked.

The dungeon floors were damp and the walls cold. The entire thing smelled like a swamp. They passed several metal doors until the guard stopped at one and placed his hand on the door. The lock popped open.

Luna put her hand on his arm once again. "Wait out here for us, please."

Then she rushed into the room. Phoenix sat on a chair on the far side of the room with his head hung. He looked up at the sound of Luna running for him, but he found Zwaantie's eyes. She held his gaze, losing herself. She would never love another. She didn't know what had happened yesterday, but he was her one and only. In that moment, she knew she'd do whatever she needed to be with him. She knew what this meant. He would only ever be her lover, but she'd do it for him.

Chapter Twenty-Two

THE FOOL

Luna pulled Phoenix up off his chair in an embrace. He squeezed her back and closed his eyes, his ratty hair falling into his face. Zwaantie stayed near the door, not wanting to interfere or startle him. She fiddled with her necklace.

Luna held Phoenix's face.

"Are they treating you alright?" she asked.

"No," he croaked.

"What can we do for you?"

"I don't know. I'm just so cold all the time. Can you bring me a blanket?"

"Of course, we'll make sure you get one. Anything else?"

"Zwaantie," he croaked. "I'm so sorry. I don't know what happened."

Her heart broke. She'd been wrong about him, and here he was in the horrible dungeon.

Zwaantie took a step forward, and Luna spun. "Of course, you two need to talk." She fixed Zwaantie's collar and fussed with her hair a bit. Zwaantie hesitated for a moment. He tried to kill her the last time they were together. Did he really mean he was sorry?

Go to him.

Zwaantie hand flew to her neck. Her necklace was gone.

Go to him now. You love him. The Voice was stronger than she'd ever felt. She did want to go to him. What had made her think she didn't?

She stepped around Luna and rushed for Phoenix and wrapped her arms around him. She needed to feel his embrace and know he still loved her. But he was limp in her arms. Without warning, he shoved her hard. She flew into the wall, cracking her head on the concrete.

She didn't even have a chance to call out before he whipped out his hand and punched her in the jaw. She crumpled onto the ground, and he slammed his foot into her in the back. He kicked out again, his shoe connecting with her nose. Stars exploded behind her eyes. He kicked her in the stomach, and she found her voice.

"Help," she screamed.

The floor shook as footsteps rushed into the cell. Phoenix kicked one more time, hitting her in the ear before someone pulled him away. Her vision went spotty, but just before she lost consciousness, she spotted her necklace lying on the other side of the cell.

Chapter Twenty-Three

THE NECKLACE

Zwaantie awoke to a screeching sound and blinked her eyes open. She was back in Sage's room. She didn't know how she got there. The last thing she remembered was Phoenix punching her in the face.

He really did hate her. There was no question now. She loved him, and now she would have to learn to live without him. Maybe she could just sleep the rest of her life and not have to think about anything ever again.

A man with bright blue eyes hovered over her. Blue eyes were rare in Stella. He flashed a light in her eyes.

"How are you feeling?" he asked.

She shifted. Every muscle screamed. "Not good."

"You're lucky to be alive. I can heal you, but it will take several hours." He placed a hand on her forehead. She felt something seep into her veins, but didn't feel any better.

"You should be fine in the morning. For now, it's important that you stay still." He pulled a potion out of his pocket.

"Before I give you this, I want you to understand what it does. You'll be able to move your head, but your limbs will not move. It will help you to heal. I can give you something to sleep as well."

"That would be good. Thanks."

He tipped the first bottle into her mouth. It was sickly sweet and ice cold. Her limbs immediately went limp. She tried to lift a finger and couldn't. He dug around in his pockets.

Filthy potions. Evil magic. Go home. Zwaantie tried to ignore the Voice. It'd been so long since she'd heard it, which made it hard to ignore. She had to find her necklace.

"Oh stars, I don't have any sleep potion. Give me a moment, and I'll get some more." The healer rushed out of the room.

She let her eyes drift shut, but she was too distracted by the disconcerting feeling of not being able to move. Plus the Voice was bothering her. How had she ever had any peace when she was in Sol? Her bed sank, and her eyes flew open. Sage sat there with a frown.

"That was stupid. What were you thinking?"

"I love him. I had to see if it was just a mistake."

Sage shook her head. "Still incredibly dumb. Promise me you won't do that again. Leo's going to kill me when he finds out."

It was an easy promise to make. Zwaantie's eyes had been opened. She would never see Phoenix again. "I promise. I just had to see, you know."

She felt a tear slide down her cheek. She couldn't lift her hands to wipe it away. Sage did it for her.

"I know. You'll make it through this. Maybe now you'll even let yourself fall in love with Leo."

Zwaantie gave her a fake smile. "Maybe."

"I bet you're tired."

"I'm waiting for the healer to bring me a sleeping potion. He couldn't find any."

"I have some if you want."

Zwaantie snorted. "No, I'm not taking any potions from you. I'll just wait for the healer."

Sage sighed. "Fine. I'll wait with you until he returns."

A knock sounded on the door, and Luna approached the bed. Her face was tear streaked. "I'm so, so sorry. I had no idea he'd hurt you."

"It's okay."

Sage looked from Zwaantie to Luna. "I'll leave you two alone. Zwaantie, I'll see you in the morning. We'll have a spa day."

Zwaantie had no idea what that was, but she wanted to talk to Luna as well. "Okay. See you tomorrow. Thanks for checking on me."

Luna waited until Sage left the room. "I've never seen him like that. I don't know what's wrong with him."

"Maybe he was better off in Sol. We need to send him back." Zwaantie didn't see any other option. With him there, she'd be safe. She supposed he could just say in prison, but she'd feel better if he was far, far away.

"That still won't make him love you," Luna said with a glare.

"I know, but at least he won't try to kill me."

You should go with him. You belong in Sol.

She needed her necklace. She didn't like the Voice being in her head.

Luna fussed with Zwaantie's blankets. "Are you comfortable? You look awful."

Zwaantie swiveled her head around. "Not really, but they gave me a potion to prevent me from moving my arms and legs. I could use another pillow under my head."

"Of course." Luna gave her sympathetic smile.

Luna reached across and grabbed another pillow. "Oh, that's not a good one." She dropped the pillow right on Zwaantie's face and leaned over to get another one. Zwaantie couldn't breathe, and she couldn't move. She tried to call out but felt the breath being stolen from her body. She was going to suffocate under Luna all because she let that stupid healer give her a potion that prevented her from moving.

The weight lifted, and the pillow disappeared. She gasped for breath. Luna played with her hair and slid another pillow under head.

"I'm so sorry. I wasn't thinking. Are you okay?"

"Yeah. That was scary."

Ari stood next to Luna, looking concerned. He held up a potion. "Ran into the healer. He asked me to bring it to you since I was coming this way anyway."

Luna gave Ari a wary glance and then slipped out of the room. Ari sat in the place that had now held three of her well-wishers. At least she was well-loved.

"How are you?"

"You mean besides the love of my life intentionally tried to kill me and my best friend accidentally almost finished the job."

He chuckled. "So, not well."

"No. Not well at all. I just want to sleep and forget this."

"Well, I have two presents for you." He held up the necklace Leo had given her.

"This was found in Phoenix's cell. My guess is he ripped it off before he attacked you."

Zwaantie tried to recall the attack. She didn't remember him going after the necklace, but it was a blur. Ari leaned into her and slid the necklace around her, clasping it. His fingers were soft and warm on her skin.

The Voice immediately ceased. She let out a breath of relief.

"Thank you." She needed to talk to someone about what the Voice was doing, but she didn't know who. Sage and Ari wouldn't understand. Leo maybe.

"You're welcome. Now are you ready to sleep?"

"Yes please," Zwaantie said with a grateful smile.

"Open up."

She did as he commanded, and he tipped the lavender-tasting potion into her mouth. Just before she closed her eyes, he leaned over and kissed her on the forehead. She enjoyed the warmth his kiss brought.

"Sleep safe."

Chapter Twenty-Four

THE SPA

Something landed on Zwaantie's stomach, waking her up. Andromeda meowed at her. Zwaantie stretched her arms out. Nothing hurt, but she was stiff. Her muscles protested as she moved. She rolled over to her side, knocking Andromeda onto the bed. The kitten rubbed her face against Zwaantie's cheek, and Zwaantie pushed her away.

She almost sat up but froze at the sound of Leo's voice. She turned her head and saw his face on the wall. Sage stood in front of him. Both were speaking in low, angry voices.

"You were supposed to protect her. You're her guard. That's the third time she's almost died in your care," Leo said.

Sage threw her hands up. "I've never been with her when she's been attacked. Keep in mind if it wasn't for me, she'd be dead by vipers already. If I was trying to be with her every second of the day, she'd get suspicious. Unless you want me to tell her."

Guard. Sage was her guard? Sage had denied it when Zwaantie asked and Zwaantie had accepted it. Zwaantie thought through the last few days. It made her sad. She'd wanted Sage to just be her friend. She wanted to be angry, but she couldn't. This was Sage.

"No, don't tell her. She needs a friend here. I know I'm angry, but I wouldn't trust her with anyone else. Just tell Ari to give her some space, will you?"

Sage giggled. "Worried?"

"A little. She doesn't love me."

"Give her time. Ari knows the stakes. He won't try anything. Besides he keeps her company when I can't be around."

"Ari's no guard. He can't protect her like you can."

"He does just fine."

Leo sighed. "Okay, I've gotta run. Keep her alive. Please."

"Doing my best, brother. She doesn't make it easy."

Zwaantie kept her eyes closed, not knowing if it was a good idea to tell Sage she'd overheard their conversation. She needed to process what Sage was.

The bed bounced, and suddenly Sage's face was in hers. "Get up."

"I was nearly murdered yesterday. Let me sleep."

"Nope. I'm not letting you mope, and I know you will. You need good old-fashioned spa therapy. Now get up."

She flung off the covers, and Zwaantie glowered at her. Sage could give Luna a run for her money.

Zwaantie swung her legs out and groaned. "Okay, let me shower."

"Not necessary." She flung a light dress at Zwaantie and pointed at the bathroom. "Change and let's get going."

Zwaantie staggered to the bathroom and splashed water on her face. She stared at herself in the mirror. Despite having her face smashed in the day before, she looked no different.

The dress Sage picked out was silky and soft. It fit her well, had no sleeves, and settled just before her knees. She could never wear those Solite dresses again. Even when she became queen, she'd wear clothes from Stella.

Thirty minutes later she stared up at a bright pink building shaped like a giant cloud.

"What's this?" Zwaantie asked.

"The Spa."

As they entered, the door said, "You are beautiful," in a deep sexy voice.

"What was that?"

Sage giggled. "Feels good, doesn't it?"

Sage collapsed onto a bright white couch. Zwaantie followed. "You have a very nice figure," the couch said in the same voice.

"Does everything in here talk?" Zwaantie asked.

"Just about."

The couch was the most comfortable thing Zwaantie had ever sat on. She'd be happy just parking there the rest of the day.

A woman in a pink dress the same shade as the building approached them. She had on a small nametag that said *Nysa*.

"Sage, Zwaantie, are you ready?"

"Of course we are," Sage said and pulled Zwaantie up off the couch.

"I'll miss you," it whispered.

Zwaantie followed Sage and Nysa into a long pink hallway with white doors. She opened the door with Zwaantie's name on it and directed Zwaantie to go inside.

"I'll be in the room next door. We'll be able to talk to each other when we get to the soak," Sage said.

Zwaantie had no idea what she was talking about, but figured she'd go with it. Right now, she didn't really care what anyone did to her.

Nysa followed her into the room, picked up Zwaantie's hand, and examined it. Then she studied Zwaantie's face, her nose inches away. Zwaantie nearly backed up. Nysa went to a panel on the wall and pushed a few buttons.

"I'll be leaving. You need to strip and lie down. Your body will be scrubbed and then wrapped. You'll be alone for about twenty minutes. Then you'll be let down for a soak. The wall between you and Sage will disappear, and you'll be able to talk. Any questions?"

Zwaantie shook her head. She was getting nervous, but she didn't even know what kind of questions to ask. Nysa slid out of the room, closing the door softly behind her, and Zwaantie stood there for a moment unsure of what to do.

"It's okay, dear. No one is watching," the wall said.

"Except you," Zwaantie muttered as she pulled her dress off and laid it down on the table. Then the entire thing disappeared, and she was left floating in midair. It felt as if tiny rocks were scrubbing all over her body. It should've hurt, but didn't. The smell was amazing too, like flowers in the spring. She let her eyes close and just enjoyed the sensation. She wanted to get lost in it and forget about Phoenix and responsibilities.

Why had she gone to see him after he'd tried to kill her the first time? If this is what love did to people, then she was through with it. The tear in her heart would never heal, and she didn't want it to. She needed to be reminded of what it meant when you opened your heart to someone and got hurt.

The rubbing rocks stopped, and bright white cloths bound her body. They smelled of coffee and vanilla. She still floated in the air, her head supported by what felt like a fluffy pillow.

She let her eyes shut, and she drifted in between consciousness and sleep, Phoenix alive in her mind. Her heart twisted.

After a while, her body began to sink, and she found herself in a deep tub. The cloths dissolved. Sweet smelling flowers and leaves floated in the water.

"Nice, huh," Sage said.

Zwaantie's eyes flew open, and she turned toward the voice. Sage was in her own tub.

"It is nice. I could stay here forever."

"I've tried. They kick you out before midnight."

"That's too bad. There's no boys here."

Sage flung and arm over the side of her tub. "You still thinking about Phoenix?"

"How can I not? I was, still am, completely in love with him. It doesn't just go away because he tried to kill me."

Sage gave a snort. "That should make the love go away pretty quickly."

"You would think. But it doesn't."

"Well, what he did was awful. You need to move on."

Zwaantie played with a rose floating in the water. "How?"

"I've never been in love. Perhaps you should focus on Leo. It can't hurt, right?"

Zwaantie didn't want to think about loving Leo. How could she possibly force herself to love someone else? She had so many questions and few answers. Why did Leo ask Sage to guard her anyway? She hesitated for a moment.

"I woke up while you and Leo were talking this morning. I know you're my guard."

Sage didn't say anything for a long moment. Zwaantie hadn't really planned on telling her she knew, but she didn't see how things would change if she didn't. Besides, she needed to tell someone about what had happened with Phoenix, and if Sage was really her guard, then she was the best one to talk to.

Sage let out a long breath. "I'm sorry I didn't tell you. Leo didn't want me to. He thought if you knew I was your guard, you wouldn't trust me."

"He might've been right. But you're my friend now, so it doesn't really matter."

Sage reached over and gripped Zwaantie's hand. "Thanks. I'm glad you're not mad."

Zwaantie shook her head. "I don't know how anyone could be mad at you. Why do I need a guard anyway? It's not like Stella is unsafe."

"It can be. Especially with the Ticker and everything. Leo just wanted to make sure you were okay."

She'd never felt unsafe in Sol before, so the idea of needing a guard to protect her was a little new. Though, near the end, she wasn't so sure Sol was the safest place for even her.

"Do you know about the Voice in Sol?"

"Yeah, I do. I've actually been to Sol."

"You what?"

"I go over with the traders sometimes. I met you before you even came here."

"I don't remember you."

"I was heavily disguised, but you tried to buy the dome from me."

Zwaantie thought back to that day. The female mage was the one who shoved those necklaces into her pocket.

"You were selling those necklaces."

"You bet I was."

"Why?" When Sage had hidden them, Zwaantie had desperately wanted to know what they were. Now she might have some answers. That day seemed so long ago. She'd actually thought Stella was going to invade.

"I can't tell you. I'm sorry. Maybe I'll be able to tell you eventually, but for now, I'm bound to secrecy."

Those necklaces turned off the Voice. If enough of them got into Sol, the Voice would be useless, meaning Sol could easily be overtaken by Stella.

"Are you going to invade Sol?"

"No, nothing like that. I still can't tell you though."

"Well, you should know the Voice followed me here. Every time I take off my necklace, I hear it."

Sage's mouth dropped open. "What's it saying?"

"It's telling to me go home." She chewed on her lip, not sure if she should press forward. "Sage, I think it wants me dead."

"Why?"

"It encouraged me to go to Phoenix. There were a few things that happened in Sol too that make me suspicious."

"Like what?"

"After it found out I didn't want to be queen, it tried to get me to walk into the wall. Oh, and a guard tried to kill me just before midnight, but as soon as the bells rang, he stopped and ran off."

"I have to tell Leo."

"No. Please don't. I don't want anyone else knowing." She didn't want anyone else thinking she was crazy or that something was wrong with her. Sage would be bad enough.

Nysa walked in with another woman, cutting off their conversation. She stood on the far side of the tub with a towel. "Out you go."

Zwaantie stepped out, not self-conscious in the least. Something about the treatments she'd been receiving made her bolder, more carefree. She didn't care anymore. Nysa patted her down and gave her a fluffy robe and slippers. After Zwaantie secured the knot, Sage looped her arm through Zwaantie's.

"I'm glad you'll be my sister."

Zwaantie let out a sigh. "Me too."

This room was purple instead of pink and had two chairs sitting in the middle. Sage settled in one and Zwaantie in the other. Nysa lowered the head of the chair and started rubbing some sort of salt on Zwaantie's face.

Zwaantie wasn't sure if she'd made the right decision in telling

Sage, but she hoped so. It did feel good to get it off her chest, but their conversation left her uneasy. Why had Sage been in Sol selling those necklaces? Sage obviously knew more than she was letting on. Zwaantie was about to be queen of Sol. She needed answers.

Chapter Twenty-Five

THE DEATH

A fter the spa, Zwaantie felt incredibly relaxed, but at the same time she felt anxious about the future. She still had no answers, but Sage knew her secret.

A guard met them at the doors to the castle.

"Your father needs to see you," he said to Sage.

She nodded. "I'll see you at dinner. Please try to not get yourself killed." She had her hands on her hips like an exasperated mother.

"No promises." Zwaantie gave her a half grin, but Sage still glowered at her.

Zwaantie made her way to Sage's room, collapsed on the couch, and pulled out her disc. If she called Leo, it would make him think she was interested, which was absolutely the right thing to do. She didn't want to, though. A cat jumped on her lap, but she pushed it off, stood up, and stretched. She wanted to see the stars. The tower would be safe. No murdering boys.

~

ZWAANTIE BLINKED HER EYES OPEN, WONDERING HOW LONG SHE'D slept. The stars spread out in every direction, a sight she'd love to wake up to every morning. High above her was Leo's constellation.

She searched for Ari's but couldn't find it. Her eyes drifted shut again, but she forced them open and groggily made her way down the stairs and pushed the elevator button to the sixth floor.

She slogged down the hall toward her room, turned the corner, and met the very angry eyes of Sage.

"Where in the depths have you been?"

"I was up in the tower. I fell asleep. Sorry."

"We looked everywhere for you, and you were nowhere to be found. We were so worried." She crossed her arms and shot daggers at Zwaantie.

"Why?" Zwaantie asked. Though that was a stupid question.

Sage grabbed Zwaantie by the wrist and dragged her to Ari's room. "She's fine," Sage said.

"Thank the stars," said Ari. He gathered her up in a hug. "We thought someone had finally gotten to you."

"What are you talking about?" She hadn't meant to scare them, and she hoped nothing happened.

He let go of her and collapsed on his couch, running a hand through his hair.

"Someone attacked Sage while she was getting ready for dinner. We assumed they'd gotten to you."

"Are you okay?" Zwaantie asked. She looked Sage over carefully. She didn't seem to have a bruise or scratch on her. Zwaantie sighed in relief.

"I'm fine. I know how to defend myself."

"Who was it?"

"He wore a mask, but as soon as he got a look at my face, he said, 'You're not Zwaantie,' and he ran away. You were his target. Who else wants you dead?"

Zwaantie let out a long breath.

"I don't know. Someone wanted to kill me in Sol too."

She sat next to Ari and told them the whole story. "I thought it was the Voice that was trying to kill me because I didn't want to be queen. Maybe he's still trying to kill me."

The screen across from Ari's couch flashed on, and Leo appeared. Nope. She certainly wasn't telling Leo the truth, especially with that look on his face. He looked like he'd seen a ghost. Maybe he overheard their conversation.

"Leo," Ari said. "Is everything okay?"

"No. Candace's nephew is dead."

Zwaantie felt the blood drain out of her face. "How?" she asked.

"The vipers. Somehow they got into the bedroom last night."

"Was he still sleeping with his parents?" Zwaantie asked.

"In the same room? Yes. But the baby is the only one who was taken. They don't even know how they got in. The vipers are the only explanation. It's just like all the rest of the deaths."

"There could be some other explanation, couldn't there?" Ari asked.

"Maybe, but there have been reports of three other deaths. All on the eve of their first birthday."

Zwaantie's heart went cold. "It sounds like the prophecy."

Leo ran his hand through his hair. "Exactly. It's scary that suddenly one-year-olds are dying."

"But we're getting married, so how could this have anything to do with the prophecy?"

"Maybe it doesn't. I'm just trying to piece together what's happening."

Sage scrolled through something on her disc. "Leo, it's all over the Ticker. No one knows what to make of it, but people are panicking."

"I know. I've already talked to Viggo. He's going to try to calm the public. But if more babies die tomorrow, we're going to have a crisis on our hands."

"Are you coming back?" Zwaantie asked.

"No. This is where everything started. I need to stay here and figure out how to stop this. I'll be back for the lock-in. I swear. Sage, can you make sure she gets a dress?"

"Of course. Leo you have to come though. This is Zwaantie's big entrance. She can't do it without you."

"I know. I will. Maybe it will even distract people from what's going on. Make her dress shopping a big event."

"That's a good idea. I'll get Viggo to come with us."

"How's Candace?" Zwaantie asked. She didn't want to talk about herself anymore.

"Scared and sad. She came to the same conclusion we did about the prophecy. She thinks maybe we're not doing something right."

Zwaantie thought about that for a moment. She was marrying Leo, there was no question of that. What else could go wrong?

～

Viggo and a handful of photographers followed her and Sage around the dress shop. Zwaantie supposed she should be happy and excited, but she just couldn't muster it. She smiled for the camera though.

She tried on dress after dress. Showing them off for Sage and Viggo. She played her part well, giggling and oohing and ahhing, but inside she felt dead.

Finally after what felt like hours, she found the dress. It was dark green, smelled like a forest, and fell in layers to her ankles. The straps were wide and soft, and while it plunged low, Zwaantie didn't feel like she was revealing too much.

Sage gasped when she stepped out.

"That's the one sister. Leo's going to love it."

She hoped so. She felt as if she were botching everything with Stella, but she could at least do what she could to make Leo happy.

One of them should be.

Chapter Twenty-Six

THE GUILT

Over the next week, Zwaantie rarely left Sage's room. She didn't want to face anyone. Somehow she felt as if this was her fault, though she couldn't figure out why. Guilt plagued her, and so she stayed in Sage's room, and Sage made sure no one came to visit her. She even helped her turn off her disc.

Zwaantie even ate there. She'd taken to the cats and shared her food with Andromeda. Late in the afternoon, Ari entered the room. She hadn't seen him since the babies started dying. Every day there was another one or two.

He sat in a chair across from her. Usually he sat near her, but the cats covered the couch, including the two on her lap.

"You're hiding." He raised his eyebrows at her.

Zwaantie scratched Andromeda behind her ears. "I don't like the attention. Besides, I'm scared."

"You can't hide forever. People keep trying to come talk to you, but Sage blocked everyone from coming in."

Zwaantie gave a small smile. "She's a good friend."

"Yes, she is. But it's time for you to face the stars. Come on, I want to take you for a walk."

"What if I don't want to?"

"Too bad. I'm not leaving here without you, even if I have to carry you."

Zwaantie narrowed her eyes. "Fine." She shifted, but as she tried to stand up, Andromeda dug her claws in. "I have to get up," she said to the kitten, gently removing it from her lap.

Ari chuckled.

"What?" she asked.

"You're covered in cat fur."

She shrugged. She didn't care what she looked like.

He waited for a moment. "Do you want to change?"

"No."

He gave a slow nod. "Okay then. Let's go."

He held her hand and led her out of the room. There wasn't anyone else in the hallways, which Zwaantie was grateful for.

He pulled her into the elevator and pushed a button.

"Where are we going?" Zwaantie asked.

"Tower. I thought we could watch the stars as we talked."

"Thanks, I like it there." Maybe she should've gone up there this week. It would've gotten her out of the room.

His lips formed a tight line, but he didn't say anything. After they got out of the elevator, they climbed the dizzying stairs once again and sat on the platform where Zwaantie could see the thousands of tiny stars in the sky. Ari sat so close to her their legs were pressed up against one another.

"Tell me what's wrong," he said.

"How about everything?"

"Yes, but what is bothering you the most?"

"Candace's nephew. I feel like it's my fault."

"How could it be your fault?"

"I don't know. If I don't marry Leo, little Raaf will die as well. I hate having so much pressure on my shoulders. What if I do something wrong? What if I've already done something wrong and those babies are dying because of it."

The guilt ate away at her insides. She knew it shouldn't. She planned on marrying Leo and not allowing little Raaf to die, but the death of Candace's nephew weighed on her.

"I don't see how it could be your fault."

"Neither do I. But the guilt sits right in the pit of my stomach. If we were in Sol, I'd be begging the chancellor to encourage the Voice to remove it."

"Really? It can take away your guilt?"

"Yeah. Most of the time the Voice is all about lecturing and telling us what to do, but when you do something wrong, it can remove the guilt and bad feelings associated with it. Life was easier then."

Ari nudged her. "But not as fun."

In spite of herself she gave a small laugh. "No, not nearly as much fun."

"Is it possible you're feeling guilty about something else?"

She let out a breath. "Like what?"

"Maybe it's time for you to come clean with Leo and tell him about Phoenix."

"Maybe you're right. He's going to be so angry though."

"Probably. But it's the right thing to do."

Zwaantie knew this. She didn't want to know this, but she did.

"Fine, but if I'm going to do the right thing, then so are you."

"What's that supposed to mean?"

"When I return to Sol, I'll become queen. You'll be king of Stella. You need a queen."

"Have we not been over this?"

"Yep. The way I see it, you need to find your true love. Then you won't want to sleep around."

"You're making sacrifices for the sake of the kingdom, I suppose I could too. You first though."

"Fair enough. Let's go call Leo and get this over with."

Chapter Twenty-Seven

THE TRUTH

They found Sage in her room, deep in her closet tossing clothes around.

"What's up?" Zwaantie asked.

"Lots of people are coming in for the lock-in. Appearances must be kept. Leo should be back early tomorrow morning."

Neither Ari nor Zwaantie replied. Sage spun around and stared at both of them.

"What's going on?" Sage asked.

"I'm going to tell Leo everything about Phoenix."

Sage frowned. "Why?"

"Because I need to."

Sage turned around and pulled out a dress.

"Yeah, that's probably a good idea. You wanna do it here?"

"Yes. Will you two stay with me?"

Sage laughed. "Oh no way. You are on your own, sister. We'll make sure you can get him on the wall though. Oh and we have an appointment this afternoon."

"With who?" Zwaantie asked.

"It's about the Voice and stuff. I have news."

"Good news?" Zwaantie asked, hopeful.

"You'll just have to wait and see. Let's get this call over with first."

Zwaantie sank down on the couch, took out her disc, and said, "Call Leo."

Nothing happened.

"That's odd. He never turns his disc off," Ari said. They waited another twenty minutes and tried again. He still didn't answer.

"Try Candace," Sage said.

Ari pulled out his own disc. "Call Candace."

Her face appeared on the screen. It looked as if they'd woken her up. "What do you want?" she asked groggily.

"We need Leo."

"He left. He should be on his way home."

Zwaantie's disc buzzed, and Leo's face floated above her disc. "Sorry about that, I was busy."

"I'm going back to sleep," Candace said, and her face disappeared from the wall. Leo's replaced it.

"We'll be in my rooms if you need us," Ari said.

Zwaantie nodded. "Okay. Thanks."

Leo smiled at her. "How are you doing?"

Zwaantie let out a breath. "I'm fine, just struggling with all this death."

He ran a hand through his hair. "Me too."

"Are you coming back?" Zwaantie asked.

"Yeah, I'm just trying to finish some things up here."

She needed to forge on, or she was going to lose her courage. "I have something to tell you."

Leo interrupted. "I already know you aren't in love with me."

"There is more to it."

"What?" he asked, frowning.

She wrung her hands and hesitated. She opened her mouth to speak and closed it again. This would not be easy. She had to tell him the truth. "I'm in love with someone else."

He looked as if she'd slapped him.

"I don't understand."

She launched into her tale about how she fell for Phoenix and how she used Leo to get him over here. She even told him of her plans to run away. Leo didn't say anything, but as Zwaantie got further into her story, she couldn't look at him. The anger on his face was too much.

When she finished, she finally dared to meet his eyes. Hatred burned behind them.

"I can't believe you used me. All because you wanted to run away with a lover, and you couldn't do it under your mommy's nose."

"I'm sorry."

"There is more than one way to join kingdoms. We don't have to get married. Go home, Zwaantie. We're through."

Chapter Twenty-Eight

THE SURPRISE

Zwaantie fled back to her own rooms. She flung open her closet and pulled out her old clothes. The ones she brought from Sol. She dumped them on her bed and searched for her trunks. She had no idea what they had done with them, but she needed to get out of there. Go home and forget this whole mess.

Her door opened, and she spun around to find Luna.

"What are you doing?" she asked.

"Going home. Are you coming with me?"

"No. I'm having my baby here. We already talked about this."

"Okay. I will see what I can do about sending Pieter over."

Luna sunk down on the bed next to the clothes.

"Why are you going home?"

"Because Leo told me to. I told him about Phoenix, and he said there was more than one way to join a kingdom."

Luna frowned as she fiddled with the corset strings on one of Zwaantie's dresses. "You know what this means, right?"

"No, I don't." Zwaantie rubbed at her temples. She felt another headache coming on.

"War."

"No." Zwaantie had known this was a possibility, but she hadn't thought about it in a while. She couldn't see Stella declaring war at this point.

"How else would they make Sol part of their kingdom? It's war or marriage."

Oh stars. She was right. She needed to get home and warn her father. Forget her stuff, she was going to catch a carriage and go home right now, even if the Voice was a threat. She'd just keep her necklace on and hope the Voice didn't tell someone else to kill her.

She flung her door open and nearly ran into Ari. "What are you doing in here?"

"Packing. Leo told me to go home."

Ari rolled his eyes. "Let's not be hasty. Really."

"He told me there is more than one way to join a kingdom. That means war. I have to go home and warn my father."

Ari shook his head. "We're not going to invade Sol."

"Right, and Sage was just selling those necklaces in Sol out of the goodness of her heart. This was the plan all along if I didn't marry him."

"Listen, I know you're upset right now, but we can work this out. First though, you need to come with me. There's someone you need to talk to." He looked past her to Luna, who still sat on the couch. "You should come as well."

Zwaantie scowled at him. "I'm going home."

"Fifteen minutes. Please. Also, let me talk to Leo. He's probably just angry."

Zwaantie let out a breath. She trusted Ari. More than she should. War was the last thing she wanted, but maybe she was overacting.

"Fine. What do you want to show me?"

He placed his hand on her back and led her out of the room. Luna followed.

The first thing Zwaantie noticed in his room was the sheer number of guards. Ari's room always felt large, but with the ten guards it felt small. Suddenly, Zwaantie felt the urge to run. If they were planning on a war, this was one way to capture her.

She backtracked, but Ari pushed her farther into the room. "Don't be scared. He can't hurt you."

Zwaantie looked at the guards. In the middle of them sat Phoenix with Sage right next to him.

"What's he doing here?" Zwaantie asked. Luna pushed past her and threw her arms around him.

"Sage has been visiting him. She thought she would try a visit with you."

"Why?"

"Have a seat," Sage said.

Zwaantie sat as far as she could from Phoenix and his guards. He gave her a small smile, but she couldn't return it.

"You mentioned being able to hear the Voice, right?" Sage asked. "I got to thinking maybe Phoenix could as well. His behavior didn't make sense, so I went to the prison, put a necklace on him, and his entire attitude changed. We've talked at length about the Voice and its influence. So far, it appears to only influence you and Phoenix. I've talked with Luna and a few other slaves, and no one else hears it."

Zwaantie spun on Luna. "You haven't heard the Voice even once since we've arrived?"

"No, of course not." Luna's face was earnest. She was telling the truth.

"Why would it just follow Phoenix and I?"

"I don't know. I still have a ton of questions, none of which have easy answers. We needed to meet to see if the necklace really changed Phoenix. Both times when he attacked you, he was completely out of control," Sage said.

Zwaantie wasn't sure what to make of Sage's words. She didn't move. She was terrified to go to Phoenix.

"Really, he won't hurt you. And if he tries, there are ten guards around to make sure he can't."

Zwaantie stood up and took two steps forward. Phoenix smiled at her, and her heart melted. She'd missed him. She took a few more steps, and he stood. She cautiously reached for him. He wrapped her in a tight hug, his body warm and comforting.

"I'm so, so, sorry," he whispered in her ear. "I should've resisted, but the Voice was so strong." Zwaantie pulled away, but he grasped her hands. "When Sage put that necklace on me, everything changed. My eyes were opened, and for the first time since we arrived, I was able to relax. I slept for forty-eight hours straight. I spent some time with healers, and Sage moved me to the hospital instead, but I was still heavily guarded. I've been wanting to apologize. I hope you can forgive me."

"Of course I can. It wasn't you. This does bring up a bigger problem though."

"What's that?" Sage asked.

"We now know for sure the Voice wants me dead. I can't go home."

Sage creased her eyebrows. "Why would you go home?"

"Leo told me to."

Sage laughed. "He'll get over it. Ari and I will talk to him tonight. Trust me, by tomorrow morning, he'll be begging you to stay."

"And if he still wants me to leave?"

"We'll figure it out. Sit. I'm sure you and Phoenix have a lot to discuss. These guards are sworn to secrecy, so they won't tell anyone what they hear. Phoenix will have several guards with him at all times for the foreseeable future. We can't risk him taking off or losing the necklace and trying to kill you again."

Soon they were laughing and talking like nothing horrible had ever happened between them. She wondered what their futures held. If she married Leo, could she keep Phoenix as a lover? If Leo didn't forgive her, would he marry her? Could she risk keeping Phoenix as a lover?

She met Phoenix's eyes, and she knew she would. In a heartbeat.

Chapter Twenty-Nine

THE COMPROMISE

The next morning, just after Zwaantie finished getting ready, Ari poked his head in Sage's room.

"Leo's on the wall in my room. He wants to talk to you."

Zwaantie's palms began to sweat. Ari had told her he'd work something out, but this seemed too easy. As she walked down the hall, she wondered what Leo could possibly have to say to her. His hatred had been real.

She looked at Ari's wall with trepidation. Leo's anger had slipped away and was replaced with resolve.

"Hi," she said meekly.

"I'm sorry I exploded earlier. I was very hurt."

"I know. I shouldn't have used you."

"No, you shouldn't have. What's done is done though, and there is nothing we can do to change the past. After taking some time to think about things, I don't want you to go home."

"You don't?"

"No. The fastest way to secure the safety of the people of Stella is for us to get married. If you are still willing to marry me, I'd like to move forward."

"It doesn't change the fact that I don't love you."

"I know. That's irrelevant."

He seemed so flippant about it. Like it didn't matter.

"Do you still love me, even after what I did?"

"You don't just turn off love. But I hate you as well."

His words stung, but she supposed it was to be expected. She clasped her hands together. "I understand."

"I'm still really hurt and angry. I won't be back for the lock-in. I have too much work to do here, and I'm not sure I could pull off being lovestruck right now."

"That's fine. I'll just go with Sage and Ari. Is Candace coming?"

"No. She's still comforting her sister-in-law. Parties are the last thing on their minds."

"Okay. Thank you for still being willing to marry me."

"Sure. I gotta go. Bye, Zwaantie." He turned off before she could reply. She stayed in Ari's room for a long while, thinking over things. This was working out better than she could've planned. Phoenix was back. She could still be with him and fulfill her responsibility as queen. Which she would do as soon as she learned how to take care of the Voice. Before she left Sol, she never would've thought about having a lover. But here in Stella she could do the right thing and still be happy. That was never a possibility in Sol.

Chapter Thirty

THE REVELATION

Phoenix was staying in a room right next to Luna's, and Zwaantie needed to see him. Two guards stood outside his door.

"May I see him?" she asked.

One of the guards nodded and let her in.

"Princess. Come in."

Phoenix was sitting on a couch fiddling with a disc. He looked up and gave her a smile. "What are you doing here?"

"I had to see you."

"Come, sit."

She sat on the couch next to him and inhaled his scent. She'd missed him so much. She reached for his hand and grasped it tight.

"I need to talk to you about something. I have to marry Leo."

"I know. Sage told me about the prophecy."

"But there is a way we can still be together."

He creased his eyebrows. "What do you mean?"

"Lovers are common here. Leo pretty much hates me right now, so I don't think it will be a problem here."

Phoenix let out a breath. "I wasn't expecting you to say that."

"I know. It's absurd, but I love you."

"Zwaantie, I know this will probably hurt you, but I just got my mind back for the first time in years. I don't fully understand what has happened in the last few months, but I don't think I love you."

Zwaantie gripped his hand. "How can you say that?"

"I look at you, and I see a beautiful girl, but I have no intense feelings. I need time to figure out who I am, but I don't see a future for us. Maybe someday, we can be friends again, but I need time."

"Are you saying the Voice told you to love me?"

Phoenix shrugged. "I think so. All the feelings I have for you are tied to it."

"But why?" Was it possible the Voice wanted her to love Phoenix? No, that couldn't be. The feelings she had were real. Plus, even after she put on the necklace, she still wanted him.

"The ways of the Voice are a mystery. Maybe it doesn't want you to marry Leo. Maybe that is somehow a threat to him."

"What difference does it make to the Voice if I marry Leo or not?" Zwaantie rubbed her head. She had no idea what to make of this news. For some reason, though, thinking that maybe the Voice didn't want her to marry Leo didn't bother her as much as the news that Phoenix didn't love her.

That he never did.

Chapter Thirty-One

THE DINNER

Zwaantie spent most of the next day in Sage's room. Honestly, she was so tired of everything. At this point she just wanted to marry Leo and get it out of the way. She supposed she could learn to love him. She had to. Little's Raaf's life depended on it.

For the first time in her life, she was also ready to take her place as the leader of Sol. As soon as she got rid of the Voice, because as long as it wanted her dead, she could never take her place as queen.

She needed to understand how Stella worked. By marrying the two kingdoms together, there would be a lot more going back and forth across the wall, and she needed to make sure she could handle the ramifications.

Just before dinner, Sage came into the room carrying two long dresses.

"What's that?" Zwaantie asked.

"Dresses for dinner tonight. Lots of people in town for the lock-in. The Ticker will be all over it. We have to dress up. Let's go get our hair done first."

Zwaantie didn't argue as Sage dragged her down to the beauty mages. They put her hair up in a twist and painted her face. Every time she looked in the mirror, she was startled because she barely recognized herself.

Once back in Sage's room, she changed into the blood red dress. Sage's dress looked a lot like Zwaantie's but was a deep royal blue.

"Ari's not going to be able to keep his hands off you tonight. He loves red," said Sage.

Zwaantie cocked her head at Sage. "I'm engaged to Leo."

Sage laughed. "Do you think that matters to Ari? I've seen the way he's been looking at you. He would consider it a colossal failure if he didn't manage to get you in bed at least once before Leo comes back."

"But I have no intention of sleeping with him." She looked down at her hands. She would never get used to how casually people spoke of intimacy here.

"That's part of the problem. You are untouchable, and that makes him want you more."

"But you've left me alone with him plenty of times."

"If you have sex with Ari, you will be one happy girl. I have no reason to keep him away from you."

"But what about Leo?"

"Ari is my favorite brother. And Leo will get over it. No one can resist Ari. Leo knows this."

She grabbed Zwaantie's hands. "Come on, it's time for dinner. You look amazing. Relax a little."

Ari met them at the door.

"Hey, pretty ladies. I think the dressmakers have gotten better."

"It's because Zwaantie is here. They want to impress her."

"Well, they've impressed me," said Ari.

He offered Zwaantie his arm, and she tucked her hand in it reluctantly. Sage took his other arm.

Cameras were flashing as they entered the large dining room. They paused in the doorway and smiled. Zwaantie wondered briefly what the public thought about Leo missing.

Ari found Zwaantie's name card on a place setting right next to his father. She sat, and Ari pushed her chair forward. His hand lingered over her bare shoulder, and he leaned down and whispered into her ear.

"You belong here. In Stella, not Sol."

Then he walked around the table and took his place between Sage and Pius. It didn't matter what he thought. She would have to go home to Sol no matter what. Leo would be king of Sol once she married. That meant their home would be there. Not here. But only if the Voice cooperated.

A man with a camera stopped in front of her. "Where's Leo tonight?" he asked.

"Still in Deep Sky. He's working on the viper case."

The man nodded. "Will he make it back in time for the lock-in?"

"I don't think so." The man walked away. Hopefully he couldn't find anything scandalous in those words.

The king sat down a few moments later. She hadn't really talked to him since she'd had breakfast with Sage weeks ago.

"You look lovely tonight," the king said.

"Thank you."

They chatted about the kingdom for a little while. Though she was looking for information, she was able to keep the tone light and her true motives hidden. She wanted to eke out every boring detail about how it worked. She had her own kingdom to protect. There were a lot of things she loved about Stella, but there were other things she wouldn't allow. The king changed the subject after Zwaantie pressed him on the details of how the jobs master worked.

"What do you think of Leo?" he asked. Apparently he wasn't shy about being direct. She'd have to remember that the next time they spoke.

"He's nice."

"And Ari?"

"Intense, but friendly enough."

"You seem to be spending a lot of time with him." The king seemed awfully curious about her relationship with Ari. Did he want it to be something more? She thought about how to ask without being overly direct.

"He and Sage are close, and I enjoy spending time with Sage. But, sir, can I ask you something?"

"Sure."

"Why did you send Leo to Sol instead of Ari?"

"Ari doesn't want to marry."

"I heard he was upset you sent Leo."

"He was. He likes power and wants to be king, despite anything he says to the contrary. I imagine there was quite an internal battle when he found out Leo got to court the high princess of Sol. Sol's a large kingdom."

"So why didn't you let him come?"

"Ah, well, Leo's a bit more reserved than Ari. I assumed the high king and queen of Sol would've taken one look at Ari and thrown him out."

Zwaantie giggled. "Maybe. But then why didn't you send Pius?"

"Pius is too young, and Leo deserves a kingdom. And because he is smart, I knew he'd find a way to be successful."

By now, dessert had come and gone, and people were beginning to leave. Sage swooped down on her father and planted a huge kiss on his cheek.

"We've got to get our sleep tonight. Tomorrow will be a very long day."

The king nodded. "You have fun tomorrow night."

"Won't you be there?" Zwaantie asked.

"Oh no. Lock-ins are for the young and adventurous. Most married couples do not attend."

"But Candace wanted to go."

"She's barely married. I imagine she won't even consider it next year."

Zwaantie followed Sage out of the room. She still didn't understand how most of Stella worked. Even if they did allow magic in Sol after she and Leo were married, she wanted nothing to do with the Ticker and the pressures it brought.

Chapter Thirty-Two

THE POTIONS

They slept late the next day and spent most of the afternoon in the spa. They ate an early dinner in Sage's room, and the dresses were delivered just as they finished eating.

Zwaantie was excited for this dress. She'd loved the way it felt and looked when she'd picked it out. She unzipped the bag and frowned. It wasn't the dress she'd chosen.

This one had a corset in bright red, but was striped with black. The top of the corset was heart shaped and covered in black lace. Along the bottom was a short, but poufy black skirt. It was beautiful, but where was the one she picked out?

Sage held up her own. It was almost identical except the colors were reversed.

"These are not the dresses we chose," Zwaantie said, still trying to understand what happened.

Sage snorted. "Of course not. Everyone saw those on the Ticker. I ordered these after we got back from shopping. We needed something completely unexpected for your grand entrance. What do you think?"

"It's short and very revealing."

"I know. That's the point. No one will expect you to step out in that. Everyone will be talking about you. It's perfect."

"Why did you get a matching one?"

"Because we'll make our entrance together. Ari will have a black vest and red pants. We'll look incredible together."

Zwaantie changed in Sage's closet. The dress fit well. She wished for a second Phoenix could see her, but then remembered he never loved her. Zwaantie's face fell when she looked in the mirror.

Sage snuck up behind her. She looked stunning in her own dress. "What's the matter?"

"Nothing."

"You look sad."

"I'm fine. We need to get our hair done before we leave, right?"

Sage gave her a frown. "Yes." She drug Zwaantie out of the room. Zwaantie was grateful Sage allowed the change of subject.

They visited the beauty mages who painted Zwaantie's lips a bright red and made her hair a deep black, but when she swung it back and forth, red flared from the end. The mage did something with her eyelashes that made them appear nearly an inch long. The whole effect was a little disconcerting.

Ari met them in the entry hall.

"What in hades took—" He stared at Zwaantie.

He looked at Sage for a second, opened his mouth to say something, and then closed it.

Sage laughed. "You've left Ari speechless. Leo doesn't stand a chance. Come on, we need to hit Party Potions before we go." She handed Zwaantie a cape.

"What's this?"

"No one sees our dresses until we get there."

Ari stayed close to her as they walked outside and climbed into a carriage. Ari sat across from the both of them and glared at Sage. "Did you have to pick a dress that was so revealing?"

"Since when do you care what I wear?" Sage asked.

"It's not you I'm worried about. It's Zwaantie."

"Why?" Zwaantie asked.

Ari scoffed. "Everything about the way you look screams 'I'm hot, and I'm not scared to flaunt it. Oh, and I'm too good for mere mortals, so don't bother.' Which I suppose is a good thing. But that doesn't mean there aren't fools who won't try. You need to be careful tonight."

The carriage stopped in front of a small shop that glowed green.

Ari climbed out and held his hand out for Zwaantie and Sage. Then held open the door.

The shop was bright with colored lights, but tiny and perfectly square. Narrow shelves lined each wall from floor to ceiling, except for a spot in the corner with a long black curtain covering a doorway. Tiny bottles filled every shelf. In the middle of the room sat a counter with four bar stools and a tall blonde woman on the other side. She was arguing with a ragged looking man who slumped on one of the bar stools.

"I don't have what you want. I told you before, nothing in here is habit forming or dangerous. Go somewhere else." Her voice was hard, commanding, but the man didn't seem to care.

"Then do you at least have Painfree? I'll take anything. My potion maker disappeared last night, and I don't know where else to go." He pulled at his greasy hair.

"I don't do medicine either. This is a place for party potions."

The black curtain moved, and a tall bald man stepped out. His shoulders were wide, and his arms were the size of melons. He grabbed the scruffy man by his bicep and pulled him out the door. He nodded to Ari as he passed.

As the door thudded shut, the tall and willowy woman came out from behind the counter. She wore a long green dress that trailed on the floor. She came forward and gave Sage a big hug.

"Sagie. And Ari. It's so good to see you. I suppose you are here because of the lock-in. We've been busier tonight than in a long time. But don't worry, Max will keep out anyone until you leave. What a pleasure to have the new princess," she said, turning to Zwaantie. "I hope you are enjoying your stay in Stella."

"Yes, very much."

"I'm Xandria. It's nice to meet you. Come sit." She pointed to the chairs.

Sage started talking as soon as they sat down.

"We'll all need Cool and Awake. I want Giggle and Black Wings, large."

Xandria pulled out bottles from under the counter and then moved over to the shelf on the right and reached up to grab a bottle from the top.

Sage didn't open the bottles.

Xandria looked at Ari with a wicked glint in her eyes. "What'd you think of Lover Clone?"

"That was a nasty bit of revenge. I finally went home and hid in my room until it wore off."

Sage giggled. "It was hilarious. And what was even funnier was when I looked at him, I saw Corvus. I got all nervous and shy around him, even though I knew it was Ari."

"Why did you hide?" Zwaantie asked, confused.

"Party potions create illusions. Good ones. If you take Lover Clone, anyone who looks at you will see his or her lover instead of you. So, if I took it tonight, I imagine I'd look just like…" He paused and looked at Xandria.

"Like Leo." Zwaantie finished for him, getting to the point.

"Exactly. Now you can imagine the trouble this would cause. If you saw Leo kissing or flirting with another girl, you'd be mad, right?"

"Yes. I suppose."

"Well, I got yelled at, slapped, and spit on all in the period of an hour. I won't be taking that one again."

Xandria laughed. "You deserved it."

His eyes sparkled. "You knew what you were getting into."

She shrugged. "Yes, but that doesn't mean I couldn't exact a little revenge. You can go look in the back room and pick out a few potions if you want."

"Well, consider the revenge exacted. No more potions that put me through hell please. And I'm not interested in the back room tonight. I've got to keep an eye on my sisters."

"Suit yourself. What do you want?"

"Dry, Touch Me, Soul Mate, and Truth."

"Oh yeah," Sage interrupted. "I want Lie."

Everyone turned to Zwaantie.

"What do you want?" Xandria asked.

"What do these do again?"

Sage and Ari started to speak over one another. Xandria shushed both of them. "Seriously," she said. "Being with them is like being with overgrown children. All my potions do one of three things. They either act on you, how people see you, or what you see. Most of them are illusionary, but a few do other things."

She held up a bottle. "Cool will make sure you don't get hot. That's important at the lock-in. Awake will keep you awake. Black Wings will make it appear as if Sage has wings. She won't, but everyone will think so. Giggle will make her laugh at anything anyone says. Dry prevents sweating. Touch Me makes people want to touch you. I wouldn't recommend that one for you. Truth makes it so you cannot speak anything but the truth, and Lie is the opposite." She turned to Sage.

"I don't think you should do Lie tonight. If this is Zwaantie's first time in a club, she'll need you to keep her out of trouble, and if everything you tell her is a lie, that will be hard."

Sage frowned. "I guess."

"Wait a minute, so if Ari takes Touch Me, and I don't want to touch him, will it make me want to?"

Xandria gave a low chuckle. "No, nothing that sinister. Everyone wants to touch Ari, but most won't because that would be weird or awkward, but with something like Touch Me, it removes that inhibition. It allows you to touch him without fear of being rejected. If someone took Touch Me that no one wanted to touch, it wouldn't work."

Zwaantie thought through the potions again. This was incredibly bizarre.

"What's Soul Mate?" Zwaantie asked. It was the only one they ordered that Xandria hadn't explained.

Ari grimaced.

"Ari's obsessed with finding his one true love. Soul Mate creates a glow around that person. He takes it every time there is a party or they go to a club, and he has yet to find her."

"It's pretty unreliable. A lot of people take Glow, and so I can't tell if they are glowing because they are my soul mate or because of their own potion. But it certainly narrows the field."

"You have thousands of potions in here. How can I even begin to tell you what I want?"

"Anything is possible. Tell me your wildest imaginations, and I probably have a potion that can create it."

Zwaantie wanted Phoenix to love her again. A potion couldn't do that for her.

"Glow sounds good. And I've never danced in public before. I want to be uninhibited. Not embarrassed."

"So, Cool, Awake, Glow, and Total Confidence." She placed four small bottles in front of Zwaantie.

Zwaantie drank all four of them. The first had no flavor, but the blood in her veins cooled almost immediately. The second tasted strongly of coffee, and the third was fruity. Total Confidence was odd. It was minty with a hint of strawberries and chocolate.

They left Party Potions at half past ten.

"Why are we going to a party so late if the magic stops at midnight?"

"That's what's cool about a lock-in. Potions still work, and they use gas lanterns from Sol to light the place up. The really awesome thing is the music is natural, not enhanced by magic."

Zwaantie had never felt more comfortable in her life. Maybe Ari was right. Maybe she did belong here.

Chapter Thirty-Three

THE LOCK-IN

They arrived at the building lit up with multicolored lights around eleven. People were everywhere, all dressed in elaborate costumes. Nearly everyone glowed. The carriage stopped in front of a guarded, roped path up to the door.

"You ready?" Ari asked.

Zwaantie let out a breath. "No."

"We'll let Sage get out first. Then, we'll wait for the shouts to die down before we step out."

At home, everyone bowed, but here it looked as if they were about to be mobbed. Sage stepped out, and screams erupted.

"It's the princess!" a girl screamed.

"Sage!" someone else called. Sage paused and dropped her cape.

Zwaantie peeked out the door and watched Sage wave to those who lined the path. She hugged a couple of girls and kissed another on the cheek. Sage grabbed the hand of a young man and pulled him under the rope that kept people out. He was all smiles as she tucked her arm into his elbow, and they escaped into the building.

"Why did she just pull that guy in from behind the ropes?" Zwaantie asked.

"They aren't going to the party. They are probably all having their own parties nearby, but they come to watch those with invitations.

Sage just allowed him to come into the party. She does it every year." Ari waited for another few moments for the crowd's cheers to die down. "It's time."

He stepped out, and young women screamed his name. He turned and offered his hand. Zwaantie took it, and cringed at the bright lights shining on them. She tucked her arm into Ari's, and he put his hand over hers.

"Breathe. You'll be okay," he whispered.

She hadn't realized she'd been holding her breath. She smiled wide and waved to the crowd.

"Zwaantie!" a few of them yelled. She fumbled with the tie around her neck and dropped the cape. There were a few whistles and catcalls.

They walked to the door, and Zwaantie tried to ignore the noise. Ari left her at the door. "Wait here. I'll be right back."

She spun around and watched him dash out. He approached the rope at the same place Sage had been. He chatted with the people there, gave a few hugs, and helped a girl cross over. They strutted to where Zwaantie stood, the girl beaming from ear to ear.

Ari took Zwaantie's hand with his free one and pulled both of them inside. They found Sage waiting near an interior door. The girl Ari had brought in squealed when she saw Sage, but she flung her arms around the boy.

"Thanks for letting us come in," the boy said after he extracted himself from the girl.

"Don't mention it. Have fun," Ari said.

The couple disappeared down the hall.

"That was clever. Grabbing his girlfriend," said Sage.

"You know I try. Come on. Let's go have fun."

They entered a large open room with an enormous crowd. The music beat a hard rhythm in Zwaantie's head, and it made her want to move. Ari stopped her and spoke loudly into her ear.

"Remember most of what you see is an illusion. Don't get caught up in what someone looks like. Also, don't take offense if someone says something rude. They might've taken Lie or Insult. People do it to be funny. If you've done this before, you hardly even notice, but since this is your first time, you need to be careful. Kids in our kingdom grow up having illusion birthday parties, so they won't understand if you don't get it."

Zwaantie nodded and thought she should be nervous, but wasn't. Must've been the Total Confidence. She followed Sage onto the dance floor, and immediately they were moving with a hundred other bodies. The music was completely natural. A large stage had been set up on the far side of the room with a few dozen musicians, and drums lined the walls. The feeling was exhilarating, but the whole experience was odd. No one was dancing with another person, yet none of them danced alone either.

Then the music changed, and suddenly everyone broke into partners. She found herself in the arms of a man whose skin was blue and who had eyes that sparkled like crystals. He smelled of sweet strawberries, and his voice was musical.

"You are the princess. Welcome."

Zwaantie giggled, more out of habit than anything else. The touching still bothered her, and this stranger had Zwaantie in what her mother would call an inappropriate embrace.

"Thank you."

He raised his eyebrows. "Have you ever been to a party like this before?"

She shook her head.

"Well then, let me explain how this works. This dance is called the Lovers' Chance. We change partners every time you hear a bell ring. In the old days, before the vipers got bad, this used to be the last song of the night. Whoever's arms you ended up in, that's who you went home with. Now they do it several times a night. It's fun and allows you to get to know a lot of people."

The bell rang then, and he spun Zwaantie away into the arms of a guy who didn't say much. He growled a couple times, and Zwaantie was grateful for the bell ringing again. This time she ended up with Ari.

Zwaantie smiled up at him, glad to be with someone familiar.

"Having fun?" he asked.

"Yeah. It's different."

She was very aware of Ari's hand on her hip, the way his eyes sparkled when he looked at her, and his gorgeous smile. She wondered what it'd be like to kiss this unreachable man. Would it mean anything? He'd already told Zwaantie he wouldn't commit to anyone. She'd be signing up for a one-night affair. Yet, still she wondered.

Then a long bell rang. Ari let her go and backed up. Sage came up to them smiling wickedly with a group of four girls who all looked identical. They had the palest of skin and bright black hair, red lips, and rainbow colored eyes.

"You two looked cute together. By the way, this is Lizzy, her illusion is so neat. I want to try it next time."

"What is it?" asked Ari.

"There are four Lizzys, but only one is real. All four will do the exact same thing at the exact same time. Watch."

Lizzy spun in a circle, and so did the rest.

Ari pulled Sage away and whispered something in her ear. She frowned and shook her head. Ari scowled. Zwaantie couldn't take her eyes off him.

"It's so nice to meet the famous princess," said the four Lizzys.

"Thank you."

"You know, I dated Leo once. He's a good sort. Do yourself a favor, though. Don't sleep with Ari."

Zwaantie immediately dropped her gaze. "I have no intention of sleeping with Ari, but why?"

"Because that was my mistake. One night with Ari, and Leo just didn't compare. Which was a shame because before that I was happy with him. And I wasn't the first girl to dump Leo after spending a night with Ari."

Poor Leo. Why would he leave her with Ari when that had happened to him? The music changed again. An extremely fast, extremely loud beat.

Behind her, Sage yelled. "Lizzy, what color is Zwaantie's glow?"

"Yellow."

"See," Sage said to Ari.

Ari shook his head and stomped away. Sage grabbed Zwaantie's and the real Lizzy's hands. "Come on, this is the girls' dance."

Something very strange happened when Sage grabbed Lizzy's hand. Sage multiplied into four, and so did Zwaantie by extension.

She didn't recognize herself. Nobody from Sol would recognize her, and she wondered if Leo would.

Most of the dancing that night was done in groups, but three times the Lovers' Chance played. Zwaantie danced with many different men. Most were polite and handsome. Some were a little scary, and some were overly friendly. Then there was Ari.

He danced with Zwaantie every chance he got. He rescued her a couple times from the overly friendly men. Most of the time he didn't talk, but he did hold her close, and she was very aware of the way his body felt against hers.

"Do you still love Phoenix?"

She hesitated. Phoenix had ripped her heart to shreds. Did she love him? "I don't know. It's very hard for me to connect the Phoenix I know now and the Phoenix I knew in Sol. To me they are hardly the same person. But then I've changed since I've come here. I'm not sure Phoenix and I would even be compatible anymore. There are things Stella's offered me that I won't give up even after Leo and I move back to Sol."

"Like what?"

"Like the clothes. And I'm bringing a beauty mage home with me."

He pulled Zwaantie closer so she was pressed against his body and his lips were right near her ear. They danced silently for a moment, and then the bell rang to signal a change of partners, but he didn't let her go. The music shifted at that point, slower, a ballad, and Ari sang quietly in her ear.

"You have a nice voice," Zwaantie said.

"Thank you. What does love feel like?"

Zwaantie pulled back and looked up at him. His eyebrows creased together in a look of concern. "I just want to know what it feels like."

"Why? I thought you were happy in all your lustful adventures."

He grimaced. "I can trust you, right?"

"Of course."

He pulled her close to him again and spoke low into her ear. "At first, it was about the sex and the fun. But for the last several years, I've been searching for the one person who I can be with forever. I'm tired of different girls. I want a best friend and a lover as one. But to me, they all feel the same. I'm attracted to them, sure, but I can't seem to care about them beyond that."

"I thought you never wanted to marry."

"I don't. I'd resent my wife forever if I did, but it doesn't mean I can't be with just one person. I want to know what love feels like."

"Why would you resent your wife?"

"Because then I'd have no choice but to remain faithful. At first I probably wouldn't care, but over time I'd resent her. Please. Tell me about love."

Zwaantie sighed. She was about to admit something to him that she hadn't even admitted to herself.

"I don't think I was ever in love with Phoenix. I mean, I thought I was, but I'm not sure it really was love. I think I was infatuated. Here, in Stella, I feel things so much more intensely. Phoenix seems like a dream. I'm not sure I ever really knew him. I think I was in love with the idea of him. Plus, I so desperately wanted to marry for love that I latched onto him, thinking he was the one. But now I'm not so sure."

Since Zwaantie had arrived in Stella, her emotions had taken such a beating. She hardly knew what she felt anymore. She couldn't imagine not fulfilling her duty and marrying Leo. She had to save that baby.

She also knew she liked the feel of Ari's arms around her, and once again, she was left confused.

Chapter Thirty-Four

THE OLD MOTHER

The bell rang, and Ari gave Zwaantie up to a man with horns growing out of his head. As the night wore on some people disappeared behind closed doors. Others lounged on couches and chairs that were spread out around the edge of the dance floor.

The illusions were starting to wear off. Zwaantie could see the tiger still had a tail, but his face was beginning to resemble a man. Sage danced with a blue man, and her wings were gone, and Zwaantie's body was fighting to stay awake. She spotted an open cushion and decided that maybe she'd go sit for a while, but Ari caught her arm.

"Last dance?"

Zwaantie smiled and nodded. The music was slow and soft. The incessant beating of the drums had stilled, leaving only several pianos playing a haunting melody. Ari pulled her close to his body, and his heart beat against hers. It struck Zwaantie again how odd it was to be so close to someone who weeks ago she would've considered naked, even though he was wearing pants.

Ari bent his head down to Zwaantie's ear and whispered. "Tell me a secret."

This again. Oh well, at least now she was prepared. "I don't want to go back to Sol. I want stay here. Forever."

He grinned. "Why don't you?"

"Because I have a country to run. I will be queen."

He was quiet for a few minutes.

"Your turn," Zwaantie said. "I want a secret from you."

This time he didn't lean down to whisper. He didn't have to. The music had faded to nearly nothing, and they were almost alone on the dance floor. He looked Zwaantie straight in the eyes, and she was startled by how bright they were.

"When people take Glow, they glow yellow. I asked Sage what color you were because I was having trouble believing it. She said you were yellow."

"That's not a secret."

Ari leaned closer so that his nose practically touched hers. "But I don't see yellow. For me, you glow pink."

He leaned down, and Zwaantie knew he was about to kiss her. She wanted this kiss, and yet she didn't.

"You're my soul mate," he breathed against her lips.

Zwaantie tightened her grip on him, knowing she was about to delve into something she shouldn't. Something forbidden.

Someone grabbed her shoulder and whipped her around. An old woman glowered at her. She had a weather-beaten face and wore an old tattered coat. Zwaantie squinted.

"Wilma?"

She cackled. "You never learn, do you girl?"

"Excuse me?"

Ari gripped Zwaantie's arm and pulled her close to him. "That's the Old Mother," he hissed.

"No. That's Wilma, the midwife in Sol."

Wilma closed the distance. Zwaantie looked around. No one else seemed to notice the intruder.

"You're both correct. Shame I'm bound by prophecy at the moment, or you'd be dead."

Wilma's eyes had taken on a cold glare. Zwaantie still wasn't sure what was going on.

"I...I don't understand."

Wilma gave her a sugary smile. "Tell me, how do you feel about Prince Leo?"

"We're in love. Everyone knows that."

"Don't lie to me, girl." Wilma took a step toward her. "The vipers attacking people. All your fault. They know you don't really love the prince and that your marriage will be a sham. Not a true union. The wedding will change nothing if you don't love him."

Zwaantie felt as if a fist had slammed into her chest. The deaths. Her fault. How was this possible?

"A prophecy," Ari whispered in a low voice. "Do you have one?"

She turned her glare on Ari. "Ever the meddlesome one, aren't you? The union between Stella and Sol must be unshakable. Right now, it is weak. The vipers are warming up. They are restless, and they know their time is coming. They are ready to take the child prince and unleash their wrath against the people of Stella. As long as they sense the weak union, they will become bolder. You're failing, princess."

Without warning, she disappeared.

Zwaantie stood frozen to the spot.

She'd been willing to sacrifice her happiness. Her shot at true love. Her freedom for the people of Stella. But now destiny demanded more.

It demanded her heart.

The End

~

THE NEW PROPHECY PROMISES MORE DEATH...

And Zwaantie is sick of it.

Every choice has been taken away from her. In the depths of her despair she finds the one thing she never expected.

Love.

She must once again decide if she's going to step up and do the right thing or follow her heart.

Deceit, love, and betrayal will take you on an emotional ride through this exciting third installment of Stella and Sol.

Thank you for reading!

KIMBERLY LOTH

KING
of the
STARS

THIRD BOOK IN THE STELLA AND SOL SERIES

Stella and Sol

King of the Stars
Volume 3
By Kimberly Loth

For A.J.
You've been with me since you lived among the stars. Return as
a king.

Chapter One

THE ATTACK

Lights shone above Zwaantie's head. The music started again in earnest. The room felt infinitely smaller than it had moments earlier when the Old Mother had told Zwaantie she was responsible for every death by viper.

Ari put his arm around her as they inched toward the doors. Ari—the boy who told her she was his soul mate. Her head spun. This was too much.

People swirled around them, all heading the same direction. No one shoved or pushed. Everyone was happy and giddy. Everyone except Zwaantie. Discs flashed in her direction, and she tried to keep a smile on her face. The room was too hot with the cooling potion in Zwaantie's veins having worn out. She felt lightheaded and nauseous, desperately wanting to escape everything around her.

An arm snaked through hers. Sage laid her head on Zwaantie's shoulder. Zwaantie didn't know what to do. Everything felt surreal.

Leo could come home now. There was no reason for him to continue the investigation. She pressed her hands against her stomach, fighting to keep down the bile.

He'd spent all that time searching for the reason why vipers were killing people, but Zwaantie was at fault. She didn't love Leo enough.

How did one force love? She couldn't magically change her feelings, though she wanted to.

"Come on, it's after six. We can go home and sleep in our beds," Sage said, tugging Zwaantie around a group of laughing Stellans.

At least Ari had been the only other one who heard she was murdering the people of Sol by not giving her love to Leo.

"Let's go home," Ari said. He put a hand on her back and led them both outside. They staggered out onto the street, and Zwaantie struggled to put one foot in front of the other, her heart heavy with guilt.

"Are we taking a carriage?" Zwaantie asked. She brought death to the people of Stella. The responsibility placed on her wasn't fair. She never asked for this. Her stomach rolled.

Sage shook her head. "We're close to the castle. We only took one last night to make an entrance." Sage handed her the cape Zwaantie had worn last night. "Here, put this on and put the hood up. We don't want Ticker pictures before we've had time to clean up."

Zwaantie did as she was told, grateful for Sage's foresight. Dealing with the heat was better than having to stop and deal with people.

Sage held Zwaantie's hand and led her along, so Zwaantie didn't have to think about where she needed to go. On the building in front of her, the Ticker played lots of pictures of her, Ari, and Sage arriving to the lock-in. Was that only a few hours ago? It felt like years.

They were stunning in their black and red outfits, but she was sure she appeared pretty rough now, not having slept. She stared at the current picture of her standing in the middle of Sage and Ari with a wide smile on her face. She tried to focus on herself, but all she could see was Ari.

When those pictures were taken, she bore no responsibility for the deaths of the people of Stella, and Ari hadn't yet proclaimed she was his soul mate. Things had been complicated before, when she had to worry about Phoenix and marrying a man she didn't love, but this was so much worse. She'd never have peace.

Zwaantie risked a glance to Sage's other side. The draw to him was almost overwhelming. Ari strolled along with his hands in his pockets. His face was serious, contemplative, and devastatingly handsome as usual. Zwaantie wanted to know what he was thinking. Surely he had an opinion about what she said.

The Old Mother. Wilma. Zwaantie's mind struggled to make sense of how those two could be the same woman. She'd worked alongside Wilma for years and even spent the night in her cottage a few times when a birth went too long. Next to Luna, this woman had been her best friend. Why would Wilma want her dead? The betrayal was too much. Could Zwaantie have misunderstood? Maybe Wilma was under the influence of the Voice as well.

There were too many unanswered questions. Though they didn't really matter. Friendships were a luxury she couldn't worry about. What mattered was what Wilma said. The wedding wasn't enough. She had to *love* Leo. She didn't even know how to begin. He wasn't around enough for her to love. All those deaths were her responsibility, and if she didn't start loving him soon, more people would die. The wedding wouldn't change anything.

She let out a breath. The good news was that the only other person who knew was Ari. Thank Sol for small blessings. Zwaantie needed to talk to him about it. Maybe he could help her. But then the truth slammed into her. She couldn't talk to him. Not ever. Not since he'd told her she was his soul mate.

Her insides squirmed. Those words had touched her in ways she couldn't even understand, making her want Ari in a way she'd never wanted anyone. But she couldn't be with him. She had to learn to love Leo. Ari should've kept his mouth shut. It wasn't fair of him to put her in this position. She had to love Leo, and Ari would be a distraction.

The smart thing would be to forget the words and focus on Leo. It'd be much easier if he were here with her. There had to be a way to get him to return. The truth about her role in the viper deaths would be the easiest. But also, the hardest.

Leo knew she didn't love him, but how could she possibly call him up and say, "All those people who died. That was my fault. You need to come home so I can learn to love you." He'd probably send her back to Sol.

The crowd pressed in around them, but thankfully there were no screams about princesses and no discs were flashing. Zwaantie wanted to blend in for a bit and not worry about things. Once she got home, she was going to hide in Sage's room and take a nice long nap.

A woman leaned into her side and whispered, "Baby killer."

Zwaantie jerked her head around, but the woman was already gone. Had she imagined it, or did someone else know? This wasn't possible. No one could have heard. The Old Mother had talked to her and Ari alone. Doubt wiggled in. Perhaps someone was listening after all.

No, her mind was overthinking things, working too hard. She must've imagined it. That was what she was though, wasn't she? A baby killer.

Ari gave Sage a nod and dodged into a small alley with no people. Sage followed, dragging Zwaantie along. Zwaantie stumbled over her feet.

"We should stop and get pastries before we return," Ari said.

Sage clapped her hands. "Oh, yes. Let's go to the Little Kitten."

Zwaantie glanced away to avoid Ari's eyes, which had strayed to her. She'd never be able to meet them again. Maybe the castle wasn't so safe after all.

She wanted to go home, go to bed, and try to make sense of what happened. Alone. Because she couldn't tell anyone, and talking to Ari was out of the question.

"We are not going to a cat café. They always try to drink my coffee. How about the Minty Road?" Ari asked. Zwaantie's heart beat a little faster at the sound of his voice. This was absurd. She couldn't even listen to him talk without reacting. She spun around and tried to watch the pictures on the Ticker, which was worse because half of them had Ari in them. His shaggy brown hair and piercing gray eyes made her swoon.

"No way. That place reeks of bad dates. Please, can we go to the Little Kitten? I want to get pancake balls," Sage said.

"It's way out of the way. At least the Minty Road is on our way. Zwaantie, what do you want to do?"

"Hmm?" She'd been trying not to listen, but the sound of her name on his lips sent shivers down her spine. She didn't care what they did. She had monumental weights on her shoulders, and here they were arguing over where to eat. She longed for that kind of carelessness.

"Where do you want to eat?" Ari asked, his voice sweet. Oh Sol, he needed to leave the city.

KING OF THE STARS

No, leaving the city wouldn't be enough, he needed to leave the country.

"It doesn't matter. You two decide," Zwaantie answered, her eyes trained on the Ticker so she didn't have to look at him.

"Fine," Sage grumbled. "We'll go to the Minty Road."

They plunged into the people surging on the street, and Zwaantie welcomed the distraction. The street grew more crowded, and Zwaantie had to pay attention to where Sage was going. People jostled around her as shop doors opened. A particularly fat woman shoved in between them to get to the fruit market. Zwaantie had to let go of Sage's hand and then couldn't find her again.

Zwaantie shrugged and continued on her way, needing to think. A walk would do her good, and when she was done, she could find a carriage to bring her to the castle. At least now, she could think outside of Ari's influence.

All around her, buildings lit up. Bright greens and blues were common, but most colors were represented. Down an alley she spotted a shimmer like the one Leo brought her through on her first day in Stella—the one that turned into a forest in the middle of the city. She made a left and stepped into the shimmer, hoping to find another forest—a place where she could sit and enjoy peace and quiet.

A bright sun hung in the corner. Fields of tulips spread out as far as the eye could see. The scent was not quite the same as the fields at home. A small sign was perched on the edge of the field. "Field of Lovers. Step through for the memories."

This wasn't what she was hoping for, but she reveled in the sun. She wandered through the pink tulips first and caught a whiff of Phoenix. The field smelled of trees and grass. Memories of their time near the pond surged in her mind. Her heart ached knowing their relationship was over—had been a lie, really. Not real. At least Ari had given her someone else to pine over so the pain of Phoenix wasn't so fresh.

The flowers shifted from pink to yellow, and Phoenix's scent disappeared, only to be replaced by salt, sand, and coconut. Leo. She was supposed to love him, and every part of her wanted to. Except the part that longed for Ari. The fate of Stella rested on falling in love with Leo, but for some reason, she couldn't do it. Leo was comfortable. Warm. Friendly. He'd make a spectacular husband, but he didn't ignite her soul.

She told him about her love for Phoenix, and he was angry, but that would pass. Given enough time, she could learn to love him.

She wandered farther into the field and found herself among the red tulips. Ari. His scent overwhelmed her. Oranges and sandalwood. The almost kiss tickled at her lips. She remembered the way her body felt pressed against his. Desire like she'd never known filled her stomach. She nearly stopped walking. Was this love? Or lust? She had no idea. As long as he was around, she'd never be able to love Leo.

Without warning, she stumbled out of the illusion. The intense feelings of desire disappeared. Everything was dark. She waited a second for her eyes to adjust. When they did, she noticed she'd come out on the other side of the alley.

The darkness seemed oppressive somehow, and she was ready to go to the castle and sleep. Fear snuck into her chest because she had no idea where she was. She crept out to the main road and searched for a carriage, but could find none. She wandered a few more blocks, keeping her hood up and head down.

People still rushed around, the illusion still haunting her. She'd have passion with Ari, but she couldn't give up on Leo. Not now. Ari would lead her to the same choices she'd had with Phoenix. Honor or love. It always came down to those two choices but there had never been a real choice. Her mother had been right. Honor was more important.

She was done being a child, but she couldn't be an adult with either Ari or Sage around. Ari for obvious reasons, and Sage because she was reckless and irresponsible, even if she were Zwaantie's guard. Besides, where Sage went, Ari did too. If Zwaantie was to fulfill her duties, she would do those things her mother would do. She needed to act like a queen and learn how to love Leo. Maybe she'd even be able to prevent a few deaths.

Instantly, she felt better. Everything would work out because she was making the right choice.

The street cleared, and she found herself in what was undoubtedly the poor part of town. In Sol, it would've been the slave district. The houses were run-down, and the streets smelled of refuse. The lights were faded, and buildings crowded in oppressively. Thank goodness this part of town had yet to wake up because she feared what the people might do to her. She needed to find a carriage.

A hand gripped her elbow. A tall thin man with light skin held her. He wore a hood, and she couldn't see his face clearly, but a dagger glowed blue in his hand.

Before Zwaantie could get out a scream, he growled and thrust the knife straight at Zwaantie's heart.

Chapter Two

THE DEFEAT

Zwaantie dodged out of the way, the knife grazing her arm. She backed up, and the man pressed her against a wall. *Think.* She wasn't trained how to defend herself. Glimpses of Phoenix flashed before her eyes. But this wasn't Phoenix. She squinted at the face of her attacker.

He was slightly taller than she, with pale skin—a Solite. Probably one of those slaves. Was the Voice influencing him? If so, then he was programed not to stop until he succeeded. She wouldn't be able to reason with him or fight him off. He would fulfill his mission or die trying.

She frantically searched for help, but they were utterly alone. Stars. The one time she actually wanted people around, and they'd disappeared. She fought against his body, but he held her tight.

The man smiled, showing bright white teeth. For a second, Zwaantie pitied him. Then she shoved against him, but it did no good. He was too strong.

He raised his arm, the knife glinting in the eerie light. Zwaantie whipped her arm up into his, jarring her bones and leaving the tip dangerously close to her face. If he moved even an inch, she'd lose her eye.

His other arm pressed against her neck, and she struggled to breathe. There was no way out of this. She clawed at his arm, but it did no good.

She kicked him in the shin, and he backed away, clutching his leg. Zwaantie fell over, trying to catch her breath. She crawled away as fast as she could, knowing she wouldn't be able to stand. The man grabbed her foot, and with one swift movement, flipped her over. The victory in his eyes was clear. Zwaantie was about to die.

"Please, don't do this," she pleaded.

He raised the knife.

She flailed, not caring if the knife got her arm or anything else. She hit his face, and he grunted. His arm came down, and her shoulder screamed out in pain. The knife stuck out of her flesh. Zwaantie cried out and grappled at the handle. The man shoved the knife farther in and twisted.

She screamed. Pain she'd never before known filled her body. Stars flashed in her eyes, and she knew she was about to black out.

He twisted the knife again, and she yelped.

Footsteps pounded the pavement. The man jerked his head up, scrambled off her, and ran away. Tears flowed down her face, and relief flooded her stomach. She was saved.

"Whoa, don't move," Ari said, leaning over her. He'd saved her. She'd be okay.

"Thank you," she croaked. She'd never been happier to see him.

Sage knelt down next to her, her face full of worry.

"I'm so sorry. We lost you. Leo is going to kill me. What kind of guard am I, if people keep getting to you?" She patted at Zwaantie's body. "Are you okay?"

Zwaantie squeezed her eyes shut, grunting against the pain. "My shoulder."

Sage let out a squeak, and Zwaantie opened her eyes, but they swam with tears fogging her view. She was having trouble breathing. Ari placed his hand on her good shoulder. "I'm going to help you sit up."

Zwaantie nodded, and he gently lifted her up. She hissed at the pain.

After she was in a sitting position, Ari inspected the dagger, but didn't touch anything.

"A few inches lower and he'd have gotten your heart. I don't want to take it out yet though. A healer needs to do that. Sage, call a healer van." He gave Zwaantie an encouraging smile.

Sage took out her disc and said, "Healer van." Then she pocketed it and stared at the knife. "This is getting ridiculous."

"What? The attempts on my life?" Zwaantie's breath was uneven. She had trouble getting the words out. The pain was too much.

"Was it a Solite?" Sage asked.

"Yes," Zwaantie said, her teeth gritted.

"Leo needs to put someone on this." Sage creased her eyebrows and frowned. She continued to watch Zwaantie as if she was about to pass out at any moment, which was entirely possible.

"No. We promised we wouldn't tell him about the Voice. Please. He has enough to worry about. I don't want him to worry about this as well," Zwaantie said.

Ari grinned like he knew something Zwaantie didn't, and Zwaantie glanced between the both of them. She adjusted her position and yelped with the pain.

"Are you okay?" Ari asked, moving her face so she had to look directly at him.

"Yes," she said through shallow breaths.

"You know, Sage, you're the best. You could investigate without Leo even realizing it," Ari said.

"He'll figure it out. He's not stupid. We have to tell him. Besides, I can't go out and leave Zwaantie unguarded."

"I'll be okay," Zwaantie said, her head light. "I want this solved. If nothing else, you can get necklaces on all those slaves, and maybe they'll stop trying to kill me."

Sage chewed on her bottom lip. "What about protecting you?"

"I'll watch her," Ari said, holding her a little tighter.

"No. You won't. Sage, I'll be fine. I promise. Get to those other slaves and figure out how far the Voice has spread."

Sage stomped her feet. "Your safety comes first."

"Zwaantie needs someone to keep an eye on her, but you've cracked more cases than even Leo. In fact, I'm surprised he's handling the vipers on his own. Usually, that's the sort of case he'd send you out on," Ari said.

Sage shrugged and picked at her nails. "He did ask me. I said no."

"What? Why?" Ari asked, his eyes wide.

"The original case was only a viper spotting. They creep me out, so he went instead."

"Are you and Leo partners or something?" Zwaantie was having trouble putting all of this together. Sage was her guard, and Leo was investigating the vipers, but she didn't fully understand what it meant. No one ever gave her a straight answer when she asked, and Leo never told her exactly what his job entailed.

Right now though, her pain was close to causing her to black out. She squeezed her eyes shut and opened them again.

A carriage careened to a stop right in front of them, and two healers got out. Great, now she still wouldn't know what Sage and Leo did.

Ari stepped in front of Zwaantie before they could get to her. "Not a word of this reaches the Ticker, or we will throw both of you into the dungeon. Do you understand?"

Zwaantie let out a breath of relief. She wouldn't have thought to demand that.

"Of course, Prince Ari, now what is the problem?"

"The princess has been stabbed." Ari moved away, and the healer gasped at the knife sticking out of her shoulder.

They rushed Zwaantie inside the carriage. They were gentle, but she cried out in pain. She glanced at Sage and Ari, who were both watching her. She'd been ready to leave them behind, move on to more responsible friends so she could take her place as queen, but when she needed help the most, the two of them came to her rescue.

Chapter Three

THE MESS

Three hours later Zwaantie was in Sage's bed, her shoulder fixed up, with three cats curled next to her. The healer said her shoulder would be good as new in the morning, but she had to take it easy until then, which was no problem since she was exhausted from the lock-in. They napped for a couple of hours, Sage on Zwaantie's right and Ari on the left.

Zwaantie didn't have the heart to tell him to go away. Not after he rescued her, but they would have to talk about boundaries. Especially if Sage ran off to investigate the Voice and the slaves.

Her mind wandered to the attack. Why did the Voice want her dead? She'd never done anything that would warrant such an extreme response. She couldn't even reason with the Voice.

By now she should be used to the attempts on her life.

Zwaantie woke before either of them. Ari had his arm slung casually over her waist, his fingers brushing against the exposed skin between her shirt and skirt. She was scared to move. She wanted to cuddle into him and let those fingers wander. Stars, that'd feel nice.

No. She couldn't think this way. He was to be her brother-in-law.

He hadn't said a word yet about her being his soul mate, and he wasn't acting any different. To Zwaantie, those words changed everything. She was so aware of him. She had to tell him they couldn't hang out anymore. It would break his heart, but she didn't have time to be nice. Leo had to be her everything.

"Oi, Ari," yelled a voice from the wall. "What are you doing in bed with Zwaantie?"

Ari shot up, his hand sliding across her skin. Zwaantie gasped.

"Leo," he said, slowly removing his hand. His shoulders were a little too tense for him to be relaxed. Maybe his words had affected him more than he'd let on earlier. "How goes the investigation?"

"We're still no closer to figuring out how the vipers are killing people who are locked up tight. People in Deep Sky and the surrounding small islands are panicking. They are sleeping with machetes. So far, no one has been able to kill a viper. I want to come home, but I need to stay here."

Zwaantie should tell him everything. She sat up gingerly. Leo's pinched face projected on the wall.

Sage popped her head up "I've missed you, bro. We had a ball at the lock-in."

"I hope you're keeping her safe." A muscle in Leo's jaw flexed.

Sage rolled out of bed and plopped down on the couch in front of the screen. "You should've seen Zwaantie last night. Hot."

"I know, I saw the Ticker." He looked at her. "You were beautiful. I'm sorry I couldn't be there for it."

Sage proceeded to fill him in on the details of the party. Not only about Zwaantie but gossip about others as well. Leo listened, but his eyes kept flicking to Ari and Zwaantie, who were still on the bed. Zwaantie wanted to ignore the electricity flowing between them and get up, but her shoulder hurt too bad.

Ari's hand brushed her hair to her other shoulder, where Leo couldn't see it. He played with her hair, sending shivers down her spine and warmth into her belly. Her eyes fluttered shut, focusing on his touch. This was impossible.

Leo coughed, and her eyes flashed open. He wasn't watching her, but she had to stop this. She climbed down next to Sage, hoping Ari would sit on Sage's other side, but he followed and settled next to her, resting his arm behind her on the couch. He wasn't touching her, but she found it hard to breathe.

As soon as they got Leo off the wall, she'd be having words with

Ari. He'd heard the Old Mother as clearly as she had. He could not pursue her, no matter what some stupid potion said.

Ari's fingers brushed her arm and traced slow circles. Zwaantie closed her eyes, feeling guilty for enjoying the feel of his hand. He was so close to her. If Ari was trying to hide his feelings from Leo, he wasn't doing a very good job. Maybe he was trying to egg his brother on.

Zwaantie listened to Sage prattle on and tried to think of Leo.

Her fight with him still lingered. She had to tell him how much she wanted to marry him, and beg for his forgiveness. If his love waned for her as well, they'd be in more trouble. But Sage never stopped talking and never gave Zwaantie an opening to apologize.

"And then, this morning we lost Zwaantie." Sage cowered into Zwaantie as if that would lessen the blow.

Zwaantie understood now. Sage was trying to hide her attack in the middle of other events in the hopes it might not seem so bad. It didn't work.

"You what?" bellowed Leo.

"There were a lot of people. She disappeared." Sage shrunk even farther into Zwaantie, pushing her into Ari. His bare skin seared against hers. She leaned forward, away from the both of them, hoping Sage wouldn't bring up the Voice.

Leo turned his gaze to Ari. "What the dark happened?"

"Brother, you have no idea. We hit a crowd, and Sage let go of Zwaantie. She disappeared. I'm not sure what happened after that, but somehow she ended up in North Bode, and a creep tried to kill her."

Leo's eyes got wider still. "Kill her? You said she just disappeared." He glared at Sage. "You're better than this. I thought you were going to take care of her," he yelled.

Sage sat up taller. "Calm down. She's still alive, isn't she?"

"She's pale. What happened to her?"

"Got stabbed. People keep trying to kill her. You know this isn't the first time. She must have a price on her head. Sage is going to start investigating," Ari said.

Leo ran a hand over his face. "Is there more to it?"

"Nothing you don't already know, but they all have to be

connected. The slave that tried to strangle her and the vipers in her room."

"What makes you think the vipers in her room are connected to the other attempts?"

"Someone had to let them in. In the other viper attacks, the doors were locked, right?"

Leo nodded.

"What'd the attacker look like?" he asked.

"I don't know. I didn't get a good look at his face." It was a lie, but she didn't want him rounding up the slaves and sending them to Sol.

"Maybe I should come lead the investigation and give the vipers to someone else. I'm not making much progress anyway."

Zwaantie felt a twinge of guilt. If she told him the vipers were her fault, he could come back. But she couldn't bring herself to say anything. Coward.

"Don't be stupid, Leo," Sage said. "I can handle this. No one else knows the viper case better than you. I'm the best, and you know it."

He sighed. "Yeah, I do. Someone needs to protect Zwaantie though."

"I can still be her guard. I won't be out often."

"I can take care of her when Sage is gone," Ari said, pulling Zwaantie against him. She dropped her hand to balance herself, and grabbed his knee. He sucked in a breath.

"You're not a guard, Ari." Leo glared at both of them. He had to know something was going on. Except it wasn't. Not yet, anyway. Zwaantie couldn't let Ari take care of her when Leo wasn't around. It was too dangerous. She wiggled out of Ari's grip.

"I can still manage when Sage isn't around. Besides, you'll be back soon, right?"

"I don't know. Nothing with the vipers is adding up. Sage, I want you to let me know everything you find. Be very careful. This cannot end up on the Ticker. Things are bad enough for Zwaantie as it is."

They continued to chatter about the investigation, and Zwaantie leaned back and closed her eyes. Her shoulder ached, but she was still aware of Ari's arm slung across the couch once again. She tuned them out and thought about everything that had happened in the last twenty-four hours. She still didn't understand what Sage and Leo did, but anytime she asked for clarification, they deflected.

They didn't have an equivalent role in Sol. Major investigations like this were rare since the Voice controlled things so tightly. If small crimes were committed, the guards or the lower chancellors dealt with the criminals. Zwaantie had never even heard of a crime that wasn't solved within a day or two because of the Voice.

After a while, the conversation grew quiet, and Zwaantie opened her eyes. Leo smiled. Apparently he'd been watching her.

He flicked his eyes to Ari.

"So explain to me why you have your arm around my fiancée?" Leo asked with raised eyebrows.

Took him long enough to notice.

"I'm not treating her any differently than I do my other sisters. And as a good brother, I think I'll let you talk to her for a while." Ari turned to face Zwaantie, his gorgeous gray eyes boring into hers. "You'll be okay?"

Zwaantie nodded, grateful Ari was leaving. She couldn't think straight with him around.

"I'm going to shower. I'll be back in a little bit."

"Me too. You guys enjoy your alone time," Sage said with a wiggle of her eyebrows.

When Ari and Sage left, Leo brightened considerably. Zwaantie wanted to get this over with. She needed his forgiveness so they could move on.

"How was the lock-in?" he asked.

Zwaantie smiled. "It was wonderful and magical. I've never seen so many illusions. The potions were amusing."

The conversation was light and fake. Neither one spoke of her betrayal or about how someone was trying to kill her. Instead, he told her about the things they would see after they were married and how they would travel to the other kingdoms so she could meet the people.

When the conversation died, she took a deep breath and plowed forward.

"I met Lizzy last night." The lock-in seemed so long ago, but if she didn't bring this up now, she'd never be able to ask.

His face went pale. "Oh, did you like her?"

"She was nice, but she said something that bothered me."

He rubbed his face but didn't say anything. It was time to be blunt and put him out of his misery. If she didn't attack this head-on, Ari was going to be the death of her. Leo had to know. Good relationships were built on honesty and trust.

"We are going to be married, right?" Zwaantie asked.

"I hope so," he replied.

"We've already established I'm not here because I love you, but I need to apologize for what happened with Phoenix. I betrayed you. I can only hope you will someday forgive me, because I intend to make the best of this situation. Can you find it in your heart to forgive me? Start over fresh?"

He rubbed his chin and stared hard at Zwaantie for a few moments. She met his gaze and allowed him time to think, time to consider her. She needed his answer to be yes. If he were angry with her, it would make it harder for her to love him.

Eventually he dropped his hand into his lap and looked over her shoulder instead of in her eyes. It saddened her a little that he couldn't meet her gaze.

"You know, you captured my heart the moment I laid eyes on you. I'm still so hurt. I only ever wanted your love."

Zwaantie's heart broke. She had not been fair to him. She shifted and brought her knees up onto the couch so she was sitting on her legs. She leaned forward and studied him for a second.

"I'm sorry. I'll make more of an effort. I didn't mean to hurt you."

"Thank you."

She steeled herself. Now she would tell him the truth. "If you love me that much, why in the sun's name did you leave me with Ari? Lizzy told me she left you after he got his hands on her, and she wasn't the first one. I hate to be so bold, but if we are going to be married, then I need to understand these things."

He laughed, and she sat back, surprised.

"You are so much more than a pretty face, aren't you?"

Zwaantie crossed her arms and glared at him. This wasn't going at all like she planned. He gave her a crooked grin that would have sent her swooning if she wasn't thinking of Ari.

"Ari and I have a great relationship and certain understandings where girls are concerned. But that is besides the point. I didn't leave you with Ari, I left you with Sage. Not only do I trust her as your guard, but she is the best person to introduce you to Stella. She is never far from Ari's side. As far as Lizzy and those other girls are concerned, Ari simply took them off my hands with my blessing and encouragement when I got tired of them. I'm not too prideful to admit that I'm horrible at breaking up with girls. I trust Ari, and I thought I could trust you too."

"Then why did you yell at him for having his arm around me?"

He chuckled. "Because he's my brother, and I want to make sure he doesn't forget you are mine."

She wondered how he would respond if he knew what Ari confessed to her last night. That, according to some magic potion, she was his soul mate. Or how she felt about it. Not that she really understood how she felt about it. She wanted Ari, in spite of everything. No, she would not be telling Leo about that.

"Can you forgive me? Please?" She couldn't think of anything else to say. Leo probably thought she was asking for forgiveness for her sins with Phoenix, but really, she was asking for her feelings over Ari.

He stared hard at her. "I can. Under one condition."

She let out a breath of relief. "Anything."

"Will you promise me you'll do your best to learn to love me? I can't imagine spending my life with someone who will never love me."

"Of course. That's not even a question. I promise." She had to. The Old Mother had made that clear. She should just tell Leo about Ari. It would make everything easier, but the words would not come out.

A knock sounded on his door, and he yelled, "Come in."

Candace walked in, baby in arms. She gave Zwaantie a glare. "Oh, it's you."

"Candace, be nice," Leo said.

She plopped on the couch next to Leo. "Why should I? Everyone knows it's her fault Castor is dead."

"What's that supposed to mean?" Zwaantie asked, terrified of what people might know.

"Candace, stop. Zwaantie, she doesn't mean it. She's just upset."

"It's true. None of the deaths started until she showed up. People are talking, and you know it. It's time she learned it as well."

Leo shook his head. "Don't listen to her. This isn't your fault. We're going to go. I'll find out the real cause, and then Candace will owe you an apology." Candace snorted. "We'll talk tomorrow. I love you."

He turned off the screen before she had a chance to answer. She expected he didn't want to hear the silence when she didn't return his love. Because she wasn't about to lie to him.

She might be a coward, but she wasn't a liar.

Chapter Four

THE PLAN

"We're going to eat lunch in Ari's rooms and figure out how to run the investigation," Sage said.

Zwaantie nodded, her heart still heavy with Candace's words. She'd just stepped out of the shower and dressed. She didn't particularly want to hang out with Ari, but he was one of the few who knew what was going on. He had to be involved.

Sage didn't bother knocking and led Zwaantie into Ari's bedroom. She followed Sage past the bed and down a small hall into a dining room. She'd never been down here before. Her own suite had several rooms as well, but she usually only spent time in her bedroom—when she was there anyway. Most of time Sage's room was better.

She froze in the doorway. Phoenix sat next to Ari, flanked by two guards. Zwaantie hadn't seen him since he admitted he didn't love her. What was Sage up to?

Zwaantie gave him a weak smile and sat on the other side of the table, as far from him as she could without being obvious. She noted the necklace. As long as he had it on, she was safe.

Waiters brought in salad, sandwiches, and cut fruit.

"What's the plan?" Zwaantie asked. She wanted to ask what Phoenix was doing there but figured this was a safer way to start the conversation. She took a small bite of the sandwich.

Ari put his fingers to his lips. "We'll talk later." He waved his hand at the waiters.

Zwaantie stabbed at her wilted and soggy salad. She couldn't wait until she could go home and eat good food.

As soon as the waiters left, Sage shut the door and locked it. She waved her hand over the door and something shimmered.

"What'd you do?" Zwaantie asked.

"Made the door impenetrable. No one will be able to hear what we're up to."

"You've never been concerned with our privacy before."

Sage snorted. "No, you just never noticed. I put non-listening spells around us all the time. Sometimes even un-seeing ones. How do you think we get around Stella without being mobbed?"

Zwaantie was taken aback. She'd never realized they'd put spells on her. What else had they done without her knowledge? A lot probably.

She was about to ask, but Sage kept talking.

"I've invited Phoenix here because I think he can help me."

Zwaantie wasn't sure this was the best idea considering he'd tried to kill her multiple times. She still wasn't convinced the guards could stop him.

"With what?" Phoenix asked, his brow furrowed, but a small smile on his lips.

"You're not the only one who has tried to kill Zwaantie."

His eyes flicked in Zwaantie's direction. "What do you mean?"

"I was stabbed in an alleyway this morning." Her shoulder had mostly healed, but it still ached.

Pain flashed behind his eyes. "I'm so sorry. You look okay."

"Sage and Ari rescued me before the attacker succeeded. He was another slave."

"You think it's the Voice?" Phoenix pointed to his head.

"I don't know what else it would be."

"Good thing Solites can't really cross the wall without permission from the Voice," Phoenix said and popped a grape into his mouth before grimacing. Zwaantie smiled. At least she wasn't the only one who missed their food.

"Except we have fifty of them running around already," Sage said.

"So what do you want to do? Send them back?" Phoenix asked with a sneer.

Sage shook her head. "No, I want to disarm them."

Phoenix creased his eyebrows. "How?"

"By putting necklaces on them like you have and requiring them to check in with a guard once a week to make sure they don't take it off."

"We could make it unremoveable," Ari said, drawing Zwaantie's eyes. She'd been avoiding looking at him. He leaned back lazily in his chair, his dark hair hanging in his eyes. He smiled when he caught her smiling.

"We could," Sage said.

Phoenix shook his head. "That'd be like the bondage bands in Sol, and it's not fair to them."

"But it's not the same thing. We'll be protecting them from the Voice," Sage argued.

"It still takes away their free will."

Sage looked over at Zwaantie. "Up to you. Your life is the one on the line."

"Phoenix is right. They still deserve their free will. We can't take it from them. Having them check in with a guard should be good enough." At least she hoped so, but she wasn't about to do something to them that would be reminiscent of the horror in Sol. When she became queen, one of her first acts would be to do away with the slave system.

"Okay, then. Phoenix, I'd like you to come with me," Sage said.

"Why?"

"Because they won't trust me. They know you. They'll listen to you. If you can explain to them what you've already gone through, they'll be more likely to listen to us."

"They won't do this willingly. You're going to have to wrestle the necklace on them. The Voice will be telling them how evil and wicked it is. They might even try to kill us for trying."

"I'll do what I did to you."

"Which was?"

"Immobilized him," Sage said matter-of-factly.

"With magic?" Zwaantie asked in a soft voice, suddenly unsure of Sage.

"Yep."

"Can anyone do that?"

"Not really. It's hard to force someone else to do something with magic, but it's one of my specialties. Ari can't do it."

"And this has to do with your job?" The wheels turned in Zwaantie's head. If she could learn how to do magic, then she'd be able to protect herself and stop being a burden on those around her.

"Yes."

"When will I learn magic?" Zwaantie asked. This would fix everything, and then she would no longer need a guard.

"Stars, you haven't been tested yet, have you? Ari, you should bring her to the jobs master to get tested while Phoenix and I take care of the slaves."

"Sounds like a great plan," Ari said with a wicked grin.

Zwaantie wasn't sure how she felt about spending more time with Ari, but she wanted to learn magic. Though maybe she should focus on the current goings-on instead.

"We need to leave. The sooner those slaves are disarmed, the better I'll sleep at night," Sage said.

"Are you going to use your un-seeable spell?" Zwaantie asked.

Sage shook her head. "We need them to see us."

She snapped her fingers. Her hair turned brown, a few wrinkles appeared on her face, and her clothes were those of the lower class. Then she snapped her fingers again, and Phoenix was balding.

Zwaantie couldn't help but grin. "That's incredible."

"Thanks, I'm pretty awesome at disguises. Time's a-wasting. Oh wait."

She handed Zwaantie a necklace. "Can you get this to Luna? She'll need one as well."

"Sure." Zwaantie gripped the necklace. Luna was difficult to find as she was always out with Viggo and his crew. Zwaantie only really saw her on the Ticker these days.

Sage spun and disappeared out the door. Phoenix followed her without a backwards glance, his guards trailing. She should be relieved, but she was sad to see the love missing from his eyes. Why, she wasn't sure. She no longer loved him.

Zwaantie slowly became aware she was alone with Ari. She set down her napkin, trying to ignore the tension in the room. Ari drank from his glass, letting his gaze fall on her.

"We should go," she said, needing to be in public and away from those eyes that made her stomach buzz.

"There's no rush," he said with a lazy grin. "We could hang out here, talk for a bit."

"You know that would be a bad idea."

"Why?"

She met his eyes. The electricity between them was undeniable and thick in the air now. One touch and she'd lose it. Him too, from the smolder in his eyes. At least he was several seats away from her.

Zwaantie stood. "Because, I'm engaged to your brother, and I have to love him. Are you going to take me to get my magic tested or not?"

He frowned, but nodded.

She swept from the room and was nearly to the main hallway before he caught up with her. If he'd stopped her while they were alone in his room, they wouldn't be walking out of the castle. Her fingers itched to touch his.

Ari flagged down a carriage and held the door open. He climbed up behind her, closer than he should have, and brushed her hair away from her neck, his fingers sending a shiver down her spine.

He leaned forward and whispered in her ear. "You are so beautiful."

She deliberately sat across from him. The last time she took this journey with Sage, it had taken about ten minutes. She stared out the window at the people scurrying by.

She could feel his eyes on her, but she didn't dare look at him. His foot brushed against hers, and she gasped, drawing her gaze away from the window. Ari took off his sandals and stretched his legs out, running his toes along her foot and calf. A thrill buzzed through her, but she jerked her legs away.

He chuckled. She would not give him the satisfaction of commenting on his forwardness. Instead, she scooted closer to the window to avoid eye contact and continued her study of the people outside. Not that she saw them. Not really. Not with his eyes on her.

Time moved excruciatingly slow. When she was certain they were close, she finally dared look at him, and sparks flew between them. She ignored the desire in her belly.

"Why are you staring at me?" Zwaantie asked.

"You look different now, and I'm trying to figure out what it is."

"Different how?"

"I'm used to wanting beautiful girls. But when I look at you, I want more. Everything about you calls to me, from the light in your eyes, the curve of your breasts, the way you say my name, the small gasp you give off every time our skin touches. So I seek to understand what it is you do to me, because before the lock-in, I saw only a beautiful girl, and now I see more, which is torturous because you will never be mine."

She stopped breathing. She had no words to respond.

The carriage came to an abrupt stop, and she scrambled out, sucking in the fresh air. Ari's words hung in her ear as they walked into the same building she and Sage had visited before. Why did Ari have to make this so difficult?

They entered a different room. On the door hung a sign that said "Testing."

The room was bright yellow and orange with toys strung out everywhere. Kids squealed and ran around. Most couldn't have been older than three or four.

"Why do I feel so out of place?" she asked Ari, who stood a few feet from her.

Ari chuckled. "Because usually children are tested at a young age. It won't be bad. Promise."

"Right."

She followed Ari through the maze of toys and screaming children. He approached the desk on the far end. A woman looked up and beamed.

"Prince Ari, what brings you here? I wasn't aware you had any children." Her fingers crept closer to the disc that lay on the desk. Oh yeah, she wanted to send that out to the Ticker right away.

Ari reached for Zwaantie, his hand grabbing hers. She gasped before she could help herself.

"I don't. You know Zwaantie."

The woman fanned her face. "Of course. Princess, it's so nice to meet you."

"You too." Zwaantie gave her a smile.

"Zwaantie needs to be tested for magic. They don't have magic in Sol."

The woman glanced down. "I'll move you to the front of the line. It should only be a few minutes."

Zwaantie withdrew her hand from Ari's, and they sat in the bright blue chairs not far from the front desk. Ari casually slung his arm on the back of her chair. She sat forward so she didn't have to feel it. He had said he could never have her, but he kept acting like he could.

"You can relax. There's nothing to be scared of," he said.

"I'm not scared of the testing."

"Then what's wrong?"

"You."

He laughed. "I'm not going to bite. Unless you want me to."

She crossed her arms and swiveled in her seat so she was facing him. "Really? How can you joke about this? You can't say things like you did and expect everything to be comfortable."

He leaned forward, too close for her comfort, and dropped his voice low. "I didn't know I'd made such an impression, princess. Besides, I don't want things to be comfortable."

She sucked in a breath. She wasn't expecting him to be so bold. She should back away, but she didn't want to. He was so close.

"Zwaantie," someone called. She jerked away from Ari and saw an old woman with silver hair standing a few feet away.

Zwaantie stood and followed her. Ari did not come with, thank the stars. She needed to put distance between them and that unbelievable electricity.

She entered a small room. "What do I have to do?" Zwaantie asked.

The woman chuckled. "You don't have to do anything. Just sit there and let me check you out."

The woman took Zwaantie's hands in hers and closed her eyes. After what seemed like ages, the woman opened her eyes and clucked.

"Well?" Zwaantie asked.

"No magic. Most of the slaves from Sol were the same way."

"So I can't do anything like everyone else can?"

"I'm afraid not. But don't worry. I won't say anything. You can function quite well without it. Potions and magical devices will work for you, so you can adapt. No one has to know."

Zwaantie tried to hide the disappointment. She'd been looking forward to learning, but now she would be incapable of any magic. She trudged out of the room and found Ari playing catch with a little boy.

He jerked his head up when she approached. "Well?"

"Nothing."

He furrowed his brow. "At all?" He handed the boy the ball and grabbed her hand, and her stomach buzzed. She needed to get far, far away from him. "I'm sorry. It's not the end of the world. Luckily for you, we all do magic, so you can still enjoy the benefits."

The tension from earlier was gone. Zwaantie wasn't sure what to make of their feelings. They needed to talk about how to handle being in the same room together without their feelings getting in the way, but right now, she didn't want to deal with it.

The carriage wasn't waiting for them when they got out on the street, and Ari did something with his disc. "They'll be here soon."

Zwaantie watched the Ticker as they waited. Most of the stories had nothing to do with the royal family, and the pictures were things she'd never seen before. The stories were almost mean.

"Hey, Ari, what's wrong with the Ticker?"

He glanced up and rolled his eyes. "There is more than one Ticker. That one isn't used by most people, and it's full of conspiracy theories. I'm surprised to see it up on a building. The owner must be a fan. Honestly, I haven't seen that one in years."

"How many Tickers are there?"

"Four or five big ones. An infinite number of smaller ones. A lot of groups have their own so they can keep up with their families. We never saw the need to create one for our family since the main Ticker is almost always about us."

The carriage pulled up, and Zwaantie glanced up at the Ticker once more. A story at the top caught her attention. "The princess: Stella's savior or baby killer?"

Before she could alert Ari, the words disappeared.

Chapter Five

THE PROBLEM

A ri planted a light kiss on his mother's cheek. She sat tall in
her chair with Ari to her left. It was only the two of them for
lunch. His mother preferred it that way. He had very few
people he trusted, and his mother was his closest confidant.

Sage was a close second, but he didn't always tell her everything
because she worried too much. His mother, he told her everything
because he'd long since stopped caring if she worried.

"I haven't seen you much in the past couple of weeks," she said.

"I know. I've been out with Sage—"

"Please don't talk about that abominable girl."

He grinned. One of his favorite things to do was to see how many
insults she could toss out about Sage. It wasn't very productive, but it
was entertaining. He still didn't know if his mother really disliked
Sage or if she just said things to make him laugh. Either way, Sage
couldn't handle her insults, so she never came with him when he
spent time with his mother.

"You know she's my best friend."

Astrid brought her hand to her chest. "I thought I was your best
friend."

"You're my mother. You can't be. Unless you want to start partying
with me. The Ticker would have a field day with that."

She laughed. "Oh yes, I could just see it. Queen teaches all the youth how to do potions."

"Father would have a fit."

"That he would. Speaking of the Ticker. Tell me about the lock-in."

"It was fun." Ari fiddled with his fork. He wanted to talk to his mother about Zwaantie, but he didn't know how she would react. He knew he had to stop thinking about her, but she consumed him. He'd been a little too bold with her on the way to see the jobs master, and he was afraid he'd pushed her away. Which he should do, but he wanted her more than he fully understood.

"You can give your poor mother more. Tell me about it."

"There's not much to tell. We danced."

She pursed her lips. "Fine. Who'd you dance with?"

"A lot of girls."

"Any of them glowing?" Astrid's eyes sparkled.

He groaned. He shouldn't have told her about the potion.

"All of them."

"Anyone who strikes your fancy?" she asked. Ari squirmed, and her face lit up. "Tell me about her. I've never seen you like this. You're blushing. She must've really made an impression. When can I meet her?"

Ari ran his hand through his hair. "You know, Xandria failed to tell me Soul Mate actually made them glow pink. She just said glow."

Astrid gasped. "You mean you found her?"

Ari nodded, but didn't elaborate. This wasn't the way he imagined finding his true love.

"Out with it. Who's the lucky gal that's going to make an honest man out of you?"

He snorted. Even if he would consider marrying her, she'd never agree. She was promised to his brother. He couldn't ask her to abandoned Leo. Not after what the Old Mother said. Fate had a twisted sense of humor. Some would say he deserved it. Not that he would ever marry anyone. He'd been dead set against it before, but that stupid funhouse room had confirmed it. Marriage was out of the question.

"It's complicated."

"All the best love stories are. Who is she?"

He met his mother's eyes. He needed to see her reaction. "Zwaantie."

He mother began cackling. He'd hoped for a shocked gasp, but not laughing. He should leave.

"Thanks. Love you too."

She wiped her eyes. "I'm sorry. It's so ironic. She's beautiful and a crown princess. How are you going to steal her away from your brother?"

"I'm not."

Astrid leaned forward, her laughter gone. "Of course you are. Zwaantie is your best chance for happiness. You need to take it. Besides, have you thought about the power?"

"What are you talking about?"

"She'll be the queen of Sol. You'll be the king of Stella—the entire world."

He let out a sigh. "I don't want her kingdom, Mother. I just want her." It said a lot about the power she had over him that he hadn't considered what it would mean if they married.

"Does she know?" Astrid asked.

"Yes."

"And?"

"She told me to stay away from her." He should listen to Zwaantie, but nearly every thought he had was about her. She was lucky he hadn't ended up in her room overnight.

"Are you saying she doesn't feel the same way?"

"I honestly don't know how she feels. After I told her she was my soul mate, the Old Mother showed up and said if she didn't start loving Leo, the vipers were going to kill everyone. Marriage isn't enough."

"You tell the Old Mother to go off herself. What does she know? This is true love. Not many people get this opportunity. You shouldn't waste it."

"So I should just let the people of Stella die?"

Astrid rolled her eyes. "No. She's not always right. Zwaantie could fall in love with Leo, and people could still die. This could be a giant coincidence."

Ari clenched his fists. "You're telling me to risk the entire kingdom for one girl?"

"No, I'm telling you to go after your one shot at true happiness. Not many people get this chance. You should take it. But for goodness sakes, Ari, marry the poor girl."

This was the one thing they never talked about. The curse. They'd mended their relationship years ago and left this unsaid. They had to. Otherwise, he'd never speak to her.

He wanted to follow his mother's advice. Every fiber of his being did. Zwaantie made his blood sing. Even before the potion told him she was his soul mate, he'd been attracted to her. He thought it was because she was untouchable, but the closer he got to her, the more he liked her. She was interesting in a way most of the girls he knew were not. The potion heightened everything that was there.

"Mom, I can't."

Astrid sighed. "Fine, I'll drop it for now. Tell me about her though. I haven't had the privilege of spending any time with her.

"Please don't. She needs to marry Leo. That's important. We should stop talking about her."

"I didn't say anything about her upcoming marriage. I want you to tell me about her."

"You already know she's beautiful. She's quiet, but funny. She laughs at me and is always getting into mishaps, so I'm constantly having to rescue her, and yet, she holds herself like a queen. She loves fiercely and is incredibly loyal. Don't ever say anything bad about Sage in her presence. They're very close."

"Noted. I'm not allowed to say anything about the whore."

He frowned at her. "Mom, that was neither funny nor true."

"Says you. Have you kissed Zwaantie?"

"No." His mother should stop putting ideas in his head.

"You should."

"How will that be helpful?"

"It won't be, but it will make you happy."

"When are you going to stop worrying about my happiness? I'm fine."

She dropped her eyes, suddenly serious. "I just... Never mind."

He reached across and gripped her hand. "What?"

She jerked her hand out of his and gave a forced smile. "Regret. That's all. I want you to have your heart's desire." Before he could respond, she shook her head. "Whew, it almost got serious there, didn't it? Come, let's go take a walk in the garden."

Ari followed her out of the room, regret in his heart. He'd never have Zwaantie. She belonged to Leo. This wasn't fair.

Chapter Six

THE EGGS

Zwaantie slept in her own bed for the first time since she'd started sleeping with Sage. They'd cleared out the vipers days ago, and she'd made sure her door was locked tight. Sage had been staying out late, and Zwaantie wanted to be alone and reflect on what had happened. She hadn't seen Ari since they returned from the magic testing, which was good. Maybe she could simply avoid him until Leo returned. She'd tried to find Luna and give her the necklace, but she was nowhere to be found.

The next morning the cows mooed softly on her wall as she perused her closet. She put on a long, but lightweight, silver skirt and a bright red sleeveless shirt that was tight when she slid it over her head, but when she looked in the mirror, it was nice.

She twisted her hair up and glossed her lips. She thought of the conversations with Leo and Ari. She'd been agonizing over the possibilities, but really, there was only one choice.

Today she would choose honor. She would forget about Ari and the way he made her feel. There was too much at stake for her to do anything else. She would do whatever it took to learn to love Leo and take her place as the queen of Sol.

Her door flew open, and Sage bounded in and whistled. "Classy and hot. Come, we're going to the gamehouse."

Zwaantie held her hands behind her back. "Not today. I don't have time to play anymore. I need to start making plans for after the wedding. I'm sorry." This would make sure she avoided Ari as well, because she was fairly certain Sage's invitation involved Ari.

Sage's face fell. "Well, what are you going to do? I'm supposed to guard you, remember?"

"Probably find the king and queen and ask them for advice on diplomatic matters. I'll be fine without you." Her words were harsh, but she had to get rid of Sage. Being with her was too easy.

Sage screwed up her face. "Sounds boring. That shouldn't take too long. We can go out after lunch."

Zwaantie took a few steps back from Sage. She stood tall, like she'd seen her mother do and kept her arms stiff at her side. "No. Sage. You understand. I'm not going to be playing anymore. I don't have time for such frivolities." She hated to do this to Sage, but she didn't have any other options.

"I have to protect you."

"I know. But as long as I stay in the castle, I'm fine. If I leave, I'm sure I can find a castle guard to protect me. It's time for me to get to work."

Sage twisted her lips. "Fine. I'll be around if you want a break." She turned and trudged out the door, her shoulders slumped. Zwaantie felt bad for hurting her feelings, but she had to do the right thing, and Sage and Ari were not a part of that.

Zwaantie still got lost in the castle, but hoped she could at least find the king's office. She stopped at Luna's room first, but of course she was out. Zwaantie wondered if she'd been there at all. She thought about simply leaving the necklace for her, but figured Luna would have to be coerced to wear it. She didn't seem to like Zwaantie's company much anymore.

The halls were quiet. She found a stairwell and tried to remember. Up or down? She went down one flight and got lost in the maze. Eventually she'd find a servant who could direct her, but for a castle, there were very few servants. A door to her right opened, and Ari stepped out. She stopped abruptly, her breath catching.

"What are you doing here?" she asked, trying to not get lost in his eyes. This was what she was avoiding, not Sage. She wasn't sure why she didn't tell Sage, though Sage would probably tell her to kiss him and move on. Zwaantie didn't think there was any moving on from Ari. He'd grab hold of her heart and never let go.

He gave her a grin. "Just visiting the library. I'm glad I ran into you. Sage wants to go to the gamehouse today. You haven't been there. It should be fun."

Zwaantie let out a breath. "No, I'm sorry. I'm going to stay here and visit with the king and queen. Playtime is over."

"Father and Mother are out today. What were you planning on doing?"

She dropped her eyes so she didn't have to look at him. "I don't know, but it's time for me to stop playing and start stepping up. In a few short weeks, I'm going to be queen. It's time I owned that."

Ari scratched his head. "Well, I can help you. I'm going to be king." He held out his arm. "Come, let me show you all the boring and diplomatic parts of Stella."

Zwaantie squeezed her eyes shut. She had to be rude and blunt, or he'd never get the hint. "Ari, I'm sorry. I can't hang out with you."

He dropped his arm, and his face fell. "Why not?"

Zwaantie wrung her hands. "Because my feelings are all mixed up. I can't have you around. It's imperative I fall in love with Leo. You know this. I'm sorry."

She raised her head and met his eyes. He closed the distance between them, and she thought for a moment he was going to kiss her. His chest rose and fell, and he ran a light finger down her cheek. She wanted him to press his lips against hers, and she hated herself for wanting it. Instead, he dropped a kiss on her forehead and walked away without a word.

She almost went into the library, thinking maybe she could read up on Stellan history. Running into Ari made her confused. She needed to focus on Leo. How did one go about loving someone they didn't? Maybe she could learn more about him.

The problem was the person who probably knew him best was Candace, and she was on a different island and not really speaking to Zwaantie at the moment.

Zwaantie continued her walk and went down another flight of stairs. She turned right, but saw Lyra and another mage talking at the end of the hall, and she swiveled around and headed the other direction. She did not want to speak to that woman ever again.

Smells of baking bread floated out through a door. She entered the enormous kitchen with shiny metal boxes everywhere. She'd rarely gone into the one at her own castle, but it had pale wooden tables, the occasional live chicken, and it was thick with smoke. Stella's castle kitchen was clean and slick.

Zwaantie took a tentative step forward. People were milling about. Some were cooking, but most were chatting. A tall man with a very sharp face looked up. His mouth split into a grin.

"Princess. How can we help you?"

She spotted a bowl of brown eggs and remembered how Leo had told her his mother used to make him colored eggs. Perhaps she could learn how to make eggs for him.

"I've never cooked before. I'd like to learn how to make eggs."

The man held out his hand. "I'm Atlas, and I can certainly teach you how to do eggs."

He spent a good hour showing her how to make every kind of egg. From fried, to poached, to scrambled. She didn't touch anything, but he was good at explaining things.

"Leo told me his mother used to make colored eggs. Can you?"

"Of course." He held his hand over the plate of eggs, and they turned green, purple, and blue.

Zwaantie clapped her hands. "Can you show me how?"

"Have you learned how to do any magic?"

She shook her head. "I was tested, and I have none."

Atlas gave a small frown. "Then there is no way. I'm sorry."

"Is there a potion or something?"

"You know, there might be. Why don't you see if you can scramble a couple more eggs. I'll see if I can find colored potions."

He left her, and she stared at the eggs. She picked up an egg and cracked it into a metal bowl. Then she added two more. So far, so good. She mixed the eggs with a metal whisk. They didn't get as fluffy as they had when Atlas had done them, but they looked good enough. She added some milk, probably too much. She stirred the mixture, but the eggs were way too white. Oh well, they should still work.

She poured the mix into a pan and twisted the knob she'd seen

Atlas turn. A flame burst out, and she turned it all the way up. Atlas had waited at least a minute before he stirred anything in the pan. The disc in her pocket vibrated. She jumped. She pulled it out and pressed the blinking green light. Leo's face popped out.

"Whatcha doing?" he asked.

She grinned. "Trying to learn how to make eggs. Look." She tilted the disc so Leo's head was staring at the eggs.

"I think you need to stir those."

"Oh yeah." She set the disc down and ran a spoon over the eggs. Nothing changed. It was still soup.

"Why are you trying to learn how to make eggs?" Leo asked as Zwaantie continued to stir. The pan smelled funny, and the eggs didn't look like Atlas's.

"I wanted to surprise you. You said your mom used to make colored eggs. I don't have any magic, so I can't color them, but I still wanted to see how it worked."

He didn't say anything, but he creased his eyebrows. He watched the eggs instead of her. The eggs started smoking and smelled putrid. Atlas rushed back and yanked the pan off the burner.

"Goodness gracious, girl, what are you doing?"

"Making eggs."

"No, you are burning eggs." Then he laughed. Leo joined him. Zwaantie felt her face flush.

"I guess I wasn't cut out for cooking." She grabbed the disc off the counter and raced out of the kitchen, Leo's laughter following her.

Chapter Seven

THE YOUNGEST

Leo couldn't stop laughing long enough to say anything else, so eventually Zwaantie shut the disc down. So much for trying to get to know him. She needed him here. How was she going to learn to love him like this? Especially when he was laughing at her. At the moment she didn't like him much.

Ari probably wouldn't have laughed at her. Well, he might have, but then he would've shown her how to do it right. After chasing her down, of course. She shivered at the thought of his hand on hers, stirring the eggs. On second thought, maybe they'd burn anyway. She and Ari were far too likely to get carried away doing something they shouldn't.

She was doing everything wrong, and it centered around her heart not being where it needed to be, but she didn't know how to fix that. Everything she tried had failed.

She wanted to hide from everyone, so she found her way to the library. She planned on perusing the books, but she saw Leo's youngest brother sitting in an armchair in a corner. She took the seat to his left.

Pius glanced up from the book, but immediately dropped his eyes.

"I'm Zwaantie," she said. Pius would be a good ally to have. Aside from seeing him at dinner a couple of times, she hadn't spoken to him.

If she focused on making new friends, maybe she'd be able to avoid Sage and Ari.

"I know," he muttered. Of course he knew. This was a dumb way to start a conversation. Leo had mentioned Pius would be better off in Sol. Maybe they could bond over their shared desire for order and rules.

"We haven't had a chance to talk."

"So?" He wouldn't look up from the book he was reading. If he was like Solites, he certainly wasn't very polite.

"So, I thought maybe we could get to know one another a bit."

He rolled his eyes, and she nearly laughed. He reminded her a little too much of herself.

"Don't you have other friends?" he asked, finally meeting her eyes. They were a deep piercing green—an unusual color in Stella. After seeing all the illusions, she wondered if it was real, or if he colored his eyes on purpose. Either way, if he managed to drop his scowl, sit up straight, and do something with his hair, he'd probably have girls falling at his feet.

"Sure. But that doesn't mean we can't be friends."

"Sorry, not interested in being your friend." He turned his chair so he wasn't facing her anymore.

"Why?" Now she was just irritated. He had no reason to talk to her like that.

He slammed his book shut and glared at her. The hatred there was real and unnerving.

"Maybe because you're responsible for the viper deaths, and now you're running around with Ari. You're never going to love Leo. Candace is my favorite sister, and you're going to kill her baby. Maybe that's what Sol wanted, and you're just sacrificing yourself. You don't care about Stella at all."

She furrowed her brow. "You really think that?" She wanted to ask how he knew about her role in the viper deaths, but needed more information from him first.

"You should hear the rumors. You're not well-liked in our king-dom. Maybe you should go home."

Zwaantie felt like she'd been slapped. "What are you talking about?" Everything she'd ever heard from the Ticker was how beloved she was.

She remembered the other Ticker. Maybe there was truth to what he was saying. If people thought she wasn't really in love with Leo, the main Ticker would change, but right now, she was the public's darling. Plus, everyone had been nice to her. Why would they act like they loved her if they didn't really?

"You think everything you read on the Ticker is true? It's not. I'm not the only one who is suspicious of your intentions."

His words stung. She stood and made for the door, no longer wanting to make new friends. Candace's words came back to her. Perhaps there was truth to what she said.

Viggo was the one who managed the Ticker for the family. Was he hiding the truth from her? She thought back to that other Ticker. Maybe what Viggo and his family were looking at wasn't the whole truth. Were they as blind as she'd been? No, they probably knew everything and simply kept the truth from her.

Just as she was nearly out the door, Pius raised his voice and called after her.

"Baby killer. That's what they call you."

Chapter Eight

THE MISTAKE

Zwaantie fled to her room and paced back and forth in front of her cows. Baby killer. That was the third time she'd heard the phrase. Was that really what people were calling her? How many knew? She had to fix this. But how? She could no longer deny that somewhere, someone knew, and word would soon leak out to all of Stella.

She was ruining everything. Even when she was trying to be responsible, she was blowing it.

Leo was softening toward her, which was good. But the person she really needed to apologize to was Candace. She was responsible for the death of Candace's nephew. She should own this and take concrete steps toward ending the deaths.

That meant confessing to Candace what the Old Mother said. If anyone was owed the truth, it was Candace. This would be scary, but Zwaantie had to do it. She was certain Candace wouldn't forgive her, but she needed to try.

Zwaantie took a deep breath and tapped her wall. "Candace," she said and waited, her palms sweating.

Moments later Candace's face appeared on the wall.

"What do you want?" she asked. She was sitting on a couch ramrod straight with her arms crossed. Her hair was a mess. Maybe she'd been having a harder time than Zwaantie thought.

"I need to tell you something. You were right. Castor's death was my fault."

Candace blew a strand of hair out of her eye. "What are you talking about? I was just angry. We're still mourning Castor, but I don't blame you."

Zwaantie wrung her hands. "At the lock-in, the Old Mother came to visit me. She told me the reason people were dying was because I didn't love Leo enough. I'm so sorry."

Candace jerked back. "You mean it really is your fault? Why the dark are you telling me this?"

"Because I owe you the truth."

"This is supposed to make it better?" The venom in her voice was real.

"No. But I thought you should know."

"Who else knows?"

"Ari and me."

Candace rolled her eyes. "You think just because you told me this, I'm supposed to forgive you."

"No, of course not." Perhaps this was a bad idea.

Candace sneered at her. "What do you want me to say?"

"You don't have to say anything. But I needed to apologize. I'm going to do everything I can to love Leo. I won't let your baby die."

"What about Castor? He's never coming back."

"I know. I'm sorry."

"Just because you keep saying those words doesn't change anything."

"I know. I don't know what else to say. Those are the best words I have."

"Ha. You think there are words that can bring Castor back? There aren't. Believe me, I looked. I think it would be best if you didn't call again. I don't want to talk to you." Then she signed off.

Zwaantie's stomach clenched, and pain started behind her eyes. She pressed a palm to her forehead, lost as to what she could do next. Nothing was going as planned. She felt claustrophobic in her room.

She needed to see the sky. What she wanted was the sun, but she'd settle for the stars.

Things weren't working with Leo. The people of Stella were suspicious of her motives. Candace hated her. Phoenix was gone to her. The Voice was trying to kill her. Everything was going wrong. Would she ever find peace again?

She ran out of her room, found the elevator, and punched the top floor button. She'd made a mess of everything. Her only option was to love Leo. How was she going to do that? She couldn't muster up the feelings for him it required. No one could force feelings of love. She associated feelings of love with Phoenix. Ari too, but she wasn't sure that was really love.

The elevator door opened, and she raced to the stairs and right into solid flesh.

Ari looked down at her, his eyes serious.

"Sorry, I wasn't—"

Ari cut her words off by pressing his lips against hers.

Chapter Nine

THE CONFESSION

Stars exploded behind her eyes. Every part of her body buzzed with excitement. Zwaantie didn't hesitate. She eagerly leaned into the kiss. She wanted this. Far more than she should. Thought disappeared. Guilt was gone. This was pure passion.

Ari pushed her against the wall, pressing himself against her. Zwaantie held him tight, her hands woven in his hair, never wanting to let him go. She'd never been kissed like this before. Not from Leo or Phoenix. This was different, stronger somehow. She felt more alive than she ever had. At this moment nothing else mattered. She needed this.

He broke away suddenly and stared in her eyes for a few moments. Neither said anything, their breathing heavy. He leaned down once again and gave her a soft, sweet kiss on the lips and then escaped into the elevator without a word.

Zwaantie stood there for a beat, her hand on her chest, not quite sure what had happened. Every bad feeling and thought she'd had disappeared. Every fiber of her being burned for Ari. Why was she letting him get away?

She didn't need the stars right now. She needed him. He could kiss her fears and doubts away.

She punched the elevator button. Several moments passed before the doors opened. He couldn't have gone far. She pressed the number six and raced to Ari's room. She entered without knocking, but he wasn't there. She ventured deeper into the rooms, searching the dining area and closet. Stars. Where had he gotten to?

She pushed open the door to Sage's room, not sure what she'd do if he were in there. Zwaantie couldn't kiss him in front of Sage.

Maybe he didn't want to kiss her again. Maybe he was just letting off steam. Maybe she'd completely misread the situation. No, his words in the carriage were sincere. He wanted her.

"Meow," said Andromeda. Zwaantie picked the kitten up, her racing heart starting to calm.

"I've missed you," she said to the kitten.

Sage came out of her closet. "Oh, it's you," she said with a frown and stalked back into her closet. Zwaantie put down Andromeda and followed her. After all the events of the afternoon and her recent encounter with Ari, Zwaantie forgot she'd blown Sage off this morning.

"Sage, I'm sorry." Zwaantie said that a lot lately. She was tired of it. Her decision-making skills were lacking. "I'm so confused. I want to do the right thing, but I don't know what it is."

Sage put a hand on her hip and stared up at Zwaantie. "Now you've decided being friends with me might be okay?"

Zwaantie gripped Sage's hands. "I was trying to be all adult and stuff. It didn't work. I want to be your friend. That was never in question. I've run from responsibility my whole life, and now I'm trying to find it, but I'm thoroughly blowing it."

Sage's lips twitched. "I'll say." Then she squeezed Zwaantie's hands. "Okay, you're forgiven, but I'm going out."

"Can I come?"

"Sorry. No. We only found half the slaves so far. We need to find the rest. You get that necklace on Luna yet?"

"No. I still haven't seen her. How long until you leave?"

"A half hour. I need to get ready."

"Do you mind if I stay here while you do?" She needed to stay there so she didn't do something dumb, like seek out Ari. That was the last thing she needed to do. Moments of passion were so fleeting. She saw that now. Her feelings for Ari were pure lust and were exactly the opposite of what she should be seeking with Leo. She needed love.

"Sure."

Zwaantie watched Sage flip through her dresses. "Can you keep a secret?" Zwaantie asked, already knowing the answer.

Sage barely looked away from the dresses she was perusing. "Normally I can. Keep a secret, I mean. But I tell Ari most things. So if this is something you don't want him to know, then you probably shouldn't tell me."

That was not the answer Zwaantie was looking for. She sighed, left the closet, and sunk onto the couch. She needed someone to help her make sense of the things she was feeling, and she usually worked best if she could talk it out. That's what she loved so much about Luna. She listened and never spoke a word to anyone. Most of the time she didn't even offer her opinion up. Zwaantie missed having her around, but try as she might, she couldn't find Luna alone. Not that she'd been trying very hard.

Sage came out of the closet wearing a strapless blue dress.

"You look like an adult," Zwaantie said.

Sage smirked. "Good, that was the point. What's up?" Sage admired herself in the mirror. Zwaantie creased her eyebrows. Sage was going out hunting for the Solite slaves. That was hardly an evening gown occasion. Maybe she was lying to her.

"Why are you dressed up?"

Sage let out a sigh. "Because some of the slaves are hiding. We have to talk to people who might know where they are. There's a party we need to hit up. It's not for kids, and I have to wear clothes like this. Now, what do you have to tell me?"

"I'm not telling you. I don't want Ari knowing." Zwaantie studied her nails. They were in need of a painting.

"Is this about Ari?" Sage asked, sitting next to Zwaantie.

Zwaantie nodded and ran a hand through her hair.

"Okay then, I promise I won't tell him."

"You sure?" She wasn't sure if she trusted Sage, but what other choice did Zwaantie have?

"Yeah. Has he done something to you? Cause I can kick his ass if you need me to."

"Sort of. Sage, he kissed me." Zwaantie's lips burned with the memory, and her chest buzzed.

Sage raised an eyebrow. "And?"

"And it was amazing. Leo doesn't kiss like that." Zwaantie flung herself on the couch. This was impossible.

Sage giggled. And even though she was dressed up like a starlet, she appeared much younger.

"Duh. That's Ari. He's my brother, so I don't know from experience, but I've been told he's unforgettable. One night in bed with him, and you'll never be happy with anyone else. Ever. Girls line up for the chance for a single night. Not one has left disappointed."

Sage was not being helpful. Zwaantie didn't need to hear how good Ari was at anything.

"It's more than that. I really like him. A lot more than I like Leo. And I feel guilty."

"You should. But, to be fair, you hardly know Leo. He should be around more. Maybe you can go stay with him in Deep Sky. Then you can get away from Ari."

"I hardly know Ari. Yet, if he asked, I'd go to the moon for him. Why?"

Zwaantie played with the fringe on a pillow, not wanting to meet Sage's eyes. She felt ashamed for her feelings, especially in light of the Old Mother's revelation. What was she supposed to do?

Sage gripped Zwaantie's hand and put on a serious face, something Zwaantie rarely saw. "I love Ari. More than any of my siblings. Ari's not going to marry you, and he's not going to commit to you. Leo will, and you can save Stella that way. Ari won't help. He will never love you. "

Zwaantie let those words sink in. Ari was a distraction she couldn't afford. Even if he did claim she was his soul mate. Even if she knew he was right.

When she saw Ari again, she'd tell him this couldn't continue. If she was going to find a way to love Leo at all, Ari could not be in the picture. Just the thought of seeing him made her skin tingle. She had to get away.

"Maybe I should go see Leo."

"Yes. That's the smartest thing you've said since you walked into my room. Call Leo. Tell him you're coming to visit. I'll put you on a boat tomorrow."

Zwaantie nodded. This was a good idea. She pulled out her disc.

"Call Leo."

His face popped up. "Hey, beautiful. I'm sorry I laughed at you earlier."

"It's okay. Can I come see you?"

He pursed his lips. "Sure. Why?"

She shrugged. "I don't know. I want to see you. I'm missing you."

His face split into a grin, and she felt so guilty for allowing him to think she might want to be with him. She had to if this was going to work.

"Sure. I'll be busy with work, but you can tag along. When are you coming?"

"Sage said she can put me on a boat tomorrow morning."

"Okay. I'll see you then."

She suddenly felt sick. She'd be going to see him. He'd expect her to kiss him and maybe do more. Things were easy between her and Leo when they tried to be friends, but when she forced her feelings, everything was strange and wrong.

This was going to be a disaster.

Chapter Ten

THE SECRET

Ari needed his mother. She might've joked around a lot with him, but she always helped him. The problem was she'd made her opinion of Zwaantie clear, and she probably wouldn't give him the most prudent advice. She'd tell him to run away with Zwaantie and ignore what damage that might cause to the kingdom. If only to assuage her guilt from years before.

Before Zwaantie came around, he pretty much did what he wanted and didn't think about consequences. Now, she had his thoughts in complete turmoil. Everything about her was complicated. The kiss still lingered on his lips.

He pushed Sage's door open. Zwaantie would probably be there, and he needed to see her. He didn't have to bring up the kiss. Though if she was alone, there would definitely need to be a repeat.

He shouldn't be thinking about the kiss. Zwaantie didn't love Leo, and as long as Ari kept screwing with her, she never would. Unless she didn't feel the same way about Ari. No, the way she pulled him close, she wanted him. This was a nightmare.

Sage was alone in her room, playing with her cats on the floor. Ari sank down onto the couch.

"Hey, bro," Sage said as a kitten attacked her foot.

"Hey. Where's Zwaantie?"

"You shouldn't be asking that."

He creased his eyebrows. "Why not?"

"You're an idiot. We're doing everything we can to save the kingdom, and you're not thinking with your brain."

He let out a sigh. "You got that right. My heart's never been a problem before. Not sure how to handle this."

Sage snorted. "Heart. Right. Anyway, I just put Zwaantie on a boat to Deep Sky to spend time with Leo. So she can fall in love with him. And marry him. And save the kingdom."

He clenched his fists. He didn't like thinking about her with Leo, who would kiss her when he saw her. Then tonight. He frowned. How long would he have to watch Zwaantie and regret not having her? He couldn't do this. He would have to leave.

"Did Zwaantie tell you what happened at the lock-in?" he asked.

"No, she told me you kissed her in the tower. Which was stupid, by the way. What happened at the lock-in?"

"She's my soul mate. I confirmed it with Xandria. Soul mates glow pink."

Sage gaped. "Stars, Ari. Really? You couldn't pick a different girl?"

"It's not like I had control over it. What am I going to do?"

"Stay away from her."

He wasn't sure he could do that. "You're not helping."

Sage scrambled across the floor and sat up on her knees so she was looking him directly in the face. "Bro, I love you so much, and I want nothing more than for you to be happy, but Zwaantie has to marry Leo, and we have to support her in this even if we don't want to."

"This has never happened to me before. How am I supposed to deal with this?"

"For now, it's not a big deal. She's in Deep Sky. Go party, drown yourself in potions, sleep with whoever, and stay away from her." At least Sage offered better advice than his mother. He still didn't like it.

A knock sounded on the door.

"Come in," Sage called.

Phoenix strolled in. He'd been an enigma because he was Stellan, but he'd grown up in Sol. He tried to kill Zwaantie, so Ari wasn't crazy about him. That wasn't really his fault, but Ari still didn't like him. Even if there was an evil voice whispering in his ear, Ari would never hurt Zwaantie.

Sage's face lit up. "Hey, let me change. Then we'll go."

"Where you going?" Ari asked.

"We're down to the last three slaves. We're not coming home until we find them, right?"

Phoenix gave her a smile. "Well, we might end up not coming home for a few weeks, but sure."

Sage disappeared into her closet.

"You on the payroll yet?" Ari asked.

"With Lyra? Yeah. She's hoping to train me to do some undercover work in Sol."

"That'd be good. You going to smuggle in more of the necklaces?" Every necklace placed in Sol weakened the Voice's power.

"If I've learned anything here, it's that the Voice needs be stopped. Look what he did to me with Zwaantie. Once we're done here, I'm going back and will do whatever it takes to get rid of him."

"That might put you at odds with Zwaantie."

"Maybe at first, but she'll see the wisdom eventually. She might even right now. She knows the Voice wants to kill her."

Ari wasn't sure Zwaantie would be happy about what they were doing behind her back. He'd almost told her once, but he didn't want to die a slow death from angering Lyra, who insisted Zwaantie could know nothing.

Someday though, he'd talk them into telling her. She was on their side.

Sage came out of the closet and put her hands on her hips. "Whatcha gonna do about loving Zwaantie, Ari?"

"I'm not going to do anything. But it's not fair."

She planted a kiss on his forehead. "I know."

Ari watched her and Phoenix leave the room. He needed to find something to occupy his time so he didn't have to be in the same room as Zwaantie. She was gone for now, but she'd be back soon enough. Maybe Father would send him to one of the other kingdoms on a diplomatic mission of some kind.

He might have told Sage he was going to do nothing, but deep down he knew if he and Zwaantie were ever alone, a lot more than nothing would happen.

Chapter Eleven

THE BABY KILLER

Candace waited on the dock. Zwaantie took a deep breath and stepped out to meet her. Last time they talked, things hadn't ended well.

"I thought you weren't speaking to me anymore," Zwaantie said.

"You're here, aren't you? Thank you for coming." Candace's face was tight, and her fists clenched, but at least she was trying. That was probably the best Zwaantie was going to get from her.

The docks in Deep Sky weren't nearly as busy as City of Stars. This island was a mountain, and the city crawled up the hillside. Perched on the top was a castle similar to the king's but slightly smaller.

She and Candace climbed into a carriage, and Zwaantie stared out the windows at the shops. The buildings here were shorter.

"Are all the outlying kingdoms small like this?"

"No. Mine is the only one that is built on a mountain, and I think it's the prettiest."

Zwaantie gave her a smile. "It is pretty."

"Thank you." Candace seemed to relax.

"Where's little Raaf?"

"At home. I don't take him out much because I don't want to worry about anything happening to him."

"Of course. What about Leo?"

"Busy. He'll be back in time for dinner. Another baby died last night." She creased her eyebrows but didn't elaborate. Zwaantie's stomach fell. That baby's death was on her, and she was grateful Candace wasn't blaming her.

~

LEO RUSHED INTO THE ROOM SHORTLY BEFORE DINNER AND SWOOPED her up into a hug. She returned it. He was warm and safe and sweet, so very different from Ari. She pulled away before he could try and kiss her.

"I'm so glad you're here," he said, beaming.

"Me too." She tried to match his smile, but she was certain she failed. "How are things going?"

He furrowed his brow. "Not well. We're no closer to finding a solution on how to stop the vipers than we were when this started."

She should tell him what the Old Mother said, but then he'd expect her to love him. Try as she might, she couldn't turn it on.

"What are you going to do?"

"I have no idea. I'm working closely with a few other mages to see if the protection spells around the houses will last through the night. They're tricky and difficult and take forever to cast. We're starting with homes that have children turning one soon. So far, none of those houses have been attacked, but we don't know if it's because of the spells, or if we just got lucky."

"I hope it works." If they could find a workaround, then maybe it would give her more time to fall in love with Leo.

"Me too. We're going to have dinner in here if you don't mind. I want some alone time with you." He smiled, but it didn't quite reach his eyes. He was lying about something.

"What are our plans after dinner?"

"We could go up to the tower. The stars are brighter here."

As appealing as that sounded, she didn't want to be alone with him. She wouldn't be able to muster up strong feelings in such a short time. They needed time to get to know one another. If he tried to force romance, she'd end up resenting him. Love wouldn't grow in that environment.

"Maybe we can go see some of Candace's kingdom. This is new to me."

He led her to the table set with dinner. "I don't think that's a good idea," he said with a frown.

"Why not?"

He let out a breath. "Because the people of Deep Sky aren't crazy about you."

Her chest tightened. "What do you mean?"

Leo played with the food on his plate. "Did anyone explain to you about the different Tickers?"

"Yes." She wasn't sure if she liked where this was going.

"A few of the more, uh, negative ones, blame you for the babies' deaths. A lot of people here want someone to blame. You're an easy target since it started after you arrived."

Zwaantie slammed her fork down. "I'm here because I want to make sure it stops." She was so sick of being blamed for everything. This wasn't fair. Though true.

He put his hand on her arm. "I know. But you can't reason with some people. They're going to believe what they want, and this won't change until the deaths stop. I'm sorry."

If only there was an easy solution. Marry Leo, sure. Love him, not so easy.

"This seems ridiculous." What would happen if the people knew the truth? She'd be crucified.

"I know. As long as you're in Deep Sky, it would be best for you to stay in the castle. If you don't want to go see the stars, maybe we can watch a movie."

She nodded numbly. She didn't like the thought of people hating her. Though she did deserve it.

Leo tried to keep the conversation light during dinner, but her mind kept wandering to the babies.

"What kind of movie would you like to watch?" Leo asked

"A funny one." Anything that would take her mind off the events of the day.

She sat on his couch and watched him play with his disc. The wall lit up, and he collapsed next to her. He put his arm around her and kissed her temple.

"Thanks for coming to see me. It really does make me happy."

She was surprisingly okay with his affection. It wasn't any more than she'd shared with Sage. There was no fire, but that was okay. It was comfortable. She allowed herself to relax into him. Maybe this wouldn't be as hard as she thought it would be.

The movie made her laugh. After it was over, the nerves in her belly started. They would be retiring to bed soon. She was in Leo's room. That meant she had to share a bed with him.

"So, I have to go," Leo said. "I'm sorry."

"Go?"

"Yes. We're staying in the homes with children who are turning one tomorrow."

Relief flooded through her, but she didn't let it show on her face. "That's too bad. Who's we?"

"Myself and a few other mages."

He leaned in and kissed her. She kissed him back, not wanting to cause suspicion, but he deepened the kiss. It felt odd. Wrong. Why couldn't the Old Mother have said she needed to love him as a friend? That was doable. This wasn't.

He pulled away and gave her a sheepish grin. "See you tomorrow."

She locked the door after he left and collapsed into bed. She missed Ari. The way he touched her. His smile. His kiss.

She felt bad for Leo. If it weren't for Ari, she might actually be able to love him, but there was no way to know now, because her feelings for Ari were stronger than ever.

∽

LEO'S FACE HOVERED OVER THE DISC. "I'M SORRY. I KNOW YOU HAVE TO go home tomorrow, but I don't think I'll be able to get back until late tonight."

Zwaantie let out a breath. This wasn't working. "How about I bring you lunch?"

"That would be great. Just stay out of sight and wear a cloak. Ask

Candace to get you a carriage. I'm at the cottages. Call me when you get here, and we'll have a picnic."

Picnic. Okay. Now she needed to find the kitchen. She slipped out into the empty hallway.

She turned the corner and found a woman rushing by with a handful of towels. Zwaantie stopped her with a touch.

The woman jerked away. "Don't touch me. Baby killer."

Zwaantie resisted the urge to snap back.

"I'm looking for the kitchen. Can you point me in the right direction?"

The woman glared at her for a second. "Second floor. Third level."

"Thank you."

Zwaantie tried to walk away with her head held high, but she wasn't sure she succeeded. She didn't dare stop anyone else, and after a few wrong turns, she found the kitchen. They gave her the food without too much fuss, and before she knew it, she was climbing out of the carriage at the cottages where Leo waited for her.

He pulled her close as soon as she stepped out and kissed her hard. It felt all kinds of wrong. She wiggled away. "Here's your food."

He frowned. "Thank you."

She didn't know how to make this work. She laid her head on his shoulder. "Where should we eat?"

"We're on the beach, so the sand makes sense, yeah?"

"Sure."

She spent all of the lunch pretending to be interested in what he had to say, but her heart wasn't in it. She was fairly certain that if Ari had greeted her with a kiss, they would've ended up back in the carriage, lunch forgotten.

Chapter Twelve

THE DRESS

On the boat ride home, Zwaantie was reflective. She was unsure of how the rest of her life would be. She'd barely seen Leo, and the moments they were together were incredibly awkward. She worried things could never be easy between them.

Her stomach buzzed at the thought of seeing Ari. She shouldn't be thinking about him, but she couldn't help herself. She wondered what she could do to avoid him, because it would be the only way she would ensure she didn't do something she'd regret.

During her stay in Deep Sky, Zwaantie had spent a good amount of time reading about Stellan customs and history. The more she learned, the more she wanted to stay and rule here, not in Sol. She felt like she now knew more about Stella than she did about Sol. From the rulers to the magical customs. At home, the Voice kept a tight rein on what people knew. Her own library wasn't nearly as extensive. In every way Sol was stifling; Stella was free.

So far, Sage hadn't found much about how the Voice worked in Stella. But if it wanted her dead, then Zwaantie couldn't very well go home. Then again, she didn't want to sit in fear either that something could happen to her. She'd never been one to run from a problem or let it stop her from doing what she wanted. If she stayed in Stella, would the Voice win?

If she wanted to return to Sol, she would have to figure out how to defeat the Voice. It seemed like such a daunting task, but the people of Sol were trapped under his tyranny. Perhaps she could remain in Stella and still get rid of the Voice.

The boat docked, and she rushed out. She was slightly disappointed to see Sage standing there.

"Where's Ari?" she asked before she could help herself.

Sage rolled her eyes. "I haven't seen him in a couple of days. But I told him to stay away from you."

Zwaantie scowled. "I could've told him myself."

"Uh huh, until he kissed you again. It's better this way. Trust me. We have an appointment anyway."

It wasn't Sage's job to keep Ari away from her. But it was better this way. Sage had a far steadier hand than Zwaantie had known before. Perhaps the crazy partying girl was an act.

"An appointment?"

"We're getting your dress made."

Zwaantie's heart stilled. It was one thing to think about Leo and having to spend the rest of her life with him. It was quite another to think of the actual wedding.

"Are we going to use a castle dressmaker?" She'd gotten used to shopping in the Stellan shops, but she expected this wasn't something she could go out and buy.

"Uh, no. There is only one dressmaker in town if you want an awesome wedding gown. Let's go."

Sage dragged her off the docks and into a carriage. Fifteen minutes later Zwaantie blinked at a deep black, perfectly square building.

"I feel like it should be shaped like a wedding dress or something," Zwaantie said. She was almost disappointed. She'd gotten used to everything in Stella being grand in some way.

"Not Nash. He likes things classy."

They entered the building where a short man in a bright green suit greeted them. He had a severe face and was balding.

"It's about time you came calling," the man said to Sage, his voice light and happy. Then he turned to Zwaantie. "Princess, I'm Nash. I was beginning to think you'd picked another dressmaker. Less than three weeks until the big day."

"Nonsense," said Sage. "There is no one else." Sage kissed him on the cheek.

Nash straightened his tie and raised an eyebrow. "That's what I thought. Oh, I'm excited about this one. Whatever you choose will be the wedding dress fashion for months or even years to come." His eyes twinkled a little. "And I will be the only one they come to. Ah, I can hear the money rolling in."

Sage gave him a grin. "We'll get pictures of you two together before we leave. Viggo will put it at the top of the Ticker."

Nash brought a hand to his chest. "Ah, you do know how to make my day, don't you?" He looped his arm through hers.

Zwaantie followed them up a short flight of stairs and through a curtain into a circular room. A few silvery blue couches were scattered about the room, facing a three-foot round dais situated in the middle. Silver and pink curtains covered every wall. Classy.

Sage plopped down on a couch. Nash pointed to the dais. "Take your place, dear."

Zwaantie took a small step up onto the dais while Nash circled her.

"Take off your clothes," he commanded, his light and happy voice gone.

Zwaantie threw a panicked look at Sage, who shrugged.

Nash snapped his fingers. "Don't be shy. I haven't got all day. I can't make you a dress if I can't see your figure."

Zwaantie tentatively pulled her shirt over her head and slid off her skirt. She crossed her arms over her chest, feeling extremely exposed as Nash studied her. He snapped his fingers again.

A long, silky black dress appeared on her body. She looked down in shock and relief. At least she wasn't naked anymore, but no one had magicked clothes on her before. Nash waved his arm, and the curtains disappeared. Every inch of the circular walls were mirrors.

The dress was plain and loose. It reminded her of the dresses in Sol but with no sleeves.

Nash continued to circle her.

"What do you think of the color, dear? Black looks good on you."

"In Sol, we wear white." Black was for funerals. White symbolized purity and new beginnings. She wanted a white dress.

Nash frowned. "Here wedding dresses are very dark. Only a few are black, most are navy, deep purple, maroon, or dark green. I always start with black and go from there."

Zwaantie clenched her fists. She'd always pictured wearing a white wedding dress. She didn't see why just because she was in Stella it had to be different. They were in the process of merging their cultures. Maybe this would be one way to show it.

"I'd still like a white dress." There, she was standing up for herself. Something she didn't do often enough in Stella.

Nash rubbed his head. "Sage, talk to her. I'll be the laughing stock of the country. I can't do white."

Sage wrinkled her nose. "White is for babies and little kids, not adults. You're getting married."

"I want a white dress. In Sol, I would've worn white. I'm still the Solite princess. If I wear your colors, I'm giving up my identity."

Sage tapped her chin and studied Zwaantie. She spun and faced Nash. "She has a point. Maybe it will start a new trend. Can you at least try to do a white dress. For her?"

"This could ruin me." Nash snapped his fingers and the dress on her changed suddenly from black to bright white. He walked around her. "That white isn't quite right for you skin. It washes you out."

He fingered the edge of the fabric, and it went a slight different shade of white. "Nope, not that one either."

He continued massaging the fabric. Zwaantie stared in the mirror as the dozens of shades of white flashed by. She didn't know white was so diverse. Finally, he nodded. "That's workable. Sage, what do you think?"

Sage nodded. "I wouldn't want ivory for myself, but I like it on her. Are you sure you want white? Maybe we could do yellow instead. Look like the sun."

Zwaantie shook her head. "This is a good color."

"Good. Now for style. Do you have a preference?"

"I don't know what the different styles are. In Sol all the wedding dresses looked the same." And they did. Like a tent. Aside from the color, she wanted the style to be wholly Stellan. It would be neat to see the two cultures combined. She felt inadequate as he stared up at her reflection. She didn't know what to say.

"Okay, I'll show you several different styles, and you say yes or no. That will give me a better idea of where to go. We can do this quickly if you don't hesitate with your answers."

He snapped his fingers, and an enormous gown with a twelve-foot train appeared on her body. She shook her head. The train disappeared, and the bodice became a little tighter.

"Better, but no."

The dress clung to her body but poofed out on the bottom.

Sage started laughing. "She looks like a mermaid."

Zwaantie tried to move her legs but couldn't and was reminded of the day Ari took her to the funhouse. "I don't think I could walk, but it's pretty."

He snapped his fingers, and the entire dress nearly disappeared. The new dress had no sleeves and a slightly poofy skirt that landed just above her knees.

"No, but we're getting closer."

"You like the short? I didn't think Solites did short."

"I don't want a Solite dress. Just a white one."

"Nothing short," Sage called. "It's a wedding dress."

Nash winked at Zwaantie. "What do you think, dear?"

Zwaantie pursed her lips. "I like it, but a little longer wouldn't be bad."

He circled her and tapped his fingers on his lips. Then his eyes lit up. "Yes, I have it."

He snapped his fingers again, and this time Zwaantie knew he'd done it. The front of the dress was above her knees, but got progressively longer until it stretched into a six-foot train.

"Yes," Zwaantie said before Sage could say a word. "This is the one."

"Perfect. Now stay still."

Then Nash really got to work. Zwaantie enjoyed watching him. He never once touched her, and yet her dress changed constantly. He created a pattern of flowers all over the dress that changed color, but all were shades of purple and pink. Zwaantie loved it.

He played with scent. Roses. Lilies. Oranges. Mint. She finally settled on a light tulip. She blushed when she thought of the tulip fields where she imagined the kiss with Ari. She had to stop thinking about him.

After what felt like hours, he stepped back. "Perfect."

It was. The ivory color of the dress was stunning against her pale skin. The flowers created a rainbow of purples and pinks that wound around to the train. Sage was all smiles.

"Leo is going to faint when he sees you in that thing."

Zwaantie forced a smile—she wasn't thinking of Leo.

The door across the room opened, and all eyes flew to it.

Ari strolled in, followed by his mother.

He stopped dead when he saw her, and his eyes traveled the length of the dress.

"You look beautiful," he said. There was no cockiness in his face, and Zwaantie was nervous he would do something stupid in front of everyone, but he made no move toward her.

"No one else is supposed to see it," Nash replied. "How did you get in here?"

"Your assistant let us in."

Nash snapped his fingers, and the dress disappeared. Zwaantie wasn't prepared, and she scrambled to put her clothes back on as Ari gave an appreciative chuckle.

"White, Nash? Really?" the queen asked.

"My dear Astrid, she insisted. But don't you think it turned out fantastically?"

The queen snorted. "I suppose that one over there gave you pointers." She jerked her thumb at Sage.

"I didn't say a word," Sage said with a glower.

"In that case, it's lovely and will be the talk of the town." Astrid batted her eyes at Nash. Zwaantie had never seen this side of the queen before and now understood where Ari got his personality.

Sage rolled her eyes and looked pointedly at Ari. "What are you doing here?"

"I'm heading to The Black City to visit my sister tomorrow, and I wanted to see if the princess would join us for lunch," Astrid replied.

"In that case, I'm outta here. You guys have fun," Sage said and rushed from the room.

Ari and Zwaantie waited outside the door while Astrid talked with

Nash about a dress she wanted. The simmer that always existed between them was thick in the air.

"How was your visit with Leo?" Ari asked.

"It was nice. Thanks." She gave him a grin, hoping he'd believe her. But he closed the distance between them and brushed her hair out of her face. Her skin burned where he'd touched her.

"That doesn't sound very convincing." He whispered right in her ear, "Did he kiss you?"

His closeness made it hard for her to breathe, let alone answer the question. He backed away.

"Of course he did." She hated the way her voice trembled.

He glowered. "I see."

"Ari, you know—"

"Okay, dears," Astrid said. "Let's go have some lunch. I'm dying to get to know the princess."

The queen looped her arm into Zwaantie's, reminding her of an adult version of Sage. Maybe that's why they didn't get along. They were too much alike.

Chapter Thirteen

THE POTIONS

They took a carriage and stopped by a small building that shifted shapes, but instead of changing shapes like the funhouse, this one changed settings—an ocean, a park, a castle, and an island.

"Not another funhouse," Zwaantie said.

Ari chuckled. "No. This isn't nearly as disconcerting, but it's fun. Come on."

The well-dressed man standing in the entryway gave a tiny bow. "Queen Astrid, Prince Ari, Princess Zwaantie, it is a pleasure to see you today. Just the three of you?"

"Yes," Ari replied.

"Very well. Please give me a moment to get it set up. Any requests?"

"No, I trust you to put together something spectacular."

It was rare for Zwaantie to see any of the Stellans pay respect to their royalty. Normally they treated them like friends.

Astrid fussed with Ari's hair while they waited.

"The beauty mages don't only do work on the women. I'm sure if you visited them, they could help you manage this."

"I like my hair, Mother."

She frowned as the host returned.

"Follow me, please." They followed him down a long corridor. He pushed open the door to room number five and pulled three vials out of his pockets. "Potions?"

The queen cackled. "Oh goodness, I haven't played potion roulette in a very long time. We should definitely do this."

Ari eyed his mother. "Are you sure?"

"Only if the princess wants to play."

"I don't understand," Zwaantie said.

"You take a potion, but you have no idea what it does. Generally there is a boring one like Cool, a moderate one like Lie, and one funny or extreme one like Giggle or Touch me. You never know what you'll get," Ari said.

Zwaantie debated for a moment. There were a thousand ways this could go wrong, but why not. She was used to doing dumb things when she was around Ari. Besides, she didn't really feel like she could tell the queen no. "Sure."

Zwaantie plucked one of the vials from the host's hand, and Ari and his mother did the same.

They drank them at the same time. Zwaantie's tasted like sugar and cinnamon. She had no idea what it would do.

"Oh man," Ari said. He was glowing. "I got the boring one."

Astrid looked the same, and Zwaantie didn't feel any different.

"Your favorite, Your Highness," the host said, ushering them into the room. "Enjoy your meal."

"Thank you, Vulcan."

Zwaantie was almost disappointed in the room. She'd expected something otherworldly. Instead, a simple table sat in the middle. Astrid sat first, with Ari and Zwaantie on either side of her.

"Ari, dear, your hair is ratty. You must get a haircut when we arrive home."

"Hm. Did you get Truth or Insult?"

She raised her eyebrows. "Good question." She turned to Zwaantie. "You look stunning. I don't know why my son is even hesitating."

"Yep. She got Truth. This is going to be fun. I wonder what you got."

She wasn't sure. If Ari got the boring one, and Astrid got a moderate, that meant Zwaantie got something extreme. Maybe she could keep her mouth shut. Somehow though, she couldn't.

"Astrid, why did you put that curse on Ari?"

Ari's eyes opened wide. Zwaantie couldn't believe she'd just asked the queen such a forward question.

Before Astrid could answer, the entire room changed. Instead of sitting at a table, they were now on a blanket on the ground, surrounded by thick trees. Ari had his head in Zwaantie's lap. He beamed up at her, and she had her hand in his hair. At first, it felt so natural and normal, and she didn't process that he shouldn't have his head in her lap.

In the middle of the blanket was an enormous platter with meats and cheeses and a few bowls of fruit.

Ari sat up and popped a grape into his mouth. "The scene will change at random. It's never quite the same. Though a park seems to appear at least once."

The queen still hadn't responded to Zwaantie's question. "Why did you put that curse on Ari?" she asked again, unable to help herself.

"I didn't mean to. Not really. I'm horribly impulsive."

"Mom, you really don't need to do this," Ari said, and Zwaantie shoved a grape into her mouth in the hopes that she wouldn't say anything more.

"I want to know, Astrid. Please tell me," Zwaantie said and gripped Ari's arm. "What the dark kind of potion did he give me?"

"Probably Secret. It makes you ask questions you would never dream of asking otherwise. Be careful though. If someone asks you for one your secrets, you won't have any choice but to tell them." Astrid shoved a few crackers in her mouth with the cheese.

Ari gave a dark chuckle. "As long as she keeps eating, she doesn't have to answer. Truth makes her tell you the absolute truth. These two potions are a deadly combination."

Astrid took a sip of wine and gave a small smile. "It was time it came out anyway, right?"

"It's really not. We've moved past it."

Without warning, the park disappeared, and they were sitting at a small round table with bowls of clear soup. All around them was the night sky. The table and chairs were floating.

Astrid set down her glass. "No, I want you to understand. I felt so betrayed every time your father spent a night away. My own family was pretty conservative, and my parents were faithful to one another. They taught me marriage was special. After I got angry about all of his children, Ajax promised me he wouldn't have any other kids, but he still slept around. I couldn't handle it. I wanted him to feel the pain I felt, and I took it out on you. I thought if your father saw how important it was to me, he'd change. Of course he didn't."

Pain flashed across Ari's face. "Stop. I don't want to know any more."

"But I do," Zwaantie said. She clapped her hands over her mouth. This was impossible.

Astrid sipped at her soup and was quiet for a few long moments.

The scenery changed again. Now they were on a beach with bowls of shrimp resting in the sand. Waves crashed onto the shore.

Astrid leaned back and stared out over the fake ocean.

"I'm so sorry, Ari. I should've never made you make the promise. I couldn't see clearly then, but I do now."

"You don't seem so conservative. What changed?" Zwaantie asked.

Astrid snorted and picked up a shrimp. She dipped it in the bright red sauce.

Ari waved another shrimp in front of Zwaantie's face. "Here, eat."

She swatted it away. "I'm not hungry." She wanted to hear the stories she so foolishly asked about.

Astrid chewed and swallowed. "After Ajax still denied me his fidelity, I paid Xandria a visit. She made a potion that allowed me to not care what he did. It had some interesting side effects. I'm...less inhibited. I have my own lovers now. I only have one regret in my life, and that is what I did to Ari."

The setting changed, and now they were in a bubble in the ocean, brightly colored fish swimming all around them. A platter with fried fish sat in the middle of a small table.

The space in the bubble was more confining and claustrophobic. She met Ari's eyes, and he shook his head. "Don't you dare open your mouth. I don't know what you are about to ask, but I won't want to answer it."

"You said I'm your soul mate. If things were different, would you marry me?"

"No. I wouldn't."

His words stung. She ate her fish and didn't say anything else. Astrid and Ari were quiet as well. She supposed no one wanted more secrets to come out.

The scenery changed one more time, and they were in the middle of a field of tulips, ice cream cones in hand. The smell was intoxicating and reminded her far too much of her fantasies of Ari. She wandered away from him and ate her cone. They needed to get out of this place.

Just as she was finishing up, Ari grabbed her hand and tugged her into him, his lips right next to her ear. "Tell me, princess, how do you feel about me?"

Her heart constricted. She had to tell him the truth. She had no choice. Her secret would be revealed. She tried to keep it in, but her body betrayed her. She gripped his vest, stood up on her tiptoes, and whispered, "I love you."

Chapter Fourteen

THE OTHER MOTHER

Ari avoided Zwaantie for the next two days, and Zwaantie was absolutely beside herself. She'd told him exactly how she felt, and he'd run.

Zwaantie had been ornery and unpleasant, but Sage didn't seem fazed. She suspected Sage knew why she was grumpy. Maybe Zwaantie could go ask Xandria for a special potion as well.

"We should keep working on the wedding. What do you want to plan next? Flowers? Foods?" Sage asked.

Zwaantie tossed a toy mouse across the room, and four cats fought over it. "I don't know. What kinds of things does Leo like? I don't want to make this all about me." She felt so guilty for her feelings about Ari. She couldn't stand this. The wedding should be all about Leo.

"You're asking the wrong person. If you want to know what he likes, Candace is the one to ask. She knows more about him. Leo and I hang, but I don't know what his favorite colors are or what kind of food he'd want at his wedding."

Zwaantie blinked at her. "Candace is still dealing with everything in her kingdom. I doubt she's going to be up to helping with the wedding. Plus, even though we sort of made up, we're not on the best of terms."

"Riiiiight. Well then, maybe Leo's mother. She should know that kind of stuff, right? Maybe you can talk to her, and I'll track down the wedding planner."

"Oh, yes. I haven't met his mother yet." Mothers were an important part of any man's life. She'd been too focused on herself to think of his mother. She had to start looking outward.

Sage gave a chuckle. "Oh yes you have."

Zwaantie furrowed her brow. Now she was confused. "Who is she?"

"Lyra, the head mage."

Dread filled Zwaantie's heart. "What the dark? Why did you never tell me?"

Sage shrugged.

"You told me Lyra was the scariest woman in all of Sol." She had been avoiding the head mage since they last met.

"She is."

"And she's Leo's mother?" Leo was so sweet. How could his mother be this awful woman?

"Yep."

Zwaantie hadn't made a very good impression on Lyra the first time they met.

"Why didn't anyone ever say anything?" Zwaantie wanted to know everything she could about this woman before she spent any time alone with her.

"I don't know. It's not widely known. They like to keep it under wraps. With Lyra being the head mage, and Leo basically her second in command, they don't like to advertise things."

Zwaantie gaped at Sage. "What do you mean second in command?"

"You know, Leo is the spymaster."

Dread filled Zwaantie's heart. The leaders of Stella had been sneaky. "No, I thought he was in charge of investigating tragedies in Stella." Spymaster. For the love of Sol. "Seriously? They sent the spymaster over to Sol to marry the princess?" Her mind spun with the possibilities. Was Stella up to something more sinister?

"Well, yeah. He had the best shot. Plus, he did it for Candace."

Zwaantie shook her head. At this moment she didn't understand the implications, but she was sure once she had time to mull it over, she would.

They hadn't sent a prince to her kingdom. They'd sent a spy.

What had he learned that he could use against her? Spies were the best liars out there. Had he been lying every time he told her he loved her? Maybe nothing he'd ever done had been honest. Sage too. She worked with him.

"We should go see her and get it over with. Seriously, she'll know everything you want to know," Sage said.

Zwaantie let out a breath. "I'm not sure about this."

Sage tugged on her arm. "Come on. If you don't do this now, you never will. The longer you have to think about it, the harder it will be."

Zwaantie reluctantly allowed Sage to drag her down a couple of flights of stairs.

Before Zwaantie could ask any questions, Sage knocked on the door, alarming Zwaantie to what she was about to do. She wasn't ready for this.

"Good luck," Sage said and took off in the opposite direction. Oh no, she wasn't going to leave her here.

"Sage," Zwaantie hissed after her. "Where are you going?"

"Anywhere but with Lyra. I'll see you when you're done. If you're alive." She gave Zwaantie a wicked grin and disappeared around the corner. Brat. She'd get her back for this one. That was if Zwaantie survived. Zwaantie wiped her sweating palms on her skirt. Then she straightened her shirt.

The door opened, and Zwaantie sucked in a breath.

"Princess. What are you doing here?" Lyra held the door open only a crack. Who knew what she was hiding.

Zwaantie held her head high. "I came to talk to you about your son."

Lyra raised her eyebrows. "Which one? I have three."

"You know which one. May I come in?" Zwaantie could not let her fear show. Now was the time to make sure she acted like a queen.

Lyra considered her for a moment. "Of course."

One hurdle crossed, now to win her over.

Lyra sat behind a large desk, and Zwaantie took a chair across from her. Lyra didn't say anything and simply stared at Zwaantie, making her feel uncomfortable. Lyra's features were hard, and her arms were crossed. This would not be easy.

Zwaantie squirmed in her chair. "I was hoping you could help me. Leo and I had very little time to get to know one another. Sage and I were working on wedding plans, and I want to make sure I do something for him. What kinds of food does he like? Does he have people you think he would like for certain roles? What sort of venue would he want to get married in?"

Lyra uncrossed her arms and leaned on the desk, staring down at Zwaantie menacingly. Oh Sol, this woman was terrifying. Zwaantie shrunk in her chair.

"Why do you care?" Lyra's voice was full of venom.

"Excuse me?" Why was Lyra being so nasty? She'd been prepared for a tongue-lashing, but a question like that was strange.

"Why do you care what my son wants? I was under the impression you didn't want to marry him. Why do care about his input?"

"Why would you think I don't want to marry him?" Zwaantie was certain only Leo, Sage, and Ari knew about her relationship with Phoenix.

Lyra snorted. "I am the head mage. I know about Phoenix. Including that he tried to kill you. Twice. That's the only reason you are still willing to marry my son. Otherwise, you'd be off in some poor village with your precious Phoenix."

Zwaantie felt the blood drain from her face. "I wasn't aware that was public knowledge." Who else knew? Was the Ticker blaring with news of her betrayal? She didn't look at the Ticker very often because she didn't like it, so she wouldn't know if it was saying nasty things about her or not.

"It's not. Leo told me. Now go ahead and plan your wedding the way you like, and stop trying to pretend you care. I have work to do."

Lyra waved a hand at her and picked up a paper from her desk and perused it.

Zwaantie sat up straighter. This woman didn't scare her. She needed to show Lyra she meant business. Besides, Zwaantie was certain Leo only shared his side of the story.

"No," she said.

"No?" Lyra sneered at her.

"I know what you're thinking, but Leo showed up in my kingdom begging for my hand out of the blue. Phoenix and I had already fallen in love, and there was zero hope for our romance. I was trapped in my own home. I had no options, so when Leo presented one, I took it. I'll not apologize for that."

Zwaantie was sick of telling everyone how sorry she was. Sick of being treated like an evil shrew. She knew this woman could obliterate her, but at this moment, she didn't care. Her words were right on the edge of her tongue. Ready to spill everything. This moment, she was in control, not under the influence of any potion.

Lyra didn't say a word as Zwaantie took another breath. "If I was presented the same choice today, I would take it. Phoenix betrayed me, and I was left with an excruciating decision. Stay and marry a man I don't love but save Stella, or go home and have my freedom but know I've condemned my friends to death."

Lyra's face did not give any indication she cared or was softening.

"I may have chosen to marry Leo under false pretenses, but then so did he. He didn't come to Sol and ask for my hand because he loved me. He did it to save his kingdom. I'm doing this to save Stella. This requires me to love him, so I'm doing my best to learn about him and come to love him. Tell me. What's wrong with that?"

Zwaantie waited for the blow. The sharp words she knew Lyra would throw at her because Lyra was looking for a fight. A knot had loosened in Zwaantie's chest. It felt amazing to get out the words she should've said to Leo but didn't. Instead, she told his murderous mother. Maybe she should've thought this through.

Lyra glared at her. "You think it will be easy? Poor Zwaantie has to learn how to love my son. Not just, 'I do,' sweetheart. The prophecy was very clear. You need to join the kingdoms. Stella and Sol must become one, and it will take more than a wedding. You're too busy nursing your broken heart."

Zwaantie sat back, stunned. Sure, the Old Mother spoke of love, but beyond that, Zwaantie hadn't given much thought on how to truly join the kingdoms. She hadn't even realized it was necessary.

"I figured we would work that out after we were married. Focus on the wedding first." And love. She had to do that as well. The day-to-day operations of her kingdom wasn't something she thought of often. Obviously, Leo's mother had given it a great deal of thought. Had Leo?

Lyra gave a tiny smile, got up, and pulled a small bottle and two goblets off a shelf. She poured wine into both glasses and handed one over. Zwaantie took it but didn't say anything. She was still waiting for Lyra to scold her. She didn't drink. Perhaps Lyra planned to poison her.

"We're going to have to work together, so for now, I'm going to pretend to like you. But know this, if you hurt my son again, I will kill you."

Ari's face flashed across Zwaantie's mind. "Of course. From here on out, my heart belongs to Leo." Even as she said the words, she knew it was a lie, but she kept a smile plastered on her face and her mouth shut. She could pretend as well.

Lyra took a sip of wine. "Leo's been overlooked most of his life. He's nearly the same age as his four elder siblings. Having Candace take a kingdom was hard for him."

"Why, how was that different than the others?"

"Candace is also my daughter. I gave him a job so he would feel appreciated, but I don't want him to have the life of a spymaster. It's hard and lonely work. The eventual outcome is head mage." She paused, took a sip of her wine, and raised her eyebrows at Zwaantie. "But now he'll be king in Sol. He won't have any real power because you're the heir. Don't shove him to the side. Give him responsibility and a job. Make him feel important. He needs that."

Zwaantie thought for a moment. This woman had given her a lot of good information. Perhaps she could trust Lyra as well. No one knew Zwaantie couldn't return home, but to fulfill the prophecy, she had to. She couldn't put the kingdoms together if no one from Stella could step foot on Solite soil because the Voice was feeling murderous.

Maybe Lyra could help her find a way to return to Sol without being killed by the Voice. Sol was her kingdom, and she wasn't about to give it up.

"The longer I'm in Stella, the less I like the influence of the Voice. I guess I should've seen it, but those necklaces Leo brought were made by you or someone close to you. It takes powerful magic to turn off the Voice."

"I don't see how this is relevant. The Voice doesn't exist in Stella."

So Sage hadn't told Lyra about the Voice following Zwaantie and the others. She and Sage would need to talk about this. Perhaps Sage was the most trustworthy of the whole lot. Zwaantie grinned at the first impression she had of Sage. No one would believe she was a spy. She played the part of a carefree partying teen well.

"It's very relevant. How do you create them?"

Lyra snorted. "You're asking me for secrets? You aren't as smart as I thought."

Zwaantie leaned forward. "No, I don't think you understand. If all Solites were given a necklace, then the Voice would no longer have any influence. We would have free will. Our entire lives would change. It's possible magic would even work."

She hadn't realized what she was going to say until the words were out of her mouth. Magic in Sol. It would be incredible.

"Why would you want to do this?" Lyra narrowed her eyes.

"You have free will. We don't. I don't know who or what the Voice is, but he's the biggest threat to my future reign, and so I no longer have any respect for him. What good is a queen if someone else is truly calling the shots?"

"I don't understand what any of this has to do with Leo."

Ah, ever the meddling mother looking out for her son. "I haven't a clue how to manage a kingdom that isn't under the Voice's influence. I'll need someone to do it with me. It will be an enormous job. Leo will be good at it, and that would fulfill the prophecy of joining the kingdoms"

Lyra smiled at Zwaantie. "We should also have free trade. Throw the borders wide open. Put up several more rods. Allow people to cross at will."

Zwaantie gulped. This was moving too fast. She needed time to process. Lyra was basically proposing pushing Stella into Sol. Zwaantie needed the Voice to disappear, but she didn't want to do away with their entire culture and kingdom. She didn't know what else to say, so she smiled and nodded. This was a long ways away. She had time to make these decisions, but at least she'd be on speaking terms with Leo's mother.

Chapter Fifteen

THE SPY

Z waantie had a ton on her mind as she made her way to Sage's room. She felt like she was being manipulated by everyone in Stella, including Sage, but she knew from experience she could never stay mad at Sage for long.

Zwaantie pushed the door open. A giggling Sage jerked her head up and immediately shut down whatever she was looking at on her disc.

"How did the visit go with Lyra?" Sage asked with an innocent smile. She wasn't going to get away with this. Even if Zwaantie knew she could trust her more than she could Lyra and Leo, Sage still lied to her. A lot.

Zwaantie tentatively sat on the couch near Sage. "You're not my guard, are you?"

"What do you mean?"

"You were assigned to spy on me."

Sage pursed her lips. "Sort of. My main purpose was to make sure you stayed safe, but if I were to find out anything, um, pertinent, I was to pass the information on to Leo and Lyra."

"Did you tell Leo about Phoenix when I first told you?"

"No," Sage said, staring straight into Zwaantie's eyes. She had to be telling the truth.

"Why not? That's part of your job, isn't it?" Zwaantie's stomach rolled. She'd fallen into such a treacherous den. Could she trust anyone?

Sage let out a long breath. "My job is complicated. I don't trust Lyra and so by extension, Leo sometimes. I'm a hoarder of information. I reveal what I want when I'm ready. I probably know more secrets about those in the kingdom than anyone else. Lyra knows this. She would never force me to tell her anything I didn't want to."

Zwaantie sat back stunned. She'd been wrong. Lyra wasn't the most dangerous person in the kingdom. Sage was.

"You said you don't trust her, so how do you know she'll never force you to do anything?"

"Because she trusts me. I've proved myself time and time again. She's willing to allow me to withhold information as long as I get the job done."

"Until you don't."

"I don't know what you mean."

"The first time you mess up, it's over. She'll no longer trust you. Seems like a precarious position for you to be in."

Sage shrugged. "Maybe, but it works for now."

"You're known for partying hard with potions. How do you never accidentally reveal something you shouldn't?"

"Oh, I give out a lot of potions, but I don't actually drink that many. Enough that people think I do, but I don't take potions that would put me in an awkward position."

"How do you prevent someone from giving you one you weren't expecting?"

"I can tell what a potion is from touching the bottle. I've spent a lot of time with Xandria. She taught me how to identify potions."

Zwaantie had completely underestimated Sage.

A knock sounded on the door, and Sage jumped up. "That's the wedding planner."

Zwaantie nodded, still unsettled by the things she learned from Sage and Lyra. She had to reassess all of her knowledge about the people of Stella.

The wedding planner was a short woman with spikey green hair and hardly any clothes. Very Stellan. Zwaantie's mother and father would be attending the wedding. What would they think of such a woman? Truly blending Stella and Sol would not be an easy feat. If Lyra interpreted the prophecy correctly, then it would take them months or even years to truly join the two kingdoms. Marriage and love might not be enough to save little Raaf.

The woman sat down and stared at Zwaantie with bright purple eyes. "Tell me, dear, what do you want?"

"I want a wedding that has the best of both Solite and Stellan cultures." She had to start somewhere.

The woman's eyes lit up.

"Oh yes, that will be the talk of the century. Tell me about Solite weddings."

Chapter Sixteen

THE DINNER

That evening, Zwaantie zipped up her dress, a pretty black and pink strapless with a flared skirt. She couldn't believe she'd started thinking about how it would look in pictures. Maybe she really was becoming Stellan. Maybe that wasn't a bad thing.

Leo's face appeared on her wall.

"Hey," she said with a smile. For once, she was glad to see him. Ari hadn't been around, and Zwaantie wanted to make a real go of things with Leo. Her life and kingdom depended on it.

"If I'd been a few seconds earlier, I'd have had quite a view." He wiggled his eyebrows. She laughed. She really should learn how to turn the screen off so she wouldn't accidentally get popped in on. Sage told her there was a way, but she didn't know how. There had been too many other things occupying her time.

"Yeah, you wish." She settled down on the couch and stared up at him. She needed to love this man. Try as she might, she couldn't muster up feelings for him. She wanted to. He was handsome, friendly, funny. He lacked nothing, and yet, her heart burned for Ari. She let out a breath.

Astrid had gone to Xandria for a potion to allow her to live with the king's infidelity, so maybe Xandria could help Zwaantie rid herself of her feelings for Ari.

"What are you up to?" she asked.

"Missing you. Mom said you came to visit her."

Of course his mother told him. "I did. She's not as scary as everyone makes her out to be."

He snorted. "Well, you are the only one who thinks that. I'm terrified of her most of the time."

"She's your mother!" Zwaantie said with a laugh.

"Exactly. I'm glad you like her. It will make our lives easier." Like was a stretch, but if Leo wanted to believe that, she'd let him.

"Yes it will. I got my wedding dress."

"Really. Wow. This still feels a bit surreal, you know." He ran a hand through his hair and glanced away from her. She'd been nervous about everything, but she didn't realize he was as well. He was getting a shoddy deal with her.

"Planning is fun. Do we really have to rule in Sol when it's over?"

"That's up to you. It's your kingdom." He furrowed his brow.

"I talked to your mom about how to make it easier."

"She mentioned that."

Geesh. Did this woman tell Leo everything? Perhaps Zwaantie should take a page out of Sage's book and not talk about anything real with anyone.

The door flew open, and Sage bounded in, wearing the same dress as Zwaantie, except hers had blue instead of pink. Of course. Pictures. Maybe this was how they dealt with the enormous pressures of royalty. Pictures and matching dresses allowed one to forget about the real pressures of life.

"Late! We're late for dinner," Sage said.

Zwaantie peered at Leo. "I gotta go. Can't be late for dinner."

He gave her a sad smile. "I know. We'll talk later. Love you." He usually signed off after he said the words, but this time he waited.

Zwaantie steeled herself. She couldn't say the words yet, even though she should. "You too."

Close enough. He gave her a tight smile and clicked off. Zwaantie closed her eyes and took a couple of deep breaths. How long would it be before she did something that made him happy instead of sad or stressed.

Sage grabbed her hand. "Late, seriously. Let's go." In the hallway, Sage wiggled her eyebrows. "'You too.' You're really going out on a limb there."

"I'm trying. Give me a break." She needed to get Sage off her love life. Thinking of the Voice and her death was easier. "Any word on my assassination attempts?"

"Not really anything new. All roads lead to the Voice. He must not like you much."

Zwaantie's heart sank. As long as there was a Voice, she could never go home. How was she supposed to run a kingdom where the Voice wanted her dead? She could use the necklaces, but they'd have to be dispersed before she ever arrived, and she couldn't guarantee each and every person would wear them. Keeping track of fifty people was one thing. Thousands would be impossible.

Everyone was already at dinner, including Luna. It'd been a while since Zwaantie had seen her. She still didn't have on a necklace, and Zwaantie had left hers in the room. Though Zwaantie wasn't sure why she bothered. Luna hadn't shown any inclination she wanted to kill Zwaantie, and she had the most opportunity.

The photographers were already making the rounds. She and Sage must've missed the group pictures, and she wondered what the Ticker would make of that. Probably something dramatic. She could smooth it over by saying she got stuck on a long conversation with Leo, because the public seemed fascinated with their relationship. Personally, she'd never cared much what others did unless she was close to them.

The two empty seats were several chairs away from one another. One was next to the king and the other next to Ari. Zwaantie assumed she'd be sitting next to the king, and so she strode right past Ari without even glancing at him. She couldn't afford to.

He grabbed her hand, and she froze, her heart racing.

"You're sitting here," he said, pointing at the placard.

Sage squeezed past Zwaantie. "It's okay. We'll switch."

"I do believe Father wants you next to him," Ari said, nodding his head toward the king.

"I can sit here." Zwaantie slid into the seat before Sage could argue. Her brain told her to sit by the king. Her heart said otherwise. Besides, she needed to learn how to be around Ari. If she couldn't be in the same room with her brother-in-law, it would raise a lot of red flags. Her fingers itched to touch his, and her face flushed as she thought of his kiss.

"You're late," Ari said with that devastating grin of his. Those lips called to her. This was impossible

"I know. I was talking to Leo." She hoped it would throw him off for a few moments.

Ari took a sip of his wine. "And how is Leo?"

"Fine. Lonely. He's looking forward to us being together again."

"I can imagine. I've had more action with you than he has."

"Ari," Zwaantie hissed. "Shut it." Now her face was really red. She'd die if anyone heard them. Ari would ruin her and any hope she had of appeasing the public.

A photographer appeared in front of them then. "Picture?"

Ari slid closer to Zwaantie and put his arm around her shoulder. She smiled because it was expected, but she was incredibly aware of his soft musky cologne and how his skin felt on her shoulder. The way his fingers stroked her arm, light enough to send shivers down her back but discreet enough so no one else noticed.

The photographer moved away, and Zwaantie shrugged off his arm. She had to find a way to be friends with him, but if he kept reminding her of their indiscretions, that would never happen. He was going to be King of Stella and she Queen of Sol. If they couldn't be civil with one another, they'd never make any progress in joining the kingdoms.

She folded her hands in her lap. "Ari, I want to be your friend."

He met her eyes. "Well, I don't."

His words stung. "That's mean."

He put a hand on her bare knee. "No, Zwaantie I..."

Zwaantie knocked his hand off. If Ari wasn't willing to be her friend, then she'd ignore him until he came around. If she had to deal with him concerning affairs of the state, she'd make sure she always had people with her. She could always send Leo to deal with him.

She turned to the person on her left. Viggo. King of the Media.

Maybe she could see what the public was really saying about her. He might prove a more powerful ally than Ari.

"Usually you and Luna aren't far from one another," Zwaantie said. Luna was several seats away talking animatedly with the princesses on either side of her. It was true. Anytime Zwaantie had caught a glance of Luna, she was always with Viggo.

"The king and queen decide where everyone sits. I am quite fond of Luna, but tonight they put her near the princesses. Perhaps the queen thought she needed to make new friends. We're meeting up later and partying in the gardens."

"I've never been to the gardens." Zwaantie was a little envious of Luna. She had no worries or concerns about what the future held. It wasn't fair.

Ari slid closer and slung his arm across the back of her chair. His fingers lingered on her shoulder. Her chest tingled. Her reactions to him were distracting. "Then you are missing out. Can Zwaantie and I join your little party?"

Zwaantie let out a deep breath. She couldn't make any moves that would lead Viggo to think something was going on. If she made it seem like she didn't want to be around Ari, Viggo might get suspicious.

"Of course. We're going to spend the night there," Viggo said.

Zwaantie wanted to argue, to get out of spending the night in the same place as Ari, but she didn't want to be rude. Viggo said party though, so there would be a lot of people. A lot of pictures would be taken, and she hoped Ari wouldn't risk her reputation.

Zwaantie could make sure Sage went as well, and then she'd avoid Ari and surround herself with princesses like Luna had. This might be good. She hadn't spent much time with Viggo before, and these relationships were important. No matter what happened, Viggo was her connection to a good image with the people. If she won him over, he could do wonders for her.

Dinner flew by. Viggo was hilarious, and Zwaantie managed to avoid Ari's roaming hands. By the time dinner was over, Ari was sulking and nudging her with his foot.

"I'm going to get Sage. We'll meet you in the gardens," Zwaantie said to Viggo. Sage would be a good ally and buffer. She wouldn't let Ari pester her.

"Of course. See you there. Make sure Sage brings her potions," Viggo said with a wink.

Just as Zwaantie stood, so did Ari, and he followed her to Sage.

"Hey, we're going to party with Viggo and friends in the gardens," Zwaantie said, standing as far from Ari as she dared.

Sage's face fell. "That sounds like so much fun, but I have to help Daddy with some stuff."

"We're going to spend the night. Maybe you'll come later."

"Yeah, that sounds great," she said. Her face told a different story. Her jaw was tense and her eyes sad. Zwaantie wondered what was going on.

"Viggo said to bring your potions."

Sage recovered and raised her eyebrows. "You sure, princess? You've never really partied with me before. The lock-in was tame."

Zwaantie shrugged. "Something new, I guess." Now that she knew how Sage really operated, it would be interesting to watch her work. She was fairly certain every move Sage made was calculated to gather information, no matter how innocent it seemed.

"See you around midnight," Zwaantie said.

Ari put his hand on Zwaantie's back and a thrill went up her spine. "Come on, I'll show you where it is."

She liked the feel of his hand and knew she shouldn't. What she really wanted was more of it, but that was out of the question. No matter how badly she wanted him, Ari would never be hers.

Chapter Seventeen

THE GARDEN

By the time she and Ari left the dining room, there was no sign of Viggo or Luna. Zwaantie took a few steps away from Ari. She couldn't afford to be close to him.

Ari shoved his hands in his pockets. Maybe he was feeling the same way. She snorted. Yeah, right. Ari had only one goal, and that was Zwaantie. If he was withdrawing from her, it was because he thought it would further his ability to win her over.

"They must've already gone down. I'll go with you," Ari said.

Zwaantie didn't say anything as they walked down the hallway, and neither did he. Though he did keep glancing her way. They entered the elevator, and she finally let herself meet Ari's eyes. That was a mistake.

"You look beautiful," he said.

A thrill buzzed in her chest, and she squirmed. "Thank you."

He shook his head and leaned back against the glass, holding her gaze, the tension between them through the roof.

"You know it's not fair. If I had been the one sent to Sol, I wouldn't have to fight against these feelings," he said.

"You never would've come to Sol, because then you would've been committing to marriage." At least she knew where he drew the line.

He scowled, but didn't respond. She wondered about his words. If he had come and agreed to marry her, they would be creating the strongest bond possible between the two kingdoms. She was surprised she hadn't thought of it before. It presented an intriguing possibility.

The gardens were located in the middle of the castle on the third floor. They stopped in small room lined with glass bottles like the potion shop.

"These are all glow. We have to take them, or we won't see each other. The garden is pitch black except the plants. The darkness makes them stand out more. Here." He handed Zwaantie a small bottle, and she drank it while he downed another one. Maybe she should've checked it first in case he'd given her more than glow. "Oh and take your shoes off."

Ari glowed faintly in front of her. He looked like an angel.

"Just so you know, Viggo and the others won't be here until close to midnight."

"What?" she asked, regretting allowing him to bring her. Before she could argue, he pushed open the door and gave her a nudge.

The first thing she noticed was the smell of roses, lilies, and tulips mixed into one. Plus pine and the faint smell of the ocean. The room was pitch black, and they were completely alone. They had nearly four hours until midnight. This would not end well.

She stopped in the doorway, and Ari pressed up behind her. Stars, he felt nice.

"You need to move," he whispered into her ear, sending a shiver down her spine.

"I don't want to run into anything." Her voice was breathy and weak. She hated how he did this to her.

"You won't. The garden doesn't start until several feet in. Just a couple of steps, you'll be fine."

She took a reluctant step forward, and Ari moved with her, his hand resting on her hip. The ground beneath her feet was cool and soft. Like grass.

"Are you ready?" Ari asked.

"For what?" She worried he was going to kiss her then and there. She wouldn't stop him either.

"We're going to turn the garden on."

"Okay."

"Here. I'll show you how." He ran his fingers down her arm and gripped the back of her hand, pressing it against the wall behind her. Her fingers brushed up against a small button.

"When you are ready, push it," he breathed into her ear. She hated how much she loved his voice. She took a couple of deep breaths to calm her racing heart, and then she pressed down.

"Oh," she gasped. Everything glowed. The grass beneath their feet was a soft green. The flowers, the trees. Even the butterflies gave off light. They glowed rainbow, and the color shifted as they fluttered in the air.

Ari wrapped his arms around Zwaantie's stomach. She barely noticed because it felt so natural. That was almost worse than the constant energy between them. At least with the tension, she was on her guard. She'd be lulled into the comfort and not even notice she was falling.

"Pretty amazing, huh?"

Amazing didn't even begin to describe it.

"Are these real?" Zwaantie asked, feeling a petal on an enormous lily bloom. She'd never seen anything like this before. It was as if someone looked at a flower and said, "How can I make this better?"

"No, the plants are magical. But the mages studied natural gardens. They've taken some liberties, obviously. And they change it up quite a bit. This is one of my favorite places in the castle. Sometimes Sage and I sleep down here when we're feeling blue. I'm surprised we haven't brought you here before."

The grass felt real beneath her feet, but softer. She walked along a small path and admired the too-large roses and blinking bees. Several butterflies landed on her arm, and she stopped to watch them change colors.

Ari led her to the center of the garden where an enormous oak tree stood. Every few moments she was struck by how comfortable she was with Ari. In the garden, time felt endless as if she and Ari simply were together. There was no beginning and no end.

The leaves of the oak tree glowed different colors. They were fall colors, so the leaves were red, orange, and yellow. Ari pulled her under the tree and lay down. The ground was soft and warm.

She threw caution to the wind and scooted closer to him, pressing up against his side, staring up into the magical tree.

"This feels like the fairy stories my slave nanny used to tell me as a little girl. I never knew this was real."

He laughed.

"I guess we are both having our realities changed today."

She didn't want to hear how his reality had changed because she had a sinking feeling it had everything to do with her. Tears threatened. She couldn't love him. Not now. Though, she desperately wanted to. She didn't know what was happening to her, but she felt like she loved him. More than she'd ever loved Phoenix. Why couldn't Ari have just left her alone?

He brushed her hands with his fingers. "I never thought it would be possible to feel this way, you know. I mean I've kissed hundreds of girls and slept with most of them, but I've never once had the desire to want anything more. But you, you make me want more." He sighed and withdrew his hand. She missed it immediately.

"I wonder if it's because maybe I'm getting tired of sleeping with a different woman every night, or if it's because you are unattainable. I've never hesitated in sleeping with a married woman before, but you are Leo's. He's my brother. I feel guilt for being attracted to you. That's a new feeling too. Guilt. I don't know what's real anymore."

Neither did she, but she couldn't say that to him as much as she wanted to. If she admitted her feelings, a dam would break, and the flood that followed would kill them both. This wasn't right.

He rolled over and faced her, his expression full of anguish. She knew she should say something, anything, but her words were lost.

"Oh stars, I can't even look at you without wanting to touch you." He ran his fingertips down her bare arm and then brought her fingers to his lips. He kissed them lightly. Goosebumps rose on her arms. Ari stared at Zwaantie with those intense eyes of his.

"Am I crazy? Maybe I've bared my soul to you, and you don't even feel the same way."

Zwaantie should've said she didn't. It would make everything easier and was the only way out of whatever this was. She wasn't allowed to want him. She needed to tell him they could never be together no matter how badly either one wanted it. She'd admitted she loved him when she'd taken that secret potion, but he still seemed insecure of the way she felt. So she said the one thing she knew she shouldn't.

"Leo doesn't kiss me the way you do."

He groaned. "You weren't supposed to make this harder for me. You were supposed to tell me you've grown to love Leo, and I need to get over it."

"I should," she said, placing a hand on his face, thrilled with her own boldness. "You know I don't love Leo. I planned on marrying him in the hopes someday I would learn to love him. I'm marrying him for the sole purpose of joining our kingdoms. I'm marrying him to save little Raaf."

That was it. The only reason. But Ari was a prince too. Right? Not just any prince either. The heir to the Stellan throne. Oh stars. She could have him.

"Remind me of the prophecy," she said.

"If Stella and Sol aren't joined by little Raaf's first birthday, he'll die." He recited it like he memorized the words. "Then there's the new part that you have to love Leo, or it won't work." The Old Mother didn't say Leo. She said prince. Zwaantie had to love the prince and love him she did.

"You know, the same purpose could be served if I married you instead."

Ari's face turned hard. "Not happening. I'm never marrying anyone. Even if I choose to be completely faithful to someone, we won't be married. I would forever resent my wife."

Zwaantie's smile faltered. The purpose was to join the kingdoms. Stella would not be saved if they pretended, and she couldn't be with him otherwise. The Old Mother had been clear about what she had to feel. Love. The only obstacle between her and Ari was marriage.

"Then I guess our conversation is over. I have to love my husband, and you won't marry me."

He clutched at his hair. "Do you know what you're asking of me?"

"Of course. What I don't understand is how hard it is to give me your fidelity. If you love me, then you'll marry me. We have more to think about than ourselves."

"Seriously, woman. Why couldn't we just be together?"

"Oh, and let little Raaf die? Also, in case you forgot, I have a kingdom I have to run. Our children would be bastards. Is that what you want? In my kingdom they would not even be recognized as true heirs to the throne."

He scoffed. "They won't want to rule in Sol anyway. There are plenty of places for them to rule over here. Besides, I am heir to the throne here. I have to rule here. We wouldn't go back to Sol."

Ugh. He was infuriating. It didn't matter anyway.

"Well, that argument is not worth having because you won't marry me. Did you forget what happens to your kingdom if we don't merge them?"

Zwaantie wasn't sure how they got from not being sure of their feelings to declaring a love so deep they were willing to risk everything just to have it. At least she was. He wouldn't consent to marry her, which meant that he didn't feel the same way.

His breathing was deep, and anger marred his beautiful features, but she could tell he was thinking.

"Okay, okay. I'll tell you what. We'll rule in Sol. I'll give up my right to rule here. Leo can have it. And we'll pretend to be married. We'll tell everyone we got married here. I can give up Stella for you."

He really thought that would make it okay. They'd just pretend. Yeah, right.

"Oh, so you can sleep with my slaves? You know, when we fight and stuff, you'll make sure you'll still get laid. This is absurd. I can't believe I thought you loved me. You don't. If you did, you wouldn't be thinking about the stupid curse because you'd know you would never cheat on me."

He squeezed his eyes shut. "You do understand that even if you marry Leo, he will probably have affairs from time to time. And he'll expect the same from you. It's part of our culture. There is nothing wrong with an occasional fling on the side."

"Apparently your mother felt differently."

"Yes, well, there are a few people who disagree, but they are in the minority."

"I'd rather be cheated on by someone I didn't love than someone I did. It doesn't matter anyway. I have to marry a prince of Stella. That's crucial to joining our kingdoms. Do you think the vipers will care if we pretend?"

"You are impossible." He stormed from the oak tree. A few minutes later the door slammed.

Chapter Eighteen

THE DOOR

Zwaantie wandered around the garden for a while thinking about Ari and Leo. They were so different, and while Leo was growing on her and she was sure they'd have a happy marriage once she got over Ari, it wouldn't have the fire a marriage with Ari would have. Probably wouldn't have the fights they had either.

How she wanted Ari. He was everything she'd never known she wanted, and she had to ignore her feelings because she was not allowed to have him. In another life, maybe, but with the prophecy hanging over their heads, no way.

Who was she kidding? She understood now how the prophecy worked. It could only ever be Leo. He was the one who would marry her and properly join the kingdoms. She needed to forget about Ari and focus on Leo. He was safe and would save his kingdom. Her heart ached at the thought of marrying Leo. What if she never loved him? What if she could never figure out how to force her feelings? Little Raaf would die anyway.

Eventually her glow wore off so she reluctantly left the enchanted garden and wondered why no one else had shown up. Perhaps she hadn't been down here as long as she thought. She was in no mood to party, and she was certain the others would arrive soon. She wanted to sleep. Sage would have to tell her about it in the morning.

She'd just shut the door to the garden when Luna, surrounded by a group of people, waved to her from down the hall. Zwaantie had to figure out how to get out of this. She had hoped to make it upstairs before she saw anyone.

Luna rushed up and gave her a big hug. Zwaantie returned the embrace, surprised. She'd missed her dear friend.

"I missed you," Luna said. "I know you are off doing all those princessy things."

"Not really. You should come out with me tomorrow." After this mess with Ari, she wanted to do something that wouldn't remind her of him. Then she could give Luna the necklace and explain what was happening. Luna would understand her inner turmoil in a way her Stellan friends could not.

"Yeah, I will. Are you coming to the party? We can hang in there. I bet it's totally amazing inside the garden."

"It is."

Viggo came over to them. "Princess, you ready?"

"I'm sorry. I'm not feeling well. I'm going to bed."

Luna's face fell, and Zwaantie felt a tinge of guilt. She hadn't spent much time with Luna at all, and she'd hoped to change that, but after her fight with Ari, she didn't have it in her. Tonight she needed to sleep. Clear her head and focus on how to fall in love with Leo. The thought filled her with dread.

"Picture before you leave." Viggo said, pushing the girls together.

Zwaantie agreed, but she was certain her smile was fake. She hoped it wouldn't come across that way on the disc.

She waved goodbye and made her way to the elevators. The hallways were unusually empty. Zwaantie wondered what time it was. She and Ari had arrived at the garden just after dinner. Surely she hadn't been in there for four hours. A servant hurried down the hall.

"Princess, you only have a few minutes until the vipers come out. Hurry," the servant said.

Oh, Stars, time flew. She thanked him and rushed toward her room. She'd never been out this late. She'd always worried about death by the vipers, and so she always made sure to get to her room on time.

She passed Ari's room on the way. She paused by his door and almost knocked, but the five-minute warning bell sang. This was cutting it way too close. She shouldn't be thinking about him, but she couldn't help herself.

She had barely gone around the curve when she heard a door open. She peeked back and saw a girl slip out of Ari's room. She was thin, and her clothes barely covered her breasts. She scurried down the hall. Anger burned in Zwaantie's chest. Ari couldn't even handle one night alone. She couldn't believe she thought she was falling for him. He couldn't keep his hands or other body parts to himself for even a second. It just reaffirmed in her heart that Leo was the one she should focus on, the one who loved her and would save the kingdom.

Time was slipping away. She turned the handle to her door, but it wouldn't budge. Locked. She shoved harder. What the dark? These doors only locked from the inside. There was no reason to lock it when you weren't inside. She tried again. Nothing.

She pounded on the door. Maybe Sage was in there.

"Sage," Zwaantie yelled. "Let me in."

Silence. This was stupid. Sage never hung out in Zwaantie's room.

The clock began to chime the twelve bells of midnight. On the last bell, the vipers would come out, and Zwaantie would die.

She rushed to Sage's room, but her door wouldn't open either. Zwaantie pounded and yelled but no one responded. Stars. She paused to think, knowing she only had one option if she wanted to survive.

On chime six she ran down the hall to his room, hating herself for needing him to rescue her. This was the last thing she wanted. She would be sleeping on the couch and not speaking to him more than necessary. Bad things would happen otherwise.

She beat on his door.

"Ari, Ari, let me in!" she yelled and slapped the door again.

The ninth bell chimed. He stuck his head out. His eyes bloodshot and his hair a mess.

"What do you want?" he slurred. Oh great. While she'd dawdled in the garden, he'd been busy getting drunk with the blonde girl who just left. Had Zwaantie really wanted him? Why?

The tenth bell chimed.

"I'm about to get stuck out here. I need to come in. My door is locked."

The eleventh bell chimed. Zwaantie didn't wait. She pushed past him. He stumbled and glowered at her. She slammed the door behind her, locking it.

The twelfth bell chimed, and she slid down next to his door, breathing hard. The pounding on the other side began almost immediately. She'd brushed death so many times now. She'd forgotten what it was like to feel safe.

"That was close," she breathed and rubbed her temples. Now she was safe from one kind of monster. Would she survive the night with another?

Chapter Nineteen

THE LOST CAUSE

Ari staggered to his couch and slouched down on it. On the small table in front of him sat ten small potion bottles and two empty wine bottles. She'd never taken liberties with wine before. Maybe she'd have to in order to get through the night with him. Though, then she might do something stupid. Maybe she'd get lucky, and he'd just go to sleep.

He squinted at the potion bottles and shoved them toward Zwaantie. "Find the one that says Sober."

She raised her eyebrows at him. "Maybe I should let you stay drunk." If he passed out, then she'd have nothing to worry about.

"Please," he murmured and pinched his nose. "My head is pounding."

Zwaantie sorted through them. She found Lust, Awake, and a few others that made her blush. The seventh bottle was called Sober. She handed him the bottle, and he tipped it into his mouth.

He grimaced.

"Thanks," he said without looking at her. He staggered to the bathroom and turned on the shower. Zwaantie had no idea what the night would bring, now that he was sober and awake.

She was stuck here, for better or for worse. She had two goals. First, she didn't want to fight with Ari. Second, she was not going to kiss him. Though if she had to choose one of the two, it would be safer to fight with him.

She searched for an extra blanket. There were plenty of pillows on the couch. Her dress wasn't terribly comfortable, but she could sleep in it. Not finding one, she sat on the couch and waited for Ari to come out. Mentally she prepared herself. She would only talk to him to get a pillow and blanket so she could sleep. Then she would go to sleep and be out of his room before he woke the next morning.

Twenty minutes later Ari returned wearing a robe and smelling of raspberry soap. His eyes were clear again, and Zwaantie had trouble not getting lost in them. Her plan seemed futile.

He settled on the couch next to her, closer than he should've. "Sorry about that. I was trying to, uh, forget about our fight."

"Did it work?" Zwaantie asked, attempting to be civil, and slid back a few inches. This was better. If she could continue arguing with him, then she wouldn't do something stupid, like kiss him.

He shook his head.

"What about the girl who left your room before I showed up. Did she help you forget?" Zwaantie didn't even try to hide the venom in her voice. So much for not fighting. Everything about Ari stirred up emotions in her, both good and bad. It was exhausting.

Ari ran a hand along his face. "If it makes you feel any better, nothing happened. I don't think I even kissed her."

"Right, with..." Zwaantie picked up a bottle. "Orgasm, and all these others sitting out here." She was disgusted with him.

Ari gave her a crooked grin. "They are all full, in case you haven't noticed. You could take that one if you want. It'll make you happy." He raised his eyebrows at her expectantly.

She set it back down, her hands shaking. She wasn't sure if it was from nerves or anger.

"Not on your life." She didn't even know what that meant, but she had taken a chance that it had something to do with sex.

Ari slid closer to her. She should move away, but everything about him drew her in.

"I've been thinking," Ari began.

"Before or after you 'didn't' have sex with that girl." What was wrong with her? She needed to close her mouth and get away from him, but she couldn't. She didn't want to, not really.

Ari scowled. "Nothing happened. I wanted something to, believe me. But all I could think about was how disappointed you'd be if I slept with her." His voice dropped, and he searched Zwaantie's eyes. He gripped her hands, and Zwaantie didn't bother pulling away. "She wasn't the one I wanted. Not by a long shot. I want you and only you. She didn't hold an ounce of attraction for me. Even after I drank two bottles of wine. I searched her face, and all I could see was you."

Zwaantie couldn't take her eyes off of his lips. The way they moved. She wanted to press her mouth against his and forget about Leo. This wasn't fair of Ari to do to her. He was saying all the right things and looking at her in a way that made her lose sense.

"I asked her to leave. I think tonight may be the first night in several years I haven't had sex. Which is so unbelievable because this is the first time in a long time that I have a girl in my room I desperately want to be with. And I know you won't."

She met his eyes. In that moment, all of her fears disappeared. This was the man she should be marrying. This was her only desire.

Zwaantie scrambled across the couch and kissed him. She had to have him, no matter the consequence.

He didn't react for a moment. But then he kissed her back, embracing her. His body was warm against hers, his hands eager. They fit together so well. Their lips moved easily and with a hunger she didn't even know was possible. Why did fate have to be so cruel?

Screw fate.

Just for one night. Tomorrow, she'd take responsibility. She didn't know what the night would bring, but tonight, she'd let herself know what it was like to be truly loved.

After a while her lips were sore, but she was happy. She laid her head on his shoulder. Neither said anything for a long time. She reveled in the comfort.

"Are you tired?" Ari asked, massaging the back of her neck.

"Yes. No." She laughed. "I don't know."

"Let's find you something more comfortable to sleep in."

Zwaantie stumbled a little bit as she stood, and fell into his arms. They both laughed, and she tried to ignore the butterflies in her stomach. Questions flew through her head about the repercussions of tonight. What did it mean? Perhaps it would extend to more than one night. If so, would they have to tell Leo? Only if Ari would marry her. If he didn't, they would have to keep this secret. But the prophecy.

Ari gave her an extra-large t-shirt. He left the closet, and she slid out of her dress and put on the shirt. Ari was already in bed when she came out. Even though they had slept in the same bed several times over the last few weeks, it made her nervous tonight. This was the first time she'd slept with him after a heavy make-out session, and she wasn't sure where things would go.

"No expectations, just sleep. Come on," Ari said.

She slipped into bed with him, and he wrapped his arms around her. He smelled musky and sexy. She nuzzled into him. Everything about him was warm and safe. She knew she wouldn't have trouble falling asleep even though thoughts raced through her mind. He was too comfortable. Too easy. This was where she was meant to be.

Chapter Twenty

THE ALLY

"Why is it every time I appear, you are in bed with my fiancée?"

Waking up to Leo's voice was not the way Zwaantie wanted to be roused. She took a second to regroup and think about where she was.

Ari jumped out of bed and settled on the couch in front of Leo. Zwaantie smoothed her hair and joined him, sitting several inches away from Ari. He made no move to touch her and acted like everything was normal. Was this what the future would bring? Lies and hiding?

At least she and Ari had clothes on. She had no idea how they would've explained that away. Though, then everything would be out in the open. She blushed at the thought of Ari naked and grinned at the irony. Never once when she was in Sol would that thought have ever crossed her mind. If she were to take the necklace off now, the Voice would have a lot of words for her. A nasty headache probably as well.

"This is easily explained. Your fiancée returned to her room last night minutes before midnight and found her door locked. She couldn't get in. She also tried Sage's room, which was also locked. She had no choice but to come here."

Zwaantie let out a breath. Part of her had hoped Ari would tell Leo. That he'd consent to marrying her. Leo looked from Zwaantie to Ari. Zwaantie kept her eyes on Leo and gave him a sheepish smile.

"It's true. I tried to sleep on the couch, but it was impossible. I'm sorry."

He frowned. "Not sure I like seeing you in Ari's t-shirts."

"I couldn't very well sleep in my dress."

He seemed satisfied with the explanation. "What were you doing out of your rooms so late?"

"I was in the gardens and lost track of time." That, at least, was the truth. She wondered how many lies she would have to tell. She was tired of the deception.

"Where's Sage?" Leo asked. He crossed his arms.

"She's dealing with Zwaantie's assassination attempts," answered Ari. This was news. Zwaantie thought she was doing something for her father.

"Has she found anything yet?"

Ari shook his head. "Not yet, but we haven't heard from her since last night. I'll have her call you as soon as she knows something. Honestly, I figured she'd contact you before she returned."

"She hasn't called me. As soon as you see her, please tell her I need to talk to her."

"Done, brother. Now I suppose you want some time to visit with Zwaantie."

Leo's eyes flicked to her. Ari played his part well. She wasn't convinced she'd be able to keep up with the lie if she had to talk to Leo by herself. She didn't want to hide anymore.

"I wish. But I'm due at breakfast with Jem. I'll have some time this afternoon. Love you."

He didn't wait for Zwaantie's response and clicked off. He probably didn't want to hear her lame "You too." She was glad because she wasn't sure she could even manage that. If it were Ari, she'd be able to say the words to him.

Ari clicked off the screen and then pushed a small button on the wall.

"Is that how you turn it off?" Zwaantie asked. "I haven't been able to figure it out."

"Yep. No one will be able to call. Your device may buzz, but you have to physically answer it."

She would need to find that button in her own room.

He collapsed next to her, and she snuggled into him. She had a decision to make. She could leave Ari and never look back. Leave last night an amazing memory and forget all about Ari. Go to Leo and force herself to love him. Or she could stay here and be foolish, but happy.

"Where were we last night before we got tired, huh?" he asked and planted a soft kiss on her neck. Foolish looked nice right about now. He trailed his lips up near her ear. She shivered.

"I can't remember. Maybe you should refresh my memory." This moment would forever change their trajectory. They were on a slippery slope, and it would end badly, but their feelings were too strong. She couldn't deny them.

"Oh yeah? You want a repeat?"

"Very much so." She meant every word.

His hungry lips met hers. There was more passion to this kiss, as if he'd finally let his guard down and allowed himself to have what he wanted. He pushed Zwaantie back on the couch so he was lying on top of her. His hands moved everywhere. It was thrilling and amazing and not at all guilt-ridden, now that she'd allowed herself to love him.

Maybe they could stay locked in his room forever and not worry about anything that happened out in the real world.

The door behind them opened, and Ari made no move to get up, but he lifted his head to see who came through the door.

"Why the hell is my door locked?" Sage's irritated voice floated from the other side of the couch. Real life was coming way too quickly.

"Don't know," Zwaantie replied, ready to get this encounter over with.

Sage squeaked and ran over.

For a second Sage didn't say anything. Zwaantie didn't want to hear the chastisement. Sage didn't approve, and she knew the repercussions.

Sage sank down onto the ottoman and stared at them. Zwaantie shifted under Ari's weight, and he sat up, pulling Zwaantie with him and into his lap, his arms wrapped tightly around her.

"Did you sleep here?" Sage asked cautiously.

"Yeah, I couldn't get into your room. Or my own." Zwaantie tried to justify her night with Ari, but she knew Sage wasn't buying it. Even if it was the truth.

Ari turned Zwaantie's face toward his and kissed her lightly on the lips. "We're not keeping this a secret from Sage."

Sage kept looking from Zwaantie to Ari. "Are you going to marry her?"

Zwaantie had avoided that question this morning, afraid of the response.

Ari shook his head. Zwaantie's heart sank. Reality wasn't fun.

"You do understand if you don't marry her, she still has to marry Leo." Sage said the words Zwaantie couldn't. Not now.

"I know," Ari said.

She couldn't quite believe he was acting so casual about this, and now she wondered exactly what his plan was to deal with their relationship.

Zwaantie stood up. "So you want me to marry Leo, but sleep with you." No way. He was such a cow-hole. He just expected her to give up everything for him, but he wouldn't for her.

"You were willing to do that for Phoenix."

This was different. She didn't know why, but it was. She didn't have any other options with Phoenix. "Leo is your brother."

"So? I've cleaned up plenty of his messes. He'll let me have this."

Zwaantie moved away from him. "Excuse me? I think I'll be the one who decides that." He was so arrogant. Her blood boiled just thinking about what he was asking of her.

Ari shrugged. "Okay. Sure. I'm willing to wait, but I love you, Zwaantie."

She pinched the bridge of her nose. She was so sick of people expecting her to love them simply because they thought she should. She was to marry one man, love him, and then when the mess was cleaned up, love another.

"I can't do this," Zwaantie said.

"Wait," he said, grabbing for her hand. "I know this isn't ideal, but I don't see any other options."

"No other options? How about you marry me, you idiot!"

"I've already told you I won't do that."

"How am I supposed to fall in love with Leo if all I can think about is you?"

Ari started to argue, but Sage interrupted him. "Zwaantie's right. Maybe you should go away for a while. You know, stay at The Black City or something until after Zwaantie and Leo are married. I can make an excuse for you at the wedding. Then after they've been married and the threat is gone, you can come back, and you and Zwaantie can figure out what you're going to do."

Sure, deflect the hard decisions until later. "Sounds good to me," Zwaantie said. She needed Ari away. As it was, she wasn't sure how she was going to muster up feelings for the man she was supposed to love. Though she was fairly certain if Ari left and she fell in love with Leo, she'd never be able to love Ari again.

"No," Ari said and crossed his arms.

Sage stalked over to him. "Then marry her."

"No."

"You're impossible," Sage said. "If Zwaantie doesn't fall in love with Leo, everyone in Stella dies. Is that what you want?"

Ari ran his hand through his hair. "No, that's not what I want. There has to be a way to make everything work out."

The door flew open and a servant rushed in. "Prince Ari, you must come at once. The king demands it."

"I'm a little busy here."

"It's urgent."

Ari sighed and stood up. "This conversation is not over. I'll be back soon. Don't go anywhere. We'll figure this out, and I will be with you, Zwaantie."

She resisted the urge to scream "Then marry me" behind his back. Sol, he made her mad.

Chapter Twenty-One

THE CONSEQUENCE

Sage sank back into the couch. "What were you thinking?"

"I wasn't. That's the problem. I had nowhere else to go. If my door hadn't been locked, we wouldn't be having this conversation."

"Yeah, right. I saw the way he was looking at you. Ari has his eyes set on a prize, and that prize is you. We may not be having this conversation today, but it would have come eventually." Sage crossed her legs and gave Zwaantie a look she probably only used on those she was interrogating. For a second, Zwaantie understood how Sage did her job.

Zwaantie let out a breath. "I gave him an option to have me, and he refused."

"This isn't going to end well, trust me. Why don't you let me handle Ari, and you take care of Leo."

"I can't stop thinking about him."

"I know, and I'm fairly certain he feels the same way. Leo needs to come back for good and not let you out of his sight. Maybe I'll suggest he take you out for a romantic weekend or something. That way you two can give love a shot."

"Sure, that sounds nice." No, it didn't. Not really. But she had to try, or she'd be condemning a lot of people to death. Curse her feelings.

It was time to change the subject.

"Why are you still out looking for assassins? I thought you gave them necklaces."

"We did. Now I'm trying to figure out how to stop the Voice from being in Stella altogether." She chewed on her bottom lip. "I think I need to go to Sol."

"What? Why?"

"Because I'm missing a big piece of the puzzle, and I won't figure it out from here."

"I'm not sure that's safe."

"I'm not the one the Voice wants dead. We need to do this for you."

"I don't see how going to Sol will fix that."

"Because I can talk to people there that I can't here. I want to find the source of the Voice."

"You'll get killed."

"Nah. I'm resourceful." Sage stood and fluffed her skirt. "I'm hungry. Let's go get ready for breakfast." She had dark circles under her eyes, and her normal smile had settled into a frown. She was carrying too much weight on her shoulders. Sage rarely talked about her own problems, but between trying to find Zwaantie's assassins and keeping Ari away from her, Sage had more than enough going on.

They showered, changed, and made their way to the king's empty dining room. Were they early? No. If anything, they were late. Maybe they missed breakfast.

Sage stopped a servant. "Where is the king?"

The servant pointed to a closed bedroom door.

"What's he doing in there? It's time for breakfast."

The servant shrugged and hurried out of the room.

Sage didn't bother to knock and barged in. The king sat shaking on the couch, his face in his hands. Ari had his arm around his shoulders.

"Daddy, what's wrong?" Sage sunk down on the other side of the king. Zwaantie stayed by the door. Something serious had happened, and she wasn't sure if she should be involved. She was still an outsider in this family. "What's going on? Talk to me."

Lyra entered the room. She took a seat across from the king. Zwaantie sat next to her, feeling awkward standing there.

Lyra looked down her nose at Sage. "Three days ago, the queen went to visit her sister in The Black City. No one is quite sure what happened, but the vipers killed her in the middle of the night. The whole household is dead."

Sage gasped. The king let out a sob. Zwaantie's heart froze. She glanced at Ari, who had his head buried in his father's shoulder. Zwaantie wanted to go over and comfort him, but she couldn't under the watchful eye of Lyra. Not to mention this was because of her.

Guilt settled in Zwaantie's stomach. She'd been considering loving Ari instead. Now his mother was dead. Zwaantie really had liked her, and her heart broke for Ari. He was so close to Astrid.

Lyra swept from the room, and the king resumed his silent sobbing. Zwaantie sat helpless, not sure what she could do.

ZWAANTIE SPENT THE NEXT COUPLE OF DAYS IN THE LIBRARY AND THE gardens and avoided Ari. Queen Astrid would still be alive if Zwaantie had tried harder to love Leo. Anytime she saw Ari, he wouldn't even look at her. Maybe he was feeling some guilt as well, or maybe he blamed her. Either way, she wasn't about to add to his misery by trying to talk to him.

The morning of the third day, the king held the funeral. Zwaantie dressed in a long black dress Sage picked out for her. The bodice was tight and the skirt loose. Zwaantie felt like she should be going to a ball instead of a funeral. Sage looped her arm through Zwaantie's and laid her head on Zwaantie's shoulder.

"How are you feeling?" Zwaantie asked.

"I'm fine. I didn't get along with the queen, but Ari is stricken. It's been hard watching him."

"I know. I'm sorry. I thought about talking to him, but didn't know if it would be appropriate."

Sage rubbed her forehead. "Yeah, probably not."

Zwaantie was surprised when Sage led her out of the castle and flagged down a carriage.

"Isn't the funeral here?" The castle made the most sense for a funeral. At least in Sol that was where it would've been held.

"No. The beach. We burn our bodies, and we can't do that inside. Plus, like it or not, the funeral feeds the Ticker. It's a huge social affair."

Zwaantie felt sick to her stomach. How could people use a funeral for gossip? Funerals should be respectful and small, quiet affairs for only close friends and family. Even royal funerals.

They arrived at the beach. People were everywhere. Thousands of chairs had been set up. Zwaantie trailed after Sage. She didn't feel right sitting with the royal family, but she didn't know where else she would sit. Sage slid in next to Ari. His head hung, and Sage gripped his hand. Zwaantie wanted to reach out and comfort him, but she knew it would be the wrong thing to do. Instead, she sat behind him. Ari's shoulders were tense.

On the stage, next to the queen's body, sat the king. With bloodshot eyes, he stared out over the crowd. His face was impassive. The only indication he was feeling any stress at all was his hands clenched into fists on his lap. He had no one to comfort him.

Discs fluttered around, taking pictures. Zwaantie nearly plucked one out of the air that flashed next to Sage and Ari. This was a time to mourn, not to plaster pictures all over the Ticker.

Lyra settled next to her and pursed her lips. Zwaantie didn't say anything because she knew whatever she said, it would be the wrong thing.

"The vipers are getting worse," Lyra finally said.

"I know." Zwaantie began to sweat. Could Lyra possibly know about Ari? "Has Leo found anything in The Black City?"

"This was the first attack outside of Deep Sky. He's baffled. Have you talked to him?"

"I've tried. He's very busy. I know he's talking to you because you are a part of the investigation, but he's not confiding in me." Not that she'd tried very hard. She had called a few times, but she wasn't persistent.

"The next time you talk to him, see what you can do to cheer him up. Don't mention the vipers or anything else. He's under an extraordinary amount of stress. The king blames him for not finding a solution fast enough."

"That must be awful for Leo." Zwaantie knew a thing or two about unrealistic pressures. Perhaps Leo felt the same guilt she did, that this was somehow his fault. The only difference was that this really was her fault. Leo's guilt was unfounded.

"It is. He's handling it well, but I can tell he's struggling. Maybe we should send you to The Black City to keep him company."

Zwaantie thought for a moment. The last time she'd visited Leo, things had been a little bizarre, but she wasn't about to mention that to Lyra. "That's a good idea. I'll suggest it the next time I talk to him and see if he'll let me."

Lyra snorted. "Let you? Honey, you have a lot to learn about handling men. You tell him you're coming."

Zwaantie wrung her hands. Going to see Leo would get her away from Ari and make it easier to forget him.

The king stood and a hush fell over the crowd. Zwaantie had never seen him so sad. His normal regal stature drooped. Zwaantie was going to stop the deaths. She would learn to love Leo if it was the last thing she did.

Chapter Twenty-Two

THE LULL

Zwaantie arrived in The Black City that afternoon. She proceeded alone to Leo's room to meet him, her palms sweating. She wasn't sure how she would approach him.

She knocked on the door, and he opened it, his hair a mess and his clothes wrinkled. He stared at her. She stood there and waited for him to say something.

"Zwaantie?" Leo asked with a frown.

"Hi," Zwaantie said. "I, um, thought I'd come for a visit."

He bit his bottom lip. "Of course. I'm sorry, come in."

She entered the room, surprised at how much it looked like his room at home, full of gray and sharp lines. He gave her an awkward grin. Zwaantie let out a breath of relief.

She tried not to think about what Ari was doing, even though he'd been on her mind during the entire ride over. She also tried to forget about the danger Sage was in. She could get killed in Sol.

Zwaantie came here for one purpose and one purpose only. To get closer to Leo and fall in love. Though she'd tried quite a bit, and so far nothing had worked.

"What are you doing here?" Leo asked.

She should kiss him, but she couldn't bring herself to.

"I wanted to see you."

"Right." He sank down on the couch. Zwaantie sat as close as she dared and grasped his hand in hers.

"I really did."

She put her finger on his chin and turned his face so he was looking right at her. His eyes were full of pain and stress. She longed to take it away from him and would do whatever it took.

She leaned forward and pressed her lips against his. She focused on how to make Leo's kiss mean something to her. His lips were soft, gentle, and sweet.

His hands pushed her away.

"I can't do this right now. You shouldn't be here." He ran a hand through his hair and exhaled.

Zwaantie's face flushed with embarrassment. "I wanted to spend time with you. We're going to be married in ten days, right?"

He laid his head back and closed his eyes. "Yes. We're going to be married, but I have bigger things to think about at the moment."

She gripped his hand. "Tell me. Let me shoulder some of this burden with you."

"I don't know if you can. My people are dying. You can't even imagine. Everyone goes to bed in a panic, thinking they might not wake up in the morning, and we're no closer to understanding why."

Zwaantie knew it was because she decided to give her heart to Ari. How could she tell Leo she was responsible? She couldn't. He'd never forgive her if he knew she could've ended the vipers long ago.

She was here now, ready to make this work and end the deaths. The problem was that she felt no different about him than when she arrived in Stella.

"Maybe you can use me a sounding board. I can help you sort out your thoughts. I'm a good listener."

He frowned. "I don't think so. You should go home. I have work to do."

"I'll wait here." He wasn't kicking her out. Not now. "Sage is doing some business here. I'll go home with her in a few days. Don't worry about me. I'll stay out of your way." She didn't want to lie to him, but she was already concerned about Sage in Sol. She didn't want Leo to be as well.

He pinched his nose and squeezed his eyes shut. "You shouldn't be here. It's dangerous."

"It's dangerous in the City of Stars as well. I belong here, by your side." She put a hand on his shoulder. It didn't mean anything to her, but maybe it would to him.

"Why the sudden interest in me?"

"Our wedding is in ten days. We belong together. I don't want to marry a stranger."

His face softened, and he drew her into his side and kissed the top of her head. "I know. I'm sorry. I'm very stressed. I have to go back out. I don't know how much I'll even see you."

"It's okay. I'll take what I can get." She snuggled close into him and felt guilty for not enjoying it.

~

A FEW DAYS LATER, SAGE SWOOPED INTO THE ROOM. "WHERE'S LEO?"

Zwaantie shrugged. She'd only seen him a few times, and he'd been cordial but distant. At least she was here, and that was what mattered. She spent a lot of time reading and exploring the castle and figured as long as she wasn't actively avoiding Ari, life was easier.

"What'd you find in Sol?"

"Not much. We have a few spies planted there. Sorry, but they haven't heard any word of the Voice crossing the wall. It alarmed them, quite frankly."

Everything was at a standstill. Leo's investigation. Sage's. Zwaantie's love. The world was holding its breath, just waiting to exhale and allow everything to fall down. The future was grimmer than ever.

The three days passed quickly, and she barely saw Leo. Just before she headed out to her boat, Leo managed to find time for her. He kissed her quickly. "I'm sorry we didn't get to see much of each other."

She let out a breath. "Come back, please. Let someone else handle this. We're going to be married in days, and we barely know each other. Don't you think this is just as important?"

"I can't. This is my responsibility. I'll be home the day before the wedding. We'll just have to make the best of it."

Zwaantie trudged down to the boat alone. What was she doing? She felt so lost. Her wedding would not be a happy occasion. It would be full of honor and duty, but it would be missing love.

This was her life now.

Chapter Twenty-Three

THE FATHER

When Zwaantie arrived to the castle, she went straight to her rooms. She didn't want to accidentally see Ari. As long as she avoided him, she might be able to pull this off, but then again, maybe not. Things with Leo didn't exactly go well.

A knock sounded on her door not more than fifteen minutes later. Luna stood there with a couple of bottles and glasses.

"I've been missing you. How are you doing?" Luna asked, pushing past her.

"I'm okay." Zwaantie followed Luna to the sitting area, where she unstopped both bottles, pouring wine into one glass and orange juice into the other one.

"I can't drink wine, but I figured you might want some. You just got back from Leo's, right? How'd it go?"

Zwaantie sat across from her and picked up her glass. She swirled the liquid around. She'd missed Luna, but she was surprised to see her here.

"It was okay. He was busy. It's going to be a sham of a marriage, but I'm doing my best."

"Phoenix seems to be doing better."

"Do you see him often?"

"Sometimes. He's made a lot of new friends."

"I'm happy for him." She should tell Luna about Ari, but didn't want to rehash the Ari argument with anyone again.

"Are you happy?" Luna asked.

Zwaantie snorted. "No, not by a long shot." She lifted the glass to her lips. Luna lunged for her and grabbed the glass out of her hand. Wine sloshed all over Zwaantie's face, and she wiped at her eyes. Luna gripped the glass tight and swallowed it in one gulp.

She dropped the glass, and it shattered at Zwaantie's feet. Tears flowed down Luna's face, and she embraced Zwaantie in a tight hug. "I'm so sorry," she whispered in Zwaantie's ear.

Zwaantie wiggled out of her grip. Panic settled in Zwaantie's stomach. Something was definitely not right. "What are you talking about?"

Luna took shallow breaths. "I don't know how long it will take before the poison takes effect, but the Voice. He was too strong. I love you, Zwaantie. I'm so sorry."

Luna sank onto the couch, and Zwaantie joined her, her mind spinning. "I don't understand."

Luna's breath became more labored. "I was the one who left the door open for the vipers and locked you out of your room. I tried to stay away, hoping if I wasn't with you, he couldn't tell me to kill you. But lately he's become more insistent, and I couldn't fight it. I'm sorry."

Zwaantie's heart raced. Luna was dying in her arms. She closed her eyes for a moment. She pushed down the sadness that threatened to overwhelm her. She didn't have time, and crying wouldn't stop the flow of poison in Luna's veins.

"Do you know who the Voice is? Can we stop him?"

Luna gripped Zwaantie's arm. "He's the father of my child." She collapsed, her last breath gone.

"No, Luna. No." She patted Luna's face and pulled Luna to her chest, silent tears flowing down her cheeks. Her heart tightened, and an ache formed in her belly. She sobbed over her body. Her best friend was dead.

Very gently, she laid Luna back down on the couch. This wasn't fair to Luna. She'd been a victim of the Voice.

She ran out of the room and burst into Sage's room. Sage jumped up off the couch.

"Zwaantie, are you okay?" Sage rushed to her and brushed away Zwaantie's tears.

"Luna, she's dead." Zwaantie's voice cracked, and she had to blink back more tears.

Phoenix rose from the couch with wide eyes. "What? How?"

Zwaantie took a couple of deep breaths. Nothing felt real. "She... she tried to kill me. Poison. At the last minute she took the glass from me and drank it herself." Zwaantie covered her mouth, unable to go on. Luna was dead because of her. Because of the Voice. She met Phoenix's eyes. "She told me who the Voice is."

"What?" Sage asked, gripping her hand. "Who?"

"Pieter."

"Her husband?" Sage asked, her eyebrows furrowed.

Phoenix nodded. "It makes sense. He had full access to the castle. We all thought he was always around because the king kept him too busy, but maybe it was a cover."

Sage looked between the both of them. "Zwaantie, go tell Lyra everything. Including about the Voice. I'm going to back to Sol."

"Why?" Phoenix asked.

"I'm going to capture Pieter and bring him back here. I have to go now though. If he knows that she told you, he'll act quickly to avoid being discovered. Phoenix, keep her safe."

Chapter Twenty-Four

THE ALLIANCE

"**P**hoenix, I'm so sorry," Zwaantie said.

He reached for her, and she hugged him. His body shuddered, and she held tighter, knowing he needed this. After several moments, he pulled away, wiping his eyes. "Can I see her?"

"Of course." She held his hand and led him to her room. He collapsed next to Luna's body. Zwaantie could barely look at her. Every time she did, a sob escaped. Luna was dead. She'd never smile, never bear the child growing in her belly, never return to Sol and see the sun. Zwaantie would be dead right now if Luna hadn't overpowered the Voice. She owed Luna her life.

Zwaantie dropped her hand to Phoenix's shoulder. "I'm going to find someone to help us take care of the body. Will you be okay with her?"

Phoenix nodded. "Yeah, I want some alone time with her anyway."

She kissed him on the cheek and rushed out of the room. She wove through the complex halls, down a couple flights of stairs, and pounded on Lyra's door.

Lyra jerked the door open. "You don't have to beat—"

Zwaantie shoved past her.

"What's the matter?" Lyra furrowed her brow.

"My best friend. My servant from Sol. She tried to poison me but killed herself instead."

"What? Where?"

"She's in my room. Can you have someone take care of her?"

"Yes. Sit. I'll be with you in a moment."

Zwaantie pressed her hands against her eyes while she waited. Luna was dead. So much death. The Voice was behind it all. Maybe not all. The vipers were doing their fair share as well. Perhaps they were connected somehow. Maybe Lyra could help her sort out her thoughts.

The ache in Zwaantie's chest grew. Luna's death would haunt her for years to come. She'd still be alive if not for Zwaantie. No. She couldn't take this guilt upon herself. This was on the Voice. He would pay. Zwaantie would hunt him down herself if she had to and avenge Luna's death. The Voice would regret the decision to take on Zwaantie. He'd gone too far.

Lyra returned a few minutes later, took the chair across from Zwaantie, and gripped her hands. "Tell me."

Zwaantie launched into the tale about the Voice. Everything she could remember from the first assassination attempt in Sol with the poisoned slave to Luna revealing the Voice was Pieter.

"Sage is on her way to Sol to see if she can capture him. Do you think she'll be okay?" Sol was a dangerous place for any Stellan at the moment. The Voice knew Zwaantie and Sage were close. If he caught wind she was on his turf, he could have her killed. Zwaantie wouldn't be able to handle another death hanging over her head.

Lyra nodded. "If anyone can get him, Sage can. That girl is stealthy, deadly, and a survivor. She's not power hungry at all, but if she were, she'd have overthrown her father and taken the crown."

If a hollowness hadn't filled her chest, Zwaantie would've laughed, but right now nothing was funny, even Sage as Queen of Stella.

"What if she can't get him?"

"We'll continue to be vigilant. Let's increase your guard. Sage can't fulfill that role anymore. We'll also employ official tasters for your food and drinks."

Zwaantie clenched her fists. "I don't want to live like a prisoner."

"It's that or risk death. Go back to your room. I'll send guards."

Lyra was obviously used to being listened to, but she didn't yet know that Zwaantie wasn't good at following directions. She would not be a prisoner in her own home, not when she had a Voice to hunt down.

"Can we keep this from Leo?" Zwaantie asked.

Lyra leaned away, contemplative. "Why?"

"We'll have to tell him about Luna and the poison, but I don't want him to know about the Voice. The more people who know, the more dangerous things will be. It will be better if we just let Leo think it's a run-of-the-mill assassin."

"You have a point. Besides, he needs to focus on the vipers. I have to tell him, but I won't mention the Voice."

Zwaantie left Lyra's office and went to the tower. She needed air. The tower was the only place she could be alone. Contrary to what Lyra thought, Zwaantie didn't need the guards. She needed solitude.

Chapter Twenty-Five

THE PROPOSAL

O nce up in the tower, she lay down in the middle of the circle and put her arms behind her head. Those stars. She couldn't get enough of them. Perhaps Luna had taken her place among them. Zwaantie searched to see if she could find a new one, but there were millions of stars. She'd never know.

If she ever made it home, she'd sure miss them. Though, as long as the Voice was around, she wouldn't be able to return. What if Pieter was simply a small part of a bigger problem, and by eliminating him, the Voice would still be there, trying to kill her. She wished she could talk to someone from home. She could write a letter to Raaf. He might know more about how things worked, but he wouldn't want to have anything to do with getting rid of the Voice.

She would be queen soon. How could she not return to her own kingdom? While she loved the stars, she wasn't sure she could live with never seeing the sun again. She closed her eyes and imagined its warmth on her skin. Life had been so simple in Sol. When had things changed?

They changed when Raaf and Phoenix arrived home from Raaf's training, and she fell in love with Phoenix, and the attempted murders had began. Leo showing up only increased the severity of the attacks.

How her life would be different if she had married Prince Moo-for-me.

She'd be miserable. But alive.

A clatter sounded beneath her, and she poked her head up to see Ari climbing out of the hatch. She hadn't talked to him since his mother's funeral.

His face was full of sadness and sorrow. He didn't look like the Ari she'd come to love. Zwaantie's stomach clenched. It'd been a week since the funeral of his mother, and now she was dealing with grief of her own, but she still didn't know what to say or do. Death leaves holes in hearts that do not heal. She sat up.

"I'm so sorry," she said.

He collapsed next to her. She reached over and squeezed his hand, and he let out a sob. She'd never seen him so vulnerable. She gathered him in her arms and let him cry. Her heart broke for him.

After a several minutes, he calmed, wiped his bloodshot eyes, and took a deep shuddering breath. "You know, I've never cried before."

"Ever?" Everyone cried occasionally, even if only in private. Though she supposed his normal unending carelessness was part of Ari's charm. His mother's death would change that. He'd become someone different. Grief did that to a person. Luna's death would change her.

"Since I was a child." His breathing was still ragged, but his eyes were starting to clear.

"You didn't cry at the funeral?"

"No. I've just been numb. I can't believe she's gone. She was the one person I told everything to. She never judged me, and she always supported my decisions. You know I came up here because I knew you'd be here. I heard about Luna. I needed to make sure you were okay. Sorry I hijacked your grief."

She gave him a small grin. "It's okay. I'm still a little in shock." She squeezed his hand. "You shouldn't be here."

"I need you. Not my father. Not Sage. You." He balled his hands into fists. "I don't know how to do this without you."

"Do what?" Butterflies fluttered in her stomach. Her emotions betrayed her. When she was done here, she was getting on a boat back to The Black City and not leaving Leo's side. Even in grief and death, she and Ari were walking a dangerous line.

"Life. I was doing so good before you came around, and then you go and turn everything upside down."

"I don't know what you want me to say. I can't love you." Yet she did. She loved him more than she'd loved anyone. She refused to look at him because she'd give in to something she shouldn't.

"There's nothing to say. The moment I laid eyes on you, I was lost. I tried to deny it, but I couldn't stop thinking about you. Then at the lock-in, I wasn't surprised when Soul Mate revealed you even though I should've been. After I kissed you, I knew my life would never be the same."

Zwaantie didn't respond. She couldn't. She knew that whatever she said, it would be the wrong thing.

"Marry me." He spoke the words without hesitation. Like he'd planned this. Like it would be that easy.

Zwaantie's heart froze. If he had uttered those words a week ago, she would've been ecstatic, but now, she wasn't so sure. If they got this wrong, the consequences could be catastrophic.

"Last week you were adamantly against marriage. What if you resent me for it?"

"At this point the resentment won't be toward you but against my own country."

"So, you'll marry me not because you love me but because of your country. I'm sorry your mother died, but I can't bring her back. I'm not sure I want to marry you under these circumstances." She knew she was being mean, but this proposal was unexpected. She had a plan in her head for how to deal with the prophecy and Leo, and now she had to figure out how to change it. She needed time to absorb.

He ran a hand through his hair. "You don't understand. People are dying and will continue to die unless we get married. I suppose I could let you marry Leo, but I don't think you want that either."

"Maybe that's what I'm supposed to do." If she'd learned anything in the past several weeks, it was that she wasn't allowed to do what she wanted. Duty and honor came first, and marrying Ari would be foolish.

"I was considering proposing even before Mother died. I know I didn't say it, but the more I thought about things, the more I realized it was the best option. I want to marry you and not only because my mother died."

"Are you lying to me?" A spark of hope bloomed in her chest. Was this possible?

"No, I swear."

"I need to think about it." She didn't want to mess anything up or be responsible for any other deaths, so she would not rush into this. If she married Ari, it would be because it was right decision. Not just because she wanted him.

He let out a breath. "Okay. But don't think too long." He leaned over and kissed her lightly on the lips. "I love you, Zwaantie."

"I love you too," Zwaantie replied with conviction.

Chapter Twenty-Six

THE CONUNDRUM

Zwaantie nodded at the guards posted outside her room and stopped dead in the doorway. She couldn't go in. Luna had died in there only a few hours before. Not only would it be eerie, but it would be too quiet. She needed a companion.

She needed Sage, but Sage was in Sol, risking her neck for Zwaantie.

She met the eyes of one of the guards. "I'm going to stay in Sage's room." The guard nodded and put his hand on the small box on his hip. "What's that?" Zwaantie asked.

"A backsnipe. Better than my sword."

Ah, yes. Zwaantie remembered the magical crossbow Leo brought to Sol when he came seeking her hand.

She left her room, guards trailing after her, and hesitated in front of Ari's door, but knew staying with him would be a mistake. Instead, she found herself surrounded by a dozen cats and Andromeda on her lap, her thoughts in turmoil. Processing Luna's death was one thing. Ari's proposal was quite another.

Zwaantie's disc buzzed, and Sage's face flashed up on her wall.

"I'm not surprised to find you here," Sage said.

"I couldn't go back to my own room. Where are you?" Zwaantie would've thought Sage would be in Sol by now.

"In Sol. A pub."

"Your disc works?" Zwaantie asked. Potions worked in Sol. Things like discs should not.

"Um. Yeah. I'm not explaining how."

Zwaantie shook her head, not allowing one more thing to enter her already confused thoughts. "Have you found anything?"

"No. I thought you might know where Pieter lives. I can get him tonight. Sol is easy to sneak around after midnight."

Zwaantie's voice caught in her throat, and the reality of Luna's death slammed into her. "I gave him and Luna a home." Zwaantie squeezed her eyes shut and explained to Sage how to get to Pieter.

"It will get easier," Sage said.

"I know. I can't believe she's gone." Zwaantie wiped away her tears.

"I wish I could be there for you. Maybe you should talk to Ari."

Sage wouldn't usually suggest something so reckless. But it made sense in a twisted kind of way since they were both grieving. "I already have."

"How'd that go?"

Zwaantie let out a long breath. Sage would help her work through the different options. She was wise beyond her years.

"He proposed," Zwaantie said.

Sage's eyes popped open, and she squeaked. "Really?"

"Yeah."

"What are you going to do?" Sage was all grins. Zwaantie should've known better than to ask her for advice. Her answer would be absolutely marry Ari. Maybe Zwaantie had misjudged her wisdom.

"I have no idea. This whole thing. The prophecy. Leo. Ari. I don't know what to do. Whatever I do, it needs to be the right thing. But what is the right thing? How do I know?" If she messed this up, she'd never forgive herself. No one else would either. She'd end up executed if she got this wrong. She'd deserve it too. She'd probably welcome death at that point.

Sage stared at Zwaantie for a long moment. "I'm pretty smart, you know."

Zwaantie snorted. "Yeah, I know." It was as if Sage could read her mind.

"The prophecy. It was very specific. The kingdoms of Stella and Sol must be joined, right?"

"Right." She'd heard the words a thousand times. She didn't know why Sage needed to point it out again. Plus, Zwaantie had made the same argument to Ari in the garden.

"Well, if you marry Ari, then both Stella and Sol will fall under the same reign. You will be queen of both Sol and Stella. Likewise, Ari will be king. How could they be more joined? Plus, you're madly in love. Bam. Prophecy fulfilled."

That sounded too easy. She felt like she was missing something. "I know. But for so long, anything I've wanted has been wrong. What if I'm supposed to be miserable, and the only possible path is marriage to Leo."

"Don't be stupid. If you want to marry Ari, marry Ari."

Zwaantie appreciated how Sage didn't pull any punches. Though it might just be because that's what Zwaantie wanted to hear.

"But what if I'm wrong? So many people have died already. I can't be responsible for any more." This was the crux of any decision she was about to make.

"I actually think it's the smarter choice. We can spin it that way for the public too. We don't know what's going to happen when the kingdoms join, just that the vipers will stop killing people."

"You really think this is the best path?" She wanted this to be the answer, but she needed someone else to confirm it.

"I do."

A weight lifted off of Zwaantie's chest. She so desperately wanted to make the right choice. By having Sage on her side, she felt a little better.

"What about Leo?" He'd be crushed. She could split their family by marrying Ari.

"He'll survive."

"Candace is going to kill me." She didn't want to hurt Candace. She had so many people to think about besides herself.

"No. She's going to be happy her baby will live."

"And Lyra? She's going to be furious."

"Are you really going to base this decision on what Lyra thinks?"

"And avoid a slow and painful death? Absolutely." Maybe that wasn't entirely true, but Lyra was someone she had to consider.

"No. Let Ari and I take care of Lyra. She'll be fine."

"You seem pretty strongly opinionated on this." Sage had been so against them when things first started happening. Now she acted as if there was no other choice. Maybe there wasn't. Maybe that was the point.

"Well, I want you to be happy. Ari too. You won't be happy with Leo. That much is clear."

"I hardly know Leo. That can't be determined yet."

"Can you honestly tell me you'll be fine married to Leo, knowing Ari is still out there and available?"

"No. I can't." Of course she wouldn't. Ari stole her heart, so she'd never be able to give it to Leo, no matter how hard she tried. Maybe that was her problem. As long as she'd known Leo, her heart had always belonged to another. She hoped Leo would someday find the kind of love she had. He deserved it.

"There. That's your answer. Now you get some sleep. You have a big day ahead of you tomorrow."

"What do you mean?"

"You need to change the wedding plans. Your wedding is scheduled in less than a week. Your family is coming. You need to make sure everyone knows of the change. This will not be easy, sister, but you'll get it done. I'll help as soon as I get back."

"How can you think about the wedding with everything else going on?"

"Because that wedding is the key to our salvation. Nothing else matters. I'll get Pieter tonight and be back in City of Stars by noon tomorrow. We'll lock him up, plan your wedding, and end this curse. I'm out."

She clicked off, and Zwaantie scratched Andromeda behind the ears.

Sage seemed to think their plans were completely changed even though Zwaantie hadn't confirmed anything. Deep in her heart though, Zwaantie knew it was the right thing to do. Was that the answer then? Would she really marry Ari? She wanted this to be the right answer. All she could think about was Leo. This wasn't fair to him.

She allowed herself to feel a little bit of happiness. In spite of the bad things raining down upon her, she was about to marry the love of her life. She allowed thoughts of Ari to fill her head as she drifted off to sleep.

Chapter Twenty-Seven

THE VIRGIN

Zwaantie blinked her eyes open and met the gorgeous gray ones of Ari. She stretched and smiled at him.

"How'd you get in here?" she asked sleepily. "I have guards."

"They let me in."

"Not very good guards then." She rubbed her eyes.

"Nope, certainly not. Maybe I need to sleep with you from now on. Keep you safe."

"Maybe you should."

He pulled her into him, and her entire body buzzed. "Does that mean you've made a decision?"

She leaned into him and planted her lips on his before saying anything because she couldn't stand it anymore. He returned the kiss and pulled her on top of him. His hands wandered over her body, and she pressed herself into him. Then she slowly broke away and smiled down at him.

"You haven't given me an answer yet," he said with a cocky grin.

"Yes, Ari. I would be honored to marry you."

He kissed her, but she wiggled away, climbed off of him, and shrugged on a robe. They still had a lot of decisions to make, and she didn't want to get carried away first.

"We're not waiting," Ari said, sitting up. Leo's face flashed on the wall.

"Leo," Zwaantie said and spun around to face him. She flushed as she sat on the couch. "How are you?"

His eyes flashed to Ari on the bed. "I'm fine. I wanted to apologize for my behavior while you were here. I should've paid more attention to you."

She ran a hand through her hair. Could he tell she'd been kissing Ari?

"No, it's okay. I understand."

He furrowed his brow. "Mother said Luna died yesterday. Poisoned."

"Yes, she did."

"I'm so sorry. She also said the poison was meant for you."

"Yes. Your mother increased my guard, and Ari is staying with me when Sage cannot."

"Where is Sage?"

"Out searching for the assassin."

He looked between her and Ari and pursed his lips. Perhaps he wasn't easily convinced. "Well, I need to get back to my own investigation. Have Sage call me if she finds anything."

As soon as Leo clicked off, Ari pushed the button that turned off the screen.

"I'm really surprised Sage has this turned on."

"Not anymore," Zwaantie said with a smirk.

Ari lowered himself next to her. "That was a close call."

"It would've made it easier to tell him. We need to."

"Maybe, but it would've hurt worse for him to find out this way. No worries now. We have a couple of hours before Sage returns. Any ideas what we should do?"

Zwaantie placed her hands on his chest. "Oh yes, I can think of a lot of things we can do."

～

"DON'T YOU HAVE YOUR OWN ROOM, ARI?" SAGE ASKED WHEN SHE walked in later.

Ari grinned at her as Zwaantie untangled herself.

"We were already here. Where's the prisoner?"

"In the interrogation room. I think you both should come. Zwaantie, you'll probably understand more of what he says than I do. We should get Phoenix as well."

Ari went to fetch Phoenix as Sage and Zwaantie made their way to the interrogation room.

"Has he told you anything?" Zwaantie asked.

"I haven't asked. I drugged him to get him across the wall, so he's just now waking up."

The interrogation was in a large inner stone room with several chairs surrounding the prisoner. Aside from a handful of lights floating around, the room was very dark and cold. The dampness seeped into Zwaantie's bones. She shivered. Pieter's head hung, and he fought against the chains.

Anger swelled in her chest. This was the man who was responsible not only for Luna's death, but her own terror for the past couple of months.

He jerked his head up.

"Princess. Get me out of here. What is this madness?"

Zwaantie didn't answer, afraid of the words that would come out of her mouth. She wanted to slap him across the face. Sage sat directly across from Pieter, and Zwaantie settled on her left. Pieter continued to fight.

"Please, Princess. Why have you kidnapped me? I have no information on the king, I swear. Why would you send a Stellan to capture me? Help me."

She crossed her arms and glared at him. If he wasn't the Voice and wasn't responsible for all the trouble she'd had in the last several months, she might feel inclined to help him. For now, she kept her mouth shut and watched him, disgusted.

Once Ari and Phoenix arrived, Sage spoke in a low voice. "Tell me about the Voice."

"The Voice? He's all powerful, all knowing, and keeps us in check." He searched the faces around them. "Where's Luna?"

How dare he ask such a question, when he knew that he killed her.

"Tell me more," Sage said. Zwaantie studied Pieter.

He jerked his hands. "No. Not until you tell me where Luna is."

"She's dead, and it's all your fault," Zwaantie spat, losing control. She couldn't help herself.

Sage glared at her. "Let me do the interrogations, please. I'll let you know if I need your input."

Her words stung, but Zwaantie focused on Pieter. His face went white.

"Dead?"

"Yes," Sage said. "By your hand. She drank the poison you sent for Zwaantie."

"What are you talking about?" Silent tears flowed down his cheeks. His grief was real. Of course, he'd expected Zwaantie to die, not Luna. Perhaps he'd been unable to see the death.

"Just before she died, she told us you were the Voice and you told her to poison Zwaantie."

"Me? No, I would never. I'm not the Voice. How can the Voice be a person?"

"Why would she say it was you?"

"I have no idea." He creased his eyebrows together.

Sage looked at Zwaantie. "Exactly what did she say?"

"She said it was the father of her child."

"Luna's pregnant?"

"Was."

Pieter squeezed his eyes shut, and a red flush crawled up his face. "I'm not the father."

"What do you mean?" Zwaantie asked. Luna and Pieter had been married. How could it be anyone else? Even if Luna had slept with someone else, there was no way for Pieter to rule himself out.

He let out a breath. "Luna and I had a whirlwind romance, but we never consummated the marriage."

"Why?" Zwaantie asked.

He narrowed his eyes at Zwaantie. "Because you never let her sleep at home. Okay, you did a couple of times, but she came home so exhausted nothing ever happened."

What? No. Zwaantie always sent Luna home. Early sometimes.

"For the love of all the stars. We got the wrong person? For real?"

Sage dug a necklace out of her pocket. "Do you have any desire to kill the princess?"

"Zwaantie? No. Why would I? Is Luna really dead?"

"I'm afraid so. Though I'm not sure I believe you about Zwaantie. I'm going to put this necklace on you. Then you're going to tell us who the father of Luna's child is." Sage fastened the necklace on him.

"I never kept Luna up at the castle. Not even once," Zwaantie said.

The freckles on Pieter's face paled, and he let out a breath. "She was sleeping with someone else. Not with me."

"Then who?" Sage asked.

Pieter didn't respond, but Zwaantie's mind raced through her memories of home. "No, wait, she couldn't spend the night with someone because of the Voice. The one time Phoenix slept in my room he couldn't even stand up because of his headache."

"Phoenix slept in your room?" Ari asked with a glare at Phoenix.

"Yes," Zwaantie replied. She didn't owe him an explanation. Not with his past.

"She said the Voice was the baby's father. Obviously he could make it so she didn't feel any guilt," Phoenix said.

"We're still not any closer to finding out who it is," Sage muttered.

"Someone at the castle," Zwaantie said.

"Oh Sol," Phoenix muttered.

"What?" Zwaantie asked.

"I often stayed in the castle. I had a bed in Raaf's rooms. It was easier. One time I was late, just before midnight, and I saw Luna running down the hall. I didn't think much of it at the time. I figured she'd be staying with Zwaantie. Except I found it odd that she wasn't going toward Zwaantie's rooms."

"Where was she going?"

"Down a hall that only had one door. The king's."

Chapter Twenty-Eight

THE WEDDING: PART 1

Zwaantie fled. Her father would never sleep with Luna and impregnate her. Bile rose in Zwaantie's throat. How could he do such a thing? So many questions and no possible answers. She'd never seen her father even look at Luna. Perhaps he caught her one night and coerced her.

She stopped a little ways down the hall and closed her eyes. Her father was a sick, sick man. She would make sure he paid for not only Luna's death, but that baby as well.

They'd never been terribly close, but to think he wanted to kill her. This wasn't possible. Her head spun. Why would he want her dead? He couldn't be that desperate to hang on to his reign. If he had been, then he wouldn't have encouraged her marriage.

The attempts had started before Leo showed up though. Maybe he wanted Raaf on the throne. She could think of no other motive. What would she do now?

Hands caressed her arms. "Are you okay?" Ari asked.

"No." She opened her eyes and met his.

"We're getting married today."

"What? I just found out my father is the Voice, and he wants me dead. He's the king of Sol. We can't think of marriage now. We need to think of how we can assassinate him. I'm going to invade my own country." She took a deep breath. "How can you think of marriage?"

"Our marriage will strengthen that position. I'll take my place as the king of Stella, which will make you queen, which will give us more power when we take him on. You will claim your own kingdom. I'll see to it. But nothing can happen unless we get married. Today."

Zwaantie searched his face. He wanted this more than she did. Her heart belonged to him, and she couldn't wait to begin their life together, but she felt like there were too many other things to worry about. Weddings were supposed to be happy, not just something they did out of necessity. Though perhaps princesses didn't have that luxury.

He pulled out his device. "Sage. Meet Zwaantie in your rooms."

"Are you sure this is the right thing to do?" Zwaantie asked. Was Phoenix really telling the truth? Of course he was. He wouldn't lie, but did it mean that her father was the Voice? She suddenly doubted everything. They were wrong about Pieter. They could be wrong about this. Though probably not. However, she couldn't base an entire war on *probably*. How could she think about getting married now?

"Yes. I'm off to find a discreet marriage mage. I love you, Zwaantie. Together, we will fix this."

Thoughts hung heavy in her mind, but Ari placed a light kiss on her lips sending shivers down her spine.

A COUPLE OF HOURS LATER, SHE AND SAGE WERE JUST SITTING DOWN with the beauty mages when Ari showed up. Zwaantie was shocked at how fast things were going. Sage had kept up with Ari via their discs, and she hustled Zwaantie all over the city. They went back to Nash and had a last minute simple white dress made. Sage paid him an exorbitant amount of money not to ask any questions. The circumstances that brought the marriage together weren't ideal but Zwaantie was excited to marry Ari. Sage promised she would worry about the Voice while Zwaantie focused on her wedding. Sage reassured her that this was the best course of events.

Ari sat across from her as the beauty mages worked on her hair.

They didn't know what was going on, though it would take an idiot not to recognize the look of sheer sappiness on Ari's face. Zwaantie tried not to stare at him, but she couldn't keep her eyes off him. She clung to the feelings of love they had, and the thousands of other worries didn't plague her.

After her hair and makeup were done, Ari took Zwaantie out of the castle and toward the docks.

He kept a tight grip on her hand as they walked and spoke in low voices. "This is going to be done in secret. We can't tell anyone yet because of Leo. I haven't figured out how to tell him yet. But we can't wait any longer. I want to be with you and save our kingdom. Leo will understand in the end."

Zwaantie knew Leo would be crushed. She couldn't think about him because she had to save not only her own life, but the lives of all those in Stella. Plus, if her father was the Voice, who knew what kind of terror he was wreaking on the citizens of Sol. If he was going to such lengths to murder her, he was capable of so much more. She still couldn't wrap her head around that it was him.

"Where are we going?" Zwaantie asked as Ari hopped down into a boat. He placed his hands on her waist and lifted her in. A small thrill went up her spine. She'd have only his hands on her for the rest of her life. She liked those hands.

"We are going to get married under the stars. Sage, the marriage mage, and Xandria are already out there on a different boat."

"Why is Xandria coming?"

"She creates the binding potion."

After they climbed down into the boat, Ari pushed a few buttons, and they were off. It was amazing to Zwaantie how quickly the stars appeared.

She liked this boat, with only her and Ari on it. She slid her arm around his waist and stood up on her tiptoes to give him a kiss. Her problems seemed a thousand miles away out here on the water.

"Calm down there, princess. We have a ceremony to complete first."

She raised her eyebrows at him. "You sure? Maybe we can change the order."

He snorted and planted his lips against hers briefly. "You are going to be such a fun wife."

After about thirty minutes, they arrived next to another boat in the middle of the ocean. Ari lashed the boats together and helped Zwaantie onto the other boat.

The marriage mage fiddled with his glasses. Sweat beaded on his forehead. "Are you sure about this, Prince Ari? Shouldn't we tell the king?"

"No, I'll tell the king when I'm ready."

The mage nodded, and Sage squealed with excitement.

Xandria stepped forward. She had a long sharp needle in her hand. Zwaantie backed away. Next to Xandria sat a wooden table filled with small bottles of all different colors.

"Before the ceremony, we will do the parting of the potions. Ari will drink yours, and you will drink his. It connects your souls. Your arm, please."

Zwaantie hesitated but held out her shaking arm. She hoped that wouldn't mess things up for Xandria. She was surprised by the idea of blood. It seemed so barbaric.

She almost smiled. Not so long ago she thought of Stella as a barbaric country that she would never set foot in. Xandria stuck the needle in the crook of Zwaantie's elbow.

"Ouch," she yelped from the pain.

Xandria drew out a small amount of blood into a tube. Then she did the same with Ari, but used a different needle. Zwaantie rubbed the spot where she'd been poked. No one had told her the wedding would be painful.

In a porcelain dish, Xandria deposited Zwaantie's blood. She stirred it with a silver spoon, stuck her nose in the dish, and inhaled. Her hands found a tiny gold bottle, and she set it aside. Then she waved her hands above the bowl, and the blood floated in front of her.

Ari dropped his head next to hers. "Isn't this cool? It's one of the only times we get to see potion makers work. Normally they insist on complete privacy, but the wedding ceremony calls for the work to be done in front of everyone," Ari whispered in Zwaantie's ear.

Xandria jerked her head up and glared at him. "Silence, please."

Ari took Zwaantie's hand and squeezed. She smiled up at him and watched Xandria again. It was fascinating.

Zwaantie's blood separated into seven multicolored strands. Xandria waved her hand, and the strands disappeared among the dozens of potion bottles. She plucked out six different bottles, each of which had a strand of Zwaantie's blood wrapped around it.

Xandria creased her eyebrows and searched for another bottle. Finally she found what she was looking for. She frowned and hesitated before she placed the seventh bottle with the others. She snapped her fingers, and the blood left in the bowl disappeared.

She took the seven potions and mixed them together in a red chalice. Then she did the same for Ari, but his potion went in a purple chalice.

Xandria brought both cups to them and gave Ari the red cup first.

"Ari, Zwaantie gives you a foundation of honor. To that she adds love, peace, laughter, passion, affection, nurture, and sacrifice. Do you accept this gift that she has given you and take it upon yourself?"

"I do," he said and took a sip from the red chalice.

"Zwaantie, Ari gives you a foundation of passion. To that he adds friendship, love, amusement, compassion, honor, selflessness, and desire." Her lips twitched on the last word. "Do you accept this gift and take it upon yourself?"

"I do," Zwaantie said and raised the glass to her lips.

"Don't drink it all, just a sip," Xandria said.

The sweet fruity liquid slid across her tongue and down her throat. She grinned up at Ari.

Xandria moved back to her table and poured both chalices in a small gold dish. She handed the dish to the marriage mage, then backed away and stood by Sage.

The marriage mage stood in front of them, the bowl held out. "Grasp hands and hold them up."

Ari took Zwaantie's right hand into his own and turned to face her. They held their hands up at chest level. The marriage mage took the bowl and began to slowly pour the contents over their hands. It was a warm clear silvery color.

"Do you promise to love each other unconditionally?" The marriage mage asked.

"Yes," they both responded, and the liquid turned a deep red. The potion continued to flow into their hands.

"Do you promise to respect and honor one another till the end of your days?"

"Yes." The liquid turned a royal blue.

"Do you promise to stay together throughout eternity and dwell together among the stars?"

"Yes." The liquid turned bright white, and the little bowl was empty, the potion disappearing into their hands. Zwaantie hoped they would live a long time before they would dwell together in the stars.

"Kiss your wife," the marriage mage said.

Ari held her gaze as he placed his lips on hers. She never kissed with her eyes open before, but an energy flowed through them. It was as if she was connected with Ari in ways she couldn't understand. She melted into him, allowing her eyes to close. This moment would be one she'd never forget. The moment she and Ari became one.

Sage squealed and threw her arms around the both of them.

Chapter Twenty-Nine

THE HONEYMOON

Ari led Zwaantie over to the other boat, and Sage left with the marriage mage and Xandria. Butterflies danced in Zwaantie's belly. Was this the part where they went back to real life? Told Leo, dealt with her father, and became king and queen?

"What are we doing?" she asked.

Ari ran his hands down her arms. "We are spending some time alone on a small island the royal family uses as a retreat. There are no other inhabitants. I know how much you love the stars, so I figured we'd stay out there for the few days. We should get back two days before Leo does. While we're gone, Sage is going to do some reconnaissance concerning your father. We need some time before life starts, because I have a feeling after this, it will be a very long time before we find true peace."

Two days alone with Ari. Yes, please. She wanted to forget about all the attempts on her life and the responsibilities of being a queen. She was grateful for his foresight.

The little boat didn't go much farther before Ari drove it up onto a sandbar. A small castle sat perched several hundred feet away. Zwaantie made to go up the path, but Ari caught her around the waist. "We're not going in there until we have to."

He spread a blanket out on the beach and gently laid her down. He looked deep into her eyes and kissed her lips with the lightest of touch, but held so much tenderness. His slid his hand along her bare thigh, and she shivered. He smiled. Her heart filled, and she was ready to become his. Forever.

They made love under the stars. It was everything she dreamed it would be and more. She wished for a moment that time could stop.

Later in the evening Ari led her into the small castle. It had no windows and only one heavy steel door. It was tiny inside, with only four rooms. After they sealed off the door, she followed Ari into the bedroom, and they snuggled under a blanket.

"I don't want to go home," Zwaantie said. "I want to stay in Stella. Maybe Raaf can become king once we get rid of Father."

Ari shook his head. "That won't work. Part of ending the curse is joining the kingdoms. Which won't happen if you decide to let the kingdom go to your brother."

"But the same thing will happen if you give Stella to Leo."

He chuckled and ran his hands along her ribs. They were incredibly distracting.

"You misunderstand. I have no intention of living in Sol or giving Stella away to anyone. What if you gave Sol to Leo? Then we would be crossing the kingdoms."

Zwaantie frowned. "I don't think Leo would be very happy in Sol. What about Pius? Raaf would be so angry though. I'm not sure I'm comfortable giving up my kingdom."

He kissed her nose, his fingers tracing circles on her stomach.

"Well, we'll figure it out later. When we get back, we'll discuss this with my father. He's good at finding solutions. We've got to do something about Leo too. We owe him that after I stole you away from him."

Zwaantie didn't know how he could think about politics at a moment like this. His hand was driving her crazy. She leaned forward and kissed him. "Let's not talk about this right now."

Zwaantie stared at the dark and foreign water skeptically.

"You want me to go in there? Don't the vipers come from the ocean?"

Ari sighed with exasperation. "I've been swimming in here hundreds of times, and I've never seen a viper. Come on, you have no idea what you're missing."

She took a few steps forward, letting the water lap up on her feet. It was warmer than she expected, but she still wasn't convinced.

Ari drew her close and kissed her, pulling her farther in until the water was up to her calves. Nothing had brushed up against her leg yet, so she was still okay.

"You're trying to distract me."

He reached down and swooped her up into his arms. "You bet I am. Do you know how to swim?"

"Yes. I swam in the lake at home a lot. This is different." She clutched onto the back of his neck, nerves coursing through her body.

He continued his descent. Cold water hit her back, and she squealed. She clung tighter to him.

"Ari. Take me back." This wasn't fun. Not at all.

"Nope, you'll thank me. I promise."

He leaned down and planted a light kiss on her lips, and then he tossed her into the air.

She screamed as she hit the water and came up gasping. She wiped her eyes and spun in circles looking for Ari. He snaked an arm around her waist and tugged her against his body. "See, this isn't so bad."

"Until I get eaten by a viper." They had to tread water to keep from sinking.

"Look up there." He pointed to a star that lit up blue.

"Yeah." She clung to him. She wanted out. She could look at the stars safely from the shore.

"That's Sigma. He's the god of water. He will protect you." Ari ran his hand over her eyes and nose. "Now you can breathe and see underwater."

"What?" she asked.

"I spelled you to see and breathe underwater. Come, a whole different world exists under there."

He gripped her hand and plunged into the water.

It was as if someone had turned on the sun. She could see everything as if it was clear as a Solite day. She nearly laughed out loud. Shiny fish swam just underneath her. Bright coral dotted the floor. A massive octopus floated not twenty feet from them. She couldn't quite believe her eyes. This wasn't glow. She could see clearly.

Ari gave her a thumbs up, and she smiled. Something brushed her foot, and she startled. A giant turtle swam up and looked her right in the eyes. Then he swam away. She couldn't possibly take it all in.

Later, she and Ari lay on the sand, Zwaantie's head on Ari's shoulder, her hand on his stomach. He traced circles on her bare back.

"Do we have to go and deal with people?" Zwaantie asked. "We should stay on this island forever. Just me and you. This is perfect."

He chuckled. "Naw, we need people. If we don't have others to get angry with, we'll eventually get mad at each other."

Zwaantie snorted. "We'll get mad anyway." She snuggled closer to him. "I'm so glad we found each other."

He kissed her forehead. "Me too. It's going to be hard for a while, but after that, we'll be happy."

"We'll be happy anyway. We have each other. Nothing can hurt us now."

In spite of all the awful things that had befallen them lately, she truly believed that she and Ari would be fine as long as they were together.

Chapter Thirty

THE LAST CHANCE

The Voice looked at those forty-nine orbs that should've killed the princess by now. They mocked him with their very glows. He was running out of options. Phoenix, was completely unresponsive. Luna was dead because of her own conscience. He should've known better than to force her hand. She fought harder than the rest, but he'd still managed to get to her a couple of times. He'd thought she was his best bet. Poor girl thought she meant something to him. Sure, he liked her well enough, but she wasn't worth his survival.

He was getting desperate.

Zwaantie could hang herself if she ever took the wretched necklace off. She never did though. He wondered when she discovered he could still control her. Zwaantie would never dare set foot back in Sol. If only that were good enough. The wretched Old Mother had made it clear that if she married Leo, his life would end.

He'd tried everything, and nothing was working. It was time for drastic measures. He needed to go to Stella and kill her himself before the wedding.

But how? He had responsibilities here.

Could he entrust the Old Mother with the orbs? She knew how to work them. He could set it up in such a way that wouldn't involve an actual person, but she seemed the best one in case something went wrong. Zwaantie would be so upset when she found out he'd betrayed her. But then, maybe she'd be dead before the thought even registered. He needed to kill her fast and without fuss. Before she married that prince.

She didn't have to know her own brother wanted her dead.

Chapter Thirty-One

THE SURPRISE

Forty-eight hours later they reluctantly steered the boat back to the shore. Zwaantie regretted having to wear something more than a swimsuit. She would also miss the stars. She supposed if she and Ari lived in the big castle, she'd always have the tower, but it wasn't quite the same as when they were out in the middle of the ocean. They'd have to take a lot of trips out to the island. Maybe once a month.

"You know, I thought all of Stella had stars. I'm actually really disappointed that we have to go on a boat to see them."

"There are some places where you can see them. Candace's kingdom has some outlying areas where there are not as many lights. After the dust settles, we'll go spend some time there."

Zwaantie doubted that. Candace would be upset with her for ditching Leo, no matter what Sage said. She'd be grateful little Raaf lived, but that didn't mean she'd want to talk to Zwaantie.

Sage met them at the docks, wringing her hands.

"Why'd you turn your disc off, Ari?"

"I didn't want to be disturbed."

"Too much crap is going on for you to do that. I know you wanted a couple of days of peace. But did you forget that Zwaantie is still engaged to Leo? Maybe he'd find it odd Zwaantie was alone on an island overnight with another man who regularly takes advantage of women?"

"You were going to cover for her. Tell Leo she's in different places when he called. It was two days. How hard was that?"

She sighed and rolled her eyes. "That would've worked if Leo was just calling by disc. But he showed up yesterday, and he's livid."

"Wait, Leo's here?" Zwaantie asked. He'd been very clear that he couldn't come home for several days.

"Yeah, he managed to get your mother and brother to come a few days early, and he's moved up the wedding to the day after tomorrow. I didn't know what the hell to tell him other than that you two had gone off to watch the stars. I told them you were planning on spending a couple of days out on the island. He couldn't figure out why I didn't stay with you. I'm afraid I wasn't very convincing. He nearly got on a boat and came to the island to find you. He doesn't know about the wedding, but he suspects you are sleeping together." Sage ran a hand over her face. "And Zwaantie's mother. She can't figure out why you'd spend time alone with another man. I tried to explain to her that it wasn't that big of a deal. Though Leo's expression may have nixed anything I said."

Zwaantie looked at Sage. "Father didn't come?"

"No, thank goodness. We're keeping a close eye on your brother and mother. Do you think your father would send one of them to kill you?"

"Why didn't my father come?" This was looking more and more like he was the one responsible.

"Your mother said he was ill."

Ill. Yeah, right.

"Did you give them necklaces?"

"Yes. I explained it would keep them safe from hidden dangers in Stella. Your mother latched it on without another thought. Raaf was hesitant, but he took it anyway. We'll keep you well-guarded, in case one of them takes it off."

"Okay." Zwaantie let out a deep breath. She wasn't on shore for more than thirty seconds, and already they had things to deal with. She wondered if she'd ever have peace in her life. She hated making her mother and brother wear necklaces. She couldn't take any chances though. If Father were still controlling them, they would do things they wouldn't do otherwise.

"What are we going to do?" she asked Ari, panic starting to set in.

Ari took her hand. "I'll deal with Leo. You deal with your mother and brother. Try to pretend everything is still as planned. We need to proceed cautiously. As soon as Leo is informed, we'll make a plan to deal with the public and your family."

"But why? This gives us a perfect opportunity to get everything out in the open. It will be painful, but we can deal with it."

"I'd like to try to see if we can have a public wedding as well. That way your family won't be upset they couldn't be there for it. Plus, we need to appease the public, and the rest of my family is probably in town by now. If we can keep this quiet for a couple more days, we can probably salvage our reputations and relationships. Leo is the only one who won't be happy, but I can deal with him. Sage is Candace here?"

"Yeah."

Ari kissed Zwaantie one more time. "Remember you are in love with Leo. Candace will see through you. Sage, maybe you can head her off."

Zwaantie let out a breath. This was not how things were supposed to go. She was married to the man she loved more than life itself, and she was supposed to pretend she was in love with another one. This had disaster written all over it.

Ari started back for the castle.

Sage called after him. "Take a shower first. You stink."

He made a rude gesture and continued walking. Then she looked at Zwaantie with resignation.

"So do you for that matter. Come on, let's go to Xandria's. You can shower and change your clothes."

Xandria gave Zwaantie a potion for nerves after her shower. Then they snuck back into the castle and went immediately to the king's quarters where Sage had left Zwaantie's mother and brother. Zwaantie steeled herself. These two were not going to be easy to deal with, but they'd be better than Leo. Maybe she wouldn't have to talk to Leo at all. Maybe Ari would make everything okay with him. She could hope.

Zwaantie interrupted their lunch. Mother nodded to Zwaantie and then continued her conversation with Ajax. Zwaantie was certain it took a lot of self-control on Mother's part.

"Ah, the missing princess. Come, eat with us and tell us of your adventures on the ocean and our remote islands," the king said and winked at Zwaantie, but no one could see. Did he know?

Zwaantie crossed to her mother and gave her a polite kiss on the cheek. "Hello, Mother."

"Zwaantie, how was your trip?"

"It was very nice. The stars are bright out there. We went swimming in the ocean as well, and the fish are incredible."

"I'm happy to see you."

Zwaantie slid into a chair next to Raaf, who barely looked at her. There were dark circles under his eyes, and his skin had a yellow sheen.

"What happened to you?" Zwaantie asked.

"What are you talking about?" He continued eating without taking his eyes off of his food. She wasn't sure what was going on. Maybe he was having trouble with the Voice as well. She checked and he had a necklace on. Hopefully he'd feel better after being here for a few days.

"You look sick."

"I'm fine. You're the one who needs help." Raaf's voice was gruff and mean. She'd never heard him talk to her like that.

Zwaantie looked from him to Mother, who averted her eyes.

"Why?" she asked, not wanting to hear his response, but needing to.

"Let's see." He put his fork down. "Well, you are dressed like a slut, and you just spent the last two days alone on an island with a man who has a reputation for sleeping with anything that moves. I'd say you are the one who needs help. Not me."

Zwaantie drew herself up to her full height. His argument was weak. True, but weak, so she'd be able to talk her way out of this.

"Ari's my friend, and he took me out on the boat so that I could see the stars. You know how obsessed I was with them before I left home. That's all."

Mother released a huge breath, but Raaf didn't look convinced. Neither did the king.

"Why didn't Sage go with you two?" asked King Ajax with a furrowed brow.

"She had an investigation that needed her attention."

"Hmm," said the king. "Yes, I'd forgotten about that. I wonder if she made any progress."

Before Mother or Raaf could ask the king to elaborate, Sage opened the door.

"Hi, Daddy," she said and planted a kiss on his cheek. She then sat down next to Zwaantie.

Sage smiled at Mother and then attacked the food in front of her. Mother looked down her nose at Sage. If Sage had been entertaining them for the last twenty-four hours, Mother probably had a lot of opinions about her. Zwaantie was sure she'd hear about them when they were alone.

The subject of Ari didn't come up again, and Mother and Ajax resumed speaking about the affairs of the kingdoms.

After they ate, Zwaantie stood. "Mother, would you like to see my rooms? We can discuss the goings-on at home."

"Oh, yes. Of course. Raaf?"

He nodded and both followed her down the hall. Two guards trailed behind them.

Mother brushed her fingers along the edge of Zwaantie's shirt. "Did you really have to adopt their style?"

"Aren't you stifling, Mother? It's so hot."

"You have a point. But you're wearing so few clothes."

"I'm much more comfortable." Zwaantie pushed open the door and watched her mother's reaction to the room. A slow smile crawled across her face.

"It's almost like being at home again. They did this for you?"

"Leo did. Go touch one of the cows."

She did, and it mooed. Mother chuckled.

Raaf sank down on the couch and looked around with a bored expression.

"What have you been up to, besides running around with the king's playboy son?" Raaf asked.

"Learning about the magic of Stella. It's incredible. I wonder if it would be possible to bring some of it home."

Raaf screwed up his face. "No. That would be awful. Do you see what they have here? No way."

Mother sat across from them. "Those monsters last night. I thought I was going to have a heart attack."

"I know. As long as we are in before midnight, we're safe."

Raaf leaned forward and touched her necklace. "Yours looks different than ours. Can I see it?"

Zwaantie gripped the necklace. "No. I never take it off."

"Why not?"

"Because it protects me from danger. I've had too many close calls to risk it."

"I don't blame you," Mother said. "Without the Voice, I bet the dangers are prevalent."

Zwaantie nodded. She wasn't about to tell Mother that the real danger came from Sol. From the king himself.

The conversation turned to lighter things. Seeing them here, Zwaantie never wanted to step foot on Solite soil again. She didn't miss it. Perhaps the food and definitely the sun, but nothing else. Sol was far more dangerous than Stella ever was.

Chapter Thirty-Two

THE SCORNED

After a half hour, Leo came into the room followed by Ari. Leo seemed pacified. Which was good. And bad.

What if Ari hadn't told him the truth?

Leo swept down and lifted Zwaantie up out of the chair in an embrace. Oh no. Ari stood behind Leo and mouthed the word, "Sorry."

Oh stars. How was she supposed to keep this charade up?

Leo let go and kissed her full on the lips. She kissed him back, mostly because if she didn't, he'd know something was up. It was nice, but it didn't hold a candle to Ari's kisses. Plus, she felt dirty kissing another man in front of her husband. Though this was his fault. Maybe she should pretend a little harder with Leo and make Ari jealous.

Leo pulled away, all smiles. She couldn't do this.

"I missed you so much. I'm never leaving you alone again. I know you haven't seen your mother in a couple of months, but I would really like some time with you. Especially after how we left things in The Black City. Will you go for a walk with me?"

Zwaantie shot Ari a look, and he shrugged.

"Okay," she agreed reluctantly. Leo took her hand and led her out into the hallway. She gave Ari one last fleeting look and trailed after Leo.

He chattered all the way out of the castle. She was so angry with Ari that she didn't even realize where they were heading. He had put her in an impossible situation. She should tell Leo. She worried that she'd do the wrong thing though. So much of Stella relied on the Ticker and reputations.

"I felt so bad after you left. I totally ignored you, and you were trying so hard. I am so sorry. After we get married, I'd like you to come on my investigations with me if you want. Are you excited for the wedding?"

Zwaantie nodded, words completely lost on her.

He stopped and kissed her again. His kisses were filled with longing, and suddenly she pitied him. He had no idea what was going on. How could she lead him on like this? How was it that Ari didn't deal with it? Oh, she was so angry. The second she got Ari alone, she was going to let him have it. How could he put her in this position?

She hated faking it, but she had no choice at the moment. Leo smiled at her, and she tried to smile back as they went on an incredibly awkward walk. She didn't see Ari again that day. She went to his room, but he never came home. Either he was avoiding her, or something else was going on. The next morning she searched the entire castle for him, but he was nowhere to be found. Sage didn't seem concerned and instead kept Zwaantie busy with flowers, food, and her family so she didn't have to spend much time with Leo. She had no plan for escaping this. Tomorrow was her wedding, and she was already a married woman. So far the marriage mage hadn't said anything, but if she tried to marry Leo tomorrow, surely she would say something.

Stars. Where was Ari?

Chapter Thirty-Three

THE BETRAYAL

T hat evening they had a huge dinner with the entire family. Little Raaf was getting big. Zwaantie had hoped Raaf would've been pleased she'd named the baby after him, but he didn't seem all that impressed. Discs flashed everywhere.

Ari came in right before dinner started and sat clear across the table. He didn't even look her way.

Candace kept up a running commentary on all the gossip, which distracted Zwaantie from trying to catch Ari's eye. Candace followed her eyeline.

"He looks a little miserable, huh. Maybe he finally fell in love and can't have her. Serves him right."

"No, it doesn't."

Candace frowned. "Excuse me? He's slept with half the kingdom, and he left a string of broken hearts. Of course he deserves it."

Zwaantie couldn't stand it anymore. The pretending. The fakeness. But she couldn't defend her husband without revealing her secret. She had to get out of there.

"I'll be back." Zwaantie shoved the chair out and rushed toward the door hoping no one would notice. She went for the one place she knew she could hide. The entire royal family was upstairs having dinner. No one would think to look for her here.

She didn't even take glow before she pushed the door open and found the tree. She curled up under the golden leaves and let herself cry. It wasn't until arms were around her that she realized someone else was there.

"I'm so sorry. I caused this," Ari said in a strained voice.

He curled up behind Zwaantie and kissed her neck.

"Where have you been?"

"Trying to find a solution."

"By hiding from me? How could you let this continue?" she asked, her anger building. "It's not fair of you to put me in this position. I'm going back upstairs, and I'm going tell him everything." It was time. The consequences would not be pleasant, but this had to come out. She was sick of pretending.

"I'll go with you. We'll tell everyone and let the chips fall where they may."

Zwaantie rolled over to face him. "Thank you."

Ari kissed Zwaantie, and their hands were all over each other, and before she knew it, their clothes were off.

Twenty minutes later they lay under the tree appreciating the beauty of the colors and the afterglow of their lovemaking. So much for staying angry with him. They were both procrastinating over what needed to be done.

"Come on," she muttered. "We have some people to tell."

Ari reached a hand over and pulled her close to him. "One more time and then we'll go upstairs."

She giggled and kissed him. Another thirty minutes wouldn't make any difference. At least that's what she told herself. Maybe they'd stay in the gardens forever and never face reality. Every time she was with Ari, everything around her disappeared.

Footsteps crunched on the fake leaves that had fallen to the ground.

Ari's eyes widened, and they both scrambled for their clothes.

Leo's head appeared under the tree. "What the hell is going on?"

Of all the people who could find them in the garden, he was the worst. Zwaantie would've rather seen her mother or Candace or even Lyra. She had managed to get most of her dress back on, but Ari was still searching for his pants, and he clambered up to talk to Leo.

Zwaantie stood a few feet from Ari. She didn't know what to say.

"I can explain," Ari said.

"No," Leo roared. His face was red, and he gripped his hair. "You knew how I felt about her, and you had to have her anyway."

Ari took two steps closer to him. "It wasn't like that. I swear. Neither one of us expected this to happen."

Leo stared past Ari to Zwaantie, and his eyes were so sad. She didn't mean to hurt him.

"I'm sorry," she said. "I fell in love. I didn't mean to. I intended to marry you, and I figured eventually I would love you. But then I fell in love. I couldn't deny it, and neither could he." She didn't know what else to say. This wasn't okay.

"And what," he snarled, "do you expect him to do? Marry you? He won't. You'll be a mistress your whole life. I can give you a marriage. He can't."

"Actually, I already did," Ari said.

"What? Screw her? I know that."

Zwaantie winced at the crude words.

"No, I married her. A few days ago. On the boat."

"You what?" The blood drained from Leo's face. He flicked his eyes between the both of them, and when neither responded, he stormed from the room.

"I should follow him," Ari said.

Zwaantie nodded, knowing Leo wouldn't want to see her. He probably wouldn't want to see Ari either, but at least they might be able to reconcile.

"I'll go to Sage's room. If you need me, send someone."

Ari gave her a quick kiss and raced from the garden.

Zwaantie took her time. She didn't want to deal with what lay on the other side of the door.

Sage was already in her room reading something on her disc.

She looked up when Zwaantie shut the door, and a blush crept across her cheeks.

"Leo's pissed," Zwaantie said. At least she was on Zwaantie's side. No one else would be.

"I know. Ari's talking to him, right?"

"How do you know?" Zwaantie asked.

"They locked themselves in Ari's room. Wouldn't let me come in. I figured Ari finally found the balls to tell him."

"Not exactly."

Sage raised an eyebrow. "What do you mean?"

"Leo walked in on me and Ari in the gardens."

Sage giggled. "What were you doing in the gardens?"

Zwaantie threw a pillow at her. "You know what we were doing. Should I try to go talk to them?"

"No, they'll figure it out."

Zwaantie took a shower and put her pajamas on. She should've gone and attended to her mother, but she couldn't deal with the judgment after what happened with Ari and Leo. Her mother didn't know about Ari yet, but she was sure to harp on something about either Zwaantie or Stella.

Zwaantie was grateful she didn't have to worry about a wedding the next day. Though she did feel a little guilty when she saw a wistful Sage standing next to the wedding dress.

"What do you think is going to happen?" Zwaantie asked.

Sage shrugged and locked her door.

They curled up in her bed and waited for the lights to go out. When they did, Zwaantie felt her eyes slowly close. For a mere second though, she registered there was no sound on the other side of the door. The vipers were gone.

Chapter Thirty-Four

THE WEDDING: PART 2

The next morning Ari woke to Sage glaring at him.

"Get up. The both of you," Sage said.

Leo was sound asleep on the couch across from him. They stayed up most of the night talking. In the end, Leo hadn't punched him, but he should've.

"Sage," Leo grumbled. "Get out."

"Nope. We have a wedding to plan."

"Stars, Sage. Everyone knows," Ari said.

"Nope. No one knows except us and Zwaantie. Father might. He seems suspicious. Did you notice how quiet it was last night?"

"What are you talking about?"

"No vipers. That's what everyone is talking about."

"You mean it worked?"

"What I can't figure out is why it took so long. You guys have been married three days."

"They're like gone, gone?"

"I doubt anyone will risk going out for a few nights, but it's all over the Ticker. Not a single person heard the vipers last night."

Leo sank into the couch. "Thank the stars. At least that's over."

Sage shuffled her feet. "Now. Wedding. I say we leave it. Except switch the groom and not tell a soul. The public will eat it up. The

Ticker will be buzzing for weeks about this, maybe even months. What do you say?"

"Only if we change the location."

"What? No."

"Please. The beach will be better."

"The point is to not give anyone a reason to be suspicious."

Ari sighed. He'd been trying to avoid a wedding at the castle. The vision from the funhouse still haunted him. It was why he married Zwaantie out on the boat. It ensured that what he saw couldn't possibly come true. If he argued too much more, Sage would start asking questions.

"Only if Leo is okay with it." Ari said.

"If it will make things easier in the long run, sure. But then I'm leaving for a while. I do not want to see you and Zwaantie suck face." His face was stony, but at least he was attempting to make it light.

"Can do, brother. Sage, go get our bride ready."

Most of the guests were already there when Ari and Leo arrived. They posed for pictures. Leo put on a good face. Everyone kept asking him if he was ready to get married. He just smiled and nodded. This wasn't fair to him, but he went along with it anyway. Maybe he deserved Zwaantie more than Ari did.

The room was incredible. The ceiling glittered with stars, and flowers floated around the room. People stood along the path in the middle where Zwaantie would walk down. Ari and Leo took their places at the front of the aisle, next to the marriage mage.

This would be the story of the century. Though the vipers might override it. Ari wondered like Sage why it had taken three days. Was something different now than before? Ari couldn't possibly see what.

Music began, and the entire crowd stood. Sage made her way up the walkway in a very pretty pink dress. He wondered when she'd settle down. He hoped soon. He chuckled to himself. That was a thought he would've never had a few weeks ago. Now, he wanted everyone to be as in love as he was.

Zwaantie appeared at the end of the aisle, her face beaming. Her blonde hair hung in ringlets around her face. She practically glowed in her white dress, though he barely took his eyes off her smile. She stared directly at him. His chest swelled. She was his. Forever. Discs flashed all over the room.

She had to climb three stairs to get to him. She took the first step, and her eyes sparkled. Out of the corner of his eye, Zwaantie's brother stepped around his mother. In his hands he held, oh stars, no. A back-snipe pointed at Zwaantie.

Ari didn't hesitate.

"No," he shouted as he lunged for Zwaantie. He shoved her out of the way as a bolt shot straight for her.

Chapter Thirty-Five

THE SOUL MATE

Zwaantie's ankle twisted, and her dress tangled around her legs. Leo leaped over her. Her head cracked against the stairs as she was forced to the ground. Zwaantie scrambled to get up, but Ari lay on top of her. She blinked and shook her head. She forced herself into a sitting position, which was difficult because Ari was lying across her legs. She gripped at his torso.

She saw but didn't believe the short arrow that stuck out of his chest. The blood that bloomed around it.

"I love you," Ari said, his pained face inches away with his eyes locked on hers.

"Ari, no." Her mind raced, trying to put together what was happening.

"Take care of Sage, please." He gripped her hand tight.

Her tears started. "Don't leave me, Ari. You stay here. A healer will fix this."

"No, he won't. I love you."

His eyes fluttered shut, and his face fell slack.

She scrambled out from underneath him and grabbed his face.

"Ari, Ari, talk to me." She patted his cheeks and kissed his lips, but he didn't move.

Strong arms grabbed her from behind. "We need to get you out of here."

"No!" Zwaantie screamed. "Ari, he needs help. Help him."

Leo turned her around. She couldn't believe what was happening.

"There is nothing else we can do. You're not safe."

"But Ari."

Zwaantie collapsed in Leo's arms. He swooped her up and raced with her into the castle.

"No, no. Ari." She fought against his arms. "Ari," she screamed again. Leo held her tight as they made their way into a narrow passageway. She was in the arms of the wrong man. Ari should be holding her. She stopped fighting and sobbed. Ari would never hold her again.

Ari was dead.

The End

∼

Zwaantie doesn't know how she can keep living...

In fact, she doesn't want to.

But she discovers devastating information about both kingdoms. And she has to step up and be queen or more of her friends could die.

When the Voice takes control of both Stella and Sol, Zwaantie has to fight for the very survival of both kingdoms.

Thank you for reading!

KIMBERLY LOTH

QUEEN
of the
DAWN

FOURTH BOOK IN THE STELLA AND SOL SERIES

Stella and Sol

Queen of the Dawn
Volume 4
By Kimberly Loth

For Xandi
You've been my beautiful princess for so long.
You're going to rock being a queen.

Chapter One

THE PAIN

Zwaantie didn't pay attention to where they were going. She couldn't see beyond the tears. A pain settled deep in her chest, and she could barely breathe. Leo led her deep into the castle, the concrete walls crowding in on her. They wove around and around, going up stairs and down. She was certain wherever they were going, she'd never been there before.

Ari would never return. Never again smile at her. Never kiss her. Never drive her crazy with his touch. Never make her laugh. Gone.

She hyperventilated and was unable to move. She sucked in long deep breaths, and sobs overtook her.

"Zwaantie, stay with me. We've got to get you somewhere safe." Leo tugged on her hand.

She jerked her hand out of his, collapsed, and curled into a ball, the pain in her chest too much. She could still feel Ari's lifeless body in her arms, the way his eyes fluttered shut and how his smile fell slack. The blood on his chest. She howled. Ari was dead.

Leo stooped down, swung her up against his chest, and raced down a set of stairs. She cried into his shoulder, clutching and soaking his vest, needing to hang on to something.

Eventually he stopped, pushed open a door, and set her down carefully on a couch. Her sobs were calming now, an emptiness slowly replacing the pain. Would she ever be happy again? The bigger question was, would she ever be free of sadness? It didn't seem possible.

Leo locked the door and sat next to her. She stared blankly at him. He wiped at his own tears and dropped his head into his hands. The circular room was small but had couches and chairs scattered about. There were no windows, no pictures or tapestries on the walls, only bare stone. Zwaantie rubbed her arms, a chill settling over her.

Leo's body was deathly still, and for a half second Zwaantie worried that he might be dead as well, but he turned and stared at her.

"I can't believe he's gone." Leo kept a hand over his mouth, and his eyes spoke of the pain she was certain reflected in her own eyes.

"Me either," she muttered and pulled her knees to her chest, resting her head on them, her eyes still leaking.

Leo dropped his arms and scooted closer to her, his face stony. "I know this is hard, but I need to know what happened."

He put a hand on her knee, and she jerked away from him. "What happened? Ari's dead." The ache in her chest swelled. How could he ask these questions of her? She didn't have a clue what happened to Ari.

"Did you see who killed him?"

Pain shot through her body. Surely everyone saw who killed him. "It was Raaf," she choked out. Her brother killed the love of her life.

Leo gave a slow nod. "Okay, just making sure we saw the same thing. I didn't want to accuse him if my eyes had deceived me. Why would Raaf want to kill you?"

A sob escaped. "He didn't kill *me*." Raaf loved her. She was closer to him than she was to her parents. Sure, he'd been different when he came home from training, but he was still Raaf. How could he betray her?

"I know, but you were his target. Any ideas why?" Leo asked. She could see the wheels turning in Leo's head as he took out his disc. "Probably for the throne, don't you think?"

"I said I don't know," she screeched. Panic crept across her veins, and she felt as if she was going to crawl out of her skin. She was nearing hysteria. Ari was dead. Raaf killed him. Who else in her life would betray her? From Phoenix, to Wilma, to Luna, to Raaf. Could she trust no one from Sol?

It came down to the Voice. Whoever or whatever it was, it had to be destroyed because it had killed everyone she loved. Her mind cleared a little. It was good to have something to focus her rage on. As long as the Voice existed, she would be in danger—as well as those around her.

"Raaf wouldn't want to kill me. It's the Voice." Which was her father, or at least that's what they thought. Maybe it wasn't. Maybe they were wrong. Did he want her dead so much that he sent Raaf to kill her? How barbaric.

"The Voice?"

She'd forgotten she'd told Sage not to tell him. His mother knew of course, but Zwaantie had asked Lyra to keep it quiet as well. She felt stupid for keeping this a secret. If they'd tried harder to eliminate the Voice before now, maybe Ari would still be alive. This was her fault. She gripped her sides and leaned over, the tears coming in earnest again.

Someone knocked hard on the door, and Zwaantie cowered.

Leo moved to the door and placed his hand on the wood. "Call first."

Leo's disc buzzed. Zwaantie curled into herself once again and stared at the stone walls. She heard the king say, "It's me."

Leo undid the locks, clicking and clanking. The sound jarred Zwaantie's ears. Several voices floated in from the hall. Zwaantie didn't recognize any of them. Sage collapsed on the floor and wrapped her arms around Zwaantie. Her hands were warm and welcome.

Zwaantie's well burst again, and Sage sobbed with her. Zwaantie cried for the loss of her husband. Sage for the loss of her best friend. A hole opened up in their lives and would never be filled again.

People spoke in low voices around them, but Zwaantie didn't pay attention. She only wanted to escape the pain. Nothing else existed. It was so raw and real and would never go away.

A voice rose above the rest.

"Unhand me at once," Zwaantie's mother yelled. "This is an outrage. How dare you humiliate me like this."

Zwaantie untangled herself from Sage. This was a problem she had to handle even if she didn't feel like it was possible to handle anything at the moment.

King Ajax hovered over Mother, his face filled with rage. "Your son killed my son. You're lucky you aren't locked up in the dungeon. Sol just became an enemy of Stella."

Zwaantie had trouble comprehending his words. Did that mean they were going to kick her out as well? Mother sputtered. "I saw no such thing. Raaf would never kill anyone."

Zwaantie jumped up and spun towards her mother. This was too much. She might not know the details, but she knew exactly how her husband died. "Yes, he did. But he was trying to kill me. Not Ari. Ari saved my life." She turned to the guards. "Get her out of here and lock her up." Raaf was acting under the influence of the Voice, but Mother was being spiteful. Zwaantie wouldn't let anyone distort the reality of Ari's death.

Mother turned to Zwaantie, her face a mask of anger. "How dare you."

Zwaantie clenched her clammy fists. "The Voice wants me dead. He can control anyone—including you. I'm not safe with you in this room. Get her out." The guards didn't move. Perhaps they were suspicious of her as well.

Mother's bright blue eyes bored into Zwaantie's. Sage climbed off the couch and fished a necklace out of her pocket. She clasped it around Mother's neck. They must've taken them off before the wedding. Fools.

"Why did you remove that necklace? We told you it was for your own safety," Zwaantie said.

Mother smoothed her skirt. "It didn't match my dress. I'm Queen of Sol. I had to make a good impression."

Zwaantie gripped her own hair. "If you'd kept them on, Ari would still be alive. This is your fault." She couldn't even begin to fathom their stupidity. For the first time in her life, Mother expressed some vanity, and now Ari was dead.

Mother snorted. "You think Raaf did this? You must've seen it wrong. You were focused on your groom and distracted."

Zwaantie grabbed her mother's shoulders and shook her. "Raaf killed Ari. I saw it with my own eyes."

The annoyance in Mother's face didn't change, and they stood staring at each other for a few moments, neither one saying anything. Zwaantie's fingers dug into her mother's shoulder.

Mother glanced down. "Let. Go. Of. Me."

Zwaantie shoved her away. "Get her out of here," she commanded the guards.

Mother struggled as they dragged her out of the room. Zwaantie should feel some guilt, but instead she felt relief. This was one less thing she'd have to deal with, one less complication she didn't need. Especially now after defending Raaf.

"Have they caught Raaf?" Zwaantie asked the king.

"No. We'll be staying in here for the time being. He could be halfway to Sol by now, though, if he had people in town hiding him. If not, we'll find him. Guards are scouring the castle."

Zwaantie let out a breath. She worried this would be her life. Constantly hiding from others who might want to do her harm. Even her own father wanted to hurt her if he was the Voice. She'd never say that out loud to Mother. Not without proof. She hoped she was wrong.

Zwaantie's mother was stuck in Stella for now. Zwaantie wanted the border sealed up tight. Solites would stay on their side as long as she was in danger. The ones she loved were dying. But a sealed border would mean the kingdoms weren't truly joined, and the vipers might start killing people again. One night of peace did not mean they were gone for good.

She couldn't wrap her head around anything. She needed Ari. He always knew what to say and would comfort her. But Ari was dead.

Zwaantie looked around at those with her. The king, Leo, Sage, and Lyra.

She wiped her eyes and let out a breath, ready to tackle the problem at hand. Anything to distract her from the pain. "How are we going to find Raaf?"

King Ajax put a hand on her shoulder. "You aren't going to do anything but stay safe. We'll find him."

"Excuse me? He's my brother." She saw Raaf kill Ari, but she planned on asking Raaf how the Voice had gotten to him to discover exactly what drove him to shoot at her.

"He wants to kill you."

Zwaantie clenched her fists, knowing she would be fighting an uphill battle. "What will you do to him when you find him?"

"That depends on how we find him," King Ajax said with a frown.

She squeezed her eyes shut. "He's under the influence of the Voice. You can't hurt him."

Leo snorted. "He killed Ari. How can you be thinking of him?"

She wrung her hands. She didn't know how to explain how powerful the Voice could be. "I know, but it's not his fault. It's the Voice."

"She's right," Sage said. "Can I lead the investigation?"

"Yes," Zwaantie said, relieved Sage was helping her. This had to count for something. The two people who loved Ari the most, defending Raaf together. "Sage knows everything, and she'll make sure Raaf doesn't get hurt in the process."

The king ran a hand along his face. "I don't understand anything about this Voice. We're stuck here until they determine Raaf is no longer in the castle or even City of Stars. The guards should finish their search sometime this evening. We need to get some rest, and then I need a briefing on everything. We can't make any decisions right now."

"No. We need to make a plan to find the Voice and destroy it." Zwaantie needed purpose, a job. Something to move her forward, or she might fall apart. The Voice had taken everything from her. It had to go.

Sage tugged on Zwaantie's hand. "We can't do anything in here. Come, I have a sleeping potion. When you wake up, we'll gather everyone together and make a real plan."

Zwaantie wanted to argue, but no one else wanted to fix the problem now. Except her. Though it wouldn't bring Ari back. Her heart clenched again. He was really gone. Maybe she would let Sage give her a potion, and she'd wake up and find Ari alive and breathing.

Zwaantie collapsed next to Sage onto the couch, took the potion, and swallowed it before she could change her mind.

Sage wrapped her arms around Zwaantie. Ari filled her thoughts as she fell into the darkness.

Chapter Two

THE LOST LOVE

Leo watched the love of his life sleep in the arms of his sister. He should be the one holding and comforting her. That was impossible though because that love of his life was grieving the love of *her* life. Not to mention that he was still furious with her.

He clenched his fists. He still wanted to be angry about Zwaantie's betrayal. He wanted to yell and scream and tell her how much she'd hurt him because she'd taken his heart and torn it to shreds.

How could he though? Ari was dead, something Leo could barely even begin to process. He knew the ache in his chest was minor compared to hers. The world would be a dimmer place without Ari. He could hardly fathom that not long ago, no one was dying. The prophecy given by the Old Mother changed everything.

"Do you think she's asleep?" Leo asked Sage, who kept wiping at her own tears.

"She won't wake up for several hours," Sage replied in a quiet voice. She twirled Zwaantie's blonde locks around her fingers and stared off into space.

Leo glanced around the room. His father and mother sat in the opposite corner whispering in low voices. His dad probably was wrestling with his own grief. Two weeks ago, his wife died and now his oldest son. Yet, he was completely put together. Leo wasn't sure he'd be able to do the same.

Perhaps Lyra was briefing him on the Voice. He was glad they'd shut Zwaantie down. As much as he wanted the Voice gone and Ari's murderer brought to justice, they'd make bad decisions in the state they were in. They needed to take a deep breath and think about things first.

"Are you okay?" he asked Sage. He was worried about her. She'd never lost anyone close to her before, and Ari was her best friend.

"I took a numbing potion, so I don't feel anything. But no, I'm not okay." Of course she took a potion. That was her solution for everything. One of these days she'd run into something a potion wouldn't solve.

"How long do you think we'll be stuck in here for?" Leo asked, itching to get out and do something.

"Too long. You want a potion?"

He shook his head. He didn't want to lose control of his own thoughts and feelings. "She really loved him, didn't she?"

Sage rested her chin on Zwaantie's head. "Yeah, but their relationship was really about how much Ari loved her. She stole his heart. I still can't believe he married her."

Leo swallowed. This was going places he didn't want it to. "You know, I loved her too."

"I know. People can't control their feelings, though. Ari made it easy for her to love him."

"And I didn't?"

Sage snorted. "No. You didn't. You were gone. Also, your mind works too hard. Once Ari decided he had to have her, every action he had was for her, and when she was in the room, he saw no one else."

"That's dangerous." Leo couldn't imagine risking his entire kingdom for love. Though Ari did. He put his own feelings above what was best for the kingdom.

"That's love."

Leo scowled. Maybe he didn't love Zwaantie the way he thought he did. He didn't really want to talk about this, but if it kept Sage's mind off Ari's death, he'd do that for her. She was one of his favorite sisters because she told him the truth. Candace did as well, but Sage was nicer about it.

"What do you know about love?" he asked, in hopes to change the subject. But one thing Sage hated doing was talking about herself.

"More than you think."

He hadn't expected an answer. This was new. Sage had a fling now and again, but she never got too close to anyone. She couldn't. Not with her job.

"Oh yeah. Who?" He wanted to bring things back to work, but he also wanted to subdue his curiosity.

"Who, what?" Sage asked with a raised blue eyebrow.

"Who are you in love with?"

"Who said I fell in love with anyone? Even if I did, it's none of your business. I don't want to talk about me. Let's talk about you."

"What about me?"

"You still in love with Zwaantie?"

"Of course." His insides still ached for the loss of his brother, and here she was bringing up old hurts.

"Are you going to marry her?"

"What? No." How could she even think that? After everything Zwaantie had put him through. From pretending to love him, to Phoenix, to Ari. Marrying that woman would be like asking for his heart to be broken time and time again. Plus, she was Ari's bride. It would be an insult to his memory to marry her. Also, she'd never go for it, even if he wanted to.

"You have to." Sage dropped her eyes and fiddled with the edge of her wrinkled dress.

"Why?" Leo asked. He'd expected her to argue that Zwaantie would be lonely, and that they could find solace in one another. Not that he had to marry her.

Sage stroked Zwaantie's hair. "Stella's still unsafe. You have to marry her, otherwise little Raaf—oh stars, she's going to need to change his name. Anyway, he could still die."

Leo rubbed his forehead. He hadn't thought about the ramifications. She'd betrayed him not once, but twice. He did love her, but he also hated her. A lot. There had to be another solution. Her marriage with Ari surely fulfilled the prophecy. There was no reason to think otherwise.

Leo was grateful he'd forgiven Ari before he died. They'd stayed up talking the night before the wedding. Ari said how hard he tried to stay away from Zwaantie and couldn't. He'd tried to do the right thing, but Zwaantie consumed him. While Leo loved her, he didn't understand the all-consuming love, but he saw it in his brother's eyes.

Zwaantie, on the other hand—she might have fallen for Ari—but she knew better. She knew the stakes, and she did it anyway and lied to Leo on several occasions. He wanted to move on with his life and forget this whole nightmare.

"The vipers stopped though." He'd make Sage see reason. He needed to quell her idea before it got out of hand. Once Sage latched onto an idea, she didn't let go, and she was very good at persuading others. If left unchecked, she'd convince everyone, including his father and Zwaantie, that they needed to marry.

Sage shrugged. "The prophecy didn't say anything about the vipers stopping. Only that they would kill little Raaf. Maybe the vipers stopping all together was something deeper than the prophecy. That doesn't mean they won't kill little Raaf."

Sage made a good point.

No, he couldn't think this way. Zwaantie would shatter him.

"She might not agree to marry me."

"She will. Trust me, after Ari, she'll toe the line. Though it wouldn't surprise me if vengeance will be the first thing on her mind."

"The Voice you mean?"

"Yeah." Sage chewed on her lip. "Do you really think it's her dad?"

"Maybe. Though, wouldn't it have made more sense to come and kill her himself? Why send Raaf and pretend to be sick? If he is the Voice and is looking for power, an invitation to Stella would be a great opening. I don't know. Maybe Luna meant someone else."

"Unless he was worried about how things would work if he crossed the wall."

"We can't prove anything."

"We still aren't any closer to destroying it."

"We need to. Ari wasn't the first, and he won't be the last. We can't risk Zwaantie dying." Her safety was paramount. She was also the only link they had to Sol. If something happened to her and the Voice discovered how to cross the wall, Stellans could be slaughtered or enslaved.

"Yeah. She loved her brother a lot. She probably hasn't had much time to process anything, but this is going to mess her up pretty good. I mean Ari dying would've done it, but Raaf pulled the trigger. That makes it much harder for her."

Leo didn't know how to respond. He had been hoping to simply move on with his life without worrying about Zwaantie. She had a lot of people who loved and supported her. But because of the prophecy, he would probably still have to marry her. He'd have to be her comforter, and she would need him in the coming months. He wanted to be clear across the kingdom from her.

He squeezed his fists. He didn't know if he was up to this.

"It'd be easier to figure out how to kill the Voice. If we capture Raaf, we might be able to get answers out of him."

"Unlikely. Phoenix didn't have a clue the Voice was influencing him when he went after Zwaantie. Luna fought it. Why couldn't Raaf? He was her brother. He should've been aware."

"No clue. Maybe Luna was stronger. I can't imagine he'd really want to murder his own sister. We fight sometimes, but I'd never hurt any of you. The Voice must be incredibly powerful to overcome him."

"We might get some answers from her mother. I can't believe she denied Raaf killed Ari. I was afraid Zwaantie was going to kill her."

"She still might. You think she knows something?" Zwaantie's mother always made him nervous. She was the most judgmental woman he'd ever met. When he was in Sol, he loved pushing her buttons. He still remembered the look on her face when Zwaantie stepped out in a Stellan dress.

Sage shrugged. "Maybe. We'll let her sit in the dungeon for a few days before we question her. I'm glad she's not my mother."

"Me too." He would have run away for sure. Maybe that explained some of Zwaantie's poor decisions.

"This could cause a war between Stella and Sol."

"I've already thought about this. If Zwaantie wasn't the crown princess, it would've. But I doubt she'll allow it to get that far. All we need to do is assassinate her father, and she'll become queen of Sol. It was probably a good thing Ari hadn't ascended to the throne yet."

Sage let out a breath. "Can you imagine? Prince of Sol murders King of Stella. It's going to be bad enough as it is. People are going to be crying for blood. Hopefully they don't take it out on Zwaantie."

"I'm sure Viggo can figure out how to swing it so she doesn't take any blame. She'll need to make a statement."

"She can't defend Raaf. People here won't understand he was under the influence of someone else. I'll talk to her."

"I can't believe we have to think about these things. We'll barely have time to mourn him." He wanted to hide in his room and cry for the brother he would never see again. He couldn't though. Leo had to hunt Ari's murderer and worry about protecting Zwaantie.

That would have to drive him. Revenge. Otherwise he wasn't sure he'd get through this. Maybe when the Voice was dead, he'd have time to grieve.

Chapter Three

THE WORST-CASE SCENARIO

Raaf wandered around his orbs. The glowing lights comforted him. He'd missed them when he'd been in Stella.

Wilma had kept them safe, and no one had been the wiser. She'd enjoyed it too much. He'd have to be careful, or she might like the position for herself. After he eliminated Zwaantie as a threat, he might have to find a way to eliminate Wilma as well.

He stopped in front of the large orb, the one that controlled the collective conscience. The orb was taller than him, and it spun slowly about a foot off the ground. It didn't hurt to look at, and swirls of light pulsed within. He wanted to place a hand on it and allow it to comfort him, but he'd been warned to never touch it or risk contamination. He nearly had a heart attack when Wilma touched one of the smaller ones.

Raaf needed a backup plan. He'd barely escaped from Stella. What if he hadn't made it? What would have happened to the Voice? The Voice was bigger than him. He had to protect it at all costs, even if it meant risking his own life, and he couldn't leave it unattended. He needed to train someone to replace him.

The old chancellor was dead. Aside from himself and Wilma, no one else knew the nature of the Voice. If Raaf died, the Voice would eventually fade away. He wouldn't let that happen. The Voice was life.

He let out a breath. The Voice was the reason for everything. Without it, life would be over, and chaos would reign. It was his task to protect the Voice no matter what. Which was why, although he loved her, Zwaantie had to die. At first he'd struggled with the guilt of having to kill his own sister, but now he was resigned to it.

The prophecy Wilma had given him so long ago said if Zwaantie ascended to the throne and became queen, she'd destroy the Voice. This was why he encouraged Phoenix to love her. He'd hoped to get away with not killing her. If she'd given up the throne for love instead, she'd still be alive. But fate had other ideas.

Maybe he was fighting a losing battle. Maybe the time of the Voice was over.

"No," Raaf shouted. He had to do this. She had to die. A tear escaped. It'd been a long time since he'd cried. Two years at least, but he was about to lose his entire family.

His father was not long for this earth. As soon as he died, Zwaantie would be queen. It happened as soon as death happened. A coronation usually occurred a few days later, but her transition from Your Highness to Your Majesty would happen instantly. Raaf wondered briefly if he could trust his mother if she returned to Sol. She usually listened to the Voice, but she loved Zwaantie. If she'd seen him try to kill Zwaantie, she'd turn against him.

He gave a small smile. It was a shame really. If he wasn't the one trying to kill Zwaantie, he'd be fighting for her life. She'd been his best friend. His only confidant. If only she understood what kind of threat she posed to him. Maybe she'd abscond. Maybe not. She'd taken on many of the Stellan ways. At this point death was his only option.

Though there had never really been another option.

Chapter Four

THE HEIR

The guards cleared everybody to return to their rooms just before midnight. Leo had to carry Zwaantie as she couldn't walk out on her own. Partly because of the potion Sage gave her and partly because she felt so defeated. Zwaantie and Sage slept next to one another, clinging to each other as they cried themselves to sleep. Zwaantie wanted the pain to go away. She would never see Ari again. How long would she mourn his death? How long would the pain consume her? It felt so infinite.

The next morning Zwaantie took a long shower. Her tears had subsided, but the ache in her chest was raw. She scrubbed at her body, turning it red. She'd hoped the pain on the outside would drive away some of the internal pain, but it didn't help.

She stepped out of the bathroom, wrapped in a towel. Sage handed her a floor-length, deep black dress.

"How long do I wear black?" Zwaantie asked, more out of a desire to fill the void of silence than really wanting to know.

Sage let out a sigh. Her face held none of the joy it normally did. Even the kittens were more subdued, napping along the couch. It was too quiet in the room.

"As his sister, I will wear black for a month. As his wife, you would wear it for six months. But no one knows you are his wife, so the people will expect you to dress normally after a few weeks. You weren't even his sister yet."

Zwaantie clenched her fists and squeezed her eyes shut. She would not let the Ticker dictate her life. "I want people to know. I will mourn him as his wife."

"I'll talk to Viggo. We'll see how we can spin this."

Zwaantie took a few deep breaths as she stared in the mirror. The events of yesterday played in her mind. From walking down the aisle, to watching Ari fall, to holding his body, to arguing with her mother. Her mother. Zwaantie was going to put an end to her nonsense right away.

"I want to see my mother."

Sage cocked her head. "I don't think that's a good idea. We need to give her some time to settle."

"She's my mother. I have to see her." Zwaantie pressed her hand to her stomach. She had to know if her mother still thought Raaf was innocent. Which he was, but he killed Ari, and Zwaantie needed her mother to at least acknowledge that something wasn't right. Mother didn't need time to come to her senses. She needed to face reality like the rest of them. A few tears escaped. Reality was overrated.

Sage pursed her lips. "I can have her brought back to the castle. It will be safest in the interrogation room. I'm still not sure about this, but I understand your desire. Are you positive? This could make things worse."

Zwaantie squeezed Sage's hand, glad Sage never asked too many questions. Zwaantie didn't want to explain everything. She simply didn't have the energy. "I'm certain. I need her to understand what Raaf did and what this means for the Voice. If she can acknowledge something is wrong with the Voice, then we could have a powerful ally on our hands. Mother is key to understanding the situation in Sol."

~

ZWAANTIE AND SAGE WALKED INTO THE SMALL ROOM. MOTHER WAS shackled in the same dress she wore to the wedding. Her head held high, she glowered as Zwaantie took a seat across from her.

"This is an outrage," she growled and fought against her restraints. Zwaantie was certain her mother had never been treated this way before. She should feel bad, but she didn't.

"We have to take precautions. Yesterday a prince of Sol killed the crown prince of Stella and tried to kill me." Zwaantie's voice cracked. She cleared her throat to hold back the tears. She didn't want her mother knowing how much Ari meant to her. Not to mention that she needed to be strong like a queen. This would be her role soon in Sol, and she couldn't show weakness. Not even to her own mother.

Mother strained against her bonds, her face hard. "That is ridiculous. He did no such thing."

Zwaantie closed her eyes for a moment. This was not going as she had planned. She really thought her mother would see reason. "Mother, I watched him. He was aiming for me."

"Raaf would never do that. He loves you." Mother's face softened a bit. Maybe there was hope. Zwaantie leaned forward.

"Raaf tried to kill me because he was under the influence of the Voice. It is the Voice who wants me dead. He's wanted me dead for quite some time. Phoenix tried to kill me, and so did Luna. A handful of other Solites as well. All of them did so because of the Voice."

Mother's eyes flashed. "You speak blasphemous words."

The anger rose in her chest. This had gone too far. Mother was being unreasonable. Even if Zwaantie had Raaf in front of her with a necklace on, he wouldn't deny the truth. She knew this. "The Voice is not a god. He's just a man who is using magic to control all of Sol. He must be stopped. He's responsible for more than one death. Luna for one."

Mother shook her head vigorously. "This is not true. How can you turn on us and accuse Sol of such horrible things?"

Zwaantie was about to lose it. She took a few deep breaths so she could control her words and tone.

"Not Sol, Mother. Just the Voice."

"They are one and the same."

"They are not." Zwaantie's voice rose a few octaves. "How can you be so unreasonable?"

Zwaantie stood and paced in front of her mother, who appeared completely unrepentant. She truly believed the Voice couldn't be evil.

She would watch her own daughter die and still deny it. She'd pay for this. Zwaantie would see to it. In her eyes, Mother was just as responsible as Raaf, if not more, because she refused to acknowledge the Voice was capable of murder even when she was not under its influence.

Sage touched her elbow, and Zwaantie jumped. She'd forgotten there was anyone else in the room. Slowly she brought her eyes away from Mother and looked into Sage's concerned face.

"Maybe we should go," Sage said.

Mother rattled her chains. "What about me?"

Sage looked down her nose at Mother. "You're going home."

"Oh, thank Sol. When will you release me?"

"What? She can't go home." Rage coursed through Zwaantie's veins. Why did they want to let her go?

"Yes, I need to. Your father is ill. I need to take care of him." She spoke to Zwaantie but looked at Sage.

Sage crossed her arms. "She's done nothing wrong. Plus, she's in danger here. The people of Stella will call for her head since she's queen of Sol, so unless you want to go to war with your own country, we need to send her back."

Zwaantie stormed out of the room. They were going to let her mother go. How could they do that? Someone needed to pay for Ari's death. Someone needed to feel the pain she felt. A knot formed in her throat.

Sage caught up with her and grabbed her arm.

"I know this isn't ideal, but we don't really have any other choice. She'll be guarded to the border, and we'll have spies keep an eye on her once she crosses."

Zwaantie shook off Sage. Her nostrils flared as she took deep breaths. She wanted to blame her mother for Ari's death, but she shouldn't. It wasn't any more her fault than it was Raaf's. But Mother was so sure that the Voice was innocent. Zwaantie couldn't look past that.

A servant rushed down the hall. "The king wishes an audience with High Princess Zwaantie. Alone."

Zwaantie gave Sage a look and then followed him, a bit bewildered. She was curious about what he wanted. She worried he might send her home. But she couldn't go. Not with the Voice and the assassination attempts and everything.

Was Father really ill, or was it a story? Perhaps Mother knew he was the Voice and was trying to protect him. If that was the case, then sending her home would be a horrible idea. Though Sage had a point. Zwaantie didn't want to go to war with her own country. When Stella won, the people of Sol would hate her. There was so much to consider when kingdoms were at hand. She didn't want to think about these things. She just wanted revenge for Ari's death.

The king sat with a blank expression at the big table. Poor man. He'd lost his wife a few weeks before and now his firstborn. He glanced up when Zwaantie entered and waved her over to the chair across from him. She sat cautiously, still unsure what the meeting was about.

His dark eyes held so much sorrow. He was normally jovial—to see him without a smile was disconcerting. He grasped her hand and stared deep into her eyes.

"How are you?" He said it with such sincerity, like a father should. Her affection for this man swelled.

Zwaantie let out a breath, trying to ignore the pain in her chest. "As good as can be expected. I miss him."

A few tears leaked out of the king's eyes. "Me too."

"I would like to stay here in Stella for a while if that is okay." She was afraid he'd send her home. Her life was on the line, and she was terrified. She was fairly certain Lyra, Leo, and Sage would help her stay in Stella, but she'd feel better with the king's support.

The king gave a slow nod, leaned back, and took a sip of his drink. "Yes. That is what I brought you here to discuss. Ari was my favorite son. I'd never tell the others, but he was. I always felt guilty for the curse his mother laid on him and so I encouraged his playboy ways. He changed when you showed up. I've never seen him happier. I suspected you two were involved long before Ari informed me. I knew this would hurt Leo, but I was so happy for Ari, and I rationalized Leo would be okay. But I see the way Leo looks at you. He's absolutely smitten. What would you say to marrying him anyway?" He said the last few words in a rush and raised his sleek eyebrows.

Zwaantie wrung her hands. The thought of marrying Leo never

occurred to her. It made no sense. "Your Majesty, I don't see what purpose that would serve. The vipers have already stopped. I don't love Leo."

He sighed and nodded, scooting closer to her. "You noticed the lack of the vipers, did you? I suspect they're gone because you are with child. A true union of the kingdoms."

Zwaantie gasped. Instinctively, she put her hand to her belly. She was carrying Ari's baby. He lived on even in death. A lump formed in her throat. This poor baby would never know his incredible father. She wouldn't be going home for a very long time, even if the Voice was eliminated. Ari's child would be born in Stella, probably raised here. Ari would never see his baby, but his baby would know him.

"I see. I still don't understand why I need to marry Leo. The kingdoms have been joined." Apparently more than she'd been aware.

The king tapped his chin and studied her. "Perhaps I should tell you a few things about the magic here. It runs deep. It's in the very soil this castle is built upon. Magicians have been imbuing the earth with spells for hundreds, if not thousands of years. We can't just change the spells with the snap of our fingers. Though it would make things easier.

"The succession of kings works as follows. Ari, as my firstborn, was heir to the throne. The next three claimed kingdoms, thereby negating their right to the throne. Which meant that if Ari died, then the natural heir would be Leo. However, marriage holds a great deal of weight in our magic. Ari became king when he married you even if the people didn't know it. Very few people know this. Leo doesn't even know. No one would recognize Ari as king until he was crowned, but I could tell instantly. Since the people knew no differently, I continued to rule, figuring eventually the traditions could be upheld, and then we could go through with the ceremony of transferring the kingship. That's just for show. The land and the magic recognized Ari as king. I wouldn't have been able to rule for long before things would start going wrong."

Comprehension dawned. "Then that would mean the heir to the throne would be Ari's child."

"That is correct. Leo cannot rule. The magic would behave erratically."

"How so?"

"Things would simply cease to work the way they should. People would cast a green spell and get yellow. Lights would darken, carriages would carry you to the wrong place, and discs would malfunction."

"But then who holds the right to rule Stella now? An unborn baby cannot rule."

"In Sol, spouses do not inherit the throne, am I correct?"

"Yes, if my father dies before I ascend, I would become queen, even if my mother were still alive. By the way, as soon as that happens, the people will call me queen. Even without a ceremony. But my father can choose to give me the kingdom anytime he wants."

Ajax nodded; his lips pursed. "Things are different in Stella. If Ari were still alive and I died, my wife would be queen until Ari married or she died."

Zwaantie stopped breathing. This couldn't be possible. She couldn't do this. "That would mean…"

"You are queen." He paused and watched her. She wasn't sure how to react, so she forced a smile, but inside she was horrified. Queen of Stella. She was the Solite princess. The king let out a breath and continued. "Very few know about the secret marriage. The people will revolt if they find out. They are already angry Raaf killed Ari. They will think Sol has taken over, and they won't understand. That scandal alone would leave the Ticker talking for weeks, but since the Solite prince killed him—well, that's the stuff wars are made of. Plus, my own children don't understand that Ari became king when he married."

Zwaantie sat back, taking in what he said. She should be in bed, grieving Ari, not worrying about a possible war. "I'm sorry," she finally said because she didn't know what else to say.

"Don't you see? The only option you have is to marry Leo. Make love to him and let him think the child is his. No one needs to understand any of this but you, me, and handful of others who have been sworn to secrecy. I've already had them bound by death to not tell a soul. I know you don't love him, and I know this causes you pain, but as rulers and royalty we have an obligation to choose honor over love. The honorable thing to do is marry Leo."

Zwaantie nodded. For the past several weeks she'd been chasing her own happiness without any thought of honor. When she lived in Sol, her honor meant nearly everything to her. She'd lost that here.

She didn't want to marry Leo. Loving him would be painful, especially since she was supposed to pretend for the public she was happy and completely in love with him. Not only that, she'd have to convince Leo she loved him in private as well. That would not be easy, but necessary. Otherwise she wouldn't be able to convince him that the baby was his. Her stomach rolled. She wasn't sure if she was strong enough for this. The logical part of her brain told her to, but her heart hurt, so she hesitated and stalled.

"If I agree, how do you know he will marry me?"

Ajax gave a sad smile. "Because he's still in love with you."

Zwaantie let out a breath, thoughts of Ari filling her head. She couldn't marry Leo. But the entire kingdom of Stella depended on her decision. Ari would want her to. It was the only way to protect his kingdom and his child. "Okay."

The king let out a huge sigh. "Thank you." The relief on his face was obvious. Zwaantie wondered what he would have done if she'd refused.

The king pulled out his disc. "Leo, please see me in my rooms." He wasn't wasting any time. Zwaantie needed a few moments to prepare herself.

She met his eyes. "I'm sorry he's dead. I really loved him."

The king put his hand over hers, his eyes kind. "I know. You have no idea how much pain I'm in. I miss both him and Astrid so very much. Part of me wishes it had been me instead of him."

The king launched into a tale of Ari as a young man, and Zwaantie fought tears. Thankfully, Leo poked his head in only a few minutes later. Zwaantie wasn't ready to relive Ari's life. She needed to hang on to her own memories of him.

"Zwaantie, I didn't expect to find you here." Leo's face was stony.

"Your father and I were discussing my options."

Leo sat. "Your options?"

"Yes, whether I should stay in Stella or go home."

Leo creased his eyebrows. "That's up to you." At least he wasn't telling her to go home.

Ajax leaned forward. "We think the best thing for both Stella and Sol is for you to marry Zwaantie."

Leo's face fell, and he sank into his chair. "The vipers have stopped. Why bother?"

Zwaantie clutched at her skirt. He wouldn't even consider the idea. She should've expected his rejection, but it stung all the same.

"They may return. We don't want to risk anything. If you and Zwaantie marry, you will rule over Stella and Sol. Zwaantie and I think this is a good thing for both kingdoms. You will naturally become king regardless."

Leo sighed. "What if I don't want it?"

"It is your duty. You are next in line."

Leo rubbed his face. "And if I refuse?"

"That would not be wise."

"This still doesn't explain why you want me to marry Zwaantie." His face was so serious. Zwaantie wondered what he was thinking.

"We still don't know if the prophecy is completely fulfilled. When Zwaantie's father passes on, you will rule over both Stella and Sol. This is a true union. It will be a position of great power and influence. Your skills are needed."

Leo looked down his nose at Zwaantie.

She wrung her hands. "I'm so sorry, Leo. I didn't mean to hurt you."

"You don't love me." His words were cold, unfeeling. She took a moment to gather her thoughts before speaking. She would be key in convincing him to do the right thing without alerting him to the real issue.

"But I do love these people, and I've come to accept Stella as my home. A marriage between our countries is a good thing. I don't want to risk the vipers returning with a vengeance. Little Raaf's life is still on the line. Plus, I have to contend with the Voice, and it is safer for me here than in Sol. If we do not marry, people will wonder what it is I am doing here. They may even blame me for Ari's death. I promise I will learn to love you. Right now I ache, but that will fade, and I think we could be happy together." Zwaantie attempted a smile.

He looked at her for a long moment, leaned forward, and kissed her lightly on the lips. She closed her eyes, and when she opened them, she expected to see Ari sitting in front of her. The kiss wasn't as passionate as Ari's, but he'd given her quick kisses before. When she saw Leo, it was all she could do to not cry.

"Okay. I think we can pull this off. We will need to be affectionate in public so the Ticker does not get suspicious," Leo said.

The king stood up. "I'll call the marriage mage. There is no reason to do anything big at this point, and we should move forward quickly. The people will understand because of Ari's death. Let's get you two married so we can get on with our lives."

Leo raised his eyebrows but didn't argue. Zwaantie wanted to. She wanted days, weeks, months, years to mourn first.

That was a luxury a queen did not have.

Chapter Five

THE FINAL WEDDING

Zwaantie watched Sage dress her for the wedding. A black dress this time in true Stellan fashion. The same one she wore to Astrid's funeral. The same one she'd wear to Ari's tomorrow. She wondered if the Stellans would think she was mourning or dressing normal. Sage sniffed and wiped her eyes.

After Zwaantie dressed, Sage wrapped her arms around her and held her tight. Her touch was comforting but still did not drive away the real pain.

"You are a better person than me. I wouldn't do it. Thank you for being brave." Sage's voice broke.

Zwaantie didn't feel brave. She felt numb. But she was doing the right thing and didn't really care about the rest. She was more important as a monarch than she was as a person, which had been a fear of hers since she was young. She never imagined it would come about by so much death.

A knock sounded on the door, and Sage opened it. Phoenix gave Zwaantie a small smile as he came into the room. It seemed so long ago that they'd been in love.

"The king sent me to get you. How are you doing?"

"Not well," Zwaantie said.

He dropped his eyes. "I know. Me neither. Here, I have something for you."

In his hand was a blue ribbon. It was somewhat worn, but shiny. There was something familiar about the ribbon, but Zwaantie couldn't identify what it was. "I don't understand."

"It was Luna's. She wore it at her own wedding. You gave it to her, and I found it in her things. She'd want you to have it."

Tears pricked Zwaantie's eyes. In her grief over Ari, she'd nearly forgotten Luna. "Thank you." A gift like this was rare and special.

Sage took the ribbon and tied it onto the end of Zwaantie's braid. Phoenix held out his arm, and Zwaantie took it, grateful he was there. Sage took his other side, and he gave her a wide grin.

The walk to the king's chambers was long, and dread built in Zwaantie's stomach. The irony of Phoenix escorting her was not lost on Zwaantie. Part of her felt like this was so frivolous. They should be planning how to destroy the Voice, not having a wedding.

She'd have none of her own family present at her wedding. Her mother was still locked up. She'd be going home the next day even if Zwaantie didn't want her to. Who knew where Raaf was. Zwaantie hoped he was still safe. And her father. Was he really responsible for all the death? Zwaantie tightened her grip on Phoenix's arm. If he was, he would pay. Zwaantie would see to it. If he wasn't, they needed to find the real culprit and fast.

Phoenix pushed open the door, revealing a handful of people, including the king and Lyra. Leo narrowed his eyes at Phoenix, and Zwaantie took her place next to him. She wasn't about to explain Phoenix's presence, especially since it wasn't like she went and sought Phoenix out. Besides, he was her friend and would probably always be.

During the ceremony, Leo barely looked at her. When Xandria sliced open Zwaantie's hand, she welcomed the pain, watching the blood drip into the chalice. The tears that escaped could be explained by the pain in her hands.

A well-placed photographer stood by. No one expected Zwaantie and Leo to be extremely happy, which was good. Ari's death would cause the entire country to mourn for weeks.

Xandria brought the chalice to Zwaantie, and she tried to compose herself.

"Leo gives you a foundation of love. To that he adds honor, peace, joy, sacrifice, friendship, and safety. Do you accept this gift he has given you and take it upon yourself?"

"I do," Zwaantie said and took a sip. Leo's gifts were different. Love was good. Passion was better.

Xandria held the other chalice out for Leo. "Zwaantie gives you a foundation of sacrifice. To that she adds friendship, affection, honor, selflessness, nurturing and peace. Do you accept this gift she has given you and take it upon yourself?"

Leo hesitated just long enough that only Zwaantie noticed. Finally, he said yes. He took a sip, and she worried about his hesitation. Was it because he didn't love her or because he felt like he was betraying Ari? Or perhaps he was unhappy with the gifts she gave. There was no way she could give love. She wasn't even sure the blood had been right about affection.

They clasped hands. The marriage mage then took the bowl and began to slowly pour the contents over their hands. The liquid was gold this time. Zwaantie had expected the color to be the same as when she married Ari. Silver, but it was not.

"Do you promise to love each other unconditionally?" Xandria asked.

"Yes." they both responded, and the liquid turned a deep red. It flowed into their hands and disappeared. The remaining potion continued to flow into their hands.

"Do you promise to respect and honor one another till the end of your days?"

"Yes." The liquid turned a royal blue.

"Do you promise to stay together throughout eternity and dwell together among the stars?"

Leo said yes. Zwaantie did not. She mouthed the word so it appeared as if she did, but she would join Ari in the stars. Not Leo. She wondered how long she would have to wait. Not long if the Voice had its way.

The liquid turned bright white.

"Kiss your wife," the marriage mage said.

Leo pressed a soft kiss onto her lips. She held the kiss for the pictures. When she pulled away, she saw the agony in Leo's eyes. He took her hand and grinned. She did the same, trying to look like a happily married woman. She wasn't sure if she'd succeeded.

Inside she was still a grieving widow.

Zwaantie left Leo with his father and found Xandria alone, cleaning up the potions. She wanted to understand how this worked.

"How do you feel?" Xandria asked, placing a hand on her shoulder, concern in her eyes.

"Not good, but I suppose that's to be expected." She hesitated. "Why was the liquid gold instead of silver?"

Xandria gave a small smile. "You noticed, didn't you? It's because you're queen."

"What?"

"The magic recognizes you as queen."

"Why wasn't anyone else surprised?" This was not good. Their carefully crafted lie was already unraveling. There were so few who were supposed to know about her marriage to Ari.

"Because the original color of the potion is different for everyone. Most people don't think much of it. I understand the significance of the colors, but that's because I'm a good potion mage. There are only a few of us this powerful in the entire kingdom. Only kings and queens get gold. Princes and princesses get silver."

"What about the other colors?" Zwaantie was now curious about the whole process.

"They usually signify the type of relationship people have. Red is passionate. Green means they don't love each other. Blue signifies a deep friendship. There are others and different shades mean different things." Xandria looked across the room, and Zwaantie knew the conversation was over.

"Thank you," Zwaantie said.

Xandria snapped her eyes back to Zwaantie. "When will the coronation be?"

"I'm not sure."

"Soon, I hope. My potions haven't been behaving properly. I was worried about today, but it seemed to go fine."

"You mean because the old king is still ruling." Xandria knew more than most. Zwaantie hoped Ajax was aware.

"Yes. Most people won't notice, but those of us who work complex magic do. Few understand it has to do with the monarch. The sooner Leo and you are crowned the better."

Chapter Six

THE FIGHT

L
eo led Zwaantie to his room and kept close to her, wanting to keep her safe. Viggo and photographers followed. Both Leo and Zwaantie gave big grins when they shut the door in the photographers' faces. As soon as the door closed, Zwaantie's smile disappeared. His did as well. This was not how he'd envisioned his life. Trapped in a loveless marriage. He didn't really have much of a choice though. His father had not so subtly implied that if he didn't marry Zwaantie, the kingdom would fall apart.

Zwaantie leaned against the door and closed her eyes. Molly greeted her by nosing her hand. To his surprise, instead of pushing Molly away, Zwaantie laid her hand on the dog's head.

Part of him ached to comfort her, but a bigger part was still angry. He loved her, but he couldn't bring himself to like her. Plus, he still felt pain over Ari's death. How was it fair that Leo was with Zwaantie when Ari was dead? It wasn't. Ari should be here with her, leaving Leo to be pissed in peace. But now he had to reconcile his anger and sadness at once. It was something he didn't know how to do, and he vacillated between soul-sucking grief and white-hot anger.

Sometimes he still couldn't quite believe Ari was dead. Leo expected him to walk through the door or call him up and insist Leo go out with him.

Zwaantie sniffed, and he met her eyes but didn't say anything. He couldn't imagine what she was going through. Here she was married to him days after she married Ari. He knew why he agreed to it. What he couldn't figure out was why she did.

"Do you want a glass of wine?" he asked, saying anything to fill the silence but not bring up Ari.

"Sure."

She followed him to his living area and sank into a chair, her face still a mask. He poured her a glass and sat on the couch across from her. She swirled the liquid and frowned.

"Do you know the details on how my mother will be sent home?" she asked.

He'd heard her mother was going home but hadn't bothered to ask many questions. Quite frankly, he didn't care.

"I don't. My mother is in charge. She will be heavily guarded as long as she remains in Stella. Once she crosses the border, there is nothing we can do." Zwaantie's mother was in danger, but she should be safe in Sol. Though if someone put an arrow in her neck on that side of the wall, he wouldn't cry. There was a lot of corruption in the leadership in Sol, and it needed to be purged. With the exception of Zwaantie.

"Why send her home?" Zwaantie wouldn't look up, so he had no idea if she was concerned or just making conversation.

"In the hopes to avoid an all-out war."

"But Father isn't even aware something is going on. Why can't we keep her here until the Voice is eliminated?"

"Your father is ill. He's probably not the one managing the day-to-day affairs of the kingdom. Eventually someone will get suspicious, and if it appears that we are keeping her against her will, we could lose our food. No one wants to risk that." He might not have asked many questions about Zwaantie's mother, but he knew enough about running the kingdom to understand the necessary pains that must be endured to keep the peace with Sol so they wouldn't risk their food supplies.

Zwaantie nodded but didn't look up.

"You must be tired," Leo said, eager to end the conversation.

"I am."

"I think Sage had some of your clothes moved into my closet. I'm sure she put some nightdresses in there."

Zwaantie reached out and squeezed his hand and then disappeared into the closet. He appreciated that little bit of affection but was puzzled as to why. She hadn't been particularly affectionate even before Ari had been in the picture.

Leo figured she'd basically leave him alone as long as they weren't in front of the discs. He changed into his night shorts and crawled under the covers. He wasn't sure what tonight was going to bring, but he wasn't about to kick her out of his bed.

He'd have to let her know he had no intention of doing anything with her for a very long time. Maybe not ever. Though the idea she'd want to do anything with him anytime soon was laughable. She probably wouldn't even look his way until at least a year had passed. Maybe even longer. As long as their marriage kept the kingdom intact, that's all he cared about.

She stepped out of the closet wearing a black, very short nightgown that was sheer in all the wrong places. Or right, depending on who you asked. What was she thinking?

He busted up laughing. He couldn't help himself. It was the last thing he expected and certainly a joke on her part. He didn't think she had it in her. Sure, she was going to flaunt her entire self in front of him and not let him touch her. It seemed unnecessarily cruel. But maybe she felt the need to remind him he was not her first choice.

Hurt flashed across her face as she crossed the room and shut down his laughter. Everything about this was absurd. Why was she doing this? It didn't make sense.

She sat on the edge of the bed, closer to him than she should. "You find my appearance amusing?"

"On the contrary. But I do find it amusing you'd tease me like this."

She crawled across the covers to him, her face serious. "I'm not teasing."

He stopped her before she climbed into his lap. "Don't do this. I have no expectations. I know you're in love with Ari, and you will mourn him for a very long time. Go put on something decent. Please."

She jerked back. "Decent? Since when did you turn into the Voice of Sol?"

He creased his eyebrows. She was behaving so bizarrely. "Zwaantie, what are you doing?"

She dropped her gaze to her hands. "I just thought, you know, it'd be a good distraction."

Distraction? "Sorry, I thought sex was about love. If you want a distraction, go find Phoenix. You seemed pretty cozy with him before the wedding."

She rolled her eyes. "Phoenix brought me a gift from Luna. There is nothing between us. But ever since I arrived in Stella, I've learned sex has nothing to do with love."

"It does to me. I'm not doing this." She seemed so blasé about everything. This was not the Zwaantie he knew.

"Why not? You married me."

"I don't know what your relationship with Ari was like, but I don't do sex for the sake of sex."

She slapped him across the face. He brought his hand up to the sting.

"You know nothing about my relationship with Ari." Tears fell as she ran back to the closet.

He didn't have a clue what had gotten into her. He followed her, still frustrated, but knowing she was hurt. He had to get to the bottom of this so it didn't happen again.

She stood in the middle of the closet, her face in her hands, her back to him, her shoulders shaking. If he were a real man, he'd wrap her in a hug and hold her, but at the moment, he wasn't feeling very charitable. She'd hurt him. Deeper than he'd admit to anyone.

He loved her with every fiber of his being. Her love for Ari hadn't changed that. He was better at suppressing his feelings for her though, so no one would ever know.

He watched her for a moment, then reached above her head and pulled out a sheet and blanket. She didn't turn around.

He draped the sheet across the couch, pulled a couple of pillows off the bed, and settled in. She'd be happier alone than with him, in spite of her advances. She didn't want him. Not really. She wanted to close her eyes and pretend Ari was still here, and that thought made his stomach sour.

He pressed his hand against his chest. The pain of losing Ari was so hard. He wanted his brother here. He wanted to be angry and fuming because Zwaantie slept with Ari instead of him.

Anger was a thousand times better than grief.

Chapter Seven

THE FUNERAL

Zwaantie woke in the morning with crusty eyes. She rubbed at them, sat up, and wrinkled her nose. While Leo had slept on the couch, Molly had not. Dog smell. Yuck. Feet in the air, she snored softly.

Zwaantie wasn't sure what was worse, the prospect of sleeping with Leo or his dog. She sat up taller to see if he was still on the couch. He was gone. Thank Sol. She let out a breath of relief and flopped back.

Last night had been a disaster. She had to sleep with him, but he was having none of it. Maybe she'd been too forward, but really, what was she supposed to do? He'd never believe she loved him. She was quite mortified he'd laughed at her. He did that a lot. Maybe marrying him had been a mistake. She'd successfully buried some of the pain of Ari's death, and Leo threw it in her face.

Her heart sank. Today was the funeral. After this, Ari would be nothing but a memory. She wasn't even allowed to sit in a place of honor as his wife. She'd have to sit next to Leo and pretend she wasn't completely broken up.

Zwaantie found the black wedding dress she'd worn the day before and put it on after her shower. Everything felt so empty. She missed having company around. Especially Sage. Perhaps this was her life now. Married and alone.

A soft knock sounded on the door.

"Come in," Zwaantie called.

Sage poked her head in. Her eyes were red as well. She shuffled in and embraced Zwaantie. How many more nights would they cry themselves to sleep?

"Since when do you knock?" Zwaantie asked.

"Since you're married, and I don't want to walk in on anything." Normally a phrase like that would elicit a grin from Sage's face, but there was nothing but sadness.

"Nothing to walk in on."

"It will come with time." Sage patted her arm but stared off into space. Sage had so much to think about, and here she was worrying about Zwaantie.

She couldn't tell Sage about the baby even though she wanted to. The king made her swear she wouldn't tell a soul, including Leo. Especially Leo. She hated shouldering the secret and responsibility alone.

Zwaantie lost it, and Sage held her tight.

Sage let out a breath. "We're sending your mother home during the funeral."

"Why?" Zwaantie didn't really care one way or another.

"Because most of the country will be distracted, and she'll be safer that way."

"I don't care about her safety." Zwaantie was being cruel, but if Mother and Raaf had kept on those necklaces, Ari would still be alive. It didn't make sense to blame her mother, but she had to blame someone.

Sage frowned. "Her safety is important. We rely on Sol for our food, and we need to maintain a good relationship. People are angry with Sol because Raaf killed Ari. They don't understand how precarious our position is."

"Do people blame me?" Zwaantie's heart tightened. As if she needed one more thing to worry about.

"No. There is a Ticker video of the death, and everyone sees how you cared for Ari. People see you as practically Stellan now. It's a good thing. I know this is hard, but before we go to the funeral, I need you to talk to your mother."

"What? Why?" Zwaantie clenched her jaw. She didn't want to have anything to do with her wretched mother.

"You need to pretend that everything is okay. We need her to go home and not cut us off. We rely on that food."

One more thing she had to do because of her position. Pretty soon she wouldn't be allowed to have any of her own opinions. She hadn't realized how much Stellans relied on Sol. She'd always worried about what Stella could do to Sol, but really, Sol could starve Stella if it chose to do so.

Zwaantie closed her eyes and took a deep breath. "Okay. Let's get this over with."

They met Mother just outside the castle doors, surrounded by several guards.

Zwaantie stood a few feet away from her. "I'm sorry you were locked up. You understand we had to take every precaution."

Mother stood tall, her face hard. "This was unnecessary."

Zwaantie sighed and tried to keep her voice light. "Raaf killed Ari. It was necessary."

"This is a mistake. Raaf wouldn't do this." Mother clasped her hands in front of her.

Sage stepped up. "Yes, he did. Excuse my forwardness, Your Majesty, but Raaf killed my brother. Probably at the behest of the Voice. Zwaantie is in danger as is all of Stella. You must go home and arrest him. Let us come and interrogate him. Perhaps we can discover who the Voice is."

Zwaantie was grateful for Sage stepping in. Zwaantie wouldn't have been as nice.

Mother sputtered and took two steps back. "Don't be absurd. You can't come into Stella and interrogate anyone, especially not my son. Stay on your own side of the wall."

Sage clenched her fists, but Zwaantie spoke. "Mother, we're sending you home with a disc. They work in Sol. When you find Raaf, please, call me, and I will talk to him and find out why he tried to kill me."

Mother's lips formed a tight line. "He wasn't trying to kill you. You saw it wrong. It was someone else. It had to be."

Zwaantie was losing her patience. "Just because you didn't see it doesn't mean it didn't happen. There were witnesses. The Ticker has pictures." Zwaantie rubbed her forehead. "Just go home."

Mother turned on her heel and climbed into her carriage. Zwaantie pinched her nose. "Did someone pack a disc for my mother? At some point she's going to believe me, and then she'll want to call me."

Sage pulled out her own disc, typed a few words, and slid it into her pocket. "One of the guards will make sure she has what she needs. How are you feeling?"

"Like the love of my life just died." She didn't want to talk about her mom. Today was Ari's day. His last one. Everything should be about him.

Sage gripped her hand. "I know. Everything feels empty without him, doesn't it?"

Before Zwaantie could respond, Leo appeared at the doorway. "It's time to go."

Zwaantie refused to meet his eyes. She tucked her hand into the crook of his elbow, and Sage hung onto her other side. She was grateful she had Sage because Leo would be no comfort at all.

~

THE AIR WAS HEAVY AND SMELLED OF THE SEA. DISCS FLASHED everywhere. Zwaantie tried to keep her head down, not wanting her face in any pictures. This time she sat in the front row, with the royal family, which was her right as Leo's wife. She glanced up and saw the king sitting next to Ari. King Ajax stared at the body. Zwaantie should be up there with him. Ari was her husband.

The Ticker wouldn't know what to make of her being next to Ari. This was so unfair.

Leo grasped her hand and leaned down. "I'm so sorry for your pain. I may not be happy about this, but I wouldn't wish this on anyone."

She let out a breath and met his eyes. "Thank you."

Hurt crawled across his face. She'd been so caught up in her own grief that she forgot about his. Ari was his brother and close friend. Ari had left hearts crushed all over Stella.

The king stood and began speaking, but Zwaantie didn't hear a word. She stared at the lifeless face of her beautiful husband. He looked so peaceful in death. She half-expected him to sit up, give her a grin, and say, "Just kidding. I'm not dead." She wished for it desperately, but of course it didn't come true. He was truly gone.

Tears flowed freely as they lit the logs beneath Ari's body. The flames exploded to life, and Zwaantie had to cover her face from the heat. Leo pulled her close to him. The stench of burning flesh hit her next, and she covered her nose with a scarf. She remembered this from Astrid's funeral, but she wasn't prepared for it. A few moments later, and it was done. The flames disappeared, and all that was left was ash.

The king scooped a small handful and trudged to the ocean. Ari's siblings followed. Zwaantie and the other spouses went next. As she scooped a small amount into her hands, she liked to think she'd gotten his heart.

She stood next to the king and scattered the ash into the sea. Ajax put his arm around her shoulder and pulled her into him. He dropped a kiss on the top of her head. His affection was comforting. She was grateful to have a parent who actually cared about her, even if it was just an in-law.

"He loved you more than anything. He died a happy man."

Zwaantie sniffed. "Thank you. I loved him too. He took my heart with him."

"I know, mine too."

Zwaantie watched as the rest of Ari's close friends and distant family scattered his ashes. She and the king stayed long after everyone else left, staring out into the sea.

Ari was truly gone.

Chapter Eight

THE SECRET

Zwaantie cried herself to sleep, but the tears weren't as bad as the night before. Leo still slept on the couch, and Molly snored next to Zwaantie.

She slipped out before Leo woke up because didn't want to face him and reality. Figuring out how to sleep with him and convince him that Ari's baby was his plagued her. Part of her wondered if she should just tell him, but she didn't want to betray Ajax's trust.

She went to Sage because Sage always gave her good advice. She pushed the door open.

"Sage," she called, the meows of a dozen cats greeting her. Maybe she was still sleeping. Zwaantie picked up Andromeda, who sniffed her shoulder accusingly. She could probably smell Molly.

The bed was still made up. Sage spent the night elsewhere. Zwaantie frowned. Sage often partied pretty hard, but she usually slept at home.

Zwaantie sank onto the couch, and three cats jumped up next to her. She couldn't blame Sage for wanting to forget about the day's events, but she was curious where she had been. Zwaantie played with the kittens until the door creaked open, and Sage slipped in barefoot, wearing only a long shirt, her hair a mess.

She jumped at the sight of Zwaantie. "What are you doing here?"

"I wanted to get away from Leo."

Sage leaned against the wall and scratched her head. "Is he getting handsy already? I can talk to him."

"No. He's not Ari. I don't love him, and I'm tired of pretending. I don't have to pretend with you." She felt comfortable in Sage's room. The emptiness in her heart was a little less here.

Sage picked up one of the kittens. "Let's watch movies and forget about everything."

Zwaantie shook her head. Movies would be a band-aid. "No. I need more than that. Astrid said that Xandria gave her a potion to help her cope. Do you think she could do the same for me?"

Sage didn't answer for a second, her face blank. "Are you sure? Astrid was never the same after that potion. Some would say she was more relaxed and fun, but it fundamentally changed her. Is that what you want? Because I like Zwaantie just the way she is."

Zwaantie let out a breath. "Maybe not something permanent, but something to help me deal with things now. Ari's dead, which is going to take me a long time to get over. But I can't take long because I need to deal with the affairs of the kingdom. We still don't know where we are on the Voice. Sure, we think it is my father, but we don't have evidence. Not really. Phoenix watching Luna go down the wrong hall once isn't enough. Zwaantie said this in a rush. Everything had been hanging over her head, and the second she tried to think of solutions to the Voice, Ari rushed back into her head. "I can't think about any of this because the pain is too much. Please. Take me to Xandria's."

Sage gave a slow nod. "While you are here, we need to talk about something."

"What?" Zwaantie prepared for the worst. *We need to talk* had become dreaded words to Zwaantie.

"Are you ready for the coronation?"

This wasn't so bad. "It's a ceremony."

"It's where you become queen of Stella."

According to Ajax, she was already queen. The actual act of succession was kept from everyone except the king and queen. Though that meant at some point Leo would find out eventually she was already queen. Zwaantie wondered when Ajax would impart that knowledge. Hopefully not for a few years.

"I know. But Leo will be king. I'll just be his queen."

Sage shook her head, frustration on her features. "No. You'll hold as much power as him. Have you guys talked about Sol yet?"

"What do you mean?"

"Eventually you'll be the king and queen of Sol as well."

Zwaantie rubbed her head. "No. See, I can't think about any of this right now. All I think about is Ari. Please. Take me to Xandria." That much power seemed so unbelievable. King and queen of the whole world. She already had a target on her back. What would power like that bring?

Sage looked like she wanted to say something else but bit her lip. "Okay, we'll go see Xandria. Can I shower first?"

Zwaantie relaxed. She was going to get help. She wanted to change the subject and not think about taking her place as queen until she was able to put Ari out of her mind. "Where were you anyway? Obviously you didn't sleep here."

"Out," Sage said and disappeared into her bathroom before Zwaantie could press her. That wasn't suspicious at all. Maybe this would prove a good distraction for Zwaantie.

A knock sounded on the door. "Come in," Zwaantie called.

Viggo strolled through the door with a handful of assistants. A visit from Viggo was never really a good thing. Usually it meant she did something wrong for the Ticker.

"Where's Sage?" Viggo asked.

Oh, good. Maybe it was Sage who was in trouble. "Shower."

He shooed the cats off the other couch and sat across from her. "I wanted to talk to you anyway. I need help."

Oh, no. Zwaantie creased her eyebrows. "With what?"

"The Ticker. It's a mess with these deaths. We need to bring it back to normal. The coronation is tomorrow, and we need to put Ari's death behind us. You are the key."

One more thing she was responsible for. There were dozens of royalty that could bring the Ticker back to happier things. "Why me?"

"You are the Solite princess who killed the vipers, but all people can talk about is Ari's death. Tomorrow you'll be our queen."

"That means I shouldn't have to do anything." She said the words more brusquely than she intended, but her patience was thin.

Viggo didn't seem fazed. "Except, you're not helping the situation. I know Ari was your friend, but you're grieving too hard. Every picture out there of you is sad. The most prominent one is you and the king standing by the ocean with his arm around you. Which is sweet, but people are speculating you and the king are having an affair."

"What?" Of all the things for people to think, that was the last one Zwaantie wanted. She missed the simple days of Sol where no one gossiped about the love lives of the royalty. How could people possibly think she and Ajax had anything going on? He was a loving father-in-law, and she appreciated him.

Zwaantie closed her eyes and leaned back. Poor Leo. He would be crushed. Not only did he have to deal with her loving Ari, but now he had to contend with people thinking she was spurning him for the king. This was a mess.

"You can see where I might be concerned," Viggo said.

Zwaantie met his eyes. "Of course. I'm concerned as well. Ajax treats me more like a daughter than my own father does. I hate that I have to hide my relationship with him. But I understand. How can I help?"

"You don't have to avoid my father completely. That will be just as suspicious since the rumors are out there. But go out with Sage today and get a knock-out dress from Nash. I'll send him a message telling him what I want. He'll be dressing Leo for the coronation as well. You'll have to match. If there is any way possible for you to make it look like you are comforting Sage and trying to cheer her up, that would be amazing. I know you were close with Ari as well, but the last thing we need is for the people to think you were sleeping with him too. Don't wear black today."

"The funeral was yesterday." Once again, she wished she'd been born a peasant instead of royalty. It was such a curse to always have to be someone you were not.

"I know. But given the circumstances, it will look better if you don't mourn him as we do. People might read more into your mourning than we want. Besides, it will help Stellans move on if they see their queen doing so."

Zwaantie squeezed her eyes shut and pinched her nose. She was taking something from Xandria today, no matter what the cost. This was ridiculous. If she was going to pretend Ari meant nothing to her, then she needed help. Forget the Voice. The Ticker was going to be the death of her. Once she succeeded in destroying the Voice, she was going to see what she could do about the Ticker.

Viggo stood, took Zwaantie's hand in his, and kissed the back of it. "Thank you for saving our kingdom. I'm not sure I fully understand the depth of your sacrifice, but I do know you have had loss. I will be honored to call you my queen."

Zwaantie was lost for words. His declaration meant more than he realized. She was queen of Stella and already her freedom was taken from her. It was nice to be recognized even if Viggo didn't fully understand. She wondered if things would change after the coronation. Would people treat her differently? In Sol they certainly would.

"Thank you," she finally said after blinking back tears.

"You do a good job taking care of Sage. If possible, try to get her to smile today." Viggo gave her a forced smile, and she attempted to return it.

He and his entourage swept out of the room, and Zwaantie trudged into Sage's closet. If they were to appease the public today, then she and Sage would need to match in some way. Sage would be wearing black. What could Zwaantie wear?

Sage's closet was enormous, and there was no reasoning for where any of the clothes were placed. The red dress Zwaantie wore to the lock-in caught her eye. Ari loved red.

That was it. She might not be able to mourn him properly, but she would mourn in her own way. She would wear red for Ari instead of black, and no one would know differently.

She found a long blood-red skirt, which she paired with a sleeveless white shirt. She almost chose a black one, but Viggo's words haunted her. People would think she was still mourning, and she had to pretend Ari meant nothing to her.

She checked herself. The girl in the mirror looked stunning and put together. The girl on the inside was a mess.

If Ari had been alive, his hands would be all over her. She missed those hands. A few tears escaped, and she brushed them away. If she were to fulfill her duty as queen, she needed to put on a fake smile and stay away from Ajax. It was a shame because she liked him, and he was one of the few who knew everything about what happened with Ari. She wanted him to explain more about what being queen meant, but now she'd have to find her information elsewhere.

She shivered at the thought of someone posting a picture of her sneaking away from the king's chambers. She'd seen enough pictures on the Ticker of people doing things without realizing others were watching.

Sage wandered into the closet, wrapped in a towel. She stopped dead when she saw Zwaantie, and a slow smile crept along her face.

"Good thinking, Z. Maybe I should wear red as well."

Zwaantie smoothed her skirt. "No, Sage. Let me have this. If people think I'm wearing red for Ari, then it won't work. This has to be my private declaration. Only you will understand what it means."

Sage pursed her lips and thumbed through her clothes. She pulled out a skirt just like Zwaantie's, but in black. "Leo might know what it means."

Zwaantie let out a breath. "Leo will have to understand. I won't wear red for a full year, but I get at least a month. Maybe longer. I need to mourn him."

Sage was in full black, but they still made a stunning pair. "I know. This isn't fair to you. I wish we could somehow let the public know without it being a scandal."

Zwaantie studied both of them in the mirror. "That will never happen. Viggo stopped by. He wants us to go to Nash today and get dresses made for the coronation tomorrow."

"Did he talk to you about my father?" Sage didn't betray any emotion, just kept fluffing her hair.

"How do you know about him?" Zwaantie asked with a glare. Maybe she needed to start reading the Ticker so she wasn't the last person to know everything. She hated learning gossip about her friends and family though. She didn't need to know all that stuff. Based on the things it said about her, she was certain at least half of what was on the Ticker was probably false.

"I read the Ticker." Sage pulled out her disc and pressed a button. Zwaantie didn't want to see what it said, so she put her hand over it, hiding the hologram. Now that she knew about the rumor, she wanted to make it go away. She certainly didn't want to see the damning headlines.

"Yes, he talked to me. I don't know what else to do but stay away from the king."

Sage put her hand on Zwaantie's arm. "Fawning over Leo would help. I know it's hard, but the public is going to see what it wants. We have to lead them in the right direction."

Zwaantie slipped on a pair of strappy heels. "Can't I have a week at least?"

Sage pursed her lips. "Yeah, let's go see Xandria. She'll have something that will help. You need it." Sage grabbed Zwaantie's hand and dragged her out of the room.

~

ZWAANTIE AND SAGE WERE GREETED WITH HUGS FROM XANDRIA. THEN she locked the shop before returning to the other side of her counter.

"I can guess why you are here," she said soberly. She wore black as well. It wasn't fair that Xandria was allowed to mourn Ari, but Zwaantie was not.

"If you have something that will take away the pain, I would be very grateful," Zwaantie said.

Xandria frowned. "I don't do things like this very often, and I usually regret them when I do."

"My situation is unique." Zwaantie wrung her hands, silently begging Xandria to understand.

Xandria's lips twitched. "I do understand, but everyone's situation is unique. I saw the Ticker. People can be so petty sometimes. The truth would almost be better. I figured you'd be coming to see me, so I made something, but I can't give it to you now."

"What? Why?"

Xandria's eyes flicked to Sage, then back to Zwaantie. "Do you have secrets?"

"No, of course not. Sage knows everything."

"I don't give potions to expectant mothers."

"What?" Sage yelled, throwing her hands up. "You're pregnant?"

Zwaantie dropped her head on the counter. She couldn't believe she'd forgotten about the baby. Too many other things had been going on.

"Yes. I'm sorry I didn't tell you. The king made me swear not to tell anyone."

Sage gasped and brought her hand to her mouth. "Oh my stars. That's when the vipers stopped. It's why it took three days. You didn't get pregnant until that day."

"Yeah. I'm supposed to sleep with Leo to convince him the baby is his. I don't think I can pull it off." A blush crept across her face.

Xandria smirked. "Now that I can help with."

"Oh, please, no. I should be able to do this on my own."

"He's still angry about Ari, I'm sure. It may take longer than you think. Let me go find something that will increase his, uh, need. Hang on."

Xandria slipped into the back room.

"This is so embarrassing." Zwaantie sat back up.

Sage had her arms crossed and wouldn't look at Zwaantie.

"Oh, come on, Sage, don't be mad at me."

"You have baby Ari in there, and you should've told me. That's kind of important."

"I know. I wanted to tell you, but I couldn't. No one knows."

"Yeah, people with the gift can tell."

"Like Xandria?"

"Yeah."

"But most people will think it's Leo's baby."

"You should've told me." Sage pouted and dropped her eyes.

"I know. I wanted to, believe me. Forgive me."

Xandria returned carrying three bottles.

"I don't want something that will force him to sleep with me."

"You know I don't do that. None of these will force him to do anything." She held up the first bottle. "This one will make him less inhibited. Make sure you only give him these when you two are alone, or you might see your husband going home with someone else." She raised another one. "This one increases his desire." Then she held up the last one. "This one will make it go fast. That's for your benefit. I know this won't be a happy experience. Pour all three of these into his wine before bed, and voila, pregnant," she said with a wink.

Zwaantie put the potions in her bag. She wasn't convinced she'd use them, but she couldn't wait too much longer, or he'd know it wasn't his.

Xandria gripped Zwaantie's hands. "I'm not going to give you anything. You're a strong, strong woman. Draw on that strength to deal with all of this. I have faith in you. After all, you saved all of our lives, even if most of the people can't see that."

They chatted with Xandria for a while, and then Sage looped her arm through Zwaantie's. "It's time to see Nash."

Zwaantie was nervous that Sage would still be angry with her, but she didn't seem to be. Nash met them in the lobby of his building. He embraced Zwaantie first, then Sage.

"First Astrid, then Ari. We're losing all the good ones. You ladies need to be careful." He shook his head and ascended the stairs, with Zwaantie and Sage following.

He took them into a different room this time. This one had two daises. Sage stood on one, and Zwaantie took the other one.

"Clothes, off," Nash snapped, and circled them as they undressed. "You can't be matching for this one. Zwaantie will be crowned queen, and, Sage, you will still be a princess. Perhaps we can do a similar style, but make Zwaantie's long and Sage's short."

"That sounds good," Zwaantie said. "Sage's will obviously need to be black. I would like red."

"Always messing with my colors, aren't you, dear. I was going to do a royal blue or purple. Those will be more fitting for a coronation."

"No. I want red."

Nash sighed and snapped his fingers, and a bright red sheath appeared on her body. He massaged the fabric until the red was a little deeper and he put a black sheath on Sage.

He stood back, and Zwaantie watched the changes in the mirror. She wasn't sure she'd ever get used to this kind of magic. It was fascinating to watch. The top of her dress turned into a tight corset decorated with ruby's and diamonds. Sage's was exactly the same except he used black sapphires. Then he went to work on the skirt. Ruffles exploded all the way to the floor. Sage's stopped at her knees.

Nash made small subtle changes that Zwaantie had trouble detecting. Finally, he stepped back. "Well, ladies, what do you think?"

"It's gorgeous, Nash. You've outdone yourself," Sage said.

"Try not to die in this dress. Please. People might think my dresses are cursed."

Zwaantie gave him a small smile. "I'll try. Promise."

He snapped his fingers, and the dresses disappeared. "I'll have these sent up to the castle."

They dressed, and Nash gave them both kisses on the cheeks. "I'll see you at the coronation. I expect a good seat."

"I'll let Viggo know. He'll put you as close to the front as he can. Right behind the royal family," Sage said.

"Atta girl. Thank you."

Just before they left the room, the memory of the last time they were there struck Zwaantie. Ari and Astrid had come and taken her to lunch. Now they were both dead, and she was still here, getting dresses made. Her dress last time was supposed to signify a new beginning for both Stella and Sol.

Fate had a twisted sense of humor. This new beginning wasn't what she imagined.

Chapter Nine

THE LAST RESORT

Raaf devoured the baked chicken and rolls Wilma brought him. It seemed so silly, really, that he had to eat, but it was difficult to concentrate when the hunger pains hit.

Wilma stared at him, disgust in her eyes. He wiped his mouth. "Is there a problem?"

She sniffed. "Zwaantie's still alive. You couldn't even finish the job yourself."

He let out a breath. "She's also still a princess, so we have time."

"How much? Your dad is worse than they are telling the public. His illness could kill him."

Raaf gripped the edge of his table. "Will the Voice disappear when Zwaantie becomes queen? The prophecy wasn't exactly clear."

Wilma shrugged. "I only say the words that are given to me. I have no way to interpret anything."

Raaf rolled his eyes. "Then get out. You're no help."

Wilma crossed her arms and then spun on her heel and stomped out of the room.

Raaf pulled out the same book he used to allow the Voice to cross the wall with the slaves. He'd stolen it when he was angry with his trainers.

He'd spent four years in a tower in the middle of the woods being taught everything there was to know about the Voice but never actually seeing its source. No, he wasn't allowed to witness the orbs until after he'd been crowned grand chancellor.

The same day Wilma had visited him for the first time and told him Zwaantie had to die.

He'd been horrified. Zwaantie had been his best friend. But the whole purpose of his training in the woods was to teach him the importance of the Voice. They drilled the message into his head every day. Protect the Voice at all costs.

In the beginning, the training wasn't too bad. Mostly just boring old men teaching and testing him. But then two years in, the grand chancellor showed up.

He was a wizened old man with a long white beard. His eyes were friendly, and Raaf thought he'd be more exciting than the other old men.

The grand chancellor came in and dropped a hand on Raaf's shoulder while he was reading. "They say your training is going well."

Raaf met those eyes and smiled. "I'm learning a lot."

"Yes. You've learned everything you can from books."

Raaf sat up straight. "Does this mean I can come back with you and train?"

The old man chuckled. "No. But I will oversee some of your training here." He held out a small ball. "Go hide this somewhere where you think no one can find it and come back."

Without question, Raaf ran up several flights of stairs and found a loose stone. He pried it out and hid the ball behind it. He replaced the stone and returned quickly to the grand chancellor.

"Are you going to find it?" Raaf asked with an excitement he'd never experience again.

"No, you will tell me where to find it."

"But then why did I hide it?" This was stupid. He asked Raaf to hide it. Why would he now demand to know where?

"The Voice has many enemies. Your job is to protect it."

Raaf rolled his eyes. It's all he'd learned in the two years he'd been there. "Yes. I know."

The old man stuck a fire poker into the fire and left it there. He spun on Raaf. "Pretend the ball is the Voice. No matter what happens, do not tell me where it is."

Raaf nodded.

"Also take off your shirt."

"Why?"

"Do not ask questions." His eyes had gone hard.

Raaf pulled off his shirt, unsure of why, but he'd been taught to listen and not question.

The old man pulled the poker out of the fire, its tip glowing red. Raaf scooted back as the man shoved the poker in Raaf's face. "Tell me, where is the ball?"

Raaf gulped. "I'm not telling you."

"Are you sure?"

The poker hovered only an inch from his nose. The heat nearly burned him. What if the grand chancellor slipped and took off his nose? Raaf's heart raced. "Yes, I'm sure. I won't tell you."

The old man dropped the poker to Raaf's shoulder. Pain flared through his muscles, and Raaf cried out, dropping to the ground. The old man shoved the poker back in his face.

"Tell me. Where is the ball?" the chancellor asked in a deathly quiet voice.

Raaf squeezed his eyes shut and shook his head. The poker came down on his other shoulder, and he collapsed from the pain.

The poker appeared in his face again.

"Tell me."

"Behind the loose stone, three flights up."

The old man threw the fire poker across the room. "You fail. Go hide it somewhere else."

Raaf stumbled up the stairs, tears pricking his eyes.

And so went the next year. He was burned, punched, kicked, cut, given poisons that made him vomit, nearly drowned, and other things he didn't like to think about. He was always given a respite for however long he held out. So if he went a whole day without telling them where the ball was, he was given a day's rest. The chancellors didn't stop until he held out for a whole month. That was the worst month of his life, but he earned his right to control the Voice.

He had to protect it.

Even if people he loved died.

Chapter Ten

THE CORONATION

Leo slept on the couch once again. Zwaantie was positive if this kept up, she'd never get him to sleep with her. Perhaps she'd need to use the potions after all, though she dreaded having to resort to that.

Leo stopped her before she left for Sage's rooms. "We need to talk about today."

"Sure."

"Have you heard about the Ticker?"

"You mean the rumors I'm sleeping with the king?" She dropped her eyes. She couldn't look at him. Guilt over Ari and Phoenix settled in her stomach. She might not be sleeping with the king, but she'd done enough to hurt Leo.

"Yes." His lips formed a tight line. This couldn't be good for him. "Would it be too much to ask you to help me put those rumors to rest today? I'm about to be crowned king, and I can't have the people thinking my wife is sleeping with my father."

Zwaantie shuddered. "That is not what I want. You know that."

"I know. It doesn't make this any easier. It would be helpful if we were happy and affectionate with one another today."

"I'm not the one trying to stop this marriage from moving forward." It was a low blow, but maybe it'd get him thinking.

"It's been only a few days. Really, Zwaantie, is it that easy for you to forget Ari?"

She felt as if he'd slapped her. "You have no idea what I'm going through, so stop acting like this is easy for me. I'm getting ready with Sage. I promise I will make sure the Ticker thinks we are madly in love."

Leo's face fell. "I'm sorry. It's just… This is hard for me as well. I know you loved Ari, but so did I. Every time I look at you, I'm reminded that you were his wife."

Zwaantie didn't trust herself to speak. She didn't want to think of his pain. Hers was enough to deal with.

"I'll come get you from Sage's room, and we'll go to the coronation together."

Zwaantie nodded and swept from the room. They would never be happy if both of them always brought up Ari. Their marriage was doomed from the beginning.

~

LEO TOOK A DEEP BREATH AS HE KNOCKED ON SAGE'S DOOR THAT evening. He wasn't handling Zwaantie very well. Part of it was his grief.

Every time he looked at her the image of the two of them under the oak tree haunted him. He wasn't sure he could ever go into those gardens again.

He felt like a fool. When she'd come to see him in The Black City, he'd really thought she meant the things she'd said. But she lied to him. He let the guard around his heart down—the one put up after Phoenix—and she'd crushed it again. He didn't trust her, not by a long shot.

But now Zwaantie was his life, his wife, and his soon-to-be queen. Someday, he'd have to get over her infidelity. Not today, though.

Sage opened the door, and he gave her a quick kiss on the cheek. "You look lovely this evening."

"Thanks," Sage said, playing with one of the ruffles on her dress. "Nash really outdid himself. Wait until you see Zwaantie."

She probably looked stunning, not that he wanted to care.

She stepped out of the closet, and his breath caught in his throat. A ruby necklace lay on her creamy skin, drawing attention to her breasts that nearly spilled out of her red dress.

Red. Ari's favorite color.

This was no accident. He swallowed, anger building in his chest. "You're not wearing black." He clenched his fists. How could she do this to him? It was bad enough he had to be reminded she loved Ari. Now she was going to make sure he never forgot it either.

She placed a hand on her stomach. "Viggo told me I wasn't allowed to."

Viggo was smart. Was it possible he knew about her relationship with Ari? Even if he did, he'd never let anyone know. Viggo's whole purpose in life was to protect the royal family from scandal, and he was damn good at what he did.

The red bothered Leo, but he shouldn't let it. Ari was her husband, and they weren't allowing her time to mourn. As long as she wore it though, she reminded him she belonged to Ari, and today he needed to pretend she was his.

"What can we expect from the ceremony?" Zwaantie asked.

"I don't know. I'm told it's much like the wedding ceremony."

Zwaantie scowled. "More blood?"

He chuckled. "Probably."

She met his eyes, and he forgot for a second that she wasn't really his. There was anxiety there and sadness, but beauty in the stunning blue color. He took her hands in his, pulled her close, and kept eye contact. "I'm so sorry for the way things have gone. If I could go back and put myself in Ari's spot, I would."

She squeezed his hands. "I know. Me too."

A flash ruined the moment. He glared at Sage. "What was that?"

"Feeding the Ticker. Look."

The picture hovered on the top of her disc. If Leo didn't know better, he'd think Sage had captured a truly tender moment between lovers. It was sweet and intimate. He didn't want this floating all over the Ticker. That was a moment for him and Zwaantie alone.

Zwaantie gave Sage a wide smile. "That's incredible, Sage. Throw it up there. If we're lucky, by the end of the evening, no one will ever remember they thought I was sleeping with the king."

Just like that, Zwaantie ruined it.

He held out his arm. "Shall we?"

She tucked her hand into the crook of his elbow. He took a deep breath just before they stepped out of the room. He had to pretend they were happy. That she was the love of his life.

Which she was. But he wasn't hers, and it made this unbearable.

The great hall was crowded. Commoners and royalty alike mingled. He and Zwaantie entered from the front and only greeted a handful of people before taking their places on the stage.

The thrones were empty. They would take them after the ceremony was complete and talk to people of Stella until dinner, where they would entertain the entire royal family. Invitations were extended to anyone with royal blood, which was over two thousand.

His brothers and sisters stood in the front. He met Sage's eyes and was surprised to see Phoenix standing by her side.

The crowd quieted when Xandria took the stage. She was dressed in a midnight blue dress with diamonds that sparkled like the stars. She didn't say a word but waved her hands in the air. A clear bubble formed in front of her.

"Prince Leo, please join me on my right. Princess Zwaantie, my left."

He did as she instructed. Not a sound was heard in the hall. Only those older than his father would have witnessed this before. The crowd was made mostly of Leo's peers.

Xandria grabbed his right hand and drew out a strand of blood, which she dropped into the bubble. Then she did the same for Zwaantie.

She placed both of her hands on the bubble, and the blood inside swirled around, coating the ball in red. The color changed to purple, then blue, silver, and finally a deep gold.

Xandria pulled her hands apart, and the bubble split in two, leaving a ball in each hand.

"Kneel before your people," Xandria commanded.

Leo reached for Zwaantie's hand, and they both dropped to their knees. Xandria moved around behind them.

"Good people of Stella, your king and queen give you a foundation of honor. Do you accept this gift?"

The people shouted out a resounding yes. Leo felt a weight on his head, but he didn't dare look up.

"To honor, they add loyalty, safety, love, joy, peace, and prosperity. Do you accept this gift?"

Again the crowd shouted yes.

"King Leo, Queen Zwaantie, arise."

They stood and found Xandria in front of them facing the crowd.

"Stella, meet your new king and queen."

The entire crowd dropped into a bow. Leo looked over at Zwaantie. An intricate gold crown perched on her head. He guessed he had one on his as well.

He was now king. A position he never wanted. Next to him stood his queen who deserved so much more. A real king. His brother. This was not supposed to be his place.

He had to force his smile. This was what so many dreamed of, and yet he felt completely undeserving of it. King of Stella was a title he didn't want.

Xandria walked behind him and whispered, "Kiss your queen. Make it a good one."

He tried to imagine what he would do if Ari had never been in the picture. How would he react?

He pulled Zwaantie into a tight hug. Her eyes sparkled as she looked at him. Maybe she was imagining Ari as well, but he tried not to think of that. Leo dipped her down, and she gasped.

"You make a stunning queen," he said and pressed his lips on hers. She returned the kiss, and for a moment he forgot he was pretending. He was kissing his bride, his queen.

He brought her up and was shocked into reality with the flashing discs. This was for show only. Not real.

~

DINNER WAS PLEASANT. LEO AND ZWAANTIE RARELY LET GO OF ONE another, though they talked with many people. Every once in a while, he'd drop a chaste kiss on her lips, and she smiled. He knew the smile wasn't real, but it pleased him all the same.

By the time they headed back to their rooms, he was almost happy.

He pushed the door open, and he expected her to go icy on him, but she made no move to let go of him once the discs were gone.

She pressed herself into him.

"That was fun tonight, wasn't it?" Leo asked.

"It was," she said, removing her crown. "We should put these away."

"We should. One kingdom down, one to go."

"I wonder how long we have."

"Not long if your mother is to be believed."

"I'm not convinced she was being honest."

He took his crown off. It looked very similar to Zwaantie's, but a little larger.

She slipped off her shoes and rubbed her feet. "I wasn't expecting the crowns to be made of our blood."

"Me either..." He was about to say more, but his words were lost. The way she bent over, he could see down her dress, far more of her than he'd planned on seeing quite yet. He averted his eyes and swallowed.

"I'll keep these in the armoire."

"Okay. I'm going to get out of this dress."

He put the crowns on pillows on a shelf and took deep breaths. The wall around his heart was falling, and he couldn't afford to let it. She'd crushed him twice. He wouldn't be able to handle a third.

He changed out of his own clothes and put on a pair of pajama bottoms. He would love to sleep in his own bed tonight. He didn't have to touch her. Plus, she'd seemed upset he hadn't slept with her so far. If Molly slept in between them, then there wouldn't be any issues. He didn't want to sleep on the couch again.

"Leo, can you help me?" Zwaantie called from the closet. A strange sense of déjà vu crept over him. He leaned against the closet door. She was still fully dressed. "It's been a long time since I couldn't get out of a dress on my own. Can you get the buttons in the back?"

She turned around and brushed her hair to the side. He stared at the top button. He dropped his head and whispered into her ear, "Do you remember the first time I undressed you?"

She didn't answer for a moment. His fingers continued to work away the buttons, every once in a while brushing her skin.

"I do. That feels so long ago." Her voice was breathy.

His fingers lingered for a moment near the bottom of her spine. He wanted to slide his hands inside her dress and pull her against him.

"Tell me something," he said, running his finger softly along her back. "Did you feel anything for me then?"

She spun around, clutching her corset to her chest. "I would've never admitted it, not even to myself, but I did. You were handsome, exotic, and forbidden. I felt guilty for liking the attention you gave me."

She grabbed his hand with her free one and pulled herself close to him.

He brushed a piece of hair out of her eye, "Zwaantie, I..."

Her disc buzzed on a shelf in the closet, and she jumped back. "Oh goodness, it's my mother. Could you answer this while I change quickly?"

He took the disc and exited the closet, both relieved and frustrated. He didn't particularly want to talk to her mother

He answered, and the queen's face floated above the disc.

"What do you want?" Leo asked, irritated she'd interrupted their moment.

Tears streamed down her face.

"Where's Zwaantie?" she asked. Maybe she realized Zwaantie was right.

"Changing."

She brought a tissue to her nose. "Please. I need to talk to her."

"If you'll wait just a minute, she'll be right out." He didn't want to ask what was wrong or pretend like he actually cared.

Zwaantie took the disc from his hands. "Mother, what's wrong?" Her voice was low and tight. She must still be angry. Good.

"It's your father. He's dead."

Zwaantie paled. "Dead?"

"Yes. Zwaantie, you're queen now. It's time to come home."

"It's not that simple. I'm queen of Stella as well."

The implication hit Leo in the gut. He was king of both Stella and Sol, of the entire world. Nothing was out of their jurisdiction. This was unprecedented. Nowhere in their histories was the entirety of Stella and Sol under one ruler.

They knew this day was coming, but they'd assumed they would have time before it happened. Plus, they had been preoccupied with Ari's murder and the Voice trying to kill Zwaantie.

Zwaantie met his eyes, and he knew she'd realized the same thing. What would they do now?

Chapter Eleven

THE REALITY

A fter Zwaantie hung up with her mother, she sat stunned for a full minute before she said a word. She'd known this was a possibility but wasn't prepared for it. She'd really thought everyone was lying about her father being sick.

She was fairly certain her father was the Voice, but he was still her father. Maybe she could wear black without drawing suspicion now.

If her father was the Voice, did that mean it was gone? She wouldn't know until she was able to talk to someone from Sol. Maybe they could take off Phoenix's necklace and test it. Not in her presence of course. She could also take hers off, but she didn't want to risk hearing that Voice for even a second.

Leo gave a chuckle, bringing her out of her thoughts. "That put a damper on things, didn't it?"

She snorted. Here she was worried about the future of their kingdoms, and he was busy thinking about sex. She rubbed her forehead. "What? You thought something was really going to happen? It was all for the Ticker."

She crossed her arms. She wasn't going to admit to him he'd stirred up real feelings. She had planned on using those feelings to get him in bed. Tonight had been her best shot. They were a little tipsy and happy. She'd hoped she'd be able to get away with not using those potions.

But now her father was dead, and the full implications hadn't yet manifested. She had no idea what those would be. Getting Leo in bed now would be impossible.

Leo frowned. "I forgot. You only love men you aren't supposed to. I don't stand a chance."

She didn't want to fight with him tonight. She needed to prepare for what tomorrow would bring. Everything would be different. She'd be useless if they stayed up all night fighting.

She grabbed her bag and searched for a sleeping potion. Xandria told her those were safe. She couldn't find it, and so she dumped the bag on the couch next to her. The three bottles from the potions shop rolled next to Leo.

Oh, stars. Not now.

He picked all of them up and read the labels. "What are these?"

She shrugged, moving things around, still searching for Sleep, hoping he'd drop it.

"Were you going to use these on me?"

She shrugged again.

"Why?"

She met his eyes and saw both pain and anger there. It mirrored her own. "You won't sleep with me."

"Are you really that desperate?"

She could feel the hysteria building up. Ari's death, having to hide her true feelings, becoming queen, her father's death, the Voice, the baby, everything.

"Desperate," she said in a soft voice. "No. I'm not that desperate. I don't really want to sleep with you. Every time I look at you, I'm reminded you're not the man I love, the man that I want to call my husband, the man whose child I carry."

The words were out of her mouth before she even realized she said them.

He drew back. "You're pregnant?"

Tears streamed down her face, the weight of everything catching up with her. "Yes."

"With Ari's child?"

"Who else?"

He looked down his nose at her. "I don't know who else you've been screwing in the castle. It could be any number of men."

Her hands trembled. "Every time you open your mouth you say something cruel. Why did I marry you?"

He rolled his eyes and shook his head at her, his irritation evident. "The same reason I married you, because we had no choice. What am I supposed to do now?"

"What do you mean?"

"I'm not raising your and Ari's love child and pretending it's my own."

"This child is the heir to the throne, so you will. I tried to do this in such a way you'd never know, but you refused to even give me a chance."

"Because every word out of your mouth is a lie." He stormed toward her. "Listen to me. We will play nice in front of the discs. We will smile, and we will pretend we are deeply in love, but when we are alone, we will not touch, will not kiss, I will *never* sleep with you. Once some time has passed, we will each have our own quarters and live separate lives. You will raise Ari's child on your own."

He mercifully stopped talking, but he breathed deeply, hatred in his eyes. Zwaantie spun on her heel and raced out of the room.

She almost went to Sage but didn't want to explain herself to anyone. Instead, she headed for the tower. Once on the top, she stared up at the stars. Ari was up there somewhere. She ran a hand along her belly. Did he know about his child?

Leo said hurtful things. Perhaps he meant them, perhaps he didn't. It didn't matter. He'd never trust her, and their marriage would always be what it'd always been. A marriage of convenience and treaty. Their purpose was to join the kingdoms, and that is exactly what they did.

Happiness would be too much to ask for.

Chapter Twelve

THE DAWN

Zwaantie couldn't sleep up on the tower, but she didn't want to go back to bed. Tomorrow would bring all kinds of questions that had no answers and responsibility she wasn't ready for. She was queen of a kingdom she couldn't set foot in.

These thoughts would drive her crazy, and she couldn't solve any of them anyway. So instead, she took out her disc and studied the stars to distract her. Her disc told her what the stars were called and what purpose they served. Every once in a while, it would find a star that it couldn't identify, and Zwaantie would pretend it was Ari or Luna.

As the hours wore on, Zwaantie saw something odd on the horizon. A pink light appeared. At first she thought it was some sort of magic far off in the city, but it grew brighter, turning slightly orange.

Zwaantie stopped studying the stars and watched the light. Soon a yellow crescent appeared and the stars grew dim.

Oh. My. Sol.

She whipped out her disc and called Leo. He didn't answer, and she rolled her eyes. He was obviously still angry. Or asleep. Either way, she needed him.

"Sage," she said into her disc.

"It's early. Go back to bed," Sage said groggily, her hair completely messed up.

Zwaantie couldn't keep the smile off of her face. "No. Go get Leo and come up to the tower. It's urgent."

Sage's eyes flashed open. "Who else died?"

"No one, just get up here. But get Leo first."

"This better be good."

Zwaantie hung up on her before she could say anything else. Zwaantie hadn't thought anything could ever make her happy again, but she felt twinges of happiness now. This was a moment she never thought she'd see in her lifetime.

The yellow circle continued to rise. If Sage and Leo took too much longer, they'd miss it. A few minutes later the trap door clattered open.

Sage squealed and grabbed onto Zwaantie. "Is that the sun?"

Zwaantie didn't look at them. She couldn't take her eyes off the yellow light in front of her. "It is."

Leo stood on her other side, not saying a word.

"What does this mean?" Sage asked.

"Leo and I are king and queen of the whole world. My father died yesterday."

Sage gasped. "That means the kingdoms are truly one."

Leo scratched his head. "How does this play into the prophecy?"

"The prophecy had nothing to do with the sun rising, only the vipers."

"Yeah, but why did they stop early then?"

Zwaantie brought her hand to her stomach. "Because of the heir."

Leo crossed his arms and nodded.

"Now what?" Sage asked.

Leo frowned. "I don't know. I'm not sure any of us will know until this evening. Have the kingdoms reversed? Or will we get both sun and stars?"

"The wall..." Sage said, cocking her head.

"What about it?" Zwaantie asked.

"Do you think it's still there?"

"I don't know. Maybe. We should go check it out."

"Stars," Leo said as sunlight bathed the city below. "This is incredible. I never knew Stella looked like this."

The entire city appeared different in the sunlight. The buildings, which lit up with different colors in the dark, were various shades of brown or gray. Zwaantie was certain that it wouldn't take long for the Stellans to find a way for them to be just as colorful in the daylight. They stayed up on the tower for longer than they should have. Zwaantie reveled at the feeling of the sun on her face. She really thought she'd never see it again.

Sage grabbed both her and Leo's hands. "Let's go. I want to see if the wall is gone."

Zwaantie didn't look at Leo, but she eagerly followed Sage.

Even if the wall was still there, the lives of everyone in Stella and Sol were about to change. Hopefully for the better.

Chapter Thirteen

THE PARTY

Ajax, Phoenix, and Lyra joined them on the boat to The Black City. It would be several hours until they arrived, but all six of them were glued to the Ticker the entire ride. The wall had indeed fallen. Stellans were dancing in the streets. They spent quite a bit of time on the disc with Tauro, lower king of The Black City, discussing the party that would last for the next twenty-four hours or so. No one wanted to miss the sunset or the sun rising the next day.

"We should have you guys officially declared king and queen over both lands," Sage said. "Right where the wall used to be."

Leo nodded. Zwaantie wasn't so sure. "Sol is probably not going to take to this so well. Where the Stellans are excited, Solites are going to be scared when it gets dark."

"Well, then we'll show them it's not scary after dark. This is the best time to lay claim to both lands before someone else decides to complicate things like declare your mother queen or something," Sage said.

"Any word on the Voice?" Leo asked.

"No. But that doesn't mean it's gone. We've no word from Sol at all," Sage said.

~

THE BLACK CITY WAS IN ABSOLUTE CHAOS. NOT A SOUL WAS INDOORS. Some people ran in the streets, laughing. Others stood still, eyes closed, their faces turned up to the sun. People stopped when Leo and Zwaantie passed by and bowed deeply.

"Why are they bowing?" Zwaantie hissed.

"Because we're king and queen."

"They never did before."

"That's because we were still a prince and a princess. Do you see how they treat my father now?"

Zwaantie turned around. People were shaking his hand and kissing his cheek.

"I don't understand. I've rarely been around him when he was in public."

"He's no longer king. He's approachable. We are not."

Zwaantie wasn't sure which she preferred. Leo flagged down a carriage. "Let's go visit Tauro's castle and get ready for tonight."

Four hours later Zwaantie and Leo arrived at a huge open arena that had been put up. A large grassy area sat in the middle of large risers. It could seat thousands. On the far side of the arena were two large thrones.

"It's incredible to think that a few hours ago, this was a wall of mist," Leo said.

"I know. What is all this?" Zwaantie asked, studying the arena.

"A show. Tauro said they've been preparing all day. It will be magical. I hope we get several Solites. This will be a new experience for them."

People were already starting to arrive and fill the seats. They bowed low to Leo and Zwaantie. A small building had been erected next to the arena with a handful of guards.

"We should wait in here until it is time." Leo said

"What's with the guards?" Zwaantie asked.

"We still aren't sure how safe you are."

The inside of the building was spacious with a handful of white couches. Zwaantie sat down, still worried about her own safety. It was hard to think of serious things when everyone was so incredibly happy.

Sage and Phoenix burst in. Zwaantie jumped and placed a hand on her chest. "You guys know how to make an entrance, don't you?"

Sage grinned and flopped down on the couch. She pulled a bag of grapes out of her bag and popped one in her mouth.

"Mm. Real food."

"Were you in Sol?"

"Yeah. Phoenix and I went to see if we could rustle up a few Solites for tonight's party, but everything was locked up tight. There was no one out. Not even guards."

"That's not good."

Leo sat next to Zwaantie. "Maybe you should call your mother."

Zwaantie made a face because she still blamed her a little for Ari's death and didn't really want anything to do with her.

"I know, but she's the only one who can explain," Leo said.

Zwaantie pulled out her disc and said, "Mother."

Mother's face appeared almost instantly. Her face was full of fear. "Are you safe?"

Zwaantie creased her eyebrows. "Of course I am. Why are all the Solites locked up?"

"Because the wall fell. We aren't safe."

"Safe from what?"

"Stella!"

"I'm the queen of Stella. You have nothing to fear." Her mother was exasperating, and Zwaantie really had no patience for her fear. She should, but she didn't like her mother at the moment.

"What happens when it gets dark?"

"Nothing. It just gets dark. Why is everyone locked up? Surely someone is curious."

"The Voice. It says we can't go anywhere."

Zwaantie exhaled. "Of course. Okay, Mother, we'll talk later."

"Are you coming home? Sol needs you now more than ever."

"I'm claiming the throne tonight. You are welcome to come. We've built an arena where the crossing was."

Mother hesitated for a moment. "No. I can't."

"Okay." Zwaantie hung up before she could say anything else, and she really didn't want to argue with her mother anymore. The offer for Mother to come was a polite gesture. Zwaantie didn't really want her here.

The four of them stared at each other for a long minute before anyone spoke.

Sage finally broke the silence. "So. The Voice wasn't your dad."

"Maybe it was, and it's simply operating on its own." Zwaantie wasn't quite sure what to think anymore.

"That doesn't explain the new order to stay inside."

Leo put his hand over hers. "Maybe we should not join the party tonight."

"What? No," Sage yelled.

"Sage is right. I'm queen. I cannot hide."

"But the Voice wants you dead, and we know it's still alive."

"I'll be fine. We still have guards. If there are no Solites, then there should be no threat, right?"

Leo let out a breath. "I suppose."

A knock sounded on the door, and everyone jumped.

Leo cracked it open cautiously. Then his face split into a grin, and he opened it wider.

Nash and Xandria strolled in. Nash immediately found Zwaantie and dropped into a low bow. He grasped her hand and kissed her knuckle. "You brought the sun, my queen."

Zwaantie gave him a smile. "I can't..." Zwaantie started, but Leo kicked her foot.

"We will be forever indebted to the queen for her gift," Leo said.

Zwaantie looked at him quizzically but didn't respond. Nash stood up and gave Leo a short bow. "My king."

"What brings you here?" Zwaantie asked.

He spun and faced her. "Your dress of course."

⁓

Two hours later, Zwaantie clutched Leo's arm, ready to enter the chaos. Nash dressed her in a bright yellow dress with a short swishy skirt. Leo wore a bright blue suit. Xandria placed their crowns on their heads and smiled at both of them.

"Night and day. How can I be of assistance this evening?"

"Perhaps you could simply introduce us," Leo said.

"Very well, after you."

There weren't many people outside the arena. Those that were snapped pictures on their discs.

Leo and Zwaantie entered at the back of the arena. Zwaantie took a deep breath, and as they stepped into the light, the stadium erupted into cheers. Flowers rained down on them.

Zwaantie waved to the crowd, and more cheers followed.

"You are their hero. Let's keep it that way," Leo said, squeezing her hand.

"Because they think I brought the sun?"

"Yes. They don't realize your father died. They simply think that once you were crowned queen, the wall fell."

"I guess that makes sense."

They climbed up a few stairs to their thrones and waved to the crowd for several moments. Xandria stood in front of them, and the crowd silenced.

"Ladies and gentleman," she said, her voice far louder than Zwaantie thought was possible. "I present to you the king and queen of Stella and Sol."

The crowd roared once more, and tears pricked at Zwaantie's eyes. A few months ago, she would've never imagined such a phrase would've been possible. Now, here she was. Queen of the whole world that had both a sun and stars.

Chapter Fourteen

THE INVASION

The party lasted long into the night. The next morning Sage and Zwaantie left for the City of Stars early. Ajax wanted to explore the border with Leo, so they decided to take a later boat back.

Leo and Ajax took a carriage along where the edge of the wall used to be.

"I never thought I'd see this in my lifetime," Ajax said.

"Sol or sun in Stella?" Leo asked.

Ajax gave a small smile. "Both."

"So much change. I didn't expect to be king," Leo said.

"I know." Ajax rubbed his face. "I wasn't quite ready to give up the throne. I planned to reign for several more years. I'm not quite sure what to do with my time now."

"I'm sure Zwaantie and I can find something for you to do if you want."

"I would appreciate that."

Leo had his father alone for the first time in a long time. He hesitated, wanting to ask something, but he was scared of what he might learn.

"Did you…did you know about Zwaantie and Ari?"

"You mean the affair or the wedding?"

"Both."

"I suspected, but I didn't know the extent of it until they got married."

"And you approved of this?" Leo felt foolish for being the only one out of the loop.

"No. I only knew because the magic of the kingship transferred the moment he got married. You'll feel it as well when your firstborn marries."

"You mean Ari's child." He clenched his fists. He was trying to forget about that.

"Yes. I didn't realize she told you."

Leo furrowed his brow. "So you were in on it as well."

"I counseled her to let you think the child was yours. I thought it would make things easier."

He couldn't believe his father was in on part of the plan. Treachery from both him and Zwaantie. "Yes, it would've if I'd slept with her, but I haven't yet. Probably never will. Once things settle, she and I will live apart. She'll probably live in Sol, and I'll stay in the City of Stars."

Ajax leaned forward, his face serious. "Son, you've always had a clear head and made good decisions, but this is absurd. Both you and Zwaantie deserve happiness, which you will only find within yourselves."

"She's carrying my brother's child."

"Who will never know his father. Don't blame the child. You will be a good father."

"I'm supposed to forget everything that happened?" Leo asked.

"Yes, you are. Ari is dead. If nothing else, he showed us life is fleeting, and we need to forgive, and embrace what is in front of us. Zwaantie deserves a chance to be loved by you."

"She's had two," Leo grumbled, but knew his father was right.

"You'll regret it if you hold onto that anger."

Neither Leo nor Ajax spoke for several moments. Perhaps he could rule with her, but just as friends for now. He wasn't ready to give up his heart. She'd crushed it too many times.

~

LATER THAT EVENING, AFTER EVERYONE ARRIVED BACK IN THE CITY OF Stars, Zwaantie ran into Leo and Ajax in the hallway outside of her room. She and Sage were on their way to talk to Lyra.

"Oh, good, you're back. We need to talk about Sol," Zwaantie said, meeting Leo's eyes. She could finally look at him without wanting to slap him. Perhaps the wall falling would have more effects than she thought.

"Yes, we do," Leo said.

A guard approached them. "Your Majesty," he said with an incline of his head to Leo. He looked Zwaantie in the eye, and something changed in his face. He gripped his sword and whipped it toward her. "The queen must die," he growled.

Sage touched his forehead, and he dropped to the ground.

Leo grabbed Zwaantie's hand. "You need to hide."

Zwaantie didn't fully understand. "What's going on?"

Leo didn't answer as he rushed her into their rooms, Sage and Ajax right behind him. He slammed the door and locked it.

Zwaantie spun on them. "Why did he just try to kill me?"

"I imagine the Voice. He must've figured out how to get into Stella. Stars. Zwaantie, you won't be safe anywhere." Leo picked up his disc. "Lyra."

Within seconds her face bobbed up and down on his disc. "Well done, you two," she said.

"Not exactly, Mother. Are you wearing your necklace?"

She touched the disc on her throat. "Of course. Why wouldn't I?"

"The Voice is now influencing Stellans. We need to get necklaces on everyone. Zwaantie will not be safe until we do. Not to mention that once the Voice realizes he has control over the people of Stella, he could do something drastic and have us all killed."

Lyra cocked her head. "We prepared for this."

"You did?" Zwaantie asked.

Lyra snorted. "We were planning a full-scale invasion of Sol. We needed enough necklaces for our entire army and most of Sol. We'll start distributing the necklaces immediately. Leo, will you help, or will you protect your bride?"

"I'll help. Sage needs to come as well. She's more valuable out there than she is in here. We'll put necklaces on the guards first and post them both inside and outside of the room."

"Very well. I'll see you in a few. Hurry," Lyra said.

There was no way Zwaantie was going to hide here while her friends got to go around handing out necklaces. This was her life on the line.

"This isn't fair," she said to Leo.

"It's the only way. You won't be safe otherwise. We do need your help though."

"How?"

"I'm going to send Sage into Sol with a carriage full of necklaces. Will your mother cooperate?"

Zwaantie shrugged. "Probably not."

It was what she wanted to talk to Leo about. She'd need to stay in Stella as long as the Voice existed, but she would need a regent, someone to rule in her place. If Mother was cooperative, that would make the most sense, but she would not be.

"Then we'll have trouble doing anything in Sol."

"Not if I appoint a regent to act in my stead."

"Who did you have in mind?"

"I have no idea. I asked Sage, but she said no."

Sage snorted. "Not on your life."

Ajax stepped forward. "I could do it."

Zwaantie cocked her head. She hadn't thought of him, but he knew what it took run a country. He'd do a good job.

"Yes. I like it. Let me write a letter."

Leo pulled a box out from under the bed. He propped open the lid. It was full of plain necklaces like the ones the slaves wore.

"Why would you keep those here?" Zwaantie asked.

"After we discovered the Voice followed the slaves, several of us keep boxes of these under our beds in case something like this happened. I always thought it would be because the Voice figured out how to cross the wall, not that the wall would actually fall. Sage will help me get these on the castle guards. Once I feel like you're protected, we'll head outside. I'll stay here in the city. We have an efficient distribution system. The entire city should be pretty well protected by nightfall."

"But that means I can't go outside."

"There is always tomorrow. Your safety comes first. Sage will go with my father. They'll have a harder time in Sol."

He unlocked the door and slipped into the hallway. Sage stayed with Zwaantie.

"Why will you have a harder time in Sol? There are fewer people."

"Here, we can motivate by money. We'll get the necklace on around a hundred people, and they'll each receive at least ten necklaces to put on someone else. The more necklaces they put on a person, the more gold they earn. Trust me, by the time the sun sets, every person in the city will be protected from the Voice. We have no way to incentivize the citizens of Sol."

It was pretty ingenious. "You could do the same thing in Sol. It will take longer because we don't have the magic and discs. But we have enough physical gold that we can hand out. Maybe make it different. Every person who checks in with a necklace on gets gold."

"Okay, we'll do our best. But your mother is going to be a problem," Sage said.

"I know."

"She needs to be careful because more than likely, someone close to her is the Voice. I still can't believe it's not your father. We were so sure."

"We were, but it's not."

"Is it possible it's your mother?" Sage asked.

"Luna said he was the father of her child. I don't think that's possible."

"Unless Luna was mistaken."

"I guess so. I don't think it's my mother though. She'd had plenty of opportunity to kill me, and she didn't."

Leo entered with three guards.

"They will stay with you until I return this evening. There are five more posted outside your door. I know you want to help, but you have to stay here."

"Do you think the Voice figured out what's going on yet?" Zwaantie asked.

"We're not sure. It seems the only command anyone has been

given is to kill you. Perhaps the Voice knows, but it's not taking advantage of anything."

"Well, get those necklaces on people before he figures it out."

Zwaantie wrote a quick letter and sealed it with her seal so her mother couldn't argue. Mother would be furious. She might even call Zwaantie.

Sage and Ajax left with Leo, and Zwaantie collapsed on her couch and opened the Ticker. She didn't look at it often, but she wanted to see what was going on.

The first picture was of Leo kissing her at the coronation. She had to suppress a smile. In spite of everything that was said between them that night, she'd enjoyed the kiss.

She'd enjoyed the entire evening.

Ari still hung heavy in her heart, but she'd seen a glimpse of what her and Leo's life could be like if they were to move past their issues. Though she'd ruined it when she spilled the beans about the baby.

Leo was distracted right now, but he'd remember eventually, and then he'd stop speaking to her. She wished they could move beyond this place where they were trying to love each other. They could live happily like that. Maybe now that she wasn't trying to sleep with him, they could be friends.

Several pictures on the Ticker were of the sun. The Stellans were fascinated. Magic still worked, but the sun shone brightly overhead. Temperatures were rising, which meant it was even more stifling.

People speculated on what this meant for food. They'd be able to grow it now. Others talked about crossing the border. Everyone felt it was safe since Zwaantie was queen of Stella.

The news of Ari's death had been pushed aside. The people of Stella were happy. The vipers were gone, the sun was shining, and life was good.

Zwaantie's heart felt heavy. Life was not good for her.

She turned off the Ticker and found a movie. If she was to be stuck here, then she might as well make the time go by faster. Six movies later, Leo burst into the room, just after midnight.

"As far as we can tell, everyone is protected. You should probably still go out with a guard, but you won't have masses trying to assassinate you." He collapsed next to her. "You're safe."

"That's good." She was a bit dazed from her movie binge.

"Did you watch movies all day?"

"I had nothing better to do."

He chuckled. "You look bushed."

"Thanks a lot. You don't look so hot yourself."

"It was a long day. I'm going to shower, and then we should go to bed. You can go out tomorrow and enjoy the sun."

She changed while he was in the shower, and slid into bed. Molly curled up next to her, and Zwaantie scratched her behind her ears.

She thought she'd doze off, but Leo climbed under the covers, and Zwaantie's eyes flashed open. They hadn't slept in the same bed since they'd been married.

He gave Molly a pat. "Tomorrow, we'll need to talk about the implications of a sun and other things."

"It will change our rule quite a bit."

"Do you plan on ruling from here?"

"I don't see how we could avoid it, unless you were willing to move to Sol. Both kingdoms belong to both of us. It's not only my decision or yours." Zwaantie pulled a pillow out from behind her and set it on her lap.

"Our people will more than likely move around quite a bit in the next few years as they learn about the different ways of life."

"Yes. I expect in fifty or a hundred years, you won't be able to distinguish Stella from Sol." Zwaantie looked at him, hoping for a sign that things might be warming up for the both of them.

He grinned. "That's pretty amazing to think about. Our children will grow up in a very different world than we did."

She was shocked he'd mentioned "our" children. Two nights ago he made it seem as if a future for them would be impossible. She didn't want to bring it to his attention.

"How long do you think the fascination will last?"

Leo put his hands behind his head. "You mean before they decide the novelty is not fun, and they want things to go back to normal? I give it two weeks."

"No way. It will take at least a month, maybe two."

"You overestimate people."

"I like to think the best of them," Zwaantie said.

"I hope you're right. If we have a month or two for things to settle, it will make things much easier when people get restless."

"Whatever happens we can deal with it." Listening to him talk made her optimistic. The past had been difficult, but the future was wide open with possibilities.

Leo flipped around so he was facing her, his head propped up. "I think we'll rule well together. Especially in this situation where we both have experience from the different lands."

He seemed so casual, like the fight they had didn't mean anything. At some point, they were going to have to deal with their relationship.

For now though, the affairs of Stella and Sol would keep them together.

Chapter Fifteen

THE FAILURE

Raaf looked around his workroom. Overnight, it had exploded with five times as many orbs as it had before the sun set. The entire population of Stella was now under his control. Stella had a greater population than Sol. To have that many people under him was a rush. He could come out of this wretched room and walk among his people once again, since everyone would be his.

He sat back and watched his universe. Up in the corner something strange happened. An orb turned black, like Zwaantie's and the slaves who went to Stella.

No.

A few more darkened. Raaf slid off the table and walked into the middle of his orbs, standing before the big one, and looked up. One by one, each and every orb went dark. Raaf couldn't move, couldn't even fathom what was happening.

This was Zwaantie's fault.

Damn her and that king for getting in the way.

It had to be those necklaces. He gave a command to rip off the necklaces if they were spotted. Most of the new orbs were dark, but almost all of Sol still seemed to be under his influence. If Stellans crossed the border, the Solites would remove the necklaces, and gradually he would gain power over the world. He could be patient.

Shoes clattered on the floor, and he spun around.

"You failed," Wilma said. "Now we wait for our death."

"You're so optimistic," Raaf said.

"You had every opportunity. Though I'm not surprised. You can't change the future, no matter how hard you try." She stared up at the balls. "My sisters are dead. I'm all that is left, and my days are numbered."

"Your sisters?" Raaf asked, curious.

"Yes. There were three of us. The past, the present, and the future."

"You were the future."

"Yes. When the wall went up years ago, the past became the wall."

"And the present?"

Wilma cackled. "Oh, that was rich. She was angry at the mages who insisted on creating the wall. She became the monsters of Stella. Do you not know the story of the three sisters?"

Raaf frowned. "I don't really care."

"Sure you do. Sit. This is a story that might help you in the coming days."

Raaf sat, not sure what else he would do at the moment anyway.

"Before the prophecy came, I could feel the changing in the earth. I am the last of my kind, left behind from the old magic that used the earth, not the sky. This magic controls things outside the realm of physical and mental magic as you understand it. The earth magic controls time. The past, present, and the future. We three were on the earth since time began. One who could change the past, one who controlled the present, and one who saw the future."

She cackled. "I do miss them. My sisters of the present and the past died when the sun and star mages decided to change the world. They died protecting it. The sister of the past became the barrier, and the sister of the present became the vipers. She was angry that she died after all the warnings she gave the people, but they didn't listen, and now they must pay. I saw the future and knew it could not be changed. I begged my sisters to reconsider their movements, but in my heart I knew they would not. I could not see so far as their eventual demise, but I did see what they would become. The day the barrier was erected they refused to stop."

"Just because your sisters didn't listen doesn't mean we have to be beholden to your vision. We can still succeed."

"Come now, you're smarter than that. How many times have you tried and failed? It's time to let it go. The time of the Voice is over."

He slammed his fist down on the table. "No. I will not lose. It may take some time, but with the people of Sol still under the influence, Stella will fall. You just wait."

Chapter Sixteen

THE QUEEN

Over the next few days, Zwaantie managed to get out and enjoy the sun. She and Leo even went swimming once. She didn't tell him she'd done it already with Ari. So far nothing had been said about their fight or the baby. Plus the sun was an exciting enough event. The Ticker was full of fun and happiness.

She spent most of her time planted on her couch talking with either Sage or Ajax. Getting the necklaces on Solites was proving more difficult than the Stellans. But they were making slow and steady progress.

Friday afternoon, she and Leo took a private lunch in their rooms. He held up an apple. "Soon we'll be able to grow these on our own. Can you imagine?"

"I know, it's going to be pretty incredible."

"I'm going out to see one of the new farms after lunch. Would you like to go with me?" A farm. Imagine!

"Very much so. We should bring a few Solites over to help establish the farms since they've been doing it for years."

Leo picked up the fork. "That's a great idea. Let's talk to Sage about it when she calls this evening."

"That is, if she doesn't call earlier."

Leo chuckled. "She doesn't understand the people of Sol. She expected them to be just like you."

"She didn't realize I wasn't like the rest of them." It seemed so long ago that Zwaantie snuck away from the castle to go running around the forest with Phoenix.

"She's learning fast."

"Not fast enough. Dad's having trouble as well. Your mother is defying him at every turn. She'd got most of the guards listening to her."

"I don't know what to do about that, short of locking her up."

Leo ran a hand over his face. "Believe me, Dad would like to, but that would cause trouble with the Solites."

Zwaantie's device buzzed, and she spun around. Sage stood there with a scowl. Dirt was smeared over her face. Grass and straw stuck out of her hair. Her pants were ripped. Zwaantie stifled a giggle. "What happened? I just talked to you two hours ago."

Sage stomped her foot. "Horses are the devil."

"You tried to ride a horse?" Zwaantie couldn't help the laughter in her voice. It was the first time she'd laughed since Ari died.

Sage pulled a piece of straw out of her hair. "Not successfully, mind you. I want to come home." She let out a breath.

Leo coughed to cover his own laugh. "How are things going with the necklaces?"

"I think we're close. I didn't see anyone without one today. A few more days and we should be safe." Sage brushed at dirt on her pants.

"Leo and I were talking. When you come home, you need to bring a delegation of farmers to teach the Stellans how to grow food."

Sage nodded. "We should send a tester out here and see who can do magic. They're fascinated by what I can do. I taught a girl how to make light, and now they all want to know."

"I think that's a great idea. We need people from both sides to teach."

"I'll get the delegation together and let you know when I'm coming home."

Sage clicked off, and Leo creased his eyebrows. "She called just to tell you she can't ride a horse."

"You have no idea. She called me when she pulled a carrot out of the ground, milked a cow, and found the stinky pond I used to hang out by. At least your father calls about real issues. Though Sage's calls are more entertaining."

Phoenix had gone with Sage and threatened to throw her in their old pond. Zwaantie's heart pinched just a little bit. She missed home, more than she thought she did.

"I'm going to go home with the Stellan delegation. Just for a little while." Zwaantie wouldn't meet his eye. She knew he wouldn't like the idea.

Leo dropped his fork. "What? No. You need to stay here."

"Why? What good am I here? I can help my people as they adapt. Show them the different kinds of magic and help them adjust to not having the Voice. I'm the best person for them. Plus, I'm their queen. They need to see me."

Leo came around the table and took her hand in his. It was the first time he'd been so affectionate. "Listen. I know Sage managed to get most of the necklaces out, but that doesn't mean it's safe."

"I'm just as safe there as I am here. You could come with me."

"I'm needed here. You know that."

Her voice rose a couple of notches. He was being unreasonable. "Why shouldn't I be needed in my own kingdom?"

"We may have tuned out the Voice, but he still wants you dead, and he's in Sol. Possibly even in the castle."

"Fine. Then we need to destroy him."

"What do you think we're doing?"

"No one seems to even know how to find him, let alone kill him." Zwaantie slumped in her chair. "I'll never be able to go home at this rate. Please, I need to go. I have guards. Stellan guards. They'll protect me."

He closed his eyes for a moment. "They couldn't stop your own brother from trying to kill you. Besides, it's not just you I'm worried about."

Her heart clenched at the thought of Raaf. He was still out there somewhere, hunted by Stellans. No matter how often she said he was innocent, no one believed her.

"Then who are you worried about?"

"Your baby."

"What's that supposed to mean?" She brought her hand to her stomach.

"He's the heir to the throne. The first royal child who will be truly both Stellan and Solite. You can't risk his life."

"You didn't seem to care much about him when I told you." She was surprised he even brought it up.

He let out a breath. "I've had time to think about it. That child was conceived the day I caught you and Ari in the garden. He's the reason the vipers stopped. We can't risk his life."

She snorted. "Nice. So you don't care much about him other than to make sure he doesn't mess things up for Stella."

"You should be pregnant with my child, not his." His words were said through clenched teeth.

"How's that supposed to happen if you won't even touch me?"

"That ship sailed a long time ago. I thought we'd been over this already. Since the wall has fallen, I've realized we work well together, and I expect we can develop a decent friendship as long as you don't keep trying to force something that isn't there. I will raise him as my own. He will never know."

He will never know. The truth slammed into Zwaantie, and she pressed her hands against her stomach. Ari's son would never know who his father really was. She couldn't share stories with him and encourage him to be like his dad. This wasn't fair.

She scowled at Leo. This was his fault. Not only that, he'd just told her they would have marriage without love. She was prepared for a year or so of recovery from Ari, but she hoped eventually she and Leo would have something. But the way he was talking, it was as if they'll never have anything.

"I thought you loved me. Or at least that's what you told me. Multiple times, in fact." Zwaantie held her head high. She wasn't going to let him win this one.

"You think that after you betrayed me, not just once, but twice, that I'm going to take a chance with you again. I'm sorry. It won't be happening. Also, you are not going to Sol. End of discussion."

She stood up tall. "I am going, and you can't stop me. You've made it clear you care for me as an ally and nothing else. You have no claim on me. I will make my own decisions. Now, if you'll excuse me, I have some packing to do."

He gave her one last glare and stormed out of the room.

Zwaantie fiddled with her necklace. It was not lost on her that as long as they were discussing how to run the kingdoms, they got along wonderfully, but the second they brought feelings into it, all hope was lost.

She supposed she was still grieving and would be for some time. He probably was as well. The excitement of the week didn't change the fact that Ari was dead, and she was now stuck in a marriage that would never have love.

That didn't matter, anyway. She was going home.

As a queen.

Chapter Seventeen

THE LIE

Leo woke the next morning to an empty bed. Even Molly was gone. Dammit. He couldn't let Zwaantie go to Sol. She would be in more danger than she knew. While Sage had been giving Zwaantie the happy version of what was going on in Sol, she'd kept Leo up on the reality and the truth.

Sage. There was another thing. She was keeping a pretty big secret herself. A secret that even his father wasn't aware of.

They could've sent anyone to Sol to hand out the necklaces. Sage was in Sol doing what she did best.

She was there to assassinate the Voice.

Leo, as spymaster, and his mother, as the head mage, were the only ones who knew what Sage's real title was. Not even Ari or his father knew. Sage was the country's assassin, and her sole purpose was to protect the kingdom.

It was why Leo had Sage stay with Zwaantie in the beginning. If she had discovered Zwaantie had ulterior motives for being in Stella, she would've poisoned her.

The identity of the assassin was to be unknown, even to the king, in case a sitting king or queen became a threat. Leo supposed his mother would find another assassin. But he also knew too much about the spy network, so he'd figure out who it was anyway.

Sage never had trouble finding her target. In fact part of the reason she was off riding horses and playing with chickens was that she was frustrated.

He didn't tell Zwaantie Sage's true mission because they strongly suspected someone in the castle was the Voice. Probably someone close to Zwaantie. She'd want to talk to them and have a trial. The future of the kingdom depended on the death of the Voice. He or she was the biggest threat to their joined kingdom. Zwaantie would be angry when she discovered they went behind her back, but she would be safe, as would the child she carried.

He wasn't sure how he'd feel about the child, but as he and his father talked at length about how that child was the future of Stella and Sol, and needed to survive and thrive.

Leo would have to pretend. Which he could do for the sake of the child, but he didn't have to pretend to like Zwaantie. Not anymore. He would not give her his heart to have her shatter it.

He scrambled out of bed to find Zwaantie. She was serious about going back to Sol, and he had to stop her. He used his disc first, but she didn't answer. He opened the door and found only two guards.

"Where did the queen go?"

"Back to Sol."

"How long ago did she leave?"

The guard stroked his beard. "Maybe five, six hours ago. She took ten guards with her. I'm surprised you slept through the whole thing."

"What time is it?"

"Near noon."

How had he slept through it all? He sat at the couch and fiddled with his wine goblet from the night before. A tiny bottle on the floor caught his eye, and he picked it up.

Deep Sleep.

She'd drugged him. Lovely. What next?

He'd never catch up with her now. He could have the guards stop her at the border, but there was no clear border anymore. At some point, they would have to address the lack of a border. If she survived.

He could go over himself and bring her back, but Sage warned him his neck was on the line as well. Their union threatened the Voice.

Leo doubted the Voice knew about the child, or he'd be doubling his efforts to kill Zwaantie. Though he'd been fairly persistent.

She was walking into a mess. Between necklaces being ripped off, to her mother refusing to recognize his father as regent. Not to mention that Leo was still terrified her brother was going to come out of whatever hole he was hiding in and finish the job he started.

Zwaantie had no idea how much danger she was in.

Chapter Eighteen

THE MEDDLER

Zwaantie stepped carefully out of the carriage following her guards. She inhaled deeply and smiled. She was home. The air smelled of grass and cows.

Ajax waited on the steps, and people filled the stairs and the courtyard. They'd come to see their new queen.

She'd been careful when she'd chosen her outfit that morning, making sure it had elements of Stella but wasn't too shocking for the residents of Sol. Her dress was dark blue with purple flowers, long but sleeveless.

As soon as her feet hit the dirt, the people around her dropped into a low bow. A few peeked at her. She crouched down in front of a child of about ten who had a streak of pink in her hair.

"Hello, what is your name?"

The little girl slowly met Zwaantie's eyes. "I'm Katarina, Your Majesty."

Zwaantie fingered the streak in her hair. "Where did you get this?"

"Sage, Your Majesty. She gives them to anyone who asks."

Zwaantie chuckled and stood, making her way to Ajax. He smiled wide and embraced her.

"I'm glad you are here. We've been busy."

"I see that." Zwaantie arrived before the delegation of mages, but evidence of magic was everywhere, though it wasn't as clean as Stella. On her way she'd seen a dog race across the street, his behind a bright green. A few colored lights hung awkwardly in the streets. The door behind the king opened and closed on its own at a fairly regular interval.

"How many Solites can do magic?" Zwaantie asked.

"Enough," Ajax said with a sigh. "I hope the testing mages are on their way."

"They should be here in a few days. Where is Sage?"

"Who knows? I hardly ever see the girl. Did she know you were coming?"

"No. I snuck away this morning. Leo didn't want me coming."

"Why?"

"He said it was unsafe for me here. But really, it's unsafe for me everywhere. It was time for me to come home for a bit." She was happy to be breathing Solite air again. She was home.

Ajax frowned. "He called and told me you were on your way, but he didn't tell me he disapproved."

"That was nice of him." She waved to the door. "Should we go in?" She wanted to get away from all the eyes.

"Yes."

Ajax stepped back and let her go first. She chewed on her lip. She'd have to call Leo when she got a free moment. She should feel guilty for drugging him, but she didn't know how else she would get out of there. He wouldn't listen to her.

He had a lot to learn.

Before stepping into the castle, Zwaantie inhaled the fresh air. It didn't have the sweet smell of the air in Stella, but it smelled natural and clean.

She crossed the threshold, and slaves bowed as she passed. A knot she hadn't realized she had relaxed in her chest. She was home. As much as she had come to love Stella, this was where she belonged. She would be Queen of Sol and Leo King of Stella, and they would reign together but live apart.

Slaves followed with her trunks and brought them to her room.

"When is Sage bringing a group of farmers to Stella?" Zwaantie asked Ajax.

"Next week, I think. Sage doesn't seem in any hurry to go home."

"She did when she called me. I'm going to freshen up. Shall I meet you in the king's office?"

Ajax gave a small smile. "Of course. Will you be taking the queen's office?"

"I'm not sure how long I'll be here, but maybe."

"Just so you know, your mother is still using it."

Zwaantie rolled her eyes. "I'll deal with her. Thank you for acting as regent."

"My pleasure, Your Majesty." He gave a small bow and retreated. She thought his behavior was oddly formal, but then she noticed all the slaves around them watching. Ajax was a smart man.

She pushed the door open to her room, leaving her guards behind. So much had happened since she'd left. She'd change things in this room, for sure. She'd have a shower installed and lights. Maybe she'd even adopt a kitten or two.

A slave followed her in and dropped into a deep bow. "Can I get you anything, Your Majesty?"

Zwaantie studied the slave. She was young and wore a necklace that signified she wasn't under the influence of the Voice.

"Join me in my room for a few minutes. I have some questions."

The slave would not look up. "Of course, Your Majesty."

"Sit, please. Tell me, how have things been since the stars appeared."

The girl sat on the edge of her seat and wouldn't meet Zwaantie's eyes. "For me. Not much different. I can't hear the Voice anymore, but no one freed the slaves."

No one should be a slave. She was surprised Ajax still allowed this to go on. Freeing them would be her first order of business, but she needed to know other things as well.

"How are people being kept in line?" This was the one thing Zwaantie worried about most. She didn't want Sol descending into chaos.

"The guards. They are quite cruel. I wouldn't dare cross them."

Zwaantie frowned. That wasn't a good answer. She had hoped things were better in her country than this. Perhaps change took longer than she thought.

"Ajax approves of this?"

The girl shrugged. "I'm not sure. As far as I know, the guards only answer to your mother."

"My mother has no authority." Anger swelled. She and her mother would have words, and from now on, those guards would answer only to Zwaantie or Ajax.

"She thinks she does."

Zwaantie let out a breath. This was not good. "How is Ajax doing as regent?"

"He's most gracious. The people love him." The girl fiddled with her dress.

Zwaantie was glad they'd sent him to Sol.

"How do you feel about the magic?"

Her lips twitched. "It is fun. I have some. But I don't see how it's good for much."

"What can you do? Show me."

A blush crept up the girl's cheeks. "No, I couldn't. Not in front of you."

"Don't be silly. I want to see."

The girl screwed up her face, and her hair turned bright blue.

"Stars," Zwaantie said. "I'd say you're destined to become a beauty mage."

"Oh, no. I'm a slave. I'll stay in the castle."

"The wall falling opens new doors for you. You can do whatever you want."

"Not as long as I have the bands."

Zwaantie hated those bands. That will end now. Slaves were a thing of the past. The Solites would struggle for a bit, but perhaps the magic would help soften the blow.

"This is true. I'll talk to Sage about removing yours right away. Thank you for your information, you've been most helpful."

Zwaantie rubbed her forehead. Sol was as she expected, but she didn't know the next steps in truly freeing her people. She needed Leo's help. Perhaps she should've waited and convinced him to return with her. He was much better at this diplomatic stuff than she.

He was probably angry, but he'd talk to her. She turned her disc on. Thirty messages blinked at her. She ignored them and called him.

He answered right away. "What in the dark were you thinking?"

"I told you I wanted to go home."

"It's not safe for you there. Don't you get that?"

She rolled her eyes. "It's not more dangerous here than it was in Stella."

"Yes, it is." He sighed. "But I understand. You wanted to see your home again. Sage should be returning with the farmers in a few days. You can ride back with her."

"No. My people need me. They have not yet moved into the realm of Stella. Until then, we both have kingdoms to think about. I'm staying here."

He pinched his nose. "What happened to trying to work out our marriage?"

"You made it clear you weren't interested in that."

"Please, just come back. Did you consider what the Ticker might say now that you are living with my father and not me?"

She drew back, not prepared for that argument. "I didn't. I'm sorry." Her voice was soft. He'd taken the wind out of her sails.

"It is a concern, but not the one I'm really worried about. You're not safe."

"I'm fine, but I need some help."

He sighed with exasperation. "With what?"

"I need to free the slaves. Can Sage do that?"

"Yes, of course. But that's a huge job for just her."

"When you send the mages, can you make sure they have the ability to as well? That way, it will go quickly, and we won't be dependent on Sage."

He nodded. "Yes. I'll do that because it's best for the people, but then you'll come back, right?"

"Leo," Zwaantie warned. "Give me one good reason why it's safer for me in Stella than Sol."

"We know the Voice is in Sol. Probably in the castle. You're feet from him, and we don't know who he is. You could die."

Zwaantie didn't want to argue with Leo anymore. "Just send the mages, and we'll work this out when they are done. Thanks, Leo. We'll talk later."

He sighed and waved. He'd lost. Zwaantie stood up and smoothed her dress. It was time for a visit with her mother. This would not be a fun conversation, but once it was over, she could council with Ajax and Sage.

She glided down the hall. People stopped in their tracks and bowed. She hadn't missed this at all. Around a dozen guards mingled outside of Mother's door. They were both Stellan and Solite. They stopped talking and stood at attention when she approached.

"All guards from Sol are dismissed. You will no longer guard my mother."

Four of the guards marched away. Zwaantie waited until they were out of earshot.

"The Solite guards are not to be trusted. I do not want to see them anywhere near my mother. Do you understand?"

"Yes," the guards shouted. The guard on the far right stepped forward. "Excuse me, Your Majesty, but all of the guards inside her chambers are Solite."

"How many?" she asked.

"Four."

Zwaantie thought for a moment. She spun around to the ten Stellan guards who followed her everywhere she went. She knew she was in danger, but she'd made sure she was well protected.

"When we enter my mother's chambers, you will all come with me. I will instruct the Solite guards to leave. If they refuse, you may remove them by force. Saros, Cosmos, and Jupiter. You will remain with my mother as her personal guards. There must always be at least two of you with her at all times. Each night, one of you will report to me what she's up to."

They nodded. Zwaantie exhaled, took three steps forward, and pushed open her mother's door.

Mother sat on her couch fanning her face. Her guards stood next to the doors. Zwaantie faced them before she said anything to her mother.

"You are all dismissed. Go find the head guard and ask for a new assignment on order of your *queen*."

The guards looked to her mother. Mother stood and stalked over to Zwaantie. "Those are my guards. What do you think you're doing?"

Zwaantie refused to acknowledge her. "I'm waiting. If you do not leave right now, I will have you hung for treason." She really hoped they would leave because she didn't know if she was ready to act on that order, but she wanted them to know she was in charge and not her mother.

They hesitated for another second, and then they marched out of the room. Zwaantie plastered a smile on her face and turned to greet her mother.

"Hello, Mother. How are you?"

"You took my guards." Mother's voice was tight and angry. Good. This was exactly what Zwaantie wanted.

Zwaantie kept her voice deliberately sugary. "I know. Meet your new guards, Saros, Cosmos, and Jupiter. They are more than capable of keeping you safe."

Mother clenched her fists. "You and I both know the guards are not there for my safety."

Zwaantie widened her smile. "Well, then you'll understand why I insisted on Stellan guards. Shall we sit and discuss things?"

Zwaantie wasn't sure how much longer she could keep up her fake sweetness. The only reason she did was because she knew it drove her mother nuts. She could see the fury in her eyes, but since she'd been trained to not lose her cool, she wouldn't retaliate.

They sat across from one another. "Tell me what you think of the changes since the wall fell," Zwaantie said.

"It's been pretty chaotic. But that has more to do with you turning off the Voice."

"We wouldn't have had to do that if he wasn't trying to kill me."

Mother rolled her eyes, and Zwaantie dropped her carefully placed smile.

"You have no idea what I've been through. How dare you roll your eyes at me."

"I don't care if it wanted to murder all the Stellans. It's lawless out there. People doing whatever they want. Young girls are taking cues from Sage on fashion. I even saw a farmer in the field not wearing a shirt. The guards can't keep up with it."

Zwaantie desperately wanted to address the Voice's murderous thoughts, but she knew that wouldn't be productive.

"I hope you aren't having the guards policing clothes. Surely they have more to worry about than that."

Mother frowned. "If they were, you'd be locked up. I thought you'd at least put on a decent dress."

"If the guards aren't policing clothes, then what are they doing?"

"They're dealing with theft mostly. A few fights. Nothing major. I expect it will get worse when people realize what they are allowed to do. The midnight hours are still relatively quiet. I even heard some families are packing up and heading for the border because they think life will be better in Stella."

Zwaantie nodded. "We expected that. People from Stella will try to come here as well."

Mother leaned forward. "We need to find a way to seal the border. Otherwise we'll be overrun."

"Good thing you don't have to make that decision since you are no longer queen."

Mother sputtered. "But they're my people."

"Not anymore. Also, you are no longer allowed to speak to Solite guards. They will report to me or Ajax. You are done. If you try anything at all, I will have you locked up."

Mother opened her mouth, but a knock sounded on the door, and Sage burst into the room followed by three giggly teenage girls. She threw herself at Zwaantie in a hug. "You're in big trouble, missy. Leo told you not to come. Now I have to keep an eye on you."

"I have guards."

"Amateurs."

Sage's hair was a mess, and she reeked. "You smell like a farm."

"I know. It's so much fun. I'm moving to Sol."

"Does Leo know this?"

"No. He'll deal. The horse and I made up."

Zwaantie laughed, grateful for Sage's interruption. "Good."

She looped her arm through Sage's and left the room. Part of her hoped she never had to see her mother again.

Chapter Nineteen

THE SPELL

Raaf was close to a breakthrough. He had to use magic, which he despised, but he had no other choice. He was losing. Magic always had the upper hand. So he would use his enemy's weapon against them. Wilma had brought him a necklace the day they invaded Sol, and he'd been studying it nearly non-stop ever since.

He'd been testing the magic it used and found a handful of spells he thought would work. He drew one of the darkened orbs to him.

It was late. Long past midnight. He should sleep, but when at war, there was little time for that. Zwaantie would die one way or another. She had to. Chaos had already begun in his beautiful country. He rubbed at the scars on his arms.

The door slammed behind him, and he spun around and glared at Wilma. "Don't you ever knock, woman?"

"Who else would bring you food?"

"I'm fine."

She leaned on the counter next to him, ruffling his papers. "I have news."

"What news?" he asked, flipping through a book.

"Zwaantie is in town."

He shrugged.

Wilma nudged his arm. "I thought that would make you happy. She's under this very roof. You could take her out easily."

"She's going to die soon enough anyway. It doesn't matter where she is." He wanted this wretched woman out of his workroom. She was distracting him.

Wilma gave him a look. "You've said that before."

He flicked her necklace. "Why are you wearing one of those?"

"It's not real. I got sick of people trying to force one on me."

"Makes sense. You don't have to worry much longer. Soon, everyone's necklace will be as useless as yours."

Wilma's eyes lit up. "You've figured out how to turn them off?"

"I'm very close. If you leave me alone, I might actually finish."

She cackled. "I'll believe it when I see it. Good luck, Raaf."

She clacked out of the room, and he continued working on his spell. He wasn't sure what time it was. Late. Maybe two, when he nearly gave up. He threw the necklace into the air in frustration.

It fell through the orb in front of him. The clatter of the necklace dropping to his desk never came.

He stared at the orb. The necklace floated inside of it, and suddenly the orb lit up bright white.

He laughed and snatched the necklace out of the orb, running to the large orb in the middle of the room. He tossed the necklace inside and watched it sink into the milky center.

For a moment, nothing happened, and he held his breath. A small light flickered out of the corner of his eye. Then another. Soon lights were turning on all over the room. He sank to his knees. He'd succeeded. Tears of relief flowed down his face.

He waited until nearly every orb was lit and called out.

"Kill the queen," he commanded.

Tomorrow would be a very different day.

Chapter Twenty

THE COMPLICATION

L eo couldn't sleep. He was worried about his and Zwaantie's shared future. He paced late into the night and didn't arrive to his room until near two. His guard stopped him before he went in and bowed. Leo was already tired of being king.

The guard stood tall again and hesitated. "Your Majesty, something is wrong."

"What do you mean?"

"There's a voice in my head, like before."

Leo gripped his arm. "Do you still have your necklace on?"

"I do. The Voice is telling me to kill the queen."

Leo felt the blood drain out of his face. He pushed open the door where two more guards sat, looking confused.

"Can you hear it? The Voice telling you to kill the queen." Leo was being rude and urgent, but he didn't care.

Both hurriedly stood as he entered.

"Yes, Your Majesty."

Dammit. Zwaantie wasn't safe. He flew out the door with only one goal. He had to save her.

He might already be too late.

~

IT WAS STILL THE MIDDLE OF THE NIGHT WHEN LEO HOPPED ON THE boat and headed out. He hoped against hope everyone was still sleeping. It would take him several hours to arrive, but he should be able to get a hold of Sage or Ajax when they woke up, and maybe they'd protect her. He'd tried both of their discs on the carriage ride to the boats, but neither answered. He tried Zwaantie as well, but she must've still been sleeping.

He collapsed on the couch in the hull of the boat and pulled out his disc once more. He had to talk to someone. There was no telling how far this had spread. Everyone he'd spoken to had the Voice. Why didn't he?

"Call Mother."

Lyra appeared almost instantly.

"What's wrong?" she asked.

"The Voice turned off the necklaces."

She fiddled with her own. "I don't hear a voice."

"I don't either, but everyone else does."

Lyra tapped her chin for a moment. "Our necklaces are different."

"What do you mean?"

"Well, they have the spell to turn off the Voice, but they also contain protection and other spells."

"Mine is a little different than yours though, right?"

"Yes."

Leo let out a breath. "Okay, this is good news. Zwaantie's is different as well. Ajax and Sage too."

"Zwaantie's guards don't have different ones though."

Leo clenched his fists. He had to get there before everyone woke up.

"Mom, can you get to the necklace maker and see if he can make a few different ones and test them. If they work, get the mass production started. Maybe we can fix this whole problem in a few days."

Lyra nodded. "Let's hope so, or Zwaantie will not survive."

Chapter Twenty-One

THE RESCUE

Zwaantie woke late the next morning, the vipers still pounding at her door.

Vipers. No. That couldn't be right. She was in Sol. She sat straight up. The thumping continued. Wait. What?

She grabbed her disc. She needed Sage, but it buzzed in her hand before she could do anything.

"You're in danger," Leo said as soon as she answered. "The Voice turned off the necklaces."

"What?" she hissed. Then reality hit her. The people banging on the door wanted her dead. She thought for a half second before she jumped out of bed. "I have to go. Don't call me again. I'm going to hide. I'll send you a message when I'm safe."

She ran to her wall where she had a secret passage and pressed the brick that opened the small door, then ducked in and quietly shut it. She hadn't been in the passageway since she was a small child. As far as passages went, it was useless since the exit had caved in centuries earlier. But it had its advantages when playing hide-and-seek.

She hoped none of her assassins would find their way inside because then she'd be trapped. Her hope was that if they searched her room and found her gone, they would assume she escaped and would search for her elsewhere.

She heard a clatter on the other side. "We know you're in here, Zwaantie. Come out and play."

She snorted. Yeah, right.

A silent message from Leo appeared on her screen. "Where are you?"

"Safe."

"Are you in your room?"

"Yes. Secret passage."

"Stay there. I'm about two hours away."

Two hours. She'd only survive if they didn't find their way inside.

Gruff voices sounded on the other side. "All these old castles have secret rooms. She must be hiding in one."

Zwaantie stopped breathing. She wouldn't be able to hide if they found the brick. She heard banging on the bricks. It was far from her, thank goodness. They'd never find her.

She held her breath as the banging got closer. Her heart raced. If they got lucky, they'd hit it. Even if they couldn't find it, if the brick echoed, they would know she was on the other side, and they might break the door down.

A loud thud sounded way too close to her, and she jumped. She clutched at the necklace she wore. How was this happening? How come she couldn't hear the Voice?

Another loud thud, and she jumped again.

"There's nothing here. She must've climbed out the window."

Loud footsteps led away from her, and she let out a sigh of relief. Now she had to hope no one else would search her room.

Time crawled by. She froze at each tiny noise. She wondered how Leo would get in there and why he didn't have the Voice in his head either.

If the Voice figured out how to turn the necklaces off, she was somehow immune. Now more than ever she needed to find a way to destroy him. She'd have to disguise herself, but she'd find a way to kill him.

Something scratched on the wall, and she held her breath. The door opened, and she pressed herself as far into the passage as she could get. She picked up a stone in the hopes she might be able to knock her attacker out.

Footsteps crunched down the hall. A small part of her hoped it was Leo, but the face that appeared was unfamiliar.

"Lookie here. I found the queen." He didn't have a sword, but held a deadly curved dagger. She kept the stone next to her side, knowing her only advantage would be surprise. He advanced, and she pressed herself against the wall, planning to use it as leverage.

He lunged, and she moved right, putting all her strength behind the stone in her hand. She crushed it on top of his skull. The dagger grazed her arm, but the blow she'd delivered caused him to drop. Hard. She scrambled over him and out into her room, no idea where she would hide next.

She stopped dead. There were five soldiers, each with a sword pointed at her.

"Please don't hurt me. I have no weapon. Take me to the Voice. Let me talk to him." Maybe she could reason with him. Maybe she'd find a way to kill him. Maybe this was better than being skewered.

One of the guards cocked his head. "Kill the queen," he said and advanced. Zwaantie stumbled backwards into the tunnel, knowing it was a dead end, and she was about to die. She squeezed her eyes shut, not wanting to see the sword come at her.

She heard a squelching sound, but no stab came. She peeked. The guard fell to the floor, and Zwaantie met Leo's eyes. She scrambled over the guard and threw herself at him. He held her tight.

"I was so worried. Are you hurt?"

"No," she mumbled into his shoulder.

"Okay, lovebirds, let's get you out of here."

Zwaantie let go of Leo and found Sage standing near the entrance with four more guards dead at her feet. "Where have you been?" Zwaantie flung herself at Sage.

"Around." Sage pushed her away. "We need to get out of here before anyone else comes." She placed a finger on Zwaantie's forehead and then Leo's.

Zwaantie's arms had gone wrinkly, and Leo was now as pale as a Solite.

"These illusions don't last very long, but it should get you back to Stella. Leo, take her somewhere safe. I'll stay and see if I can figure out how to make the necklaces work again."

"Why do ours still work?" Zwaantie asked.

"Probably because they are different than everyone else's. Lyra is working on testing other kinds. If they work, we'll get them distributed in the next few days," Leo said.

Sage nodded and motioned for them to follow. "Go hide. We'll keep in touch."

"Don't they want to kill me there too?" Zwaantie asked.

"Yes, but I know where to hide in Stella. Let's hurry," Leo said.

Chapter Twenty-Two

THE FLIGHT

Leo didn't breathe easy until they were on the boat. Sage's spell had held well enough that no one looked twice at them. Once he was far enough away from land, he sat next to Zwaantie, who hadn't said a word.

Her illusion had fallen, and her beautiful eyes stared at him. He wasn't used to feeling such panic. He'd been terrified he'd lost her. At first he thought his fear was because of losing the heir and the future of Stella. But as he traveled to Sol, he'd come to realize the carefully constructed wall he'd put around his heart had crumbled.

He loved this woman.

She'd crushed him more than once, and she could do it again, but he couldn't imagine his life without her. She was a brilliant queen, gorgeous, and wonderful in ways she probably didn't even understand. She was also reckless, but that was part of her charm.

He resisted the urge to kiss her. That wouldn't go over well, not yet. He needed to give her time to grieve Ari. But he wanted a full life with her, and for the first time in a long time, he saw their future.

He took her hand in his own. "How are you?"

She let out a breath. "Scared."

"I can imagine. Lyra, Sage, and those who work with them will get this all fixed. It should be safe for us in a few days."

Zwaantie snorted. "Right, she'll fix the necklaces until the Voice does something else, and then I'll still die."

"Have faith."

"Faith? How can I have faith right now? My life is a living hell." Her face twisted in pain, and he ached to comfort her but didn't know how without crossing boundaries she might not want crossed.

He placed his hand over hers. "At some point, things will start getting better."

She pulled her hand out from under his and crossed her arms. "Or I'll die. It might be an act of mercy at this point."

"You can't mean that." Leo couldn't lose her. Not now.

She rubbed her forehead. "I know. It's so frustrating to be constantly on edge. Never knowing what's around the corner."

"I'm taking you somewhere safe."

Her face softened, and she scooted closer to him, putting her hand on his knee. He tried not to read too much into it. "Thank you for rescuing me. It means more than you know. I would be dead right now if not for you."

"I will always rescue you. As long as you are alive, I will protect you."

She gave him a sad smile. "I'm worried about the others. Will Ajax be safe?"

"He's hiding as well. He'll return to Stella if the Voice is still a threat after a few days. We can't risk the Voice putting an assassination order on him as well."

"The Voice needs to be destroyed."

"We'll find a way. I'm having several books that we can use to research possibilities delivered to our hiding place," Leo said.

"Books on what? I thought you didn't know much about Sol."

"Old books. Histories of how things were before the wall was even created. If we can find the source of the Voice, we can learn where it is and how to get rid of it."

"That's a good idea. Everyone I love is in danger."

"Everyone is taking precautions. At the moment, you and I are the most at risk."

She nodded. "Where are we going?"

"To a private island. Just me and you until they work things out."

Her jaw clenched. "You know, Ari and I stayed on an island right after we got married."

He hated thinking about that time. "Yes, I know."

"Is this the same island?" Her eyes were full of tears.

"No. This is one near Deep Sky. It's Candace's retreat. The castle is larger than the one you and Ari stayed in."

Her shoulders relaxed. "Okay. Good. I'm sorry. I can't go back there." She wiped away a few tears.

"I understand." It had actually been his first choice, but when he remembered she'd been there, he wrote it off. He didn't want to stay in their love shack either. He wasn't sure how long they'd be there, and he didn't want it tainted with memories of Ari.

"Is this wise for you? Obviously, I need to go into hiding, but shouldn't you be supporting your people."

"This is the best thing I can do for them. I'm no good to my people dead."

"It feels sort of wrong hiding when there is work to do."

"We'll be doing work. Trust me. But until we find a way to free them from the Voice, we'll need to stay safe."

"I need to go make sure the magic is guiding the boat correctly. I'll be right back."

"Thank you," she said and looked out over the ocean.

He only had been gone a few minutes, but when he returned to her, her shoulders were shaking.

He forced her to look at him. Tears were streaming down her cheeks. "I'm sorry." She sniffed. He pulled her into him and just held her.

"It's okay. I understand."

She clutched at his vest. "I miss him so much."

Those were not the words he wanted to hear, but he understood her pain.

"I know. Me too."

Her blonde hair blew in the breeze. He wasn't sure what the future would hold for the two of them, but he did know one thing. He'd do everything he could to keep Zwaantie alive. She was his everything.

Chapter Twenty-Three

THE ISLAND

Several hours later the boat docked, and Zwaantie took a tentative step onto the island. It was different than the one she visited with Ari. For one thing, the sun beat down, and everything shone bright. The island she and Ari went to was mostly beach, but this one was very jungle-like. There was only a few feet of sand before lush green trees grew up around her.

"Are these real?" Zwaantie asked.

"Yes, a mage managed to grow them. We had no idea if they were natural or anything though. This island was always bright." He pointed to an orb in the sky. "You'll find those all over the island. The trees grew from the bright heated lights. It's why I picked this island. The castle is hard to find."

Zwaantie had to admit that growing trees in that way was pretty ingenious. "I bet it's amazing in there."

"It is. Maybe we'll have some time to explore later. Let's get to the castle now and check in with everyone and see if there are any new developments."

Zwaantie followed Leo down a well-hidden path. Water from leaves dripped on them, and birds twittered in the trees. The path was smooth and unnatural, but everything else was so alive.

They walked for around ten minutes before a small castle

appeared. It was circular, like the main castle, but it only had one level.

Leo pushed open the door and waited for her to enter. She stopped dead in the entryway, feeling like she was out in the jungle once again with bright birds and green trees painted on the walls.

"It's beautiful," Zwaantie said.

Leo placed his hand on her back and led her in a few more steps. "It is. The whole castle is painted. It will smell like the outside as well."

"Why doesn't the mage who created it still live here?"

"She died before I was born. This was her home. She never married, so she gifted it to the royal family when she died. She was very reclusive. Few even know this island exists."

"Sounds safe." She gave him a tentative smile, and he smiled back. She was so grateful he rescued her. She appreciated his comfort as well. He made her feel safe. There were fleeting moments where she could see their future. A future where the pain of Ari's death wasn't so fresh.

"Let me show you to your room. Mine will be next door, so if you need anything, I'll be there. The bedroom doors have multiple locks, so no one can get in."

Zwaantie cocked her head. "Why?"

"I'm not sure. I would assume the vipers. Maybe they were worse out here."

At least she'd be safe. Leo stopped in front of a door with a bright red flower painted on it.

"If the smell is too much, we can put you on the other side, but I thought you'd like this one best."

He pushed the door open, and Zwaantie gasped. Paintings of different flowers covered every inch of the walls. The floor appeared to be strewn with rose petals. A soft pink blanket covered the bed. She stepped in and inhaled. Rose, lily, and wisteria. For some it would be too much, but for her it was perfect.

She grasped Leo's hand. "Thank you. It's beautiful." She leaned up and placed a kiss on his cheek. "You know me better than I thought."

He blushed. "Well, it was this or the fish room."

Leo had trouble getting Zwaantie to come out of her room over the next several days.

They were always on the discs with someone, from the moment they got up until they went to sleep. They barely had time to eat.

Ajax returned to Stella after Zwaantie's mother ordered him to. She was in charge again. The Voice commanded it. At least she hadn't tried to kill his father. In fact, no one tried to kill anyone. Everyone was safe at the moment, but the Voice controlled both kingdoms. Leo wondered how Zwaantie's parents ever thought they had any control. Obviously the Voice had been in charge.

Sage and Lyra had a new necklace created that contained both a simple protection spell and the spell that turned off the Voice. It worked on the few people they tested it on. Today was the day they would try to mass distribute them.

They were more cautious this time though, as the Voice would probably expect a trick like this and fight aggressively the second he figured out what they were doing.

Leo knocked on Zwaantie's door. They were going to watch on the Ticker as the necklaces went out. She didn't respond. He waited for another few seconds and then pushed the door open a little.

"Zwaantie," he called, stepping carefully into the room.

"Back here," she yelled. He crossed the room, inhaling the various floral scents. It was a little overwhelming for him, but she liked it.

He turned the corner and stopped dead. Zwaantie was in the bathtub, purple water up to her neck, her leg flung casually over the side. She turned her head and beamed at him. "This is heaven."

He wiped his palms on his pants and cautiously made his way over to her. He didn't want to make her feel uncomfortable.

He sat on the vanity chair next to the tub, grateful he couldn't see into the water. She'd leave him speechless, and avoiding awkwardness would be out of the question.

He picked up her hairbrush and fiddled with it.

"Can you brush my hair?" she asked. Her long blonde hair flowed over the back of the tub, and he moved around, not quite sure what to do.

"I've never done this before."

She chuckled. "Just run it over my hair."

He brushed down along her hair, and she sighed. "It's been so long since someone has done that for me. Luna used to do it all the time, but once we got to Stella, the mages always did my hair, and they don't use brushes."

He wasn't sure if he was doing it right, but a smile crept across her face. The motion was relaxing for him as well. There was something methodical in brushing.

His disc buzzed, jarring him. He put the brush down and picked up the disc.

You ready? It was from Sage.

"Sage says it's time."

"I guess. It's easy to pretend nothing bad is going on when I'm in the tub. Just me and you and nothing else exists."

Leo tried not to read too much into her words even though they made his stomach flip-flop.

"I'll let you get dressed, and I'll meet you in the dining room." He didn't wait around for her response because if she stood up before he left the room, they'd never make it out.

The dining room was a perfect circle in the middle of the castle. A table for twelve sat in the center. Pictures of exotic animals covered the walls, which Leo always found creepy. The best thing about the room was that more than one disc could connect to the screens on the walls.

Leo covered the walls with video feeds of various parts of Stella. He called his sister and connected Zwaantie's disc with Lyra. They were ready to take their country back. With any luck, he and Zwaantie would be on a boat to the City of Stars by morning.

Several hours later Leo, cracked open a new bottle of wine and lifted his glass to his queen. They'd succeeded in getting the necklaces distributed. They'd done it once, so they were more efficient this time around.

Zwaantie leaned into him. "No more Voice, at least for now."

He put his arm around her and rested his hand on her hip. Every-thing about this felt natural and comfortable. Maybe life was finally looking up. People all over Stella were celebrating. They remembered everything they'd done under the influence of the Voice, and they were now free from his tyranny. Leo and Zwaantie watched the scene play out across the screens. Sage had finally signed off and went to get dinner. Mother was still connected, and they watched the people celebrating on the Ticker over several screens.

Suddenly everyone on the streets stilled. Stopped dead in their tracks. Zwaantie stiffened next him. Every person reached up and ripped off their necklaces.

"No," Leo muttered. "No." This couldn't be happening. They hadn't won at all. They'd lost.

"Lyra, what's going on?" Zwaantie asked.

Lyra dropped her head into her hands. "We failed. My guess is as soon as the Voice figured out what was occurring, he found a way to turn off the new necklaces."

"I'm coming home. We're fighting this," Leo said. He wasn't letting this Voice rule. He was king. Stars, this was awful.

"Calm down. Let us take stock of the situation. Once we know where things stand, then we'll discuss whether or not you can return."

Leo kicked the table. He'd been hopeful. He hadn't been king more than a week, and already his kingdom was under another's rule.

~

THE NEXT FEW WEEKS WERE DIFFICULT FOR ZWAANTIE. SHE WATCHED Leo sink into a depression that she would've never thought possible for him.

Once the Voice came back, it ordered not only her death but Leo's as well. He was stuck on this island with her. He spent hours on the disc with Lyra and Ajax discussing the fate of his people.

Zwaantie tried to comfort him, but she didn't know how. Ari flooded her thoughts. She felt so lost and isolated. Leo often made dinner but then ate in his own room, leaving her in the dining room alone.

The books made things easier. She read so much about the history of Stella and Sol before the wall was created. Magic had been around from the beginning in both kingdoms.

But so far, she couldn't find anything about the time when the wall went up. It was as if they went from together and happy to separate with no memory of what it was like before. There were over a hundred books though, and she was determined to find something in one of them. But she was tired of working alone.

She waited until Leo was busy in the kitchen. He wouldn't abandon the food.

He glanced up when she walked in. His face was unreadable.

"Are you looking for something?" Leo asked.

She stood closer to him than she should've, given his avoidance, and peered into the pot he was stirring.

"What are you making?" Zwaantie asked.

"Spaghetti."

"Yum." She didn't move, craving his closeness.

"Zwaantie, what do you want?"

"Company, I'm lonely. Why are you avoiding me?"

He took a step back and ran his hand through his hair. "Because I don't deserve your company."

"What are you talking about?"

"I have completely and utterly failed at being king and your husband."

She climbed onto the counter next to the stove. "I don't understand. You've only been my husband and king for a few weeks. Little early to call it a failure."

He stirred the noodles in tight, fast circles. The muscles in his arm tense. "My kingdom is under the influence of a being we can't find or even identify, and my wife is in love with my brother."

"We will find a way to take our kingdoms back. I don't know how, and I don't know when, but we will. As far as me, of course I love Ari, but that does not mean I cannot love you as well."

He jerked his head up. "Do you?"

"What?"

"Love me?"

"In a romantic way, no, not yet. It will come with time. But I do like and respect you." She hopped off the counter and dipped her finger in the sauce. She sucked it off her finger. "Needs more salt." She leaned into him, placing her hands on his stomach. "But there is no way I'm going to fall in love with you if you keep avoiding me."

She withdrew, because she couldn't go any further than that. Not yet.

Leo stared at her for a long moment. "I'm sorry."

"Will you eat with me tonight?"

"Yes, of course."

"Very well. I'll set the table."

Zwaantie set the plates next to each other, and Leo came out a few minutes later, spaghetti in hand. He dished the food up for her. She barely had the food to her mouth, and he spoke.

"I really am sorry. This has all been too much for me, and I needed time to process. In some ways I needed to grieve Ari as well, and I haven't had time to do that. I'll be better. I promise."

"I could use some help reading those books," Zwaantie said.

"Have you found anything?"

"Other than that life before the wall was amazing. No, I haven't found anything."

He raised his eyebrows. "Sounds interesting."

"It is."

They continued to eat and talk, and for the first time since the wall fell, Zwaantie felt hopeful that life might actually be taking a turn for the better.

THE NEXT COUPLE OF WEEKS LEO AND ZWAANTIE SPENT EVERY WAKING moment with those books. Every once in a while they would find something that was close to the time the wall was created and get excited, but it always concluded with a dead end.

One night, Leo was exhausted, and the words on the page blended together. "I can't read another thing. You wanna go watch a movie?"

Zwaantie looked up at him, her eyes sparkling. "No."

He rubbed his forehead. "No? Come on, we've been reading for hours."

"I found it," she said with a grin.

"You what?" Leo rushed to her side.

"Look." She held out the book, and they read together.

Physical magic was created first—the magic that controlled and manipulated the physical environments, but as the years waned, a new magic emerged—magic that controlled the mind. Soon a division formed among the people. Those who were drawn to the mental magics worshiped the sun, and those drawn to the physical magics worshiped the stars.

As new stars were discovered, along with the powers that came from them, those who worshiped the sun found themselves in the minority. As rulers came into power, the sun magicians felt abandoned and unheard. They withdrew from the main cities and built small villages where they would be left alone. There, they were able to focus on their own magics and learn the nuances of the magic of the sun.

One day a mage discovered that he had the ability to control another's actions. After much discussion among their Solite elders, they determined that they could finally have a voice in the government of earth. The Stellan elders had cut them out, but they could control the actions of the elders.

At first they only did it occasionally, when a law or rule would unfairly affect them, but as time went on, they felt they deserved more, and within a few years one of the Solite mages made himself King of Earth and called himself the Voice. A few of the Solite mages were uncomfortable with the way he gained his power, feeling that he had violated the Solite code of honor. They approached the Stellan elders and explained what the king had done.

The Stellan elders were angry with the king, but found themselves unable to defy him due to his ability to control their actions. For ten years they worked with the Solite elders who disagreed with the Voice and researched and experimented until they found a spell that would protect them from the Solite king. It was risky, and they did not know the effect the spell would have, but they did know they had to be free of his power.

Together the mages erected a barrier, one that would separate the Stellans and Solites forever.

"That's it. What's next?" Leo asked.

"Nothing. The book is finished."

"Well, it did tell us something incredibly important."

"What's that?" Zwaantie asked.

"The Voice is human. It's just a spell. He can be killed."

Zwaantie sank into her chair. "Do you think it's the same person from years ago?"

Leo shook his head. "That would make him immortal, and this says nothing about that. No, I'm guessing he simply passed on his skills to someone new when he was close to death."

"What are these Solite elders the book speaks of? I know nothing about them." Zwaantie let out a breath of frustration.

"I suppose it is possible they still exist, but it sounds like they were unhappy with the king. See, this makes it seem like the Voice would carry on with each king, and therefore it would be your father, but he died," Leo said.

"Maybe my father trained someone else, but the threat on my life was personal. No, my father was not the Voice. Maybe the Voice went underground over the years," Zwaantie said.

"If we found this, I bet there's more somewhere else." Leo thumped the book.

"I bet there is."

They both turned and stared at the stack of books that looked no smaller than it had on day one. He took Zwaantie's hand and drew her near to him. "Why don't we worry about that tomorrow? I can't read another thing. We deserve to relax a little."

Zwaantie smiled up at him. "At least we found something."

He ran a thumb across her cheek. "You look beautiful when you're excited." He was being bold, bolder than he'd been since they arrived on the island, but he was tired of holding back.

She didn't respond, but she didn't pull away either. He dipped his head toward her and let his eyelids flutter shut, and he inhaled her floral scent. Then she was gone.

He opened his eyes and found her standing a few feet from him.

"I'm sorry. I couldn't. I'm not ready." She wrung her hands and wouldn't meet his eyes.

He closed the distance, grabbed her hand, and pulled her into him again. She had a hint of fear in her eyes. He'd never been aggressive with her before. He lifted her chin so she was looking him right in the eyes. "I'll wait as long as you need."

She gave a tiny nod and rested her cheek on his chest. He wasn't sure how long they stood there like that, but he wanted that moment to last forever.

～

ZWAANTIE AND LEO SPENT THREE MONTHS ON THE ISLAND. IN SOME

ways it was a relief to Zwaantie. She didn't constantly worry someone was about to kill her.

Every few days an unmanned boat would come from Deep Sky with food and more books. They kept up with Sage, Lyra, and Ajax via their discs. Sage got different necklaces on the spies and the guards. They had to be very careful because they didn't want to bring the necklaces to the attention of the Voice. Lyra said nearly every necklace was unique in some way. The theory was that if the Voice discovered if the necklaces all had to be the exact same spell, then the Voice could turn them off.

King Ajax and Zwaantie's mother ran the day-to-day operations of the kingdoms. Ajax called Leo nearly every day. Zwaantie's blood boiled every time she thought of her mother ruling over her kingdom.

No one was fooled though because the real ruler was the Voice. His influence was everywhere, and people were docile and obedient. Stellans changed their style so they looked more like Solites. Magic was tempered. The people learned fast that if they disobeyed the Voice, pain was imminent.

The Ticker was downright boring.

Zwaantie and Leo read as many books as they could get their hands on, but most of them didn't contain any new information. When they couldn't keep the words straight, they would watch movies and cuddle. He'd made no more moves to kiss her.

Her belly swelled. At night, she would talk to her baby and tell him stories about his father. He would grow up thinking Leo was his dad, but for now, Zwaantie could pretend otherwise.

"Let's go swimming," Leo said, late one afternoon.

Her hand went to her stomach. She'd been wearing clothes that hid it from him. If they went swimming, he would see it.

"I don't know."

"Come on. It's hot. We're not finding anything in these books."

She let out a breath. "Okay."

She changed and put on the only swimsuit Leo had brought over. It was bright blue and tiny. She threw a sundress over it, suddenly self-conscious. What would he think when he saw her? She let out a breath. This was silly. Why did she even care?

Leo stood in the entryway with a couple of towels slung over his shoulder. He took her hand, and they strolled outside. Zwaantie tried not to think too much of him holding her hand. He'd done that a lot since they'd been on the island. He was ready for things to go beyond just friends, but Zwaantie wasn't. In the last few days though, she'd been increasingly aware of him.

Ari still lingered in her mind, but the pain had lessened. Her future lay with Leo, and it could be a future cut short by any number of things. The thought of running the kingdoms on her own wasn't a pleasant thought. Though, she was more likely to die than he was. After the Voice turned off the necklaces, she didn't take anything for granted.

Down on the beach, Leo dropped the towels and slid off his sandals. She gathered up her sundress and pulled it over her head. A blush crept up her cheeks as she met Leo's eyes.

Leo stared openly but didn't say a word. She wished she could tell what he was thinking. He took two steps toward her and slowly reached out his hand and placed it on her belly. It was warm against her skin.

"There's a baby in there," he whispered. His face was so serious.

"Yes, there is." His touch was gentle and sent a shiver down her spine.

He met her eyes, searching them. "We're going to raise this baby together, right?"

"As far as the child will know, you are his father." She wanted nothing more than for Ari's child to grow up happy.

"If it's a boy, we should name him Ari."

She blinked back tears. Her heart hurt, but she could feel it starting to heal. "We should."

"And if it's a girl, we'll just name our first boy after him."

Zwaantie's breath caught in her throat. He was speaking of future children. Of future love and happiness between the two of them. Words failed her, so she nodded, afraid tears would come if she opened her mouth. For the first time in a long time, those tears would be of happiness, not sorrow.

He dropped to his knees so his face was level with her stomach, his hands on her hips. He planted a kiss on her belly, and warmth flooded her.

"You're going to be very loved, little baby."

He pulled her close to him, searching her face, and brushed a strand of hair out of her eyes. "So will his mother. You look stunning, by the way."

Leo had kissed her many times before they were married, but Zwaantie hadn't enjoyed them. This time, as he dropped his lips toward hers, she knew it would be different. She was ready to be loved again.

"Hey," a voice called, and Leo leapt away, pushing her behind him. She crouched down. No one had set foot on the island since they arrived. It wasn't safe for Zwaantie if they did. Everyone knew this. Fear crept into her heart. They'd been safe for so long. Would the Voice finally succeed in assassinating her when she'd finally started allowing herself to be happy again?

Chapter Twenty-Four

THE TRUTH: PART 1

Zwaantie peeked around Leo. Sage and Phoenix strolled up the beach. Relief flooded Zwaantie. She rushed around Leo and crushed Sage in a hug.

"I've missed you so much," she whispered into Sage's ear.

"Me too," Sage said, her voice flat.

Zwaantie pulled away. Dark purple lines were under Sage's eyes, and where her lips were normally turned up into a smile, they formed a tight line.

"What's wrong?" Zwaantie asked, searching for some clue as to what might be going on.

Sage wiped sweat off her forehead. "A lot. I want to get out of the sun though. Can we go inside?"

"Sure."

Zwaantie put her sundress back on and looped her arm through Sage's. They pulled ahead of the boys onto the path in the middle of the trees. Soon they couldn't even hear Leo and Phoenix talking.

"I'm glad you're here. Things were getting rather dull with just Leo," Zwaantie said.

Sage raised an eyebrow. "It didn't look like things were very dull to me."

Zwaantie giggled. "Maybe things were just about to get exciting."

She expected Sage to come back with something funny, but she was quiet. This was so unlike Sage. "Please, tell me what happened."

Sage shook her head. "No, not until we're inside and can talk. This is going to take a while. Plus, I'm starving. We rushed out of there so fast we didn't even bring food with us."

Something horrible must've happened. Though, everyone she loved was either on the island or already dead.

"You could've stopped in the City of Stars or something."

"No, I couldn't. I'm in as much danger as you now."

Zwaantie wanted to press her for details, but she had a feeling that Sage wouldn't give up anything until they were together.

Once inside the castle, they settled in at the dining room table. Leo brought in fruit and sandwiches. Sage and Phoenix scarfed down the food before they said anything. Zwaantie wasn't sure what Phoenix was doing here. He'd tried to kill her twice and was susceptible to the Voice. If he was here, things were really bad.

"What's going on?" Zwaantie asked, now impatient.

Sage met Leo's eyes. "I can't tell her the story without telling her the truth."

Zwaantie's stomach fell. "What truth?" Just when she was starting to feel like they were being honest with her, she discovered more secrets. This was so unfair. She was queen of the entire world. There should not be secrets anymore.

"You might as well tell her. When this mess is cleaned up, we'll have to replace you anyway, since as king, I'm not supposed to know who you are."

Zwaantie furrowed her brow, now thoroughly confused, her anger slowly building. "What is that supposed to mean?"

"I'm not a spy," Sage said.

"Well then, what are you?"

"I'm Stella's assassin. I work for the head mage and only do what is in the best interest of Stella. I kill powerful evil people. The king if necessary."

Zwaantie's head spun. "You assigned your assassin to be my guard?" she asked Leo.

Leo shrugged. Red crept up his neck. "Yeah. If you posed any threat, she would've taken you out. I know this seems brutal, but

Zwaantie, when I came to Sol, I knew nothing about you. I was slightly suspicious of your intentions in Stella, especially because you rebuffed me so thoroughly when I arrived. Your sudden decision to marry me was unnatural. By the time I felt comfortable with you, Sage had become your friend and refused a reassignment."

Zwaantie dropped her head into her hands. This was unbelievable. From the very beginning, her life had been on the line. Not just from the Voice but from Sage as well. They could've easily told her the whole truth when she found out Sage was a spy.

She brought her head up and met Phoenix's eyes. "Why does he know?" It came out whinier than she'd intended.

"He didn't until a few hours ago. He thought I was a spy, just like you did. He's been working with Lyra and me. It's why he had a different necklace when everything fell apart. The entire spy network is intact, which is the only reason we're all still alive."

Zwaantie wanted to stay angry, but this was not the news Sage came to tell.

"Explain," Zwaantie said.

"I found the Voice," Sage said with a grimace.

Zwaantie paled. "And did you kill him?"

"No. I tried, but failed. He is far stronger than any of us could anticipate."

Zwaantie's anger disappeared. They were finally close to killing the Voice. She wanted to know everything. "Back up. Please, tell me the whole story."

Sage let out a breath. "Phoenix and I had been watching the castle and studying the comings and goings. There was an old woman who came quite frequently, but as far as we could tell, she had no real reason. Today, we followed her. She went deep into the castle into a secret passageway."

"Which one?"

"The door is next to the king's rooms."

"That's where Luna was going," Zwaantie said, finally understanding.

"Yep. As soon as she pushed open that door, we knew we were close to the Voice. The entire hallway hummed with energy. The door led down a winding hall that ended at an ancient wooden door. We let the woman go first, and we listened at the door and heard two voices. I'm very good at what I do, so I thought it would be easy to take on just two people, but, while the Voice can probably be killed, it will never happen in his own room."

Sage paused and took a sip of her water. Zwaantie wanted to ask questions but thought it might be better to wait until Sage spilled the whole story.

"I put an invisibility spell on both me and Phoenix, and we slipped into the room. But as soon as we crossed the threshold, the spell broke."

Sage scooted her chair close to Zwaantie and gripped her hand. "Zwaantie, when we crossed the threshold, we found the old woman with Raaf."

Zwaantie couldn't breathe. "Are you saying my brother is the Voice?"

"I am. I wasn't sure at first, thinking maybe it was the old woman. I took nothing for granted, but once the fight started, it was obvious it was him."

The Voice, her own brother? How could this be? He loved her and she him. Even when he tried to kill her at the wedding, she thought it was because of the influence of the Voice. This was so much worse than her father. How many times had she confided in him? How long had he been trying to kill her? This was impossible.

Zwaantie let out a breath. "What happened?"

"The old woman attacked me first, and I killed her. Then Raaf attacked me. It was the strangest thing. He never laid a hand on me, but I could feel his blows anyway. I've got bruises all over my body. I couldn't even get close to him. When Phoenix started bleeding from his eyes, I grabbed him and escaped. We didn't stop running until we got on a boat. Raaf's got wicked magic like I've never seen before. I'm so sorry."

Zwaantie pushed up and away from the table. "I need to be alone."

She made it to her room before she lost it. She slammed the door and slid down and let herself cry. Her brother wanted her dead. She'd never done anything to him. Yet, here she was exiled because she became queen, a job she never wanted in the first place. If he wanted to be king, why didn't he just ask? She would've gladly given him the position, married Phoenix, and everyone would've lived happily ever after.

Phoenix.

He only loved her because the Voice told him to. Raaf had been trying to dethrone her even before Leo had come into the picture. How could he want power that much?

Now, he held the entire world in his hands. He had to be stopped. Zwaantie was still upset Sage hadn't been honest with her, but she wished Sage had succeeded in killing Raaf. His death was their only hope. She couldn't believe she'd defended and pitied him after Ari died. He was a monster and had to go.

She wasn't ready to face her friends, and she'd have to come to terms with Raaf's betrayal. Trust was so hard to give, and now she wasn't sure who else to give it to. She felt herself becoming hardened, and she didn't like that. She longed for the time before she met Leo and came to Stella. When she was innocent and carefree.

She took a shower and let the hot water soothe her aching eyes and stiff shoulders. When she was ready, she went in search of Sage. Together they were going to devise a plan to kill Raaf. They would make sure he never hurt another person.

She headed toward the dining room, but heard Sage's voice coming from one of the guest bedrooms. She paused next to the door and then pushed it open.

She froze in the doorway. Phoenix had his arm around Sage and his lips pressed against her cheek. It wasn't indecent by any means, but that was definitely not the way friends or colleagues treated one another. This was a lovers' embrace. Sage looked up and met Zwaantie's eyes. Zwaantie didn't even say a word. She turned and ran. She thought nothing else could hurt. But this cut deep into her soul. She had no idea why.

Her relationship with Phoenix had been over for months. But he had been her first love. She didn't begrudge Sage's love for him, but this felt so wrong. She understood now how Leo must've felt when he caught her and Ari in the garden.

An anger welled in her chest like she'd never before felt. All reason left her. She had the urge to break something. She picked up a small dish from the table and threw it across the room. It shattered, but she didn't feel any better.

All the betrayal. It was too much. The rage in her heart roared. She picked up a fire poker and smashed a lamp on her bedside. That was for Raaf.

Her own brother turned his back on her. Made her life a living hell. She lashed out again, leaving a wide gash in the wall. Seeing the destruction to the pretty flowers only encouraged her. She let out a yell and slashed again.

Sage was not who Zwaantie thought she was, and now she was sleeping with Phoenix. Phoenix! Zwaantie went after the flower statues on the top of the fireplace, smashing one after another until they were gone.

She collapsed on the floor and sobbed. She couldn't believe she had come to this. A powerless queen who trashed her bedroom. A large vase caught her eye, taunting her. She stood above it, letting her rage build. All her anger at Raaf, Sage, and Ari. She was mad he'd died and left her here to deal with this. She knew he hadn't done it on purpose, but rage felt good.

She yelled out again and put every ounce of energy she had into destroying the vase. It shattered in a satisfying crack.

"Zwaantie," Sage said.

She spun and found Sage taking a few cautious steps into the bedroom.

Zwaantie was certain she looked like a deranged housecat. Her eyes were wide, her hair was half out of a braid. Tear streaks stained her cheeks. The fire poker in her hand. She glanced around, seeing this as they would. Her room was trashed. Lamps were shattered, a small chair was in smithereens, and pillows were strung about the room.

"Would you like me to come back later?" Sage asked and backed toward the door.

"No," Zwaantie shouted and lunged at her. "You stay here, and you listen to me." She stood about three feet from Sage, fire poker pointed right at her face. She wasn't sure what she was going to do, but Sage was the only one here to yell at. Everyone else she was angry with was out of reach.

"You won't hurt me," Sage said with her hands up.

Zwaantie wiggled her stick. "Don't be so sure. How could you do this to me? You know how I felt about him. There are thousands of good men in Stella, and you fell for the one that I loved. You're my best friend. How could you do this to me?"

"Zwaantie, I'm sorry," Sage said.

"No, you're not," Zwaantie screamed and threw the fire poker across the room. It left another wide gash in her wall.

She stood in front of Sage, breathing deep, and Sage stared back. Zwaantie's anger flushed out of her. She loved Sage. Her real anger lied with Raaf. Zwaantie reached out and pulled Sage into a hug. Sage returned the hug with force, and they fell to the floor.

"I like what you did with the place. It needed a new decorator." Sage gave Zwaantie a toothy grin.

Zwaantie lost it then, laughing hysterically, and so did Sage. It wasn't that funny, but the release of her anger left only laughter.

Chapter Twenty-Five

THE PLAN

S age and Zwaantie lay on the bed. Zwaantie couldn't quite bring herself to stay upset with Sage, and she felt a hundred times better getting out all of her anger. She would need to clean up her room eventually, but for now, the mess was there to stay.

"Sorry," she said to Sage. "You and Phoenix, that was kind of a last straw." It was. She was happy for both Sage and Phoenix, but in the moment, it seemed like one more betrayal.

"I understand. I'm sorry I didn't tell you about us. It's just been so much lately. I didn't want to add to it."

"How long has this been going on?" Zwaantie wanted to hear about their relationship, but she also wanted the distraction. If Sage was talking about Phoenix, Zwaantie didn't have to think about Raaf.

"Mmm. He didn't kiss me until after you married Ari. But I've had a thing for him since I wrestled that necklace onto him."

Zwaantie was surprisingly okay with this. So many bad things had happened. There was no reason one couldn't take advantage of the good things. Plus, she wanted her friends to be happy.

"So what's next?" Zwaantie asked, curious how serious they were. Maybe this was just a fling.

"What do you mean?" Sage asked, not meeting her eyes.

"Are you going to marry him?"

Sage screwed up her face. "I'm not a queen. I don't have to think about those things. For now, I'm gonna enjoy him. We'll see where it goes."

"Good. You should." Zwaantie rolled onto her back and stared at the ceiling, thinking of the Voice in spite of trying to forget about it. They had to destroy him. "What are we going to do about Raaf?"

"I don't know." Sage's eyes went wide with fear. "Zwaantie, I've never been so scared in my life. I'm pretty sure we can beat him if we get him out of his room, but there was so much power in there. Thousands of glowing orbs. It was such a strange sight."

"What do you think the orbs were?" Zwaantie asked, trying to picture the room.

"Probably the source of the Voice. My guess is if we destroy those, the Voice goes away."

"So maybe then we don't have to kill Raaf." She knew this was foolish, but she loved him.

"He's been trying to kill you for months, and he killed Ari."

Zwaantie rolled over onto her back. "I know. But he's my brother." She squeezed her eyes shut. She'd been so sure he was under the influence of the Voice that she was having trouble reconciling he was, in fact, responsible for Ari's death.

Sage let out a breath. "I have an idea, but you aren't going to like it."

"What's that?"

Sage hesitated. "We bring down the castle. The room is deep inside. He won't survive and neither will the orbs."

"I don't care about the castle. We'll have to evacuate it though." It was actually a great idea. They could rebuild.

"We can't evacuate."

"What? Why?" That changed everything. She was fine with the castle, but not killing everyone else inside.

"Because the Voice will figure out what we're doing, and then we'll have dozens of people trying to kill us."

"But we'll kill everyone else inside."

"I told you that you wouldn't like it." Sage's face was so serious. Zwaantie wanted this to be over so she could have her carefree Sage back.

Zwaantie closed her eyes. They would kill dozens of people. Plus, she had no clue how they could take down an entire castle.

"I don't like it. We can't kill innocent people just to get rid of him." She couldn't believe Sage even proposed such an idea. Though, now that she knew Sage was Stella's assassin, she shouldn't be surprised.

"Dozens of people dead or thousands under his tyranny. Pick your poison," Sage said matter-of-factly.

"I refuse to believe there isn't another way."

"There probably is a way to kill him, but we won't get close enough to find out. We could lose dozens of people just attempting to kill him. We simply don't have time. The longer we wait, the worse things get out there."

Zwaantie wasn't convinced. "I need time to think about this. How do you bring down an entire castle anyway?"

"A lot of magic, you wouldn't understand the logistics. Since none of the spies have fallen, they can help. It will take several people."

"I still need time to process this. I'm not going to okay this yet."

"I know, but, Zwaantie, we don't need your approval."

How dare she. "Excuse me, I'm queen."

"Leo is king. If he's okay with it, we'll move forward."

Zwaantie clenched her jaw. "Leo and I will have words about that."

They both grew quiet, lost in their own thoughts. If Zwaantie authorized bringing down the whole castle, she'd have the deaths of all the innocents inside on her head for the rest of her life. Would she be able to live with herself? Would she forgive Leo if he went ahead and did it without her permission?

She needed answers. Answers she would never receive without talking to Raaf. She didn't want him dead. Not really. She just wanted him to stop controlling the country. He would pay for what he did to her and Ari, but there had been too much death already.

Chapter Twenty-Six

THE ALLIES

The next day three more people arrived on the island. Nerves settled in Zwaantie's stomach. She never knew who wanted to kill her. Sure Leo said they were safe, but there was no real way to tell until they were around her.

Ajax and Lyra stepped off the boat first. A woman Zwaantie had never met threw her arms around Sage.

"Zwaantie, meet Titania, my mother," Sage said.

She smiled, and Zwaantie instantly saw Sage in Titania's face.

"It's a pleasure to meet you," Zwaantie said.

"Likewise. I've heard so much about you, my queen." She gave a small bow and followed Sage up to the castle. Zwaantie wondered how many people were hiding from the Voice. She hoped it was a lot.

Once inside, they gathered around the dining room table, with Leo at the head and Zwaantie next to him.

"Thank you for coming. You've all been briefed on the situation. We're here to discuss how to take out the threat with minimal loss of life. We'd like to hear any and all ideas," Leo said.

Sage stood up first and presented her idea to take down the castle.

"No," Zwaantie argued. "Too many innocent people die. Find another way."

"You're right," Lyra said. Zwaantie turned to her. She hadn't expected Lyra to agree. "What about taking out only the room. We don't have to be in the room to do that, just get close. A handful of mages could destroy the room from the hallway."

"That would work, except the Voice has increased his guard after Sage's failed attempt to assassinate him," Titania said. "I've been in touch with a few of the spies we left there. The hallway into the king's quarters has anywhere between eight and ten guards at any given time."

"So murder the guards and take out the room," Zwaantie said. There had to be a way to do this without killing so many people. A few guards would be a small price to pay.

"The spell takes time. If we do anything that draws attention to ourselves, we risk the Voice finding out and retaliating," Sage said. "It's much easier outside of the castle where we don't risk detection."

Zwaantie exhaled. This wasn't going well.

"What about Raaf's room? Surely there is a way in from there. He didn't go near the king's chambers every time he went to his room," Leo said.

"There are guards as well. Not as many as by the king's chambers, but they are there. Plus it might take too long to find the way to the room with the orbs from there. The entryway must be hidden from Raaf's rooms," Sage said. Zwaantie sat back and crossed her arms.

"Sage, you said the room was tall. Is there a window on the roof?" Ajax asked.

Sage squeezed her eyes shut and clenched her fists. "I think so. It was hard to tell. Most of the castle roof is windows though, so it would be difficult to find."

"But not impossible. We could use no magic, break the window, and send an arrow right into his head," Ajax said.

"Possible," Zwaantie said. "But that runs a lot of risk of discovery. Look what he did to Sage. If we open the roof, does that allow out more of his power?"

Lyra rubbed her forehead and frowned. "We don't know. His power is unknown to us, so we have no idea how it will behave. We also can't risk killing him and leaving the orbs intact. For all we know, if we kill him, someone else will take over and use the power. We need to kill the source. I would say that's more important than killing Raaf himself."

Which meant they had to destroy the room. Now Zwaantie understood why Sage told her ahead of time. This was the only viable plan. The others continued to bounce around ideas, each shot down for one reason or another. Eventually the table quieted.

"This leaves us with only one option," Leo said.

"What?" Zwaantie asked, already knowing the answer.

"We have to take down the castle."

Zwaantie closed her eyes. Part of her knew this was coming. But it still made her sick. She would live with those deaths for the rest of her life. She would never forget.

She stood, needing to get away from everyone. "If that is what you think is best. I will have no part of this, but I will not stand in your way. Excuse me. I will be in my room while you finalize your plans."

Zwaantie made it to her bathroom and threw up her lunch. So many people would die. This was wrong, but also, as Leo pointed out, it was the only option.

Chapter Twenty-Seven

THE WALK

It was late when a soft knock came at her door. Zwaantie threw on a light robe and answered it, worrying that something bad had happened.

Leo stood there with a bottle of wine, two flutes, and a crooked grin. "Come for a walk with me."

She let out a breath of relief and gave him a small smile. "Of course. Let me get dressed."

She moved to shut the door, but he grabbed her wrist. "Don't be silly. Who are we going to see? There are only seven of us on this island, and I can guarantee three of them are asleep."

"What about the others?" Zwaantie asked.

"I heard Sage giggling in her room. I don't expect she or Phoenix has any intention of leaving."

Zwaantie frowned. Though she was okay with Phoenix and Sage together, she didn't want to think about that.

He tugged on her hand, and she stumbled out of the door.

"If you insist. Do I need shoes?"

"Nope, we'll just be walking on the sand."

He didn't let go of her hand as they snuck outside quietly. Though Zwaantie had been sorely tempted to bang on Sage's door.

Her hand tingled where Leo held it. She shivered at the thought of what might happen on the beach. This was not just a friendly visit.

Zwaantie was very slowly falling for him. If Sage hadn't showed up when she did, Zwaantie would probably be feeling very different about things.

The feelings she had for Leo were real though. What had been so hard when Ari was around was suddenly much easier. She'd tried to love Leo before, but not really. Ari had taken ahold of her heart, and it wasn't possible for her to love another. Ari still held onto her heart, but she was beginning to see that there was life after him.

They walked out to the water's edge and sat on the sand so the water lapped at their feet. The water was warm and relaxing. Zwaantie wondered how this would feel if the world wasn't falling apart. Leo poured her a glass and handed it to her.

She sipped at the sweet liquid and laid her head on his shoulder, suddenly needing his affection. She wanted to be loved again, and she wanted to fill the empty void in her chest that Ari left.

"The stars are still so beautiful. Do you remember showing me the stars for the very first time?" Zwaantie asked.

Leo nodded. "I do. I consider it one of the best days of my life."

She exhaled. "We ought to replace that."

"Why?" he asked, looking her deep in the eyes. His eyelashes were so long.

"Because it wasn't one of my best days. I was in a new country and terrified. That was the first time I heard the vipers, and I delivered Candace's baby. I was scared, not happy. Let's make a new best day together."

He traced a finger down her cheek and looked away, taking a sip of his wine. Her skin burned where he touched her. Why was he taking so long to kiss her? Perhaps she'd need to take things into her own hands.

"I would like tonight to be that night, but it won't be," he said.

"Why not?" she asked, nervous and grateful she hadn't tried anything. She didn't want to be laughed at again.

"Because today we decided to take down your home. I don't feel right about it. I want to say I'm sorry, but we still have to do it."

She snuggled into his side. "I know. I understand. There was no other good solution."

He put his arm around her and placed his finger under her chin, lifting her face so she was only a breath away.

"I want desperately to kiss you right now and make this a memorable night though."

"Why don't you?" she whispered, feeling vulnerable. She was nervous about what the future would look like after tonight.

"Because I need to show you something." He turned his head, but kept her tucked into him.

"I'm pretty close with a mage who discovers the magic and gods associated with various stars, so I asked for some help."

"And?"

"They found Ari's star."

Zwaantie let out a gasp. "Where?" She searched the sky. She'd been looking for so long.

A green light lit up high in the sky. "It's the star just above the light."

Zwaantie stared at the star, which was much bigger than the lights around it. "It's bright." She couldn't take her eyes off of it. That was Ari.

"Did you expect anything less?" Leo asked with a chuckle.

She studied the area around his star. She wanted to burn the memory of that spot in her head. She would find it every night before she went to sleep and talk to him. It was a large star, right above a cluster of tiny ones.

"Do you know what magic it controls yet?" She didn't care if she had zero magic. She'd figure out how to do Ari's.

Leo grinned. "Not completely. But in true Ari fashion, it has something to do with sex."

"Oh my Sol. How do they know that, but not the exact magic?"

"Because magic funnels. You can typically use any magic to do what you want, but it won't work very well. If you want it to work better, you need to try several different broad categories, like light or love, and then you can funnel further. The furthest they've gone with Ari's was sex, but everyone finds it amusing."

Zwaantie would've liked to have been in the room that day. They probably laughed and raised their glasses to Ari. He would appreciate that.

"Thank you for showing me this. I know it has been hard for you." She wanted him to know she understood not only his own grief but his struggle to trust her.

He didn't say anything, but held her tight as they watched the stars. After several moments, he let out a breath. "I counted him among my closest friends."

"That makes me feel worse." She'd been so stupid, playing Leo like that. How was it possible for him to love her now? If the tables were turned, she wouldn't have been as nice.

"Don't. Ari and I talked long into the night the day before he died. The way he spoke of you wasn't like anything I've ever seen in him before. He was completely and entirely smitten and happy. Ari was carefree most of his life, but I'd never seen him extremely happy. He was with you. I don't begrudge that. I forgave him, and I forgive you."

Tears pricked at her eyes. "Thank you." She hoped it would be adequate enough to express how much his forgiveness meant to her, because no other words would be possible right now.

There was another beat of silence, and then Leo chuckled. "You know, one time, he almost locked me out after midnight."

"What? No." The vipers had been a bad nightmare to her for a short time, but to the Stellans, midnight hours had been full of danger and death for years.

"Yep." Leo launched into his tale of Ari and continued with the stories until far into the night. Part of Zwaantie was sad, but a bigger part of her liked learning everything there was to know about Ari. It was like getting to know him all over again.

Chapter Twenty-Eight

THE TRUTH: PART 2

Leo woke up the next morning entangled in the arms of the woman he loved. It was something he had never really experienced before. She'd been the only one he ever loved, and this was the first time they'd really been close. It would also be the last, and that saddened him.

They lay in the sand, her bare leg thrown over him, her head on his chest. As much as he wanted to stay here and love her, he was leaving with the others to destroy the castle. He didn't really want to, but he'd invented the spell to destroy large buildings, and they couldn't take any chances. He had to be among them. He wasn't a fool though. He wouldn't survive.

He planned on leaving Titania with Zwaantie. She was the best babysitter around. Plus, then, when the news of his death came, Titania would be good at comforting her. It was the reason he brought her over instead of someone else like Candace.

The rest of their party would meet up with several others before they crossed the Solite border. If they were lucky, this time tomorrow, the entire kingdom would be free of a madman. It was a sacrifice he had to make.

He shifted a little, and Zwaantie pressed closer into him. Her whole body was warm against his, and his heart began to race. Oh, yeah, he was completely slayed. He didn't have to move yet; he could stay in her arms.

He'd barely closed his eyes again when sand sprayed across his face. He rubbed his eyes as Sage plopped down next to him.

"Have fun last night, bro?"

He smiled up at her and then spit out the sand from his lips. "Did you?"

"You know it. We could all die today. Gotta make the best of things."

He looked down at Zwaantie, sand on her face. She hadn't so much as flinched. She was out.

"You scared?" he asked.

"You sure she's asleep?" Sage asked.

"Yeah. She hasn't moved, and her breathing is still steady."

"Okay, well, we've never done this before. With the probability the magic will probably take us out, yeah, I'm scared."

"It's a sacrifice we have to make. Raaf can't be allowed to keep enslaving people, even if it means we all die."

Zwaantie moved against him, and he put a finger to his lips. She would never let him go if she thought he could die. He and Sage probably shouldn't have been so open, but he was fairly certain Zwaantie was still asleep.

"We've got to go. Everyone else is up and getting ready. We want to make it to Sol before the sun sets."

Leo gently shook Zwaantie awake. She blinked, stretched, and gave him a smile. He let out a breath of relief. She hadn't heard a thing.

"Morning, you sleep good?" Leo asked.

She nodded. "We should sleep in the sand more often."

"We should. Listen, I have something to tell you."

She sat up and stared out over the sea, not meeting his eyes. She'd probably heard that phrase one too many times. "What's that?"

"I have to go with them."

"Will you be safe?" She turned and searched his face. There was something in her eyes that he couldn't place, but he wasn't sure what.

He put his arm around her and pulled her into him. "Yeah, of course. I just need to make sure they really take him out. Nothing will happen to me." He couldn't tell her the real possibilities. He couldn't let her know it was dangerous.

"You promise? I lost Ari. I can't lose you too." Her voice was pleading, her eyes panicked.

"Yes, I promise." He hated lying to her, thinking of what she'd have to go through when this was over.

Her face went stoic. "Well, then I guess you better get going. I'm going to shower and get this sand out of my hair. You go and come back safe. Is anyone staying here with me, or will I be alone?"

"Titania will be staying with you."

"Okay." She embraced him hard and whispered in his ear, "Come back to me. Please."

Then she spun and jogged back up to the castle. She'd given in too easily. Maybe she had heard him. No. That was the guilt that plagued him. If he died, she'd never let anyone out of her sight again. He let out a breath. It didn't matter.

If Raaf died, it would be worth it.

Chapter Twenty-Nine

THE ESCAPE

Zwaantie locked her door and flung open her closet. She'd heard every word Leo and Sage said on the beach, and she wasn't about to let them both go and kill themselves for her. The biggest threat Raaf presented was to her, so she would either kill him or die trying. Part of her was angry they were hiding one more thing from her, but a bigger part of her understood.

She wouldn't have told them either if she was doing something that could get her killed. Like now, for instance. But she'd never forgive herself if they died protecting her. Too many people had died already.

She pulled on black shorts and a tank and stuffed a Solite dress and cloak into her bag. She'd stowaway on the boat and get to the castle before all of them. She'd send a message to Leo on his disc just before she went in so he wouldn't try to bring down the castle on her.

She turned on her shower so everyone thought she was in there and snuck into the hallway. Low voices came from the dining room. If she was lucky, they would stay in there until she slipped out the front door. She tiptoed down the hall. She heard her name a couple of times, but she didn't stop to find out why.

Once out the door, she raced to the boat, not bothering to be quiet since everyone was inside. This boat was bigger than the one she and

Leo came in on. It had a large hull with several Zwaantie-sized cupboards. She opened a few until she found an empty one and slipped inside. It smelled musty, and the wood was rough. This would be the most uncomfortable ride of her life, but at least she was able to sit down.

She adjusted herself until she was sitting with her back against a wall and her bag on her lap. Maybe she'd manage to get a nap in. Though with her nerves on high alert, she doubted sleep would come.

It wasn't long before she heard Leo and Sage's voices.

"Who's driving the ship?" Sage asked.

"Mother. She'll get us there the fastest," Leo replied. Zwaantie's heart squeezed at the sound of his voice. He'd be so angry with her when he found out what she'd done.

More footsteps clattered down the stairs.

"This is so nerve-wracking. Six hours to go to what is probably our death," Phoenix said. Zwaantie could almost see the anxiety on his face.

"Eight hours. It's six from the City of Stars. Don't think like that. We could survive," Leo said. His voice wasn't very convincing. Zwaantie was doing the right thing. She couldn't let them die.

"Right. Sage told me what happened the first time you did this spell and brought down a small building. They almost burned you on the funeral pyre. That's how close to death you were," Phoenix said.

"There are five of us," Leo said.

"And a massive castle," Phoenix replied.

"We're sacrificing for our kingdom. It's what leaders do. If we succeed, Zwaantie will live to rule, and our people will be free," Ajax said.

Zwaantie didn't regret a minute of her decision. Leo lied to her. He would not come home from this safely. She had no intention of ruling alone. If they all died to protect her, she'd never be happy again.

This was her mess, not theirs. She'd clean it up.

Zwaantie waited a good fifteen minutes after everyone left the boat before she crawled out of her cupboard. Leo and the others weren't planning on attacking until the middle of the night. This gave her several hours to take care of Raaf. Maybe she wouldn't even have to alert Leo to what she was doing.

She threw the green Solite dress over her tank and shorts, slid on her wooden shoes, and tied her cloak at the neck, with the hood up. Hopefully no one would look twice at her since she looked just like everyone else in Sol. She clattered onto the dock. It'd been so long since she wore Solite shoes. She was making a racket, but no one glanced her way.

The Stellans and Solites were busy. Zwaantie admired how well they worked together. When Raaf died, it wouldn't be hard to merge the kingdoms. She was ready for the challenge.

She didn't arrive at the castle for another hour. Her feet ached. She wasn't used to walking that long anymore while wearing unyielding shoes.

There were fewer people near the castle, but nobody really noticed her. She kept her hood up so her face wasn't visible, but then so did most of the others. She dug around her pockets for some of the Solite gold she'd brought with her and stopped at a fruit stand.

She picked up a basket and filled it with apples, grapes, and bananas. The food would provide a nice distraction for the guards so she could get into Raaf's room. After she paid for the food, she stopped at the bakery and bought a few rolls. She nibbled on one as she approached the castle.

Leo and Sage stood near the edge of a field, talking in low voices. She recognized their disguises from before. Zwaantie averted her eyes and pulled her hood down a little more. If they caught her, she'd never make it inside. She took the path to the slave entrance. Several others trudged along with her. A few were free, but most still had the bands on.

She would free the slaves as soon as she did away with Raaf. Her pity for him was gone. He killed Ari and Luna. He would pay.

She blended well. The basket helped. Once inside, she headed up the stairs to her old room. She wasn't going in there, but she wouldn't be able to get to where Raaf was by going down the hall to the king's chambers. That would be too well guarded. No, she had a better idea.

She'd go through Raaf's rooms. When they said it had fewer

guards, Zwaantie knew this was the place to get to Raaf. She could find her way through his room. Quickly too.

She peeked around the corner. Three guards sat outside his door. She ducked into a cove, pulled out her bottle of Deep Sleep, and poured it over the fruit and bread. It seeped into the food, but the food still looked exactly the same. Xandria was good at what she did.

She approached the guards with her head bowed.

"Your lunch, sirs."

"Thank you," one of them grunted and took the basket from her. She waited nearby and shuffled her feet.

"What are you waiting for?" One asked Zwaantie with a mouthful of food.

"I need to take the basket back to my mother." She needed this to happen quickly. If they didn't eat fast or if one passed out before the other, she'd be made.

The guard rolled his eyes, but they all scarfed down the food and shoved the basket back into her hands.

"Tell your mother we want more bread next time."

She nodded and slipped around the corner. She'd been just as rude to Luna at times, though never rough. She wished she'd been nicer. The hole in her heart by Ari overshadowed everything, but a big part of her missed Luna as well.

Less than a minute later, she heard the first thump, then a second and third.

She peered around the corner. All three were out on the floor. She wouldn't have much time. Once someone discovered the guards, they would come after her. She stepped over them and slipped into Raaf's rooms. Then she locked the door and slid the couch in front of it. She whipped off her dress and noisy shoes. She still had on her black tank and shorts. She'd maneuver better this way.

Now all she had to do was find the secret passageway. When she was a child, they'd played hide-and-seek so many times, and no one ever found Raaf. She'd searched his room high and low, pushing bricks and pulling out books, but never found him or caught him going in and out of his hiding place. Usually she or Raaf would win the game because Luna and Phoenix never knew of the secret passages.

It took the guards hours to find her holed away in her own passageway when the Voice turned off the necklaces, so Raaf's trigger was probably not a brick, or he would've instructed them to press all of the bricks. She searched the bookshelf first, thinking maybe she missed something as child, but nothing seemed unusual there.

Perhaps, the secret passageway wasn't in his bedroom, but deeper in his rooms. She slid open the door that led to the hallway. She hadn't been down here in years. She crept down the hall, past his private dining room and library. The room on the left used to be his toy room. She'd spent hours playing with his toy swords and building blocks. They were much more interesting than her dolls and tea sets. If only they could turn back time and be kids again. Maybe then she could teach him to not be a ruthless killer.

At the very end of the hall was an old stone door with an empty box outside of it. Of course. This was where he went. The grand chancellor title was a cover for what he really was doing. He was either controlling or was in fact the Voice. She'd find out soon enough which one it was.

This would be too easy.

She shoved the door, and it opened to a small closet. She felt along the walls, but still nothing. She ran her hands along the stones on the floor, but it was an ordinary closet.

She frowned and stepped back into the hall. Everything looked normal. She examined the small table. It was so useless sitting there. Why even bother with it?

She crouched down, not quite sure what she was looking for. In the corner, there was a small nub on the leg of the table. She pressed it, and the floor under the table gave way, revealing a ladder.

Stars. She found it.

She shimmied down the ladder and into a long dark passageway. She pulled out her disc.

"Light," she commanded, and it lit right up.

She started down the hall and found the door Sage spoke of. This was it, her last chance. She could turn around, climb up that ladder, and live to see another day.

Or she could save the world.

She turned the knob and pushed open the door.

Chapter Thirty

THE MISSING QUEEN

"I'm telling you that was Zwaantie," Sage said, her disguised face full of concern. She looked weird as an old Solite woman.

"No way could you tell because of the way she walked." Leo glanced down and startled again at his pale hands. The disguise was necessary, but he hated not looking like himself. It was disconcerting.

Sage stomped her foot and glared at him. "Yeah, I could. Seriously. Call my mother and ask her where Zwaantie is. Please. We can't go through with this if she's in there. Do you really think she'll be able to defeat Raaf on her own?"

Leo groaned. "This is impossible. We left her in Stella. She's not here."

Sage shoved a disc in his face. "I'm calling my mother."

"Mom," Sage said.

"Hey," Titania said groggily. Her head hovered above his disc, but her eyes were still closed.

"Where's Zwaantie?" Leo asked, not concerned.

She rubbed her eyes. "I'm not sure. She left a note on her door that she wanted to be alone, so I went out to swim. I spent a few hours in the water, went for a hike, and then I fell asleep on the beach. Give me a moment, and I'll go check on her. Sorry."

Dread filled his stomach. He'd expected her to say they'd been together all day, but if she hadn't seen Zwaantie since they left, it was possible. Why would Zwaantie come to Sol?

"Hurry, please."

He bounced back and forth on his feet. If Sage was right, that changed everything.

"Why would she be here?" he asked Sage.

"Maybe she overheard us talking, and she doesn't want you to die." Sage glared at him.

He swallowed. He really thought she'd been asleep. "No. Titania's going to call back and say she's safe and sound."

"Believe what you want. We've got three hours to find her, and if she was heading into the castle, she won't be easy to find."

A few minutes later Sage's disc buzzed. Titania's face floated over the disc, her eyes wide with panic. "Her shower was still running, so I opened her bathroom door. She wasn't there. I don't know where she is."

"Search the castle and the beaches and call me immediately if you find her." He turned off his disc. "We need to see if she's in there. Call the others and tell them the plan is on hold for the moment."

Sage nodded and clicked open her disc. Leo stared at the castle. Why would Zwaantie go in there? If she was going after Raaf, he worried she wouldn't be able to go through with actually killing him. He was her brother. If the tables were turned, Leo wasn't sure he'd be able to kill one of his own siblings, no matter the crime, and he had eleven of them. Zwaantie only had one.

Though that didn't really matter because Raaf would kill her before she had a chance to kill him.

Chapter Thirty-One

THE VOICE

Zwaantie didn't immediately see Raaf. The room was tall, with glowing orbs floating around the entire thing. She was mesmerized. She walked right into the middle of them. Most of the balls were small, a little larger than a chicken's egg, but the one in the middle, it was enormous. She was drawn to it.

The orbs whispered all around her. The big one pulsed light, and wisps shot out occasionally. It reminded her eerily of the wall. She reached a hand out.

"Don't touch that."

She spun around and found Raaf standing several feet from her. She felt like she should feel fear, but there was something comforting about the orbs. It was like coming home.

"Raaf."

He looked healthier than he had when he'd been in Stella. His red hair glowed with the orbs. His face was tight and angry, but underneath she could still see the little boy he'd once been. That boy grew up to become a murderer. She clenched her fists. This was her chance to avenge Ari. She had no weapon. No way to fight him. She wasn't sure what the plan was. She hadn't thought much past getting in.

No normal weapon would work. Sage told her how strong Raaf had been. If Sage hadn't been able to fight him off in this room, neither would Zwaantie. Her only hope was to talk to him and get him away from the orbs.

Raaf stopped a few feet from her. "You've been hiding from me. Every person in the kingdom would kill you on sight. You knew this, so what are you doing here?"

Zwaantie took a step forward, reaching for him, but he pulled back. She dropped her hand. "This has to stop. The wall has fallen. The Voice needs to as well."

"Ah, so you are here to destroy me. The Old Mother warned me of this."

"Wilma warned you?"

He laughed. "Ironic, isn't it? I never wanted you dead, you know. But when she told me it was either the Voice or you, I had to choose the Voice. There was no choice. I really am sorry." His face held the remorse he spoke of.

Zwaantie moved back. "Why didn't you talk to me? Surely we could've worked something out."

He snorted. "Talk? Look what you've done since you moved to Stella. You dropped the wall and shut down the Voice. You don't want to talk. You want to win."

"That's not true. I don't want anyone else to die, but the Voice needs to go away."

He laughed, and it reverberated around the room. "That's all I needed to hear. It's time to die, Zwaantie."

He held out his hand and squeezed. Nothing happened.

He made the same motion. What in the star gods was he doing? Zwaantie raised her eyebrows.

"Is that supposed to do something?" she asked. Even though fear coursed through her veins, she was able to remain calm. She had to. She didn't want to provoke him.

"Why aren't you dead?" His face contorted in anger.

"Maybe the Voice doesn't want you to kill me."

She took a step forward, and he shoved his hands out toward her. Again, nothing happened. She moved around him, and he grabbed her arm.

"Maybe my magic doesn't work on you, but I can still kill you."

"Why do you think your magic doesn't work on me?" Her heart raced, but she kept her voice deliberately calm.

He squeezed her bicep and wrenched her closer. "Blood. I read about it, but didn't understand. You and I share the same blood. I can't attack you with the Voice, because the Voice sees you as part of me in this room."

She tugged her arm, but he held tight. "Let me go."

"I hope you've made your peace, because you are not going to walk out of this room alive."

He dragged her away from the main orb, and she stumbled intentionally. She fell to the floor, and Raaf tumbled on top of her. Zwaantie untangled herself, stood up, and tried to run, but Raaf grabbed her hair. She jerked backwards, and he growled in her ear. "Nice try."

She twisted, not caring about the pain in her head. She gripped his wrist that held her hair and squeezed. Then she kicked him in the stomach. He let go and fell backwards into the large glowing orb.

Zwaantie should've run, but she stared in horror as Raaf floated lifelessly in the orb, his eyes shut. Had she killed him?

The small orbs all around the room flew toward the one in the middle. Wisps whipped past her, leaving whispers in their wake. The room roared as the orbs rushed to the large one. It swelled, and Zwaantie flew back, covering her eyes from the brightness. Soon, the only orb left in the room was the large one with Raaf floating in the middle.

Raaf's Voice filled the room. Be Polite. Respect your parents. Don't talk back. Control your thoughts. Cover your ankles. Don't steal. No kissing. Work hard. Don't lie. Die, Zwaantie, Die.

Zwaantie covered her ears and shrunk away.

The light in the room dimmed, and the Voice quieted. Zwaantie peeked through her fingers to the orb. It was shrinking rapidly. After a few moments, Raaf became clear, the orb glowing faintly around him. Then it was gone, and Raaf was curled up on the ground.

Oh, Sol. She'd done it. She'd destroyed the Voice.

She went to Raaf and placed her hand on shoulder. "Are you okay?"

He jerked his head up at her and glared at her. "What have you done?" he growled. She backed away, and he scrambled up and looked around "What have you done?" he screamed.

"I don't know," Zwaantie stammered.

He rushed to his work tables and gripped his head for a moment. Then he turned and gave her a twisted smile.

"The Voice is in me. It's telling me what to do. It's a failsafe to protect the Voice. It still exists. All I need to do is find another room like this, and I can put it all back. In the meantime, I am the Voice. All who hear my voice have no choice but to follow my directions."

Dread filled Zwaantie's heart. He was a man possessed. She had no way to escape. He was between her and the door.

He searched his worktable, picked up a jagged dagger, and approached her. She tried to run.

"Stop," he commanded.

She was forced to stop, though she willed herself to move, but her feet wouldn't budge. Raaf twirled the dagger in his hands.

She was going to die. She closed her eyes. At least now she would meet Ari in the stars. Maybe Leo or Sage would kill Raaf before he could do any more damage.

"Open your eyes," he commanded. She did and met the blue eyes that once were friendly. Now they held hatred and anger.

"Get it over with."

"Why would I get my hands dirty when I can have you do it for me. You'll kill yourself."

He handed her the dagger, handle first. "Take it," he commanded.

She did, and then she moved before she could think. She had one goal. Shut him up. She lunged and pushed the dagger right into his throat. It slid in easily, and blood spurted everywhere. Zwaantie stumbled backwards as she watched Raaf grasp at the knife. Then his eyes rolled up into his head, and he fell. A bright light flashed from his body, and Zwaantie covered her eyes. As quickly as the fight started, it was over.

The Voice was dead.

Chapter Thirty-Two

THE COMPROMISE

Zwaantie didn't even get a chance to take a step toward the body when the door to the workshop burst open. Sage and Leo rushed in. They stopped dead in their tracks when they saw her and Raaf.

Leo ran for her and crushed her in a hug. "I was so worried. Are you hurt?" He pulled away and looked her up and down.

"A little bruised and sore, but I don't think I have any injuries." Her hands were shaking. She'd just killed her brother. She looked around Leo to where Raaf's body lay. Sage hovered over it.

"He's dead, right?" Zwaantie asked.

Sage glanced up. "Yes. Remind me not to get near you when you hold a dagger. How did you know to stab him in the throat? Most people go for the heart. Throat is quicker though."

"The Voice went inside of him, and I acted before I could think. I didn't want him speaking because then he would have made me do whatever he wanted."

"I'm glad you're alive," Sage said.

Leo pinched his nose. "What were you thinking coming here by yourself?"

Zwaantie rubbed her forehead. "Me? You were the one who was

about to kill not only yourself but your father, mother, and sister. I risked only myself."

"And your baby." The irritation in his voice was evident. She killed the Voice and her own brother, and here he was lecturing her about safety. She did what she had to.

"Don't make this about me. You lied to me. Again."

His face hardened. "Lied? You are one to talk. Nearly every word to me out of your mouth has been a lie."

And just like that they were fighting again. It was as if the last three months on the island disappeared in an instant.

~

Two days later Sage burst into her room in Stella without warning. Zwaantie had been sound asleep under the stars blanket with the cows mooing on the wall.

Zwaantie sat straight up. "Can't you come in a little quieter next time?"

"No. It's time for you to stop sulking." Sage bounced onto the bed, her hair a bright purple. She looked almost normal again, no longer wearing black for Ari.

"I'm not sulking." Zwaantie was hiding though. The guilt of Raaf's death hung over her. She replayed that moment in her head over and over again and tried to see if there was another way it could've ended.

Leo was still avoiding her. Or maybe she was avoiding him. Ultimately he was right. She shouldn't have gone after Raaf on her own. That was foolish. She could've told Leo and Sage about the other way in, and they could've gone after him together, but she went in blind. She was lucky she was alive.

"Yeah, you are. I can't figure out why. We defeated the Voice. The people are rejoicing. Stellans are teaching the Solites all about the Ticker and party potions. Seriously, we're going to be celebrating for weeks. You act like the world ended."

"I killed my own brother. My heart hurts, but it's different than when Ari died. I took Raaf's life. I don't know how to recover from that."

Sage sat on the edge of Zwaantie's bed. "I've killed a lot of people."

"That's not comforting."

Sage snorted. "I know. I remember the first time I killed someone. I puked up everything I ate for a week. It was awful. He was a bad man, and he had to die, but still the idea of taking a human life was so horrific. The only way I got over it was by getting out and living my life. I couldn't let the end of his life end mine. You can't either."

"I love you, Sage."

"Me too. I'm glad we all survived. I promised Leo I would get you to come out."

"He's still mad at me."

"No, he was just giving you space. He wants to see you."

"Can't I just start by hanging out with you?"

"He's your husband, and he's up in the tower with breakfast."

"I don't know." She still wanted to hide and stay out of the public eye. If Leo came to her, she probably wouldn't be as nervous.

Sage crossed her arms. "You don't have a choice. Go shower, and I'll tell Leo you're on your way."

Zwaantie thought about arguing but realized it was pointless. She slipped into the bathroom and took her time in the shower. Before Sage had showed up on the island, she and Leo were getting along fairly well. Things had almost gotten romantic, but now she felt numb, and she wasn't sure she'd be able to face him. She needed time to find herself and come to terms with what she did. Adding romance into the mix of it would just complicate things. Plus she was starting to feel weird about her pregnancy.

How could she love Leo while she carried Ari's child? On the island, none of the rest of the world existed, but here, life smacked her in the face.

She dried her hair and perused her closet. She grabbed a skirt that flared out mid-thigh and a pink tank top. Stella was hotter than ever with the sun. The tower would be scorching.

In the elevator she contemplated what she would say to him. Would he try to kiss her? She wasn't ready. When she and Leo moved past being friends, she wanted it to be intentional. Would he understand, or would he just accuse her of lying to him again?

She pushed the trap door open and was pleasantly surprised by how cool it was.

Leo sat in the center on a picnic blanket.

"How is it cool out here?" Zwaantie asked, settling a few feet from Leo.

"We created a spell. Otherwise no one could come out here."

"If I had known that, I would've dressed more appropriately."

His eyes raked over her body. "You look fine to me. I've missed you these past few days. I'm sorry for what I said."

She wiped her sweaty palms on her skirt. "Me too. I'm just happy this is all over."

He scooted closer to her and put his hand over hers. She pulled it out from under his. "We need to talk about us." She hoped he'd understand. He'd been so patient so far.

"What's there to talk about?"

"I think we need to wait before we try to become romantically involved."

His face fell. "Why?"

She looked down, not wanting to see his face. "It's just too much right now. All of this change. Plus, I still think of Ari often. I want to give you my all, but I can't do that yet. It's not fair to you."

"And making me wait is?" He propped up on his knees and looked her right in the eyes. "Zwaantie, I love you. When I knew you'd gone after Raaf, I thought for sure you were dead. I was terrified. I don't want to lose you again. I know part of your heart is with Ari and will be for some time. I'll take you even if it's just a small part."

Tears pricked at her eyes. "Then I need you to just be my friend for right now. Can you do that?"

He exhaled and deflated. "Yes. For you."

"Thank you."

A MONTH LATER, ZWAANTIE STARED AROUND THE TABLE. ALL THE lower kings and queens from both Stella and Sol were present. Plus Sage, Lyra, and Leo's brother Scorpion. Sage didn't know why she was there, but Zwaantie was excited to tell her, though she wasn't sure Sage would be as eager. Whether Sage knew it or not, this would be the best thing for all of them.

Zwaantie stood and addressed them. "The celebrations are ending. Real life has come back into play. It is time to discuss the future of our land. All of you who currently hold lower kingdoms will keep them. No changes will be made. We imagine that the Solite kingdoms will have the most difficulty changing, and so for the past few weeks, all the lower chancellors were tested for magical abilities. With the exception of one, all showed great capacity for magic. They will stay in the City of Stars for several weeks and train with Lyra, who will train them to be head mages over their city. They will then train others. In time, magic will become commonplace and normal in Sol."

There were a few titters among the Solite kings and queens, but no one argued. Prince Moo-for-me had replaced his father, and he was sufficiently cowed in her presence. She snorted at her silent joke.

Zwaantie sat down and let Leo address them. For the past few weeks she and Leo mapped out a plan to run the kingdom. She hoped the lower kings and queens would be happy with it.

"We have decided to establish a new capital city on the border of Stella and Sol, just north of both Zonnes and The Black City, where the wall used to be. It will be called the City of the Dawn. This, in effect, causes both the City of Stars and Zonnes to become lower kingdoms. Libby has refused the crown, and so Scorpion will become the new lower king of City of Stars. Sage will become lower queen of Zonnes."

Sage squeaked, and Zwaantie gave her a grin. Things were definitely changing for the better.

～

THAT EVENING, THEY MINGLED IN THE GRAND HALL AFTER BOTH Scorpion and Sage were crowned. Phoenix nudged Zwaantie.

"You still mad at me?" he asked. She hadn't really had a chance to speak to him since she'd caught him and Sage kissing.

"No. You make Sage happy."

"Yeah, and you made her queen. Talk about putting her out of my reach."

Zwaantie smirked at him. "Hardly. You know, if you marry Sage, you'll be king in the same castle where you were a slave."

His eyes widened. "I hadn't thought of that."

"Maybe you should. You have my blessing. Go and take that throne."

He left her with a grin that used to make her stomach buzz so long ago. A lifetime, really.

Leo slipped his arm around her. "How are you doing?"

"I'm fine."

He put his hand on her ever-growing belly. "You're not too tired?"

"No. I'm good. Today's been fun. New beginnings, right?"

He nodded. "New beginnings."

Leo kissed her on the top of her head, and she froze. They were still strictly in friend zone, and she didn't want that kiss to shift into something more. She wasn't ready to move on yet. But there were appearances that needed to be kept, unfortunately.

"Let me know when you are ready, and I'll make sure you get back to your room."

"You don't have to do that anymore. The threat is gone."

"Zwaantie, for as long as I've known you, your life has been in danger. I'm not sure I'll ever feel at ease with your safety. I've come too close to losing you too many times."

There was great deal of truth to his statement, but for the first time in a long time, she felt utterly safe.

Chapter Thirty-Three

THE CASTLE

T he next several months passed with very little hiccups. Leo and Zwaantie still slept in separate rooms in the City of the Stars and he'd managed to keep that out of the Ticker. The joining of the kingdoms preoccupied everyone.

Things were moving too slowly for him, but he let her set the pace. She grew more and more beautiful every moment. His favorite time of day was the early mornings when he would sneak into her room and snuggle with her and feel the baby kick. It was the only time she didn't brush off his affections.

He hated it when the mornings came to an end. Which usually happened because she was either hungry or they had an early meeting.

She was his, and yet, she wasn't.

Today, they had no plans, which was something that didn't happen often. He curled up behind her, and she pressed his hand against her stomach.

"You feel that?" she asked.

"I do. It's very hard."

"It's his foot, I think. He's trying to push his way out. I've been awake for hours."

He brushed her hair away and buried his nose into her shoulder. "Maybe I should've come earlier."

"Maybe you should just sleep here tonight."

His stomach buzzed. Were things finally beginning to change? "You sure?"

She rolled onto her back, her face dangerously close to his. "Yes, I'm sure. He calms at your touch. Maybe I'll actually get some sleep."

It wasn't the reason he wanted, but he'd take what he could get.

"Okay, I will do my best to be a sleep knight and make that little baby stop moving."

She scooted away from him, and he knew he'd lost her for the day.

"What's the plan for today?" Zwaantie asked.

"I thought we'd go scout out a spot for our castle in the new capital."

"I think that's an incredible idea. Then can we meet with the design mages? I want to do a combination of Stellan and Solite castles." She sat up and waddled over to the table, popping a grape into her mouth.

"The Stellan castle doesn't make sense. The vipers are no longer a threat. We can have outer rooms," Leo said.

"True, but I like it. A curved window in our bedroom could have spectacular views." She rubbed her back and cringed.

"Everything okay?"

"Yeah, but my back hurts."

"Has the healer told you when they thought the baby might come?"

"She said a month or so."

Leo joined her at the breakfast table. "Sage wants to come with us to scope out locations."

"That's fine. I didn't realize she was here. I swear, she spends more time in this castle than she does her own."

"She had an appointment with Nash this morning."

"That's right. How could I forget? She's going to have the wedding of the century since mine failed epically." Zwaantie cringed, and Leo was sorry he brought up Sage's wedding at all.

She didn't talk about the day Ari died very often, but when she did, she was grumpy the rest of the day. Just when he'd thought things were going so well.

After breakfast, Sage met them at the carriage and squeezed Zwaantie so hard Leo thought she was about to pop.

"I wanna move back to Stella," Sage said, climbing up after them.

Zwaantie ignored her. He'd agreed with her decision to give Zonnes to Sage even if Sage complained about it all the time. The people of Sol needed someone like Sage, and Sage needed a new job. This was perfect because she wouldn't get bored.

"How did your dress appointment go this morning?" Zwaantie asked.

"Good. I wish you could've been there, but I understand. My dress is going to be bright pink."

Zwaantie pressed her lips together. "Nash approved this?"

"You got to have white. I told him it was only fair."

"What did he say?"

"He said he's going to be the laughing stock of both Stella and Sol."

Zwaantie laughed. "I can't wait to see it. How's being queen?"

Sage groaned. "Awful. Do you have any idea how needy people are? I can't wait until we get married and Phoenix can take over the boring stuff. He already does a lot of it. He loves it."

They climbed out of the carriage and into a boat.

"At least we'll be closer to you once we build the new castle," Zwaantie said, collapsing on the couch in the hull.

"That is good. I'm sick of you being so far away. Hopefully people like Nash and Orion will move with you. A brand new city. This will be incredible."

～

THEY RODE UP AND DOWN FOR HOURS ALONG WHAT USED TO BE the wall.

For each spot they found, someone liked it, and someone else did not. Sage was very vocal about her opinions. Leo wanted Zwaantie to pick the spot, but so far she didn't seem excited about any of them.

Zwaantie rubbed her back again and grimaced as they stood in a spot that had pretty hills off in the distance.

"Are you feeling okay?" Leo asked her.

"Not really, but I never feel okay these days."

He rubbed her shoulders. "We can do this another day."

"No. I want to get started on our castle. This spot would work, but I'd like to keep looking."

In other words, she didn't like the spot.

Fifteen minutes later the ocean came into view on their right. To their left, far off into the distance, cows and horses grazed in the farmlands.

"Stop," Zwaantie said, and the carriage shuttered. She climbed out and spun in a circle. "This is it. This spot right here. I get cows and the ocean."

Sage wandered around the backside of the carriage and down to the beach. After several yards, she yelled back, "You'll probably need to move inland a bit, but this is pretty."

Leo pulled her into him. "You sure? This is what you want?"

"Positive. This is perfect." She gripped the edges of his vest and pulled him closer. "We can start a new life here. One that isn't tainted by horrible memories."

He tried not to get too excited by her affection. "They weren't all horrible."

She blinked up at him, and he was lost in that bright blue.

"Leo, I'm sorry I've pushed you away. I just needed time, but I'm ready to move forward. This is our life, and I want it to be a happy life."

He dipped his head forward, ready to take that kiss he'd wanted for so long. "Then let's start. Right now," he whispered against her lips.

"Oh," she groaned and jerked away from him, gripping her stomach.

"What's wrong?"

Her face screwed up in a grimace. "My water broke," she said, through clenched teeth. Stars. What was he going to do?

"Oh no, that's bad. We're hours from the nearest city." He put his arm around her and guided her back to the carriage. "Sage!" he yelled. "Get back here!" He couldn't think too much about what was happening. Her life was in danger out here in the middle of nowhere.

Sage showed up at the door just as he helped Zwaantie onto one of the wide benches.

"What's up?"

"Zwaantie's in labor." He spat the words out, panic setting in.

Sage paled. "What? No. What are we going to do?"

"Get to The Black City as soon as possible." That was the only plan that made sense. He had to get her to safety.

Sage scrambled in, and the carriage took off. Zwaantie held her stomach. Her whole body tensed, and she let out a groan. Leo held tight to her.

"Sage, I need you to help me," she said once the contraction released.

"What? No."

"Yes. I need you to check how far I am."

Leo was speechless. Here he was close to a full-blown panic, and she was calm as anything.

Sage grew wide-eyed. "I don't think I can do that."

Leo was glad she'd asked Sage instead of him. He felt like he was about to pass out.

"Sage you've killed dozens of people, spied on countless others, and nearly died protecting me. You can check and see how much time we have left."

Sage gave a solemn nod.

"Okay, Leo, can you hold me from behind. This is too crowded, but I think we can make it work."

He climbed around behind her, and she pressed her back into him. This he could do. He could hold her and hope she didn't die.

She propped her knees up, and Sage checked her.

"What do you see?" Zwaantie asked. Leo was grateful Zwaantie had been a midwife in Sol. Otherwise she'd probably be a lot more upset.

"Um, the head."

"You're sure?" Zwaantie asked, resigned. Leo wasn't exactly sure what this meant, but he was fairly certain they wouldn't make it to The Black City in time.

"Pretty sure."

"Okay, Sage, get ready. You're delivering my baby."

The blood drained out of Sage's face. "No. No. I can't do that."

"You have to," Leo said, suddenly resolved. "Her life is in our hands."

Another contraction came, and Zwaantie clutched her stomach and grunted. After it passed, she took a couple of deep breaths. "I'm going to push now. You catch the baby. That's all."

A few minutes later Zwaantie crushed Leo's finger, and Sage squealed. "I have his head. Now what?"

Leo's hands started to sweat. He wasn't ready for this. He watched Sage with admiration. She jumped right in without fear.

Zwaantie breathed hard again. "Just a minute and I'll push again." Her grip tightened, and suddenly a wail filled the carriage.

"It's a boy!" Sage yelled over the cry and handed the pink child to Zwaantie. Leo looked down at the last connection they had to Ari. He would always know this child belonged to Ari, but Leo would do his best to raise him as Ari would.

Chapter Thirty-Four

THE FUTURE

It only took a few weeks for them to build the castle. Zwaantie was shocked when Leo walked into her room two days ago and announced it was finished. He offered to wait until she was ready to move, since the baby was only a few weeks old, but she started packing that very afternoon.

She'd grieved for the past several months and was surprised to find her feelings growing for Leo. A quiet spark had flared, and she allowed herself to explore it. Leo hadn't kissed her yet, but she was eager to move forward. She and Leo had a kingdom to run.

She gathered baby Ari in her arms and stepped out of the carriage. Leo had gone on ahead, just to make sure everything was ready. He said he didn't want her to have to do anything but take care of the baby once she arrived.

He was too good for her. She'd come to understand that.

The castle rose up in front of her. It was larger than either castle she'd lived in. A dozen turrets were scattered about. Some were short, and others disappeared into the sky. In a way, it looked haphazard, but every room had a purpose, and it would provide hours of exploring for their children and nieces and nephews.

It exceeded her expectations.

She had hoped Leo would greet her, but instead the nanny waited and took Ari from her.

"The king is up in your rooms, Your Majesty. He asked that you meet him there."

Zwaantie smiled. "Thank you, please bring Ari up in a half hour or so."

"Of course."

Zwaantie climbed up the stairs and found the elevator that would take her to her rooms. It went up and sideways, and she nearly fell over.

She laughed, thinking of the first time she'd ridden in one and had a similar experience. The elevator opened into the entryway of their room. Leo offered to give her a room of her own, but she refused. They would start this life together.

She stepped into the sunlight and immediately rushed to the balcony. Their room was on the top of a tower, with a balcony that went all the way around. She found herself on the side that faced the fields of farm animals. She breathed in the clean air. Slowly she walked around, taking in the sun and the distant hills. On the other side, Leo stood overlooking the ocean. She stopped and watched him for a moment.

She must've been quiet because he didn't look her way.

The last year had not been easy for either of them. At times she hated him and what he represented, but he'd been so patient with her. Even when she was in the depths of grief, he gave her the space she needed.

As time went on, she came to treasure those quiet moments they had together. Those early mornings when he would come in and hold her were her favorites. It was pure love untainted by lust or anger. Her love for him had grown quite unexpectantly.

It was quiet. It was safe. It was Leo.

There were times though, when she could feel a fire in her belly or when she shivered at his touch. The guilt would follow, and so she always shut it down and withdrew. Deep down, she knew Ari wouldn't want her to be miserable. That he would want her to love again, but it'd been hard to allow herself that joy.

She approached Leo and put her hand into the crook of his arm, noticing how warm his skin was against hers. He dropped a kiss on the top of her hand and slid his arm around her waist. Her stomach buzzed. She was a little nervous about how to tell him she was ready.

"This is gorgeous. You picked a good spot," he said.

"I know. I'm not sure we'll ever need to leave our rooms."

He grinned. "Except for Sage's wedding. She'll never forgive us if we miss that."

Zwaantie sighed. "I guess. Though I'd be happy if it were just you, me, and little Ari, alone for the rest of our lives."

"Me too, but we're the king and queen. No rest for us."

She wiggled around so she was facing him, her back against the balcony's ledge. Leo pressed into her, and her arms held him close. He raised his eyebrows. "This is new."

She wished he'd shut up and go with it. This was hard enough for her as it was.

"I know. Listen, I... I..."

His dark eyes met her. "You don't have to say it. I know. I love you too."

She shook her head. "No. that's not it. Of course I love you."

"That's the first time you've said it." His face was serious, and his eyes questioned her motives.

"I'm sorry. I think it a lot."

He dropped his head, his nose practically touching hers. "So if that wasn't what you meant, what did you want to say?"

She clenched her fists against his back. This was so difficult to say out loud, and she wasn't sure why. She was ninety-nine percent sure he wouldn't reject her. But that one percent still remembered how he laughed at her on their wedding night.

"Leo, I want you."

He chuckled, and her cheeks burned. He brought his lips to her ear. "You want me, huh? Maybe we can lock ourselves in our tower for a few months. We have nearly a year of marriage to make up for."

He brought his lips to her neck, and desire filled her belly. He trailed kisses across her jaw and stopped just before her lips. His breath was soft, and she wondered what he was waiting for.

"Tell me again," he whispered.
"I want you," she said.
"No, the other one."
"I love you."

The End

Loved the Stella and Sol series? Check out the first book in the completed Sons of the Sand series!

Genies are only good for one thing....Devouring.

Liv is everything any genie could want in a mistress. Beautiful, young, and naïve. And she unknowingly summons Gabe from his three thousand year imprisonment.

Now Gabe has only one thought.

Elicit the death wish from her beautiful lips. But Liv doesn't cooperate.

Instead she does the impossible...she steals Gabe's heart.

Gabe is now torn between two powerful desires because he needs to kill her. But he wants to love her. The longer he is with her the stronger the desire to kill becomes until he can't resist anymore...

This exciting series is available at
Kimberlyloth.com

Acknowledgments

Another series finished. Thank you to all my readers who stuck out the whole thing.

Thanks go first to my very patient editors, Kelley and Suzi. This would not be nearly as good without you. You gals changed my life. Thank you.

Jaye, thanks for doing the formatting. I rest easier knowing it's in your hands.

Brittany, once again, thanks for your awesome proofing skills.

Virginia, thank you so much for all you do. I'm where I am today because of you.

Will, thanks for your unwavering support. I love you.

Xandi and AJ, thanks for being patient with your mom. Love you.

Tiffany, thank you for being my sister. Love you.

Superfans!!! You guys rock. Thank you.

Astrid Rudloff, Brianna Snowball, Sara Groenheide, Laurie Murray, Patti Hays, Anne Loshuk, Samantha Murphy, Ashley Martinez, Sherry Beasley, Jennifer LaRocca, Tera Comer, Cortnee Hancock, Jennifer McIntosh, Ola Adamska, Andrea McKay, Kristen Rummerfield, Debbie Rodriguez, Linda Longo,Faydra Fuller, Darcy Whitaker, Julie Hainsworth, Leslee Lusk, Dora Zeno, Isis Ray-Sisco, Ksandra Unangst, Pansy Mesimer, Andrea Hubler, Seraphia Sparks,

Yolanda Johnson, Bev Christensen, Jai Henson, Alicia Arana, Stephanie Pittser, Shelly Small, Mary Martin, Diane Norwood, Zoe Cannon, Shelby white, Amanda Showalter, Denise Austin, Angela Hogate, Sandra Singleton, Marie Rice, Linda Levine, Belinda Tran, Dawn Foster, Christine Stokes, Anita Hanekom, Victoria Palmer, Rosemary Lekman

Also by Kimberly Loth

All Kimberly Loth novels are part of the Amazon Kindle Unlimited
Program (Learn more)

The Thorn Chronicles (Young Adult Paranormal)
Kissed: www.kimberlyloth.com/kissed
Destroyed: www.kimberlyloth.com/destroyed
Secrets: www.kimberlyloth.com/secrets
Lies: www.kimberlyloth.com/lies
The Thorn Chronicles Boxed Set

The Dragon Kings (Young Adult Paranormal)
Obsidian: www.kimberlyloth.com/obsidian
Aspen: www.kimberlyloth.com/aspen
Valentine: www.kimberlyloth.com/valentine
Skye: www.kimberlyloth.com/skye
The Kings: www.kimberlyloth.com/kings
The Dragon Kings Boxed Set

Omega Mu Alpha Brothers (Sweet Romance Series)
Snowfall and Secrets: www.kimberlyloth.com/snowfall
Pyramids and Promises: www.kimberlyloth.com/pyramids
Folly and Forever: www.kimberlyloth.com/folly
Monkeys and Mayhem: www.kimberlyloth.com/monkeys
Roadtrips and Romance: www.kimberlyloth.com/roadtrips
Omega Mu Alpha Brothers Boxed Set

Stella and Sol (Young Adult Fantasy)
God of the Sun: www.kimberlyloth.com/sun

Prince of the Moon: www.kimberlyloth.com/moon

King of the Stars: www.kimberlyloth.com/stars

Queen of the Dawn: www.kimberlyloth.com/dawn

Stella and Sol Box Set

Sons of the Sand (Young Adult Paranormal)

The Smoking Lamp: www.kimberlyloth.com/smoking

The Blazing Glass: www.kimberlyloth.com/blazing

The Glowing Sands: www.kimberlyloth.com/glowing

About the Author

Kimberly Loth has lived all over the world. From the isolated woods of the Ozarks to exotic city of Cairo. Currently she resides in Tucson, Arizona with her family including an old grumpy cat named Max.

She's been writing for ten years and is the author of the Amazon bestselling series The Dragon Kings. In her free time she volunteers at church, reads, and travels as often as possible.

She loves talking to school groups and book clubs. For more information about having her come speak at your school or event contact her at kimberlyloth@gmail.com.

Made in the USA
Monee, IL
07 February 2022

90840739R10426